Liz Buh

D0374872

Days of Dreams and Laughter

The Story Girl and Other Tales

Days of Dreams and Laughter

The Story Girl and Other Tales

The Story Girl
The Golden Road
Kilmeny of the Orchard

By Lucy Maud Montgomery

Illustrated

GRAMERCY BOOKS
NEW YORK • AVENEL, NEW JERSEY

The works in this collection were originally published in three separate volumes: *The Story Girl, The Golden Road,* and *Kilmeny of the Orchard.* This volume contains the complete and unabridged texts of the original editions. They have been completely reset for this volume.

This 1990 edition is published by Gramercy Books, distributed by Outlet Book Company, Inc., a Random House Company, 40 Engelhard Avenue, Avenel, New Jersey 07001.

Printed and bound in the United States of America

Library of Congress Cataloging-in-Publication Data

Montgomery, L. M. (Lucy Maud), 1874–1942.
    Days of dreams and laughter : The story girl and other tales / by
Lucy Maud Montgomery.
        p.   cm.
    Contents: The story girl. The golden road. Kilmeny of the orchard.
    ISBN 0-517-05137-0
    1. Children's stories, Canadian.   [1. Storytelling—Fiction.
2. Prince Edward Island—Fiction.]   I. Title.
PZ7.M768Day   1990
[Fic]—dc20   90–48681
                                                                                   CIP
                                                                                    AC

ISBN 0-517-05137-0
8   7   6   5   4   3

CONTENTS

INTRODUCTION

HAVE YOU ever experienced *real* storytelling? Not stories being read from a book, not an actress performing in a one-character play, but those enchanted moments when a true teller of tales draws her audience close, looks into their eyes, and speaks from her heart to theirs? *The Story Girl* and its sequel, *The Golden Road*, by Lucy Maud Montgomery, are about such a storyteller, fourteen-year-old Sara Stanley, better known in her home, on Canada's Prince Edward Island, as "The Story Girl." Sara's family and friends are drawn under the spell of her tales, classic stories of love and loss as well as whimsical anecdotes about local eccentrics. It is a wonderful way to grow up, listening to stories—in fact, I think, the best way. For it is a way my brother and I shared many years ago in Brooklyn, when we were surrounded by not one talespinner, but by many—relatives and long-cherished family friends—all masterful raconteurs. Like the Story Girl, they "probably would have known a story and tried to tell it if [they] were being led to the stake."

As the Story Girl says, ". . . there are two kinds of true things—true things that *are,* and true things that are *not,* but *might* be." Whether she becomes a Greek god or her own Great-Aunt Edith, Sara enters into the skin of each character in her stories "so thoroughly," her cousin recalls, "that it was a matter of surprise to us when she emerged . . ." When asked how she does it, she replies, "It just does itself." The Story Girl shares this intensity of concentration with her creator, Lucy Maud Montgomery.

Recovering from a frightening experience, the Story Girl remarks, "But it'll be a good story to tell sometime." Sara knows that our lives are stories waiting to be told. And, indeed, there is another tale to tell about *The Story Girl*—a story that happened to me. I hope, had she known it, it would have given the author pleasure.

As a child, I loved L. M. Montgomery's novels about Anne of Green Gables, who often has to come to terms with the effects of her full-blown imagination, as does the Story Girl. And, as an adult, I became a storyteller and visited the "Green Gables" house in Prince Edward Island. In the bookstore there, I was intrigued by an old copy of *The Story Girl* that was displayed in a glass case, but was not for sale. There were new editions of other Montgomery books I bought, but, as the Story Girl herself says when a friend gives her an old, beloved book of poetry,

> I'd ten times rather have this than a new book. It's one of his own . . . one that he has read a hundred times and loved and made a friend of. A new book, just out of the shop . . . . wouldn't *mean* anything.

The thought of *The Story Girl* nagged at me. Returning home, I rummaged in my bookshelves, and found the identical book, a first edition, buried at the bottom. I took it with me to the neighborhood coffee shop where I went for breakfast.

I sat down at a small table next to a slim, unassuming woman. We were soon involved in conversation—at least, as I realized with surprise, *I* was talking a lot—and all about Lucy Maud Montgomery—not typical small chat.

The woman was one of the editors of the company that published this book, and at that particular time, she happened to be looking for someone to write an introduction to a collection of three of the *Anne of Green Gables* stories.

That was five years ago. I wrote that introduction—to *Anne of Green Gables, Three Volumes in One* (Avenel Books, New York, 1985)—and have since written many others for this editor's books. So, there is as often a tale behind the introduction to a book as there is in the book itself.

And now the story has come full circle: *The Story Girl* is being published, together with *The Golden Road,* and *Kilmeny of the Orchard.* It is an auspicious grouping, for all three novels tell of girls on the brink of womanhood—girls who are natural, self-taught artists; the first two books are about a superb storyteller, while the last is about Kilmeny Gordon, a gifted violinist. And all three novels take place on the island Maud Montgomery loved—where she grew up—Prince Edward Island.

The Story Girl and *The Golden Road* describe the adventures of a group of young teenagers led by the motherless Story Girl, who weaves her stories through their escapades. Sara is not pretty,

> But you'll think she is while she's talking to you. Everybody does. It's only when you go away from her that you find out she isn't a bit pretty after all.

For it is her voice that works the enchantment.

> . . . If voices had colour, hers would have been like a rainbow. It made words *live.* Whatever she said became a breathing entity . . .

Challenged by a neighborhood skeptic to recite the multiplication table, she plunges in,

> As she announced it, the fact that three times three was nine was exquisitely ridiculous, five times six almost brought tears to our eyes, eight times seven was the most tragic and frightful thing ever heard of, and twelve times twelve rang like a trumpet call to victory.

Enticing as this description is, it is a paradox of the author's achievement that the Story Girl's artistry surpasses her creator's ability to describe it, for the immediacy and the nuances of oral storytelling can almost never be captured in print.

Kilmeny of the Orchard is an unabashedly romantic love

story in which rich, young Eric Marshall unexpectedly en-
counters the "absolute, flawless purity" of mute Kilmeny, who
has learned to express herself through the music of the violin:

> . . . he believed that that wonderful music was coming
> straight from the soul of the unseen violinist . . . [It
> was] the very soul of music.

Kept isolated from village folk, Kilmeny has never learned
the pretences of society, and is "utterly unskilled in the art of
hiding her feelings." Eric realizes that here is

> A girl of eighteen who has never looked in a mirror!
> I wonder if there is another such in any civilized
> country in the world.

Beguiled by Kilmeny, Eric sets himself the task of gradually
welcoming her into both his life and that of the outside world.
He moves slowly and gently to earn her trust—it is much like
taming a deer.

Kilmeny first appeared as a magazine serial, "Una of the
Garden," during the winter of 1908. Maud Montgomery length-
ened it at the insistence of her publishers, L. C. Page. She
thought of the novel as "a love story with a psychological
interest." (*The Selected Journals of L. M. Montgomery, Volume
I: 1889–1910,* Mary Rubio and Elizabeth Waterston, editors,
Oxford University Press, Toronto, 1985.) It became her third
published book.

On November 29, 1910, Montgomery wrote in her diary
(*Journals, Volume II: 1910–1921,* Toronto, 1987),

> I had finished my book "The Story Girl." I was sorry
> to finish it. Never, not even when I finished with
> *Anne,* had I laid down my pen and taken farewell of
> my characters with more regret. I consider "The Story
> Girl" the best piece of work I have yet done. . . . It
> is an idyl of childhood on an old P.E. Island farm.
> . . . I have written it from sheer love of it . . . . up
> there by the window of my dear white room.

In *The Story Girl,* the author dealt with one of the themes she loved best—the enduring presence of the past in the lives of those living now, achieved through the power of story. Montgomery's deep feeling is clearly shown in her description of the orchard planted by the Story Girl's grandfather sixty years before,

> . . . in his mind [Grandfather King] had a vision of the years to be . . . great, leafy avenues of wide-spreading trees laden with fruit to gladden the eyes of children and grandchildren yet unborn.
> It was a vision to develop slowly into fulfillment. Grandfather King was in no hurry. He did not set his whole orchard out at once, for he wished it to grow with his life and history. . . .

"An orchard dies hard." And it is also in an orchard, this one long-neglected, that Eric Marshall first hears the "elusive, haunting" melody Kilmeny plays,

> . . . it had in it . . . all the soul of the old laughter and song and tears and gladness and sobs 'the orchard had ever known in the lost years

Unlike many children living elsewhere today, the youngsters of Prince Edward Island dwell among their roots, with their ancestors a vivid presence in their lives. With her mother dead and her father absent, Maud Montgomery herself maintained a sense of connectedness with her family by absorbing the stories told by and about her relatives and neighbors. She must have learned quickly that stories are hidden in each of us, no matter how simple we may appear to be. When the Story Girl tells the tale of the Sighing Reed, she speaks of a slender, brown reed, ignored by all, that yearns to make the music of the birds and the wind:

> Who would ever look for music in it, a plain, brown, unbeautiful thing?

More "unbeautiful" still is the Story Girl's friend, Jasper

Dale, the "Awkward Man," who, as his nickname implies, is gangling and clumsy. Yet he creates beauty, not with musical notes or the expression of his voice, but from the stuff of real life. He summons up a real person through the power of story expressed with the force of his "strange, almost mystical love," much as Aladdin might have called up the genie.

Paradoxically, the Awkward Man is able to change reality because he lives in the reality of his own dreams. He gains the fulfillment of love, without encountering the risks of love. And, just so, the Story Girl and Kilmeny do not often take risks in their art—they are almost always easily able to express their deepest feelings. Also, Sara and Kilmeny achieve the quintessential fantasy of many aspiring artists: they do not have to struggle to perfect either their art or their skills. Maud Montgomery, enduring years of physical and emotional isolation, both as schoolteacher and, later, as sole companion of her widowed grandmother, may be forgiven this wish-fulfillment.

It was also during these years of distress, as the author struggled to write, and to write well, that there grew in her an empathy for all those people who do not "fit in," those who face the dark side of human nature. Peter, the hired boy in *The Story Girl,* says, ". . . you oughtn't to believe anything just 'cause it would be more comfortable." Peg Bowen, suspected by many of being a witch, says, "Folks is too ready to call other folks crazy." And Kilmeny, too, has experienced pain,

> It is so dreadful to believe one is ugly. You get used
> to everything else, but you never get used to that.

Perhaps we hear the author's voice as she encountered her grandmother's censure. Maud may have transformed some of the desperate quality of her yearning to escape the confines of her own life into Peg's half-crazed outburst,

> "Do you hear the wind?" she asked in a thrilling
> whisper. "What is the wind? What is the wind. . . .
> I *am* afraid of it . . . When the blasts come like that
> I want to crouch down and hide me. But I can tell
> you one thing about the wind—it's the only free thing
> in the world—*the—only—free—thing.* Everything else
> is subject to some law, but the wind is free."

But Maud found freedom as well as sanctuary in her many walks through the forest. Sara's father speaks of the woods,

> When we can really feel its wild heart beating against ours its subtle life will steal into our veins and make us its own forever.

As stories mix with one's soul, like water and wine, to become part of one forever, so, too, does the spirit of nature. In *The Golden Road,* Maud writes of an "exquisite night . . . a frosty, starry, lyric of light," during which one might dream,

> feeling all the while through one's sleep the soft splendour and radiance of the white moon-world outside, as one hears soft, far-away music sounding through the thoughts and words that are born of it.

But the Story Girl's meek cousin Cecily

> dreamed that night that she saw three full moons in the sky, and wakened up crying with the horror of it.

Surrounded by stories of their past, the teenagers are led to ponder the nature of death. Walking by a graveyard at night, the Story Girl asks her cousin,

> Are you frightened to pass it, Bev?" "No . . . but I have a queer feeling." "So have I. But it isn't fear. . . . I feel as if something was reaching out of the graveyard to hold me—something that wanted life— I don't like it. . . . But isn't it strange to think of all the dead people in there who were once alive like you and me. I don't feel as if I could ever die. Do you?"

The youngsters are able to bear the idea of death just so long, says the cousin, as after death "our little identities remain unchanged." It is the author at her most ironic.

And stories can defeat death. Indeed, the strongest character in *The Story Girl* novels is Time. As one of Sara's adult friends says, there are

> people who are not soon forgotten, whose personality
> seems to linger about the scenes of their lives long
> after they have passed away.

The exhilarating experiences of the Story Girl's tale-telling are imbued with traces of her ancestors, whether they seem to haunt the places in which she tells or whether they be her heroes and heroines.

Storytelling makes the moment become substantial. Tales told in an orchard or a field capture time's transience, creating a memory from those fleeting, changeable moods of nature which often mirror our own feelings and states of mind. Through the Story Girl's artistry, it all comes together: the changing play of light and shadow in field and forest, the intriguing characters of her forebears, and the truth of her own transformation into these characters. Her tale-telling is a gift to her listeners of their present as well as their past, for these impelling moments when she works her magic will always live in their memories, together with the past of which she tells. And Lucy Maud Montgomery's implied questions linger with us, too, after we have put down her books—Whom do we remember? Do we leave stories? Who will remember us?

ELLEN S. SHAPIRO

Brooklyn, New York
1990

ABOUT THE AUTHOR

Lucy Maud Montgomery, best known for her novels about Anne of Green Gables, was a prolific writer who also penned portraits of other engaging heroines on the verge of young womanhood. The novels which comprise this volume—*The Story Girl;* its sequel *The Golden Road;* and *Kilmeny of the Orchard,* all published early in this century—are the stories of such young adults, as are the Emily, Pat, Marigold, and Jane books that the author also wrote. L. M. Montgomery also published numerous poems and short stories, as well as other novels.

Born in 1874 in a small village in Prince Edward Island, Canada, and sent to live nearby with her strict, duty-bound maternal grandparents when her mother died less than two years later, Maud (as she preferred to be called) did not have consistent contact with her father. At the age of nine, she turned to journal writing to express what was most important to her, and she continued this pattern for the remainder of her life.

Maud juggled the demands of her sense of duty with her desire to write. She spent three years as an Island schoolteacher, and also worked for nearly a year on a newspaper in Halifax, Nova Scotia. But she returned to her grandmother's home upon the death of her grandfather in 1898, and lived alone with her grandmother for the bulk of the following thirteen years, struggling with her own feelings of emotional isolation. Out of this period came *Anne of Green Gables,* her first novel, published in 1908, which was an immediate and lasting success. After her grandmother died, Maud married the Reverend Ewan Macdonald, and during the remainder of her life she squeezed her writing into the exacting life of a minister's wife. The great delight of her early married life was her two sons. Maud died in 1942, deeply discouraged by both World War II and family problems, but her spunky heroines, thrilling to the wonder of nature even as they embark on sometimes impractical undertakings, have been cherished by generations of readers.

NOTES ON THE ART
AND THE TEXT

The illustrations by George Gibbs, an American painter and book illustrator, were created originally for the first editions of these stories. Gibbs was a talented and prolific artist, who not only painted many delicate frontispieces for the early series of books about Anne of Green Gables but also authored and illustrated over forty novels and historical tales, including *American Sea Fights, The Yellow Dove,* and *Tony's Wife.*

* * *

In another dimension, the publisher notes that the modern reader may be surprised to discover old-fashioned styles of punctuation and spelling in this edition, but these have been retained in order to convey the flavor of the original works, which were published early in the twentieth century.

CLAIRE BOOSS
Editor

1990

The Story Girl

TO
MY COUSIN
FREDERICA E. CAMPBELL
IN REMEMBRANCE OF OLD DAYS, OLD DREAMS,
AND OLD LAUGHTER

OVERLEAF: "AUNT OLIVIA IS VERY PRETTY . . . JUST LIKE A PANSY—ALL VELVETY AND PURPLY AND GOLDY."

CHAPTER 1

THE HOME OF OUR FATHERS

"I DO like a road, because you can be always wondering what is at the end of it."

The Story Girl said that once upon a time. Felix and I, on the May morning when we left Toronto for Prince Edward Island, had not then heard her say it, and, indeed, were but barely aware of the existence of such a person as the Story Girl. We did not know her at all under that name. We knew only that a cousin, Sara Stanley, whose mother, our Aunt Felicity, was dead, was living down on the Island with Uncle Roger and Aunt Olivia King, on a farm adjoining the old King homestead in Carlisle. We supposed we should get acquainted with her when we reached there, and we had an idea, from Aunt Olivia's letters to father, that she would be quite a jolly creature. Further than that we did not think about her. We were more interested in Felicity and Cecily and Dan, who lived on the homestead and would therefore be our roofmates for a season.

But the spirit of the Story Girl's yet unuttered remark was thrilling in our hearts that morning, as the train pulled out of Toronto. We were faring forth on a long road; and, though we had some idea what would be at the end of it, there was enough

3

glamour of the unknown about it to lend a wonderful charm to our speculations concerning it.

We were delighted at the thought of seeing father's old home, and living among the haunts of his boyhood. He had talked so much to us about it, and described its scenes so often and so minutely, that he had inspired us with some of his own deep-seated affection for it—an affection that had never waned in all his years of exile. We had a vague feeling that we, somehow, belonged there, in that cradle of our family, though we had never seen it. We had always looked forward eagerly to the promised day when father would take us "down home," to the old house with the spruces behind it and the famous "King orchard" before it—when we might ramble in "Uncle Stephen's Walk," drink from the deep well with the Chinese roof over it, stand on "the Pulpit Stone," and eat apples from our "birthday trees."

The time had come sooner than we had dared to hope; but father could not take us after all. His firm asked him to go to Rio de Janeiro that spring to take charge of their new branch there. It was too good a chance to lose, for father was a poor man and it meant promotion and increase of salary; but it also meant the temporary breaking up of our home. Our mother had died before either of us was old enough to remember her; father could not take us to Rio de Janeiro. In the end he decided to send us to Uncle Alec and Aunt Janet down on the homestead; and our housekeeper, who belonged to the Island and was now returning to it, took charge of us on the journey. I fear she had an anxious trip of it, poor woman! She was constantly in a quite justifiable terror lest we should be lost or killed; she must have felt great relief when she reached Charlottetown and handed us over to the keeping of Uncle Alec. Indeed, she said as much.

"The fat one isn't so bad. He isn't so quick to move and get out of your sight while you're winking as the thin one. But the only safe way to travel with those young ones would be to have 'em both tied to you with a short rope—a *mighty* short rope."

"The fat one" was Felix, who was very sensitive about his plumpness. He was always taking exercises to make him thin, with the dismal result that he became fatter all the time. He vowed that he didn't care; but he *did* care terribly, and he glowered at Mrs. MacLaren in a most undutiful fashion. He had never liked her since the day she had told him he would soon be as broad as he was long.

For my own part, I was rather sorry to see her going; and she cried over us and wished us well; but we had forgotten all about her by the time we reached the open country, driving along, one on either side of Uncle Alec, whom we loved from the moment we saw him. He was a small man, with thin, delicate features, a close-clipped gray beard, and large, tired, blue eyes—father's eyes over again. We knew that Uncle Alec was fond of children and was heart-glad to welcome "Alan's boys." We felt at home with him, and were not afraid to ask him questions on any subject that came uppermost in our minds. We became very good friends with him on that twenty-four mile drive.

Much to our disappointment it was dark when we reached Carlisle—too dark to see anything very distinctly, as we drove up the lane of the old King homestead on the hill. Behind us a young moon was hanging over southwestern meadows of spring-time peace, but all about us were the soft, moist shadows of a May night. We peered eagerly through the gloom.

"There's the big willow, Bev," whispered Felix excitedly, as we turned in at the gate.

There it was, in truth—the tree Grandfather King had planted when he returned one evening from ploughing in the brook field and stuck the willow switch he had used all day in the soft soil by the gate.

It had taken root and grown; our father and our uncles and aunts had played in its shadow; and now it was a massive thing, with a huge girth of trunk and great spreading boughs, each of them as large as a tree in itself.

"I'm going to climb it tomorrow," I said joyfully.

Off to the right was a dim, branching place which we knew was the orchard; and on our left, among sibilant spruces and firs, was the old, whitewashed house—from which presently a light gleamed through an open door, and Aunt Janet, a big, bustling, sonsy woman, with full-blown peony cheeks, came to welcome us.

Soon after we were at supper in the kitchen, with its low,

dark, raftered ceiling from which substantial hams and flitches of bacon were hanging. Everything was just as father had described it. We felt that we had come home, leaving exile behind us.

Felicity, Cecily, and Dan were sitting opposite us, staring at us when they thought we would be too busy eating to see them. We tried to stare at them when *they* were eating; and as a result we were always catching each other at it and feeling cheap and embarrassed.

Dan was the oldest; he was my age—thirteen. He was a lean, freckled fellow with rather long, lank, brown hair and the shapely King nose. We recognized it at once. His mouth was his own, however, for it was like to no mouth on either the King or the Ward side; and nobody would have been anxious to claim it, for it was an undeniably ugly one—long and narrow and twisted. But it could grin in friendly fashion, and both Felix and I felt that we were going to like Dan.

Felicity was twelve. She had been called after Aunt Felicity, who was the twin sister of Uncle Felix. Aunt Felicity and Uncle Felix, as father had often told us, had died on the same day, far apart, and were buried side by side in the old Carlisle graveyard.

We had known, from Aunt Olivia's letters, that Felicity was the beauty of the connection, and we had been curious to see her on that account. She fully justified our expectations. She was plump and dimpled, with big, dark-blue, heavy-lidded eyes, soft, feathery, golden curls, and a pink and white skin—"the King complexion." The Kings were noted for their noses and complexion. Felicity had also delightful hands and wrists. At every turn of them a dimple showed itself. It was a pleasure to wonder what her elbows must be like.

She was very nicely dressed in a pink print and a frilled muslin apron; and we understood, from something Dan said, that she had "dressed up" in honour of our coming. This made us feel quite important. So far as we knew, no feminine creature had ever gone to the pains of dressing up on our account before.

Cecily, who was eleven, was pretty also—or would have been had Felicity not been there. Felicity rather took the colour from other girls. Cecily looked pale and thin beside her; but she had dainty little features, smooth brown hair of satin sheen, and mild brown eyes, with just a hint of demureness in them now and again. We remembered that Aunt Olivia had written to father that Cecily was a true Ward—she had no sense of humour. We did not know what this meant, but we thought it was not exactly complimentary.

Still, we were both inclined to think we would like Cecily better than Felicity. To be sure, Felicity was a stunning beauty. But, with the swift and unerring intuition of childhood, which feels in a moment what it sometimes takes maturity much time to perceive, we realized that she was rather too well aware of her good looks. In brief, we saw that Felicity was vain.

"It's a wonder the Story Girl isn't over to see you," said Uncle Alec. "She's been quite wild with excitement about your coming."

"She hasn't been very well all day," explained Cecily, "and Aunt Olivia wouldn't let her come out in the night air. She made her go to bed instead. The Story Girl was awfully disappointed."

"Who is the Story Girl?" asked Felix.

"Oh, Sara—Sara Stanley. We call her the Story Girl partly because she's such a hand to tell stories—oh, I can't begin to describe it—and partly because Sara Ray, who lives at the foot of the hill, often comes up to play with us, and it is awkward to have two girls of the same name in the same crowd. Besides, Sara Stanley doesn't like her name and she'd rather be called the Story Girl."

Dan, speaking for the first time, rather sheepishly volunteered the information that Peter had also been intending to come over but had to go home to take some flour to his mother instead.

"Peter?" I questioned. I had never heard of any Peter.

"He is your Uncle Roger's handy boy," said Uncle Alec. "His name is Peter Craig, and he is a real smart little chap. But he's got his share of mischief, that same lad."

"He wants to be Felicity's beau," said Dan slyly.

"Don't talk silly nonsense, Dan," said Aunt Janet severely.

Felicity tossed her golden head and shot an unsisterly glance at Dan.

"I wouldn't be very likely to have a hired boy for a beau," she observed.

We saw that her anger was real, not affected. Evidently Peter was not an admirer of whom Felicity was proud.

We were very hungry boys; and when we had eaten all we could—and oh, what suppers Aunt Janet always spread!—we discovered that we were very tired also—too tired to go out and explore our ancestral domains, as we would have liked to do, despite the dark.

We were quite willing to go to bed; and presently we found ourselves tucked away upstairs in the very room, looking out eastward into the spruce grove, which father had once occupied. Dan shared it with us, sleeping in a bed of his own in the opposite corner. The sheets and pillow-slips were fragrant with lavender, and one of Grandmother King's noted patchwork quilts was over us. The window was open and we heard the frogs singing down in the swamp of the brook meadow. We had heard frogs sing in Ontario, of course; but certainly the Prince Edward Island frogs were more tuneful and mellow. Or was it simply the glamour of old family traditions and tales which was over us, lending its magic to all sights and sounds around us? This was home—father's home—our home! We had never lived long enough in any one house to develop a feeling of affection for it; but here, under the roof-tree built by Great-Grandfather King ninety years ago, that feeling swept into our boyish hearts and souls like a flood of living sweetness and tenderness.

"Just think, those are the very frogs father listened to when he was a little boy," whispered Felix.

"They can hardly be the *same* frogs," I objected doubtfully, not feeling very certain about the possible longevity of frogs. "It's twenty years since father left home."

"Well, they're the descendants of the frogs he heard," said Felix, "and they're singing in the same swamp. That's near enough."

Our door was open and in their room across the narrow hall the girls were preparing for bed, and talking rather more loudly than they might have done had they realized how far their sweet, shrill voices carried.

"What do you think of the boys?" asked Cecily.

"Beverley is handsome, but Felix is too fat," answered Felicity promptly.

Felix twitched the quilt rather viciously and grunted. But I began to think I would like Felicity. It might not be altogether her fault that she was vain. How could she help it when she looked in the mirror?

"I think they're both nice and nice looking," said Cecily. Dear little soul!

"I wonder what the Story Girl will think of them," said Felicity, as if, after all, that was the main thing.

Somehow, we, too, felt that it was. We felt that if the Story Girl did not approve of us it made little difference who else did or did not.

"I wonder if the Story Girl is pretty," said Felix aloud.

"No, she isn't," said Dan instantly, from across the room. "But you'll think she is while she's talking to you. Everybody does. It's only when you go away from her that you find out she isn't a bit pretty after all."

The girls' door shut with a bang. Silence fell over the house. We drifted into the land of sleep, wondering if the Story Girl would like us.

--------------- C H A P T E R 2 ---------------

A QUEEN OF HEARTS

I WAKENED shortly after sunrise. The pale May sunshine was showering through the spruces, and a chill, inspiring wind was tossing the boughs about.

"Felix, wake up," I whispered, shaking him.

"What's the matter?" he murmured reluctantly.

"It's morning. Let's get up and go down and out. I can't wait another minute to see the places father has told us of."

We slipped out of bed and dressed, without arousing Dan, who was still slumbering soundly, his mouth wide open, and his bed-clothes kicked off on the floor. I had hard work to keep Felix from trying to see if he could "shy" a marble into that tempting open mouth. I told him it would waken Dan, who would then likely insist on getting up and accompanying us, and it would be so much nicer to go by ourselves for the first time.

Everything was very still as we crept downstairs. Out in the kitchen we heard some one, presumably Uncle Alec, lighting the fire; but the heart of the house had not yet begun to beat for the day.

We paused a moment in the hall to look at the big "Grandfather" clock. It was not going, but it seemed like an old, familiar acquaintance to us, with the gilt balls on its three peaks; the little dial and pointer which would indicate the changes of the moon, and the very dent in its wooden door which father had made when he was a boy, by kicking it in a fit of naughtiness.

Then we opened the front door and stepped out, rapture swelling in our bosoms. There was a rare breeze from the south blowing to meet us; the shadows of the spruces were long and clear-cut; the exquisite skies of early morning, blue and wind-winnowed, were over us; away to the west, beyond the brook field, was a long valley and a hill purple with firs and laced with still leafless beeches and maples.

Behind the house was a grove of fir and spruce, a dim, cool place where the winds were fond of purring and where there was always a resinous, woodsy odour. On the further side of it was a thick plantation of slender silver birches and whispering poplars; and beyond it was Uncle Roger's house.

Right before us, girt about with its trim spruce hedge, was the famous King orchard, the history of which was woven into our earliest recollections. We knew all about it, from father's descriptions, and in fancy we had roamed in it many a time and oft.

It was now nearly sixty years since it had had its beginning, when Grandfather King brought his bride home. Before the wedding he had fenced off the big south meadow that sloped to the sun; it was the finest, most fertile field on the farm, and the neighbours told young Abraham King that he would raise many a fine crop of wheat in that meadow. Abraham King smiled and, being a man of few words, said nothing; but in his mind he had a vision of the years to be, and in that vision he saw, not rippling acres of harvest gold, but great, leafy avenues of wide-spreading trees laden with fruit to gladden the eyes of children and grandchildren yet unborn.

It was a vision to develop slowly into fulfilment. Grandfather King was in no hurry. He did not set his whole orchard out at once, for he wished it to grow with his life and history, and be bound up with all of good and joy that should come to his household. So the morning after he had brought his young wife home they went together to the south meadow and planted their bridal trees. These trees were no longer living; but they had been when father was a boy, and every spring bedecked themselves in blossom as delicately tinted as Elizabeth King's face when she walked through the old south meadow in the morn of her life and love.

When a son was born to Abraham and Elizabeth a tree was planted in the orchard for him. They had fourteen children in all, and each child had its "birth tree." Every family festival was commemorated in like fashion, and every beloved visitor who spent a night under their roof was expected to plant a tree in the orchard. So it came to pass that every tree in it was a fair green monument to some love or delight of the vanished years. And each grandchild had its tree, there, also, set out by grandfather when the tidings of its birth reached him; not always an apple tree—perhaps it was a plum, or cherry or pear. But it was always known by the name of the person for whom, or by whom, it was planted; and Felix and I knew as much about "Aunt Felicity's pears," and "Aunt Julia's cherries," and "Uncle Alec's apples," and the "Rev. Mr. Scott's plums," as if we had been born and bred among them.

And now we had come to the orchard; it was before us; we had only to open that little whitewashed gate in the hedge and we might find ourselves in its storied domain. But before we reached the gate we glanced to our left, along the grassy, spruce-bordered lane which led over to Uncle Roger's; and at the entrance of that lane we saw a girl standing, with a gray cat at her feet. She lifted her hand and beckoned blithely to us; and, the orchard forgotten, we followed her summons. For we knew that this must be the Story Girl; and in that gay and graceful gesture was an allurement not to be gainsaid or denied.

We looked at her as we drew near with such interest that we forgot to feel shy. No, she was not pretty. She was tall for her fourteen years, slim and straight; around her long, white face—rather too long and too white—fell sleek, dark-brown curls, tied above either ear with rosettes of scarlet ribbon. Her large, curving mouth was as red as a poppy, and she had brilliant, almond-shaped, hazel eyes; but we did not think her pretty.

Then she spoke; she said,

"Good morning."

Never had we heard a voice like hers. Never, in all my life since, have I heard such a voice. I cannot describe it. I might say it was clear; I might say it was sweet; I might say it was vibrant and far-reaching and bell-like; all this would be true, but it would give you no real idea of the peculiar quality which made the Story Girl's voice what it was.

If voices had colour, hers would have been like a rainbow. It made words *live*. Whatever she said became a breathing entity, not a mere verbal statement or utterance. Felix and I were too young to understand or analyze the impression it made upon us; but we instantly felt at her greeting that it *was* a good morning—a surpassingly good morning—the very best morning that had ever happened in this most excellent of worlds.

"You are Felix and Beverley," she went on, shaking our hands with an air of frank comradeship, which was very different from the shy, feminine advances of Felicity and Cecily. From that moment we were as good friends as if we had known each other for a hundred years. "I am glad to see you. I was so disappointed I couldn't go over last night. I got up early this morning, though, for I felt sure you would be up early, too, and that you'd like to have me tell you about things. I can tell things so much better than Felicity or Cecily. Do you think Felicity is *very* pretty?"

"She's the prettiest girl I ever saw," I said enthusiastically, remembering that Felicity had called me handsome.

"The boys all think so," said the Story Girl, not, I fancied, quite well pleased. "And I suppose she is. She is a splendid cook, too, though she is only twelve. *I* can't cook. I am trying to learn, but I don't make much progress. Aunt Olivia says I haven't enough natural gumption ever to be a cook; but I'd love to be able to make as good cakes and pies as Felicity can make. But then, Felicity is stupid. It's not illnatured of me to say that. It's just the truth, and you'd soon find it out for yourselves. I like Felicity very well, but she *is* stupid. Cecily is ever so much cleverer. Cecily's a dear. So is Uncle Alec; and Aunt Janet is pretty nice, too."

"What is Aunt Olivia like?" asked Felix.

"Aunt Olivia is very pretty. She is just like a pansy—all velvety and purply and goldy."

Felix and I *saw,* somewhere inside of our heads, a velvet and purple and gold pansy-woman, just as the Story Girl spoke.

"But is she *nice?"* I asked. That was the main question about grown-ups. Their looks mattered little to us.

"She is lovely. But she is twenty-nine, you know. That's pretty old. She doesn't bother me much. Aunt Janet says that I'd have no bringing up at all, if it wasn't for her. Aunt Olivia says children should just be let *come* up—that everything else is settled for them long before they are born. I don't understand that. Do you?"

No, we did not. But it was our experience that grown-ups had a habit of saying things hard to understand.

"What is Uncle Roger like?" was our next question.

"Well, *I* like Uncle Roger," said the Story Girl meditatively. "He is big and jolly. But he teases people too much. You ask him a serious question and you get a ridiculous answer. He hardly ever scolds or gets cross, though, and *that* is something. He is an old bachelor."

"Doesn't he ever mean to get married?" asked Felix.

"I don't know. Aunt Olivia wishes he would, because she's tired keeping house for him, and she wants to go to Aunt Julia in California. But she says he'll never get married, because he is looking for perfection, and when he finds her she won't have *him.*"

By this time we were all sitting down on the gnarled roots of the spruces, and the big gray cat came over and made friends with us. He was a lordly animal, with a silver-gray coat beautifully marked with darker stripes. With such colouring most cats would have had white or silver feet; but he had four black paws and a black nose. Such points gave him an air of distinction, and marked him out as quite different from the common or garden variety of cats. He seemed to be a cat with a tolerably good opinion of himself, and his response to our advances was slightly tinged with condescension.

"This isn't Topsy, is it?" I asked. I knew at once that the question was a foolish one. Topsy, the cat of which father had talked, had flourished thirty years before, and all her nine lives could scarcely have lasted so long.

"No, but it is Topsy's great-great-great-great-grandson," said the Story Girl gravely. "His name is Paddy and he is my own particular cat. We have barn cats, but Paddy never associates with them. I am very good friends with all cats. They are so sleek and comfortable and dignified. And it is so easy to make them happy. Oh, I'm so glad you boys have come to live here. Nothing ever happens here, except days, so we have to make our own good times. We were short of boys before—only Dan and Peter to four girls."

"Four girls? Oh, yes, Sara Ray. Felicity mentioned her. What is she like? Where does she live?"

"Just down the hill. You can't see the house for the spruce bush. Sara is a nice girl. She's only eleven, and her mother is dreadfully strict. She never allows Sara to read a single story. *Just* you fancy! Sara's conscience is always troubling her for doing things she's sure her mother won't approve, but it never prevents her from doing them. It only spoils her fun. Uncle Roger says that a mother who won't let you do anything, and a conscience that won't let you enjoy anything is an awful combination, and he doesn't wonder Sara is pale and thin and nervous. But, between you and me, I believe the real reason is that her mother doesn't give her half enough to eat. Not that she's mean, you know—but she thinks it isn't healthy for children to eat much, or anything but certain things. Isn't it fortunate we weren't born into that sort of a family?"

"I think it's awful lucky we were all born into the same family," Felix remarked.

"Isn't it? I've often thought so. And I've often thought what a dreadful thing it would have been if Grandfather and Grandmother King had never got married to each other. I don't suppose there would have been a single one of us children here at all; or if we were, we would be part somebody else and that would be almost as bad. When I think it all over I can't feel too thankful that Grandfather and Grandmother King happened to marry each other, when there were so many other people they might have married."

Felix and I shivered. We felt suddenly that we had escaped a dreadful danger—the danger of having been born somebody else. But it took the Story Girl to make us realize just how dreadful it was and what a terrible risk we had run years before we, or our parents either, had existed.

"Who lives over there?" I asked, pointing to a house across the fields.

"Oh, that belongs to the Awkward Man. His name is Jasper Dale, but everybody calls him the Awkward Man. And they do say he writes poetry. He calls his place Golden Milestone. I know why, because I've read Longfellow's poems. He never goes into society because he is so awkward. The girls laugh at him and he doesn't like it. I know a story about him and I'll tell it to you sometime."

"And who lives in that other house?" asked Felix, looking over the westering valley where a little gray roof was visible among the trees.

"Old Peg Bowen. She's very queer. She lives there with a lot of pet animals in winter, and in summer she roams over the country and begs her meals. They say she is crazy. People have always tried to frighten us children into good behaviour by telling us that Peg Bowen would catch us if we didn't behave. I'm not so frightened of her as I once was, but I don't think I would like to be caught by her. Sara Ray is dreadfully scared of her. Peter Craig says she is a witch and that he bets she's at the bottom of it when the butter won't come. But I don't believe *that*. Witches are so scarce nowadays. There may be some somewhere in the world, but it's not likely there are any here right in Prince Edward Island. They used to be very plenty long ago. I know some splendid witch stories I'll tell you some day. They'll just make your blood freeze in your veins."

We hadn't a doubt of it. If anybody could freeze the blood in our veins this girl with the wonderful voice could. But it was a May morning, and our young blood was running blithely in our veins. We suggested that a visit to the orchard would be more agreeable.

"All right. I know stories about it, too," she said, as we walked across the yard, followed by Paddy of the waving tail. "Oh, aren't you glad it is spring? The beauty of winter is that it makes you appreciate spring."

The latch of the gate clicked under the Story Girl's hand, and the next moment we were in the King orchard.

CHAPTER 3

LEGENDS OF THE OLD ORCHARD

Outside of the orchard the grass was only beginning to grow green; but here, sheltered by the spruce hedges from uncertain winds and sloping to southern suns, it was already like a wonderful velvet carpet; the leaves on the trees were beginning to come out in woolly, grayish clusters; and there were purple-pencilled white violets at the base of the Pulpit Stone.

"It's all just as father described it," said Felix with a blissful sigh, "and there's the well with the Chinese roof."

We hurried over to it, treading on the spears of mint that were beginning to shoot up about it. It was a very deep well, and the curb was of rough, undressed stones. Over it, the queer, pagoda-like roof, built by Uncle Stephen on his return from a voyage to China, was covered with yet leafless vines.

"It's so pretty when the vines leaf out and hang down in long festoons," said the Story Girl. "The birds build their nests in it. A pair of wild canaries come here every summer. And ferns grow out between the stones of the well as far down as you can see. The water is lovely. Uncle Edward preached his finest sermon about the Bethlehem well where David's soldiers went to get him water, and he illustrated it by describing his old well at the homestead—this very well—and how in foreign lands he had longed for its sparkling water. So you see it is quite famous."

"There's a cup just like the one that used to be here in

father's time," exclaimed Felix, pointing to an old-fashioned shallow cup of clouded blue ware on a little shelf inside the curb.

"It is the very same cup," said the Story Girl impressively. "Isn't it an amazing thing? That cup has been here for forty years, and hundreds of people have drunk from it, and it has never been broken. Aunt Julia dropped it down the well once, but they fished it up, not hurt a bit except for that little nick in the rim. *I* think it is bound up with the fortunes of the King family, like the Luck of Edenhall in Longfellow's poem. It is the last cup of Grandmother King's second best set. Her best set is still complete. Aunt Olivia has it. You must get her to show it to you. It's so pretty, with red berries all over it, and the funniest little pot-bellied cream jug. Aunt Olivia never uses it except on a family anniversary."

We took a drink from the blue cup and then went to find our birthday trees. We were rather disappointed to find them quite large, sturdy ones. It seemed to us that they should still be in the sapling stage corresponding to our boyhood.

"Your apples are lovely to eat," the Story Girl said to me, "but Felix's are only good for pies. Those two big trees behind them are the twins' trees—my mother and Uncle Felix, you know. The apples are so dead sweet that nobody but us children and the French boys can eat them. And that tall, slender tree over there, with the branches all growing straight up, is a seedling that came up of itself, and *nobody* can eat its apples, they are so sour and bitter. Even the pigs won't eat them. Aunt Janet tried to make pies of them once, because she said she hated to see them going to waste. But she never tried again. She said it was better to waste apples alone than apples and sugar too. And then she tried giving them away to the French hired men, but they wouldn't even carry them home."

The Story Girl's words fell on the morning air like pearls and diamonds. Even her prepositions and conjunctions had untold charm, hinting at mystery and laughter and magic bound up in everything she mentioned. Apple pies and sour seedlings and pigs became straightway invested with a glamour of romance.

"I like to hear you talk," said Felix in his grave, stodgy way.

"Everybody does," said the Story Girl coolly. "I'm glad you

like the way I talk. But I want you to like *me*, too—*as well* as you like Felicity and Cecily. Not *better*. I wanted that once but I've got over it. I found out in Sunday School, the day the minister taught our class, that it was selfish. But I want you to like me *as well*."

"Well, *I* will, for one," said Felix emphatically. I think he was remembering that Felicity had called him fat.

Cecily now joined us. It appeared that it was Felicity's morning to help prepare breakfast, therefore she could not come. We all went to Uncle Stephen's Walk.

This was a double row of apple trees, running down the western side of the orchard. Uncle Stephen was the first born of Abraham and Elizabeth King. He had none of grandfather's abiding love for woods and meadows and the kindly ways of the warm red earth. Grandmother King had been a Ward, and in Uncle Stephen the blood of that seafaring race claimed its own. To sea he must go, despite the pleadings and tears of a reluctant mother; and it was from the sea he came to set out his avenue in the orchard with trees brought from a foreign land.

Then he sailed away again—and the ship was never heard of more. The gray first came in grandmother's brown hair in those months of waiting. Then, for the first time, the orchard heard the sound of weeping and was consecrated by a sorrow.

"When the blossoms come out it's wonderful to walk here," said the Story Girl. "It's like a dream of fairyland—as if you were walking in a king's palace. The apples are delicious, and in winter it's a splendid place for coasting."

From the Walk we went to the Pulpit Stone—a huge gray boulder, as high as a man's head, in the southeastern corner. It was straight and smooth in front, but sloped down in natural steps behind, with a ledge midway on which one could stand. It had played an important part in the games of our uncles and aunts, being fortified castle, Indian ambush, throne, pulpit, or concert platform, as occasion required. Uncle Edward had preached his first sermon at the age of eight from that old gray boulder; and Aunt Julia, whose voice was to delight thousands, sang her earliest madrigals there.

The Story Girl mounted to the ledge, sat on the rim, and

looked at us. Pat sat gravely at its base and daintily washed his face with his black paws.

"Now for your stories about the orchard," said I.

"There are two important ones," said the Story Girl. "The story of the Poet Who Was Kissed, and the Tale of the Family Ghost. Which one shall I tell?"

"Tell them both," said Felix greedily, "but tell the ghost one first."

"I don't know." The Story Girl looked dubious. "That sort of story ought to be told in the twilight among the shadows. Then it would frighten the souls out of your bodies."

We thought it might be more agreeable not to have the souls frightened out of our bodies, and we voted for the Family Ghost.

"Ghost stories are more comfortable in daytime," said Felix.

The Story Girl began it and we listened avidly. Cecily, who had heard it many times before, listened just as eagerly as we did. She declared to me afterwards that no matter how often the Story Girl told a story it always seemed as new and exciting as if you had just heard it for the first time.

"Long, long ago," began the Story Girl, her voice giving us an impression of remote antiquity, "even before Grandfather King was born, an orphan cousin of his lived here with his parents. Her name was Emily King. She was very small and very sweet. She had soft brown eyes that were too timid to look straight at anybody—like Cecily's there—and long, sleek, brown curls—like mine; and she had a tiny birthmark like a pink butterfly on one cheek—right here.

"Of course, there was no orchard here then. It was just a field; but there was a clump of white birches in it, right where that big, spreading tree of Uncle Alec's is now, and Emily liked to sit among the ferns under the birches and read or sew. She had a lover. His name was Malcolm Ward and he was as handsome as a prince. She loved him with all her heart and he loved her the same; but they had never spoken about it. They used to meet under the birches and talk about everything except love. One day he told her he was coming the next day to ask *a very important question,* and he wanted to find her under the birches when he came. Emily promised to meet him there. I am sure she stayed awake that night, thinking about it, and wondering what the important question would be, although she knew perfectly well. *I* would have. And the next day she dressed herself beautifully in her best pale blue muslin and sleeked her curls and went smiling to the birches. And while she was waiting there, thinking such lovely thoughts, a neighbour's boy came running up—a boy who didn't know about her romance—and cried out that Malcolm Ward had been killed by his gun going off accidentally. Emily just put her hands to her heart—so—and fell, all white and broken among the ferns. And when she came back to life she never cried or lamented. She was *changed.* She was never, never like herself again; and she was never contented unless she was dressed in her blue muslin and waiting under the birches. She got paler and paler every day, but the pink butterfly grew redder, until it looked just like a stain of blood on her white cheek. When the winter came she died. But next spring"—the Story Girl dropped her voice to a whisper that was as audible and thrilling as her louder tones—"people began to tell that Emily was sometimes seen waiting under the birches still. Nobody knew just who told it first. But more than one person saw her. Grandfather saw her when he was a little boy. And my mother saw her once."

"Did *you* ever see her?" asked Felix skeptically.

"No, but I shall some day, if I keep on believing in her," said the Story Girl confidently.

"*I* wouldn't like to see her. I'd be afraid," said Cecily with a shiver.

"There wouldn't be anything to be afraid of," said the Story Girl reassuringly. "It's not as if it were a strange ghost. It's our own family ghost, so of course it wouldn't hurt us."

We were not so sure of this. Ghosts were unchancy folk, even if they were our family ghosts. The Story Girl had made the tale very real to us. We were glad we had not heard it in the evening. How could we ever have got back to the house through the shadows and swaying branches of a darkening orchard? As it was, we were almost afraid to look up it, lest we should see the waiting, blue-clad Emily under Uncle Alec's tree. But all we saw was Felicity, tearing over the green sward, her curls streaming behind her in a golden cloud.

"Felicity's afraid she has missed something," remarked the Story Girl in a tone of quiet amusement. "Is your breakfast ready, Felicity, or have I time to tell the boys the Story of the Poet Who Was Kissed?"

"Breakfast is ready, but we can't have it till father is through attending to the sick cow, so you will likely have time," answered Felicity.

Felix and I couldn't keep our eyes off her. Crimson-cheeked, shining-eyed from her haste, her face was like a rose of youth. But when the Story Girl spoke, we forgot to look at Felicity.

"About ten years after Grandfather and Grandmother King were married, a young man came to visit them. He was a distant relative of grandmother's and he was a Poet. He was just beginning to be famous. He was *very* famous afterward. He came into the orchard to write a poem, and he fell asleep with his head on a bench that used to be under grandfather's tree. Then Great-Aunt Edith came into the orchard. She was not a Great-Aunt then, of course. She was only eighteen, with red lips and black, black hair and eyes. They say she was always very full of mischief. She had been away and had just come home, and she didn't know about the Poet. But when she saw him, sleeping there, she thought he was a cousin they had been expecting from Scotland. And she tiptoed up—so—and bent over—so—and kissed his cheek. Then he opened his big blue eyes and looked up into Edith's face. She blushed as red as a rose, for she knew she had done a dreadful thing. This could not be her cousin from Scotland. She knew, for he had written so to her, that he had eyes as black as her own. Edith ran away and hid; and of course she felt still worse when she found out that he was a famous poet. But he wrote one of his most beautiful poems on it afterwards and sent it to her—and it was published in one of his books."

We had *seen* it all—the sleeping genius—the roguish, red-lipped girl—the kiss dropped as lightly as a rose-petal on the sunburned cheek.

"They should have got married," said Felix.

"Well, in a book they would have, but you see this was in real life," said the Story Girl. "We sometimes act the story out. I like it when Peter plays the poet. I don't like it when Dan is the poet because he is so freckled and screws his eyes up so tight. But you can hardly ever coax Peter to be the poet—except when Felicity is Edith—and Dan is so obliging that way."

"What is Peter like?" I asked.

"Peter is splendid. His mother lives on the Markdale road and washes for a living. Peter's father ran away and left them when Peter was only three years old. He has never come back, and they don't know whether he is alive or dead. Isn't that a nice way to behave to your family? Peter has worked for his board ever since he was six. Uncle Roger sends him to school, and pays him wages in summer. We all like Peter, except Felicity."

"I like Peter well enough in his place," said Felicity primly, "but you make far too much of him, mother says. He is only a hired boy, and he hasn't been well brought up, and hasn't much education. *I* don't think you should make such an equal of him as you do."

Laughter rippled over the Story Girl's face as shadow waves go over ripe wheat before a wind.

"Peter is a real gentleman, and he is more interesting than *you* could ever be, if you were brought up and educated for a hundred years," she said.

"He can hardly write," said Felicity.

"William the Conqueror couldn't write at all," said the Story Girl crushingly.

"He never goes to church, and he never says his prayers," retorted Felicity, uncrushed.

"I do, too," said Peter himself, suddenly appearing through a little gap in the hedge. "I say my prayers sometimes."

This Peter was a slim, shapely fellow, with laughing black eyes and thick black curls. Early in the season as it was, he was barefooted. His attire consisted of a faded, gingham shirt and a scanty pair of corduroy knickerbockers; but he wore it with such an unconscious air of purple and fine linen that he seemed to be much better dressed than he really was.

"You don't pray very often," insisted Felicity.

"Well, God will be all the more likely to listen to me if I don't pester Him all the time." argued Peter.

This was rank heresy to Felicity, but the Story Girl looked as if she thought there might be something in it.

"You *never* go to church, anyhow," continued Felicity, determined not to be argued down.

"Well, I ain't going to church till I've made up my mind whether I'm going to be a Methodist or a Presbyterian. Aunt Jane was a Methodist. My mother ain't much of anything but *I* mean to be something. It's more respectable to be a Methodist or a Presbyterian, or *something,* than not to be anything. When I've settled what I'm to be I'm going to church same as you."

"That's not the same as being *born* something," said Felicity loftily.

"I think it's a good deal better to pick your own religion than have to take it just because it was what your folks had," retorted Peter.

"Now, never mind quarrelling," said Cecily. "You leave Peter alone, Felicity. Peter, this is Beverley King, and this is Felix. And we're all going to be good friends and have a lovely summer together. Think of the games we can have! But if you go squabbling you'll spoil it all. Peter, what are you going to do today?"

"Harrow the wood field and dig your Aunt Olivia's flower beds."

"Aunt Olivia and I planted the sweet peas yesterday," said the Story Girl, "and I planted a little bed of my own. I am *not* going to dig them up this year to see if they have sprouted. It is bad for them. I shall try to cultivate patience, no matter how long they are coming up."

"I am going to help mother plant the vegetable garden today," said Felicity.

"Oh, I never like the vegetable garden," said the Story Girl. "Except when I am hungry. Then I *do* like to go and look at the nice little rows of onions and beets. But I love a flower garden. I think I could be always good if I lived in a garden all the time."

"Adam and Eve lived in a garden all the time," said Felicity, "and *they* were far from being always good."

"They mightn't have kept good as long as they did if they hadn't lived in a garden," said the Story Girl.

We were now summoned to breakfast. Peter and the Story Girl slipped away through the gap, followed by Paddy, and the rest of us walked up the orchard to the house.

"Well, what do you think of the Story Girl?" asked Felicity.

"She's just fine," said Felix, enthusiastically. "I never heard anything like her to tell stories."

"She can't cook," said Felicity, "and she hasn't a good complexion. Mind you, she says she's going to be an actress when she grows up. Isn't that dreadful?"

We didn't exactly see why.

"Oh, because actresses are always wicked people," said Felicity in a shocked tone. "But I daresay the Story Girl will go and be one just as soon as she can. Her father will back her up in it. He is an artist, you know."

Evidently Felicity thought artists and actresses and all such poor trash were members one of another.

"Aunt Olivia says the Story Girl is fascinating," said Cecily.

The very adjective! Felix and I recognized its beautiful fitness at once. Yes, the Story Girl *was* fascinating and that was the final word to be said on the subject.

Dan did not come down until breakfast was half over, and Aunt Janet talked to him after a fashion which made us realize that it would be well to keep, as the piquant country phrase went, from the rough side of her tongue. But all things considered, we liked the prospect of our summer very much. Felicity to look at—the Story Girl to tell us tales of wonder—Cecily to admire us—Dan and Peter to play with—what more could reasonable fellows want?

--------- CHAPTER 4 ---------

THE WEDDING VEIL OF THE PROUD PRINCESS

WHEN WE had lived for a fortnight in Carlisle we belonged there, and the freedom of all its small fry was conferred on us. With Peter and Dan, with Felicity and Cecily and the Story Girl, with pale, gray-eyed little Sara Ray, we were boon companions. We went to school, of course; and certain home chores were assigned to each of us for the faithful performance of which we were held responsible. But we had long hours for play. Even Peter had plenty of spare time when the planting was over.

We got along very well with each other in the main, in spite of some minor differences of opinion. As for the grown-up denizens of our small world, they suited us also.

We adored Aunt Olivia; she was pretty and merry and kind; and, above all, she had mastered to perfection the rare art of letting children alone. If we kept ourselves tolerably clean, and refrained from quarrelling or talking slang, Aunt Olivia did not worry us. Aunt Janet, on the contrary, gave us so much good advice and was so constantly telling us to do this or not to do the other thing, that we could not remember half her instructions, and did not try.

Uncle Roger was, as we had been informed, quite jolly and fond of teasing. We liked him; but we had an uncomfortable feeling that the meaning of his remarks was not always that which met the ear. Sometimes we believed Uncle Roger was making fun of us, and the deadly seriousness of youth in us resented that.

To Uncle Alec we gave our warmest love. We felt that we always had a friend at court in Uncle Alec, no matter what we did or left undone. And we never had to turn *his* speeches inside out to discover their meaning.

The social life of juvenile Carlisle centred in the day and Sunday Schools. We were especially interested in our Sunday School, for we were fortunate enough to be assigned to a teacher who made our lessons so interesting that we no longer regarded Sunday School attendance as a disagreeable weekly duty; but instead looked forward to it with pleasure, and tried to carry out our teacher's gentle precepts—at least on Mondays and Tuesdays. I am afraid the remembrance grew a little dim the rest of the week.

She was also deeply interested in missions; and one talk on this subject inspired the Story Girl with a desire to do a little home missionary work on her own account. The only thing she could think of, along this line, was to persuade Peter to go to church.

Felicity did not approve of the design, and said so plainly.

"He won't know how to behave, for he's never been inside a church door in his life," she warned the Story Girl. "He'll likely do something awful, and then you'll feel ashamed and wish you'd never asked him to go, and we'll all be disgraced. It's all right to have our mite boxes for the heathen, and send missionaries to them. They're far away and we don't have to associate with them. But *I* don't want to have to sit in a pew with a hired boy."

But the Story Girl undauntedly continued to coax the reluctant Peter. It was not an easy matter. Peter did not come of a churchgoing stock; and besides, he alleged, he had not yet made up his mind whether to be a Presbyterian or a Methodist.

"It isn't a bit of difference which you are," pleaded the Story Girl. "They both go to heaven."

"But one way must be easier or better than the other, or else they'd all be one kind," argued Peter. "I want to find the easiest way. And I've got a hankering after the Methodists. My Aunt Jane was a Methodist."

"Isn't she one still?" asked Felicity pertly.

"Well, I don't know exactly. She's dead," said Peter rebukingly. "Do people go on being just the same after they're dead?"

"No, of course not. They're angels then—not Methodists or anything, but just angels. That is, if they go to heaven."

"S'posen they went to the other place?"

But Felicity's theology broke down at this point. She turned her back on Peter and walked disdainfully away.

The Story Girl returned to the main point with a new argument.

"We have such a lovely minister, Peter. He looks just like the picture of St. John father sent me, only he is old and his hair is white. I know you'd like him. And even if you are going to be a Methodist it won't hurt you to go to the Presbyterian church. The nearest Methodist church is six miles away, at Markdale, and you can't attend there just now. Go to the Presbyterian church until you're old enough to have a horse."

"But s'posen I got too fond of being Presbyterian and couldn't change if I wanted to?" objected Peter.

Altogether, the Story Girl had a hard time of it; but she persevered; and one day she came to us with the announcement that Peter had yielded.

"He's going to church with us tomorrow," she said triumphantly.

We were out in Uncle Roger's hill pasture, sitting on some smooth, round stones under a clump of birches. Behind us was an old gray fence, with violets and dandelions thick in its corners. Below us was the Carlisle valley, with its orchard-embowered homesteads, and fertile meadows. Its upper end was dim with a delicate spring mist. Winds blew up the field like wave upon wave of sweet savour—spice of bracken and balsam.

We were eating little jam "turnovers," which Felicity had made for us. Felicity's turnovers were perfection. I looked at her and wondered why it was not enough that she should be so pretty and capable of making such turnovers. If she were only more interesting! Felicity had not a particle of the nameless charm and allurement which hung about every motion of the Story Girl, and made itself manifest in her lightest word and most careless glance. Ah well, one cannot have every good gift! The Story Girl had no dimples at her slim, brown wrists.

We all enjoyed our turnovers except Sara Ray. She ate hers but she knew she should not have done so. Her mother did not approve of snacks between meals, or of jam turnovers at any time. Once, when Sara was in a brown study, I asked her what she was thinking of.

"I'm trying to think of something ma hasn't forbid," she answered with a sigh.

We were all glad to hear that Peter was going to church, except Felicity. She was full of gloomy forebodings and warnings.

"I'm surprised at you, Felicity King," said Cecily severely. "You ought to be glad that poor boy is going to get started in the right way."

"There's a great big patch on his best pair of trousers," protested Felicity.

"Well, that's better than a hole," said the Story Girl, addressing herself daintily to her turnover. "God won't notice the patch."

"No, but the Carlisle people will," retorted Felicity, in a tone which implied that what the Carlisle people thought was far more important. "And I don't believe that Peter has got a decent stocking to his name. What will you feel like if he goes to church with the skin of his legs showing through the holes, Miss Story Girl?"

"I'm not a bit afraid," said the Story Girl staunchly, "Peter knows better than that."

"Well, all I hope is that he'll wash behind his ears." said Felicity resignedly.

"How is Pat today?" asked Cecily, by way of changing the conversation.

"Pat isn't a bit better. He just mopes about the kitchen," said the Story Girl anxiously. "I went out to the barn and I saw a mouse. I had a stick in my hand and I fetched a swipe at it—so. I killed it stone dead. Then I took it in to Paddy. Will you believe it? He wouldn't even look at it. I'm so worried. Uncle Roger says he needs a dose of physic. But how is he to be made take it, that's the question. I mixed a powder in some milk and tried to pour it down his throat while Peter held him. Just look at the scratches I got! And the milk went everywhere except down Pat's throat."

"Wouldn't it be awful if—if anything happened to Pat?" whispered Cecily.

"Well, we could have a jolly funeral, you know," said Dan.

We looked at him in such horror that Dan hastened to apologize.

"I'd be awful sorry myself if Pat died. But if he *did,* we'd have to give him the right kind of a funeral," he protested. "Why, Paddy just seems like one of the family."

The Story Girl finished her turnover, and stretched herself out on the grasses, pillowing her chin in her hands and looking at the sky. She was bare headed, as usual, and her scarlet ribbon was bound filletwise about her head. She had twined freshly plucked dandelions around it and the effect was that of a crown of brilliant golden stars on her sleek, brown curls.

"Look at that long, thin, lacy cloud up there," she said. "What does it make you think of, girls?"

"A wedding veil," said Cecily.

"That is just what it is—the Wedding Veil of the Proud Princess. I know a story about it. I read it in a book. Once upon a time"—the Story Girl's eyes grew dreamy, and her accents floated away on the summer air like wind-blown rose petals—"there was a princess who was the most beautiful princess in the world, and kings from all lands came to woo her for a bride. But she was as proud as she was beautiful. She laughed all her suitors to scorn. And when her father urged her to choose one of them as her husband she drew herself up haughtily—so—"

The Story Girl sprang to her feet and for a moment we saw the proud princess of the old tale in all her scornful loveliness—

"and she said,

" 'I will not wed until a king comes who can conquer all kings. Then I shall be the wife of the king of the world and no one can hold herself higher than I.'

"So every king went to war to prove that he could conquer every one else, and there was a great deal of bloodshed and misery. But the proud princess laughed and sang, and she and her maidens worked at a wonderful lace veil which she meant to wear when the king of all kings came. It was a very beautiful veil; but her maidens whispered that a man had died and a woman's heart had broken for every stitch set in it.

"Just when a king thought he had conquered everybody some other king would come and conquer *him;* and so it went on until it did not seem likely the proud princess would ever get a husband at all. But still her pride was so great that she would not yield, even though everybody except the kings who wanted to marry her, hated her for the suffering she had caused. One day a horn was blown at the palace gate; and there was one tall man in complete armor, with his visor down, riding on a white horse. When he said he had come to marry the princess every one laughed, for he had no retinue and no beautiful apparel, and no golden crown.

" 'But I am the king who conquers all kings,' he said.

" 'You must prove it before I shall marry you,' said the proud princess. But she trembled and turned pale, for there was something in his voice that frightened her. And when he laughed, his laughter was still more dreadful.

" 'I can easily prove it, beautiful princess,' he said, 'but you must go with me to my kingdom for the proof. Marry me now; and you and I and your father and all your court will ride straightway to my kingdom; and if you are not satisfied then that I am the king who conquers all kings you may give me back my ring and return home free of me forever more.'

"It was a strange wooing and the friends of the princess begged her to refuse. But her pride whispered that it would be such a wonderful thing to be the queen of the king of the world; so she consented; and her maidens dressed her, and put on the long lace veil that had been so many years a-making. Then they were married at once, but the bridegroom never lifted his visor and no one saw his face. The proud princess held herself more proudly than ever, but she was as white as her veil. And there was no laughter or merry-making, such as should be at a wedding, and every one looked at every one else with fear in his eyes.

"After the wedding the bridegroom lifted his bride before him on his white horse, and her father and all the members of his court mounted, too, and rode after them. On and on they rode, and the skies grew darker and the wind blew and wailed, and the shades of evening came down. And just in the twilight they rode into a dark valley, filled with tombs and graves.

" 'Why have you brought me here?' cried the proud princess angrily.

" 'This is my kingdom, he answered. 'These are the tombs of the kings I have conquered. Behold me, beautiful princess. I am Death!'

"He lifted his visor. All saw his awful face. The proud princess shrieked.

" 'Come to my arms, my bride,' he cried. 'I have won you fairly. I am the king who conquers all kings!'

"He clasped her fainting form to his breast and spurred his white horse to the tombs. A tempest of rain broke over the valley and blotted them from sight. Very sadly the old king and courtiers rode home, and never, never again did human eye behold the proud princess. But when those long, white clouds sweep across the sky, the country people in the land where she lived say 'Look you, there is the Wedding Veil of the Proud Princess.' "

The weird spell of the tale rested on us for some moments after the Story Girl had finished. We had walked with her in the place of death and grown cold with the horror that chilled the heart of the poor princess. Dan presently broke the spell.

"You see it doesn't do to be too proud, Felicity," he remarked, giving her a poke. "You'd better not say too much about Peter's patches."

—————— C H A P T E R 5 ——————

PETER GOES TO CHURCH

THERE WAS no Sunday School the next afternoon, as superintendent and teachers wished to attend a communion service at Markdale. The Carlisle service was in the evening, and at sunset we were waiting at Uncle Alec's front door for Peter and the Story Girl.

None of the grown-ups were going to church. Aunt Olivia had a sick headache and Uncle Roger stayed home with her. Aunt Janet and Uncle Alec had gone to the Markdale service and had not yet returned.

Felicity and Cecily were wearing their new summer muslins for the first time—and were acutely conscious of the fact. Felicity, her pink and white face shadowed by her drooping, forget-me-not-wreathed, leghorn hat, was as beautiful as usual; but Cecily, having tortured her hair with curl papers all night, had a rampant bush of curls all about her head which quite destroyed the sweet, nun-like expression of her little features. Cecily cherished a grudge against fate because she had not been given naturally curly hair as had the other two girls. But she attained the desire of her heart on Sundays at least, and was quite well satisfied. It was impossible to convince her that the satin smooth lustre of her weekday tresses was much more becoming to her.

Presently Peter and the Story Girl appeared, and we were all more or less relieved to see that Peter looked quite respectable, despite the indisputable patch on his trousers. His face was rosy, his thick black curls were smoothly combed, and his tie was neatly bowed; but it was his legs which we scrutinized most anxiously. At first glance they seemed well enough; but closer inspection revealed something not altogether customary.

"What is the matter with your stockings, Peter?" asked Dan bluntly.

"Oh, I hadn't a pair without holes in the legs," answered Peter easily, "because ma hadn't time to darn them this week. So I put on two pairs. The holes don't come in the same places, and you'd never notice them unless you looked right close."

"Have you got a cent for collection?" demanded Felicity.

"I've got a Yankee cent. I s'pose it will do, won't it?"

Felicity shook her head vehemently.

"Oh, no, no. It may be all right to pass a Yankee cent on a store keeper or an egg peddler, but it would never do for church."

"I'll have to go without any, then," said Peter. "I haven't another cent. I only get fifty cents a week and I give it all to ma last night."

But Peter must have a cent. Felicity would have given him one herself—and she was none too lavish of her coppers—rather than have him go without one. Dan, however, lent him one, on the distinct understanding that it was to be repaid the next week.

Uncle Roger wandered by at this moment and, beholding Peter, said,

" 'Is Saul also among the prophets?' What can have induced you to turn church-goer, Peter, when all Olivia's gentle persuasions were of no avail? The old, old argument I suppose— 'beauty draws us with a single hair.' "

Uncle Roger looked quizzically at Felicity. We did not know what his quotations meant, but we understood he thought Peter was going to church because of Felicity. Felicity tossed her head.

"It isn't my fault that he's going to church," she said snappishly. "It's the Story Girl's doings."

Uncle Roger sat down on the doorstep, and gave himself over to one of the silent, inward paroxysms of laughter we all found so very aggravating. He shook his big, blond head, shut his eyes, and murmured,

"Not her fault! Oh, Felicity, Felicity, you'll be the death of your dear Uncle yet if you don't watch out."

Felicity started off indignantly, and we followed, picking up Sara Ray at the foot of the hill.

The Carlisle church was a very old-fashioned one, with a square, ivy-hung tower. It was shaded by tall elms, and the graveyard surrounded it completely, many of the graves being directly under its windows. We always took the corner path through it, passing the King plot where our kindred of four generations slept in a green solitude of wavering light and shadow.

There was Great-grandfather King's flat tombstone of rough Island sandstone, so overgrown with ivy that we could hardly read its lengthy inscription, recording his whole history in brief, and finishing with eight lines of original verse composed by his widow. I do not think that poetry was Great-grandmother King's strong point. When Felix read it, on our first Sunday in Carlisle, he remarked dubiously that it *looked* like poetry but didn't *sound* like it.

There, too, slept the Emily whose faithful spirit was supposed to haunt the orchard; but Edith who had kissed the poet lay not with her kindred. She had died in a far, foreign land, and the murmur of an alien sea sounded about her grave.

White marble tablets, ornamented with weeping willow trees, marked where Grandfather and Grandmother King were buried, and a single shaft of red Scotch granite stood between the graves of Aunt Felicity and Uncle Felix. The Story Girl lingered to lay a bunch of wild violets, misty blue and faintly sweet, on her mother's grave; and then she read aloud the verse on the stone.

" 'They were lovely and pleasant in their lives and in their death they were not divided.' "

The tones of her voice brought out the poignant and immortal beauty and pathos of that wonderful old lament. The girls wiped their eyes; and we boys felt as if we might have done so, too, had nobody been looking. What better epitaph could any one wish than to have it said that he was lovely and pleasant in his life? When I heard the Story Girl read it I made a secret compact with myself that I would try to deserve such an epitaph.

"I wish I had a family plot," said Peter, rather wistfully. "I haven't *anything* you fellows have. The Craigs are just buried anywhere they happen to die."

"I'd like to be buried here when I die," said Felix. "But I hope it won't be for a good while yet," he added in a livelier tone, as we moved onward to the church.

The interior of the church was as old-fashioned as its exterior. It was furnished with square box pews; the pulpit was a "wine-glass" one, and was reached by a steep, narrow flight of steps. Uncle Alec's pew was at the top of the church, quite near the pulpit.

Peter's appearance did not attract as much attention as we had fondly expected. Indeed, nobody seemed to notice him at all. The lamps were not yet lighted and the church was filled with a soft twilight and hush. Outside, the sky was purple and gold and silvery green, with a delicate tangle of rosy cloud above the elms.

"Isn't it awful nice and holy in here?" whispered Peter reverently. "I didn't know church was like this. It's nice."

Felicity frowned at him, and the Story Girl touched him with her slippered foot to remind him that he must not talk in church. Peter stiffened up and sat at attention during the service. Nobody could have behaved better. But when the sermon was over and the collection was being taken up, he made the sensation which his entrance had not produced.

Elder Frewen, a tall, pale man, with long, sandy side-whiskers, appeared at the door of our pew with the collection plate. We knew Elder Frewen quite well and liked him; he was Aunt Janet's cousin and often visited her. The contrast between his weekday jollity and the unearthly solemnity of his countenance on Sundays always struck us as very funny. It seemed so to strike Peter; for as Peter dropped his cent into the plate he laughed aloud!

Everybody looked at our pew. I have always wondered why Felicity did not die of mortification on the spot. The Story Girl turned white, and Cecily turned red. As for that poor, unlucky Peter, the shame of his countenance was pitiful to behold. He never lifted his head for the remainder of the service; and he followed us down the aisle and across the graveyard like a beaten dog. None of us uttered a word until we reached the road, lying in the white moonshine of the May night. Then Felicity broke the tense silence by remarking to the Story Girl,

"I told you so!"

The Story Girl made no response. Peter sidled up to her.

"I'm awful sorry," he said contritely. "I never meant to laugh. It just happened before I could stop myself. It was this way—"

"Don't you ever speak to me again," said the Story Girl, in a tone of cold, concentrated fury. "Go and be a Methodist, or a Mohammedan, or *anything!* I don't care what you are! You have *humiliated* me!"

She marched off with Sara Ray, and Peter dropped back to us with a frightened face.

"What is it I've done to her?" he whispered. "What does that big word mean?"

"Oh, never mind," I said crossly—for I felt that Peter *had* disgraced us—"She's just mad—and no wonder. Whatever made you act so crazy, Peter?"

"Well, I didn't mean to. And I wanted to laugh twice before that and *didn't*. It was the Story Girl's stories made me want to laugh, so I don't think it's fair for her to be so mad at me. She hadn't ought to tell me stories about people if she don't want me to laugh when I see them. When I looked at Samuel Ward I thought of him getting up in meeting one night, and praying that he might be guided in his upsetting and downrising. I remembered the way she took him off, and I wanted to laugh. And then I looked at the pulpit and thought of the story she told about the old Scotch minister who was too fat to get in at the door of it, and had to h'ist himself by his two hands over it, and then whispered to the other minister so that everybody heard him,

" *'This pulpit door was made for speerits'*—and I wanted to laugh. And then Mr. Frewen come—and I thought of her story about his sidewhiskers—how when his first wife died of information of the lungs he went courting Celia Ward, and Celia told him she wouldn't marry him unless he shaved them whiskers off. And he wouldn't, just to be stubborn. And one day one of them caught fire, when he was burning brush, and burned off, and every one thought he'd *have* to shave the other off then. But he didn't, and just went round with one whisker till the burned one grew out. And then Celia give in and took him, because she saw there wasn't no hope of *him* ever giving in. I just remembered that story, and I thought I could see him, taking up the cents so solemn, with one long whisker; and the laugh just laughed itself before I could help it."

We all exploded with laughter on the spot, much to the horror of Mrs. Abraham Ward, who was just driving past, and who came up the next day and told Aunt Janet we had "acted scandalous" on the road home from church. We felt ashamed ourselves, for we knew people should conduct themselves decently and in order on Sunday farings-forth. But, as with Peter, it "had laughed itself."

Even Felicity laughed. Felicity was not nearly so angry with Peter as might have been expected. She even walked beside him and let him carry her Bible. They talked quite confidentially. Perhaps she forgave him the more easily, because he had justified her in her predictions, and thus afforded her a decided triumph over the Story Girl.

"I'm going to keep on going to church," Peter told her. "I like it. Sermons are more int'resting than I thought, and I like the singing. I wish I could make up my mind whether to be a Presbyterian or a Methodist. I s'pose I might ask the minister about it."

"Oh, no, no, don't do that," said Felicity in alarm. "Ministers wouldn't want to be bothered with such questions."

"Why not? What are ministers for if they ain't to tell people how to get to heaven?"

"Oh, well, it's all right for grown-ups to ask them things, of course. But it isn't respectful for little boys—especially hired boys."

"I don't see why. But anyhow, I s'pose it wouldn't be much use, because if he was a Presbyterian minister he'd say I ought to be a Presbyterian, and if he was a Methodist he'd tell me to be one, too. Look here, Felicity, what *is* the difference between them?"

"I—I don't know," said Felicity reluctantly. "I s'pose children can't understand such things. There must be a great deal of difference, of course, if we only knew what it was. Anyhow, *I* am a Presbyterian, and I'm glad of it."

We walked on in silence for a time, thinking our own young thoughts. Presently they were scattered by an abrupt and startling question from Peter.

"What does God look like?" he said.

It appeared that none of us had any idea.

"The Story Girl would prob'ly know," said Cecily.

"I wish I knew," said Peter gravely. "I wish I could see a picture of God. It would make Him seem lots more real."

"I've often wondered myself what He looks like," said Felicity in a burst of confidence. Even in Felicity, so it would seem, there were depths of thought unplumbed.

"I've seen pictures of Jesus," said Felix mediatively. "He looks just like a man, only better and kinder. But now that I come to think of it, I've never seen a picture of God."

"Well, if there isn't one in Toronto it isn't likely there's one anywhere," said Peter disappointedly. "I saw a picture of the devil once," he added. "It was in a book my Aunt Jane had. She got it for a prize in school. My Aunt Jane was clever."

"It couldn't have been a very good book if there was such a picture in it," said Felicity.

"It was a real good book. My Aunt Jane wouldn't have a book that wasn't good," retorted Peter sulkily.

He refused to discuss the subject further, somewhat to our disappointment. For we had never seen a picture of the person referred to, and we were rather curious regarding it.

"We'll ask Peter to describe it sometime when he's in a better humour," whispered Felix.

Sara Ray having turned in at her own gate, I ran ahead to join the Story Girl, and we walked up the hill together. She had recovered her calmness of mind, but she made no reference to Peter. When we reached our lane and passed under Grandfather King's big willow the fragrance of the orchard struck us in the face like a wave. We could see the long rows of trees, a white gladness in the moonshine. It seemed to us that there was in that orchard something different from other orchards that we had known. We were too young to analyze the vague sensation. In later years we were to understand that it was because the orchard blossomed not only apple blossoms but all the love, faith, joy, pure happiness and pure sorrow of those who had made it and walked there.

"The orchard doesn't seem the same place by moonlight at all," said the Story Girl dreamily. "It's lovely, but it's different.

When I was very small I used to believe the fairies danced in it on moonlight nights. I would like to believe it now but I can't."

"Why not?"

"Oh, it's so hard to believe things you know are not true. It was Uncle Edward who told me there were no such things as fairies. I was just seven. He is a minister, so of course I knew he spoke the truth. It was his duty to tell me, and I do not blame him, but I have never felt quite the same to Uncle Edward since."

Ah, do we ever "feel quite the same" towards people who destroy our illusions? Shall I ever be able to forgive the brutal creature who first told me there was no such person as Santa Claus? He was a boy, three years older than myself; and he may now, for aught I know, be a most useful and respectable member of society, beloved by his kind. But I know what he must ever seem to me!

We waited at Uncle Alec's door for the others to come up. Peter was by way of skulking shamefacedly past into the shadows; but the Story Girl's brief, bitter anger had vanished.

"Wait for me, Peter," she called.

She went over to him and held out her hand.

"I forgive you," she said graciously.

Felix and I felt that it would really be worth while to offend her, just to be forgiven in such an adorable voice. Peter eagerly grasped her hand.

"I tell you what, Story Girl, I'm awful sorry I laughed in church, but you needn't be afraid I ever will again. No, sir! And I'm going to church and Sunday School regular, and I'll say my prayers every night. I want to be like the rest of you. And look here! I've thought of the way my Aunt Jane used to give medicine to a cat. You mix the powder in lard, and spread it on his paws and his sides and he'll lick it off, 'cause a cat can't stand being messy. If Paddy isn't any better tomorrow we'll do that."

They went away together hand in hand, childrenwise, up the lane of spruces crossed with bars of moonlight. And there was peace over all that fresh and flowery land, and peace in our little hearts.

CHAPTER 6

THE MYSTERY OF GOLDEN MILESTONE

PADDY WAS smeared with medicated lard the next day, all of us assisting at the rite, although the Story Girl was high priestess. Then, out of regard for mats and cushions, he was kept in durance vile in the granary until he had licked his fur clean. This treatment being repeated every day for a week, Pat recovered his usual health and spirits, and our minds were set at rest to enjoy the next excitement—collecting for a school library fund.

Our teacher thought it would be an excellent thing to have a library in connection with the school; and he suggested that each of the pupils should try to see how much money he or she could raise for the project during the month of June. We might earn it by honest toil, or gather it in by contributions levied on our friends.

The result was a determined rivalry as to which pupil should collect the largest sum; and this rivalry was especially intense in our home coterie.

Our relatives started us with a quarter apiece. For the rest, we knew we must depend on our own exertions. Peter was handicapped at the beginning by the fact that he had no family friend to finance him.

"If my Aunt Jane'd been living she'd have given me something," he remarked. "And if my father hadn't run away he might have given me something too. But I'm going to do the best I can anyhow. Your Aunt Olivia says I can have the job of gathering the eggs, and I'm to have one egg out of every dozen to sell for myself."

Felicity made a similar bargain with her mother. The Story Girl and Cecily were each to be paid ten cents a week for washing dishes in their respective homes. Felix and Dan contracted to keep the gardens free from weeds. I caught brook trout in the westering valley of spruces and sold them for a cent apiece.

Sara Ray was the only unhappy one among us. She could do nothing. She had no relatives in Carlisle except her mother, and her mother did not approve of the school library project, and would not give Sara a cent, or put her in any way of earning one. To Sara, this was humiliation indescribable. She felt herself an outcast and an alien in our busy little circle, where each member counted every day, with miserly delight, his slowly increasing hoard of small cash.

"I'm just going to pray to God to send me some money," she announced desperately at last.

"I don't believe that'll do any good," said Dan. "He gives lots of things, but He doesn't give money, because people can earn that for themselves."

"*I* can't," said Sara, with passionate defiance. "I think He ought to take that into account."

"Don't worry, dear," said Cecily, who always poured balm. "If you can't collect any money everybody will know it isn't your fault."

"I won't ever feel like reading a single book in the library if I can't give something to it," mourned Sara.

Dan and the girls and I were sitting in a row on Aunt Olivia's garden fence, watching Felix weed. Felix worked well, although he did not like weeding—"fat boys never do," Felicity informed him. Felix pretended not to hear her, but I knew he did, because his ears grew red. Felix's face never blushed, but his ears always gave him away. As for Felicity, she did not say things like that out of malice prepense. It never occurred to her that Felix did not like to be called fat.

"I always feel so sorry for the poor weeds," said the Story Girl dreamily. "It must be very hard to be rooted up."

"They shouldn't grow in the wrong place," said Felicity mercilessly.

"When weeds go to heaven I suppose they will be flowers," continued the Story Girl.

"You do think such queer things," said Felicity.

"A rich man in Toronto has a floral clock in his garden," I said. "It looks just like the face of a clock, and there are flowers in it that open at every hour, so that you can always tell the time."

"Oh, I wish we had one here," exclaimed Cecily.

"What would be the use of it?" asked the Story Girl a little disdainfully. "Nobody ever wants to know the time in a garden."

I slipped away at this point, suddenly remembering that it was time to take a dose of magic seed. I had bought it from Billy Robinson three days before in school. Billy had assured me that it would make me grow fast.

I was beginning to feel secretly worried because I did not grow. I had overheard Aunt Janet say I was going to be short, like Uncle Alec. Now, I loved Uncle Alec, but I wanted to be taller than he was. So when Billy confided to me, under solemn promise of secrecy, that he had some "magic seed," which would make boys grow, and would sell me a box of it for ten cents, I jumped at the offer. Billy was taller than any boy of his age in Carlisle, and he assured me it all came from taking magic seed.

"I was a regular runt before I begun," he said, "and look at me now. I got it from Peg Bowen. She's a witch, you know. I wouldn't go near her again for a bushel of magic seed. It was an awful experience. I haven't much left, but I guess I've enough to do me till I'm as tall as I want to be. You must take a pinch of the seed every three hours, walking backward, and you must never tell a soul you're taking it, or it won't work. I wouldn't spare any of it to any one but you."

I felt deeply grateful to Billy, and sorry that I had not liked him better. Somehow, nobody did like Billy Robinson over and above. But I vowed I *would* like him in future. I paid him the ten cents cheerfully and took the magic seed as directed, measuring myself carefully every day by a mark on the hall door. I could not see any advance in growth yet, but then I had been taking it only three days.

One day the Story Girl had an inspiration.

"Let us go and ask the Awkward Man and Mr. Campbell for a contribution to the library fund," she said. "I am sure no one else has asked them, because nobody in Carlisle is related to them. Let us all go, and if they give us anything we'll divide it equally among us."

It was a daring proposition, for both Mr. Campbell and the Awkward Man were regarded as eccentric personages; and Mr. Campbell was supposed to detest children. But where the Story Girl led we would follow to the death. The next day being Saturday, we started out in the afternoon.

We took a short cut to Golden Milestone, over a long, green, dewy land full of placid meadows, where sunshine had fallen asleep. At first all was not harmonious. Felicity was in an ill humour; she had wanted to wear her second best dress, but Aunt Janet had decreed that her school clothes were good enough to go "traipsing about in the dust." Then the Story Girl arrived, arrayed not in any second best but in her very best dress and hat, which her father had sent her from Paris— a dress of soft, crimson silk, and a white leghorn hat encircled by flame-red poppies. Neither Felicity nor Cecily could have worn it; but it became the Story Girl perfectly. In it she was a thing of fire and laughter and glow, as if the singular charm of her temperament were made visible and tangible in its vivid colouring and silken texture.

"I shouldn't think you'd put on your best clothes to go begging for the library in," said Felicity cuttingly.

"Aunt Olivia says that when you are going to have an important interview with a man you ought to look your very best," said the Story Girl, giving her skirt a lustrous swirl and enjoying the effect.

"Aunt Olivia spoils you," said Felicity.

"She doesn't, either, Felicity King! Aunt Olivia is just sweet. She kisses me good-night every night, and your mother *never* kisses you."

"My mother doesn't make kisses so common," retorted Felicity. "But she gives us pie for dinner every day."

"So does Aunt Olivia."

"Yes, but look at the difference in the size of the pieces! And Aunt Olivia only gives you skim milk. My mother gives us cream."

"Aunt Olivia's skim milk is as good as your mother's cream," cried the Story Girl hotly.

"Oh, girls, don't fight," said Cecily, the peacemaker. "It's such a nice day, and we'll have a nice time if you don't spoil it by fighting."

"We're *not* fighting," said Felicity. "And I like Aunt Olivia. But my mother is just as good as Aunt Olivia, there now!"

"Of course she is. Aunt Janet is splendid," agreed the Story Girl.

They smiled at each other amicably. Felicity and the Story Girl were really quite fond of each other, under the queer surface friction that commonly resulted from their intercourse.

"You said once you knew a story about the Awkward Man," said Felix. "You might tell it to us."

"All right," agreed the Story Girl. "The only trouble is, I don't know the whole story. But I'll tell you all I do know. I call it 'The Mystery of Golden Milestone.' "

"Oh, I don't believe that story is true," said Felicity. "I believe Mrs. Griggs was just romancing. She *does* romance, mother says."

"Yes; but I don't believe she could ever have thought of such a thing as this herself, and so I believe it must be true," said the Story Girl. "Anyway, this is the story, boys. You know the Awkward Man has lived alone ever since his mother died, ten years ago. Abel Griggs is his hired man, and he and his wife live in a little house down the Awkward Man's lane. Mrs. Griggs makes his bread for him, and she cleans up his house now and then. She says he keeps it very neat. But till last fall there was one room she never saw. It was always locked—the west one, looking out over his garden. One day last fall the Awkward Man went to Summerside, and Mrs. Griggs scrubbed his kitchen. Then she went over the whole house and she tried the door of the west room. Mrs. Griggs is a *very* curious woman. Uncle Roger says all women have as much curiosity as is good for them, but Mrs. Griggs has more. She expected to find the door locked as usual. It was *not* locked. She opened it and went in. What do you suppose she found?"

"Something like—like Bluebeard's chamber?" suggested Felix in a scared tone.

"Oh, no, *no!* Nothing like *that* could happen in Prince Edward Island. But if there *had* been beautiful wives hanging up by their hair all round the walls I don't believe Mrs. Griggs could have been much more astonished. The room had never been furnished in his mother's time, but now it was *elegantly* furnished, though Mrs. Griggs says *she* doesn't know when or how that furniture was brought there. She says she never saw a room like it in a country farmhouse. It was like a bed-room and sitting-room combined. The floor was covered with a carpet like green velvet. There were fine lace curtains at the windows and beautiful pictures on the walls. There was a little white bed, and a dressing-table, a bookcase full of books, a stand with a work basket on it, and a rocking-chair. There was a woman's picture above the bookcase. Mrs. Griggs says she thinks it was a coloured photograph, but she didn't know who it was. Anyway, it was a very pretty girl. But the most amazing thing of all was that *a woman's dress* was hanging over a chair by the table. Mrs. Griggs says it *never* belonged to Jasper Dale's mother, for she thought it a sin to wear anything but print and drugget; and this dress was of *pale blue* silk. Besides that, there was a pair of blue satin slippers on the floor beside it— *high-heeled* slippers. And on the fly-leaves of all the books the name 'Alice' was written. Now, there never was an Alice in the Dale connection, and nobody ever heard of the Awkward Man having a sweetheart. There, isn't that a lovely mystery?"

"It's a pretty queer yarn," said Felix. "I wonder if it is true— and what it means."

"I intend to find out what it means," said the Story Girl. "I am going to get acquainted with the Awkward Man sometime, and then I'll find out his Alice-secret."

"I don't see how you'll ever get acquainted with him," said Felicity. "He never goes anywhere except to church. He just stays home and reads books when he isn't working. Mother says he is a perfect hermit."

"I'll manage it somehow," said the Story Girl—and we had no doubt that she would. "But I must wait till I'm a little older, for he wouldn't tell the secret of the west room to a little girl. And I mustn't wait till I'm *too* old, for he is frightened of grown-up girls, because he thinks they laugh at his awkwardness. I know I will like him. He has such a nice face, even if he is awkward. He looks like a man you could tell things to."

"Well, I'd like a man who could move around without falling over his own feet," said Felicity. "And then the look of him! Uncle Roger says he is long, lank, lean, narrow, and contracted."

"Things always sound worse than they are when Uncle Roger says them," said the Story Girl. "Uncle Edward says Jasper Dale is a very clever man and it's a great pity he wasn't able to finish his college course. He went to college two years, you know. Then his father died, and he stayed home with his mother because she was very delicate. *I* call him a hero. I wonder if it is true that he writes poetry. Mrs. Griggs says it is. She says she has seen him writing it in a brown book. She said she couldn't get near enough to read it, but she knew it was poetry by the shape of it."

"Very likely. If that blue silk dress story is true, I'd believe *anything* of him," said Felicity.

We were near Golden Milestone now. The house was a big, weather-gray structure, overgrown with vines and climbing roses. Something about the three square windows in the second story gave it an appearance of winking at us in a friendly fashion through its vines—at least, so the Story Girl said; and, indeed, we could see it for ourselves after she had once pointed it out to us.

We did not get into the house, however. We met the Awkward Man in his yard, and he gave us a quarter apiece for our library. He did not seem awkward or shy; but then we were only children, and his foot was on his native heath.

He was a tall, slender man, who did not look his forty years, so unwrinkled was his high, white forehead, so clear and lustrous his large, dark-blue eyes, so free from silver threads his rather long black hair. He had large hands and feet, and walked with a slight stoop. I am afraid we stared at him rather rudely while the Story Girl talked to him. But was not an Awkward Man, who was also a hermit and kept blue silk dresses in a locked room, and possibly wrote poetry, a legitimate object of curiosity? I leave it to you.

When we got away we compared notes, and found that we all liked him—and this, although he had said little and had appeared somewhat glad to get rid of us.

"He gave us the money like a gentleman," said the Story Girl. "I felt he didn't grudge it. And now for Mr. Campbell. It was on *his* account I put on my red silk. I don't suppose the Awkward Man noticed it at all, but Mr. Campbell will, or I'm much mistaken."

CHAPTER 7

HOW BETTY SHERMAN WON A HUSBAND

THE REST of us did not share the Story Girl's enthusiasm regarding our call on Mr. Campbell. We secretly dreaded it. If, as was said, he detested children, who knew what sort of a reception we might meet?

Mr. Campbell was a rich, retired farmer, who took life easily. He had visited New York and Boston, Toronto and Montreal; he had even been as far as the Pacific coast. Therefore he was regarded in Carlisle as a much travelled man; and he was known to be "well read" and intelligent. But it was also known that Mr. Campbell was not always in a good humour. If he liked you there was nothing he would not do for you; if he disliked you—well, you were not left in ignorance of it. In short, we had the impression that Mr. Campbell resembled the famous little girl with the curl in the middle of her forehead. "When he was good, he was very, very good, and when he was bad he was horrid." What if this were one of his horrid days?

"He can't *do* anything to us, you know," said the Story Girl. "He may be rude, but that won't hurt any one but himself."

"Hard words break no bones," observed Felix philosophically.

"But they hurt your feelings. *I* am afraid of Mr. Campbell," said Cecily candidly.

"Perhaps we'd better give up and go home," suggested Dan.

"You can go home if you like," said the Story Girl scornfully. "But *I* am going to see Mr. Campbell. I know I can manage him. But if I have to go alone, and he gives me anything, I'll keep it all for my own collection, mind you."

That settled it. We were not going to let the Story Girl get ahead of us in the matter of collecting.

Mr. Campbell's housekeeper ushered us into his parlour and left us. Presently Mr. Campbell himself was standing in the doorway, looking us over. We took heart of grace. It seemed to be one of his good days, for there was a quizzical smile on his broad, clean-shaven, strongly-featured face. Mr. Campbell was a tall man, with a massive head, well thatched with thick, black hair, gray-streaked. He had big, black eyes, with many wrinkles around them, and a thin, firm, long-lipped mouth. We thought him handsome, for an old man.

His gaze wandered over us with uncomplimentary indifference until it fell on the Story Girl, leaning back in an armchair. She looked like a slender red lily in the unstudied grace of her attitude. A spark flashed into Mr. Campbell's black eyes.

"Is this a Sunday School deputation?" he inquired rather ironically.

"No. We have come to ask a favour of you," said the Story Girl.

The magic of her voice worked its will on Mr. Campbell, as on all others. He came in, sat down, hooked his thumb into his vest pocket, and smiled at her.

"What is it?" he asked.

"We are collecting for our school library, and we have called to ask you for a contribution," she replied.

"Why should *I* contribute to your school library?" demanded Mr. Campbell.

This was a poser for us. Why should he, indeed? But the Story Girl was quite equal to it. Leaning forward, and throwing an indescribable witchery into tone and eyes and smile, she said,

"Because a lady asks you."

Mr. Campbell chuckled.

"The best of all reasons," he said. "But see here, my dear young lady, I'm an old miser and curmudgeon, as you may have heard. I *hate* to part with my money, even for a good reason. And I *never* part with any of it, unless I am to receive some benefit from the expenditure. Now, what earthly good could I get from your three by six school library? None whatever. But I shall make you a fair offer. I have heard from my housekeeper's urchin of a son that you are a 'master hand' to tell stories. Tell me one, here and now. I shall pay you in proportion to the entertainment you afford me. Come now, and do your prettiest."

There was a fine mockery in his tone that put the Story Girl on her mettle instantly. She sprang to her feet, an amazing change coming over her. Her eyes flashed and burned; crimson spots glowed in her cheeks.

"I shall tell you the story of the Sherman girls, and how

Betty Sherman won a husband," she said.

We gasped. Was the Story Girl crazy? Or had she forgotten that Betty Sherman was Mr. Campbell's own great-grandmother, and that her method of winning a husband was not exactly in accordance with maidenly traditions.

But Mr. Campbell chuckled again.

"An excellent test," he said. "If you can amuse *me* with that story you must be a wonder. I've heard it so often that it has no more interest for me than the alphabet."

"One cold winter day, eighty years ago," began the Story Girl without further parley, "Donald Fraser was sitting by the window of his new house, playing his fiddle for company, and looking out over the white, frozen bay before his door. It was bitter, bitter cold, and a storm was brewing. But, storm, or no storm, Donald meant to go over the bay that evening to see Nancy Sherman. He was thinking of her as he played 'Annie Laurie,' for Nancy was more beautiful than the lady of the song. 'Her face, it is the fairest that e'er the sun shone on,' hummed Donald—and oh, he thought so, too! He did not know whether Nancy cared for him or not. He had many rivals. But he knew that if she would not come to be the mistress of his new house no one else ever should. So he sat there that afternoon and dreamed of her, as he played sweet old songs and rollicking jigs on his fiddle.

"While he was playing a sleigh drove up to the door, and Neil Campbell came in. Donald was not overly glad to see him, for he suspected where he was going. Neil Campbell, who was Highland Scotch and lived down at Berwick, was courting Nancy Sherman, too; and, what was far worse, Nancy's father favoured him, because he was a richer man than Donald Fraser. But Donald was not going to show all he thought—Scotch people never do—and he pretended to be very glad to see Neil, and made him heartily welcome.

"Neil sat down by the roaring fire, looking quite well satisfied with himself. It was ten miles from Berwick to the bay shore, and a call at a half way house was just the thing. Then Donald brought out the whisky. They always did that eighty years ago, you know. If you were a woman, you could give your visitors a dish of tea; but if you were a man and did not offer them a 'taste' of whisky, you were thought either very mean or very ignorant.

" 'You look cold,' said Donald, in his great, hearty voice. 'Sit nearer the fire, man, and put a bit of warmth in your veins. It's bitter cold the day. And now tell me the Berwick news. Has Jean McLean made up with her man yet? And is it true that Sandy McQuarrie is to marry Kate Ferguson? 'Twill be a match now! Sure, with her red hair, Sandy will not be like to lose his bride past finding.'

"Neil had plenty of news to tell. And the more whisky he drank the more he told. He didn't notice that Donald was not taking much. Neil talked on and on, and of course he soon began to tell things it would have been much wiser not to tell. Finally he told Donald that he was going over the bay to ask Nancy Sherman that very night to marry him. And if she would have him, then Donald and all the folks should see a wedding that *was* a wedding.

"Oh, wasn't Donald taken aback! This was more than he had expected. Neil hadn't been courting Nancy very long, and Donald never dreamed he would propose to her *quite* so soon.

"At first Donald didn't know what to do. He felt sure deep down in his heart, that Nancy liked *him*. She was very shy and modest, but you know a girl can let a man see she likes him without going out of her way. But Donald knew that if Neil proposed first he would have the best chance. Neil was rich and the Shermans were poor; and old Elias Sherman would have the most to say in the matter. If he told Nancy she must take Neil Campbell she would never dream of disobeying him. Old Elias Sherman was a man who had to be obeyed. But if Nancy had only promised some one else first her father would not make her break her word.

"Wasn't it a hard plight for poor Donald? But he was a Scotchman, you know, and it's pretty hard to stick a Scotchman long. Presently a twinkle came into his eyes, for he remembered that all was fair in love and war. So he said to Neil, oh, so persuasively,

" 'Have some more, man, have some more. 'Twill keep the heart in you in the teeth of that wind. Help yourself. There's plenty more where that came from.'

"Neil didn't want *much* persuasion. He took some more, and said slyly,

" 'Is it going over the bay the night that yourself will be doing?'

"Donald shook his head.

" 'I had thought of it,' he owned, 'but it looks a wee like a storm, and my sleigh is at the blacksmith's to be shod. If I went it must be on Black Dan's back, and he likes a canter over the ice in a snow-storm as little as I. His own fireside is the best place for a man tonight, Campbell. Have another taste, man, have another taste.'

"Neil went on 'tasting,' and that sly Donald sat there with a sober face, but laughing eyes, and coaxed him on. At last Neil's head fell forward on his breast, and he was sound asleep. Donald got up, put on his overcoat and cap, and went to the door.

" 'May your sleep be long and sweet, man,' he said, laughing softly, 'and as for the waking, 'twill be betwixt you and me.'

"With that he untied Neil's horse, climbed into Neil's sleigh, and tucked Neil's buffalo robe about him.

" 'Now, Bess, old girl, do your bonniest,' he said. 'There's more than you know hangs on your speed. If the Campbell wakes too soon Black Dan could show you a pair of clean heels for all your good start. On, my girl.'

"Brown Bess went over the ice like a deer, and Donald kept thinking of what he should say to Nancy—and more still of what she would say to him. *Suppose* he was mistaken. *Suppose* she said 'no!'

" 'Neil will have the laugh on me then. Sure he's sleeping well. And the snow is coming soon. There'll be a bonny swirl on the bay ere long. I hope no harm will come to the lad if he starts to cross. When we wakes up he'll be in such a fine Highland temper that he'll never stop to think of danger. Well, Bess, old girl, here we are. Now, Donald Fraser, pluck up heart and play the man. Never flinch because a slip of a lass looks scornful at you out of the bonniest dark-blue eyes on earth.'

"But in spite of his bold words Donald's heart was thumping as he drove into the Sherman yard. Nancy was there, milking a cow by the stable door, but she stood up when she saw Donald coming. Oh, she was very beautiful! Her hair was like a skein of golden silk, and her eyes were as blue as the gulf water when the sun breaks out after a storm. Donald felt more nervous than ever. But he knew he must make the most of his chance. He might not see Nancy alone again before Neil came. He caught her hand and stammered out,

" 'Nan, lass, I love you. You may think 'tis a hasty wooing, but that's a story I can tell you later maybe. I know well I'm not worthy of you, but if true love could make a man worthy there'd be none before me. Will you have me, Nan?'

"Nancy didn't *say* she would have him. She just *looked* it, and Donald kissed her right there in the snow.

"The next morning the storm was over. Donald knew that Neil must be soon on his track. He did not want to make the Sherman house the scene of a quarrel, so he resolved to get away before the Campbell came. He persuaded Nancy to go with him to visit some friends in another settlement. As he brought Neil's sleigh up to the door he saw a black speck far out on the bay and laughed.

" 'Black Dan goes well, but he'll not be quick enough,' he said.

"Half an hour later Neil Campbell rushed into the Sherman kitchen and oh, how angry he was! There was nobody there but Betty Sherman, and Betty was not afraid of him. She was never afraid of anybody. She was very handsome, with hair as brown as October nuts and black eyes and crimson cheeks; and she had always been in love with Neil Campbell herself.

" 'Good morning, Mr. Campbell,' she said, with a toss of her head. 'It's early abroad you are. And on Black Dan, no less! Was I mistaken in thinking that Donald Fraser said once that his favourite horse should never be backed by any man but him? But doubtless a fair exchange is no robbery, and Brown Bess is a good mare in her way.'

" 'Where is Donald Fraser?' said Neil, shaking his fist. 'It's him I'm seeking, and it's him I will be finding. Where is he, Betty Sherman?'

" 'Donald Fraser is far enough away by this time,' mocked Betty. 'He is a prudent fellow, and has some quickness of wit under that sandy thatch of his. He came her last night at sunset, with a horse and sleigh not his own, or lately gotten, and he asked Nan in the stable yard to marry him. Did a man ask *me* to marry him at the cow's side, with a milking pail in my hand, it's a cold answer he'd get for his pains. But Nan thought differently, and they sat late together last night, and 'twas a bonny story Nan wakened me to hear when she came to bed— the story of a braw lover who let his secret out when the whisky was above the wit, and then fell asleep while his rival was away to woo and win his lass. Did you ever hear a like story, Mr. Campbell?'

" 'Oh, yes,' said Neil fiercely. 'It is laughing at me over the country side and telling that story that Donald Fraser will be doing, is it? But when I meet him it is not laughing he will be doing. Oh, no. There will be another story to tell!'

" 'Now, don't meddle with the man,' cried Betty. 'What a state to be in because one good-looking lass likes sandy hair and gray eyes better than Highland black and blue! You have not the spirit of a wren, Neil Campbell. Were I you, I would show Donald Fraser that I could woo and win a lass as speedily as any Lowlander of them all; that I would! There's many a girl would gladly say "yes" for your asking. And here stands one! Why not marry *me*, Neil Campbell? Folks say I'm as bonny as Nan—and I could love you as well as Nan loves her Donald—ay, and ten times better!'

"What do you suppose the Campbell did? Why, just the thing he ought to have done. He took Betty at her word on the spot; and there was a double wedding soon after. And it is said that Neil and Betty were the happiest couple in the world—happier even than Donald and Nancy. So all was well because it ended well!"

The Story Girl curtsied until her silken skirts swept the floor. Then she flung herself in her chair and looked at Mr. Campbell, flushed, triumphant, daring.

The story was old to us. It had once been published in a Charlottetown paper, and we had read in Aunt Olivia's scrap-book, where the Story Girl had learned it. But we had listened entranced. I have written down the bare words of the story, as she told it; but I can never reproduce the charm and colour and spirit she infused into it. It *lived* for us. Donald and Neil, Nancy and Betty, were there in that room with us. We saw the flashes of expression on their faces, we heard their voices, angry or tender, mocking or merry, in Lowland and Highland accent. We realized all the mingled coquetry and feeling and defiance and archness in Betty Sherman's daring speech. We had even forgotten all about Mr. Campbell.

That gentleman, in silence, took out his wallet, extracted a note therefrom, and handed it gravely to the Story Girl.

"There are five dollars for you," he said, "and your story was well worth it. You *are* a wonder. Some day you will make the world realize it. I've been about a bit, and heard some good things, but I've never enjoyed anything more than that threadbare old story I heard in my cradle. And now, will you do me a favour?"

"Of course," said the delighted Story Girl.

"Recite the multiplication table for me," said Mr. Campbell.

We stared. Well might Mr. Campbell be called eccentric. What on earth did he want the multiplication table recited for? Even the Story Girl was surprised. But she began promptly, with twice one and went through it to twelve times twelve. She repeated it simply, but her voice changed from one tone to another as each in succession grew tired. We had never dreamed that there was so much in the multiplication table. As she announced it, the fact that three times three was nine was exquisitely ridiculous, five times six almost brought the tears to our eyes, eight times seven was the most tragic and frightful thing ever heard of, and twelve times twelve rang like a trumpet call to victory.

Mr. Campbell nodded his satisfaction.

"I thought you could do it," he said. "The other day I found this statement in a book. 'Her voice would have made the multiplication table charming!' I thought of it when I heard yours. I didn't believe it before, but I do now."

Then he let us go.

"You see," said the Story Girl as we went home, "you need never be afraid of people."

"But we are not all Story Girls," said Cecily.

That night we heard Felicity talking to Cecily in their room.

"Mr. Campbell never noticed one of us except the Story Girl," she said, "but if *I* had put on *my* best dress as she did maybe she wouldn't have taken all the attention."

"Could you ever do what Betty Sherman did, do you suppose?" asked Cecily absently.

"No; but I believe the Story Girl could," answered Felicity rather snappishly.

CHAPTER 8

A TRAGEDY OF CHILDHOOD

THE Story Girl went to Charlottetown for a week in June to visit Aunt Louisa. Life seemed very colourless without her, and even Felicity admitted that it was lonesome. But three days after her departure Felix told us something on the way home from school which lent some spice to existence immediately.

"What do you think?" he said in a very solemn, yet excited, tone. "Jerry Cowan told me at recess this afternoon that *he had seen a picture of God*—that he has it at home in an old, red-covered history of the world, and has looked at it *often."*

To think that Jerry Cowan should have seen such a picture often! We were as deeply impressed as Felix had meant us to be.

"Did he say what it was like?" asked Peter.

"No—only that it was a picture of God, walking in the garden of Eden."

"Oh," whispered Felicity—we all spoke in low tones on the subject, for, by instinct and training, we thought and uttered the Great Name with reverence, in spite of our devouring curiosity—"oh, *would* Jerry Cowan bring it to school and let us see it?"

"I asked him that, soon as ever he told me," said Felix. "He said he might, but he couldn't promise, for he'd have to ask his mother if he could bring the book to school. If she'll let him he'll bring it tomorrow."

"Oh, I'll be almost afraid to look at it," said Sara Ray tremulously.

I think we all shared her fear to some extent. Nevertheless, we went to school the next day burning with curiosity. And we were disappointed. Possibly night had brought counsel to Jerry Cowan; or perhaps his mother had put him up to it. At all events, he announced to us that he couldn't bring the red-covered history to school, but if we wanted to buy the picture outright he would tear it out of the book and sell it to us for fifty cents.

We talked the matter over in serious conclave in the orchard that evening. We were all rather short of hard cash, having devoted most of our spare means to the school library fund. But the general concensus of opinion was that we must have the picture, no matter what pecuniary sacrifices were involved. If we could each give about seven cents we would have the amount. Peter could give only four, but Dan gave eleven, which squared matters.

"Fifty cents would be pretty dear for any other picture, but of course this is different," said Dan.

"And there's a picture of Eden thrown in, too, you know," added Felicity.

"Fancy selling God's picture," said Cecily in a shocked, awed tone.

"Nobody but a Cowan would do it, and that's a fact," said Dan.

"When we get it we'll keep it in the family Bible," said Felicity. "That's the only proper place."

"Oh, I wonder what it will be like," breathed Cecily.

We all wondered. Next day in school we agreed to Jerry Cowan's terms, and Jerry promised to bring the picture up to Uncle Alec's the following afternoon.

We were all intensely excited Saturday morning. To our dismay, it began to rain just before dinner.

"What if Jerry doesn't bring the picture today because of the rain?" I suggested.

"Never you fear," answered Felicity decidedly. "A Cowan would come through *anything* for fifty cents."

After dinner we all, without any verbal decision about it, washed our faces and combed our hair. The girls put on their second best dresses, and we boys donned white collars. We all had the unuttered feeling that we must do such honour to that

Picture as we could. Felicity and Dan began a small spat over something, but stopped at once when Cecily said severely,

"How *dare* you quarrel when you are going to look at a picture of God today?"

Owing to the rain we could not foregather in the orchard, where we had meant to transact the business with Jerry. We did not wish our grown-ups around at our great moment, so we betook ourselves to the loft of the granary in the spruce wood, from whose window we could see the main road and hail Jerry. Sara Ray had joined us, very pale and nervous, having had, so it appeared, a difference of opinion with her mother about coming up the hill in the rain.

"I'm afraid I did very wrong to come against ma's will," she said miserably, "but I *couldn't* wait. I wanted to see the picture as soon as you did."

We waited and watched at the window. The valley was full of mist, and the rain was coming down in slanting lines over the tops of the spruces. But as we waited the clouds broke away and the sun came out flashingly; the drops on the spruce boughs glittered like diamonds.

"I don't believe Jerry can be coming," said Cecily in despair. "I suppose his mother must have thought it was dreadful, after all, to sell such a picture."

"There he is now!" cried Dan, waving excitedly from the window.

"He's carrying a fish-basket," said Felicity. "You surely don't suppose that he would bring *that* picture in a fish-basket!"

Jerry *had* brought it in a fish-basket, as appeared when he mounted the granary stairs shortly afterwards. It was folded up in a newspaper packet on top of the dried herring with which the basket was filled. We paid him his money, but we would not open the packet until he had gone.

"Cecily," said Felicity in a hushed tone. "You are the best of us all. *You* open the parcel."

"Oh, I'm no gooder than the rest of you," breathed Cecily, "but I'll open it if you like."

With trembling fingers Cecily opened the parcel. We stood around, hardly breathing. She unfolded it and held it up. We saw it.

Suddenly Sara began to cry.

"Oh, oh, oh, does God look like *that?*" she wailed.

Felix and I spoke not. Disappointment, and something worse, sealed our speech. *Did* God look like that—like that stern, angrily-frowning old man with the tossing hair and beard of the wood-cut Cecily held.

"I suppose He must, since that is His picture," said Dan miserably.

"He looks awful cross," said Peter simply.

"Oh, I wish we'd never, never seen it," cried Cecily.

We all wished that—too late. Our curiosity had led us into some Holy of Holies, not to be profaned by human eyes, and this was our punishment.

"I've always had a feeling right along," wept Sara, "that it wasn't *right* to buy—or *look at*—God's picture."

As we stood there wretchedly we heard flying feet below and a blithe voice calling,

"Where are you, children?"

The Story Girl had returned! At any other moment we would have rushed to meet her in wild joy. But now we were too crushed and miserable to move.

"Whatever is the matter with you all?" demanded the Story Girl, appearing at the top of the stairs. "What is Sara crying about? What have you got there?"

"A picture of God," said Cecily with a sob in her voice, "and oh, it is so dreadful and ugly. Look!"

The Story Girl looked. An expression of scorn came over her face.

"Surely you don't believe God looks like that," she said impatiently, while her fine eyes flashed. "He doesn't—He couldn't. He is wonderful and beautiful, I'm surprised at you. *That* is nothing but the picture of a cross old man."

Hope sprang up in our hearts, although we were not wholly convinced.

"I don't know," said Dan dubiously. "It says under the picture 'God in the Garden of Eden.' It's *printed.*"

"Well, I suppose that's what the man who drew it thought God was like," answered the Story Girl carelessly. "But *he* couldn't have known any more than you do. *He* had never seen Him."

"It's all very well for you to say so," said Felicity, "but *you*

don't know either. I wish I could believe that isn't like God—
but I don't know what to believe."

"Well, if you won't believe me, I suppose you'll believe the
minister," said the Story Girl. "Go and ask him. He's in the
house this very minute. He came up with us in the buggy."

At any other time we would never have dared catechize the
minister about anything. But desperate cases call for desperate
measures. We drew straws to see who should go and do the
asking, and the lot fell to Felix.

"Better wait until Mr. Marwood leaves, and catch him in
the lane," advised the Story Girl. "You'll have a lot of grown-
ups around you in the house."

Felix took her advice. Mr. Marwood, presently walking be-
nignantly along the lane, was confronted by a fat, small boy
with a pale face but resolute eyes.

The rest of us remained in the background but within hearing.

"Well, Felix, what is it?" asked Mr. Marwood kindly.

"Please, sir, does God really look like this?" asked Felix,
holding out the picture. "We hope He doesn't—but we want
to know the truth, and that is why I'm bothering you. Please
excuse us and tell me."

The minister looked at the picture. A stern expression came
into his gentle blue eyes and he got as near to frowning as it
was possible for him to get.

"Where did you get that thing?" he asked.

Thing! We began to breathe easier.

"We bought it from Jerry Cowan. He found it in a red-
covered history of the world. It *says* it's God's picture," said
Felix.

"It is nothing of the sort," said Mr. Marwood indignantly.
"There is no such thing as a picture of God, Felix. No human
being knows what He looks like—no human being *can* know.
We should not even try to think what He looks like. But, Felix,
you may be sure that God is infinitely more beautiful and
loving and tender and kind than anything we can imagine of
Him. Never believe anything else, my boy. As for this—this
sacrilege—take it and burn it."

We did not know what a sacrilege meant, but we knew that
Mr. Marwood had declared that the picture was not like God.

That was enough for us. We felt as if a terrible weight had been lifted from our minds.

"I could hardly believe the Story Girl, but of course the minister *knows,"* said Dan happily.

"We've lost fifty cents because of it," said Felicity gloomily.

We had lost something of infinitely more value than fifty cents, although we did not realize it just then. The minister's words had removed from our minds the bitter belief that God was like that picture; but on something deeper and more enduring than mind an impression had been made that was never to be removed. The mischief was done. From that day to this the thought or the mention of God brings up before us involuntarily the vision of a stern, angry, old man. Such was the price we were to pay for the indulgence of a curiosity which each of us, deep in our hearts, had, like Sara Ray, felt ought not to be gratified.

"Mr. Marwood told me to burn it," said Felix.

"It doesn't seem reverent to do that," said Cecily. "Even if it isn't God's picture, it has His name on it."

"Bury it," said the Story Girl.

We did bury it after tea, in the depths of the spruce grove; and then we went into the orchard. It was so nice to have the Story Girl back again. She had wreathed her hair with Canterbury Bells, and looked like the incarnation of rhyme and story and dream.

"Canterbury Bells is a lovely name for a flower, isn't it?" she said. "It makes you think of cathedrals and chimes, doesn't it? Let's go over to Uncle Stephen's Walk, and sit on the branches of the big tree. It's too wet on the grass, and I know a story—a *true* story, about an old lady I saw in town at Aunt Louisa's. Such a dear old lady, with lovely silvery curls."

After the rain the air seemed dripping with odours in the warm west wind—the tang of fir balsam, the spice of mint, the wild woodsiness of ferns, the aroma of grasses steeping in the sunshine,—and with it all a breath of wild sweetness from far hill pastures.

Scattered through the grass in Uncle Stephen's Walk, were blossoming pale, aerial flowers which had no name that we could ever discover. Nobody seemed to know anything about them. They had been there when Great-grandfather King bought the place. I have never seen them elsewhere, or found them described in any floral catalogue. We called them the White Ladies. The Story Girl gave them the name. She said they looked like the souls of good women who had had to suffer much and had been very patient. They were wonderfully dainty, with a strange, faint, aromatic perfume which was only to be detected at a little distance and vanished if you bent over them. They faded soon after they were plucked; and, although strangers, greatly admiring them, often carried away roots and seeds, they could never be coaxed to grow elsewhere.

"My story is about Mrs. Dunbar and the Captain of the *Fanny*," said the Story Girl, settling herself comfortably on a bough, with her brown head against a gnarled trunk. "It's sad and beautiful—and true. I do love to tell stories that I know really happened. Mrs. Dunbar lives next door to Aunt Louisa in town. She is so sweet. You wouldn't think to look at her that she had a tragedy in her life, but she has. Aunt Louisa told me the tale. It all happened long, long ago. Interesting things like this all did happen long ago, it seems to me. They never seem to happen now. This was in '49, when people were rushing to the gold fields in California. It was just like a fever, Aunt Louisa says. People took it, right here on the Island; and a number of young men determined they would go to California.

"It is easy to go to California now; but it was a very different matter then. There were no railroads across the land, as there are now, and if you wanted to go to California you had to go in a sailing vessel, all the way around Cape Horn. It was a long and dangerous journey; and sometimes it took over six months. When you got there you had no way of sending word home again except by the same plan. It might be over a year before your people at home heard a word about you—and fancy what their feelings would be!

"But these young men didn't think of these things; they were led on by a golden vision. They made all their arrangements, and they chartered the brig *Fanny* to take them to California.

"The captain of the *Fanny* is the hero of my story. His name was Alan Dunbar, and he was young and handsome. Heroes always are, you know, but Aunt Louisa says he really was. And he was in love—wildly in love,—with Margaret Grant. Margaret was as beautiful as a dream, with soft blue eyes and clouds of golden hair; and she loved Alan Dunbar just as much as he loved her. But her parents were bitterly opposed to him, and they had forbidden Margaret to see him or speak to him. They hadn't anything against him as a *man,* but they didn't want her to throw herself away on a sailor.

"Well, when Alan Dunbar knew that he must go to California in the *Fanny* he was in despair. He felt that he could *never* go so far away for so long and leave his Margaret behind. And Margaret felt that she could never let him go. I know *exactly* how she felt."

"How can you know?" interrupted Peter suddenly. "You ain't old enough to have a beau. How can you know?"

The Story Girl looked at Peter with a frown. She did not like to be interrupted when telling a story.

"Those are not things one *knows* about," she said with dignity. "One *feels* about them."

Peter, crushed but not convinced, subsided, and the Story Girl went on.

"Finally Margaret ran away with Alan, and they were married in Charlottetown. Alan intended to take his wife with him to California in the *Fanny.* If it was a hard journey for a man it was harder still for a woman, but Margaret would have dared anything for Alan's sake. They had three days—*only* three days—of happiness, and then the blow fell. The crew and the passengers of the *Fanny* refused to let Captain Dunbar take his wife with him. They told him he must leave her behind. And all his prayers were of no avail. They say he stood on the deck of the *Fanny* and pleaded with the men while the tears ran down his face; but they would not yield, and he had to leave Margaret behind. Oh, what a parting it was!"

There was heartbreak in the Story Girl's voice and tears came into our eyes. There, in the green bower of Uncle Stephen's Walk, we cried over the pathos of a parting whose anguish had been stilled for many years.

"When it was all over, Margaret's father and mother forgave her, and she went back home to wait—to *wait.* Oh, it is so dreadful just to *wait,* and do nothing else. Margaret waited for nearly a year. How long it must have seemed to her! And at last there came a letter—but not from Alan. Alan was *dead.*

He had died in California and had been buried there. While Margaret had been thinking of him and longing for him and praying for him he had been lying in his lonely, faraway grave."

Cecily sprang up, shaking with sobs.

"Oh, don't—don't go on," she implored. "I *can't* bear any more."

"There is no more," said the Story Girl. "That was the end of it—the end of everything for Margaret. It didn't kill *her,* but her heart died."

"I just wish I'd hold of those fellows who wouldn't let the Captain take his wife," said Peter savagely.

"Well, it was awful sad," said Felicity, wiping her eyes. "But it was long ago and we can't do any good by crying over it now. Let us go and get something to eat. I made some nice little rhubarb tarts this morning."

We went. In spite of new disappointments and old heartbreaks we had appetites. And Felicity did make scrumptious rhubarb tarts!

────────────── CHAPTER 9 ──────────────

MAGIC SEED

WHEN THE time came to hand in our collections for the library fund Peter had the largest—three dollars. Felicity was a good second with two and a half. This was simply because the hens had laid so well.

"If you'd had to pay father for all the extra handfuls of wheat you've fed to those hens, Miss Felicity, you wouldn't have so much," said Dan spitefully.

"I didn't," retorted Felicity indignantly. "Look how Aunt Olivia's hens laid, too, and she fed them herself just the same as usual."

"Never mind," said Cecily, "we have all got something to

give. If you were like poor Sara Ray, and hadn't been able to collect anything you might feel bad."

But Sara Ray *had* something to give. She came up the hill after tea, all radiant. When Sara Ray smiled—and she did not waste her smiles—she was rather pretty in a plaintive, apologetic way. A dimple or two came into sight, and she had very nice teeth—small and white, like the traditional row of pearls.

"Oh, just look," she said. "Here are three dollars—and I'm going to give it all to the library fund. I had a letter today from Uncle Arthur in Winnipeg, and he sent me three dollars. He said I was to use it *any* way I liked, so ma couldn't refuse to let me give it to the fund. She thinks it's an awful waste, but she always goes by what Uncle Arthur says. Oh, I've prayed so hard that some money might come some way, and now it has. See what praying does!"

I am very much afraid that we did not rejoice quite as unselfishly in Sara's good fortune as we should have done. *We* had earned our contributions by the sweat of our brow, or by the scarcely less disagreeable method of "begging." And Sara's had as good as descended upon her out of the skies, as much like a miracle as anything you could imagine.

"She prayed for it, you know," said Felix, after Sara had gone home.

"That's too easy a way of earning money," grumbled Peter resentfully. "If the rest of us had just set down and done nothing, only prayed, how much do you s'pose we'd have? It don't seem fair to me."

"Oh, well, it's different with Sara," said Dan. "We *could* earn money and she *couldn't*. You see? But come on down to the orchard. The Story Girl had a letter from her father today and she's going to read it to us."

We went promptly. A letter from the Story Girl's father was always an event; and to hear her read it was almost as good as hearing her tell a story.

Before coming to Carlisle, Uncle Blair Stanley had been a mere name to us. Now he was a personality. His letters to the Story Girl, the pictures and sketches he sent her, her adoring and frequent mention of him, all combined to make him very real to us.

We *felt* then, what we did not understand till later years, that our grown-up relatives did not altogether admire or approve of Uncle Blair. He belonged to a different world from theirs. They had never known him very intimately or understood him. I realize now that Uncle Blair was a bit of a Bohemian—a respectable sort of tramp. Had he been a poor man he might have been a more successful artist. But he had a small fortune of his own and, lacking the spur of necessity, or of disquieting ambition, he remained little more than a clever amateur. Once in a while he painted a picture which showed what he could do; but for the rest, he was satisfied to wander over the world, light-hearted and content. We knew that the Story Girl was thought to resemble him strongly in appearance and temperament, but she had far more fire and intensity and strength of will—her inheritance from King and Ward. She would never be satisfied as a dabbler; whatever her future career should be, into it she would throw all her powers of mind and heart and soul.

But Uncle Blair could do at least one thing surpassingly well. He could write letters. Such letters! By contrast, Felix and I were secretly ashamed of father's epistles. Father could talk well but, as Felix said, he couldn't write worth a cent. The letters we had received from him since his arrival in Rio de Janeiro were mere scrawls, telling us to be good boys and not trouble Aunt Janet, incidentally adding that he was well and lonesome. Felix and I were always glad to get his letters, but we never read them aloud to an admiring circle in the orchard.

Uncle Blair was spending the summer in Switzerland; and the letter the Story Girl read to us, among the fair, frail White Ladies of the Walk, where the west wind came now with a sigh, and again with a rush, and then brushed our faces as softly as the down of a thistle, was full of the glamour of mountain-rimmed lakes, and purple chalets, and "snowy summits old in story." We climbed Mount Blanc, and saw the Jungfrau soaring into cloudland, and walked among the gloomy pillars of Bonnivard's prison. Finally, the Story Girl told us the tale of the Prisoner of Chillon, in words that were Byron's, but in a voice that was all her own.

"It must be just splendid to go to Europe," sighed Cecily longingly.

"*I* am going some day," said the Story Girl airily.

We looked at her with a slightly incredulous awe. To us, in those years, Europe seemed almost as remote and unreachable as the moon. It was hard to believe that one of *us* should ever go there. But Aunt Julia had gone—and *she* had been brought up in Carlisle on this very farm. So it was possible that the Story Girl might go too.

"What will you do there?" asked Peter practically.

"I shall learn how to tell stories to all the world," said the Story Girl dreamily.

It was a lovely, golden-brown evening; the orchard, and the farm-lands beyond, were full of ruby lights and kissing shadows. Over in the east, above the Awkward Man's house, the Wedding Veil of the Proud Princess floated across the sky, presently turning as rosy as if bedewed with her heart's blood. We sat there and talked until the first star lighted a white taper over the beech hill.

Then I remembered that I had forgotten to take my dose of magic seed, and I hastened to do it, although I was beginning to lose faith in it. I had not grown a single bit, by the merciless testimony of the hall door.

I took the box of seed out of my trunk in the twilit room and swallowed the decreed pinch. As I did so, Dan's voice rang out behind me.

"Beverley King, what have you got there?"

I thrust the box hastily into my trunk and confronted Dan.

"None of your business," I said defiantly.

"Yes, 'tis." Dan was too much in earnest to resent my blunt speech. "Look here, Bev, is that magic seed? And did you get it from Billy Robinson?"

Dan and I looked at each other, suspicion dawning in our eyes.

"What do you know about Billy Robinson and his magic seed?" I demanded.

"Just this. I bought a box from him for—for—something. He said he wasn't going to sell any of it to anybody else. Did he sell any to you?"

"Yes, he did," I said in disgust—for I was beginning to understand that Billy and his magic seed were arrant frauds.

"What for? *Your* mouth is a decent size," said Dan.

"Mouth? It had nothing to do with my mouth! He said it

would make me grow tall. And it hasn't—not an inch! I don't see what you wanted it for! You are tall enough."

"I got it for my mouth," said Dan with a shamefaced grin. "The girls in school laugh at it so. Kate Marr says it's like a gash in a pie. Billy said that seed would shrink it for sure."

Well, there it was! Billy had deceived us both. Nor were we the only victims. We did not find the whole story out at once. Indeed, the summer was almost over before, in one way or another, the full measure of that shameless Billy Robinson's iniquity was revealed to us. But I shall anticipate the successive relations in this chapter. Every pupil of Carlisle school, so it eventually appeared, had bought magic seed, under solemn promise of secrecy. Felix had believed blissfully that it would make him thin. Cecily's hair was to become naturally curly, and Sara Ray was not to be afraid of Peg Bowen any more. It was to make Felicity as clever as the Story Girl and it was to make the Story Girl as good a cook as Felicity. What Peter had bought magic seed for remained a secret longer than any of the others. Finally—it was the night before what we expected would be the Judgment Day—he confessed to me that he had taken it to make Felicity fond of him. Skillfully indeed had that astute Billy played on our respective weaknesses.

The keenest edge to our humiliation was given by the discovery that the magic seed was nothing more or less than caraway, which grew in abundance at Billy Robinson's uncle's in Markdale. Peg Bowen had had nothing to do with it.

Well, we had all been badly hoaxed. But we did not trumpet our wrongs abroad. We did not even call Billy to account. We thought that least said was soonest mended in such a matter. We went very softly indeed, lest the grown-ups, especially that terrible Uncle Roger, should hear of it.

"We should have known better than to trust Billy Robinson," said Felicity, summing up the case one evening when all had been made known. "After all, what could you expect from a pig but a grunt?"

We were not surprised to find that Billy Robinson's contribution to the library fund was the largest handed in by any of the scholars. Cecily said she didn't envy him his conscience. But I am afraid she measured his conscience by her own. I doubt very much if Billy's troubled him at all.

CHAPTER 10

A DAUGHTER OF EVE

"I HATE the thought of growing up," said the Story Girl reflectively, "because I can never go barefooted then, and nobody will ever see what beautiful feet I have."

She was sitting, in the July sunlight, on the ledge of the open hayloft window in Uncle Roger's big barn; and the bare feet below her print skirt *were* beautiful. They were slender and shapely and satin smooth, with arched insteps, the daintiest of toes, and nails like pink shells.

We were all in the hayloft. The Story Girl had been telling us a tale

> "Of old, unhappy, far-off things,
> And battles long ago."

Felicity and Cecily were curled up in a corner, and we boys sprawled idly on the fragrant, sun-warm heaps. We had "stowed" the hay in the loft that morning for Uncle Roger, so we felt that we had earned the right to loll on our sweet-smelling couch. Haylofts are delicious places, with just enough of shadow and soft, uncertain noises to give an agreeable tang of mystery. The swallows flew in and out of their nests above our heads, and wherever a sunbeam fell through a chink the air swarmed with golden dust. Outside of the loft was a vast, sunshiny gulf of blue sky and mellow air, wherein floated argosies of fluffy cloud, and airy tops of maple and spruce.

Pat was with us, of course, prowling about stealthily, or making frantic, bootless leaps at the swallows. A cat in a hayloft is a beautiful example of the eternal fitness of things. We had not heard of this fitness then, but we all felt that Paddy was in his own place in a hayloft.

"*I* think it is very vain to talk about anything you have yourself being beautiful," remarked Felicity.

"I am not a bit vain," said the Story Girl, with entire truthfulness. "It is not vanity to know your own good points. It would just be stupidity if you didn't. It's only vanity when you get puffed up about them. I am not a bit pretty. My only good points are my hair and eyes and feet. So I think it's real mean that one of them has to be covered up the most of the time. I'm always glad when it gets warm enough to go barefooted. But, when I grow up they'll have to be covered all the time. It *is* mean."

"You'll have to put your shoes and stockings on when you go to the magic lantern show tonight," said Felicity in a tone of satisfaction.

"I don't know that. I'm thinking of going barefooted."

"Oh, you wouldn't! Sara Stanley, you're not in earnest!" exclaimed Felicity, her blue eyes filling with horror.

The Story Girl winked with the side of her face next to Felix and me, but the side next the girls changed not a muscle. She dearly loved to "take a rise" out of Felicity now and then.

"Indeed, I would if I just made up my mind to. Why not? Why not bare feet—if they're clean—as well as bare hands and face?"

"Oh, you wouldn't! It would be such a disgrace!" said poor Felicity in real distress.

"We went to school barefooted all June," argued that wicked Story Girl. "What is the difference between going to the schoolhouse barefooted in the daytime and going in the evening?"

"Oh, there's *every* difference. I can't just explain it—but every one *knows* there is a difference. You know it yourself. Oh, *please,* don't do such a thing, Sara."

"Well, I won't, just to oblige you," said the Story Girl, who would have died the death before she would have gone to a "public meeting" barefooted.

We were all rather excited over the magic lantern show which an itinerant lecturer was to give in the schoolhouse that evening. Even Felix and I, who had seen such shows galore, were interested, and the rest were quite wild. There had never been such a thing in Carlisle before. We were all going, Peter included. Peter went everywhere with us now. He was a regular attendant at church and Sunday School, where his behaviour was as irreproachable as if he had been "raised" in the caste of Vere de Vere. It was a feather in the Story Girl's cap, for she took all the credit of having started Peter on the right road. Felicity was resigned, although the fatal patch on Peter's best trousers was still an eyesore to her. She declared she never got any good of the singing, because Peter stood up then and every one could see the patch. Mrs. James Clark, whose pew was behind ours, never took her eyes off it—or so Felicity averred.

But Peter's stockings were always darned. Aunt Olivia had seen to that, ever since she heard of Peter's singular device regarding them on his first Sunday. She had also given Peter a Bible, of which he was so proud that he hated to use it lest he should soil it.

"I think I'll wrap it up and keep it in my box," he said. "I've an old Bible of Aunt Jane's at home I can use. I s'pose it's just the same, even if it is old, isn't it?"

"Oh, yes," Cecily had assured him. "The Bible is always the same."

"I thought maybe they'd got some new improvements on it since Aunt Jane's day," said Peter, relieved.

"Sara Ray is coming along the lane, and she's crying," announced Dan, who was peering out of a knot-hole on the opposite side of the loft.

"Sara Ray is crying half her time," said Cecily impatiently. "I'm sure she cries a quartful of tears a month. There are times when you can't help crying. But *I* hide them. Sara just goes and cries in public."

The lachrymose Sara presently joined us and we discovered the cause of her tears to be the doleful fact that her mother had forbidden her to go to the magic lantern show that night. We all showed the sympathy we felt.

"She *said* yesterday you could go," said the Story Girl indignantly. "Why has she changed her mind?"

"Because of measles in Markdale," sobbed Sara. "She says Markdale is full of them, and there'll be sure to be some of the Markdale people at the show. So I'm not to go. And I've never seen a magic lantern—I've never seen *anything.*"

"I don't believe there's any danger of catching measles," said Felicity. "If there was we wouldn't be allowed to go."

"I wish I *could* get the measles," said Sara defiantly. "Maybe I'd be of some importance to ma then."

"Suppose Cecily goes down with you and coaxes your mother,"

suggested the Story Girl. "Perhaps she'd let you go then. She likes Cecily. She doesn't like either Felicity or me, so it would only make matters worse for us to try."

"Ma's gone to town—pa and her went this afternoon—and they're not coming back till tomorrow. There's nobody home but Judy Pineau and me."

"Then," said the Story Girl, "why don't you just go to the show anyhow? Your mother won't ever know, if you coax Judy to hold her tongue."

"Oh, but that's wrong," said Felicity. "You shouldn't put Sara up to disobeying her mother."

Now, Felicity for once was undoubtedly right. The Story Girl's suggestion *was* wrong; and if it had been Cecily who protested, the Story Girl would probably have listened to her, and proceeded no further in the matter. But Felicity was one of those unfortunate people whose protests against wrong-doing serve only to drive the wrong-doer further on her sinful way.

The Story Girl resented Felicity's superior tone, and proceeded to tempt Sara in right good earnest. The rest of us held our tongues. It was, we told ourselves, Sara's own lookout.

"I have a good mind to do it," said Sara. "But I can't get my good clothes; they're in the spare room, and ma locked the door, for fear somebody would get at the fruit cake. I haven't a single thing to wear, except my school gingham."

"Well, that's new and pretty," said the Story Girl. "We'll lend you some things. You can have my lace collar. That'll make the gingham quite elegant. And Cecily will lend you her second best hat."

"But I've no shoes or stockings. They're locked up too."

"You can have a pair of mine," said Felicity, who probably thought that since Sara was certain to yield to temptation, she might as well be garbed decently for her transgression.

Sara did yield. When the Story Girl's voice entreated it was not easy to resist its temptation, even if you wanted to. That evening, when we started for the schoolhouse, Sara Ray was among us, decked out in borrowed plumes.

"Suppose she *does* catch the measles?" Felicity said aside.

"I don't believe there'll be anybody there from Markdale. The lecturer is going to Markdale next week. They'll wait for that," said the Story Girl airily.

It was a cool, dewy evening, and we walked down the long, red hill in the highest of spirits. Over a valley filled with beech and spruce was a sunset afterglow—creamy yellow and a hue that was not so much red as the dream of red, with a young moon swung low in it. The air was sweet with the breath of mown hayfields where swaths of clover had been steeping in the sun. Wild roses grew pinkly along the fences, and the roadsides were star-dusted with buttercups.

Those of us who had nothing the matter with our consciences enjoyed our walk to the little whitewashed schoolhouse in the valley. Felicity and Cecily were void of offence towards all men. The Story Girl walked uprightly like an incarnate flame in her crimson silk. Her pretty feet were hidden in the tan-coloured, buttoned Paris boots which were the secret envy of every school girl in Carlisle.

But Sara Ray was not happy. Her face was so melancholy that the Story Girl lost patience with her. The Story Girl herself was not altogether at ease. Probably her own conscience was troubling her. But admit it she would not.

"Now, Sara," she said, "you just take my advice and go into this with all your heart if you go at all. Never mind if it is bad. There's no use in being naughty if you spoil your fun by wishing all the time you were good. You can repent afterwards, but there is no use in mixing the two things together."

"I'm not repenting," protested Sara. "I'm only scared of ma finding it out."

"Oh!" The Story Girl's voice expressed her scorn. For remorse she had understanding and sympathy; but fear of her fellow creatures was something unknown to her. "Didn't Judy Pineau promise you solemnly she wouldn't tell?"

"Yes; but maybe some one who sees me there will mention it to ma."

"Well, if you are so scared you'd better not go. It isn't too late. Here's your own gate," said Cecily.

But Sara could not give up the delights of the show. So she walked on, a small, miserable testimony that the way of the transgressor is never easy, even when said transgressor is only a damsel of eleven.

The magic lantern show was a splendid one. The views were good and the lecturer witty. We repeated his jokes to each other all the way home. Sara, who had not enjoyed the exhibition at all, seemed to feel more cheerful when it was over and she was going home. The Story Girl on the contrary was gloomy.

"There *were* Markdale people there," she confided to me, "and the Williamsons live next door to the Cowans, who have measles. I wish I'd never egged Sara on to going—but don't tell Felicity I said so. If Sara Ray had really enjoyed the show I wouldn't mind. But she didn't. I could see that. So I've done wrong and made her do wrong—and there's nothing to show for it."

The night was scented and mysterious. The wind was playing an eerie fleshless melody in the reeds of the brook hollow. The sky was dark and starry, and across it the Milky Way flung its shimmering misty ribbon.

"There's four hundred million stars in the Milky Way," quoth Peter, who frequently astonished us by knowing more than any hired boy could be expected to. He had a retentive memory, and never forgot anything he heard or read. The few books left to him by his oft-referred-to Aunt Jane had stocked his mind with a miscellaneous information which sometimes made Felix and me doubt if we knew as much as Peter after all. Felicity was so impressed by his knowledge of astronomy that she dropped back from the other girls and walked beside him. She had not done so before because he was barefooted. It was permissible for hired boys to go to public meetings—when not held in the church—with bare feet, and no particular disgrace attached to it. But Felicity would not walk with a barefooted companion. It was dark now, so nobody would notice his feet.

"I know a story about the Milky Way," said the Story Girl, brightening up. "I read it in a book of Aunt Louisa's in town, and I learned it off by heart. Once there were two archangels in heaven, named Zerah and Zulamith—,"

"Have angels names—same as people?" interrupted Peter.

"Yes, of course. They *must* have. They'd be all mixed up if they hadn't."

"And when I'm an angel—if I ever get to be one—will my name still be Peter?"

"No. You'll have a new name up there," said Cecily gently. "It says so in the Bible."

"Well, I'm glad of that. Peter would be such a funny name

for an angel. And what is the difference between angels and archangels?"

"Oh, archangels are angels that have been angels so long that they've had time to grow better and brighter and more beautiful than newer angels," said the Story Girl, who probably made that explanation up on the spur of the moment, just to pacify Peter.

"How long does it take for an angel to grow into an archangel?" pursued Peter.

"Oh, I don't know. Millions of years likely. And even then I don't suppose *all* the angels do. A good many of them must just stay plain angels, I expect."

"*I* shall be satisfied just to be a plain angel," said Felicity modestly.

"Oh, see here, if you're going to interrupt and argue over everything, we'll never get the story told," said Felix. "Dry up, all of you, and let the Story Girl go on."

We dried up, and the Story Girl went on.

"Zerah and Zulamith loved each other, just as mortals love, and this is forbidden by the laws of the Almighty. And because Zerah and Zulamith had so broken God's law they were banished from His presence to the uttermost bounds of the universe. If they had been banished *together* it would have been no punishment; so Zerah was exiled to a star on one side of the universe, and Zulamith was sent to a star on the other side of the universe; and between them was a fathomless abyss which thought itself could not cross. Only one thing could cross it— and that was love. Zulamith yearned for Zerah with such fidelity and longing that he began to build up a bridge of light from his star; and Zerah, not knowing this, but loving and longing for him, began to build a similar bridge of light from her star. For a thousand thousand years they both built the bridge of light, and at last they met and sprang into each other's arms. Their toil and loneliness and suffering were all over and forgotten, and the bridge they had built spanned the gulf between their stars of exile.

"Now, when the other archangels saw what had been done they flew in fear and anger to God's white throne, and cried to Him,

" 'See what these rebellious ones have done! They have built them a bridge of light across the universe, and set Thy decree of separation at naught. Do Thou, then, stretch forth Thine arm and destroy their impious work.'

"They ceased—and all heaven was hushed. Through the silence sounded the voice of the Almighty.

" 'Nay,' He said, 'whatsoever in my universe true love hath builded not even the Almighty can destroy. The bridge must stand forever.'

"And," concluded the Story Girl, her face upturned to the sky and her big eyes filled with starlight, "it stands still. That bridge is the Milky Way."

"What a lovely story," sighed Sara Ray, who had been wooed to a temporary forgetfulness of her woes by its charm.

The rest of us came back to earth, feeling that we had been wandering among the hosts of heaven. We were not old enough to appreciate fully the wonderful meaning of the legend; but we felt its beauty and its appeal. To us forevermore the Milky Way would be, not Peter's overwhelming garland of suns, but the lucent bridge, love-created, on which the banished archangels crossed from star to star.

We had to go up Sara Ray's lane with her to her very door, for she was afraid Peg Bowen would catch her if she went alone. Then the Story Girl and I walked up the hill together. Peter and Felicity lagged behind. Cecily and Dan and Felix were walking before us, hand in hand, singing a hymn. Cecily had a very sweet voice, and I listened in delight. But the Story Girl sighed.

"What if Sara does take the measles?" she asked miserably.

"Everyone has to have the measles sometime," I said comfortingly, "and the younger you are the better."

CHAPTER 11

THE STORY GIRL DOES PENANCE

TEN DAYS later, Aunt Olivia and Uncle Roger went to town one evening, to remain over night and the next day. Peter and the Story Girl were to stay at Uncle Alec's during their absence.

We were in the orchard at sunset, listening to the story of King Cophetua and the beggar maid—all of us, except Peter, who was hoeing turnips, and Felicity, who had gone down the hill on an errand to Mrs. Ray.

The Story Girl impersonated the beggar maid so vividly, and with such an illusion of beauty, that we did not wonder in the least at the king's love for her. I had read the story before, and it had been my opinion that it was "rot." No king, I felt certain, would ever marry a beggar maid when he had princesses galore from whom to choose. But now I understood it all.

When Felicity returned we concluded from her expression that she had news. And she had.

"Sara is real sick," she said, with regret, and something that was not regret mingled in her voice. "She has a cold and sore throat, and she is feverish. Mrs. Ray says if she isn't better by the morning she's going to send for the doctor. *And she is afraid it's the measles.*"

Felicity flung the last sentence at the Story Girl, who turned very pale.

"Oh, do you suppose she caught them at the magic lantern show?" she said miserably.

"Where else could she have caught them?" said Felicity mercilessly. "I didn't see her, of course—Mrs. Ray met me at the door and told me not to come in. But Mrs. Ray says the measles always go awful hard with the Rays—if they don't die completely of them it leaves them deaf or half blind, or something like that. Of course," added Felicity, her heart melting at sight of the misery in the Story Girl's piteous eyes, "Mrs. Ray always looks on the dark side, and it may not be the measles Sara has after all."

But Felicity had done her work too thoroughly. The Story Girl was not to be comforted.

"I'd give anything if I'd never put Sara up to going to that show," she said. "It's all my fault—but the punishment falls on Sara, and that isn't fair. I'd go this minute and confess the whole thing to Mrs. Ray; but if I did it might get Sara into more trouble, and I mustn't do that. I sha'n't sleep a wink tonight."

I don't think she did. She looked very pale and woebegone when she came down to breakfast. But, for all that, there was a certain exhilaration about her.

"I'm going to do penance all day for coaxing Sara to disobey her mother," she announced with chastened triumph.

"Penance?" we murmured in bewilderment.

"Yes. I'm going to deny myself everything I like, and do everything I can think of that I don't like, just to punish myself for being so wicked. And if any of you think of anything I don't, just mention it to me. I thought it out last night. Maybe Sara won't be so very sick if God sees I'm truly sorry."

"He can see it anyhow, without you're doing anything," said Cecily.

"Well, my conscience will feel better."

"I don't believe Presbyterians ever do penance," said Felicity dubiously. "I never heard of one doing it."

But the rest of us rather looked with favour on the Story Girl's idea. We felt sure that she would do penance as picturesquely and thoroughly as she did everything else.

"You might put peas in your shoes, you know," suggested Peter.

"The very thing! I never thought of that. I'll get some after breakfast. I'm not going to eat a single thing all day, except bread and water—and not much of that!"

This, we felt, was a heroic measure indeed. To sit down to one of Aunt Janet's meals, in ordinary health and appetite, and eat nothing but bread and water—that would be penance with a vengeance! We felt *we* could never do it. But the Story Girl did it. We admired and pitied her. But now I do not think that she either needed our pity or deserved our admiration. Her ascetic fare was really sweeter to her than honey of Hymettus. She was, though quite unconsciously, acting a part, and tasting all the subtle joy of the artist, which is so much more exquisite than any material pleasure.

Aunt Janet, of course, noticed the Story Girl's abstinence and asked if she was sick.

"No. I am just doing penance, Aunt Janet, for a sin I committed. I can't confess it, because that would bring trouble on another person. So I'm going to do penance all day. You don't mind, do you?"

Aunt Janet was in a very good humour that morning, so she merely laughed.

"Not if you don't go too far with your nonsense," she said tolerantly.

"Thank you. And will you give me a handful of hard peas after breakfast, Aunt Janet? I want to put them in my shoes."

"There isn't any; I used the last in the soup yesterday."

"Oh!" The Story Girl was much disappointed. "Then I suppose I'll have to do without. The new peas wouldn't hurt enough. They're so soft they'd just squash flat."

"I'll tell you," said Peter, "I'll pick up a lot of those little round pebbles on Mr. King's front walk. They'll be just as good as peas."

"You'll do nothing of the sort," said Aunt Janet. "Sara must not do penance in that way. She would wear holes in her stockings, and might seriously bruise her feet."

"What would you say if I took a whip and whipped my bare shoulders till the blood came?" demanded the Story Girl aggrieved.

"I wouldn't *say* anything," retorted Aunt Janet. "I'd simply turn you over my knee and give you a sound, solid spanking, Miss Sara. You'd find that penance enough."

The Story Girl was crimson with indignation. To have such a remark made to you—when you were fourteen and a half—and before the boys, too! Really, Aunt Janet could be very dreadful.

It was vacation, and there was not much to do that day; we were soon free to seek the orchard. But the Story Girl would not come. She had seated herself in the darkest, hottest corner of the kitchen, with a piece of old cotton in her hand.

"I am not going out to play today," she said, "and I'm not going to tell a single story. Aunt Janet won't let me put pebbles in my shoes, but I've put a thistle next my skin on my back and it sticks into me if I lean back the least bit. And I'm going

to work buttonholes all over this cotton. I hate working buttonholes worse than anything in the world, so I'm going to
work them all day."

"What's the good of working buttonholes on an old rag?"
asked Felicity.

"It isn't any good. The beauty of penance is that it makes
you feel uncomfortable. So it doesn't matter what you do,
whether it's useful or not, so long as it's nasty. Oh, I wonder
how Sara is this morning."

"Mother's going down this afternoon," said Felicity. "She
says none of us must go near the place till we know whether
it is the measles or not."

"I've thought of a great penance," said Cecily eagerly. "Don't
go to the missionary meeting tonight."

The Story Girl looked piteous.

"I thought of that myself,—but I *can't* stay home, Cecily. It
would be more than flesh and blood could endure. I *must* hear
that missionary speak. They say he was all but eaten by cannibals
once. Just think how many new stories I'd have to tell after
I'd heard him! No, I must go, but I'll tell you what I'll do. I'll
wear my school dress and hat. *That* will be penance. Felicity,
when you set the table for dinner, put the broken-handled knife
for me. I hate it so. And I'm going to take a dose of Mexican
Tea every two hours. It's such dreadful tasting stuff—but it's
a good blood purifier, so Aunt Janet can't object to it."

The Story Girl carried out her self-imposed penance fully.
All day she sat in the kitchen and worked buttonholes, subsisting
on bread and water and Mexican Tea.

Felicity did a mean thing. She went to work and made little
raisin pies, right there in the kitchen before the Story Girl. The
smell of raisin pies is something to tempt an anchorite; and
the Story Girl was exceedingly fond of them. Felicity ate two
in her very presence, and then brought the rest out to us in
the orchard. The Story Girl could see us through the window,
carousing without stint on raisin pies and Uncle Edward's
cherries. But she worked on at her buttonholes. She would not
look at the exciting serial in the new magazine Dan brought
home from the post-office, neither would she open a letter from
her father. Pat came over, but his most seductive purrs won

no notice from his mistress, who refused herself the pleasure of even patting him.

Aunt Janet could not go down the hill in the afternoon to find out how Sara was because company came to tea—the Millwards from Markdale. Mr. Millward was a doctor, and Mrs. Millward was a B.A. Aunt Janet was very desirous that everything should be as nice as possible, and we were all sent to our rooms before tea to wash and dress up. The Story Girl slipped over home, and when she came back we gasped. She had combed her hair out straight, and braided it in a tight, kinky, pudgy braid; and she wore an old dress of faded print, with holes in the elbows and ragged flounces, which was much too short for her.

"Sara Stanley, have you taken leave of your senses?" demanded Aunt Janet. "What do you mean by putting on such a rig! Don't you know I have company to tea?"

"Yes, and that is just why I put it on, Aunt Janet. I want to mortify the flesh—"

"I'll 'mortify' you, if I catch you showing yourself to the Millwards like that, my girl! Go right home and dress yourself decently—or eat your supper in the kitchen."

The Story Girl chose the latter alternative. She was highly indignant. I verily believe that to sit at the dining-room table, in that shabby, outgrown dress, conscious of looking her ugliest, and eating only bread and water before the critical Millwards, would have been positive bliss to her.

When we went to the missionary meeting that evening, the Story Girl wore her school dress and hat, while Felicity and Cecily were in their pretty muslins. And she had tied her hair with a snuff-brown ribbon which was very unbecoming to her.

The first person we saw in the church porch was Mrs. Ray. She told us that Sara had nothing worse than a feverish cold.

The missionary had at least seven happy listeners that night. We were all glad that Sara did not have measles, and the Story Girl was radiant.

"Now you see all your penance was wasted," said Felicity, as we walked home, keeping close together because of a rumour that Peg Bowen was abroad.

"Oh, I don't know. I feel better since I punished myself. But

I'm going to make up for it tomorrow," said the Story Girl energetically. "In fact, I'll begin tonight. I'm going to the pantry as soon as I get home, and I'll read father's letter before I go to bed. Wasn't the missionary splendid? That cannibal story was simply grand. I tried to remember every word, so that I can tell it just as he told it. Missionaries are such noble people."

"I'd like to be a missionary and have adventures like that," said Felix.

"It would be all right if you could be sure the cannibals would be interrupted in the nick of time as his were," said Dan. "But sposen they weren't?"

"Nothing would prevent cannibals from eating Felix if they once caught him," giggled Felicity. "He's so nice and fat."

I am sure Felix felt very unlike a missionary at that precise moment.

"I'm going to put two cents more a week in my missionary box than I've been doing," said Cecily determinedly.

Two cents more a week out of Cecily's egg money, meant something of a sacrifice. It inspired the rest of us. We all decided to increase our weekly contribution by a cent or so. And Peter, who had had no missionary box at all, up to this time, determined to start one.

"I don't seem to be able to feel as int'rested in missionaries as you folks do," he said, "but maybe if I begin to give something I'll get int'rested. I'll want to know how my money's being spent. I won't be able to give much. When your father's run away, and your mother goes out washing, and you're only old enough to get fifty cents a week, you can't give much to the heathen. But I'll do the best I can. My Aunt Jane was fond of missions. Are there any Methodist heathen? I s'pose I ought to give my box to them, rather than to Presbyterian heathen."

"No, it's only after they're converted that they're anything in particular," said Felicity. "Before that, they're just plain heathen. But if you want your money to go to a Methodist missionary you can give it to the Methodist minister at Markdale. I guess the Presbyterians can get along without it, and look after their own heathen."

"Just smell Mrs. Sampson's flowers," said Cecily, as we passed a trim white paling close to the road, over which blew odours sweeter than the perfume of Araby's shore. "Her roses are all out and that bed of Sweet William is a sight by daylight."

"Sweet William is a dreadful name for a flower," said the Story Girl. "William is a man's name, and men are *never* sweet. They are a great many nice things, but they are *not* sweet and shouldn't be. That is for women. Oh, look at the moonshine on the road in that gap between the spruces! I'd like a dress of moonshine, with stars for buttons."

"It wouldn't do," said Felicity decidedly. "You could see through it."

Which seemed to settle the question of moonshine dresses effectually.

CHAPTER 12

THE BLUE CHEST OF RACHEL WARD

"IT'S UTTERLY out of the question," said Aunt Janet seriously. When Aunt Janet said seriously that anything was out of the question it meant that she was thinking about it, and would probably end up by doing it. If a thing really was out of the question she merely laughed and refused to discuss it at all.

The particular matter in or out of question that opening day of August was a project which Uncle Edward had recently mooted. Uncle Edward's youngest daughter was to be married; and Uncle Edward had written over, urging Uncle Alec, Aunt Janet and Aunt Olivia to go down to Halifax for the wedding and spend a week there.

Uncle Alec and Aunt Olivia were eager to go; but Aunt Janet at first declared it was impossible.

"How could we go away and leave the place at the mercy of all those young ones?" she demanded. "We'd come home and find them all sick, and the house burned down."

"Not a bit of fear of it," scoffed Uncle Roger. "Felicity is as good a housekeeper as you are; and I shall be here to look after them all, and keep them from burning the house down.

You've been promising Edward for years to visit him, and you'll never have a better chance. The haying is over and the harvest isn't on, and Alec needs a change. He isn't looking well at all."

I think it was Uncle Roger's last argument which convinced Aunt Janet. In the end she decided to go. Uncle Roger's house was to be closed, and he and Peter and the Story Girl were to take up their abode with us.

We were all delighted. Felicity, in especial, seemed to be in the seventh heaven. To be left in sole charge of a big house, with three meals a day to plan and prepare, with poultry and cows and dairy and garden to superintend, apparently furnished forth Felicity's conception of Paradise. Of course, we were all to help; but Felicity was to "run things," and she gloried in it.

The Story Girl was pleased, too.

"Felicity is going to give me cooking lessons," she confided to me, as we walked in the orchard. "Isn't that fine? In a week I ought to be able to learn something, don't you think? It will be easier when there are no grown-ups around to make me nervous, and laugh if I make mistakes."

Uncle Alec and the aunts left on Monday morning. Poor Aunt Janet was full of dismal forebodings, and gave us so many charges and warnings that we did not try to remember any of them; Uncle Alec merely told us to be good and mind what Uncle Roger said. Aunt Olivia laughed at us out of her pansy-blue eyes, and told us she knew exactly what we felt like, and hoped we'd have a gorgeous time.

"Mind they go to bed at a decent hour," Aunt Janet called back to Uncle Roger as she drove out of the gate. "And if anything dreadful happens telegraph us."

Then they were really gone and we were all left "to keep house."

Uncle Roger and Peter went away to their work. Felicity at once set the preparations for dinner a-going, and allotted to each of us his portion of service. The Story Girl was to prepare the potatoes; Felix and Dan were to pick and shell the peas; Cecily was to attend the fire; I was to peel the turnips. Felicity made our mouths water by announcing that she was going to make a roly-poly jam pudding for dinner.

I peeled my turnips on the back porch, put them in their pot, and set them on the stove. Then I was at liberty to watch the others, who had longer jobs. The kitchen was a scene of happy activity. The Story Girl peeled her potatoes, somewhat slowly and awkwardly—for she was not deft at household tasks; Dan and Felix shelled peas and tormented Pat by attaching pods to his ears and tail; Felicity, flushed and serious, measured and stirred skilfully.

"I am sitting on a tragedy," said the Story Girl suddenly.

Felix and I stared. We were not quite sure what a "tragedy" was, but we did not think it was an old blue wooden chest, such as the Story Girl was undoubtedly sitting on, if eyesight counted for anything.

The old chest filled up the corner between the table and the wall. Neither Felix nor I had ever thought about it particularly. It was very large and heavy, and Felicity generally said hard things of it when she swept the kitchen.

"This old blue chest holds a tragedy," explained the Story Girl. "I know a story about it."

"Cousin Rachel Ward's wedding things are all in that old chest," said Felicity.

Who was Cousin Rachel Ward? And why were her wedding things shut up in an old blue chest in Uncle Alec's kitchen? We demanded the tale instantly. The Story Girl told it to us as she peeled her potatoes. Perhaps the potatoes suffered— Felicity declared the eyes were not properly done at all—but the story did not.

"It is a sad story," said the Story Girl, "and it happened fifty years ago, when Grandfather and Grandmother King were quite young. Grandmother's cousin Rachel Ward came to spend a winter with them. She belonged to Montreal and she was an orphan too, just like the Family Ghost. I have never heard what she looked like, but she *must* have been beautiful, of course."

"Mother says she was awful sentimental and romantic," interjected Felicity.

"Well, anyway, she met Will Montague that winter. He was handsome—everybody says so"—

"And an awful flirt," said Felicity.

"Felicity, I *wish* you wouldn't interrupt. It spoils the effect.

What would you feel like if I went and kept stirring things that didn't belong to it into that pudding? I feel just the same way. Well, Will Montague fell in love with Rachel Ward, and she with him, and it was all arranged that they were to be married from here in the spring. Poor Rachel was so happy that winter; she made all her wedding things with her own hands. Girls did, then, you know, for there was no such thing as a sewing-machine. Well, at last in April the wedding day came, and all the guests were here, and Rachel was dressed in her wedding robes, waiting for her bridegroom. And"—the Story Girl laid down her knife and her potato and clasped her wet hands—*"Will Montague never came!"*

We felt as much of a shock as if we had been one of the expectant guests ourselves.

"What happened to him? Was *he* killed too?" asked Felix.

The Story Girl sighed and resumed her work.

"No, indeed. I wish he had been. *That* would have been suitable and romantic. No, it was just something horrid. He had to run away for debt! Fancy! He acted mean right through, Aunt Janet says. He never sent even a word to Rachel, and she never heard from him again."

"Pig!" said Felix forcibly.

"She was broken-hearted of course. When she found out what had happened, she took all her wedding things, and her supply of linen, and some presents that had been given her, and packed them all away in this old blue chest. Then she went away back to Montreal, and took the key with her. She never came back to the Island again—I suppose she couldn't bear to. And she has lived in Montreal ever since and never married. She is an old woman now—nearly seventy-five. And this chest has never been opened since."

"Mother wrote to Cousin Rachel ten years ago," said Cecily, "and asked her if she might open the chest to see if the moths had got into it. There's a crack in the back as big as your finger. Cousin Rachel wrote back that if it wasn't for one thing that was in the trunk she would ask mother to open the chest and dispose of the things as she liked. But she could not bear that any one but herself should see or touch that one thing. So she wanted it left as it was. Ma said she washed her hands of it, moths or no moths. She said if Cousin Rachel had to move that chest every time the floor had to be scrubbed it would cure her of her sentimental nonsense. But I think," concluded Cecily, "that I would feel just like Cousin Rachel in her place."

"What was the thing she couldn't bear any one to see?" I asked.

"Ma thinks it was her wedding dress. But father says he believes it was Will Montague's picture," said Felicity. "He saw her put it in. Father knows some of the things that are in the chest. He was ten years old, and he saw her pack it. There's a white muslin wedding dress and a veil—and—and—a—a"— Felicity dropped her eyes and blushed painfully.

"A petticoat, embroidered by hand from hem to belt," said the Story Girl calmly.

"And a china fruit basket with an apple on the handle," went on Felicity, much relieved. "And a tea set, and a blue candle-stick."

"I'd dearly love to see all the things that are in it," said the Story Girl.

"Pa says it must never be opened without Cousin Rachel's permission," said Cecily.

Felix and I looked at the chest reverently. It had taken on a new significance in our eyes, and seemed like a tomb wherein lay buried some dead romance of the vanished years.

"What happened to Will Montague?" I asked.

"Nothing!" said the Story Girl viciously. "He just went on living and flourishing. He patched up matters with his creditors after awhile, and came back to the Island; and in the end he married a real nice girl, with money, and was very happy. Did you ever *hear* of anything so unjust?"

"Beverley King," suddenly cried Felicity, who had been peering into a pot, *"you've gone and put the turnips on to boil whole just like potatoes!"*

"Wasn't that right?" I cried, in an agony of shame.

"Right!" but Felicity had already whisked the turnips out, and was slicing them, while all the others were laughing at me. I had added a tradition on my own account to the family archives.

Uncle Roger roared when he heard it; and he roared again at night over Peter's account of Felix attempting to milk a cow.

Felix had previously acquired the knack of extracting milk from the udder. But he had never before tried to "milk a whole cow." He did not get on well; the cow tramped on his foot, and finally upset the bucket.

"What are you to do when a cow won't stand straight?" spluttered Felix angrily.

"That's the question," said Uncle Roger, shaking his head gravely.

Uncle Roger's laughter was hard to bear, but his gravity was harder.

Meanwhile, in the pantry the Story Girl, apron-enshrouded, was being initiated into the mysteries of bread-making. Under Felicity's eye she set the bread, and on the morrow she was to bake it.

"The first thing you must do in the morning is knead it well," said Felicity, "and the earlier it's done the better—because it's such a warm night."

With that we all went to bed, and slept as soundly as if tragedies of blue chests and turnips and crooked cows had no place in the scheme of things at all.

CHAPTER 13

AN OLD PROVERB WITH A NEW MEANING

IT WAS half-past five when we boys got up the next morning. We were joined on the stairs by Felicity, yawning and rosy.

"Oh, dear me, I overslept myself. Uncle Roger wanted breakfast at six. Well, I suppose the fire is on anyhow, for the Story Girl is up. I guess she got up early to knead the bread. She couldn't sleep all night for worrying over it."

The fire was on, and a flushed and triumphant Story Girl was taking a loaf of bread from the oven.

"Just look," she said proudly. "I have every bit of the bread baked. I got up at three, and it was lovely and light, so I just gave it a right good kneading and popped it into the oven. And it's all done and out of the way. But the loaves don't seem quite as big as they should be," she added doubtfully.

"Sara Stanley!" Felicity flew across the kitchen. "Do you mean that you put that bread right into the oven after you kneaded it without leaving it to rise a second time?"

The Story Girl turned quite pale.

"Yes, I did," she faltered. "Oh, Felicity, wasn't it right?"

"You've ruined the bread," said Felicity flatly. "It's as heavy as a stone. I declare, Sara Stanley, I'd rather have a little common sense than be a great story teller."

Bitter indeed was the poor Story Girl's mortification.

"Don't tell Uncle Roger," she implored humbly.

"Oh, I won't tell him," promised Felicity amiably. "It's lucky there's enough old bread to do today. This will go to the hens. But it's an awful waste of good flour."

The Story Girl crept out with Felix and me to the morning orchard, while Dan and Peter went to do the barn work.

"It isn't *any* use for me to try to learn to cook," she said.

"Never mind," I said consolingly. "You can tell splendid stories."

"But what good would that do a hungry boy?" wailed the Story Girl.

"Boys ain't *always* hungry," said Felix gravely. "There's times when they ain't."

"I don't believe it," said the Story Girl drearily.

"Besides," added Felix in the tone of one who says while there is life there is yet hope, "you may learn to cook yet if you keep on trying."

"But Aunt Olivia won't let me waste the stuff. My only hope was to learn this week. But I suppose Felicity is so disgusted with me now that she won't give me any more lessons."

"*I* don't care," said Felix. "I like you better than Felicity, even if you can't cook. There's lots of folks can make bread. But there isn't many who can tell a story like you."

"But it's better to be useful than just interesting," sighed the Story Girl bitterly.

And Felicity, who was useful, would, in her secret soul, have given anything to be interesting. Which is the way of human nature.

Company descended on us that afternoon. First came Aunt Janet's sister, Mrs. Patterson, with a daughter of sixteen years and a son of two. They were followed by a buggy-load of Markdale people; and finally, Mrs. Elder Frewen and her sister from Vancouver, with two small daughters of the latter, arrived.

"It never rains but it pours," said Uncle Roger, as he went out to take their horse. But Felicity's foot was on her native heath. She had been baking all the afternoon, and, with a pantry well stocked with biscuits, cookies, cakes, and pies, she cared not if all Carlisle came to tea. Cecily set the table, and the Story Girl waited on it and washed all the dishes afterwards. But all the blushing honours fell to Felicity, who received so many compliments that her airs were quite unbearable for the rest of the week. She presided at the head of the table with as much grace and dignity as if she had been five times twelve years old, and seemed to know by instinct just who took sugar and who took it not. She was flushed with excitement and pleasure, and was so pretty that I could hardly eat for looking at her—which is the highest compliment in a boy's power to pay.

The Story Girl, on the contrary, was under eclipse. She was pale and lustreless from her disturbed night and early rising; and no opportunity offered to tell a melting tale. Nobody took any notice of her. It was Felicity's day.

After tea Mrs. Frewen and her sister wished to visit their father's grave in the Carlisle churchyard. It appeared that everybody wanted to go with them; but it was evident that somebody must stay home with Jimmy Patterson, who had just fallen sound asleep on the kitchen sofa. Dan finally volunteered to look after him. He had a new Henty book which he wanted to finish, and that, he said, was better fun than a walk to the graveyard.

"I think we'll be back before he wakes," said Mrs. Patterson, "and anyhow he is very good and won't be any trouble. Don't let him go outside, though. He has a cold now."

We went away, leaving Dan sitting on the door-sill reading his book, and Jimmy P. snoozing blissfully on the sofa. When we returned—Felix and the girls and I were ahead of the others—Dan was still sitting in precisely the same place and attitude; but there was no Jimmy in sight.

"Dan, where's the baby?" cried Felicity.

Dan looked around. His jaw fell in blank amazement. I never saw any one look as foolish as Dan at that moment.

"Good gracious, I don't know," he said helplessly.

"You've been so deep in that wretched book that he's got out, and dear knows where he is," cried Felicity distractedly.

"I wasn't," cried Dan. "He *must* be in the house. I've been sitting right across the door ever since you left, and he couldn't have got out unless he crawled right over me. He must be in the house."

"He isn't in the kitchen," said Felicity, rushing about wildly, "and he couldn't get into the other part of the house, for I shut the hall door tight, and no baby could open it—and it's shut tight yet. So are all the windows. He *must* have gone out of that door, Dan King, and it's your fault."

"He *didn't* go out of this door," reiterated Dan stubbornly. "I know that."

"Well, where is he, then? He isn't here. Did he melt into air?" demanded Felicity. "Oh, come and look for him, all of you. Don't stand round like ninnies. We *must* find him before his mother gets here. Dan King, you're an idiot!"

Dan was too frightened to resent this, at the time. However and wherever Jimmy had gone, he *was* gone, so much was certain. We tore about the house and yard like maniacs; we looked into every likely and unlikely place. But Jimmy we could not find, any more than if he had indeed melted into air. Mrs. Patterson came, and we had not found him. Things were getting serious. Uncle Roger and Peter were summoned from the field. Mrs. Patterson became hysterical, and was taken into the spare room with such remedies as could be suggested. Everybody blamed poor Dan. Cecily asked him what he would feel like if Jimmy was never, never found. The Story Girl had a gruesome recollection of some baby at Markdale who had wandered away like that—

"And they never found him till the next spring, and all they found was—*his skeleton,* with the grass growing through it," she whispered.

"This beats me," said Uncle Roger, when a fruitless hour had elapsed. "I do hope that baby hasn't wandered down to the swamp. It seems impossible he could walk so far; but I must go and see. Felicity, hand me my high boots out from under the sofa, there's a girl."

Felicity, pale and tearful, dropped on her knees and lifted the cretonne frill of the sofa. There, his head pillowed hardly on Uncle Roger's boots, lay Jimmy Patterson, still sound asleep!

"Well, I'll be—jiggered!" said Uncle Roger.

"I *knew* he never went out of the door," cried Dan triumphantly.

When the last buggy had driven away, Felicity set a batch of bread, and the rest of us sat around the back porch steps in the cat's light and ate cherries, shooting the stones at each other. Cecily was in quest of information.

"What does 'it never rains but it pours' mean?"

"Oh, it means if anything happens something else is sure to happen," said the Story Girl. "I'll illustrate. There's Mrs. Murphy. She never had a proposal in her life till she was forty, and then she had three in the one week, and she was so flustered she took the wrong one and has been sorry ever since. Do you see what it means now?"

"Yes, I guess so," said Cecily somewhat doubtfully. Later on we heard her imparting her newly acquired knowledge to Felicity in the pantry.

" 'It never rains but it pours' means that nobody wants to marry you for ever so long, and then lots of people do."

--------- CHAPTER 14 ---------

FORBIDDEN FRUIT

WE WERE all, with the exception of Uncle Roger, more or less grumpy in the household of King next day. Perhaps our nerves had been upset by the excitement attendant on Jimmy Patterson's disappearance. But it was more likely that our crankiness was the result of the supper we had eaten the previous night. Even children cannot devour mince pie, and cold fried pork ham, and fruit cake before going to bed with entire impunity. Aunt Janet had forgotten to warn Uncle Roger to keep an eye on our bedtime snacks, and we ate what seemed good unto us.

Some of us had frightful dreams, and all of us carried chips on our shoulders at breakfast. Felicity and Dan began a bickering which they kept up the entire day. Felicity had a natural aptitude for what we called "bossing," and in her mother's absence she deemed that she had a right to rule supreme. She knew better than to make any attempt to assert authority over the Story Girl, and Felix and I were allowed some length of tether; but Cecily, Dan, and Peter were expected to submit dutifully to her decrees. In the main they did; but on this particular morning Dan was plainly inclined to rebel. He had had time to grow sore over the things that Felicity had said to him when Jimmy Patterson was thought lost, and he began the day with a flatly expressed determination that he was not going to let Felicity rule the roost.

It was not a pleasant day, and to make matters worse it rained until late in the afternoon. The Story Girl had not recovered from the mortifications of the previous day; she would not talk, and she would not tell a single story; she sat on Rachel Ward's chest and ate her breakfast with the air of a martyr. After breakfast she washed the dishes and did the bedroom work in grim silence; then, with a book under one arm and Pat under the other, she betook herself to the window-seat in the upstairs hall, and would not be lured from that retreat, charmed we never so wisely. She stroked the purring Paddy, and read steadily on, with maddening indifference to all our pleadings.

Even Cecily, the meek and mild, was snappish, and complained of headache. Peter had gone home to see his mother, and Uncle Roger had gone to Markdale on business. Sara Ray came up, but was so snubbed by Felicity that she went home, crying. Felicity got the dinner by herself, disdaining to ask or command assistance. She banged things about and rattled the stove covers until even Cecily protested from her sofa. Dan sat on the floor and whittled, his sole aim and object being to make a mess and annoy Felicity, in which noble ambition he succeeded perfectly.

"I wish Aunt Janet and Uncle Alec were home," said Felix. "It's not half as much fun having the grown-ups away as I thought it would be."

"I wish I was back in Toronto," I said sulkily. The mince pie was to blame for *that* wish.

"I wish you were, I'm sure," said Felicity, riddling the fire noisily.

"Any one who lives with you, Felicity King, will always be wishing he was somewhere else," said Dan.

"I wasn't talking to you, Dan King," retorted Felicity. " 'Speak when you're spoken to, come when you're called.' "

"Oh, oh, oh," wailed Cecily on the sofa. "I *wish* it would stop raining. I *wish* my head would stop aching. I *wish* ma had never gone away. I *wish* you'd leave Felicity alone, Dan."

"*I* wish girls had some sense," said Dan—which brought the orgy of wishing to an end for the time. A wishing fairy might have had the time of her life in the King kitchen that morning—particularly if she were a cynically inclined fairy.

But even the effects of unholy snacks wear away at length. By tea-time things had brightened up. The rain had ceased, and the old, low-raftered room was full of sunshine which danced on the shining dishes of the dresser, made mosaics on the floor, and flickered over the table whereon a delicious meal was spread. Felicity had put on her blue muslin, and looked so beautiful in it that her good humour was quite restored. Cecily's headache was better, and the Story Girl, refreshed by an afternoon siesta, came down with smiles and sparkling eyes. Dan alone continued to nurse his grievances, and would not even laugh when the Story Girl told us a tale brought to mind by some of the "Rev. Mr. Scott's plums" which were on the table.

"The Rev. Mr. Scott was the man who thought the pulpit door must be made for speerits, you know," she said. "I heard Uncle Edward telling ever so many stories about him. He was called to this congregation, and he laboured here long and faithfully, and was much beloved, though he was very eccentric."

"What does that mean?" asked Peter.

"Hush! It just means queer," said Cecily, nudging him with her elbow. "A common man would be queer, but when it's a minister, it's eccentric."

"When he got very old," continued the Story Girl, "the Presbytery thought it was time he was retired. *He* didn't think so; but the Presbytery had their way, because there were so many of them to one of him. He was retired, and a young man was called to Carlisle. Mr. Scott went to live in town, but he came out to Carlisle very often, and visited all the people regularly, just the same as when he was their minister. The young minister was a very good young man, and tried to do his duty; but he was dreadfully afraid of meeting old Mr. Scott, because he had been told that the old minister was very angry at being set aside, and would likely give him a sound drubbing, if he ever met him. One day the young minister was visiting the Crawfords in Markdale, when they suddenly heard old Mr. Scott's voice in the kitchen. The young minister turned pale as the dead, and implored Mrs. Crawford to hide him. But she couldn't get him out of the room, and all she could do was to hide him in the china closet. The young minister slipped into the china closet, and old Mr. Scott came into the room. He talked very nicely, and read, and prayed. They made very long prayers in those days, you know; and at the end of his prayer he said. 'Oh Lord, bless the poor young man hiding in the closet. Give him courage no to fear the face of man. Make him a burning and a shining light to this sadly abused congregation.' Just imagine the feelings of the young minister in the china closet! But he came right out like a man, though his face was very red, as soon as Mr. Scott had done praying. And Mr. Scott was lovely to him, and shook hands, and never mentioned the china closet. And they were the best of friends ever afterwards."

"How did old Mr. Scott find out the young minister was in the closet?" asked Felix.

"Nobody ever knew. They supposed he had seen him through the window before he came into the house, and guessed he must be in the closet—because there was no way for him to get out of the room."

"Mr. Scott planted the yellow plum tree in Grandfather's time," said Cecily, peeling one of the plums, "and when he did it he said it was as Christian an act as he ever did. I wonder what he meant. I don't see anything very Christian about planting a tree."

"I do," said the Story Girl sagely.

When next we assembled ourselves together, it was after milking, and the cares of the day were done with. We fore-gathered in the balsam-fragrant aisles of the fir wood, and ate early August apples to such an extent that the Story Girl said we made her think of the Irishman's pig.

"An Irishman who lived at Markdale had a little pig," she said, "and he gave it a pailful of mush. The pig ate the whole pailful, and then the Irishman put the pig *in* the pail, and it didn't fill more than half the pail. Now, how was that, when it held a whole pailful of mush?"

This seemed to be a rather unanswerable kind of conundrum. We discussed the problem as we roamed the wood, and Dan and Peter almost quarrelled over it, Dan maintaining that the thing was impossible, and Peter being of the opinion that the mush was somehow "made thicker" in the process of being eaten, and so took up less room. During the discussion we came out to the fence of the hill pasture where grew the "bad berry" bushes.

Just what these "bad berries" were I cannot tell. We never knew their real name. They were small, red-clustered berries of a glossy, seductive appearance, and we were forbidden to eat them, because it was thought they might be poisonous. Dan picked a cluster and held it up.

"Dan King, don't you *dare* eat those berries," said Felicity in her "bossiest" tone. "They're poison. Drop them right away."

Now, Dan had not had the slightest intention of eating the berries. But at Felicity's prohibition the rebellion which had smouldered in him all day broke into sudden flame. He would show her!

"I'll eat them if I please, Felicity King," he said in a fury: "I don't believe they're poison. Look here!"

Dan crammed the whole bunch into his capacious mouth and chewed it up.

"They taste great," he said, smacking; and he ate two more clusters, regardless of our horror-stricken protestations and Fe-licity's pleadings.

We feared that Dan would drop dead on the spot. But nothing occurred immediately. When an hour had passed we concluded that the bad berries were not poison after all, and we looked upon Dan as quite a hero for daring to eat them.

"I knew they wouldn't hurt me," he said loftily. "Felicity's so fond of making a fuss over everything."

Nevertheless, when it grew dark and we returned to the house, I noticed that Dan was rather pale and quiet. He lay down on the kitchen sofa.

"Don't you feel all right, Dan?" I whispered anxiously.

"Shut up," he said.

I shut up.

Felicity and Cecily were setting out a lunch in the pantry when we were all startled by a loud groan from the sofa.

"Oh, I'm sick—I'm awful sick," said Dan abjectly, all the defiance and bravado gone out of him.

We all went to pieces, except Cecily, who alone retained her presence of mind.

"Have you got a pain in your stomach?" she demanded.

"I've got an awful pain here, if that's where my stomach is," moaned Dan, putting his hand on a portion of his anatomy considerably below his stomach. "Oh—oh—oh!"

"Go for Uncle Roger," commanded Cecily, pale but composed. "Felicity, put on the kettle. Dan, I'm going to give you mustard and warm water."

The mustard and warm water produced its proper effect promptly, but gave Dan no relief. He continued to writhe and groan. Uncle Roger, who had been summoned from his own place, went at once for the doctor, telling Peter to go down the hill for Mrs. Ray. Peter went, but returned accompanied by Sara only. Mrs. Ray and Judy Pineau were both away. Sara might better have stayed home; she was of no use, and could only add to the general confusion, wandering aimlessly about, crying and asking if Dan was going to die.

Cecily took charge of things. Felicity might charm the palate, and the Story Girl bind captive the soul; but when pain and sickness wrung the brow it was Cecily who was the ministering angel. She made the writhing Dan go to bed. She made him swallow every available antidote which was recommended in "the doctor's book;" and she applied hot cloths to him until her faithful little hands were half scalded off.

There was no doubt that Dan was suffering intense pain. He moaned and writhed, and cried for his mother.

"Oh, isn't it dreadful!" said Felicity, wringing her hands as she walked the kitchen floor. "Oh, why doesn't the doctor come? I *told* Dan the bad berries were poison. But surely they can't kill people *altogether.*"

"Pa's cousin died of eating something forty years ago," sobbed Sara Ray.

"Hold your tongue," said Peter in a fierce whisper. "You oughter have more sense than to say such things to the girls. They don't want to be any worse scared than they are."

"But Pa's cousin *did* die," reiterated Sara.

"My Aunt Jane used to rub whisky on for a pain," suggested Peter.

"We haven't any whisky," said Felicity disapprovingly. "This is a temperance house."

"But rubbing whisky on the *outside* isn't any harm," argued Peter. "It's only when you take it inside it is bad for you."

"Well, we haven't any, anyhow," said Felicity. "I suppose blueberry wine wouldn't do in its place?"

Peter did not think blueberry wine would be any good.

It was ten o'clock before Dan began to get better; but from that time he improved rapidly. When the doctor, who had been away from home when Uncle Roger reached Markdale, came at half past ten, he found his patient very weak and white, but free from pain.

Dr. Grier patted Cecily on the head, told her she was a little brick, and had done just the right thing, examined some of the fatal berries and gave it as his opinion that they were probably poisonous, administered some powders to Dan and advised him not to tamper with forbidden fruit in future, and went away.

Mrs. Ray now appeared, looking for Sara, and said she would stay all night with us.

"I'll be much obliged to you if you will," said Uncle Roger. "I feel a bit shook. I urged Janet and Alec to go to Halifax, and took the responsibility of the children while they were away, but I didn't know what I was letting myself in for. If anything had happened I could never have forgiven myself— though I believe it's beyond the power of mortal man to keep watch over the things children *will* eat. Now, you young fry, get straight off to your beds. Dan is out of danger, and you can't do any more good. Not that any of you have done much, except Cecily. She's got a head on her shoulders."

"It's been a horrid day all through," said Felicity drearily, as we climbed the stairs.

"I suppose we made it horrid ourselves," said the Story Girl candidly. "But it'll be a good story to tell sometime," she added.

"I'm awful tired and thankful," sighed Cecily.

We all felt that way.

———————— C H A P T E R 15 ————————

A DISOBEDIENT BROTHER

DAN WAS his own man again in the morning, though rather pale and weak; he wanted to get up, but Cecily ordered him to stay in bed. Fortunately Felicity forgot to repeat the command, so Dan did stay in bed. Cecily carried his meals to him, and read a Henty book to him all her spare time. The Story Girl went up and told him wondrous tales; and Sara Ray brought him a pudding she had made herself. Sara's intentions were good, but the pudding—well, Dan fed most of it to Paddy, who had curled himself up at the foot of the bed, giving the world assurance of a cat by his mellifluous purring.

"Ain't he just a great old fellow?" said Dan. "He knows I'm kind of sick, just as well as a human. He never pays no attention to me when I'm well."

Felix and Peter and I were required to help Uncle Roger in some carpentering work that day, and Felicity indulged in one of the house-cleaning orgies so dear to her soul; so that it was evening before we were all free to meet in the orchard and loll on the grasses of Uncle Stephen's Walk. In August it was a place of shady sweetness, fragrant with the odour of ripening apples, full of dear, delicate shadows. Through its openings we looked afar to the blue rims of the hills and over green, old, tranquil fields, lying in the sunset glow. Overhead the lacing leaves made a green, murmurous roof. There was no such thing as hurry in the world, while we lingered there and talked of "cabbages and kings." A tale of the Story Girl's, wherein princes were thicker than blackberries, and queens as common as buttercups, led to our discussion of kings. We wondered what it would be like to be a king. Peter thought it would be fine, only kind of inconvenient, wearing a crown all the time.

"Oh, but they don't," said the Story Girl. "Maybe they used to once, but now they wear hats. The crowns are just for special occasions. They look very much like other people, if you can go by their photographs."

"I don't believe it would be much fun as a steady thing," said Cecily. "I'd like to *see* a queen though. That is one thing I have against the Island—you never have a chance to see things like that here."

"The Prince of Wales was in Charlottetown once," said Peter. "My Aunt Jane saw him quite close by."

"That was before we were born, and such a thing won't happen again until after we're dead," said Cecily, with very unusual pessimism.

"I think queens and kings were thicker long ago," said the Story Girl. "They do seem dreadfully scarce now. There isn't one in this country anywhere. Perhaps I'll get a glimpse of some when I go to Europe."

Well, the Story Girl was destined to stand before kings herself, and she was to be one whom they delighted to honour. But we did not know that, as we sat in the old orchard. We thought it quite sufficiently marvellous that she should expect to have the chance of just seeing them.

"Can a queen do exactly as she pleases?" Sara Ray wanted to know.

"Not nowadays," explained the Story Girl.

"Then I don't see any use in being one," Sara decided.

"A king can't do as he pleases now, either," said Felix. "If he tries to, and if it isn't what pleases other people, the Parliament or something squelches him."

"Isn't 'squelch' a lovely word?" said the Story Girl irrelevantly. "It's so expressive. Squ-u-e-l-ch!"

Certainly it was a lovely word, as the Story Girl said it. Even a king would not have minded being squelched, if it were done to music like that.

"Uncle Roger says that Martin Forbes' wife has squelched *him,*" said Felicity. "He says Martin can't call his soul his own since he was married."

"I'm glad of it," said Cecily vindictively.

We all stared. This was so very unlike Cecily.

"Martin Forbes is the brother of a horrid man in Summerside who called me Johnny, that's why," she explained. "He was visiting here with his wife two years ago, and he called me Johnny every time he spoke to me. Just you fancy! I'll *never* forgive him."

"That isn't a Christian spirit," said Felicity rebukingly.

"I don't care. Would *you* forgive James Forbes if he had called *you* Johnny?" demanded Cecily.

"I know a story about Martin Forbes' grandfather," said the Story Girl. "Long ago they didn't have any choir in the Carlisle church—just a precentor you know. But at last they got a choir, and Andrew McPherson was to sing bass in it. Old Mr. Forbes hadn't gone to church for years, because he was so rheumatic, but he went the first Sunday the choir sang, because he had never heard any one sing bass, and wanted to hear what it was like. Grandfather King asked him what he thought of the choir. Mr. Forbes said it was 'verra guid,' but as for Andrew's bass, 'there was nae bass about it—it was just a bur-r-r-r the hale time.' "

If you could have heard the Story Girl's "bur-r-r-r!" Not old Mr. Forbes himself could have invested it with more of Doric scorn. We rolled over in the cool grass and screamed with laughter.

"Poor Dan," said Cecily compassionately. "He's up there all alone in his room, missing all the fun. I suppose it's mean of us to be having such a good time here, when he has to stay in bed."

"If Dan hadn't done wrong eating the bad berries when he was told not to, he wouldn't be sick," said Felicity. "You're bound to catch it when you do wrong. It was just a Providence he didn't die."

"That makes me think of another story about old Mr. Scott,"

said the Story Girl. "You know, I told you he was very angry because the Presbytery made him retire. There were two ministers in particular he blamed for being at the bottom of it. One time a friend of his was trying to console him, and said to him,

" 'You should be resigned to the will of Providence.'

" 'Providence had nothing to do with it,' said old Mr. Scott. "Twas the McCloskeys and the devil.' "

"You shouldn't speak of the—the—*devil,*" said Felicity, rather shocked.

"Well, that's just what Mr. Scott said."

"Oh, it's all right for a *minister* to speak of him. But it isn't nice for little girls. If you *have* to speak of—of—him—you might say the Old Scratch. That is what mother calls him."

" '"Twas the McCloskeys and the Old Scratch,' " said the Story Girl reflectively, as if she were trying to see which version was the more effective. "It wouldn't do," she decided.

"I don't think it's any harm to mention the—the—that person, when you're telling a story," said Cecily. "It's only in plain talking it doesn't do. It sounds too much like swearing then."

"I know another story about Mr. Scott," said the Story Girl. "Not long after he was married his wife wasn't quite ready for church one morning when it was time to go. So, just to teach her a lesson, he drove off alone, and left her to walk all the way—it was nearly two miles—in the heat and dust. She took it very quietly. It's the best way, I guess, when you're married to a man like old Mr. Scott. But just a few Sundays after wasn't he late himself! I suppose Mrs. Scott thought that what was sauce for the goose was sauce for the gander, for she slipped out and drove off to church as he had done. Old Mr. Scott finally arrived at the church, pretty hot and dusty, and in none too good a temper. He went into the pulpit, leaned over it and looked at his wife, sitting calmly in her pew at the side.

" 'It was cleverly done,' he said, right out loud, *'but dinna try it again!'* "

In the midst of our laughter Pat came down the Walk, his stately tail waving over the grasses. He proved to be the precursor of Dan, clothed and in his right mind.

"Do you think you should have got up, Dan?" said Cecily anxiously.

"I had to," said Dan. "The window was open, and it was more'n I could stand to hear you fellows laughing down here and me missing it all. 'Sides, I'm all right again. I feel fine."

"I guess this will be a lesson to you, Dan King," said Felicity, in her most maddening tone. "I guess you won't forget it in a hurry. You won't go eating the bad berries another time when you're told not to."

Dan had picked out a soft spot in the grass for himself, and was in the act of sitting down, when Felicity's tactful speech arrested him midway. He straightened up and turned a wrathful face on his provoking sister. Then, red with indignation, but without a word, he stalked away up the walk.

"Now, he's gone off mad," said Cecily reproachfully. "Oh, Felicity, why couldn't you have held your tongue?"

"Why, what did I say to make him mad?" asked Felicity in honest perplexity.

"I think it's awful for brothers and sisters to be always quarrelling," sighed Cecily. "The Cowans fight all the time; and you and Dan will soon be as bad."

"Oh, talk sense," said Felicity. "Dan's got so touchy it isn't safe to speak to him. I should think he'd be sorry for all the trouble he made last night. But you just back him up in everything, Cecily."

"I don't!"

"You do! And you've no business to, specially when mother's away. She left *me* in charge."

"You didn't take much charge last night when Dan got sick," said Felix maliciously. Felicity had told him at tea that night he was getting fatter than ever. This was his tit-for-tat. "You were pretty glad to leave it all to Cecily then."

"Who's talking to you?" said Felicity.

"Now, look here," said the Story Girl, "the first thing we know we'll all be quarrelling, and then some of us will sulk all day tomorrow. It's dreadful to spoil a whole day. Just let's all sit still and count a hundred before we say another word."

We sat still and counted the hundred. When Cecily finished she got up and went in search of Dan, resolved to soothe his wounded feelings. Felicity called after her to tell Dan there was a jam turnover she had put away in the pantry specially for him. Felix held out to Felicity a remarkably fine apple which he had been saving for his own consumption; and the Story Girl began a tale of an enchanted maiden in a castle by the sea; but we never heard the end of it. For, just as the evening star was looking whitely through the rosy window of the west, Cecily came flying through the orchard, wringing her hands.

"Oh, come, come quick," she gasped. "Dan's eating the bad berries again—he's et a whole bunch of them—he says he'll show Felicity. I can't stop him. Come you and try."

We rose in a body and rushed towards the house. In the yard we encountered Dan, emerging from the fir wood and champing the fatal berries with unrepentant relish.

"Dan King, do you want to commit suicide?" demanded the Story Girl.

"Look here, Dan," I expostulated. "You shouldn't do this. Think how sick you were last night and all the trouble you made for everybody. Don't eat any more, there's a good chap."

"All right," said Dan. "I've et all I want. They taste fine. I don't believe it was them made me sick."

But now that his anger was over he looked a little frightened. Felicity was not there. We found her in the kitchen, lighting up the fire.

"Bev, fill the kettle with water and put it on to heat," she said in a resigned tone. "If Dan's going to be sick again we've got to be ready for it. I wish mother was home, that's all. I hope she'll never go away again. Dan King, you just wait till I tell her of the way you've acted."

"Fudge! I ain't going to be sick," said Dan. "And if *you* begin telling tales, Felicity King, *I'll* tell some too. I know how many eggs mother said you could use while she was away— and I know how many you *have* used. I counted. So you'd better mind your own business, Miss."

"A nice way to talk to your sister when you may be dead in an hour's time!" retorted Felicity, in tears between her anger and her real alarm about Dan.

But in an hour's time Dan was still in good health, and announced his intention of going to bed. He went, and was soon sleeping as peacefully as if he had nothing on either conscience or stomach. But Felicity declared she meant to keep the water hot until all danger was past; and we sat up to keep her company. We were sitting there when Uncle Roger walked in at eleven o'clock.

"What on earth are you young fry doing up at this time of night?" he asked angrily. "You should have been in your beds two hours ago. And with a roaring fire on a night that's hot enough to melt a brass monkey! Have you taken leave of your senses?"

"It's because of Dan," explained Felicity wearily. "He went and et more of the bad berries—a whole lot of them—and we were sure he'd be sick again. But he hasn't been yet, and now he's asleep."

"Is that boy stark, staring mad?" said Uncle Roger.

"It was Felicity's fault," cried Cecily, who always took Dan's part through evil report and good report. "She told him she guessed he'd learned a lesson and wouldn't do what she'd told him not to again. So he went and et them because she vexed him so."

"Felicity King, if you don't watch out you'll grow up into the sort of woman who drives her husband to drink," said Uncle Roger gravely.

"How could I tell Dan would act so like a mule!" cried Felicity.

"Get off to bed, every one of you. It's a thankful man I'll be when your father and mother come home. The wretched bachelor who undertakes to look after a houseful of children like you is to be pitied. Nobody will ever catch me doing it again. Felicity, is there anything fit to eat in the pantry?"

That last question was the most unkindest cut of all. Felicity could have forgiven Uncle Roger anything but that. It really was unpardonable. She confided to me as we climbed the stairs that she hated Uncle Roger. Her red lips quivered and the tears of wounded pride brimmed over in her beautiful blue eyes. In the dim candle-light she looked unbelievably pretty and appealing. I put my arm about her and gave her a cousinly salute.

"Never you mind him, Felicity," I said. "He's only a grown-up."

CHAPTER 16

THE GHOSTLY BELL

FRIDAY WAS a comfortable day in the household of King. Everybody was in good humour. The Story Girl sparkled through several tales that ranged from the afrites and jinns of Eastern myth, through the piping days of chivalry, down to the homely anecdotes of Carlisle workaday folks. She was in turn an Oriental princess behind a silken veil, the bride who followed her bridegroom to the wars of Palestine disguised as a page, the gallant lady who ransomed her diamond necklace by dancing a coranto with a highwayman on a moonlit heath, and "Buskirk's girl" who joined the Sons and Daughters of Temperance "just to see what was into it;" and in each impersonation she was so thoroughly the thing impersonated that it was a matter of surprise to us when she emerged from each our own familiar Story Girl again.

Cecily and Sara Ray found a "sweet," new knitted lace pattern in an old magazine and spent a happy afternoon learning it and "talking secrets." Chancing—accidentally, I vow—to overhear certain of these secrets, I learned that Sara Ray had named an apple for Johnny Price—"and, Cecily, true's you live, there was eight seeds in it, and you know eight means 'they both love' "—while Cecily admitted that Willie Fraser had written on his slate and showed it to her,

"If you love me as I love you,
No knife can cut our love in two"—

"but, Sara Ray, *never* you breathe this to a living soul."

Felix also averred that he heard Sara ask Cecily very seriously, "Cecily, how old must we be before we can have a *real* beau?"

But Sara always denied it; so I am inclined to believe Felix simply made it up himself.

Paddy distinguished himself by catching a rat, and being intolerably conceited about it—until Sara Ray cured him by calling him a "dear, sweet cat," and kissing him between the ears. Then Pat sneaked abjectly off, his tail drooping. He resented being called a sweet cat. He had a sense of humour, had Pat. Very few cats have; and most of them have such an inordinate appetite for flattery that they will swallow any amount of it and thrive thereon. Paddy had a finer taste. The Story Girl and I were the only ones who could pay him compliments to his liking. The Story Girl would box his ears with her fist and say, "Bless your gray heart, Paddy, you're a good sort of old rascal," and Pat would purr his satisfaction; I used to take a handful of the skin on his back, shake him gently and say, "Pat, you've forgotten more than any human being ever knew," and I vow Paddy would lick his chops with delight. But to be called "a sweet cat!" Oh, Sara, Sara!

Felicity tried—and had the most gratifying luck with—a new and complicated cake recipe—a gorgeous compound of a plumminess to make your mouth water. The number of eggs she used in it would have shocked Aunt Janet's thrifty soul, but that cake, like beauty, was its own excuse. Uncle Roger ate three slices of it at tea-time and told Felicity she was an artist. The poor man meant it as a compliment; but Felicity, who knew Uncle Blair was an artist and had a poor opinion of such fry, looked indignant and retorted, indeed, she wasn't!

"Peter says there's any amount of raspberries back in the maple clearing," said Dan. "S'posen we all go after tea and pick some?"

"I'd like to," sighed Felicity, "but we'd come home tired and with all the milking to do. You boys better go alone."

"Peter and I will attend to the milking for one evening," said Uncle Roger. "You can all go. I have an idea that a raspberry pie for supper tomorrow night, when the folks come home, would hit the right spot."

Accordingly, after tea we all set off, armed with jugs and cups. Felicity, thoughtful creature, also took a small basketful of jelly cookies along with her. We had to go back through the maple woods to the extreme end of Uncle Roger's farm— a pretty walk, through a world of green, whispering boughs and spice-sweet ferns, and shifting patches of sunlight. The raspberries were plentiful, and we were not long in filling our receptacles. Then we foregathered around a tiny wood spring, cold and pellucid under its young maples, and ate the jelly cookies; and the Story Girl told us a tale of a haunted spring in a mountain glen where a fair white lady dwelt, who pledged all comers in a golden cup with jewels bright.

"And if you drank of the cup with her," said the Story Girl, her eyes glowing through the emerald dusk about us, "you were never seen in the world again; you were whisked straightway to fairyland, and lived there with a fairy bride. And you never *wanted* to come back to earth, because when you drank of the magic cup you forgot all your past life, except for one day in every year when you were allowed to remember it."

"I wish there was such a place as fairyland—and a way to get to it," said Cecily.

"I think there *is* such a place—in spite of Uncle Edward," said the Story Girl dreamily, "and I think there is a way of getting there too, if we could only find it."

Well, the Story Girl was right. There is such a place as fairyland—but only children can find the way to it. And they do not know that it is fairyland until they have grown so old that they forget the way. One bitter day, when they seek it and cannot find it, they realize what they have lost; and that is the tragedy of life. On that day the gates of Eden are shut behind them and the age of gold is over. Henceforth they must dwell in the common light of common day. Only a few, who remain children at heart, can ever find that fair, lost path again; and blessed are they above mortals. They, and only they, can bring us tidings from that dear country where we once sojourned and from which we must evermore be exiles. The world calls them its singers and poets and artists and story-tellers; but they are just people who have never forgotten the way to fairyland.

As we sat there the Awkward Man passed by, with his gun over his shoulder and his dog at his side. He did not look like an awkward man, there in the heart of the maple woods. He strode along right masterfully and lifted his head with the air of one who was monarch of all he surveyed.

The Story Girl kissed her finger tips to him with the delightful audacity which was a part of her; and the Awkward Man plucked off his hat and swept her a stately and graceful bow.

"I don't understand why they call him an awkward man," said Cecily, when he was out of earshot.

"You'd understand why if you ever saw him at a party or a picnic," said Felicity, "trying to pass plates and dropping them whenever a woman looked at him. They say it's pitiful to see him."

"I must get well acquainted with that man next summer," said the Story Girl. "If I put it off any longer it will be too late. I'm growing so fast Aunt Olivia says I'll have to wear ankle skirts next summer. If I begin to look grown-up he'll get frightened of me, and then I'll never find out the Golden Milestone mystery."

"Do you think he'll ever tell you who Alice is?" I asked.

"I have a notion who Alice is already," said the mysterious creature. But she would tell us nothing more.

When the jelly cookies were all eaten it was high time to be moving homeward, for when the dark comes down there are more comfortable places than a rustling maple wood and the precincts of a possibly enchanted spring. When we reached the foot of the orchard and entered it through a gap in the hedge it was the magical, mystical time of "between lights." Off to the west was a daffodil glow hanging over the valley of lost sunsets, and Grandfather King's huge willow rose up against it like a rounded mountain of foliage. In the east, above the maple woods, was a silvery sheen that hinted of moonrise. But the orchard was a place of shadows and mysterious sounds. Midway up the open space in its heart we met Peter; and if ever a boy was given over to sheer terror that boy was Peter. His face was as white as a sunburned face could be, and his eyes were brimmed with panic.

"Peter, what is the matter?" cried Cecily.

"There's—*something*—in the house, *ringing a bell*," said Peter, in a shaking voice. Not the Story Girl herself could have invested that "something" with more of creepy horror. We all drew close together. I felt a crinkly feeling along my back which I had never known before. If Peter had not been so manifestly frightened we might have though he was trying to "pass a joke" on us. But such abject terror as his could not be counterfeited.

"Nonsense!" said Felicity; but her voice shook. "There isn't a bell in the house to ring. You must have imagined it, Peter. Or else Uncle Roger is trying to fool us."

"Your Uncle Roger went to Markdale right after milking," said Peter. "He locked up the house and gave me the key. There wasn't a soul in it then, that I'm sure of. I druv the cows to the pasture, and I got back about fifteen minutes ago. I set down on the front door steps for a moment, and all at once I heard a bell ring in the house eight times. I tell you I was skeered. I made a bolt for the orchard—and you won't catch me going near that house till your Uncle Roger comes home."

You wouldn't catch any of us doing it. We were almost as badly scared as Peter. There we stood in a huddled, demoralized group. Oh, what an eerie place that orchard was! What shadows! What noises! What spooky swooping of bats! You *couldn't* look every way at once, and goodness only knew what might be behind you!

"There *can't* be anybody in the house," said Felicity.

"Well, here's the key—go and see for yourself," said Peter.

Felicity had no intention of going and seeing.

"I think you boys ought to go," she said, retreating behind the defence of sex. "You ought to be braver than girls."

"But we ain't," said Felix candidly. "I wouldn't be much scared of anything *real.* But a haunted house is a different thing."

"I always thought something had to be done in a place before it could be haunted," said Cecily. "Somebody killed or something like that, you know. Nothing like that ever happened in our family. The Kings have always been respectable."

"Perhaps it is Emily King's ghost," whispered Felix.

"She never appeared anywhere but in the orchard," said the Story Girl. "Oh, oh, children, isn't there something under Uncle Alec's tree?"

We peered fearfully through the gloom. There *was* something—something that wavered and fluttered—advanced—retreated—

"That's only my old apron," said Felicity. "I hung it there today when I was looking for the white hen's nest. Oh, what shall we do? Uncle Roger may not be back for hours. I *can't* believe there's anything in the house."

"Maybe it's only Peg Bowen," suggested Dan.

There was not a great deal of comfort in this. We were

almost as much afraid of Peg Bowen as we would be of any spectral visitant.

Peter scoffed at the idea.

"Peg Bowen wasn't in the house before your Uncle Roger locked it up, and how could she get in afterwards?" he said. "No, it isn't Peg Bowen. It's *something* that *walks.*"

"I know a story about a ghost," said the Story Girl, the ruling passion strong even in extremity. "It is about a ghost with eyeholes but no eyes—"

"Don't," cried Cecily hysterically. "Don't you go on! Don't you say another word! I can't bear it! Don't you!"

The Story Girl didn't. But she had said enough. There was something in the quality of a ghost with eyeholes but no eyes that froze our young blood.

There never were in all the world six more badly scared children than those who huddled in the old King orchard that August night.

All at once—something—leaped from the bough of a tree and alighted before us. We split the air with a simultaneous shriek. We would have run, one and all, if there had been anywhere to run to. But there wasn't—all around us were only those shadowy arcades. Then we saw with shame that it was only our Paddy.

"Pat, Pat," I said, picking him up, feeling a certain comfort in his soft, solid body. "Stay with us, old fellow."

But Pat would none of us. He struggled out of my clasp and disappeared over the long grasses with soundless leaps. He was no longer our tame, domestic, well acquainted Paddy. He was a strange, furtive animal—a "questing beast."

Presently the moon rose; but this only made matters worse. The shadows had been still before; now they moved and danced, as the night wind tossed the boughs. The old house, with its dreadful secret, was white and clear against the dark background of spruces. We were woefully tired, but we could not sit down because the grass was reeking with dew.

"The Family Ghost only appears in daylight," said the Story Girl. "I wouldn't mind seeing a ghost in daylight. But after dark is another thing."

"There's no such thing as a ghost," I said contemptuously. Oh, how I wished I could believe it!

"Then what rung that bell?" said Peter. "Bells don't ring of themselves, I s'pose, specially when there ain't any in the house to ring."

"Oh, will Uncle Roger never come home!" sobbed Felicity. "I know he'll laugh at us awful, but it's better to be laughed at than scared like this."

Uncle Roger did not come until nearly ten. Never was there a more welcome sound than the rumble of his wheels in the lane. We ran to the orchard gate and swarmed across the yard, just as Uncle Roger alighted at the front door. He stared at us in the moonlight.

"Have you tormented any one into eating more bad berries, Felicity?" he demanded.

"Oh, Uncle Roger, don't go in," implored Felicity seriously. "There's something dreadful in there—something that rings a bell. Peter heard it. Don't go in."

"There's no use asking the meaning of this, I suppose," said Uncle Roger with the calm of despair. "I've gave up trying to fathom you young ones, Peter, where's the key? What yarn have you been telling?"

"I *did* hear a bell ring," said Peter stubbornly.

Uncle Roger unlocked and flung open the front door. As he did so, clear and sweet, rang out ten bell-like chimes.

"That's what I heard," cried Peter. "There's the bell!"

We had to wait until Uncle Roger stopped laughing before we heard the explanation. We thought he never *would* stop.

"That's Grandfather King's old clock striking," he said, as soon as he was able to speak. "Sammy Prott came along after tea, when you were away to the forge, Peter, and I gave him permission to clean the old clock. He had it going merrily in no time. And now it has almost frightened you poor little monkeys to death."

We heard Uncle Roger chuckling all the way to the barn.

"Uncle Roger can laugh," said Cecily, with a quiver in her voice, "but it's no laughing matter to be so scared. I just feel sick, I was so frightened."

"I wouldn't mind if he'd laugh once and have done with it," said Felicity bitterly. "But he'll laugh at us for a year, and tell the story to every soul that comes to the place."

"You can't blame him for that," said the Story Girl. "I shall tell it, too. I don't care if the joke is as much on myself as any one. A story is a story, no matter who it's on. But it *is* hateful to be laughed at—and grown-ups always do it. I never will when I'm grown up. I'll remember better."

"It's all Peter's fault," said Felicity. "I do think he might have had more sense than to take a clock striking for a bell ringing."

"I never heard that kind of a strike before," protested Peter. "It don't sound a bit like other clocks. And the door was shut and the sound kind o' muffled. It's all very fine to say you would have known what it was, but I don't believe you would."

"*I* wouldn't have," said the Story Girl honestly. "I thought it *was* a bell when I heard it, and the door open, too. Let us be fair, Felicity."

"I'm dreadful tired," sighed Cecily.

We were all "dreadful tired," for this was the third night of late hours and nerve racking strain. But it was over two hours since we had eaten the cookies, and Felicity suggested that a saucerful apiece of raspberries and cream would not be hard to take. It was not, for any one but Cecily, who couldn't swallow a mouthful.

"I'm glad father and mother will be back tomorrow night," she said. "It's too exciting when they're away. That's my opinion."

------------------ CHAPTER 17 ------------------

THE PROOF OF THE PUDDING

FELICITY WAS cumbered with many cares the next morning. For one thing, the whole house must be put in apple pie order; and for another, an elaborate supper must be prepared for the expected return of the travellers that night. Felicity devoted her whole attention to this, and left the secondary preparation of the regular meals to Cecily and the Story Girl. It was agreed that the latter was to make a cornmeal pudding for dinner.

In spite of her disaster with the bread, the Story Girl had been taking cooking lessons from Felicity all the week, and getting on tolerably well, although, mindful of her former mistake, she never ventured on anything without Felicity's approval. But Felicity had no time to oversee her this morning.

"You must attend to the pudding yourself," she said. "The recipe's so plain and simple even you can't go astray, and if there's anything you don't understand you can ask me. But don't bother me if you can help it."

The Story Girl did not bother her once. The pudding was concocted and baked, as the Story Girl proudly informed us when we came to the dinner-table, all on her own hook. She was very proud of it; and certainly as far as appearance went it justified her triumph. The slices were smooth and golden; and, smothered in the luscious maple sugar sauce which Cecily had compounded, were very fair to view. Nevertheless, although none of us, not even Uncle Roger or Felicity, said a word at the time, for fear of hurting the Story Girl's feelings, the pudding did not taste exactly as it should. It was tough—decidedly tough—and lacked the richness of flavour which was customary in Aunt Janet's cornmeal puddings. If it had not been for the abundant supply of sauce it would have been very dry eating indeed. Eaten it was, however, to the last crumb. If it were not just what a cornmeal pudding might be, the rest of the bill of fare had been extra good and our appetites matched it.

"I wish I was twins so's I could eat more," said Dan, when he simply had to stop.

"What good would being twins do you?" asked Peter. "People who squint can't eat any more than people who don't squint, can they?"

We could not see any connection between Peter's two questions.

"What has squinting got to do with twins?" asked Dan.

"Why, twins are just people that squint, aren't they?" said Peter.

We thought he was trying to be funny, until we found out that he was quite in earnest. Then we laughed until Peter got sulky.

"I don't care," he said. "How's a fellow to know? Tommy

and Adam Cowan, over at Markdale, are twins; and they're both cross-eyed. So I s'posed that was what being twins meant. It's all very fine for you fellows to laugh. I never went to school half as much as you did; and you was brought up in Toronto, too. If you'd worked out ever since you was seven, and just got to school in the winter, there'd be lots of things you wouldn't know, either."

"Never mind, Peter," said Cecily. "You know lots of things they don't."

But Peter was not to be conciliated, and took himself off in high dudgeon. To be laughed at before Felicity—to be laughed at *by* Felicity—was something he could not endure. Let Cecily and the Story Girl cackle all they wanted to, and let those stuck-up Toronto boys grin like chessy-cats; but when Felicity laughed at him the iron entered into Peter's soul.

If the Story Girl laughed at Peter the mills of the gods ground out his revenge for him in mid-afternoon. Felicity, having used up all the available cooking materials in the house, had to stop perforce; and she now determined to stuff two new pincushions she had been making for her room. We heard her rummaging in the pantry as we sat on the cool, spruce-shadowed cellar door outside, where Uncle Roger was showing us how to make elderberry pop-guns. Presently she came out, frowning.

"Cecily, do you know where mother put the sawdust she emptied out of that old beaded pincushion of Grandmother King's, after she had sifted the needles out of it? I thought it was in the tin box."

"So it is," said Cecily.

"It isn't. There isn't a speck of sawdust in that box."

The Story Girl's face wore a quite indescribable expression, compound of horror and shame. She need not have confessed. If she had but held her tongue the mystery of the sawdust's disappearance might have forever remained a mystery. She *would* have held her tongue, as she afterwards confided to me, if it had not been for a horrible fear which flashed into her mind that possibly sawdust puddings were not healthy for people to eat—especially if there might be needles in them—and that if any mischief had been done in that direction it was her duty to undo it if possible at any cost of ridicule to herself.

"Oh, Felicity," she said, her voice expressing a very anguish of humiliation, "I—I—thought that stuff in the box was corn-meal—and I used it to make the pudding."

Felicity and Cecily stared blankly at the Story Girl. We boys began to laugh, but were checked midway by Uncle Roger. He was rocking himself back and forth, with his hand pressed against his stomach.

"Oh," he groaned, "I've been wondering what these sharp pains I've been feeling ever since dinner meant. I know now. I must have swallowed a needle—several needles, perhaps. I'm done for!"

The poor Story Girl went very white.

"Oh, Uncle Roger, could it be possible? You *couldn't* have swallowed a needle without knowing it. It would have stuck in your tongue or teeth."

"I didn't chew the pudding," groaned Uncle Roger. "It was too tough—I just swallowed the chunks whole."

He groaned and twisted and doubled himself up. But he overdid it. He was not as good an actor as the Story Girl. Felicity looked scornfully at him.

"Uncle Roger, you are not one bit sick," she said deliberately. "You are just putting on."

"Felicity, if I die from the effects of eating sawdust pudding, flavoured with needles, you'll be sorry you ever said such a thing to your poor old uncle," said Uncle Roger reproachfully. "Even if there were no needles in it, sixty-year-old sawdust can't be good for my tummy. I daresay it wasn't even clean."

"Well, you know every one has to eat a peck of dirt in his life," giggled Felicity.

"But nobody has to eat it all at once," retorted Uncle Roger, with another groan. "Oh, Sara Stanley, it's a thankful man I am that your Aunt Olivia is to be home tonight. You'd have me kilt entoirely by another day. I believe you did it on purpose to have a story to tell."

Uncle Roger hobbled off to the barn, still holding on to his stomach.

"Do you think he really feels sick?" asked the Story Girl anxiously.

"No, I don't," said Felicity. "You needn't worry over him. There's nothing the matter with him. I don't believe there were any needles in that sawdust. Mother sifted it very carefully."

"I know a story about a man whose son swallowed a mouse," said the Story Girl, who would probably have known a story and tried to tell it if she were being led to the stake. "And he ran and wakened up a very tired doctor just as he had got to sleep.

" 'Oh, doctor, my son has swallowed a mouse,' he cried. 'What shall I do?'

" 'Tell him to swallow a cat,' roared the poor doctor, and slammed his door.

"Now, if Uncle Roger has swallowed any needles, maybe it would make it all right if he swallowed a pincushion."

We all laughed. But Felicity soon grew sober.

"It seems awful to think of eating a sawdust pudding. How on earth did you make such a mistake?"

"It looked just like cornmeal," said the Story Girl, going from white to red in her shame. "Well, I'm going to give up trying to cook, and stick to things I can do. And if ever one of you mentions sawdust pudding to me I'll never tell you another story as long as I live."

The threat was effectual. Never did we mention that unholy pudding. But the Story Girl could not so impose silence on the grown-ups, especially Uncle Roger. He tormented her for the rest of the summer. Never a breakfast did he sit down to, without gravely inquiring if they were sure there was no sawdust in the porridge. Not a tweak of rheumatism did he feel but he vowed it was due to a needle, travelling about his body. And Aunt Olivia was warned to label all the pincushions in the house, "Contents, sawdust; not intended for puddings."

CHAPTER 18

HOW KISSING WAS DISCOVERED

An August evening, calm, golden, dewless, can be very lovely. At sunset, Felicity, Cecily, and Sara Ray, Dan, Felix, and I were in the orchard, sitting on the cool grasses at the base of the Pulpit Stone. In the west was a field of crocus sky over which pale cloud blossoms were scattered.

Uncle Roger had gone to the station to meet the travellers, and the dining-room table was spread with a feast of fat things.

"It's been a jolly week, take it all round," said Felix, "but I'm glad the grown-ups are coming back tonight, especially Uncle Alec."

"I wonder if they'll bring us anything," said Dan.

"I'm thinking long to hear all about the wedding," said Felicity, who was braiding timothy stalks into a collar for Pat.

"You girls are always thinking about weddings and getting married," said Dan contemptuously.

"We ain't," said Felicity indignantly. "*I* am *never* going to get married. I think it is just horrid, so there!"

"I guess you think it would be a good deal horrider not to be," said Dan.

"It depends on who you're married to," said Cecily gravely, seeing that Felicity disdained reply. "If you got a man like father it would be all right. But *s'posen* you got one like Andrew Ward? He's so mean and cross to his wife that she tells him every day she wishes she'd never set eyes on him."

"Perhaps that's *why* he's mean and cross," said Felix.

"I tell you it isn't always the man's fault," said Dan darkly. "When *I* get married I'll be good to my wife, but I mean to be boss. When I open my mouth my word will be law."

"If your word is as big as your mouth I guess it will be," said Felicity cruelly.

"I pity the man who gets *you*, Felicity King, that's all," retorted Dan.

"Now, don't fight," implored Cecily.

"Who's fighting?" demanded Dan. "Felicity thinks she can

116

say anything she likes to me, but I'll show her different."

Probably, in spite of Cecily's efforts, a bitter spat would have resulted between Dan and Felicity, had not a diversion been effected at that moment by the Story Girl, who came slowly down Uncle Stephen's Walk.

"Just look how the Story Girl has got herself up!" said Felicity. "Why, she's no more than decent!"

The Story Girl was barefooted and barearmed, having rolled the sleeves of her pink gingham up to her shoulders. Around her waist was twisted a girdle of the blood-red roses that bloomed in Aunt Olivia's garden; on her sleek curls she wore a chaplet of them; and her hands were full of them.

She paused under the outmost tree, in a golden-green gloom, and laughed at us over a big branch. Her wild, subtle, nameless charm clothed her as with a garment. We always remembered the picture she made there; and, in later days, when we read Tennyson's poems at a college desk, we knew exactly how an oread, peering through the green leaves on some haunted knoll of many fountained Ida, must look.

"Felicity," said the Story Girl reproachfully, "what have you been doing to Peter? He's up there sulking in the granary, and he won't come down, and he says it's your fault. You must have hurt his feelings dreadfully."

"I don't know about his feelings," said Felicity, with an angry toss of her shining head, "but I guess I made his ears tingle all right. I boxed them both good and hard."

"Oh, Felicity! What for?"

"Well, he tried to kiss me, that's what for!" said Felicity, turning very red. "As if I would let a hired boy kiss me! I guess Master Peter won't try anything like that again in a hurry."

The Story Girl came out of her shadows and sat down beside us on the grass.

"Well, in that case," she said gravely, "I think you did right to slap his ears—not because he is a hired boy, but because it would be impertinent in *any* boy. But talking of kissing makes me think of a story I found in Aunt Olivia's scrapbook the other day. Wouldn't you like to hear it? It is called, 'How Kissing Was Discovered.' "

"Wasn't kissing always discovered?" asked Dan.

"Not according to this story. It was just discovered accidentally."

"Well, let's hear about it," said Felix, "though *I* think kissing's awful silly, and it wouldn't have mattered much if it hadn't ever been discovered."

The Story Girl scattered her roses around her on the grass, and clasped her slim hands over her knees. Gazing dreamily afar at the tinted sky between the apple trees, as if she were looking back to the merry days of the world's gay youth, she began, her voice giving to the words and fancies of the old tale the delicacy of hoar frost and the crystal sparkle of dew.

"It happened long, long ago in Greece—where so many other beautiful things happened. Before that, nobody had ever heard of kissing. And then it was just discovered in the twinkling of an eye. And a man wrote it down and the account has been preserved ever since.

"There was a young shepherd named Glaucon—a very handsome young shepherd—who lived in a little village called Thebes. It became a very great and famous city afterwards, but at this time it was only a little village, very quiet and simple. Too quiet for Glaucon's liking. He grew tired of it, and he thought he would like to go away from home and see something of the world. So he took his knapsack and his shepherd's crook, and wandered away until he came to Thessaly. That is the land of the gods' hill, you know. The name of the hill was Olympus. But it has nothing to do with this story. This happened on another mountain—Mount Pelion.

"Glaucon hired himself to a wealthy man who had a great many sheep. And every day Glaucon had to lead the sheep up to pasture on Mount Pelion, and watch them while they ate. There was nothing else to do, and he would have found the time very long, if he had not been able to play on a flute. So he played very often and very beautifully, as he sat under the trees and watched the wonderful blue sea afar off, and thought about Aglaia.

"Aglaia was his master's daughter. She was so sweet and beautiful that Glaucon fell in love with her the very moment he first saw her; and when he was not playing his flute on the mountain he was thinking about Aglaia, and dreaming that some day he might have flocks of his own, and a dear little cottage down in the valley where he and Aglaia might live.

"Aglaia had fallen in love with Glaucon just as he had with her. But she never let him suspect if for ever so long. He did not know how often she would steal up the mountain and hide behind the rocks near where the sheep pastured, to listen to Glaucon's beautiful music. It was very lovely music, because he was always thinking of Aglaia while he played, though he little dreamed how near him she often was.

"But after awhile Glaucon found out that Aglaia loved him, and everything was well. Nowadays I suppose a wealthy man like Aglaia's father wouldn't be willing to let his daughter marry a hired man; but this was in the Golden Age, you know, when nothing like that mattered at all.

"After that, almost every day Aglaia would go up the mountain and sit beside Glaucon, as he watched the flocks and played on his flute. But he did not play as much as he used to, because he liked better to talk with Aglaia. And in the evening they would lead the sheep home together.

"One day Aglaia went up the mountain by a new way, and she came to a little brook. Something was sparkling very brightly among its pebbles. Aglaia picked it up, and it was the most beautiful little stone that she had ever seen. It was only as large as a pea, but it glittered and flashed in the sunlight with every colour of the rainbow. Aglaia was so delighted with it that she resolved to take it as a present to Glaucon.

"But all at once she heard a stamping of hoofs behind her, and when she turned she almost died from fright. For there was the great god, Pan, and he was a very terrible object, looking quite as much like a goat as a man. The gods were not all beautiful, you know. And, beautiful or not, nobody ever wanted to meet them face to face.

" 'Give that stone to me,' said Pan, holding out his hand.

"But Aglaia, though she was frightened, would not give him the stone.

" 'I want it for Glaucon,' she said.

" 'I want it for one of my wood nymphs,' said Pan, 'and I must have it.'

"He advanced threateningly, but Aglaia ran as hard as she could up the mountain. If she could only reach Glaucon he would protect her. Pan followed her, clattering and bellowing terribly, but in a few minutes she rushed into Glaucon's arms.

"The dreadful sight of Pan and the still more dreadful noise he made, so frightened the sheep that they fled in all directions. But Glaucon was not afraid at all, because Pan was the god of shepherds, and was bound to grant any prayer a good shepherd, who always did his duty, might make. If Glaucon had not been a good shepherd dear knows what would have happened to him and Aglaia. But he was; and when he begged Pan to go away and not frighten Aglaia any more, Pan had to go, grumbling a good deal—and Pan's grumblings had a very ugly sound. But still he went, and that was the main thing.

" 'Now, dearest, what is all this trouble about?' asked Glaucon; and Aglaia told him the story.

" 'But where is the beautiful stone?' he asked, when she had finished. 'Didst thou drop it in thy alarm?'

"No, indeed! Aglaia had done nothing of the sort. When she began to run she had popped it into her mouth, and there it was still, quite safe. Now she poked it out between her red lips, where it glittered in the sunlight.

" 'Take it,' she whispered.

"The question was—how was he to take it? Both of Aglaia's arms were held fast to her sides by Glaucon's arms; and if he loosened his clasp ever so little he was afraid she would fall, so weak and trembling was she from her dreadful fright. Then Glaucon had a brillian idea. He would take the beautiful stone from Aglaia's lips with his own lips.

"He bent over her until his lips touched hers—and then, he forgot all about the beautiful pebble and so did Aglaia. Kissing was discovered!"

"What a yarn!" said Dan, drawing a long breath, when we had come to ourselves and discovered that we were really sitting in a dewy Prince Edward Island orchard instead of watching two lovers on a mountain in Thessaly in the Golden Age. "I don't believe a word of it."

"Of course, we know it wasn't really true," said Felicity.

"Well, I don't know," said the Story Girl thoughtfully. "I think there are two kinds of true things—true things that are, and true things that are not, but might be."

"I don't believe there's any but the one kind of trueness,"

said Felicity. "And anyway, this story couldn't be true. You know there was no such thing as a god Pan."

"How do you know what there might have been in the Golden Age?" asked the Story Girl.

Which was, indeed, an unanswerable question for Felicity.

"I wonder what became of the beautiful stone?" said Cecily.

"Likely Aglaia swallowed it," said Felix practically.

"Did Glaucon and Aglaia ever get married?" asked Sara Ray.

"The story doesn't say. It stops just there," said the Story Girl. "But of course they did. I will tell you what *I* think. I don't think Aglaia swallowed the stone. I think it just fell to the ground; and after awhile they found it, and it turned out to be of such value that Glaucon could buy all the flocks and herds in the valley, and the sweetest cottage; and he and Aglaia were married right away."

"But you only *think* that," said Sara Ray. "I'd like to be really sure that was what happened."

"Oh, bother, none of it happened," said Dan. "I believed it while the Story Girl was telling it, but I don't now. Isn't that wheels?"

Wheels it was. Two wagons were driving up the lane. We rushed to the house—and there were Uncle Alec and Aunt Janet and Aunt Olivia! The excitement was quite tremendous. Everybody talked and laughed at once, and it was not until we were all seated around the supper table that conversation grew coherent. What laughter and questioning and telling of tales followed, what smiles and bright eyes and glad voices. And through it all, the blissful purrs of Paddy, who sat on the window sill behind the Story Girl, resounded through the din like Andrew MacPherson's bass—"just a bur-r-r-r the hale time."

"Well, I'm thankful to be home again," said Aunt Janet, beaming on us. "We had a real nice time, and Edward's folks were as kind as could be. But give me home for a steady thing. How has everything gone? How did the children behave, Roger?"

"Like models," said Uncle Roger. "They were just as good as gold most of the days."

There were times when one couldn't help liking Uncle Roger.

CHAPTER 19

A DREAD PROPHECY

"I'VE GOT to go and begin stumping out the elderberry pasture this afternoon," said Peter dolefully. "I tell you it's a tough job. Mr. Roger might wait for cool weather before he sets people to stumping out elderberries, and that's a fact."

"Why don't you tell him so?" asked Dan.

"It ain't my business to tell him things," retorted Peter. "I'm hired to do what I'm told, and I do it. But I can have my own opinion all the same. It's going to be a broiling hot day."

We were all in the orchard, except Felix, who had gone to the post-office. It was the forenoon of an August Saturday. Cecily and Sara Ray, who had come up to spend the day with us—her mother having gone to town—were eating timothy roots. Bertha Lawrence, a Charlottetown girl, who had visited Kitty Marr in June, and had gone to school one day with her, had eaten timothy roots, affecting to consider them great delicacies. The fad was at once taken up by the Carlisle schoolgirls. Timothy roots quite ousted "sours" and young raspberry sprouts, both of which had the real merit of being quite toothsome, while timothy roots were tough and tasteless. But timothy roots were fashionable, therefore timothy roots must be eaten. Pecks of them must have been devoured in Carlisle that summer.

Pat was there also, padding about from one to the other on his black paws, giving us friendly pokes and rubs. We all made much of him except Felicity, who would not take any notice of him because he was the Story Girl's cat.

We boys were sprawling on the grass. Our morning chores were done and the day was before us. We should have been feeling very comfortable and happy, but, as a matter of fact, we were not particularly so.

The Story Girl was sitting on the mint beside the well-house, weaving herself a wreath of buttercups. Felicity was sipping from the cup of clouded blue with an overdone air of unconcern. Each was acutely and miserably conscious of the other's presence, and each was desirous of convincing the rest of us that the other was less than nothing to her. Felicity could not succeed.

The Story Girl managed it better. If it had not been for the fact that in all our foregatherings she was careful to sit as far from Felicity as possible, we might have been deceived.

We had not passed a very pleasant week. Felicity and the Story Girl had not been "speaking" to each other, and consequently there had been something rotten in the state of Denmark. An air of restraint was over all our games and conversations.

On the preceding Monday Felicity and the Story Girl had quarrelled over something. What the cause of the quarrel was I cannot tell because I never knew. It remained a "dead secret" between the parties of the first and second part forever. But it was more bitter than the general run of their tiffs, and the consequences were apparent to all. They had not spoken to each other since.

This was not because the rancour of either lasted so long. On the contrary it passed speedily away, not even one low descending sun going down on their wrath. But dignity remained to be considered. Neither would "speak first," and each obstinately declared that she would not speak first, no, not in a hundred years. Neither argument, entreaty, nor expostulation had any effect on those two stubborn girls, nor yet the tears of sweet Cecily, who cried every night about it, and mingled in her pure little prayers fervent petitions that Felicity and the Story Girl might make up.

"I don't know where you expect to go when you die, Felicity," she said tearfully, "if you don't forgive people."

"I have forgiven her," was Felicity's answer, "but I am not going to speak first for all that."

"It's very wrong, and, more than that, it's so uncomfortable," complained Cecily. "It spoils everything."

"Were they ever like this before?" I asked Cecily, as we talked the matter over privately in Uncle Stephen's Walk.

"Never for so long," said Cecily. "They had a spell like this last summer, and one the summer before, but they only lasted a couple of days."

"And who spoke first?"

"Oh, the Story Girl. She got excited about something and spoke to Felicity before she thought, and then it was all right. But I'm afraid it isn't going to be like that this time. Don't you notice how careful the Story Girl is not to get excited? That is such a bad sign."

"We've just got to think up something that will excite her, that's all," I said.

"I'm—I'm praying about it," said Cecily in a low voice, her tear-wet lashes trembling against her pale, round cheeks. "Do you suppose it will do any good, Bev?".

"Very likely," I assured her. "Remember Sara Ray and the money. That came from praying."

"I'm glad you think so," said Cecily tremulously. "Dan said it was no use for me to bother praying about it. He said if they *couldn't* speak God might do something, but when they just *wouldn't* it wasn't likely He would interfere. Dan does say such queer things. I'm so afraid he's going to grow up just like Uncle Robert Ward, who never goes to church, and doesn't believe more than half the Bible is true."

"Which half does he believe is true?" I inquired, with unholy curiosity.

"Oh, just the nice parts. He says there's a heaven all right, but no—no—*hell*. I don't want Dan to grow up like that. It isn't respectable. And you wouldn't want all kinds of people crowding into heaven, now, would you?"

"Well, no, I suppose not," I agreed, thinking of Billy Robinson.

"Of course, I can't help feeling sorry for those who have to go to *the other place*," said Cecily compassionately. "But I suppose they wouldn't be very comfortable in heaven either. They wouldn't feel at home. Andrew Marr said a simply dreadful thing about *the other place* one night last fall, when Felicity and I were down to see Kitty, and they were burning the potato stalks. He said he believed *the other place* must be lots more interesting than heaven because fires were such jolly things. Now, did you ever hear the like?"

"I guess it depends a good deal on whether you're inside or outside the fires," I said.

"Oh, Andrew didn't really mean it, of course. He just said it to sound smart and make us stare. The Marrs are all like that. But anyhow, I'm going to keep on praying that something will happen to excite the Story Girl. I don't believe there is any use in praying that Felicity will speak first, because I am sure she won't."

"But don't you suppose God could make her?" I said, feeling that it wasn't quite fair that the Story Girl should always have to speak first. If she had spoken first the other times it was surely Felicity's turn this time.

"Well, I believe it would puzzle Him," said Cecily, out of the depths of her experience with Felicity.

Peter, as was to be expected, took Felicity's part, and said the Story Girl ought to speak first because she was the oldest. That, he said, had always been his Aunt Jane's rule.

Sara Ray thought Felicity should speak first, because the Story Girl was half an orphan.

Felix tried to make peace between them, and met the usual fate of all peacemakers. The Story Girl loftily told him that he was too young to understand, and Felicity said that fat boys should mind their own business. After that, Felix declared it would serve Felicity right if the Story Girl never spoke to her again.

Dan had no patience with either of the girls, especially Felicity. "What they both want is a right good spanking," he said.

If only a spanking would mend the matter it was not likely it would ever be mended. Both Felicity and the Story Girl were rather too old to be spanked, and, if they had not been, none of the grown-ups would have thought it worth while to administer so desparate a remedy for what they considered so insignificant a trouble. With the usual levity of grown-ups, they regarded the coldness between the girls as a subject of mirth and jest, and recked not that it was freezing the genial current of our youthful souls, and blighting hours that should have been fair pages in our book of days.

The Story Girl finished her wreath and put it on. The buttercups drooped over her high, white brow and played peep with her glowing eyes. A dreamy smile hovered around her poppy-red mouth—a significant smile which, to those of us skilled in its interpretation, betokened the sentence which soon came.

"I know a story about a man who always had his own opinion—"

The Story Girl got no further. We never heard the story of the man who always had his own opinion. Felix came tearing up the lane, with a newspaper in his hand. When a boy as fat as Felix runs at full speed on a broiling August forenoon, he has something to run for—as Felicity remarked.

"He must have got some bad news at the office," said Sara Ray.

"Oh, I hope nothing has happened to father," I exclaimed, springing anxiously to my feet, a sick, horrible feeling of fear running over me like a cool, rippling wave.

"It's just as likely to be good news he is running for as bad," said the Story Girl, who was no believer in meeting trouble half way.

"He wouldn't be running so fast for good news," said Dan cynically.

We were not left long in doubt. The orchard gate flew open and Felix was among us. One glimpse of his face told us that he was no bearer of glad tidings. He had been running hard and should have been rubicund. Instead, he was "as pale as are the dead." I could not have asked him what was the matter had my life depended on it. It was Felicity who demanded impatiently of my shaking, voiceless brother:

"Felix King, what has scared you?"

Felix held out the newspaper—it was the Charlottetown *Daily Enterprise*.

"It's there," he gasped. "Look—read—oh, do you—think it's—true? The—end of—the world—is coming tomorrow—at two—o'clock—in the afternoon!"

Crash! Felicity had dropped the cup of clouded blue, which had passed unscathed through so many changing years, and now at last lay shattered on the stone of the well curb. At any other time we should all have been aghast over such a catastrophe, but it passed unnoticed now. What mattered it that all the cups in the world be broken today if the crack o' doom must sound tomorrow?

"Oh, Sara Stanley, do you believe it? *Do* you?" gasped Felicity, clutching the Story Girl's hand. Cecily's prayer had been answered. Excitement had come with a vengeance, and under its stress Felicity had spoken first. But this, like the breaking of the cup had no significance for us at the moment.

The Story Girl snatched the paper and read the announcement to a group on which sudden, tense silence had fallen. Under a sensational headline, "The Last Trump will sound at Two O'clock Tomorrow," was a paragraph to the effect that the leader of a certain noted sect in the United States had predicted that August twelfth would be the Judgment Day, and that all his numerous followers were preparing for the dread event by prayer, fasting, and the making of appropriate white garments for ascension robes.

I laugh at the remembrance now—until I recall the real horror of fear that enwrapped us in that sunny orchard that August morning of long ago; and then I laugh no more. We were only children, be it remembered, with a very firm and simple faith that grown people knew much more than we did, and a rooted conviction that whatever you read in a newspaper must be true. If the *Daily Enterprise* said that August twelfth was to be the Judgment Day how were you going to get around it?

"Do you believe it, Sara Stanley?" persisted Felicity. "*Do* you?"

"No—no, I don't believe a word of it," said the Story Girl.

But for once her voice failed to carry conviction—or, rather, it carried conviction of the very opposite kind. It was borne in upon our miserable minds that if the Story Girl did not altogether believe it was true she believed it might be true; and the possibility was almost as dreadful as the certainty.

"It *can't* be true," said Sara Ray, seeking refuge, as usual, in tears. "Why, everything just looks the same. Things *couldn't* look the same if the Judgment Day was going to be tomorrow."

"But that's just the way it's to come," I said uncomfortably. "It tells you in the Bible. It's to come just like a thief in the night."

"But it tells you another thing in the Bible, too," said Cecily eagerly. "It says nobody knows when the Judgment Day is to come—not even the angels in heaven. Now, if the angels in heaven don't know it, do you suppose the editor of the *Enterprise* can know it—and him a Grit, too?"

"I guess he knows as much about it as a Tory would," retorted the Story Girl. Uncle Roger was a Liberal and Uncle Alec a Conservative, and the girls held fast to the political traditions of their respective households. "But it isn't really the *Enterprise* editor at all who is saying it—it's a man in the States who claims to be a prophet. If he *is* a prophet perhaps he has found out somehow."

"And it's in the paper, too, and that's printed as well as the Bible," said Dan.

"Well, I'm going to depend on the Bible," said Cecily. "I don't believe it's the Judgment Day tomorrow—but I'm scared, for all that," she added piteously.

That was exactly the position of us all. As in the case of the bell-ringing ghost, we did not believe but we trembled.

"Nobody might have known when the Bible was written," said Dan, "but maybe somebody knows now. Why, the Bible was written thousands of years ago, and that paper was printed this very morning. There's been time to find out ever so much more."

"I want to do so many things," said the Story Girl, plucking off her crown of buttercup gold with a tragic gesture, "but if it's the Judgment Day tomorrow I won't have time to do any of them."

"It can't be much worse than dying, I s'pose," said Felix, grasping at any straw of comfort.

"I'm awful glad I've got into the habit of going to church and Sunday School this summer," said Peter very soberly. "I wish I'd made up my mind before this whether to be a Presbyterian or a Methodist. Do you s'pose it's too late now?"

"Oh, that doesn't matter," said Cecily earnestly. "If—if you're a Christian, Peter, that is all that's necessary."

"But it's too late for that," said Peter miserably. "I can't turn into a Christian between this and two o'clock tomorrow. I'll just have to be satisfied with making up my mind to be a Presbyterian or a Methodist. I wanted to wait till I got old enough to make out what was the difference between them, but I'll have to chance it now. I guess I'll be a Presbyterian, 'cause I want to be like the rest of you. Yes, I'll be a Presbyterian."

"I know a story about Judy Pineau and the word Presbyterian," said the Story Girl, "but I can't tell it now. If tomorrow isn't the Judgment Day I'll tell it Monday."

"If I had known that tomorrow might be the Judgment Day I wouldn't have quarrelled with you last Monday, Sara Stanley, or been so horrid and sulky all the week. Indeed I wouldn't," said Felicity, with very unusual humility.

Ah, Felicity! We were all, in the depths of our pitiful little souls, reviewing the innumerable things we would or would not have done "if we had known." What a black and endless list they made—those sins of omission and commission that rushed accusingly across our young memories! For us the leaves of the Book of Judgment were already opened; and we stood at the bar of our own consciences, than which for youth or eld, there can be no more dread tribunal. I thought of all the evil deeds of my short life—of pinching Felix to make him cry out at family prayers, of playing truant from Sunday School and going fishing one day, of a certain fib—no, no, away in this awful hour with all such euphonious evasions—of a *lie* I had once told, of many a selfish and unkind word and thought and action. And tomorrow might be the great and terrible day of the last accounting! Oh, if I had only been a better boy!

"The quarrel was as much my fault as yours, Felicity," said the Story Girl, putting her arm around Felicity. "We can't undo it now. But if tomorrow isn't the Judgment Day we must be careful never to quarrel again. Oh, I wish father was here."

"He will be," said Cecily. "If it's the Judgment Day for Prince Edward Island it will be for Europe too."

"I wish we could just *know* whether what the paper says is true or not," said Felix desperately. "It seems to me I could brace up if I just *knew*."

But to whom could we appeal? Uncle Alec was away and would not be back until late that night. Neither Aunt Janet nor Uncle Roger were people to whom we cared to apply in such a crisis. We were afraid of the Judgment Day; but we were almost equally afraid of being laughed at. How about Aunt Olivia?

"No, Aunt Olivia has gone to bed with a sick headache and mustn't be disturbed," said the Story Girl. "She said I must get dinner ready, because there was plenty of cold meat, and nothing to do but boil the potatoes and peas, and set the table. I don't know how I can put my thoughts into it when the

Judgment Day may be tomorrow. Besides, what is the good of asking the grown-ups? They don't know anything more about this than we do."

"But if they'd just *say* they didn't believe it, it would be a sort of comfort," said Cecily.

"I suppose the minister would know, but he's away on his vacation," said Felicity. "Anyhow, I'll go and ask mother what she thinks of it."

Felicity picked up the *Enterprise* and betook herself to the house. We awaited her return in dire suspense.

"Well, what does she say?" asked Cecily tremulously.

"She said, 'Run away and don't bother me. I haven't any time for your nonsense,'" responded Felicity in an injured tone. "And I said, 'But, ma, the paper *says* tomorrow is the Judgment Day,' and ma just said, 'Judgment Fiddlesticks!'"

"Well, that's kind of comforting," said Peter. "She can't put any faith in it, or she'd be more worked up."

"If it only wasn't *printed!*" said Dan gloomily.

"Let's all go over and ask Uncle Roger," said Felix desperately.

That we should make Uncle Roger a court of last resort indicated all too clearly the state of our minds. But we went. Uncle Roger was in his barn-yard, hitching his black mare into the buggy. His copy of the *Enterprise* was sticking out of his pocket. He looked, as we saw with sinking hearts, unusually grave and preoccupied. There was not a glimmer of a smile about his face.

"You ask him," said Felicity, nudging the Story Girl.

"Uncle Roger," said the Story Girl, the golden notes of her voice threaded with fear and appeal. "The *Enterprise* says that tomorrow is the Judgment Day. *Is* it? Do *you* think it is?"

"I'm afraid so," said Uncle Roger gravely. "The *Enterprise* is always very careful to print only reliable news."

"But mother doesn't believe it," cried Felicity.

Uncle Roger shook his head.

"That is just the trouble," he said. "People won't believe it till it's too late. I'm going straight to Markdale to pay a man there some money I owe him, and after dinner I'm going to Summerside to buy me a new suit. My old one is too shabby for the Judgment Day."

He got into his buggy and drove away, leaving eight distracted mortals behind him.

"Well, I suppose that settles it," said Peter, in a despairing tone.

"Is there anything we can do to *prepare?*" asked Cecily.

"I wish I had a white dress like you girls," sobbed Sara Ray. "But I haven't, and it's too late to get one. Oh, I wish I had minded what ma said better. I wouldn't have disobeyed her so often if I'd thought the Judgment Day was so near. When I go home I'm going to tell her about going to the magic lantern show."

"I'm not sure that Uncle Roger meant what he said," remarked the Story Girl. "I couldn't get a look into his eyes. If he was trying to hoax us there would have been a twinkle in them. He can never help that. You know he would think it a great joke to frighten us like this. It's really dreadful to have no grown-ups that you can depend on."

"We could depend on father if he was here," said Dan stoutly. "*He'd* tell us the truth."

"He would tell us what he *thought* was true, Dan, but he couldn't *know*. He's not such a well-educated man as the editor of the *Enterprise*. No, there's nothing to do but wait and see."

"Let us go into the house and read just what the Bible does say about it," suggested Cecily.

We crept in carefully, lest we disturb Aunt Olivia, and Cecily found and read the significant portion of Holy Writ. There was little comfort for us in that vivid and terrible picture.

"Well," said the Story Girl finally, "I must go and get the potatoes ready. I suppose they must be boiled even if it is the Judgment Day tomorrow. But I don't believe it is."

"And I've got to go and stump elderberries," said Peter. "I don't see how I can do it—go away back there alone. I'll feel scared to death the whole time."

"Tell Uncle Roger that, and say if tomorrow is the end of the world that there is no good in stumping any more fields," I suggested.

"Yes, and if he let's you off then we'll know he was in earnest," chimed in Cecily. "But if he still says you must go that'll be a sign he doesn't believe it."

Leaving the Story Girl and Peter to peel their potatoes, the rest of us went home, where Aunt Janet, who had gone to the well and found the fragments of the old blue cup, gave poor Felicity a bitter scolding about it. But Felicity bore it very patiently—nay, more, she seemed to delight in it.

"Ma can't believe tomorrow is the last day, or she wouldn't scold like that," she told us; and this comforted us until after dinner, when the Story Girl and Peter came over and told us that Uncle Roger had really gone to Summerside. Then we plunged down into fear and wretchedness again.

"But he said I must go and stump elderberries just the same," said Peter. "He said it might *not* be the Judgment Day tomorrow, though he believed it was, and it would keep me out of mischief. But I just can't stand it back there alone. Some of you fellows must come with me. I don't want you to work, but just for company."

It was finally decided that Dan and Felix should go. I wanted to go also, but the girls protested.

"*You* must stay and keep us cheered up," implored Felicity. "I just don't know how I'm ever going to put in the afternoon. I promised Kitty Marr that I'd go down and spend it with her, but I can't now. And I can't knit any at my lace. I'd just keep thinking, 'What is the use? Perhaps it'll all be burned up tomorrow.'"

So I stayed with the girls, and a miserable afternoon we had of it. The Story Girl again and again declared that she "didn't believe it," but when we asked her to tell a story, she evaded it with a flimsy excuse. Cecily pestered Aunt Janet's life out, asking repeatedly, "Ma, will you be washing Monday?" "Ma, will you be going to prayer meeting Tuesday night?" "Ma, will you be preserving raspberries next week?" and various similar questions. It was a huge comfort to her that Aunt Janet always said, "Yes," or "Of course," as if there could be no question about it.

Sara Ray cried until I wondered how one small head could contain all the tears she shed. But I do not believe she was half as much frightened as disappointed that she had no white dress. In mid-afternoon Cecily came downstairs with her forget-me-not jug in her hand—a dainty bit of china, wreathed with dark blue forget-me-nots, which Cecily prized highly, and in which she always kept her tooth-brush.

"Sara, I am going to give you this jug," she said solemnly. Now, Sara had always coveted this particular jug. She stopped crying long enough to clutch it delightedly. "Oh, Cecily, thank you. But are you sure you won't want it back if tomorrow isn't the Judgment Day?"

"No, it's yours for good," said Cecily, with the high, remote air of one to whom forget-me-not jugs and all such pomps and vanities of the world were as a tale that is told.

"Are you going to give any one your cherry vase?" asked Felicity, trying to speak indifferently. Felicity had never admired the forget-me-not jug, but she had always hankered after the cherry vase—an affair of white glass, with a cluster of red glass cherries and golden-green glass leaves on its side, which Aunt Olivia had given Cecily one Christmas.

"No, I'm not," answered Cecily, with a change of tone.

"Oh, well, *I* don't care," said Felicity quickly. "Only, if tomorrow is the last day, the cherry vase won't be of much use to you."

"I guess it will be as much use to me as to any one else," said Cecily indignantly. She had sacrificed her dear forget-me-not jug to satisfy some pang of conscience, or propitiate some threatening fate, but surrender her precious cherry vase she could not and would not. Felicity needn't be giving any hints!

With the gathering shades of night our plight became pitiful. In the daylight, surrounded by homely, familiar sights and sounds, it was not so difficult to fortify our souls with a cheering incredulity. But now, in this time of shadows, dread belief clutched us and wrung us with terror. If there had been one wise older friend to tell us, in serious fashion, that we need not be afraid, that the *Enterprise* paragraph was naught save the idle report of a deluded fanatic, it would have been well for us. But there was not. Our grown-ups, instead, considered our terror an exquisite jest. At that very moment, Aunt Olivia, who had recovered from her headache, and Aunt Janet were laughing in the kitchen over the state the children were in because they were afraid the end of the world was close at hand. Aunt Janet's throaty gurgle and Aunt Olivia's trilling mirth floated out through the open window.

"Perhaps they'll laugh on the other side of their faces tomorrow," said Dan, with gloomy satisfaction.

We were sitting on the cellar hatch, watching what might be our last sunset o'er the dark hills of time. Peter was with us. It was his Sunday to go home, but he had elected to remain. "If tomorrow is the Judgment Day I want to be with you fellows," he said.

Sara Ray had also yearned to stay, but could not, because her mother had told her she must be home before dark.

"Never mind, Sara," comforted Cecily. "It's not to be till two o'clock tomorrow, so you'll have plenty of time to get up here before anything happens."

"But there might be a mistake," sobbed Sara. "It might be at two o'clock tonight instead of tomorrow."

It might, indeed. This was a new horror, which had not occurred to us.

"I'm sure I won't sleep a wink tonight," said Felix.

"The paper *says* two o'clock tomorrow," said Dan. "You needn't worry, Sara."

But Sara departed, weeping. She did not, however, forget to carry the forget-me-not jug with her. All things considered, her departure was a relief. Such a constantly tearful damsel was not a pleasant companion. Cecily and Felicity and the Story Girl did not cry. They were made of finer, firmer stuff. Dry-eyed, with such courage as they might, they faced whatever might be in store for them.

"I wonder where we'll all be this time tomorrow night," said Felix mournfully, as we watched the sunset between the dark fir boughs. It was an ominous sunset. The sun dropped down amid dark, livid clouds, that turned sullen shades of purple and fiery red behind him.

"I hope we'll be all together, wherever we are," said Cecily gently. "Nothing can be so very bad then."

"I'm going to read the Bible all tomorrow forenoon," said Peter.

When Aunt Olivia came out to go home the Story Girl asked her permission to stay all night with Felicity and Cecily. Aunt Olivia assented lightly, swinging her hat on her arm and including us all in a friendly smile. She looked very pretty, with her big blue eyes and warm-hued golden hair. We loved Aunt Olivia; but just now we resented her having laughed at us with Aunt Janet, and we refused to smile back.

"What a sulky, sulky lot of little people," said Aunt Olivia, going away across the yard, holding her pretty dress up from the dewy grass.

Peter resolved to stay all night with us, too, not troubling himself about anybody's permission. When we went to bed it was settling down for a stormy night, and the rain was streaming wetly on the roof, as if the world, like Sara Ray, were weeping because its end was so near. Nobody forgot or hurried over his prayers that night. We would dearly have loved to leave the candle burning, but Aunt Janet's decree regarding this was as inexorable as any of Mede and Persian. Out the candle must go; and we lay there, quaking, with the wild rain streaming down on the roof above us, and the voices of the storm wailing through the writhing spruce trees.

------- CHAPTER 20 -------

THE JUDGMENT SUNDAY

SUNDAY MORNING broke, dull and gray. The rain had ceased, but the clouds hung dark and brooding above a world which, in its windless calm, following the spent storm-throe, seemed to us to be waiting "till judgment spoke the doom of fate." We were all up early. None of us, it appeared, had slept well, and some of us not at all. The Story Girl had been among the latter, and she looked very pale and wan, with black shadows under her deep-set eyes. Peter, however, had slept soundly enough after twelve o'clock.

"When you've been stumping out elderberries all the afternoon it'll take more than the Judgment Day to keep you awake all night," he said. "But when I woke up this morning it was just awful. I'd forgot it for a moment, and then it all come back with a rush, and I was worse scared than ever."

Cecily was pale but brave. For the first time in years she had not put her hair up in curlers on Saturday night. It was brushed and braided with Puritan simplicity.

"If it's the Judgment Day I don't care whether my hair is curly or not," she said.

"Well," said Aunt Janet, when we all descended to the kitchen, "this is the first time you young ones ever all got up without being called, and that's a fact."

At breakfast our appetites were poor. How could the grown-ups eat as they did? After breakfast and the necessary chores there was the forenoon to be lived through. Peter, true to his word, got out his Bible and began to read from the first chapter in Genesis.

"I won't have time to read it all through, I s'pose," he said, "but I'll get along as far as I can."

There was no preaching in Carlisle that day, and Sunday School was not till the evening. Cecily got out her Lesson Slip and studied the lesson conscientiously. The rest of us did not see how she could do it. We could not, that was very certain.

"If it isn't the Judgment Day I want to have the lesson learned," she said, "and if it is I'll feel I've done what was right. But I never found it so hard to remember the Golden Text before."

The long dragging hours were hard to endure. We roamed restlessly about, and went to and fro—all save Peter, who still steadily read away at his Bible. He was through Genesis by eleven and beginning on Exodus.

"There's a good deal of it I don't understand," he said, "but I read every word, and that's the main thing. That story about Joseph and his brother was so int'resting I almost forgot about the Judgment Day."

But the long drawn out dread was beginning to get on Dan's nerves.

"If it is the Judgment Day," he growled, as we went in to dinner, "I wish it'd hurry up and have it over."

"Oh, Dan!" cried Felicity and Cecily together, in a chorus of horror. But the Story Girl looked as if she rather sympathized with Dan.

If we had eaten little at breakfast we could eat still less at dinner. After dinner the clouds rolled away, and the sun came joyously and gloriously out. This, we thought, was a good omen. Felicity opined that it wouldn't have cleared up if it was the Judgment Day. Nevertheless, we dressed ourselves carefully, and the girls put on their white dresses.

Sara Ray came up, still crying, of course. She increased our uneasiness by saying that her mother believed the *Enterprise* paragraph, and was afraid that the end of the world was really at hand.

"That's why she let me come up," she sobbed. "If she hadn't been afraid I don't believe she would have let me come up. But I'd have died if I couldn't have come. And she wasn't a bit cross when I told her I had gone to the magic lantern show. That's an awful bad sign. I hadn't a white dress, but I put on my white muslin apron with the frills."

"That seems kind of queer," said Felicity doubtfully. "You wouldn't put on an apron to go to church, and so it doesn't seem as if it was proper to put it on for the Judgment Day either."

"Well, it's the best I could do," said Sara disconsolately. "I wanted to have something white on. It's just like a dress only it hasn't sleeves."

"Let's go into the orchard and wait," said the Story Girl. "It's one o'clock now, so in another hour we'll know the worst. We'll leave the front door open, and we'll hear the big clock when it strikes two."

No better plan being suggested, we betook ourselves to the orchard, and sat on the boughs of Uncle Alec's tree because the grass was wet. The world was beautiful and peaceful and green. Overhead was a dazzling blue sky, spotted with heaps of white cloud.

"Pshaw, I don't believe there's any fear of it being the last day," said Dan, beginning a whistle out of sheer bravado.

"Well, don't whistle on Sunday anyhow," said Felicity severely.

"I don't see a thing about Methodists or Presbyterians, as far as I've gone, and I'm most through Exodus," said Peter suddenly. "When does it begin to tell about them?"

"There's nothing about Methodists or Presbyterians in the Bible," said Felicity scornfully.

Peter looked amazed.

"Well, how did they happen, then?" he asked. "When did they begin to be?"

"I've often thought it such a strange thing that there isn't a word about either of them in the Bible," said Cecily. "Especially when it mentions Baptists—or at least one Baptist."

"Well, anyhow," said Peter, "even if it isn't the Judgment Day I'm going to keep on reading the Bible until I've got clean through. I never thought it was such an int'resting book."

"It sounds simply dreadful to hear you call the Bible an interesting book," said Felicity, with a shudder at the sacrilege. "Why, you might be talking of *any* common book."

"I didn't mean any harm," said Peter, crestfallen.

"The Bible *is* an interesting book," said the Story Girl, coming to Peter's rescue. "And there are magnificent stories in it—yes, Felicity, *magnificent*. If the world doesn't come to an end I'll tell you the story of Ruth next Sunday—or look here! I'll tell it anyhow. That's a promise. Wherever we are next Sunday I'll tell you about Ruth."

"Why, you wouldn't tell stories in heaven," said Cecily, in a very timid voice.

"Why not?" said the Story Girl, with a flash of her eyes. "Indeed I shall. I'll tell stories as long as I've a tongue to talk with, or any one to listen."

Ay, doubtless. That dauntless spirit would soar triumphantly above the wreck of matter and the crash of worlds, taking with it all its own wild sweetness and daring. Even the young-eyed cherubim, choiring on meadows of asphodel, might cease their harping for a time to listen to a tale of the vanished earth, told by that golden tongue. Some vague thought of this was in our minds as we looked at her; and somehow it comforted us. Not even the Judgment was so greatly to be feared if after it we were the *same,* our own precious little identities unchanged.

"It must be getting handy two," said Cecily. "It seems as if we'd been waiting here for ever so much longer than an hour."

Conversation languished. We watched and waited nervously. The moments dragged by, each seeming an hour. Would two o'clock never come and end the suspense? We all became very tense. Even Peter had to stop reading. Any unaccustomed sound or sight in the world about us struck on our taut senses like the trump of doom. A cloud passed over the sun and as the sudden shadow swept across the orchard we turned pale and trembled. A wagon rumbling over the plank bridge in the hollow made Sara Ray start up with a shriek. The slamming of a barn door over at Uncle Roger's caused the cold perspiration to break out on our faces.

"I don't believe it's the Judgment Day," said Felix, "and I never have believed it. But oh, I wish that clock would strike two."

"Can't you tell us a story to pass the time?" I entreated the Story Girl.

She shook her head.

"No, it would be no use to try. But if this isn't the Judgment Day I'll have a great one to tell of us being so scared."

Pat presently came galloping up the orchard, carrying in his mouth a big field mouse, which, sitting down before us, he proceeded to devour, body and bones, afterwards licking his chops with great satisfaction.

"It *can't* be the Judgment Day," said Sara Ray, brightening up. "Paddy would never be eating mice if it was."

"If that clock doesn't soon strike two I shall go out of my seven senses," declared Cecily with unusual vehemence.

"Time always seems long when you're waiting," said the Story Girl. "But it does seem as if we had been here more than an hour."

"Maybe the clock struck and we didn't hear it," suggested Dan. "Somebody'd better go and see."

"I'll go," said Cecily. "I suppose, even if anything happens, I'll have time to get back to you."

We watched her white-clad figure pass through the gate and enter the front door. A few minutes passed—or a few years— we could not have told which. Then Cecily came running at full speed back to us. But when she reached us she trembled so much that at first she could not speak.

"What is it? Is it past two?" implored the Story Girl.

"It's—it's four," said Cecily, with a gasp. "The old clock isn't going. Mother forgot to wind it up last night and it stopped. But it's four by the kitchen clock—so it isn't the Judgment Day—and tea is ready—and mother says to come in."

We looked at each other, realizing what our dread had been,

now that it was lifted. It was not the Judgment Day. The world and life were still before us, with all their potent lure of years unknown.

"I'll never believe anything I read in the papers again," said Dan, rushing to the opposite extreme.

"I told you the Bible was more to be depended on than the newspapers," said Cecily triumphantly.

Sara Ray and Peter and the Story Girl went home, and we went in to tea with royal appetites. Afterwards, as we dressed for Sunday School upstairs, our spirits carried us away to such an extent that Aunt Janet had to come twice to the foot of the stairs and inquire severely, "Children, have you forgotten what day this is?"

"Isn't it nice that we're going to live a spell longer in this nice world?" said Felix, as we walked down the hill.

"Yes, and Felicity and the Story Girl are speaking again," said Cecily happily.

"And Felicity *did* speak first," I said.

"Yes, but it took the Judgment Day to make her. I wish," added Cecily with a sigh, "that I hadn't been in quite such a hurry giving away my forget-me-not jug."

"And I wish I hadn't been in such a hurry deciding I'd be a Presbyterian," said Peter.

"Well, it's not too late for that," said Dan. "You can change your mind now."

"No, sir," said Peter with a flash of spirit. "I ain't one of the kind that says they'll be something just because they're scared, and when the scare is over go back on it. I said I'd be a Presbyterian and I mean to stick to it."

"You said you knew a story that had something to do with the Presbyterians," I said to the Story Girl. "Tell us it now."

"Oh, no, it isn't the right kind of a story to tell on Sunday," she replied. "But I'll tell it tomorrow morning."

Accordingly, we heard it the next morning in the orchard.

"Long ago, when Judy Pineau was young," said the Story Girl, "she was hired with Mrs. Elder Frewen—the first Mrs. Elder Frewen. Mrs. Frewen had been a school-teacher, and she was very particular as to how people talked, and the grammar they used. And she didn't like anything but refined words. One very hot day she heard Judy Pineau say she was 'all in a sweat.'

Mrs. Frewen was greatly shocked, and said, 'Judy, you shouldn't say that. It's only horses that sweat. You should say you are in a perspiration.' Well, Judy promised she'd remember, because she liked Mrs. Frewen and was anxious to please her. Not long afterwards Judy was scrubbing the kitchen floor one morning, and when Mrs. Frewen came in Judy looked up and said, quite proud over using the right word, 'Oh, Mees Frewen, ain't it awful hot? I declare I'm all in a Presbyterian.' "

CHAPTER 21

DREAMERS OF DREAMS

AUGUST WENT out and September came in. Harvest was ended; and though summer was not yet gone, her face was turned westering. The asters lettered her retreating footsteps in a purple script, and over the hills and valleys hung a faint blue smoke, as if Nature were worshipping at her woodland altar. The apples began to burn red on the bending boughs; crickets sang day and night; squirrels chattered secrets of Polichinelle in the spruces; the sunshine was as thick and yellow as molten gold; school opened, and we small denizens of the hill farms lived happy days of harmless work and necessary play, closing in nights of peaceful, undisturbed slumber under a roof watched over by autumnal stars.

At least, our slumbers were peaceful and undisturbed until our orgy of dreaming began.

"I would really like to know what especial kind of deviltry you young fry are up to this time," said Uncle Roger one evening, as he passed through the orchard with his gun on his shoulder, bound for the swamp.

We were sitting in a circle before the Pulpit Stone, each writing diligently in an exercise book, and eating the Rev. Mr. Scott's plums, which always reached their prime of juicy, golden-green flesh and bloomy blue skin in September. The Rev. Mr.

Scott was dead and gone, but those plums certainly kept his memory green, as his forgotten sermons could never have done.

"Oh," said Felicity in a shocked tone, when Uncle Roger had passed by, "Uncle Roger *swore.*"

"Oh, no, he didn't," said the Story Girl quickly. " 'Deviltry' isn't swearing at all. It only means extra bad mischief."

"Well, it's not a very nice word, anyhow," said Felicity.

"No, it isn't," agreed the Story Girl with a regretful sigh. "It's very expressive, but it isn't nice. That is the way with so many words. They're expressive, but they're not nice, and so a girl can't use them."

The Story Girl sighed again. She loved expressive words, and treasured them as some girls might have treasured jewels. To her, they were as lustrous pearls, threaded on the crimson cord of a vivid fancy. When she met with a new one she uttered it over and over to herself in solitude, weighing it, caressing it, infusing it with the radiance of her voice, making it her own in all its possibilities for ever.

"Well, anyhow, it isn't a suitable word in this case," insisted Felicity. "We are not up to any dev—any extra bad mischief. Writing down one's dreams isn't mischief at all."

Certainly it wasn't. Surely not even the straitest sect of the grown-ups could call it so. If writing down your dreams, with agonizing care as to composition and spelling—for who knew that the eyes of generations unborn might not read the record?— were not a harmless amusement, could anything be called so? I trow not.

We had been at it for a fortnight, and during that time we only lived to have dreams and write them down. The Story Girl had originated the idea one evening in the rustling, rain-wet ways of the spruce wood, where we were picking gum after a day of showers. When we had picked enough we sat down on the moss-grown stones at the end of a long arcade, where it opened out on the harvest-golden valley below us, our jaws exercising themselves vigorously on the spoil of our climbings. We were never allowed to chew gum in school or in company, but in wood and field, orchard and hayloft, such rules were in abeyance.

"My Aunt Jane used to say it wasn't polite to chew gum anywhere," said Peter rather ruefully.

"I don't suppose your Aunt Jane knew all the rules of etiquette," said Felicity, designing to crush Peter with a big word, borrowed from the *Family Guide.* But Peter was not to be so crushed. He had in him a certain toughness of fibre, that would have been proof against a whole dictionary.

"She did, too," he retorted. "My Aunt Jane was a real lady, even if she was only a Craig. She knew all those rules and she kept them when there was nobody round to see her, just the same as when any one was. And she was smart. If father had had half her git-up-and-git I wouldn't be a hired boy today."

"Have you any idea where your father is?" asked Dan.

"No," said Peter indifferently. "The last we heard of him he was in the Maine lumber woods. But that was three years ago. I don't know where he is now, and," added Peter deliberately, taking his gum from his mouth to make his statement more impressive, "I don't care."

"Oh, Peter, that sounds dreadful," said Cecily. "Your own father!"

"Well," said Peter defiantly, "if your own father had run away when you was a baby, and left your mother to earn her living by washing and working out, I guess you wouldn't care much about him either."

"Perhaps your father may come home some of these days with a huge fortune," suggested the Story Girl.

"Perhaps pigs may whistle, but they've poor mouths for it," was all the answer Peter deigned to this charming suggestion.

"There goes Mr. Campbell down the road," said Dan. "That's his new mare. Isn't she a dandy? She's got a skin like black satin. He calls her Betty Sherman."

"I don't think it's very nice to call a horse after your own grandmother," said Felicity.

"Betty Sherman would have thought it a compliment," said the Story Girl.

"Maybe she would. She couldn't have been very nice herself, or she would never have gone and asked a man to marry her," said Felicity.

"Why not?"

"Goodness me, it was dreadful! Would *you* do such a thing yourself?"

"Well, I don't know," said the Story Girl, her eyes gleaming with impish laughter. "If I wanted him *dreadfully,* and *he* wouldn't do the asking, perhaps *I* would."

"I'd rather die an old maid forty times over," exclaimed Felicity.

"Nobody as pretty as you will ever be an old maid, Felicity," said Peter, who never put too fine an edge on his compliments.

Felicity tossed her golden tressed head and tried to look angry, but made a dismal failure of it.

"It wouldn't be ladylike to ask any one to marry you, you know," argued Cecily.

"I don't suppose the *Family Guide* would think so," agreed the Story Girl lazily, with some sarcasm in her voice. The Story Girl never held the *Family Guide* in such reverence as did Felicity and Cecily. They pored over the "etiquette column" every week, and could have told you on demand, just exactly what kind of gloves should be worn at a wedding, what you should say when introducing or being introduced, and how you ought to look when your best young man came to see you.

"They say Mrs. Richard Cook asked *her* husband to marry her," said Dan.

"Uncle Roger says she didn't exactly ask him, but she helped the lame dog over the stile so slick that Richard was engaged to her before he knew what had happened to him," said the Story Girl. "I know a story about Mrs. Richard Cook's grandmother. She was one of those women who are always saying 'I told you so—' "

"Take notice, Felicity," said Dan aside.

"—And she was very stubborn. Soon after she was married she and her husband quarrelled about an apple tree they had planted in their orchard. The label was lost. He said it was a Fameuse, and she declared it was a Yellow Transparent. They fought over it till the neighbours came out to listen. Finally he got so angry that he told her to shut up. They didn't have any *Family Guides* in those days, so he didn't know it wasn't polite to say shut up to your wife. I suppose she thought she would teach him manners, for would you believe it? That woman *did* shut up, and never spoke one single word to her husband for five years. And then, in five years' time, the tree bore apples, and they *were* Yellow Transparents. And then she spoke at last. She said, 'I told you so!' "

"And did she talk to him after that as usual?" asked Sara Ray.

"Oh, yes, she was just the same as she used to be," said the Story Girl wearily. "But that doesn't belong to the story. It stops when she spoke at last. You're never satisified to leave a story where it should stop, Sara Ray."

"Well, I always like to know what happens afterwards," said Sara Ray.

"Uncle Roger says he wouldn't want a wife he could never quarrel with," remarked Dan. "He says it would be too tame a life for him."

"I wonder if Uncle Roger will always stay a bachelor," said Cecily.

"He seems real happy," observed Peter.

"Ma says that it's all right as long as he is a bachelor because he won't take any one," said Felicity, "but if he wakes up some day and finds he is an old bachelor because he can't get any one it'll have a very different flavour."

"If your Aunt Olivia was to up and get married what would your Uncle Roger do for a housekeeper?" asked Peter.

"Oh, but Aunt Olivia will never be married now," said Felicity. "Why, she'll be twenty-nine next January."

"Well, o' course, that's pretty old," admitted Peter, "but she might find some one who wouldn't mind that, seeing she's so pretty."

"It would be awful splendid and exciting to have a wedding in the family, wouldn't it?" said Cecily. "I've never seen any one married, and I'd just love to. I've been to four funerals, but not to one single wedding."

"I've never even got to a funeral," said Sara Ray gloomily.

"There's the wedding veil of the proud princess," said Cecily, pointing to a long drift of filmy vapour in the southwestern sky.

"And look at that sweet pink cloud below it," added Felicity.

"Maybe that little pink cloud is a dream, getting all ready to float down into somebody's sleep," suggested the Story Girl.

"I had a perfectly awful dream last night," said Cecily, with a shudder of remembrance. "I dreamed I was on a desert island inhabited by tigers and natives with two heads."

"Oh!" the Story Girl looked at Cecily half reproachfully.

"Why couldn't you tell it better than that? If I had such a dream I could tell it so that everybody else would feel as if they had dreamed it, too."

"Well, I'm not you," countered Cecily, "and I wouldn't want to frighten any one as I was frightened. It was an awful dream—but it was kind of interesting, too."

"I've had some real int'resting dreams," said Peter, "but I can't remember them long. I wish I could."

"Why don't you write them down?" suggested the Story Girl. "Oh—" she turned upon us a face illuminated with a sudden inspiration. "I've an idea. Let us each get an exercise book and write down all our dreams, just as we dream them. We'll see who'll have the most interesting collection. And we'll have them to read and laugh over when we're old and gray."

Instantly we all saw ourselves and each other by inner vision, old and gray—all but the Story Girl. We could not picture her as old. Always, as long as she lived, so it seemed to us, must she have sleek brown curls, a voice like the sound of a harpstring in the wind, and eyes that were stars of eternal youth.

CHAPTER 22

THE DREAM BOOKS

THE NEXT day the Story Girl coaxed Uncle Roger to take her to Markdale, and there she bought our dream books. They were ten cents apiece, with ruled pages and mottled green covers. My own lies open beside me as I write, its yellowed pages inscribed with the visions that haunted my childish slumbers on those nights of long ago.

On the cover is pasted a lady's visiting card, on which is written, "The Dream Book of Beverley King." Cecily had a packet of visiting cards which she was hoarding against the day when she would be grown up and could put the calling etiquette of the *Family Guide* into practice; but she generously gave us all one apiece for the covers of our dream books.

As I turn the pages and glance over the naive records, each one beginning, "Last night I dreamed," the past comes very vividly back to me. I see that bowery orchard, shining in memory with a soft glow of beauty—"the light that never was on land or sea,"—where we sat on those September evenings and wrote down our dreams, when the cares of the day were over and there was nothing to interfere with the pleasing throes of composition. Peter—Dan—Felix—Cecily—Felicity—Sara Ray—the Story Girl—they are all around me once more, in the sweet-scented, fading grasses, each with open dream book and pencil in hand, now writing busily, now staring fixedly into space in search of some elusive word or phrase which might best describe the indescribable. I hear their laughing voices, I see their bright, unclouded eyes. In this little, old book, filled with cramped, boyish writing, there is a spell of white magic that sets the years at naught. Beverley King is a boy once more, writing down his dreams in the old King orchard on the homestead hill, blown over by musky winds.

Opposite to him sits the Story Girl, with her scarlet rosetted head, her beautiful bare feet crossed before her, one slender hand propping her high, white brow, on either side of which fall her glossy curls.

There, to the right, is sweet Cecily of the dear, brown eyes, with a little bloated dictionary beside her—for you dream of so many things you can't spell, or be expected to spell, when you are only eleven. Next to her sits Felicity, beautiful, and conscious that she is beautiful, with hair of spun sunshine, and sea-blue eyes, and all the roses of that vanished summer abloom in her cheeks.

Peter is beside her, of course, sprawled flat on his stomach among the grasses, one hand clutching his black curls, with his dream book on a small, round stone before him—for only so can Peter compose at all, and even then he finds it hard work. He can handle a hoe more deftly than a pencil, and his spelling, even with all his frequent appeals to Cecily, is a fearful and wonderful thing. As for punctuation, he never attempts it, beyond an occasional period, jotted down whenever he happens to think of it, whether in the right place or not. The Story Girl goes over his dreams after he has written them out, and puts in the commas and semicolons, and straightens out the sentences.

Felix sits on the right of the Story Girl, fat and stodgy, grimly in earnest even over dreams. He writes with his knees stuck up to form a writing-desk, and he always frowns fiercely the whole time.

Dan, like Peter, writes lying down flat, but with his back towards us; and he has a dismal habit of groaning aloud, writhing his whole body, and digging his toes into the grass, when he cannot turn a sentence to suit him.

Sara Ray is at his left. There is seldom anything to be said of Sara except to tell where she is. Like Tennyson's Maud, in one respect at least, Sara is splendidly null.

Well, there we sit and write in our dream books, and Uncle Roger passes by and accuses us of being up to dev—to very bad mischief.

Each of us was very anxious to possess the most exciting record; but we were an honourable little crew, and I do not think anything was ever written down in those dream books which had not really been dreamed. We had expected that the Story Girl would eclipse us all in the matter of dreams; but, at least in the beginning, her dreams were no more remarkable than those of the rest of us. In dreamland we were all equal. Cecily, indeed, seemed to have the most decided talent for dramatic dreams. That meekest and mildest of girls was in the habit of dreaming truly terrible things. Almost every night battle, murder, or sudden death played some part in her visions. On the other hand, Dan, who was a somewhat truculent fellow, addicted to the perusal of lurid dime novels which he borrowed from the other boys in school, dreamed dreams of such a peaceful and pastoral character that he was quite disgusted with the resulting tame pages of his dream book.

But if the Story Girl could not dream anything more wonderful than the rest of us, she scored when it came to the telling. To hear her tell a dream was as good—or as bad—as dreaming it yourself.

As far as writing them down was concerned, I believe that I, Beverley King, carried off the palm. I was considered to possess a pretty knack of composition. But the Story Girl went me one better even there, because, having inherited something of her father's talent for drawing, she illustrated her dreams with sketches that certainly caught the spirit of them, whatever might be said of their technical excellence. She had an especial knack for drawing monstrosities; and I vividly recall the picture of an enormous and hideous lizard, looking like a reptile of the pterodactyl period, which she had dreamed of seeing crawl across the roof of the house. On another occasion she had a frightful dream—at least, it seemed frightful while she told us and described the dreadful feeling it had given her—of being chased around the parlour by the ottoman, which made faces at her. She drew a picture of the grimacing ottoman on the margin of her dream book which so scared Sara Ray when she beheld it that she cried all the way home, and insisted on sleeping that night with Judy Pineau lest the furniture take to pursuing her also.

Sara Ray's own dreams never amounted to much. She was always in trouble of some sort—couldn't get her hair braided, or her shoes on the right feet. Consequently, her dream book was very monotonous. The only thing worth mentioning in the way of dreams that Sara Ray ever achieved was when she dreamed that she went up in a balloon and fell out.

"I expected to come down with an awful thud," she said, shuddering, "but I lit as light as a feather and woke right up."

"If you hadn't woke up you'd have died," said Peter with a dark significance. "If you dream of falling and *don't* wake you *do* land with a thud and it kills you. That's what happens to people who die in their sleep."

"How do you know?" said Dan skeptically. "Nobody who died in his sleep could ever tell it."

"My Aunt Jane told me so," said Peter.

"I suppose that settles it," said Felicity disagreeably.

"You always say something nasty when I mention my Aunt Jane," said Peter reproachfully.

"What did I say that was nasty?" cried Felicity. "I didn't say a single thing."

"Well, it sounded nasty," said Peter, who knew that it is the tone that makes the music.

"What did your Aunt Jane look like?" asked Cecily sympathetically. "Was she pretty?"

"No," conceded Peter reluctantly, "she wasn't pretty—but

she looked like the woman in that picture the Story Girl's father sent her last week—the one with the shiny ring round her head and the baby in her lap. I've seen Aunt Jane look at me just like that woman looks at her baby. Ma never looks so. Poor ma is too busy washing. I wish I could dream of my Aunt Jane. I never do."

" 'Dream of the dead, you'll hear of the living,' " quoted Felix oracularly.

"I dreamed last night that I threw a lighted match into that keg of gunpowder in Mr. Cooke's store at Markdale," said Peter. "It blew up—and everything blew up—and they fished me out of the mess—but I woke up before I'd time to find out if I was killed or not."

"One is so apt to wake up just as things get interesting," remarked the Story Girl discontentedly.

"I dreamed last night that I had really truly curly hair," said Cecily mournfully. "And oh, I was so happy! It was dreadful to wake up and find it as straight as ever."

Felix, that sober, solid fellow, dreamed constantly of flying through the air. His descriptions of his aerial flights over the tree-tops of dreamland always filled us with envy. None of the rest of us could ever compass such a dream, not even the Story Girl, who might have been expected to dream of flying if anybody did. Felix had a knack of dreaming, anyhow, and his dream book, while suffering somewhat in comparison of literary style, was about the best of the lot when it came to subject matter. Cecily's might be more dramatic, but Felix's was more amusing. The dream which we all counted his masterpiece was the one in which a menagerie had camped in the orchard and the rhinoceros chased Aunt Janet around and around the Pulpit Stone, but turned into an inoffensive pig when it was on the point of catching her.

Felix had a sick spell soon after we began our dream books. It was an attack of a kind to which he was somewhat subject, and Aunt Janet essayed to cure him by administering a dose of liver pills which Elder Frewen had assured her were a cure-all for every disease the flesh is heir to. But Felix flatly refused to take liver pills; Mexican Tea he would drink, but liver pills he would not take, in spite of his own suffering and Aunt Janet's commands and entreaties. I could not understand his antipathy to the insignificant little white pellets, which were so easy to swallow; but he explained the matter to us in the orchard when he had recovered his usual health and spirits. "I was afraid to take the liver pills for fear they'd prevent me from dreaming," he said. "Don't you remember old Miss Baxter in Toronto, Bev? And how she told Mrs. McLaren that she was subject to terrible dreams, and finally she took two liver pills and never had any more dreams after that. I'd rather have died than risk it," concluded Felix solemnly.

"I'd an exciting dream last night for once," said Dan triumphantly. "I dreamt old Peg Bowen chased me. I thought I was up to her house and she took after me. You bet I scooted. And she caught me—yes, sir! I felt her skinny hand reach out and clutch my shoulder. I let a screech—and woke up."

"I should think you did screech," said Felicity.

"We heard you clean over into our room."

"I hate to dream of being chased because I can never run," said Sara Ray with a shiver. "I just stand rooted to the ground— and see it coming—and can't stir. It don't sound much written out, but it's awful to go through. I'm sure I hope I'll never dream Peg Bowen chases me. I'll die if I do."

"I wonder what Peg Bowen would really do to a fellow if she caught him," speculated Dan.

"Peg Bowen doesn't need to catch you to do things to you," said Peter ominously. "She can put ill-luck on you just by looking at you—and she will if you offend her."

"I don't believe that," said the Story Girl airily.

"Don't you? All right, then! Last summer she called at Lem Hill's in Markdale, and he told her to clear out or he'd set the dog on her. Peg cleared out, and she went across his pasture, muttering to herself and throwing her arms round. And next day his very best cow took sick and died. How do you account for that?"

"It might have happened anyhow," said the Story Girl— somewhat less assuredly, though.

"It might. But I'd just as soon Peg Bowen didn't look at *my* cows," said Peter.

"As if you had any cows!" giggled Felicity.

"I'm going to have cows some day," said Peter, flushing. "I don't mean to be a hired boy all my life. I'll have a farm of my own and cows and everything. You'll see if I won't."

"I dreamed last night that we opened the blue chest," said the Story Girl, "and all the things were there—the blue china candlestick—only it was brass in the dream—and the fruit basket with the apple on it, and the wedding dress, and the embroidered petticoat. And we were laughing, and trying the things on, and having such fun. And Rachel Ward herself came and looked at us—so sad and reproachful—and we all felt ashamed, and I began to cry, and woke up crying."

"I dreamed last night that Felix was thin," said Peter, laughing. "He did look so queer. His clothes just hung loose, and he was going round trying to hold them on."

Everybody thought this funny, except Felix. He would not speak to Peter for two days because of it. Felicity also got into trouble because of her dreams. One night she woke up, having just had a very exciting dream; but she went to sleep again, and in the morning she could not remember the dream at all. Felicity determined she would never let another dream get away from her in such a fashion; and the next time she wakened in the night—having dreamed that she was dead and buried—she promptly arose, lighted a candle, and proceeded to write the dream down then and there. While so employed she contrived to upset the candle and set fire to her nightgown—a brand-new one, trimmed with any quantity of crocheted lace. A huge hole was burned in it, and when Aunt Janet discovered it she lifted up her voice with no uncertain sound. Felicity had never received a sharper scolding. But she took it very philosophically. She was used to her mother's bitter tongue, and she was not unduly sensitive.

"Anyhow, I saved my dream," she said placidly.

And that, of course, was all that really mattered. Grown people were so strangely oblivious to the truly important things in life. Material for new garments, of night or day, could be bought in any shop for a trifling sum and made up out of hand. But if a dream escape you, in what market-place the wide world over can you hope to regain it? What coin of earthly minting will ever buy back for you that lost and lovely vision?

CHAPTER 23

SUCH STUFF AS DREAMS ARE MADE ON

PETER TOOK Dan and me aside one evening, as we were on our way to the orchard with our dream books, saying significantly that he wanted our advice. Accordingly, we went round to the spruce wood, where the girls would not see us to the rousing of their curiosity, and there Peter told us of his dilemma. "Last night I dreamed I was in church," he said. "I thought it was full of people, and I walked up the aisle to your pew and set down, as unconcerned as a pig on ice. And then I found that I hadn't a stitch of clothes on—*not one blessed stitch.* Now"—Peter dropped his voice—"what is bothering me is this—would it be proper to tell a dream like that before the girls?"

I was of the opinion that it would be rather questionable; but Dan vowed he didn't see why. *He'd* tell it just as quick as any other dream. There was nothing bad in it.

"But they're your own relations," said Peter. "They're no relation to me, and that makes a difference. Besides, they're all such ladylike girls. I guess I'd better not risk it. I'm pretty sure Aunt Jane wouldn't think it was proper to tell such a dream. And I don't want to offend Fel—any of them."

So Peter never told that dream, nor did he write it down. Instead, I remember seeing in his dream book, under the date of September fifteenth, an entry to this effect:—

"Last nite i dremed a drem. it wasent a polit drem so i won't rite it down."

The girls saw this entry but, to their credit be it told, they never tried to find out what the "drem" was. As Peter said, they were "ladies" in the best and truest sense of that much abused appellation. Full of fun and frolic and mischief they were, with all the defects of their qualities and all the wayward faults of youth. But no indelicate thought or vulgar word could have been shaped or uttered in their presence. Had any of us boys ever been guilty of such, Cecily's pale face would have coloured with the blush of outraged purity, Felicity's golden head would have lifted itself in the haughty indignation of insulted womanhood, and the Story Girl's splendid eyes would have flashed with such anger and scorn as would have shrivelled the very soul of the wretched culprit.

Dan was once guilty of swearing. Uncle Alec whipped him for it—the only time he ever so punished any of his children. But it was because Cecily cried all night that Dan was filled with saving remorse and repentance. He vowed next day to Cecily that he would never swear again, and he kept his word.

All at once the Story Girl and Peter began to forge ahead in the matter of dreaming. Their dreams suddenly became so lurid and dreadful and picturesque that it was hard for the rest of us to believe that they were not painting the lily rather freely in their accounts of them. But the Story Girl was the soul of honour; and Peter, early in life, had had his feet set in the path of truthfulness by his Aunt Jane and had never been known to stray from it. When they assured us solemnly that their dreams all happened exactly as they described them we were compelled to believe them. But there was something up, we felt sure of that. Peter and the Story Girl certainly had a secret between them, which they kept for a whole fortnight. There was no finding it out from the Story Girl. She had a knack of keeping secrets, anyhow; and, moreover, all that fortnight she was strangely cranky and petulant, and we found it was not wise to tease her. She was not well, so Aunt Olivia told Aunt Janet.

"I don't know what is the matter with the child," said the former anxiously. "She hasn't seemed like herself the past two weeks. She complains of headache, and she has no appetite, and she is a dreadful colour. I'll have to see a doctor about her if she doesn't get better soon."

"Give her a good dose of Mexican Tea and try that first," said Aunt Janet. "I've saved many a doctor's bill in my family by using Mexican Tea."

The Mexican Tea was duly administered, but produced no improvement in the condition of the Story Girl, who, however, went on dreaming after a fashion which soon made her dream book a veritable curiousity of literature.

"If we can't soon find out what makes Peter and the Story Girl dream like that, the rest of us might as well give up trying to write dream books," said Felix discontentedly.

Finally, we did find out. Felicity wormed the secret out of Peter by the employment of Delilah wiles, such as have been the undoing of many a miserable male creature since Samson's day. She first threatened that she would never speak to him again if he didn't tell her; and then she promised him that, if he did, she would let him walk beside her to and from Sunday School all the rest of the summer, and carry her books for her. Peter was not proof against this double attack. He yielded and told the secret.

I expected that the Story Girl would overwhelm him with scorn and indignation. But she took it very coolly.

"I knew Felicity would get it out of him sometime," she said. "I think he has done well to hold out this long."

Peter and the Story Girl, so it appeared, had wooed wild dreams to their pillows by the simple device of eating rich, indigestible things before they went to bed. Aunt Olivia knew nothing about it, of course. She permitted them only a plain, wholesome lunch at bed-time. But during the day the Story Girl would smuggle upstairs various tidbits from the pantry, putting half in Peter's room and half in her own; and the result was these visions which had been our despair.

"Last night I ate a piece of mince pie," she said, "and a lot of pickles, and two grape jelly tarts. But I guess I overdid it, because I got real sick and couldn't sleep at all, so of course I didn't have any dreams. I should have stopped with the pie and pickles and left the tarts alone. Peter did, and he had an elegant dream that Peg Bowen caught him and put him on to boil alive in that big black pot that hangs outside her door. He woke up before the water got hot, though. Well, Miss Felicity, you're pretty smart. But how will you like to walk to Sunday School with a boy who wears patched trousers?"

"I won't have to," said Felicity triumphantly. "Peter is having a new suit made. It's to be ready by Saturday. I knew that before I promised."

Having discovered how to produce exciting dreams, we all promptly followed the example of Peter and the Story Girl.

"There is no chance for me to have any horrid dreams," lamented Sara Ray, "because ma won't let me have anything at all to eat before I go to bed. I don't think it is fair."

"Can't you hide something away through the day as we do?" asked Felicity.

"No." Sara shook her fawn-coloured head mournfully. "Ma always keeps the pantry locked, for fear Judy Pineau will treat her friends."

For a week we ate unlawful lunches and dreamed dreams after our own hearts—and, I regret to say, bickered and squabbled incessantly through the daytime, for our digestions went out of order and our tempers followed suit. Even the Story Girl and I had a fight—something that had never happened before. Peter was the only one who kept his normal poise. Nothing could upset that boy's stomach.

One night Cecily came into the pantry with a large cucumber, and proceeded to devour the greater part of it. The grown-ups were away that evening, attending a lecture in Markdale, so we ate our snacks openly, without any recourse to ways that were dark. I remember I supped that night off a solid hunk of fat pork, topped off with a slab of cold plum pudding.

"I thought you didn't like cucumber, Cecily," Dan remarked.

"Neither I do," said Cecily with a grimace. "But Peter says they're splendid for dreaming. He et one that night he had the dream about being caught by cannibals. I'd eat three cucumbers if I could have a dream like that."

Cecily finished her cucumber, and then drank a glass of milk, just as we heard the wheels of Uncle Alec's buggy rambling over the bridge in the hollow. Felicity quickly restored pork and pudding to their own places, and by the time Aunt Janet came in we were all in our respective beds. Soon the house was dark and silent. I was just dropping into an uneasy slumber when I heard a commotion in the girls' room across the hall.

Their door opened and through our own open door I saw Felicity's white-clad figure flit down the stairs to Aunt Janet's room. From the room she had left came moans and cries.

"Cecily's sick," said Dan, springing out of bed. "That cucumber must have disagreed with her."

In a few minutes the whole household was astir. Cecily was sick—very, very sick, there was no doubt of that. She was even worse than Dan had been when he had eaten the bad berries. Uncle Alec, tired as he was from his hard day's work and

evening outing, was despatched for the doctor. Aunt Janet and
Felicity administered all the homely remedies they could think
of, but to no effect. Felicity told Aunt Janet of the cucumber,
but Aunt Janet did not think the cucumber alone could be
responsible for Cecily's alarming condition.

"Cucumbers are indigestible, but I never knew of them making any one as sick as this," she said anxiously. "What made
the child eat a cucumber before going to bed? I didn't think
she liked them."

"It was that wretched Peter," sobbed Felicity indignantly.
"He told her it would make her dream something extra."

"What on earth did she want to dream for?" demanded Aunt
Janet in bewilderment.

"Oh, to have something worth while to write in her dream
book, ma. We all have dream books, you know, and every one
wants their own to be the most exciting—and we've been eating
rich things to make us dream—and it does—but if Cecily—
oh, I'll never forgive myself," said Felicity, incoherently, letting
all kinds of cats out of the bag in her excitement and alarm.

"Well, I wonder what on earth you young ones will do next,"
said Aunt Janet in the helpless tone of a woman who gives it
up.

Cecily was no better when the doctor came. Like Aunt Janet,
he declared that cucumbers alone would not have made her
so ill; but when he found out that she had drunk a glass of
milk also the mystery was solved.

"Why, milk and cucumber together make a rank poison,"
he said. "No wonder the child is sick. There—there now—"
seeing the alarmed faces around him, "don't be frightened. As
old Mrs. Fraser says, 'It's no deidly.' It won't kill her, but she'll
probably be a pretty miserable girl for two or three days."

She was. And we were all miserable in company. Aunt Janet
investigated the whole affair and the matter of our dream books
was aired in family conclave. I do not know which hurt our
feelings most—the scolding we got from Aunt Janet, or the
ridicule which the other grown-ups, especially Uncle Roger,
showered on us. Peter received an extra "setting down," which
he considered rank injustice.

"I didn't tell Cecily to drink the milk, and the cucumber
alone wouldn't have hurt her," he grumbled. Cecily was able

to be out with us again that day, so Peter felt that he might venture on a grumble. " 'Sides, she coaxed me to tell her what would be good for dreams. I just told her as a favour. And now your Aunt Janet blames me for the whole trouble."

"And Aunt Janet says we are never to have anything to eat before we go to bed after this except plain bread and milk," said Felix sadly.

"They'd like to stop us from dreaming altogether if they could," said the Story Girl wrathfully.

"Well, anyway, they can't prevent us from growing up," consoled Dan.

"We needn't worry about the bread and milk rule," added Felicity. "Ma made a rule like that once before, and kept it for a week, and then we just slipped back to the old way. That will be what will happen this time, too. But of course we won't be able to get any more rich things for supper, and our dreams will be pretty flat after this."

"Well, let's go down to the Pulpit Stone and I'll tell you a story I know," said the Story Girl.

We went—and straightway drank of the waters of forgetfulness. In a brief space we were laughing right merrily, no longer remembering our wrongs at the hands of those cruel grownups. Our laughter echoed back from the barns and the spruce grove, as if elfin denizens of upper air were sharing in our mirth.

Presently, also, the laughter of the grown-ups mingled with ours. Aunt Olivia and Uncle Roger, Aunt Janet and Uncle Alec, came strolling through the orchard and joined our circle, as they sometimes did when the toil of the day was over, and the magic time 'twixt light and dark brought truce of care and labour. 'Twas then we liked our grown-ups best, for then they seemed half children again. Uncle Roger and Uncle Alec lolled in the grass like boys; Aunt Olivia, looking more like a pansy than ever in the prettiest dress of pale purple print, with a knot of yellow ribbon at her throat, sat with her arm about Cecily and smiled on us all; and Aunt Janet's motherly face lost its every-day look of anxious care.

The Story Girl was in great fettle that night. Never had her tales sparkled with such wit and archness.

"Sara Stanley," said Aunt Olivia, shaking her finger at her

after a side-splitting yarn, "if you don't watch out you'll be famous some day."

"These funny stories are all right," said Uncle Roger, "but for real enjoyment give me something with a creep in it. Sara, tell us that story of the Serpent Woman I heard you tell one day last summer."

The Story Girl began it glibly. But before she had gone far with it, I, who was sitting beside her, felt an unaccountable repulsion creeping over me. For the first time since I had known her I wanted to draw away from the Story Girl. Looking around on the faces of the group, I saw that they all shared my feeling. Cecily had put her hands over her eyes. Peter was staring at the Story Girl with a fascinated, horror-stricken gaze. Aunt Olivia was pale and troubled. All looked as if they were held prisoners in the bonds of a fearsome spell which they would gladly break but could not.

It was not our Story Girl who sat there, telling that weird tale in a sibilant, curdling voice. She had put on a new personality like a garment, and that personality was a venomous, evil, loathly thing. I would rather have died than have touched the slim, brown wrist on which she supported herself. The light in her narrowed orbs was the cold, merciless gleam of the serpent's eye. I felt frightened of this unholy creature who had suddenly come in our dear Story Girl's place.

When the tale ended there was a brief silence. Then Aunt Janet said severely, but with a sigh of relief,

"Little girls shouldn't tell such horrible stories."

This truly Aunt Janetian remark broke the spell. The grown-ups laughed, rather shakily, and the Story Girl—our own dear Story Girl once more, and no Serpent Woman—said protestingly,

"Well, Uncle Roger asked me to tell it. I don't like telling such stories either. They make me feel dreadful. Do you know, for just a little while, I felt exactly like a snake."

"You looked like one," said Uncle Roger. "How on earth do you do it?"

"I can't explain how I do it," said the Story Girl perplexedly. "It just does itself."

Genius can never explain how it does it. It would not be genius if it could. And the Story Girl had genius.

As we left the orchard I walked along behind Uncle Roger and Aunt Olivia.

"That was an uncanny exhibition for a girl of fourteen, you know, Roger," said Aunt Olivia musingly. "What is in store for that child?"

"Fame," said Uncle Roger. "If she ever has a chance, that is, and I suppose her father will see to that. At least, I hope he will. You and I, Olivia, never had our chance. I hope Sara will have hers."

This was my first inkling of what I was to understand more fully in later years. Uncle Roger and Aunt Olivia had both cherished certain dreams and ambitions in youth, but circumstances had denied them their "chance" and those dreams had never been fulfilled.

"Some day, Olivia," went on Uncle Roger, "you and I may find ourselves the aunt and uncle of the foremost actress of her day. If a girl of fourteen can make a couple of practical farmers and a pair of matter-of-fact housewives half believe for ten minutes that she is really a snake, what won't she be able to do when she is thirty? Here, you," added Uncle Roger, perceiving me, "cut along and get off to your bed. And mind you don't eat cucumbers and milk before you go."

CHAPTER 24

THE BEWITCHMENT OF PAT

WE WERE all in the doleful dumps—at least, all we "young fry" were, and even the grown-ups were sorry and condescended to take an interest in our troubles. Pat, our own dear, frolicsome Paddy, was sick again—very, very sick.

On Friday he moped and refused his saucer of new milk at milking time. The next morning he stretched himself down on the platform by Uncle Roger's back door, laid his head on his black paws, and refused to take any notice of anything or anybody. In vain we stroked and entreated and brought him tidbits. Only when the Story Girl caressed him did he give one plaintive little mew, as if to ask piteously why she could not do something for him. At that Cecily and Felicity and Sara Ray all began crying, and we boys felt choky. Indeed, I caught Peter behind Aunt Olivia's dairy later in the day, and if ever a boy had been crying I vow that boy was Peter. Nor did he deny it when I taxed him with it, but he would not give in that he was crying about Paddy. Nonsense!

"What were you crying for, then?" I said.

"I'm crying because—because my Aunt Jane is dead," said Peter defiantly.

"But your Aunt Jane died two years ago," I said skeptically.

"Well, ain't that all the more reason for crying?" retorted Peter. "I've had to do without her for two years, and that's worse than if it had just been a few days."

"I believe you were crying because Pat is so sick," I said firmly.

"As if I'd cry about a cat!" scoffed Peter. And he marched off whistling.

Of course we had tried the lard and powder treatment again, smearing Pat's paws and sides liberally. But to our dismay, Pat made no effort to lick it off.

"I tell you he's a mighty sick cat," said Peter darkly. "When a cat don't care what he looks like he's pretty far gone."

"If we only knew what was the matter with him we might do something," sobbed the Story Girl, stroking her poor pet's unresponsive head.

"*I* could tell you what's the matter with him, but you'd only laugh at me," said Peter.

We all looked at him.

"Peter Craig, what do you mean?" asked Felicity.

" 'Zackly what I say."

"Then, if you know what is the matter with Paddy, tell us," commanded the Story Girl, standing up. She said it quietly; but Pete obeyed. I think he would have obeyed if she, in that one and with those eyes, had ordered him to cast himself into the depths of the sea. I know I should.

"He's *bewitched*—that's what's the matter with him," said Peter, half defiantly, half shamefacedly.

"Bewitched? Nonsense!"

"There now, what did I tell you?" complained Peter.

The Story Girl looked at Peter, at the rest of us, and then at poor Pat.

"How could he be bewitched?" she asked irresolutely, "and who could bewitch him?"

"I don't know *how* he was bewitched," said Peter. "I'd have to be a witch myself to know that. But Peg Bowen bewitched him."

"Nonsense!" said the Story Girl again.

"All right," said Peter. "You don't have to believe me without you like."

"If Peg Bowen could bewitch anything—and I don't believe she could—why should she bewitch Pat?" asked the Story Girl. "Everybody here and at Uncle Alec's is always kind to her."

"I'll tell you why," said Peter. "Thursday afternoon, when you fellows were all in school, Peg Bowen came here. Your Aunt Olivia gave her a lunch—a good one. You may laugh at the notion of Peg being a witch, but I notice your folks are always awful good to her when she comes, and awful careful never to offend her."

"Aunt Olivia would be good to any poor creature, and so would mother," said Felicity. "And of course nobody wants to offend Peg, because she is spiteful, and she once set fire to a man's barn in Markdale when he offended her. But she isn't a witch—that's ridiculous."

"All right. But wait till I tell you. When Peg Bowen was leaving Pat was stretched out on the steps. She tramped on his tail. You know Pat doesn't like to have his tail meddled with. He slewed himself round and clawed her bare foot. If you'd just seen the look she gave him you'd know whether she was a witch or not. And she went off down the lane, muttering and throwing her hands round, just like she did in Lem Hill's cow pasture. She put a spell on Pat, that's what she did. He was sick the next morning."

We looked at each other in a miserable, perplexed silence. We were only children—and we believed that there had been such things as witches once upon a time—and Peg Bowen *was* an eerie creature.

"If that's so—though I can't believe it—we can't do anything," said the Story Girl drearily. "Pat must die."

Cecily began to weep afresh.

"I'd do anything to save Pat's life," she said. "I'd *believe* anything."

"There's nothing we can do," said Felicity impatiently.

"I suppose," sobbed Cecily, "we might go to Peg Bowen and ask her to forgive Pat and take the spell off him. She might, if we apologized real humble."

At first we were appalled by the suggestion. We didn't believe that Peg Bowen was a witch. But to go to her—to seek her out in that mysterious woodland retreat of hers which was invested with all the terrors of the unknown! And that this suggestion should come from timid Cecily, of all people! But then, there was poor Pat!

"Would it do any good?" said the Story Girl desperately. "Even if she did make Pat sick I suppose it would only make her crosser if we went and accused her of bewitching him. Besides, she didn't do anything of the sort."

But there was some uncertainty in the Story Girl's voice.

"It wouldn't do any harm to try," said Cecily. "If she didn't make him sick it won't matter if she is cross."

"It won't matter to Pat, but it might to the one who goes to her," said Felicity. "She isn't a witch, but she's a spiteful old woman, and goodness knows what she'd do to us if she caught us. I'm scared of Peg Bowen, and I don't care who knows it. Ever since I can mind ma's been saying, 'If you're not good Peg Bowen will catch you.'"

"If I thought she really made Pat sick and could make him better, I'd try to pacify her somehow," said the Story Girl decidedly. "I'm frightened of her, too—but just look at poor, darling Paddy."

We looked at Paddy, who continued to stare fixedly before him with unwinking eyes. Uncle Roger came out and looked at him also, with what seemed to us positively brutal unconcern.

"I'm afraid it's all up with Pat," he said.

"Uncle Roger," said Cecily imploringly, "Peter says Peg Bowen has bewitched Pat for scratching her. Do you think it can be so?"

"Did Pat scratch Peg?" asked Uncle Roger, with a horror-stricken face. "Dear me! Dear me! The mystery is solved. Poor Pat!"

Uncle Roger nodded his head, as if resigning himself and Pat to the worst.

"Do you really think Peg Bowen is a witch, Uncle Roger?" demanded the Story Girl incredulously.

"Do I think Peg Bowen a witch? My dear Sara, what do *you* think of a woman who can turn herself into a black cat whenever she likes? Is she a witch? Or is she not? I leave it to you."

"Can Peg Bowen turn herself into a black cat?" asked Felix, staring.

"It's my belief that that is the least of Peg Bowen's accomplishments," answered Uncle Roger. "It's the easiest thing in the world for a witch to turn herself into any animal you choose to mention. Yes, Pat is bewitched—no doubt of that—not the least in the world."

"What are you telling those children such stuff for?" asked Aunt Olivia, passing on her way to the well.

"It's an irresistible temptation," answered Uncle Roger, strolling over to carry her pail.

"You can see your Uncle Roger believes Peg is a witch," said Peter.

"And you can see Aunt Olivia doesn't," I said, "and I don't either."

"See here," said the Story Girl resolutely, "I don't believe it, but there *may* be something in it. Suppose there is. The question is, what can we do?"

"I'll tell you what *I'd* do," said Peter. "I'd take a present for Peg, and ask her to make Pat well. I wouldn't let on I thought she'd make him sick. Then she couldn't be offended—and maybe she'd take the spell off."

"I think we'd better all give her something," said Felicity. "I'm willing to do that. But who's going to take the presents to her?"

"We must all go together," said the Story Girl.

"I won't," cried Sara Ray in terror. "I wouldn't go near Peg Bowen's house for the world, no matter who was with me."

"I've thought of a plan," said the Story Girl. "Let's all give her something, as Felicity says. And let us write a letter to her—a real nice, polite letter. Then let us all go up to her place this evening, and if we see her outside we'll just go quietly and set the things down before her with the letter, and say nothing but come respectfully away."

"If she'll let us," said Dan significantly.

"Can Peg read a letter?" I asked.

"Oh, yes. Aunt Olivia says she is a good scholar. She went to school and was a smart girl until she became crazy. We'll write it very plain."

"What if we don't see her?" asked Felicity.

"We'll put the things on her doorstep then and leave them."

"She may be miles away over the country by this time," sighed Cecily, "and never find them until it's too late for Pat. But it's the only thing to do. What can we give her?"

"We mustn't offer her money," said the Story Girl. "She's very indignant when any one does that. She says she isn't a beggar. But she'll take anything else. *I* shall give her my string of blue beads. She's fond of finery."

"I'll give her that sponge cake I made this morning," said Felicity. "I guess she doesn't get sponge cake very often."

"I've nothing but the rheumatism ring I got as a premium for selling needles last winter," said Peter. "I'll give her that. Even if she hasn't got rheumatism it's a real handsome ring. It looks like solid gold."

"I'll give her a roll of peppermint candy," said Felix.

"I'll give one of those little jars of cherry preserve I made," said Cecily.

"I won't go near her," quavered Sara Ray, "but I want to do something for Pat, and I'll send her that piece of apple leaf lace I knit last week."

I decided to give the redoubtable Peg some apples from my birthday tree, and Dan declared he would give her a plug of tobacco.

"Oh, won't she be insulted?" exclaimed Felix, rather horrified.

"Naw," grinned Dan. "Peg chews tobacco like a man. She'd rather have it than your rubbishy peppermints, I can tell you. I'll run down to old Mrs. Sampson's and get a plug."

"Now, we must write the letter and take it and the presents to her right away, before it gets dark," said the Story Girl.

We adjourned to the granary to indite the important document, which the Story Girl was to compose.

"How shall I begin it?" she asked in perplexity. "It would never do to say, 'Dear Peg,' and 'Dear Miss Bowen' sounds too ridiculous."

"Besides, nobody knows whether she's Miss Bowen or not," said Felicity. "She went to Boston when she grew up, and some say she was married up there and her husband deserted her, and that's why she went crazy. If she's married she won't like being called Miss."

"Well, how am I to address her?" asked the Story Girl in despair.

Peter again came to the rescue with a practical suggestion.

"Begin it, 'Respected Madam,' " he said. "Ma has a letter a school trustee once writ to my Aunt Jane and that's how it begins."

"Respected Madam," wrote the Story Girl, "We want to ask a very great favour of you, and we hope you will kindly grant it if you can. Our favourite cat, Paddy, is very sick, and we are afraid he is going to die. Do you think you could cure him? And will you please try? We are all so fond of him, and he is such a good cat, and has no bad habits. Of course, if any of us tramps on his tail he will scratch us, but you know a cat can't bear to have his tail tramped on. It's a very tender part of him, and it's his only way of preventing it, and he doesn't mean any harm. If you can cure Paddy for us we will always be very, very grateful to you. The accompanying small offerings are a testimonial of our respect and gratitude, and we entreat you to honour us by accepting them.

"Very respectfully yours,
                    "SARA STANLEY."

"I tell you that last sentence has a fine sound," said Peter admiringly.

"I didn't make that up," admitted the Story Girl honestly. "I read it somewhere and remembered it."

"I think it's *too* fine," criticized Felicity. "Peg Bowen won't know the meaning of such big words."

But it was decided to leave them in and we all signed the letter.

Then we got our "testimonials," and started on our reluctant journey to the domains of the witch. Sara Ray would not go, of course, but she volunteered to stay with Pat while we were away. We did not think it necessary to inform the grown-ups of our errand, or its nature. Grown-ups had such peculiar views. They might forbid our going at all—and they would certainly laugh at us.

Peg Bowen's house was nearly a mile away, even by the short cut past the swamp and up the wooded hill. We went down through the brook field and over the little plank bridge in the hollow, half lost in its surrounding sea of farewell summers. When we reached the green gloom of the woods beyond we began to feel frightened, but nobody would admit it. We walked very closely together, and we did not talk. When you are near the retreat of witches and folk of that ilk the less you say the better, for their feelings are so notoriously touchy. Of course, Peg wasn't a witch, but it was best to be on the safe side.

Finally we came to the lane which led directly to her abode. We were all very pale now, and our hearts were beating. The red September sun hung low between the tall spruces to the west. It did not look to me just right for a sun. In fact, everything looked uncanny. I wished our errand were well over.

A sudden bend in the lane brought us out to the little clearing where Peg's house was before we were half ready to see it. In spite of my fear I looked at it with some curiosity. It was a small, shaky building with a sagging roof, set amid a perfect jungle of weeds. To our eyes, the odd thing about it was that there was no entrance on the ground floor, as there should be in any respectable house. The only door was in the upper story, and was reached by a flight of rickety steps. There was no sign of life about the place except—sight of ill omen—a large black cat, sitting on the topmost step. We thought of Uncle Roger's gruesome hints. Could that black cat be Peg? Nonsense! But still—it didn't look like an ordinary cat. It was so large—and had such green, malicious eyes! Plainly, there was something out of the common about the beastie!

In a tense, breathless silence the Story Girl placed our parcels on the lowest step, and laid her letter on the top of the pile. Her brown fingers trembled and her face was very pale.

Suddenly the door above us opened, and Peg Bowen herself appeared on the threshold. She was a tall, sinewy old woman, wearing a short, ragged, drugget skirt which reached scantly below her knees, a scarlet print blouse, and a man's hat. Her feet, arms, and neck were bare, and she had a battered old clay pipe in her mouth. Her brown face was seamed with a hundred wrinkles, and her tangled, grizzled hair fell unkemptly over her shoulders. She was scowling, and her flashing black eyes held no friendly light.

We had borne up bravely enough hitherto, in spite of our inward, unconfessed quakings. But now our strained nerves gave way, and sheer panic seized us. Peter gave a little yelp of pure terror. We turned and fled across the clearing and into the woods. Down the long hill we tore, like mad, hunted creatures, firmly convinced that Peg Bowen was after us. Wild was that scamper, as nightmare-like as any recorded in our dream books. The Story Girl was in front of me, and I can recall the tremendous leaps she made over fallen logs and little spruce bushes, with her long brown curls streaming out behind her from their scarlet fillet. Cecily, behind me, kept gasping out the contradictory sentences, "Oh, Bev, wait for me," and "Oh, Bev, hurry, hurry!" More by blind instinct than anything else we kept together and found our way out of the woods. Presently we were in the field beyond the brook. Over us was a dainty sky of shell pink; placid cows were pasturing around us; the farewell summers nodded to us in the friendly breezes. We halted, with a glad realization that we were back in our own haunts and that Peg Bowen had not caught us.

"Oh, wasn't that an awful experience?" gasped Cecily, shuddering. "I wouldn't go through it again—I couldn't, not even for Pat."

"It come on a fellow so sudden," said Peter shamefacedly. "I think I could a-stood my ground if I'd known she was going to come out. But when she popped out like that I thought I was done for."

"We shouldn't have run," said Felicity gloomily. "It showed we were afraid of her, and that always makes her awful cross. She won't do a thing for Pat now."

"I don't believe she could do anything, anyway," said the Story Girl. "I think we've just been a lot of geese."

We were all, except Peter, more or less inclined to agree with her. And the conviction of our folly deepened when we reached the granary and found that Pat, watched over by the faithful Sara Ray, was no better. The Story Girl announced that she would take him into the kitchen and sit up all night with him.

"He sha'n't die alone, anyway," she said miserably, gathering his limp body up in her arms.

We did not think Aunt Olivia would give her permission to stay up; but Aunt Olivia did. Aunt Olivia really was a duck. We wanted to stay with her also, but Aunt Janet wouldn't hear of such a thing. She ordered us off to bed, saying that it was positively sinful in us to be so worked up over a cat. Five heart-broken children, who knew that there are many worse friends than the dumb, furry folk, climbed Uncle Alec's stairs to bed that night.

"There's nothing we can do now, except pray God to make Pat better," said Cecily.

I must candidly say that her tone savoured strongly of a last resort; but this was owing more to early training than to any lack of faith on Cecily's part. She knew, and we knew, that prayer was a solemn rite, not to be lightly held, nor degraded to common uses. Felicity voiced this conviction when she said,

"I don't believe it would be right to pray about a cat."

"I'd like to know why not," retorted Cecily. "God made Paddy just as much as He made you, Felicity King, though perhaps He didn't go to so much trouble. And I'm sure He's abler to help him than Peg Bowen. Anyhow, I'm going to pray for Pat with all my might and main, and I'd like to see you try to stop me. Of course I won't mix it up with more important things. I'll just tack it on after I've finished asking the blessings, but before I say amen."

More petitions than Cecily's were offered up that night on behalf of Paddy. I distinctly heard Felix—who always said his prayers in a loud whisper, owing to some lasting conviction of early life that God could not hear him if he did not pray audibly—mutter pleadingly, after the "important" part of his devotions was over, "Oh, God, please make Pat better by the morning. *Please* do."

And I, even in these late years of irreverence for the dreams of youth, am not in the least ashamed to confess that when I knelt down to say my boyish prayer, I thought of our little furry comrade in his extremity, and prayed as reverently as I knew how for his healing. Then I went to sleep, comforted by the simple hope that the Great Father would, after "important things" were all attended to, remember poor Pat.

As soon as we were up the next morning we rushed off to Uncle Roger's. But we met Peter and the Story Girl in the lane, and their faces were as the faces of those who bring glad tidings upon the mountains.

"Pat's better," cried the Story Girl, blithe, triumphant. "Last night, just at twelve, he began to lick his paws. Then he licked himself all over and went to sleep. I went to sleep, too, on the sofa. When I woke Pat was washing his face, and he has taken a whole saucerful of milk. Oh, isn't it splendid?"

"You see Peg Bowen did put a spell on him," said Peter, "and then she took it off."

"I guess Cecily's prayer had more to do with Pat's getting better than Peg Bowen," said Felicity. "She prayed for Pat over and over again. That is why he's better."

"Oh, all right," said Peter, "but I'd advise Pat not to scratch Peg Bowen again, that's all."

"I wish I knew whether it was the praying or Peg Bowen that cured Pat," said Felix in perplexity.

"I don't believe it was either of them," said Dan. "Pat just got sick and got better again of his own accord."

"I'm going to believe that it was the praying," said Cecily decidedly. "It's so much nicer to believe that God cured Pat than that Peg Bowen did."

"But you oughtn't to believe a thing just 'cause it would be more comfortable," objected Peter. "Mind you, I ain't saying God couldn't cure Pat. But nothing and nobody can't ever make me believe that Peg Bowen wasn't at the bottom of it all."

Thus faith, superstition, and incredulity strove together amongst us, as in all history.

CHAPTER 25

A CUP OF FAILURE

ONE WARM Sunday evening in the moon of goldenrod, we all, grown-ups and children, were sitting in the orchard by the Pulpit Stone, singing sweet old gospel hymns. We could all sing more or less, except poor Sara Ray, who had once despairingly confided to me that she didn't know what she'd ever do when she went to heaven, because she couldn't sing a note.

That whole scene comes out clearly for me in memory—the arc of primrose sky over the trees behind the old house, the fruit-laden boughs of the orchard, the bank of golden-rod, like a wave of sunshine, behind the Pulpit Stone, the nameless colour seen on a fir wood in a ruddy sunset. I can see Uncle Alec's tired, brilliant, blue eyes, Aunt Janet's wholesome, matronly face, Uncle Roger's sweeping blond beard and red cheeks, and Aunt Olivia's full-blown beauty. Two voices ring out for me above all others in the music that echoes through the halls of recollection. Cecily's, sweet and silvery, and Uncle Alec's fine tenor. "If you're King, you sing," was a Carlisle proverb in those days. Aunt Julia had been the flower of the flock in that respect and had become a noted concert singer. The world had never heard of the rest. Their music echoed only along the hidden ways of life, and served but to lighten the cares of the trivial round and common task.

That evening, after they tired of singing, our grown-ups began talking of their youthful days and doings.

This was always a keen delight to us small fry. We listened avidly to the tales of our uncles and aunts in the days when they, too—hard fact to realize—had been children. Good and proper as they were now, once, so it seemed, they had gotten into mischief and even had their quarrels and disagreements. On this particular evening Uncle Roger told many stories of Uncle Edward, and one in which the said Edward had preached sermons at the mature age of ten from the Pulpit Stone fired, as the sequel will show, the Story Girl's imagination.

"Can't I just see him at it now," said Uncle Roger, "leaning over that old boulder, his cheeks red and his eyes burning with excitement, banging the top of it as he had seen the ministers do in church. It wasn't cushioned, however, and he always bruised his hands in his self-forgetful earnestness. We thought him a regular wonder. We loved to hear him preach, but we didn't like to hear him pray, because he always insisted on praying for each of us by name, and it made us feel wretchedly uncomfortable, somehow. Alec, do you remember how furious Julia was because Edward prayed one day that she might be preserved from vanity and conceit over her singing?"

"I should think I do," laughed Uncle Alec. "She was sitting right there where Cecily is now, and she got up at once and marched right out of the orchard, but at the gate she turned to call back indignantly, 'I guess you'd better wait till you've prayed the conceit out of yourself before you begin on me, Ned King. I never heard such stuck-up sermons as you preach.' Ned went on praying and never let on he heard her, but at the end of his prayer he wound up with, 'Oh, God, I pray you to keep an eye on us all, but I pray you to pay particular attention to my sister Julia, for I think she needs it even more than the rest of us, world without end, Amen.' "

Our uncles roared with laughter over the recollection. We all laughed, indeed, especially over another tale in which Uncle Edward, leaning too far over the "pulpit" in his earnestness, lost his balance altogether and tumbled ingloriously into the grass below.

"He lit on a big Scotch thistle," said Uncle Roger, chuckling, "and besides that, he skinned his forehead on a stone. But he was determined to finish his sermon, and finish it he did. He climbed back into the pulpit, with the tears rolling over his cheeks, and preached for ten minutes longer, with sobs in his voice and drops of blood on his forehead. He was a plucky little beggar. No wonder he succeeded in life."

"And his sermons and prayers were always just about as outspoken as those Julia objected to," said Uncle Alec. "Well, we're all getting on in life and Edward is gray; but when I think of him I always see him a little, rosy, curly-headed chap, laying down the law to us from the Pulpit Stone. It seems like the other day that we were all here together, just as these children are, and now we are scattered everywhere. Julia in California, Edward in Halifax, Alan in South America, Felix and Felicity and Stephen gone to the land that is very far off."

There was a little space of silence; and then Uncle Alec began, in a low, impressive voice, to repeat the wonderful verses of the ninetieth Psalm—verses which were thenceforth bound up for us with the beauty of that night and the memories of our kindred. Very reverently we all listened to the majestic words. "Lord, thou hast been our dwelling place in all generations. Before the mountains were brought forth, or ever thou hadst formed the earth and the world, even from everlasting to everlasting thou art God . . . For a thousand years in thy sight are but as yesterday when it is past, and as a watch in the night . . . For all our days are passed away in thy wrath; we spend our years as a tale that is told. The days of our years are threescore and ten; and if by reason of strength they be fourscore years yet is their strength, labour and sorrow; for it is soon cut off and we fly away . . . . So teach us to number our days that we may apply our hearts unto wisdom . . . . Oh, satisfy us early with thy mercy; that we may rejoice and be glad all our days . . . and let the beauty of the Lord our God be upon us; and establish thou the work of our hands upon us; yea, the work of our hands establish thou it."

The dusk crept into the orchard like a dim, bewitching personality. You could see her—feel her—hear her. She tiptoed softly from tree to tree, ever drawing nearer. Presently her filmy wings hovered over us and through them gleamed the early stars of the autumn night.

The grown-ups rose reluctantly and strolled away; but we children lingered for a moment to talk over an idea the Story Girl broached—a good idea, we thought enthusiastically, and one that promised to add considerable spice to life.

We were on the lookout for some new amusement. Dream books had begun to pall. We no longer wrote in them very regularly, and our dreams were not what they used to be before the mischance of the cucumber. So the Story Girl's suggestion came pat to the psychological moment.

"I've thought of a splendid plan," she said. "It just flashed into my mind when the uncles were talking about Uncle Edward. And the beauty of it is we can play it on Sundays, and you know there are so few things it is proper to play on Sundays. But this is a Christian game, so it will be all right."

"It isn't like the religious fruit basket game, is it?" asked Cecily anxiously.

We had good reason to hope that it wasn't. One desperate Sunday afternoon, when we had nothing to read and the time seemed endless, Felix had suggested that we have a game of fruit-basket; only, instead of taking the names of fruits, we were to take the names of Bible characters. This, he argued, would make it quite lawful and proper to play on Sunday. We, too, desirous of being convinced, also thought so; and for a merry hour Lazarus and Martha and Moses and Aaron and sundry other worthies of Holy Writ had a lively time of it in the King orchard. Peter, having a Scriptural name of his own, did not want to take another; but we would not allow this, because it would give him an unfair advantage over the rest of us. It would be so much easier to call out your own name than fit your tongue to an unfamiliar one. So Peter retaliated by choosing Nebuchadnezzar, which no one could ever utter three times before Peter shrieked it out once.

In the midst of our hilarity, however, Uncle Alec and Aunt Janet came down upon us. It is best to draw a veil over what followed. Suffice it to say that the recollection gave point to Cecily's question.

"No, it isn't that sort of a game at all," said the Story Girl. "It is this; each of you boys must preach a sermon, as Uncle Edward used to do. One of you next Sunday, and another the next, and so on. And whoever preaches the best sermon is to get a prize."

Dan promptly declared he wouldn't try to preach a sermon; but Peter, Felix and I thought the suggestion a very good one. Secretly, I believed I could cut quite a fine figure preaching a sermon.

"Who'll give the prize?" asked Felix.

"I will," said the Story Girl. "I'll give that picture father sent me last week."

As the said picture was an excellent copy of one of Landseer's stags, Felix and I were well pleased; but Peter averred that he would rather have the Madonna that looked like his Aunt Jane, and the Story Girl agreed that if his sermon was the best she would give him that.

"But who's to be the judge?" I said, "and what kind of a sermon would you call the best?"

"The one that makes the most impression," answered the Story Girl promptly. "And we girls must be the judges, because there's nobody else. Now, who is to preach next Sunday?"

It was decided that I should lead off, and I lay awake for an extra hour that night thinking what text I should take for the following Sunday. The next day I bought two sheets of foolscap from the schoolmaster, and after tea I betook myself to the granary, barred the door, and fell to writing my sermon. I did not find it as easy a task as I had anticipated; but I pegged grimly away at it, and by dint of severe labour for two evenings I eventually got my four pages of foolscap filled, although I had to pad the subject-matter not a little with verses of quotable hymns. I had decided to preach on missions, as being a topic more within my grasp than abstruse theological doctrines or evangelical discourses; and, mindful of the need of making an impression, I drew a harrowing picture of the miserable plight of the heathen who in their darkness bowed down to wood and stone. Then I urged our responsibility concerning them, and meant to wind up by reciting, in a very solemn and earnest voice, the verse beginning, "Can we whose souls are lighted." When I had completed my sermon I went over it very carefully again and wrote with red ink—Cecily made it for me out of an aniline dye—the word "thump" wherever I deemed it advisable to chastise the pulpit.

I have that sermon still, all its red thumps unfaded, lying beside my dream book; but I am not going to inflict it on my readers. I am not so proud of it as I once was. I was really puffed up with earthly vanity over it at that time. Felix, I thought, would be hard put to it to beat it. As for Peter, I did not consider him a rival to be feared. It was unsupposable that a hired boy, with little education and less experience of church-going, should be able to preach better than could I, in whose family there was a real minister.

The sermon written, the next thing was to learn it off by heart and then practise it, thumps included, until I was letter and gesture perfect. I preached it over several times in the granary with only Paddy, sitting immovably on a puncheon, for audience. Paddy stood the test fairly well. At least, he made an adorable listener, save at such times as imaginary rats distracted his attention.

Mr. Marwood had at least three absorbed listeners the next Sunday morning. Felix, Peter, and I were all among the chiels who were taking mental notes on the art of preaching a sermon. Not a motion, or glance, or intonation escaped us. To be sure, none of us could remember the text when we got home; but we knew just how you should throw back your head and clutch the edge of the pulpit with both hands when you announced it.

In the afternoon we all repaired to the orchard, Bibles and hymn books in hand. We did not think it necessary to inform the grown-ups of what was in the wind. You could never tell what kink a grown-up would take. They might not think it proper to play any sort of a game on Sunday, not even a Christian game. Least said was soonest mended where grown-ups were concerned.

I mounted the pulpit steps, feeling rather nervous, and my audience sat gravely down on the grass before me. Our opening exercises consisted solely of singing and reading. We had agreed to omit prayer. Neither Felix, Peter, nor I felt equal to praying in public. But we took up a collection. The proceeds were to go to missions. Dan passed the plate—Felicity's rosebud plate—looking as preternaturally solemn as Elder Frewen himself. Every one put a cent on it.

Well, I preached my sermon. And it fell horribly flat. I realized that, before I was half way through it. I think I preached it very well; and never a thump did I forget or misplace. But my audience was plainly bored. When I stepped down from the pulpit, after demanding passionately if we whose souls were lighted and so forth, I felt with secret humiliation that my sermon was a failure. It had made no impression at all. Felix would be sure to get the prize.

"That was a very good sermon for a first attempt," said the Story Girl graciously. "It sounded just like real sermons I have heard."

For a moment the charm of her voice made me feel that I had not done so badly after all; but the other girls, thinking it their duty to pay me some sort of a compliment also, quickly dispelled that pleasing delusion.

"Every word of it was true," said Cecily, her tone unconsciously implying that this was its sole merit.

"I often feel," said Felicity primly, "that we don't think enough about the heathens. We ought to think a great deal more."

Sara Ray put the finishing touch to my mortification.

"It was so nice and short," she said.

"What was the matter with my sermon?" I asked Dan that night. Since he was neither judge nor competitor I could discuss the matter with him.

"It was too much like a reg'lar sermon to be interesting," said Dan frankly.

"I should think the more like a regular sermon it was, the better," I said.

"Not if you want to make an impression," said Dan seriously. "You must have something sort of different for that. Peter, now, *he'll* have something different."

"Oh, Peter! I don't believe he can preach a sermon," I said.

"Maybe not, but you'll see he'll make an impression," said Dan.

Dan was neither the prophet nor the son of a prophet, but he had the second sight for once; Peter *did* make an impression.

─────────── CHAPTER 26 ───────────

PETER MAKES AN IMPRESSION

PETER'S TURN came next. He did not write his sermon out. That, he averred, was too hard work. Nor did he mean to take a text.

"Why, who ever heard of a sermon without a text?" asked Felix blankly.

"I am going to take a *subject* instead of a text," said Peter loftily. "I ain't going to tie myself down to a text. And I'm going to have heads in it—three heads. You hadn't a single head in yours," he added to me.

"Uncle Alec says that Uncle Edward says heads are beginning to go out of fashion," I said defiantly—all the more defiantly that I felt I should have had heads in my sermon. It would doubtless have made a much deeper impression. But the truth was I had forgotten all about such things.

"Well, I'm going to have them, and I don't care if they are unfashionable," said Peter. "They're good things. Aunt Jane used to say if a man didn't have heads and stick to them he'd go wandering all over the Bible and never get anywhere in particular."

"What are you going to preach on?" asked Felix.

"You'll find out next Sunday," said Peter significantly.

The next Sunday was in October, and a lovely day it was, warm and bland as June. There was something in the fine, elusive air, that recalled beautiful, forgotten things and suggested delicate future hopes. The woods had wrapped fine-woven gossamers about them and the westering hill was crimson and gold.

We sat around the Pulpit Stone and waited for Peter and Sara Ray. It was the former's Sunday off and he had gone home the night before, but he assured us he would be back in time to preach his sermon. Presently he arrived and mounted the granite boulder as if to the manor born. He was dressed in his new suit and I, perceiving this, felt that he had the advantage of me. When I preached I had to wear my second best suit, for it was one of Aunt Janet's laws that we should take our good suits off when we came home from church. There were, I saw, compensations for being a hired boy.

Peter made quite a handsome little minister, in his navy blue coat, white collar, and neatly bowed tie. His black eyes shone, and his black curls were brushed up in quite a ministerial pompadour, but threatened to tumble over at the top in graceless ringlets.

It was decided that there was no use in waiting for Sara Ray, who might or might not come, according to the humour in which her mother was. Therefore Peter proceeded with the service.

He read the chapter and gave out the hymn with as much *sang froid* as if he had been doing it all his life. Mr. Marwood himself could not have bettered the way in which Peter said,

"We will sing the whole hymn, omitting the fourth stanza."

That was a fine touch which I had not thought of. I began to think that, after all, Peter might be a foeman worthy of my steel.

When Peter was ready to begin he thrust his hands into his pockets—a totally unorthodox thing. Then he plunged in without further ado, speaking in his ordinary conversational tone— another unorthodox thing. There was no shorthand reporter present to take that sermon down; but, if necessary, I could preach it over verbatim, and so, I doubt not, could every one who heard it. It was not a forgettable kind of sermon.

"Dearly beloved," said Peter, "my sermon is about the bad place—in short, about hell."

An electric shock seemed to run through the audience. Everybody looked suddenly alert. Peter had, in one sentence, done what my whole sermon had failed to do. He had made an impression.

"I shall divide my sermon into three heads," pursued Peter. "The first head is, what you must not do if you don't want to go to the bad place. The second head is, what the bad place is like"—sensation in the audience—"and the third head is, how to escape going there.

"Now, there's a great many things you must not do, and it's very important to know what they are. You ought not to lose no time in finding out. In the first place you mustn't ever forget to mind what grown-up people tell you—that is, *good* grown-up people."

"But how are you going to tell who are the good grown-up people?" asked Felix suddenly, forgetting that he was in church.

"Oh, that is easy," said Peter. "You can always just *feel* who is good and who isn't. And you mustn't tell lies and you mustn't murder any one. You must be specially careful not to murder any one. You might be forgiven for telling lies, if you was real sorry for them, but if you murdered any one it would be pretty hard to get forgiven, so you'd better be on the safe side. And you mustn't commit suicide, because if you did that you wouldn't have any chanct of repenting it; and you mustn't forget to say your prayers and you mustn't quarrel with your sister."

At this point Felicity gave Dan a significant poke with her elbow, and Dan was up in arms at once.

"Don't you be preaching at me, Peter Craig," he cried out. "I won't stand it. I don't quarrel with my sister any oftener than she quarrels with me. You can just leave me alone."

"Who's touching you?" demanded Peter. "I didn't mention no names. A minister can say anything he likes in the pulpit, as long as he doesn't mention any names, and nobody can answer back."

"All right, but just you wait till tomorrow," growled Dan, subsiding reluctantly into silence under the reproachful looks of the girls.

"You must not play any games on Sunday," went on Peter, "that is, any weekday games—or whisper in church, or laugh in church—I did that once but I was awful sorry—and you mustn't take any notice of Paddy—I mean of the family cat at family prayers, not even if he climbs right up on your back. And you mustn't call names or make faces."

"Amen," cried Felix, who had suffered many things because Felicity so often made faces at him.

Peter stopped and glared at him over the edge of the Pulpit Stone.

"You haven't any business to call out a thing like that right in the middle of a sermon," he said.

"They do it in the Methodist church at Markdale," protested Felix, somewhat abashed. "I've heard them."

"I know they do. That's the Methodist way and it is all right for them. I haven't a word to say against Methodists. My Aunt Jane was one, and I might have been one myself if I hadn't been so scared of the Judgment Day. But you ain't a Methodist. You're a Presbyterian, ain't you?"

"Yes, of course. I was born that way."

"Very well then, you've got to do things the Presbyterian way. Don't let me hear any more of your amens or I'll amen you."

"Oh, don't anybody interrupt again," implored the Story Girl. "It isn't fair. How can any one preach a good sermon if he is always being interrupted? Nobody interrupted Beverley."

"Bev didn't get up there and pitch into us like that," muttered Dan.

"You mustn't fight," resumed Peter undauntedly. "That is, you mustn't fight for the fun of fighting, nor out of bad temper. You must not say bad words or swear. You mustn't get drunk— although of course you wouldn't be likely to do that before you grow up, and the girls never. There's prob'ly a good many other things you mustn't do, but these I've named are the most important. Of course, I'm not saying you'll go to the bad place for sure if you do them. I only say you're running a risk. The devil is looking out for the people who do these things and he'll be more likely to get after them than to waste time over the people who don't do them. And that's all about the first head of my sermon."

At this point Sara Ray arrived, somewhat out of breath. Peter looked at her reproachfully.

"You've missed my whole first head, Sara," he said. "That isn't fair, when you're to be one of the judges. I think I ought to preach it over again for you."

"That was really done once. I know a story about it," said the Story Girl.

"Who's interrupting now?" said Dan slyly.

"Never mind, tell us the story," said the preacher himself, eagerly leaning over the pulpit.

"It was Mr. Scott who did it," said the Story Girl.

"He was preaching somewhere in Nova Scotia, and when he was more than half way through his sermon—and you know sermons were *very* long in those days—a man walked in. Mr. Scott stopped until he had taken his seat. Then he said, 'My friend, you are very late for this service. I hope you won't be late for heaven. The congregation will excuse me if I recapitulate the sermon for our friend's benefit.' And then he just preached the sermon over again from the beginning. It is said that that particular man was never known to be late for church again."

"It served him right," said Dan, "but it was pretty hard lines on the rest of the congregation."

"Now, let's be quiet so Peter can go on with his sermon," said Cecily.

Peter squared his shoulders and took hold of the edge of the pulpit. Never a thump had he thumped, but I realized that his way of leaning forward and fixing this one or that one of his hearers with his eye was much more effective.

"I've come now to the second head of my sermon—what the bad place is like."

He proceeded to describe the bad place. Later on we discovered that he had found his material in an illustrated translation of Dante's *Inferno* which had once been given to his Aunt Jane as a school prize. But at the time we supposed he must be drawing from Biblical sources. Peter had been reading the Bible steadily ever since what we always referred to as "the Judgment Sunday," and he was by now almost through it. None of the rest of us had ever read the Bible completely through, and we thought Peter must have found his description of the world of the lost in some portion with which we were not acquainted. Therefore, his utterances carried all the weight of inspiration, and we sat appalled before his lurid phrases. He used his own words to clothe the ideas he had found, and the result was a force and simplicity that struck home to our imaginations.

Suddenly Sara Ray sprang to her feet with a scream—a scream that changed into strange laughter. We all, preacher included, looked at her aghast. Cecily and Felicity sprang up and caught hold of her. Sara Ray was really in a bad fit of hysterics, but we knew nothing of such a thing in our experience, and we thought she had gone mad. She shrieked, cried, laughed, and flung herself about.

"She's gone clean crazy," said Peter, coming down out of his pulpit with a very pale face.

"You've frightened her crazy with your dreadful sermon," said Felicity indignantly.

She and Cecily each took Sara by an arm and, half leading, half carrying, got her out of the orchard and up to the house. The rest of us looked at each other in terrified questioning.

"You've made rather too much of an impression, Peter," said the Story Girl miserably.

"She needn't have got so scared. If she'd only waited for the third head I'd have showed her how easy it was to get clear of going to the bad place and go to heaven instead. But you girls are always in such a hurry," said Peter bitterly.

"Do you s'pose they'll have to take her to the asylum?" said Dan in a whisper.

"Hush, here's your father," said Felix.

Uncle Alec came striding down the orchard. We had never before seen Uncle Alec angry. But there was no doubt that he was very angry now. His blue eyes fairly blazed at us as he said,

"What have you been doing to frighten Sara Ray into such a condition?"

"We—we were just having a sermon contest," explained the Story Girl tremulously. "And Peter preached about the bad place, and it frightened Sara. That is all, Uncle Alec."

"All! I don't know what the result will be to that nervous, delicate child. She is shrieking in there and nothing will quiet her. What do you mean by playing such a game on Sunday, and making a jest of sacred things? No, not a word—" for the Story Girl had attempted to speak. "You and Peter march off home. And the next time I find you up to such doings on Sunday or any other day I'll give you cause to remember it to your latest hour."

The Story Girl and Peter went humbly home and we went with them.

"I *can't* understand grown-up people," said Felix despairingly. "When Uncle Edward preached sermons it was all right, but when we do it it is 'making a jest of sacred things.' And I heard Uncle Alec tell a story once about being nearly frightened to death when he was a little boy, by a minister preaching on the end of the world; and he said, 'That was something like a sermon. You don't hear such sermons nowadays.' But when Peter preaches just such a sermon, it's a very different story."

"It's no wonder we can't understand the grown-ups," said the Story Girl indignantly, "because we've never been grown-up ourselves. But *they* have been children, and I don't see why they can't understand us. Of course, perhaps we shouldn't have had the contest on Sundays. But all the same I think it's mean of Uncle Alec to be so cross. Oh, I do hope poor Sara won't have to be taken to the asylum."

Poor Sara did not have to be. She was eventually quieted down, and was as well as usual the next day; and she humbly begged Peter's pardon for spoiling his sermon. Peter granted it rather grumpily, and I fear that he never really quite forgave Sara for her untimely outburst. Felix, too, felt resentment against her, because he had lost the chance of preaching his sermon.

"Of course I know I wouldn't have got the prize, for I couldn't have made such an impression as Peter," he said to us mournfully, "but I'd like to have had a chance to show what I could do. That's what comes of having those cry-baby girls mixed up in things. Cecily was just as scared as Sara Ray, but she'd more sense than to show it like that."

"Well, Sara couldn't help it," said the Story Girl charitably, "but it does seem as if we'd had dreadful luck in everything we've tried lately. I thought of a new game this morning, but I'm almost afraid to mention it, for I suppose something dreadful will come of it, too."

"Oh, tell us, what is it?" everybody entreated.

"Well, it's a trial by ordeal, and we're to see which of us can pass it. The ordeal is to eat one of the bitter apples in big mouthfuls without making a single face."

Dan made a face to begin with.

"I don't believe any of us can do that," he said.

"*You* can't, if you take bites big enough to fill your mouth," giggled Felicity, with cruelty and without provocation.

"Well, maybe you could," retorted Dan sarcastically. "You'd be so afraid of spoiling your looks that you'd rather die than make a face, I s'pose, no matter what you et."

"Felicity makes enough faces when there's nothing to make faces at," said Felix, who had been grimaced at over the breakfast table that morning and hadn't liked it.

"I think the bitter apples would be real good for Felix," said Felicity. "They say sour things make people thin."

"Let's go and get the bitter apples," said Cecily hastily, seeing that Felix, Felicity and Dan were on the verge of a quarrel more bitter than the apples.

We went to the seedling tree and got an apple apiece. The game was that every one must take a bite in turn, chew it up, and swallow it, without making a face. Peter again distinguished himself. He, and he alone, passed the ordeal, munching those dreadful mouthfuls without so much as a change of expression on his countenance, while the facial contortions the rest of us went through baffled description. In every subsequent trial it was the same. Peter never made a face, and no one else could help making them. It sent him up fifty per cent in Felicity's estimation.

"Peter is a real smart boy," she said to me. "It's such a pity he is a hired boy."

But, if we could not pass the ordeal, we got any amount of fun out of it, at least. Evening after evening the orchard re-echoed to our peals of laughter.

"Bless the children," said Uncle Alec, as he carried the milk pails across the yard. "Nothing can quench their spirits for long."

———————— CHAPTER 27 ————————

THE ORDEAL OF BITTER APPLES

I COULD never understand why Felix took Peter's success in the Ordeal of Bitter Apples so much to heart. He had not felt very keenly over the matter of the sermons, and certainly the mere fact that Peter could eat sour apples without making faces did not cast any reflection on the honour or ability of the other competitors. But to Felix everything suddenly became flat, stale, and unprofitable, because Peter continued to hold the championship of bitter apples. It haunted his waking hours and obsessed his nights. I heard him talking in his sleep about it. If anything could have made him thin the way he worried over this matter would have done it.

For myself, I cared not a groat. I had wished to be successful in the sermon contest, and felt sore whenever I thought of my failure. But I had no burning desire to eat sour apples without grimacing, and I did not sympathize over and above with my brother. When, however, he took to praying about it, I realized how deeply he felt on the subject, and hoped he would be successful.

Felix prayed earnestly that he might be enabled to eat a bitter apple without making a face. And when he had prayed three nights after this manner, he contrived to eat a bitter apple without a grimace until he came to the last bite, which proved too much for him. But Felix was vastly encouraged.

"Another prayer or two, and I'll be able to eat a whole one," he said jubilantly.

But this devoutly desired consummation did not come to pass. In spite of prayers and heroic attempts, Felix could never get beyond that last bite. Not even faith and works in combination could avail. For a time he could not understand this. But he thought the mystery was solved when Cecily came to him one day and told him that Peter was praying against him.

"He's praying that you'll never be able to eat a bitter apple without making a face," she said. "He told Felicity and Felicity told me. She said she thought it was real cute of him. I think that is a dreadful way to talk about praying and I told her so. She wanted me to promise not to tell you, but I wouldn't promise, because I think it's fair for you to know what is going on."

Felix was very indignant—and aggrieved as well.

"I don't see why God should answer Peter's prayers instead of mine," he said bitterly. "I've gone to church and Sunday School all my life, and Peter never went till this summer. It isn't fair."

"Oh, Felix, don't talk like that," said Cecily, shocked. "God *must* be fair. I'll tell you what I believe is the reason. Peter prays three times a day regular—in the morning and at dinner time and at night—and besides that, any time through the day when he happens to think of it, he just prays, standing up. Did you ever hear of such goings-on?"

"Well, he's got to stop praying against me, anyhow," said Felix resolutely. "I won't put up with it, and I'll go and tell him so right off."

Felix marched over to Uncle Roger's, and we trailed after, scenting a scene. We found Peter shelling beans in the granary, and whistling cheerily, as with a conscience void of offence towards all men.

"Look here, Peter," said Felix ominously, "they tell me that you've been praying right along that I couldn't eat a bitter apple. Now, I tell you—"

"I never did!" exclaimed Peter indignantly. "I never mentioned your name. I never prayed that you couldn't eat a bitter apple. I just prayed that I'd be the only one that could."

"Well, that's the same thing," cried Felix. "You've just been praying for the opposite to me out of spite. And you've got to stop it, Peter Craig."

"Well, I just guess I won't," said Peter angrily. "I've just as good a right to pray for what I want as you, Felix King, even if you was brought up in Toronto. I s'pose you think a hired boy hasn't any business to pray for particular things, but I'll show you. I'll just pray for what I please, and I'd like to see you try to stop me."

"You'll have to fight me, if you keep on praying against me," said Felix.

The girls gasped; but Dan and I were jubilant, snuffing battle afar off.

"All right. I'm ready any time you mention," said Peter defiantly. "I can fight as well as pray."

"Oh, don't fight," implored Cecily. "I think it would be dreadful. Surely you can arrange it some other way. Let's all give up the Ordeal, anyway. There isn't much fun in it. And then neither of you need pray about it."

"I don't want to give up the Ordeal," said Felix, "and I won't."

"Oh, well, surely you can settle it some way without fighting," persisted Cecily.

"I'm not wanting to fight," said Peter. "It's Felix. If he don't interfere with my prayers there's no need of fighting. But if he does there's no other way to settle it."

"But how will that settle it?" asked Cecily.

"Oh, whoever's licked will have to give in about the praying," said Peter. "That's fair enough. If I'm licked I won't pray for that particular thing any more."

"It's dreadful to fight about anything so religious as praying," sighed poor Cecily.

"Why, they were always fighting about religion in old times," said Felix. "The more religious anything was the more fighting there was about it."

"A fellow's got a right to pray as he pleases," said Peter, "and if anybody tries to stop him he's bound to fight. That's my way of looking at it."

"What would Miss Marwood say if she knew you were going to fight?" asked Felicity.

Miss Marwood was Felix' Sunday School teacher and he was very fond of her. But by this time Felix was quite reckless.

"I don't care what she would say," he retorted.

Felicity tried another tack.

"You'll be sure to get whipped if you fight with Peter," she said. "You're too fat to fight."

After that, no moral force on earth could have prevented Felix from fighting. He would have faced an army with banners.

"You might settle it by drawing lots," said Cecily desperately.

"Drawing lots is wickeder than fighting," said Dan. "It's a kind of gambling."

"What would your Aunt Jane say if she knew you were going to fight?" Cecily demanded of Peter.

"Don't you drag my Aunt Jane into this affair," said Peter darkly.

"You said you were going to be a Presbyterian," persisted Cecily. "Good Presbyterians don't fight."

"Oh, don't they! I heard your Uncle Roger say that Presbyterians were the best for fighting in the world—or the worst, I forget which he said, but it means the same thing."

Cecily had but one more shot in her locker.

"I thought you said in your sermon, Master Peter, that people shouldn't fight."

"I said they oughtn't to fight for fun, or for bad temper," retorted Peter. "This is different. I know what I'm fighting for but I can't think of the word."

"I guess you mean principle," I suggested.

"Yes, that's it," agreed Peter. "It's all right to fight for principle. It's kind of praying with your fists."

"Oh, can't you do something to prevent them from fighting,

Sara?" pleaded Cecily, turning to the Story Girl, who was sitting on a bin, swinging her shapely bare feet to and fro.

"It doesn't do to meddle in an affair of this kind between boys," said the Story Girl sagely.

I may be mistaken, but I do not believe the Story Girl wanted that fight stopped. And I am far from being sure that Felicity did either.

It was ultimately arranged that the combat should take place in the fir wood behind Uncle Roger's granary. It was a nice, remote, bosky place where no prowling grown-up would be likely to intrude. And thither we all resorted at sunset.

"I hope Felix will beat," said the Story Girl to me, "not only for the family honour, but because that was a mean, mean prayer of Peter's. Do you think he will?"

"I don't know," I confessed dubiously. "Felix is too fat. He'll get out of breath in no time. And Peter is such a cool customer, and he's a year older than Felix. But then Felix has had some practice. He has fought boys in Toronto. And this is Peter's first fight."

"Did you ever fight?" asked the Story Girl.

"Once," I said briefly, dreading the next question, which promptly came.

"Who beat?"

It is sometimes a bitter thing to tell the truth, especially to a young lady for whom you have a great admiration. I had a struggle with temptation in which I frankly confess I might have been worsted had it not been for a saving and timely remembrance of a certain resolution made on the day preceding Judgment Sunday.

"The other fellow," I said, with reluctant honesty.

"Well," said the Story Girl, "I think it doesn't matter whether you get whipped or not so long as you fight a good, square fight."

Her potent voice made me feel that I was quite a hero after all, and the sting went out of my recollection of that old fight.

When we arrived behind the granary the others were all there. Cecily was very pale, and Felix and Peter were taking off their coats. There was a pure yellow sunset that evening, and the aisles of the fir wood were flooded with its radiance. A cool, autumnal wind was whistling among the dark boughs and scattering blood red leaves from the maple at the end of the granary.

"Now," said Dan, "I'll count, and when I say three you pitch in, and hammer each other until one of you has had enough. Cecily, keep quiet. Now, one—two—three!"

Peter and Felix "pitched in," with more zeal than discretion on both sides. As a result, Peter got what later developed into a black eye, and Felix's nose began to bleed. Cecily gave a shriek and ran out of the wood. We thought she had fled because she could not endure the sight of blood, and we were not sorry, for her manifest disapproval and anxiety were damping the excitement of the occasion.

Felix and Peter drew apart after that first onset, and circled about one another warily. Then, just as they had come to grips again, Uncle Alec walked around the corner of the granary, with Cecily behind him.

He was not angry. There was a quizzical look in his eyes. But he took the combatants by their shirt collars and dragged them apart.

"This stops right here, boys," he said. "You know I don't allow fighting."

"Oh, but, Uncle Alec, it was this way," began Felix eagerly. "Peter—"

"No, I don't want to hear about it," said Uncle Alec sternly. "I don't care what you were fighting about, but you must settle your quarrels in a different fashion. Remember my commands, Felix. Peter, Roger is looking for you to wash his buggy. Be off."

Peter went off rather sullenly, and Felix, also sullenly, sat down and began to nurse his nose. He turned his back on Cecily.

Cecily "caught it" after Uncle Alec had gone. Dan called her a tell-tale and a baby, and sneered at her until Cecily began to cry.

"I couldn't stand by and watch Felix and Peter pound each other all to pieces," she sobbed. "They've been such friends, and it was dreadful to see them fighting."

"Uncle Roger would have let them fight it out," said the Story Girl discontentedly. "Uncle Roger believes in boys fighting. He says it's as harmless a way as any of working off their original sin. Peter and Felix wouldn't have been any the worse friends after it. They'd have been better friends because the praying question would have been settled. And now it can't be—unless Felicity can coax Peter to give up praying against Felix."

For once in her life the Story Girl was not as tactful as her wont. Or—is it possible that she said it out of malice prepense? At all events, Felicity resented the imputation that she had more influence with Peter than any one else.

"I don't meddle with hired boys' prayers," she said haughtily.

"It was all nonsense fighting about such prayers, anyhow," said Dan, who probably thought that since all chance of a fight was over, he might as well avow his real sentiments as to its folly. "Just as much nonsense as praying about the bitter apples in the first place."

"Oh, Dan, don't you believe there is some good in praying?" said Cecily reproachfully.

"Yes, I believe there's some good in some kinds of praying, but not in that kind," said Dan sturdily. "I don't believe God cares whether anybody can eat an apple without making a face or not."

"I don't believe it's right to talk of God as if you were well acquainted with Him," said Felicity, who felt that it was a good chance to snub Dan.

"There's something wrong somewhere," said Cecily perplexedly. "We ought to pray for what we want, of that I'm sure—and Peter wanted to be the only one who could pass the Ordeal. It seems as if he must be right—and yet it doesn't seem so. I wish I could understand it."

"Peter's prayer was wrong because it was a selfish prayer, I guess," said the Story Girl thoughtfully. "Felix's prayer was all right, because it wouldn't have hurt any one else; but it was selfish of Peter to want to be the only one. We mustn't pray selfish prayers."

"Oh, I see through it now," said Cecily joyfully.

"Yes, but," said Dan triumphantly, "if you believe God answers prayers about particular things, it was Peter's prayer he answered. What do you make of that?"

"Oh!" The Story Girl shook her head impatiently. "There's no use trying to make such things out. We only get more mixed up all the time. Let's leave it alone and I'll tell you a story. Aunt Olivia had a letter today from a friend in Nova Scotia, who lives in Shubenacadie. When I said I thought it a funny name, she told me to go and look in her scrap book, and I would find a story about the origin of the name. And I did. Don't you want to hear it?"

Of course we did. We all sat down at the roots of the firs. Felix, having finally squared matters with his nose, turned around and listened also. He would not look at Cecily, but every one else had forgiven her.

The Story Girl leaned that brown head of hers against the fir trunk behind her, and looked up at the apple-green sky through the dark boughs above us. She wore, I remember, a dress of warm crimson, and she had wound around her head a string of waxberries, that looked like a fillet of pearls. Her cheeks were still flushed with the excitement of the evening. In the dim light she was beautiful, with a wild, mystic loveliness, a compelling charm that would not be denied.

"Many, many moons ago, an Indian tribe lived on the banks of a river in Nova Scotia. One of the young braves was named Accadee. He was the tallest and bravest and handsomest young man in the tribe—"

"Why is it they're always so handsome in stories?" asked Dan. "Why are there never no stories about ugly people?"

"Perhaps ugly people never have stories happen to them," suggested Felicity.

"I think they're just as interesting as the handsome people," retorted Dan.

"Well, maybe they are in real life," said Cecily, "but in stories it's just as easy to make them handsome as not. I like them best that way. I just love to read a story where the heroine is beautiful as a dream."

"Pretty people are always conceited," said Felix, who was getting tired of holding his tongue.

"The heroes in stories are always nice," said Felicity, with apparent irrelevance. "They're always so tall and slender. Wouldn't it be awful funny if any one wrote a story about a fat hero—or about one with too big a mouth?"

"It doesn't matter what a man *looks* like," I said, feeling that Felix and Dan were catching it rather too hotly. "He must be a good sort of chap and *do* heaps of things. That's all that's necessary."

"Do any of you happen to want to hear the rest of my story?" asked the Story Girl in an ominously polite voice that recalled us to a sense of our bad manners. We apologized and promised to behave better; she went on, appeased:

"Accadee was all these things that I have mentioned, and he was the best hunter in the tribe besides. Never an arrow of his that did not go straight to the mark. Many and many a snow white moose he shot, and gave the beautiful skin to his sweetheart. Her name was Shuben and she was as lovely as the moon when it rises from the sea, and as pleasant as a summer twilight. Her eyes were dark and soft, her foot was as light as a breeze, and her voice sounded like a brook in the woods, or the wind that comes over the hills at night. She and Accadee were very much in love with each other, and often they hunted together, for Shuben was almost as skilful with her bow and arrow as Accadee himself. They had loved each other ever since they were small pappooses, and they had vowed to love each other as long as the river ran.

"One twilight, when Accadee was out hunting in the woods, he shot a snow white moose; and he took off its skin and wrapped it around him. Then he went on through the woods in the starlight; and he felt so happy and light of heart that he sometimes frisked and capered about just as a real moose would do. And he was doing this when Shuben, who was also out hunting, saw him from afar and thought he was a real moose. She stole cautiously through the woods until she came to the brink of a little valley. Below her stood the snow white moose. She drew the arrow to her eye—alas, she knew the art only too well!—and took a careful aim. The next moment Accadee fell dead with her arrow in his heart."

The Story Girl paused—a dramatic pause. It was quite dark in the fir wood. We could see her face and eyes but dimly through the gloom. A silvery moon was looking down on us over the granary. The stars twinkled through the softly waving boughs. Beyond the wood we caught a glimpse of a moonlit world lying in the sharp frost of the October evening. The sky above it was chill and ethereal and mystical.

But all about us were shadows; and the weird little tale, told in a voice fraught with mystery and pathos, had peopled them for us with furtive folk in belt and wampum, and dark-tressed Indian maidens.

"What did Shuben do when she found out she had killed Accadee?" asked Felicity.

"She died of a broken heart before the spring, and she and Accadee were buried side by side on the bank of the river which has ever since borne their names—the river Shubenacadie," said the Story Girl.

The sharp wind blew around the granary and Cecily shivered. We heard Aunt Janet's voice calling "Children, children." Shaking off the spell of firs and moonlight and romantic tale, we scrambled to our feet and went homeward.

"I kind of wish I'd been born an Injun," said Dan. "It must have been a jolly life—nothing to do but hunt and fight."

"It wouldn't be so nice if they caught you and tortured you at the stake," said Felicity.

"No," said Dan reluctantly, "I suppose there'd be some drawback to everything, even to being an Injun."

"Isn't it cold?" said Cecily, shivering again. "It will soon be winter. I wish summer could last forever. Felicity likes the winter, and so does the Story Girl, but I don't. It always seems so long till spring."

"Never mind, we've had a splended summer," I said, slipping my arm about her to comfort some childish sorrow that breathed in her plaintive voice.

Truly, we had had a delectable summer; and, having had it, it was ours forever. "The gods themselves cannot recall their gifts." They may rob us of our future and embitter our present, but our past they may not touch. With all its laughter and delight and glamour it is our eternal possession.

Nevertheless, we all felt a little of the sadness of the waning year. There was a distinct weight on our spirits until Felicity took us into the pantry and stayed us with apple tarts and comforted us with cream. Then we brightened up. It was really a very decent world after all.

CHAPTER 28

THE TALE OF THE RAINBOW BRIDGE

FELIX, SO far as my remembrance goes, never attained to success in the Ordeal of Bitter Apples. He gave up trying after awhile; and he also gave up praying about it, saying in bitterness of spirit that there was no use in praying when other fellows prayed against you out of spite. He and Peter remained on bad terms for some time, however.

We were all of us too tired those nights to do any special praying. Sometimes I fear our "regular" prayers were slurred over, or mumbled in anything but reverent haste. October was a busy month on the hill farms. The apples had to be picked, and this work fell mainly to us children. We stayed home from school to do it. It was pleasant work and there was a great deal of fun in it; but it was hard, too, and our arms and backs ached roundly at night. In the mornings it was very delightful; in the afternoons tolerable; but in the evenings we lagged, and the laughter and the zest of fresher hours were lacking.

Some of the apples had to be picked very carefully. But with others it did not matter; we boys would climb the trees and shake the apples down until the girls shrieked for mercy. The days were crisp and mellow, with warm sunshine and a tang of frost in the air, mingled with the woodsy odours of the withering grasses. The hens and turkeys prowled about, pecking at windfalls, and Pat made mad rushes at them amid the fallen leaves. The world beyond the orchard was in a royal magnificence of colouring, under the vivid blue autumn sky. The big willow by the gate was a splended golden dome, and the maples that were scattered through the spruce grove waved blood-red banners over the sombre cone-bearers. The Story Girl generally had her head garlanded with their leaves. They became her vastly. Neither Felicity nor Cecily could have worn them. Those two girls were of a domestic type that assorted ill with the wildfire in Nature's veins. But when the Story Girl wreathed her nut brown tresses with crimson leaves it seemed, as Peter said, that they grew on her—as if the gold and flame of her spirit had broken out in a coronal, as much a part of her as

195

the pale halo seems a part of the Madonna it encircles.

What tales she told us on those far-away autumn days, peopling the russet arcades with folk of an elder world. Many a princess rode by us on her palfrey, many a swaggering gallant ruffled it bravely in velvet and plume adown Uncle Stephen's Walk, many a stately lady, silken clad, walked in that opulent orchard!

When we had filled our baskets they had to be carried to the granary loft, and the contents stored in bins or spread on the floor to ripen further. We ate a good many, of course, feeling that the labourer was worthy of his hire. The apples from our own birthday trees were stored in separate barrels inscribed with our names. We might dispose of them as we willed. Felicity sold hers to Uncle Alec's hired man—and was badly cheated to boot, for he levanted shortly afterwards, taking the apples with him, having paid her only half her rightful due. Felicity has not gotten over that to this day.

Cecily, dear heart, sent most of hers to the hospital in town, and no doubt gathered in therefrom dividends of gratitude and satisfaction of soul, such as can never be purchased by any mere process of bargain and sale. The rest of us ate our apples, or carried them to school where we bartered them for such treasures as our schoolmates possessed and we coveted.

There was a dusky, little, pear-shaped apple—from one of Uncle Stephen's trees—which was our favourite; and next to it a delicious, juicy, yellow apple from Aunt Louisa's tree. We were also fond of the big sweet apples; we used to throw them up in the air and let them fall on the ground until they were bruised and battered to the bursting point. Then we sucked the juice; sweeter was it than the nectar drunk by blissful gods on the Thessalian hill.

Sometimes we worked until the cold yellow sunsets faded out over the darkening distances, and the hunter's moon looked down on us through the sparkling air. The constellations of autumn scintillated above us. Peter and the Story Girl knew all about them, and imparted their knowledge to us generously. I recall Peter standing on the Pulpit Stone, one night ere moonrise, and pointing them out to us, occasionally having a difference of opinion with the Story Girl over the name of some particular star. Job's Coffin and the Northern Cross were to the west of us; south of us flamed Fomalhaut. The Great Square of Pegasus was over our heads. Cassiopeia sat enthroned in her beautiful chair in the north-east; and north of us the Dippers swung untiringly around the Pole Star. Cecily and Felix were the only ones who could distinguish the double star in the handle of the Big Dipper, and greatly did they plume themselves thereon. The Story Girl told us the myths and legends woven around these immemorial clusters, her very voice taking on a clear, remote, starry sound as she talked of them. When she ceased we came back to earth, feeling as if we had been millions of miles away in the blue ether, and that all our old familiar surroundings were momentarily forgotten and strange.

That night when he pointed out the stars to us from the Pulpit Stone was the last time for several weeks that Peter shared our toil and pastime. The next day he complained of headache and sore throat, and seemed to prefer lying on Aunt Olivia's kitchen sofa to doing any work. As it was not in Peter to be a malingerer he was left in peace, while we picked apples. Felix alone, most unjustly and spitefully, declared that Peter was simply shirking.

"He's just lazy, that's what's the matter with him," he said.

"Why don't you talk sense, if you must talk?" said Felicity. "There's no sense in calling Peter lazy. You might as well say I had black hair. Of course, Peter, being a Craig, has his faults, but he's a smart boy. His father was lazy but his mother hasn't a lazy bone in her body, and Peter takes after her."

"Uncle Roger says Peter's father wasn't exactly lazy," said the Story Girl. "The trouble was, there were so many other things he liked better than work."

"I wonder if he'll ever come back to his family," said Cecily. "Just think how dreadful it would be if *our* father had left us like that!"

"Our father is a King," said Felicity loftily, "and Peter's father was only a Craig. A member of our family *couldn't* behave like that."

"They say there must be a black sheep in every family," said the Story Girl.

"There isn't any in ours," said Cecily loyally.

"Why do white sheep eat more than black?" asked Felix.

"Is that a conundrum?" asked Cecily cautiously. "If it is I won't try to guess the reason. I never can guess conundrums."

"It isn't a conundrum," said Felix. "It's a fact. They do—and there's a good reason for it."

We stopped picking apples, sat down on the grass, and tried to reason it out—with the exception of Dan, who declared that he knew there was a catch somewhere and he wasn't going to be caught. The rest of us could not see where any catch could exist, since Felix solemnly vowed, 'cross his heart, white sheep did eat more than black. We argued over it seriously, but finally had to give it up.

"Well, what is the reason?" asked Felicity.

"Because there's more of them," said Felix, grinning.

I forget what we did to Felix.

A shower came up in the evening and we had to stop picking. After the shower there was a magnificent double rainbow. We watched it from the granary window, and the Story Girl told us an old legend, culled from one of Aunt Olivia's many scrapbooks.

"Long, long ago, in the Golden Age, when the gods used to visit the earth so often that it was nothing uncommon to see them, Odin made a pilgrimage over the world. Odin was the great god of the northland, you know. And wherever he went among men he taught them love and brotherhood and skilful arts; and great cities sprang up where he had trodden, and every land through which he passed was blessed because one of the gods had come down to men. But many men and women followed Odin himself, giving up all their worldly possessions and ambitions; and to these he promised the gift of eternal life. All these people were good and noble and unselfish and kind; but the best and noblest of them all was a youth named Ving; and this youth was beloved by Odin above all others, for his beauty and strength and goodness. Always he walked on Odin's right hand, and always the first light of Odin's smile fell on him. Tall and straight was he as a young pine, and his long hair was the colour of ripe wheat in the sun; and his blue eyes were like the northland heavens on a starry night.

"In Odin's band was a beautiful maiden named Alin. She was as fair and delicate as a young birch tree in spring among the dark old pines and firs, and Ving loved her with all his heart. His soul thrilled with rapture at the thought that he and she together should drink from the fountain of immortality, as Odin had promised, and be one thereafter in eternal youth.

"At last they came to the very place where the rainbow touched the earth. And the rainbow was a great bridge, built of living colours, so dazzling and wonderful that beyond it the eye could see nothing, only far away a great, blinding, sparkling glory, where the fountain of life sprang up in a shower of diamond fire. But under the Rainbow Bridge rolled a terrible flood, deep and wide and violent, full of rocks and rapids and whirlpools.

"There was a Warder of the bridge, a god, dark and stern and sorrowful. And to him Odin gave command that he should open the gate and allow his followers to cross the Rainbow Bridge, that they might drink of the fountain of life beyond. And the Warder set open the gate.

" 'Pass on and drink of the fountain,' he said. 'To all who taste of it shall immortality be given. But only to that one who shall drink of it first shall it be permitted to walk at Odin's right hand forever.'

"Then the company passed through in great haste, all fired with a desire to be the first to drink of the fountain and win so marvellous a boon. Last of all came Ving. He had lingered behind to pluck a thorn from the foot of a beggar child he had met on the highway, and he had not heard the Warder's words. But when, eager, joyous, radiant, he set his foot on the rainbow, the stern, sorrowful Warder took him by the arm and drew him back.

" 'Ving, strong, noble, and valiant,' he said, 'Rainbow Bridge is not for thee.'

"Very dark grew Ving's face. Hot rebellion rose in his heart and rushed over his pale lips.

" 'Why dost thou keep back the draught of immortality from me?' he demanded passionately.

"The Warder pointed to the dark flood that rolled under the bridge.

" 'The path of the rainbow is not for thee,' he said, 'but yonder way is open. Ford that flood. On the further bank is the fountain of life.'

" 'Thou mockest me,' muttered Ving sullenly. 'No mortal

could cross that flood. Oh, Master,' he prayed, turning beseech-ingly to Odin, 'thou didst promise to me eternal life as to the others. Wilt thou not keep that promise? Command the Warder to let me pass. He must obey thee.'

"But Odin stood silent, with his face turned from his beloved, and Ving's heart was filled with unspeakable bitterness and despair.

" 'Thou mayest return to earth if thou fearest to essay the flood,' said the Warder.

" 'Nay,' said Ving wildly, 'earthly life without Alin is more dreadful than the death which awaits me in yon dark river.'

"And he plunged fiercely in. He swam, he struggled, he buffetted the turmoil. The waves went over his head again and again, the whirlpools caught him and flung him on the cruel rocks. The wild, cold spray beat on his eyes and blinded him, so that he could see nothing, and the roar of the river deafened him, so that he could hear nothing; but he felt keenly the wounds and bruises of the cruel rocks, and many a time he would have given up the struggle had not the thought of sweet Alin's loving eyes brought him the strength and desire to struggle as long as it was possible. Long, long, long, to him seemed that bitter and perilous passage; but at last he won through to the further side. Breathless and reeling, his vesture torn, his great wounds bleeding, he found himself on the shore where the fountain of immortality sprang up. He staggered to its brink and drank of its clear stream. Then all pain and weariness fell away from him, and he rose up, a god, beautiful with im-mortality. And as he did there came rushing over the Rainbow Bridge a great company—the band of his fellow travellers. But all were too late to win the double boon. Ving had won to it through the danger and suffering of the dark river."

The rainbow had faded out, and the darkness of the October dusk was falling.

"I wonder," said Dan meditatively, as we went away from that redolent spot, "what it would be like to live for ever in this world."

"I expect we'd get tired of it after awhile," said the Story Girl. "But," she added, "I think it would be a good while before I would."

CHAPTER 29

THE SHADOW FEARED OF MAN

WE WERE all up early the next morning, dressing by candlelight. But early as it was we found the Story Girl in the kitchen when we went down, sitting on Rachel Ward's blue chest and looking important. "What do you think?" she exclaimed. "Peter has the measles! He was dreadfully sick all night, and Uncle Roger had to go for the doctor. He was quite light-headed, and didn't know any one. Of course he's far too sick to be taken home, so his mother has come up to wait on him, and I'm to live over here until he is better."

This was mingled bitter and sweet. We were sorry to hear that Peter had the measles; but it would be jolly to have the Story Girl living with us all the time. What orgies of story telling we should have!

"I suppose we'll all have the measles now," grumbled Felicity. "And October is such an inconvenient time for measles—there's so much to do."

"I don't believe any time is very convenient to have the measles," Cecily said.

"Oh, perhaps we won't have them," said the Story Girl cheerfully. "Peter caught them at Markdale, the last time he was home, his mother says."

"I don't want to catch the measles from Peter," said Felicity decidedly. "Fancy catching them from a hired boy!"

"Oh, Felicity, don't call Peter a hired boy when he's sick," protested Cecily.

During the next two days we were very busy—too busy to tell tales or listen to them. Only in the frosty dusk did we have time to wander afar in realms of gold with the Story Girl. She had recently been digging into a couple of old volumes of classic myths and northland folklore which she had found in Aunt Olivia's attic; and for us, god and goddess, laughing nymph and mocking satyr, norn and valkyrie, elf and troll, and "green folk" generally, were real creatures once again, inhabiting the orchards and woods and meadows around us, until it seemed

201

as if the Golden Age had returned to earth.

Then, on the third day, the Story Girl came to us with a very white face. She had been over to Uncle Roger's yard to hear the latest bulletin from the sick room. Hitherto they had been of a non-committal nature; but now it was only too evident that she had bad news.

"Peter is very, very sick," she said miserably. "He has caught cold someway—and the measles have struck in—and—and—" the Story Girl wrung her brown hands together—"the doctor is afraid he—he—won't get better."

We all stood around, stricken, incredulous.

"Do you mean," said Felix, finding voice at length, "that Peter is going to die?"

The Story Girl nodded miserably.

"They're afraid so."

Cecily sat down by her half filled basket and began to cry. Felicity said violently that she didn't believe it.

"I can't pick another apple today and I ain't going to try," said Dan.

None of us could. We went to the grown-ups and told them so; and the grown-ups, with unaccustomed understanding and sympathy, told us that we need not. Then we roamed about in our wretchedness and tried to comfort one another. We avoided the orchard; it was for us too full of happy memories to accord with our bitterness of soul. Instead, we resorted to the spruce wood, where the hush and the sombre shadows and the soft, melancholy sighing of the wind in the branches over us did not jar harshly on our new sorrow.

We could not really believe that Peter was going to die—to *die*. Old people died. Grown-up people died. Even children of whom we had heard died. But that one of *us*—of our merry little band—should die was unbelievable. We could not believe it. And yet the possibility struck us in the face like a blow. We sat on the mossy stones under the dark old evergreens and gave ourselves up to wretchedness. We all, even Dan, cried, except the Story Girl.

"I don't see how you can be so unfeeling, Sara Stanley," said Felicity reproachfully. "You've always been such friends with Peter—and made out you thought so much of him—and now you ain't shedding a tear for him."

I looked at the Story Girl's dry, piteous eyes, and suddenly remembered that I had never seen her cry. When she told us sad tales, in a voice laden with all the tears that had ever been shed, she had never shed one of her own. "I can't cry," she said drearily. "I wish I could. I've a dreadful feeling here—" she touched her slender throat—"and if I could cry I think it would make it better. But I can't."

"Maybe Peter will get better after all," said Dan, swallowing a sob, "I've heard of lots of people who went and got better after the doctor said they ought to die."

"While there's life there's hope, you know," said Felix. "We shouldn't cross bridges till we come to them."

"Those are only proverbs," said the Story Girl bitterly. "Proverbs are all very fine when there's nothing to worry you, but when you're in real trouble they're not a bit of help."

"Oh, I wish I'd never said Peter wasn't fit to associate with," moaned Felicity. "If he ever gets better I'll never say such a thing again—and I'll never *think* it. He's just a lovely boy and twice as smart as lots that aren't hired out."

"He was always so polite and good-natured and obliging," sighed Cecily.

"He was just a real gentleman," said the Story Girl.

"There ain't many fellows as fair and square as Peter," said Dan.

"And such a worker," said Felix.

"Uncle Roger says he never had a boy he could depend on like Peter," I said.

"It's too late to be saying all these nice things about him now," said the Story Girl. "He won't ever know how much we thought of him. It's too late."

"If he gets better I'll tell him," said Cecily resolutely.

"I wish I hadn't boxed his ears that day he tried to kiss me," went on Felicity, who was evidently raking her conscience for past offences in regard to Peter. "Of course I couldn't be expected to let a hir—to let a boy kiss me. But I needn't have been so cross about it. I might have been more dignified. And I told him I just hated him. That wasn't true, but I s'pose he'll die thinking it is. Oh, dear me, what makes people say things they've got to be so sorry for afterwards?"

"I suppose if Peter d-d-dies he'll go to heaven anyhow,"

sobbed Cecily. "He's been real good all this summer, but he isn't a church member."

"He's a Presbyterian, you know," said Felicity reassuringly. Her tone expressed her conviction that that would carry Peter through if anything would. "We're none of us church members. But of course Peter couldn't be sent to the bad place. That would be ridiculous. What would they do with him there, when he's so good and polite and honest and kind?"

"Oh, I think he'll be all right, too," sighed Cecily, "but you know he never did go to church and Sunday School before this summer."

"Well, his father run away, and his mother was too busy earning a living to bring him up right," argued Felicity. "Don't you suppose that anybody, even God, would make allowances for that?"

"Of course Peter will go to heaven," said the Story Girl. "He's not grown up enough to go anywhere else. Children always go to heaven. But I don't want him to go there or anywhere else. I want him to stay right here. I know heaven must be a splended place, but I'm sure Peter would rather be here, having fun with us."

"Sara Stanley," rebuked Felicity, "I should think you wouldn't say such things at such a solemn time. You're such a queer girl."

"Wouldn't you rather be here yourself than in heaven?" said the Story Girl bluntly. "Wouldn't you now, Felicity King? Tell the truth, 'cross your heart."

But Felicity took refuge from this inconvenient question in tears.

"If we could only *do* something to help Peter!" I said desperately. "It seems dreadful not to be able to do a single thing."

"There's one thing we can do," said Cecily gently. "We can pray for him."

"So we can," I agreed.

"I'm going to pray like sixty," said Felix energetically.

"We'll have to be awful good, you know," warned Cecily. "There's no use in praying if you're not good."

"That will be easy," sighed Felicity. "I don't feel a bit like being bad. If anything happens to Peter I feel sure I'll never be naughty again. I won't have the heart."

We did, indeed, pray most sincerely for Peter's recovery. We did not, as in the case of Paddy, "tack it on after more important things," but put it in the very forefront of our petitions. Even skeptical Dan prayed, his skepticism falling away from him like a discarded garment in this valley of the shadow, which sifts out hearts and tries souls, until we all, grown-up or children, realize our weakness, and, finding that our own puny strength is as a reed shaken in the wind, creep back humbly to the God we have vainly dreamed we could do without.

Peter was no better the next day. Aunt Olivia reported that his mother was broken-hearted. We did not again ask to be released from work. Instead, we went at it with feverish zeal. If we worked hard there was less time for grief and grievous thoughts. We picked apples and dragged them to the granary doggedly. In the afternoon Aunt Janet brought us out a lunch of apple turnovers; but we could not eat them. Peter, as Felicity reminded us with a burst of tears, had been so fond of apple turnovers.

And, oh, how good we were! How angelically and unnaturally good! Never was there such a band of kind, sweet-tempered, unselfish children in any orchard. Even Felicity and Dan, for once in their lives, got through the day without any exchange of left-handed compliments. Cecily confided to me that she never meant to put her hair up in curlers on Saturday nights again, because it was pretending. She was so anxious to repent of something, sweet girl, and this was all she could think of.

During the afternoon Judy Pineau brought up a tear-blotted note from Sara Ray. Sara had not been allowed to visit the hill farm since Peter had developed measles. She was an unhappy little exile, and could only relieve her anguish of soul by daily letters to Cecily, which the faithful and obliging Judy Pineau brought up for her. These epistles were as gushingly underlined as if Sara had been a correspondent of early Victorian days.

Cecily did not write back, because Mrs. Ray had decreed that no letters must be taken down from the hill farm lest they carry infection. Cecily had offered to bake every epistle thoroughly in the oven before sending it; but Mrs. Ray was inexorable, and Cecily had to content herself by sending long verbal messages with Judy Pineau.

"My *own dearest* Cecily," ran Sara's letter, "I have just heard the sad news about *poor dear Peter*. I can't describe *my feelings*. They are *dreadful*. I have been crying *all the afternoon*. I wish I could *fly* to you, but ma will not let me. She is afraid I will catch the measles, but I would rather have the measels *a dozen times over* than be separated from you all like this. But I have felt, ever since the Judgement Sunday that I *must obey ma better* than I used to do. If *anything happens* to Peter and you are let see him *before it happens* give him *my love* and tell him *how sorry I am,* and that I hope we will *all* meet in *a better world*. Everything in school is about the same. The master is awful cross by spells. Jimmy Frewen walked home with Nellie Cowan last night from prayer-meeting and *her only fourteen*. Don't you think it horrid *beginning so young? You and me* would *never* do anything like that till we were *grown up*, would we? Willy Fraser looks *so lonesome* in school these days. I must stop for ma says I waste *far too much time* writing letters. Tell Judy *all the news* for me.

"Your own true friend,

"SARA RAY.

"P.S. Oh I *do* hope Peter will get better. Ma is going to get me a new brown dress for the winter.

"S. R."

When evening came we went to our seats under the whispering, sighing fir trees. It was a beautiful night—clear, windless, frosty. Some one galloped down the road on horseback, lustily singing a comic song. How dared he? We felt that it was an insult to our wretchedness. If Peter were going to—going to— well, if anything happened to Peter, we felt so miserably sure that the music of life would be stilled for us for ever. How could any one in the world be happy when we were so unhappy?

Presently Aunt Olivia came down the long twilight arcade. Her bright hair was uncovered and she looked slim and queen-like in her light dress. We thought Aunt Olivia very pretty even then. Looking back from a mature standpoint I realize that she must have been an unusually beautiful woman; and she looked her prettiest as she stood under the swaying boughs in the last faint light of the autumn dusk and smiled down at our woe-begone faces.

"Dear, sorrowful little people, I bring you glad tidings of great joy," she said. "The doctor has just been here, and he finds Peter much better, and thinks he will pull through after all."

We gazed up at her in silence for a few moments. When we had heard the news of Paddy's recovery we had been noisy and jubilant; but we were very quiet now. We had been too near something dark and terrible and menacing; and though it was thus suddenly removed the chill and the shadow of it were about us still. Presently the Story Girl, who had been standing up, leaning against a tall fir, slipped down to the ground in a huddled fashion and broke into a very passion of weeping. I had never heard any one cry so, with such dreadful, rending sobs. I was used to hearing girls cry. It was as much Sara Ray's normal state as any other, and even Felicity and Cecily availed themselves occasionally of the privilege of sex. But I had never heard any girl cry like this. It gave me the same unpleasant sensation which I had felt one time when I had seen my father cry.

"Oh, don't, Sara, don't," I said gently, patting her convulsed shoulder.

"You *are* a queer girl," said Felicity—more tolerantly than usual however—"you never cried a speck when you thought Peter was going to die—and now when he is going to get better you cry like that."

"Sara, child, come with me," said Aunt Olivia, bending over her. The Story Girl got up and went away, with Aunt Olivia's arms around her. The sound of her crying died away under the firs, and with it seemed to go the dread and grief that had been our portion for hours. In the reaction our spirits rose with a bound.

"Oh, ain't it great that Peter's going to be all right?" said Dan, springing up.

"I never was so glad of anything in my whole life," declared Felicity in shameless rapture.

"Can't we send word somehow to Sara Ray tonight?" asked Cecily, the ever-thoughtful. "She's feeling so bad—and she'll have to feel that way till tomorrow if we can't."

"Let's all go down to the Ray gate and holler to Judy Pineau till she comes out," suggested Felix.

Accordingly, we went and "hollered," with a right good will. We were much taken aback to find that Mrs. Ray came to the gate instead of Judy, and rather sourly demanded what we were yelling about. When she heard our news, however, she had the decency to say she was glad, and to promise she would convey the good tidings to Sara—"who is already in bed, where all children of her age should be," added Mrs. Ray severely.

We had no intention of going to bed for a good two hours yet. Instead, after devoutly thanking goodness that our grown-ups, in spite of some imperfections, were not of the Mrs. Ray type, we betook ourselves to the granary, lighted a huge lantern which Dan had made out of a turnip, and proceeded to devour all the apples we might have eaten through the day but had not. We were a blithe little crew, sitting there in the light of our goblin lantern. We had in very truth been given beauty for ashes and the oil of joy for mourning. Life was as a red rose once more.

"I'm going to make a big batch of patty-pans, first thing in the morning," said Felicity jubilantly. "Isn't it queer? Last night I felt just like praying, and tonight I feel just like cooking."

"We mustn't forget to thank God for making Peter better," said Cecily, as we finally went to the house.

"Do you s'pose Peter wouldn't have got better anyway?" said Dan.

"Oh, Dan, what makes you ask such questions?" exclaimed Cecily in real distress.

"I dunno," said Dan. "They just kind of come into my head, like. But of course I mean to thank God when I say my prayers tonight. That's only decent."

CHAPTER 30

A COMPOUND LETTER

ONCE PETER was out of danger he recovered rapidly, but he found his convalescence rather tedious; and Aunt Olivia suggested to us one day that we write "a compound letter" to amuse him, until he could come to the window and talk to us from a safe distance. The idea appealed to us; and, the day being Saturday and the apples all picked, we betook ourselves to the orchard to compose our epistles, Cecily having first sent word by a convenient caller to Sara Ray, that she, too, might have a letter ready. Later, I, having at that time a mania for preserving all documents relating to our life in Carlisle, copied those letters in the blank pages at the back of my dream book. Hence I can reproduce them verbatim, with the bouquet they have retained through all the long years since they were penned in that autumnal orchard on the hill, with its fading leaves and frosted grasses, and the "mild, delightsome melancholy" of the late October day enfolding it.

CECILY'S LETTER

"DEAR PETER:—I am so very glad and thankful that you are going to get better. We were so afraid you would not last Tuesday, and we felt dreadful, even Felicity. We all prayed for you. I think the others have stopped now, but I keep it up every night still, for fear you might have a relaps. (I don't know if that is spelled right. I haven't the dixonary handy, and if I ask the others Felicity will laugh at me, though she cannot spell lots of words herself.) I am saving some of the Honourable Mr. Whalen's pears for you. I've got them hid where nobody can find them. There's only a dozen because Dan et all the rest, but I guess you will like them. We have got all the apples picked, and are all ready to take the measles now, if we have to, but I hope we won't. If we have to, though, I'd rather catch them from you than from any one else, because we are acquainted with you. If I do take the measles and anything happens to me Felicity is to have my cherry vase. I'd rather give it to

209

the Story Girl, but Dan says it ought to be kept in the family, even if Felicity is a crank. I haven't anything else valuable, since I gave Sara Ray my forget-me-not jug, but if you would like anything I've got let me know, and I'll leave instructions for you to have it. The Story Girl has told us some splendid stories lately. I wish I was clever like her. Ma says it doesn't matter if you're not clever as long as you are good, but I am not even very good.

"I think this is all my news, except that I want to tell you how much we all think of you, Peter. When we heard you were sick we all said nice things about you, but we were afraid it was too late, and I said if you got better I'd tell you. It is easier to write it than tell it out to your face. We think you are smart and polite and obliging and a great worker and a gentleman.

"Your true friend,

"CECILY KING.

"P.S. If you answer my letter don't say anything about the pears, because I don't want Dan to find out there's any left.

C. K."

FELICITY'S LETTER

"DEAR PETER:—Aunt Olivia says for us all to write a compound letter to cheer you up. We are all awful glad you are getting better. It gave us an awful scare when we heard you were going to die. But you will soon be all right and able to get out again. Be careful you don't catch cold. I am going to bake some nice things for you and send them over, now that the doctor says you can eat them. And I'll send you my rosebud plate to eat off of. I'm only lending it, you know, not giving it. I let very few people use it because it is my greatest treasure. Mind you don't break it. And Aunt Olivia must always wash it, not your mother.

"I do hope the rest of us won't catch the measles. It must look horrid to have red spots all over your face. We all feel pretty well yet. The Story Girl says as many queer things as ever. Felix thinks he is getting thin, but he is fatter than ever, and no wonder, with all the apples he eats. He has give up trying to eat the bitter apples at last. Beverley has grown half an inch since July, by the mark on the hall door, and he is awful pleased about it. I told him I guessed the magic seed was taking effect at last, and he got mad. He never gets mad at anything the Story Girl says, and yet she is so sarkastic by times. Dan is pretty hard to get along with as usul, but I try to bear pashently with him. Cecily is well and says she isn't going to curl her hair any more. She is so conscienshus. I am glad my hair curls of itself, ain't you?

"We haven't seen Sara Ray since you got sick. She is awful lonesome, and Judy says she cries nearly all the time but that is nothing new. I'm awful sorry for Sara but I'm glad I'm not her. She is going to write you a letter too. You'll let me see what she puts in it, won't you? You'd better take some Mexican Tea now. It's a great blood purifyer.

"I am going to get a lovely dark blue dress for the winter. It is ever so much prettier than Sara Ray's brown one. Sara Ray's mother has no taste. The Story Girl's father is sending her a new red dress, and a red velvet cap from Paris. She is so fond of red. I can't bear it, it looks so common. Mother says I can get a velvet hood too. Cecily says she doesn't believe it's right to wear velvet when it's so expensive and the heathen are crying for the gospel. She got that idea from a Sunday School paper but I am going to get my hood all the same.

"Well, Peter, I have no more news so I will close for this time.

"hoping you will soon be quite well, I remain
"yours sincerely,
"FELICITY KING.

"P.S. The Story Girl peeked over my shoulder and says I ought to have signed it 'yours affeckshunately,' but I know better, because the *Family Guide* has told lots of times how you should sign yourself when you are writing to a young man who is only a friend.

F. K."

FELIX' LETTER

"DEAR PETER:—I am awful glad you are getting better. We all felt bad when we thought you wouldn't, but I felt worse than the others because we hadn't been on very good terms lately and I had said mean things about you. I'm sorry, and, Peter, you can pray for anything you like and I won't ever object again. I'm glad Uncle Alec interfered and stopped the fight. If I had licked you and you had died of the measles it would have been a dreadful thing.

"We have all the apples in and haven't much to do just now and we are having lots of fun but we wish you were here to join in. I'm a lot thinner than I was. I guess working so hard picking apples is a good thing to make you thin. The girls are all well. Felicity puts on as many airs as ever, but she makes great things to eat. I have had some splendid dreams since we gave up writing them down. That is always the way. We ain't going to school till we're sure we are not going to have the measles. This is all I can think of, so I will draw to a close. Remember, you can pray for anything you like.

FELIX KING."

SARA RAY'S LETTER

"DEAR PETER:—I never wrote to *a boy* before, so *please* excuse *all* mistakes. I am *so* glad you are getting better. We were *so* afraid you were *going to die.* I *cried all night* about it. But now that you are *out of danger* will you tell me *what it really feels like* to think you are going to die? Does it *feel queer?* Were you *very* badly frightened?

"Ma won't let me go up the hill *at all* now. I would *die* if it was not for Judy Pinno. (The French names are *so hard to spell.*) Judy is *very obliging* and I feel that she *simpathises with me.* In my *lonely hours* I read my dream book and Cecily's old letters and they are *such a comfort* to me. I have been reading one of the school library books too. It is *pretty good* but I wish they had got more *love stories* because they are so *exciting.* But the master would not let them.

"If you had *died,* Peter, and *your father* had heard it wouldn't he have *felt dreadful?* We are having *beautiful weather* and the seenary is fine since the leaves turned. I think there is nothing so pretty as Nature after all.

"I hope *all danger* from the measles will soon be over and we can *all meet again* at the *home on the hill.* Till then *farewell.*
"Your true friend,
"SARA RAY.

"P.S. Don't let Felicity see this letter.   S.R."

DAN'S LETTER

"DEAR OLD PETE:—Awful glad you cheated the doctor. I thought you weren't the kind to turn up your toes so easy. You should of heard the girls crying.

"They're all getting their winter finery now and the talk about it would make you sick. The Story Girl is getting hers from Paris and Felicity is awful jealous though she pretends she isn't. I can see through her.

"Kitty Marr was up here Thursday to see the girls. She's had the measles so she isn't scared. She's a great girl to laugh. I like a girl that laughs, don't you?

"We had a call from Peg Bowen yesterday. You should of seen the Story Girl hustling Pat out of the way, for all she says she don't believe he was bewitched. Peg had your rheumatism ring on and the Story Girl's blue beads and Sara Ray's lace soed across the front of her dress. She wanted some tobacco and some pickles. Ma gave her some pickles but said we didn't have no tobacco and Peg went off mad but I guess she wouldn't bewitch anything on account of the pickles.

"I ain't any hand to write letters so I guess I'll stop. Hope you'll be out soon.

DAN."

THE STORY GIRL'S LETTER

"DEAR PETER:—Oh, how glad I am that you are getting better! Those days when we thought you wouldn't were the hardest of my whole life. It seemed too dreadful to be true that perhaps you would die. And then when we heard you were going to get better that seemed too good to be true. Oh, Peter, hurry up and get well, for we are having such good times and we miss you so much. I have coaxed Uncle Alec not to burn his potato stalks till you get well, because I remember how you always liked to see the potato stalks burn. Uncle Alec consented, though Aunt Janet said it was high time they were burned. Uncle Roger burned his last night and it was such fun.

"Pat is splendid. He has never had a sick spell since that bad one. I would send him over to be company for you, but Aunt Janet says no, because he might carry the measles back. I don't see how he could, but we must obey Aunt Janet. She is very good to us all, but I know she does not approve of me. She says I'm my father's own child. I know that doesn't mean anything complimentary because she looked so queer when she saw that I had heard her, but I don't care. I'm glad I'm like father. I had a splendid letter from him this week, with the darlingest pictures in it. He is painting a new picture which is going to make him famous. I wonder what Aunt Janet will say then.

"Do you know, Peter, yesterday I thought I saw the Family Ghost at last. I was coming through the gap in the hedge, and I saw somebody in blue standing under Uncle Alec's tree. How my heart beat! My hair should have stood on end with terror but it didn't. I felt to see, and it was lying down quite flat. But it was only a visitor after all. I don't know whether I was glad or disappointed. I don't think it would be a pleasant experience to see the ghost. But after I had seen it think what a heroine I would be!

"Oh, Peter, what do you think? I have got acquainted with the Awkward Man at last. I never thought it would be so easy. Yesterday Aunt Olivia wanted some ferns, so I went back to the maple woods to get them for her, and I found some lovely ones by the spring. And while I was sitting there, looking into the spring who should come along but the Awkward Man himself. He sat right down beside me and began to talk. I never was so surprised in my life. We had a very interesting talk, and I told him two of my best stories, and a great many of my secrets into the bargain. They may say what they like, but he was not one bit shy or awkward, and he has beautiful eyes. He did not tell me any of his secrets, but I believe he will some day. Of course I never said a word about his Alice-room. But I gave him a hint about his little brown book. I said I loved poetry and often felt like writing it, and then I said, 'Do you ever feel like that, Mr. Dale?' He said, yes, he sometimes felt that way, but he did not mention the brown book. I thought he might have. But after all I don't like poeple who tell you everything the first time you meet them, like Sara Ray. When he went away he said, 'I hope I shall have the pleasure of meeting you again,' just as seriously and politely as if I was a grown-up young lady. I am sure he could never have said it if I had been really grown up. I told him it was likely he would and that he wasn't to mind if I had a longer skirt on next time, because I'd be just the same person.

"I told the children a beautiful new fairy story today. I made them go to the spruce wood to hear it. A spruce wood is the proper place to tell fairy stories in. Felicity says she can't see that it makes any difference where you tell them, but oh, it does. I wish you had been there to hear it too, but when you are well I will tell it over again for you.

"I am going to call the southernwood 'appleringie' after this. Beverley says that is what they call it in Scotland, and I think it sounds so much more poetical than southernwood. Felicity says the right name is 'Boy's Love,' but I think that sounds silly.

"Oh, Peter, shadows are such pretty things. The orchard is full of them this very minute. Sometimes they are so still you would think them asleep. Then they go laughing and skipping. Outside, in the oat field, they are always chasing each other. They are the wild shadows. The shadows in the orchard are the tame shadows.

"Everything seems to be rather tired growing except the spruces and the chrysanthemums in Aunt Olivia's garden. The sunshine is so thick and yellow and lazy, and the crickets sing all day long. The birds are nearly all gone and most of the maple leaves have fallen.

"Just to make you laugh I'll write you a little story I heard Uncle Alec telling last night. It was about Elder Frewen's grandfather taking a pair of rope reins to lead a piano home. Everybody laughed except Aunt Janet. Old Mr. Frewen was *her* grandfather too, and so she wouldn't laugh. One day when old Mr. Frewen was a young man of eighteen his father came home and said, 'Sandy, I bought a piano at Simon Ward's sale today. You're to go tomorrow and bring it home.' So next day Sandy started off on horseback with a pair of rope reins to lead the piano home. He thought it was some kind of live stock.

"And then Uncle Roger told about old Mark Ward who got up to make a speech at a church missionary social when he was drunk. (Of course he didn't get drunk at the social. He went there that way.) And this was his speech.

" 'Ladies and gentlemen, Mr. Chairman, I can't express my thoughts on this grand subject of missions. It's in this poor human critter'—patting himself on the breast—'but he can't git it out.'

"I'll tell you these stories when you get well. I can tell them ever so much better than I can write them.

"I know Felicity is wondering why I am writing such a long letter, so perhaps I'd better stop. If your mother reads it to you there's a good deal of it she may not understand, but I think your Aunt Jane would.

"I remain,

"your very affectionate friend,

"SARA STANLEY"

I did not keep a copy of my own letter, and I have forgotten everything that was in it, except the first sentence, in which I told Peter I was awful glad he was getting better.

Peter's delight on receiving our letters knew no bounds. He insisted on answering them and his letter, painstakingly disinfected, was duly delivered to us. Aunt Olivia had written it at his dictation, which was a gain, as far as spelling and punctuation went. But Peter's individuality seemed merged and lost in Aunt Olivia's big, dashing script. Not until the Story Girl read the letter to us in the granary by jack-o'-lantern light, in a mimicry of Peter's very voice, did we savour the real bouquet of it.

PETER'S LETTER

"DEAR EVERYBODY, BUT ESPECIALLY FELICITY:—I was awful glad to get your letters. It makes you real important to be sick, but the time seems awful long when you're getting better. Your letters were all great, but I liked Felicity's best, and next to hers the Story Girl's. Felicity, it will be awful good of you to send me things to eat and the rosebud plate. I'll be awful careful of it. I hope you won't catch the measles, for they are not nice, especially when they strike in, but you would look all right, even if you did have red spots on your face. I would like to try the Mexican Tea, because you want me to, but mother says no, she doesn't believe in it, and Burton's Bitters are a great deal healthier. If I was you I would get the velvet hood all right. The heathen live in warm countries so they don't want hoods.

"I'm glad you are still praying for me, Cecily, for you can't trust the measles. And I'm glad you're keeping you know what for me. I don't believe anything will happen to you if you do take the measles; but if anything does I'd like that little red book of yours, *The Safe Compass,* just to remember you by. It's such a good book to read on Sundays. It is interesting and religious, too. So is the Bible. I hadn't quite finished the Bible before I took the measles, but ma is reading the last chapters to me. There's an awful lot in that book. I can't understand the whole of it, since I'm only a hired boy, but some parts are real easy.

"I'm awful glad you have such a good opinion of me. I don't deserve it, but after this I'll try to. I can't tell you how I feel about all your kindness. I'm like the fellow the Story Girl wrote about who couldn't get it out. I have the picture the Story Girl gave me for my sermon on the wall at the foot of my bed. I like to look at it, it looks so much like Aunt Jane.

"Felix, I've given up praying that I'd be the only one to eat the bitter apples, and I'll never pray for anything like that again. It was a horrid mean prayer. I didn't know it then, but after the measles struck in I found out it was. Aunt Jane wouldn't have liked it. After this I'm going to pray prayers I needn't be ashamed of.

"Sara Ray, I don't know what it feels like to be going to die because I didn't know I was going to die till I got better. Mother says I was luny most of the time after they struck in. It was just because they struck in I was luny. I ain't luny naturally, Felicity. I will do what you asked in your postscript, Sara, although it will be hard.

"I'm glad Peg Bowen didn't catch you, Dan. Maybe she bewitched me that night we were at her place, and that is why the measles struck in. I'm awful glad Mr. King is going to leave the potato stalks till I get well, and I'm obliged to the Story Girl for coaxing him. I guess she will find out about Alice yet. There were some parts of her letter I couldn't see through, but when the measles strike in they leave you stupid for a spell. Anyhow, it was a fine letter, and they were all fine, and I'm awful glad I have so many nice friends, even if I am only a hired boy. Perhaps I'd never have found it out if the measles hadn't struck in. So I'm glad they did but I hope they never will again.

> "Your obedient servant,
> "PETER CRAIG."

CHAPTER 31

ON THE EDGE OF LIGHT AND DARK

WE CELEBRATED the November day when Peter was permitted to rejoin us by a picnic in the orchard. Sara Ray was also allowed to come, under protest; and her joy over being among us once more was almost pathetic. She and Cecily cried in one another's arms as if they had been parted for years.

We had a beautiful day for our picnic. November dreamed that it was May. The air was soft and mellow, with pale, aerial mists in the valleys and over the leafless beeches on the western hill. The sere stubble fields brooded in glamour, and the sky was pearly blue. The leaves were still thick on the apple trees, though they were russet hued, and the aftergrowth of grass was richly green, unharmed as yet by the nipping frosts of previous nights. The wind made a sweet, drowsy murmur in the boughs, as of bees among apple blossoms.

"It's just like spring, isn't it?" said Felicity.

The Story Girl shook her head.

"No, not quite. It looks like spring, but it isn't spring. It's as if everything was resting—getting ready to sleep. In spring they're getting ready to grow. Can't you *feel* the difference?"

"*I* think it's just like spring," insisted Felicity.

In the sun-sweet place before the Pulpit Stone we boys had put up a board table. Aunt Janet allowed us to cover it with an old tablecloth, the worn places in which the girls artfully concealed with frost-whitened ferns. We had the kitchen dishes, and the table was gaily decorated with Cecily's three scarlet geraniums and maple leaves in the cherry vase. As for the viands, they were fit for the gods on high Olympus. Felicity had spent the whole previous day and the forenoon of the picnic day in concocting them. Her crowning achievement was a rich little plum cake, on the white frosting of which the words, "Welcome Back" were lettered in pink candies. This was put before Peter's place, and almost overcame him.

"To think that you'd go to so much trouble for me!" he said, with a glance of adoring gratitude at Felicity. Felicity got all the gratitude, although the Story Girl had originated the idea and seeded the raisins and beaten the eggs, while Cecily had trudged all the way to Mrs. Jameson's little shop below the church to buy the pink candies. But that is the way of the world.

"We ought to have grace," said Felicity, as we sat down at the festal board. "Will any one say it?"

She looked at me, but I blushed to the roots of my hair and shook my head sheepishly. An awkward pause ensued; it looked as if we would have to proceed without grace, when Felix suddenly shut his eyes, bent his head, and said a very good grace without any appearance of embarrassment. We looked at him when it was over with an increase of respect.

"Where on earth did you learn that, Felix?" I asked.

"It's the grace Uncle Alec says at every meal," answered Felix.

We felt rather ashamed of ourselves. Was it possible that we had paid so little attention to Uncle Alec's grace that we did not recognize it when we heard it on other lips?

"Now," said Felicity jubilantly, "let's eat everything up."

In truth, it was a merry little feast. We had gone without our dinners, in order to "save our appetites," and we did ample justice to Felicity's good things. Paddy sat on the Pulpit Stone and watched us with great yellow eyes, knowing that tidbits

would come his way later on. Many witty things were said—
or at least we thought them witty—and uproarious was the
laughter. Never had the old King orchard known a blither
merrymaking of lighter hearts.

The picnic over, we played games until the early falling dusk,
and then we went with Uncle Alec to the back field to burn
the potato stalks—the crowning delight of the day.

The stalks were in heaps all over the field, and we were
allowed the privilege of setting fire to them. 'Twas glorious! In
a few minutes the field was alight with blazing bonfires, over
which rolled great, pungent clouds of smoke. From pile to pile
we ran, shrieking with delight, to poke each up with a long
stick and watch the gush of rose-red sparks stream off into the
night. In what a whirl of smoke and firelight and wild, fantastic,
hurtling shadows we were!

When we grew tired of our sport we went to the windward
side of the field and perched ourselves on the high pole fence
that skirted a dark spruce wood, full of strange, furtive sounds.
Over us was a great, dark sky, blossoming with silver stars, and
all around lay dusky, mysterious reaches of meadow and wood
in the soft, empurpled night. Away to the east a shimmering
silveryness beneath a palace of aerial cloud foretokened moonrise. But directly before us the potato field, with its wreathing
smoke and sullen flames, the gigantic shadow of Uncle Alec
crossing and recrossing it, reminded us of Peter's famous description of the bad place, and probably suggested the Story
Girl's remark.

"I know a story," she said, infusing just the right shade of
weirdness into her voice, "about a man who saw the devil.
Now, what's the matter, Felicity?"

"I can never get used to the light way you mention the—
the—that name," complained Felicity. "To hear you speak of
the Old Scratch any one would think he was just a common
person."

"Never mind. Tell us the story," I said curiously.

"It is about Mrs. John Martin's uncle at Markdale," said the
Story Girl. "I heard Uncle Roger telling it the other night. He
didn't know that I was sitting on the cellar hatch outside the
window, or I don't suppose he would have told it. Mrs. Martin's
uncle's name was William Cowan, and he has been dead for

twenty years; but sixty years ago he was a young man, and a very wild, wicked young man. He did everything bad he could think of, and he never went to church, and he laughed at everything religious, even the devil. He didn't believe there was a devil at all. One beautiful summer Sunday evening his mother pleaded with him to go to church with her, but he would not. He told her that he was going fishing instead, and when church time came he swaggered past the church, with his fishing rod over his shoulder, singing a godless song. Half way between the church and the harbour there was a thick spruce wood, and the path ran through it. When William Cowan was half way through it SOMETHING came out of the wood and walked beside him."

I have never heard anything more horribly suggestive than that innocent word, "something," as enunciated by the Story Girl. I felt Cecily's hand, icy cold, clutch mine.

"What—what—was IT like?" whispered Felix, curiosity getting the better of his terror.

"IT was tall, and black, and hairy," said the Story Girl, her eyes glowing with uncanny intensity in the red glare of the fires, "and IT lifted one great, hairy hand, with claws on the end of it, and clapped William Cowan, first on one shoulder and then on the other, and said, 'Good sport to you, brother.' William Cowan gave a horrible scream and fell on his face right there in the wood. Some of the men around the church door heard the scream, and they rushed down to the wood. They saw nothing but William Cowan, lying like a dead man on the path. They took him up and carried him home; and when they undressed him to put him to bed, there, on each shoulder, was the mark of a big hand, *burned into the flesh.* It was weeks before the burns healed, and the scars never went away. Always, as long as William Cowan lived, he carried on his shoulders the prints of the devil's hand."

I really do not know how we should ever have got home, had we been left to our own devices. We were cold with fright. How could we turn our backs on the eerie spruce wood, out of which SOMETHING might pop at any moment? How cross those long, shadowy fields between us and our rooftree? How venture through the darkly mysterious bracken hollow?

Fortunately, Uncle Alec came along at this crisis and said

he thought we'd better come home now, since the fires were nearly out. We slid down from the fence and started, taking care to keep close together and in front of Uncle Alec.

"I don't believe a word of that yarn," said Dan, trying to speak with his usual incredulity.

"I don't see how you can help believing it," said Cecily. "It isn't as if it was something we'd read of, or that happened far away. It happened just down at Markdale, and I've seen that very spruce wood myself."

"Oh, I suppose William Cowan got a fright of some kind," conceded Dan, "but I don't believe he saw the devil."

"Old Mr. Morrison at Lower Markdale was one of the men who undressed him, and he remembers seeing the marks," said the Story Girl triumphantly.

"How did William Cowan behave afterwards?" I asked.

"He was a changed man," said the Story Girl solemnly. "Too much changed. He never was known to laugh again, or even smile. He became a very religious man, which was a good thing, but he was dreadfully gloomy and thought everything pleasant sinful. He wouldn't even eat any more than was actually necessary to keep him alive. Uncle Roger says that if he had been a Roman Catholic he would have become a monk, but, as he was a Presbyterian, all he could do was to turn into a crank."

"Yes, but your Uncle Roger was never clapped on the shoulder and called brother by the devil," said Peter. "If he had, he mightn't have been so precious jolly afterwards himself."

"I do wish to goodness," said Felicity in exasperation, "that you'd stop talking of the—the—of such subjects in the dark. I'm so scared now that I keep thinking father's steps behind us are SOMETHING'S. Just think, my own father!"

The Story Girl slipped her arm through Felicity's.

"Never mind," she said soothingly. "I'll tell you another story—such a beautiful story that you'll forget all about the devil."

She told us one of Hans Andersen's most exquisite tales; and the magic of her voice charmed away all our fear, so that when we reached the bracken hollow, a lake of shadow surrounded by the silver shore of moonlit fields, we went through it without a thought of His Satanic Majesty at all. And beyond us, on the hill, the homelight was glowing from the farmhouse window like a beacon of old loves.

———————— CHAPTER 32 ————————

THE OPENING OF THE BLUE CHEST

NOVEMBER WAKENED from her dream of May in a bad temper. The day after the picnic a cold autumn rain set in, and we got up to find our world a drenched, wind-writhen place, with sodden fields and dour skies. The rain was weeping on the roof as if it were shedding the tears of old sorrows; the willow by the gate tossed its gaunt branches wildly, as if it were some passionate, spectral thing, wringing its fleshless hands in agony; the orchard was haggard and uncomely; nothing seemed the same except the stanch, trusty, old spruces.

It was Friday, but we were not to begin going to school again until Monday, so we spent the day in the granary, sorting apples and hearing tales. In the evening the rain ceased, the wind came around to the northwest, freezing suddenly, and a chilly yellow sunset beyond the dark hills seemed to herald a brighter morrow.

Felicity and the Story Girl and I walked down to the post-office for the mail, along a road where fallen leaves went eddying fitfully up and down before us in weird, uncanny dances of their own. The evening was full of eerie sounds—the creaking of fir boughs, the whistle of the wind in the tree-tops, the vibrations of strips of dried bark on the rail fences. But we carried summer and sunshine in our hearts, and the bleak unloveliness of the outer world only intensified our inner radiance.

Felicity wore her new velvet hood, with a coquettish little collar of white fur about her neck. Her golden curls framed her lovely face, and the wind stung the pink of her cheeks to crimson. On my left hand walked the Story Girl, her red cap on her jaunty brown head. She scattered her words along the path like the pearls and diamonds of the old fairy tale. I remember that I strutted along quite insufferably, for we met several of the Carlisle boys and I felt that I was an exceptionally lucky fellow to have such beauty on one side and such charm on the other.

There was one of father's thin letters for Felix, a fat, foreign letter for the Story Girl, addressed in her father's minute hand-writing, a drop letter for Cecily from some school friend, with "In Haste" written across the corner, and a letter for Aunt Janet, postmarked Montreal.

"I can't think who that is from," said Felicity. "Nobody in Montreal ever writes to mother. Cecily's letter is from Em Frewen. She always puts 'In Haste' on her letters, no matter what is in them."

When we reached home Aunt Janet opened and read her Montreal letter. Then she laid it down and looked about her in astonishment.

"Well, did ever any mortal!" she said.

"What in the world is the matter?" said Uncle Alec.

"This letter is from James Ward's wife in Montreal," said Aunt Janet solemnly. "Rachel Ward is dead. And she told James' wife to write to me and tell me to open the old blue chest."

"Hurrah!" shouted Dan.

"Donald King," said his mother severely, "Rachel Ward was your relation and she is dead. What do you mean by such behaviour?"

"I never was acquainted with her," said Dan sulkily. "And I wasn't hurrahing because she is dead. I hurrahed because that blue chest is to be opened at last."

"So poor Rachel is gone," said Uncle Alec. "She must have been an old woman—seventy-five, I suppose. I remember her as a fine, blooming young woman. Well, well, and so the old chest is to be opened at last. What is to be done with its contents?"

"Rachel left instructions about them," answered Aunt Janet, referring to the letter. "The wedding dress and veil and letters are to be burned. There are two jugs in it which are to be sent to James' wife. The rest of the things are to be given around among the connection. Each member is to have one, 'to remember her by.' "

"Oh, can't we open it right away this very night?" said Felicity eagerly.

"No, indeed!" Aunt Janet folded up the letter decidedly. "That chest has been locked up for fifty years, and it'll stand being locked up one more night. You children wouldn't sleep a wink tonight if we opened it now. You'd go wild with excitement."

"I'm sure I won't sleep anyhow," said Felicity. "Well, at least you'll open it the first thing in the morning, won't you, ma?"

"No, I'll do nothing of the sort," was Aunt Janet's pitiless decree. "I want to get the work out of the way first—and Roger and Olivia will want to be here, too. We'll say ten o'clock tomorrow forenoon."

"That's sixteen whole hours yet," sighed Felicity.

"I'm going right over to tell the Story Girl," said Cecily. "Won't she be excited!"

We were all excited. We spent the evening speculating on the possible contents of the chest, and Cecily dreamed miserably that night that the moths had eaten everything in it.

The morning dawned on a beautiful world. A very slight fall of snow had come in the night—just enough to look like a filmy veil of lace flung over the dark evergreens, and the hard frozen ground. A new blossom time seemed to have revisited the orchard. The spruce wood behind the house appeared to be woven out of enchantment. There is nothing more beautiful than a thickly growing wood of firs lightly powdered with new-fallen snow. As the sun remained hidden by gray clouds, this fairy beauty lasted all day.

The Story Girl came over early in the morning, and Sara Ray, to whom faithful Cecily had sent word, was also on hand. Felicity did not approve of this.

"Sara Ray isn't any relation to our family," she scolded to Cecily, "and so she has no right to be present."

"She's a particular friend of mine," said Cecily with dignity. "We have her in everything, and it would hurt her feelings dreadfully to be left out of this. Peter is no relation either, but he is going to be here when we open it, so why shouldn't Sara?"

"Peter ain't a member of the family *yet*, but maybe he will be some day. Hey, Felicity?" said Dan.

"You're awful smart, aren't you, Dan King?" said Felicity, reddening. "Perhaps you'd like to send for Kitty Marr, too— though she *does* laugh at your big mouth."

"It seems as if ten o'clock would never come," sighed the Story Girl. "The work is all done, and Aunt Olivia and Uncle Roger are here, and the chest might just as well be opened right away."

"Mother *said* ten o'clock and she'll stick to it," said Felicity crossly. "It's only nine now."

"Let us put the clock on half an hour," said the Story Girl. "The clock in the hall isn't going, so no one will know the difference."

We all looked at each other.

"I wouldn't dare," said Felicity irresolutely.

"Oh, if that's all, *I'll* do it," said the Story Girl.

When ten o'clock struck Aunt Janet came into the kitchen, remarking innocently that it hadn't seemed any time since nine. We must have looked horribly guilty, but none of the grown-ups suspected anything. Uncle Alec brought in the axe, and pried off the cover of the old blue chest, while everybody stood around in silence.

Then came the unpacking. It was certainly an interesting performance. Aunt Janet and Aunt Olivia took everything out, and laid it on the kitchen table. We children were forbidden to touch anything, but fortunately we were not forbidden the use of our eyes and tongues.

"There are the pink and gold vases Grandmother King gave her," said Felicity, as Aunt Olivia unwrapped from their tissue paper swathings, a pair of slender, old-fashioned, twisted vases of pink glass, over which little gold leaves were scattered. "Aren't they handsome?"

"And oh," exclaimed Cecily in delight, "there's the china fruit basket with the apple on the handle. Doesn't it look real? I've thought so much about it. Oh, mother, please let me hold it for a minute. I'll be careful as careful."

"There comes the china set Grandfather King gave her," said

the Story Girl wistfully. "Oh, it makes me feel sad. Think of all the hopes that Rachel Ward must have put away in this chest with all her pretty things."

Following these, came a quaint little candlestick of blue china, and the two jugs which were to be sent to James' wife.

"They *are* handsome," said Aunt Janet rather enviously. "They must be a hundred years old. Aunt Sara Ward gave them to Rachel, and she had them for at least fifty years. I should have thought one would have been enough for James' wife. But of course we must do just as Rachel wished. I declare, here's a dozen tin patty pans!"

"Tin patty pans aren't very romantic," said the Story Girl discontentedly.

"I notice that you are as fond as any one of what is baked in them," said Aunt Janet. "I've heard of those patty pans. An old servant Grandmother King had then gave them to Rachel. Now we are coming to the linen. That was Uncle Edward Ward's present. How yellow it has grown."

We children were not greatly interested in the sheets and tablecloths and pillow-cases which now came out of the capacious depths of the old blue chest. But Aunt Olivia was quite enraptured over them.

"What sewing!" she said. "Look, Janet, you'd almost need a magnifying glass to seek the stitches. And the dear, old-fashioned pillow-slips with buttons on them!"

"Here are a dozen handkerchiefs," said Aunt Janet. "Look at the initial in the corner of each. Rachel learned that stitch from a nun in Montreal. It looks as if it was woven into the material."

"Here are her quilts," said Aunt Olivia. "Yes, there is the blue and white counterpane Grandmother Ward gave her— and the Rising Sun quilt her Aunt Nancy made for her—and the braided rug. The colours are not faded one bit. I want that rug, Janet."

Underneath the linen were Rachel Ward's wedding clothes. The excitement of the girls waxed red hot over these. There was a Paisley shawl in the wrappings in which it had come from the store, and a wide scarf of some yellowed lace. There was the embroidered petticoat which had cost Felicity such painful blushes, and a dozen beautifully worked sets of the fine muslin "undersleeves" which had been the fashion in Rachel Ward's youth.

"This was to have been her appearing out dress," said Aunt Olivia, lifting out a shot green silk. "It is all cut to pieces— but what a pretty soft shade it was! Look at the skirt, Janet. How many yards must it measure around?"

"Hoopskirts were in then," said Aunt Janet. "I don't see her wedding hat here. I was always told that she packed it away, too."

"So was I. But she couldn't have. It certainly isn't here. I have heard that the white plume on it cost a small fortune. Here is her black silk mantle. It seems like sacrilege to meddle with these clothes."

"Don't be foolish, Olivia. They must be unpacked at least. And they must all be burned since they have cut so badly. This purple cloth dress is quite good, however. It can be made over nicely, and it would become you very well, Olivia."

"No, thank you," said Aunt Olivia, with a little shudder. "I should feel like a ghost. Make it over for yourself, Janet."

"Well, I will, if you don't want it. I am not troubled with fancies. That seems to be all except this box. I suppose the wedding dress is in it."

"Oh," breathed the girls, crowding about Aunt Olivia, as she lifted out the box and cut the cord around it. Inside was lying a dress of soft silk, that had once been white but was now yellowed with age, and, enfolding it like a mist, a long, white bridal veil, redolent with some strange, old-time perfume that had kept its sweetness through all the years.

"Poor Rachel Ward," said Aunt Olivia softly. "Here is her point lace handkerchief. She made it herself. It is like a spider's web. Here are the letters Will Montague wrote her. And here," she added, taking up a crimson velvet case with a tarnished gilt clasp, "are their photographs—his and hers."

We looked eagerly at the daguerreotypes in the old case.

"Why, Rachel Ward wasn't a bit pretty!" exclaimed the Story Girl in poignant disappointment.

No, Rachel Ward was not pretty, that had to be admitted. The picture showed a fresh young face, with strongly marked, irregular features, large black eyes, and black curls hanging around the shoulders in old-time style.

"Rachel wasn't pretty," said Uncle Alec, "but she had a lovely colour and a beautiful smile. She looks far too sober in that picture."

"She has a beautiful neck and bust," said Aunt Olivia critically.

"Anyhow, Will Montague was really handsome," said the Story Girl.

"A handsome rogue," growled Uncle Alec. "I never liked him. I was only a little chap of ten but I saw through him. Rachel Ward was far too good for him."

We would dearly have liked to get a peep into the letters, too. But Aunt Olivia would not allow that. They must be burned unread, she declared. She took the wedding dress and veil, the picture case, and the letters away with her. The rest of the things were put back into the chest, pending their ultimate distribution. Aunt Janet gave each of us boys a handkerchief. The Story Girl got the blue candlestick, and Felicity and Cecily each got a pink and gold vase. Even Sara Ray was made happy by the gift of a little china plate, with a loudly coloured picture of Moses and Aaron before Pharaoh in the middle of it. Moses wore a scarlet cloak, while Aaron disported himself in bright blue. Pharaoh was arrayed in yellow. The plate had a scalloped border with a wreath of green leaves around it.

"I shall never use it to eat off," said Sara rapturously. "I'll put it up on the parlour mantel-piece."

"I don't see much use in having a plate just for ornament," said Felicity.

"It's nice to have something interesting to look at," retorted Sara, who felt that the soul must have food as well as the body.

"I'm going to get a candle for my candlestick, and use it every night to go to bed with," said the Story Girl. "And I'll never light it without thinking of poor Rachel Ward. But I *do* wish she had been pretty."

"Well," said Felicity, with a glance at the clock, "it's all over, and it has been very interesting. But that clock has got to be put back to the right time some time through the day. I don't want bedtime coming a whole half-hour before it ought to."

In the afternoon, when Aunt Janet was over at Uncle Roger's, seeing him and Aunt Olivia off to town, the clock was righted.

The Story Girl and Peter came over to stay all night with us, and we made taffy in the kitchen, which the grown-ups kindly gave over to us for that purpose.

"Of course it was very interesting to see the old chest unpacked," said the Story Girl, as she stirred the contents of a saucepan vigorously. "But now that it is over I believe I am sorry that it is opened. It isn't mysterious any longer. We know all about it now, and we can never imagine what things are in it any more."

"It's better to know than to imagine," said Felicity.

"Oh, no, it isn't," said the Story Girl quickly. "When you know things you have to go by facts. But when you just dream about things there's nothing to hold you down."

"You're letting the taffy scorch, and *that's* a fact you'd better go by," said Felicity, sniffing. "Haven't you got a nose?"

When we went to bed, that wonderful white enchantress, the moon, was making an elf-land of the snow-misted world outside. From where I lay I could see the sharp tops of the spruces against the silvery sky. The frost was abroad, and the winds were still and the land lay in glamour.

Across the hall the Story Girl was telling Felicity and Cecily the old, old tale of Argive Helen and "evil-hearted Paris."

"But that's a bad story," said Felicity when the tale was ended. "She left her husband and run away with another man."

"I suppose it was bad four thousand years ago," admitted the Story Girl. "But by this time the bad must have all gone out of it. It's only the good that could last so long."

Our summer was over. It had been a beautiful one. We had known the sweetness of common joys, the delight of dawns, the dream and glamour of noontides, the long, purple peace of carefree nights. We had had the pleasure of bird song, of silver rain on greening fields, of storm among the trees, of blossoming meadows, and of the converse of whispering leaves. We had had brotherhood with wind and star, with books and tales, and hearth fires of autumn. Ours had been the little, loving tasks of every day, blithe companionship, shared thoughts, and adventuring. Rich were we in the memory of those opulent months that had gone from us—richer than we then knew or suspected. And before us was the dream of spring. It is always safe to dream of spring. For it is sure to come; and if it be not just as we have pictured it, it will be infinitely sweeter.

The
Golden Road

TO
THE MEMORY OF
AUNT MARY LAWSON
WHO TOLD ME MANY OF THE TALES
REPEATED BY THE
STORY GIRL

AUTHOR'S PREFACE

ONCE UPON a time we all walked on the golden road. It was a fair highway, through the Land of Lost Delight; shadow and sunshine were blessedly mingled, and every turn and dip revealed a fresh charm and a new loveliness to eager hearts and unspoiled eyes.

On that road we heard the song of morning stars; we drank in fragrances aerial and sweet as a May mist; we were rich in gossamer fancies and iris hopes; our hearts sought and found the boon of dreams; the years waited beyond and they were very fair; life was a rose-lipped comrade with purple flowers dripping from her fingers.

We may long have left the golden road behind, but its memories are the dearest of our eternal possessions; and those who cherish them as such may haply find a pleasure in the pages of this book, whose people are pilgrims on the golden road of youth.

——————— CHAPTER 1 ———————

A NEW DEPARTURE

"I'VE THOUGHT of something amusing for the winter," I said as we drew into a half-circle around the glorious wood-fire in Uncle Alec's kitchen.

It had been a day of wild November wind, closing down into a wet, eerie twilight. Outside, the wind was shrilling at the windows and around the eaves, and the rain was playing on the roof. The old willow at the gate was writhing in the storm and the orchard was a place of weird music, born of all the tears and fears that haunt the halls of night. But little we cared for the gloom and the loneliness of the outside world; we kept them at bay with the light of the fire and the laughter of our young lips.

We had been having a splendid game of Blind-Man's Buff. That is, it had been splendid at first; but later the fun went out of it because we found that Peter was, of malice prepense, allowing himself to be caught too easily, in order that he might have the pleasure of catching Felicity—which he never failed to do, no matter how tightly his eyes were bound. What remarkable goose said that love is blind? Love can see through five folds of closely-woven muffler with ease!

"I'm getting tired," said Cecily, whose breath was coming rather quickly and whose pale cheeks had bloomed into scarlet. "Let's sit down and get the Story Girl to tell us a story."

237

But as we dropped into our places the Story Girl shot a significant glance at me which intimated that this was the psychological moment for introducing the scheme she and I had been secretly developing for some days. It was really the Story Girl's idea and none of mine. But she had insisted that I should make the suggestion as coming wholly from myself.

"If you don't, Felicity won't agree to it. You know yourself, Bev, how contrary she's been lately over anything I mention. And if she goes against it Peter will too—the ninny!—and it wouldn't be any fun if we weren't all in it."

"What is it?" asked Felicity, drawing her chair slightly away from Peter's.

"It is this. Let us get up a newspaper of our own—write it all ourselves, and have all we do in it. Don't you think we can get a lot of fun out of it?"

Everyone looked rather blank and amazed, except the Story Girl. She knew what she had to do, and she did it.

"What a silly idea!" she exclaimed, with a contemptuous toss of her long brown curls. "Just as if *we* could get up a newspaper!"

Felicity fired up, exactly as we had hoped.

"*I* think it's a splendid idea," she said enthusiastically. "I'd like to know why we couldn't get up as good a newspaper as they have in town! Uncle Roger says the *Daily Enterprise* has gone to the dogs—all the news it prints is that some old woman has put a shawl on her head and gone across the road to have tea with another old woman. I guess we could do better than that. You needn't think, Sara Stanley, that nobody but you can do anything."

"I think it would be great fun," said Peter decidedly. "My Aunt Jane helped edit a paper when she was at Queen's Academy, and she said it was very amusing and helped her a great deal."

The Story Girl could hide her delight only by dropping her eyes and frowning.

"Bev wants to be editor," she said, "and I don't see how he can, with no experience. Anyhow, it would be a lot of trouble."

"Some people are so afraid of a little bother," retorted Felicity.

"I think it would be nice," said Cecily timidly, "and none of us have any experience of being editors, any more than Bev, so that wouldn't matter."

"Will it be printed?" asked Dan.

"Oh, no," I said. "We can't have it printed. We'll just have to write it out—we can buy foolscap from the teacher."

"I don't think it will be much of a newspaper if it isn't printed," said Dan scornfully.

"It doesn't matter very much what *you* think," said Felicity.

"Thank you," retorted Dan.

"Of course," said the Story Girl hastily, not wishing to have Dan turned against our project, "if all the rest of you want it I'll go in for it too. I daresay it would be real good fun, now that I come to think of it. And we'll keep the copies, and when we become famous they'll be quite valuable."

"I wonder if any of us ever will be famous," said Felix.

"The Story Girl will be," I said.

"I don't see how she can be," said Felicity skeptically. "Why, she's just one of us."

"Well, it's decided, then, that we're to have a newspaper," I resumed briskly. "The next thing is to choose a name for it. That's a very important thing."

"How often are you going to publish it?" asked Felix.

"Once a month."

"I thought newspapers came out every day, or every week at least," said Dan.

"We couldn't have one every week," I explained. "It would be too much work."

"Well, that's an argument," admitted Dan. "The less work you can get along with the better, in my opinion. No, Felicity, you needn't say it. I know exactly what you want to say, so save your breath to cool your porridge. I agree with you that I never work if I can find anything else to do."

" 'Remember it is harder still
To have no work to do,' "

quoted Cecily reprovingly.

"I don't believe *that*," rejoined Dan. "I'm like the Irishman who said he wished the man who begun work had stayed and finished it."

"Well, is it decided that Bev is to be editor?" asked Felix.

"Of course it is," Felicity answered for everybody.

"Then," said Felix, "I move that the name be *The King Monthly Magazine.*"

"That sounds fine," said Peter, hitching his chair a little nearer Felicity's.

"But," said Cecily timidly, "that will leave out Peter and the Story Girl and Sara Ray, just as if they didn't have a share in it. I don't think that would be fair."

"You name it then, Cecily," I suggested.

"Oh!" Cecily threw a deprecating glance at the Story Girl and Felicity. Then, meeting the contempt in the latter's gaze, she raised her head with unusual spirit.

"I think it would be nice just to call it *Our Magazine*," she said. "Then we'd all feel as if we had a share in it."

"*Our Magazine* it will be, then," I said. "And as for having a share in it, you bet we'll all have a share in it. If I'm to be editor you'll all have to be sub-editors, and have charge of a department."

"Oh, I couldn't," protested Cecily.

"You must," I said inexorably. " 'England expects everyone to do his duty.' That's our motto—only we'll put Prince Edward Island in place of England. There must be no shirking. Now, what departments will we have? We must make it as much like a real newspaper as we can."

"Well, we ought to have an etiquette department, then," said Felicity. "The *Family Guide* has one."

"Of course we'll have one," I said, "and Dan will edit it."

"Dan!" exclaimed Felicity, who had fondly expected to be asked to edit it herself.

"I can run an etiquette column as well as that idiot in the *Family Guide*, anyhow," said Dan defiantly. "But you can't have an etiquette department unless questions are asked. What am I to do if nobody asks any?"

"You must make some up," said the Story Girl. "Uncle Roger says that is what the *Family Guide* man does. He says it is impossible that there can be as many hopeless fools in the world as that column would stand for otherwise."

"We want you to edit the household department, Felicity," I said, seeing a cloud lowering on that fair lady's brow. "Nobody can do that as well as you. Felix will edit the jokes and the Information Bureau, and Cecily must be fashion editor. Yes, you must, Sis. It's easy as wink. And the Story Girl will attend to the personals. They're very important. Anyone can contribute a personal, but the Story Girl is to see there are some in every issue, even if she has to make them up, like Dan with the etiquette."

"Bev will run the scrap book department, besides the editorials," said the Story Girl, seeing that I was too modest to say it myself.

"Aren't you going to have a story page?" asked Peter.

"We will, if you'll be fiction and poetry editor," I said.

Peter, in his secret soul, was dismayed, but he would not blanch before Felicity.

"All right," he said, recklessly.

"We can put anything we like in the scrap book department," I explained, "but all the other contributions must be original, and all must have the name of the writer signed to them, except the personals. We must all do our best. *Our Magazine* is to be 'a feast of reason and flow of soul.' "

I felt that I had worked in two quotations with striking effect. The others, with the exception of the Story Girl, looked suitably impressed.

"But," said Cecily, reproachfully, "haven't you anything for Sara Ray to do? She'll feel awful bad if she is left out."

I had forgotten Sara Ray. Nobody, except Cecily, ever did remember Sara Ray unless she was on the spot. But we decided to put her in as advertising manager. That sounded well and really meant very little.

"Well, we'll go ahead then," I said, with a sigh of relief that the project had been so easily launched. "We'll get the first issue out about the first of January. And whatever else we do we mustn't let Uncle Roger get hold of it. He'd make such fearful fun of it."

"I hope we can make a success of it," said Peter moodily. He had been moody ever since he was entrapped into being fiction editor.

"It will be a success if we are determined to succeed," I said. " 'Where there is a will there is always a way.' "

"That's just what Ursula Townley said when her father locked her in her room the night she was going to run away with Kenneth MacNair," said the Story Girl.

We pricked up our ears, scenting a story.

"Who were Ursula Townley and Kenneth MacNair?" I asked.

"Kenneth MacNair was a first cousin of the Awkward Man's grandfather, and Ursula Townley was the belle of the Island in her day. Who do you suppose told me the story—no, read it to me, out of his brown book?"

"Never the Awkward Man himself!" I exclaimed incredulously.

"Yes, he did," said the Story Girl triumphantly. "I met him one day last week back in the maple woods when I was looking for ferns. He was sitting by the spring, writing in his brown book. He hid it when he saw me and looked real silly; but after I had talked to him awhile I just asked him about it, and told him that the gossips said he wrote poetry in it, and if he did would he tell me, because I was dying to know. He said he wrote a little of everything in it; and then I begged him to read me something out of it, and he read me the story of Ursula and Kenneth."

"I don't see how you ever had the face," said Felicity; and even Cecily looked as if she thought the Story Girl had gone rather far.

"Never mind that," cried Felix, "but tell us the story. That's the main thing."

"I'll tell it just as the Awkward Man read it, as far as I can," said the Story Girl, "but I can't put all his nice poetical touches in, because I can't remember them all, though he read it over twice for me."

CHAPTER 2

A WILL, A WAY AND A WOMAN

"ONE DAY, over a hundred years ago, Ursula Townley was waiting for Kenneth MacNair in a great beechwood, where brown nuts were falling and an October wind was making the leaves dance on the ground like pixy-people."

"What are pixy-people?" demanded Peter, forgetting the Story Girl's dislike of interruptions.

"Hush," whispered Cecily. "That is only one of the Awkward Man's poetical touches, I guess."

"There were cultivated fields between the grove and the dark blue gulf; but far behind and on each side were woods, for Prince Edward Island a hundred years ago was not what it is today. The settlements were few and scattered, and the population so scanty that old Hugh Townley boasted that he knew every man, woman and child in it.

"Old Hugh was quite a noted man in his day. He was noted for several things—he was rich, he was hospitable, he was proud, he was masterful—and he had for daughter the handsomest young woman in Prince Edward Island.

"Of course, the young men were not blind to her good looks, and she had so many lovers that all the other girls hated her—"

"You bet!" said Dan, aside—

"But the only one who found favour in her eyes was the very last man she should have pitched her fancy on, at least if old Hugh were the judge. Kenneth MacNair was a dark-eyed young sea-captain of the next settlement, and it was to meet him that Ursula stole to the beechwood on that autumn day of crisp wind and ripe sunshine. Old Hugh had forbidden his house to the young man, making such a scene of fury about it that even Ursula's high spirit quailed. Old Hugh had really nothing against Kenneth himself; but years before either Kenneth or Ursula was born, Kenneth's father had beaten Hugh Townley in a hotly contested election. Political feeling ran high in those days, and old Hugh had never forgiven the MacNair his victory. The feud between the families dated from that tempest in the provincial teapot, and the surplus of votes on the wrong side was the reason why, thirty years after, Ursula had to meet her lover by stealth if she met him at all."

"Was the MacNair a Conservative or a Grit?" asked Felicity.

"It doesn't make any difference what he was," said the Story Girl impatiently. "Even a Tory would be romantic a hundred years ago. Well, Ursula couldn't see Kenneth very often, for Kenneth lived fifteen miles away and was often absent from home in his vessel. On this particular day it was nearly three months since they had met.

"The Sunday before, young Sandy MacNair had been in Carlyle church. He had risen at dawn that morning, walked bare-footed for eight miles along the shore, carrying his shoes, hired a harbour fisherman to row him over the channel, and then walked eight miles more to the church at Carlyle, less, it is to be feared, from a zeal for holy things than that he might do an errand for his adored brother, Kenneth. He carried a letter which he contrived to pass into Ursula's hand in the crowd as the people came out. This letter asked Ursula to meet Kenneth in the beechwood the next afternoon, and so she stole away there when suspicious father and watchful stepmother thought she was spinning in the granary loft."

"It was very wrong of her to deceive her parents," said Felicity primly.

The Story Girl couldn't deny this, so she evaded the ethical side of the question skilfully.

"I am not telling you what Ursula Townley *ought* to have done," she said loftily. "I am only telling you what she *did* do. If you don't want to hear it you needn't listen, of course. There wouldn't be many stories to tell if nobody ever did anything she shouldn't do.

"Well, when Kenneth came, the meeting was just what might have been expected between two lovers who had taken their last kiss three months before. So it was a good half-hour before Ursula said,

" 'Oh, Kenneth, I cannot stay long—I shall be missed. You said in your letter that you had something important to talk of. What is it?'

" 'My news is this, Ursula. Next Saturday morning my vessel, *The Fair Lady,* with her captain on board, sails at dawn from Charlottetown harbour, bound for Buenos Ayres. At this season this means a safe and sure return—next May.'

" 'Kenneth!' cried Ursula. She turned pale and burst into tears. 'How can you think of leaving me? Oh, you are cruel!'

" 'Why, no, sweetheart,' laughed Kenneth. 'The captain of *The Fair Lady* will take his bride with him. We'll spend our honeymoon on the high seas, Ursula, and the cold Canadian winter under southern palms.'

" 'You want me to run away with you, Kenneth?' exclaimed Ursula.

" 'Indeed, dear girl, there's nothing else to do!'

" 'Oh, I cannot!' she protested. 'My father would—'

" 'We'll not consult him—until afterward. Come, Ursula, you know there's no other way. We've always known it must come to this. *Your* father will never forgive me for *my* father. You won't fail me now. Think of the long parting if you send me away alone on such a voyage. Pluck up your courage, and we'll let Townleys and MacNairs whistle their mouldy feuds down the wind while we sail southward in *The Fair Lady*. I have a plan.'

" 'Let me hear it,' said Ursula, beginning to get back her breath.

" 'There is to be a dance at The Springs Friday night. Are you invited, Ursula?'

" 'Yes.'

" 'Good. I am not—but I shall be there—in the fir grove behind the house, with two horses. When the dancing is at its height you'll steal out to meet me. Then 'tis but a fifteen mile ride to Charlottetown, where a good minister, who is a friend of mine, will be ready to marry us. By the time the dancers have tired their heels you and I will be on our vessel, able to snap our fingers at fate.'

" 'And what if I do not meet you in the fir grove?' said Ursula, a little impertinently.

" 'If you do not, I'll sail for South America the next morning, and many a long year will pass ere Kenneth MacNair comes home again.'

"Perhaps Kenneth didn't mean that, but Ursula thought he did, and it decided her. She agreed to run away with him. Yes, of course that was wrong, too, Felicity. She ought to have said, 'No, I shall be married respectably from home, and have a wedding and a silk dress and bridesmaids and lots of presents.' But she didn't. She wasn't as prudent as Felicity King would have been."

"She was a shameless hussy," said Felicity, venting on the long-dead Ursula that anger she dare not visit on the Story Girl.

"Oh, no, Felicity dear, she was just a lass of spirit. I'd have done the same. And when Friday night came she began to dress for the dance with a brave heart. She was to go to The Springs with her uncle and aunt, who were coming on horseback that afternoon, and would then go on to The Springs in old Hugh's carriage, which was the only one in Carlyle then. They were to leave in time to reach The Springs before nightfall, for the October nights were dark and the wooded roads rough for travelling.

"When Ursula was ready she looked at herself in the glass with a good deal of satisfaction. Yes, Felicity, she was a vain baggage, that same Ursula, but that kind didn't all die out a hundred years ago. And she had good reason for being vain. She wore the sea-green silk which had been brought out from England a year before and worn but once—at the Christmas ball at Government House. A fine, stiff, rustling silk it was, and over it shone Ursula's crimson cheeks and gleaming eyes, and masses of nut brown hair.

"As she turned from the glass she heard her father's voice below, loud and angry. Growing very pale, she ran out into the hall. Her father was already half way upstairs, his face red with fury. In the hall below Ursula saw her stepmother, looking troubled and vexed. At the door stood Malcolm Ramsay, a homely neighbour youth who had been courting Ursula in his clumsy way ever since she grew up. Ursula had always hated him.

" 'Ursula!' shouted old Hugh, 'come here and tell this scoundrel he lies. He says that you met Kenneth MacNair in the beechgrove last Tuesday. Tell him he lies! Tell him he lies!'

"Ursula was no coward. She looked scornfully at poor Ramsay.

" 'The creature is a spy and a tale-bearer,' she said, 'but in this he does not lie. I *did* meet Kenneth MacNair last Tuesday.'

" 'And you dare to tell me this to my face!' roared old Hugh. 'Back to your room, girl! Back to your room and stay there! Take off that finery. You go to no more dances. You shall stay in that room until I choose to let you out. No, not a word! I'll put you there if you don't go. In with you—ay, and take your knitting with you. Occupy yourself with that this evening instead of kicking your heels at The Springs!'

"He snatched a roll of gray stocking from the hall table and flung it into Ursula's room. Ursula knew she would have to follow it, or be picked up and carried in like a naughty child. So she gave the miserable Ramsay a look that made him cringe, and swept into her room with her head in the air. The next moment she heard the door locked behind her. Her first proceeding was to have a cry of anger and shame and disappointment. That did no good, and then she took to marching up and down her room. It did not calm her to hear the rumble of the carriage out of the gate as her uncle and aunt departed.

" 'Oh, what's to be done?' she sobbed. 'Kenneth will be furious. He will think I have failed him and he will go away hot with anger against me. If I could only send a word of explanation I know he would not leave me. But there seems to be no way at all—though I have heard that there's always a way when there's a will. Oh, I shall go mad! If the window were not so high I would jump out of it. But to break my legs or my neck would not mend the matter.'

"The afternoon passed on. At sunset Ursula heard hoof-beats and ran to the window. Andrew Kinnear of The Springs was tying his horse at the door. He was a dashing young fellow, and a political crony of old Hugh. No doubt he would be at the dance that night. Oh, if she could get speech for but a moment with him!

"When he had gone into the house, Ursula, turning impatiently from the window, tripped and almost fell over the big ball of homespun yarn her father had flung on the floor. For a moment she gazed at it resentfully—then, with a gay little laugh, she pounced on it. The next moment she was at her table, writing a brief note to Kenneth MacNair. When it was written, Ursula unwound the gray ball to a considerable depth, pinned the note on it, and rewound the yarn over it. A gray ball, the color of the twilight, might escape observation, where a white missive fluttering down from an upper window would surely be seen by someone. Then she softly opened her window and waited.

"It was dusk when Andrew went away. Fortunately old Hugh did not come to the door with him. As Andrew untied his horse Ursula threw the ball with such good aim that it struck him, as she had meant it to do, squarely on the head. Andrew looked up at her window. She leaned out, put her finger warningly on her lips, pointed to the ball, and nodded. Andrew, looking somewhat puzzled, picked up the ball, sprang to his saddle, and galloped off.

"So far, well, thought Ursula. But would Andrew understand? Would he have wit enough to think of exploring the big, knobby ball for its delicate secret? And would he be at the dance after all?

"The evening dragged by. Time had never seemed so long to Ursula. She could not rest or sleep. It was midnight before she heard the patter of a handful of gravel on her windowpanes. In a trice she was leaning out. Below in the darkness stood Kenneth MacNair.

" 'Oh, Kenneth, did you get my letter? And is it safe for you to be here?'

" 'Safe enough. Your father is in bed. I've waited two hours down the road for his light to go out, and an extra half-hour to put him to sleep. The horses are there. Slip down and out, Ursula. We'll make Charlottetown by dawn yet.'

" 'That's easier said than done, lad. I'm locked in. But do you go out behind the new barn and bring the ladder you will find there.'

"Five minutes later, Miss Ursula, hooded and cloaked, scrambled soundlessly down the ladder, and in five more minutes she and Kenneth were riding along the road.

" 'There's a stiff gallop before us, Ursula,' said Kenneth.

" 'I would ride to the world's end with you, Kenneth MacNair,' said Ursula. Oh, of course she shouldn't have said anything of the sort, Felicity. But you see people had no etiquette departments in those days. And when the red sunlight of a fair October dawn was shining over the gray sea *The Fair Lady* sailed out of Charlottetown harbour. On her deck stood Kenneth and Ursula MacNair, and in her hand, as a most precious treasure, the bride carried a ball of gray homespun yarn."

"Well," said Dan, yawning, "I like that kind of a story. Nobody goes and dies in it, that's one good thing."

"Did old Hugh forgive Ursula?" I asked.

"The story stopped there in the brown book," said the Story Girl, "but the Awkward Man says he did, after awhile."

"It must be rather romantic to be run away with," remarked Cecily, wistfully.

"Don't you get such silly notions in your head, Cecily King," said Felicity, severely.

CHAPTER 3

THE CHRISTMAS HARP

GREAT WAS the excitement in the houses of King as Christmas drew nigh. The air was simply charged with secrets. Everybody was very penurious for weeks beforehand and hoards were counted scrutinizingly every day. Mysterious pieces of handiwork were smuggled in and out of sight, and whispered consultations were held, about which nobody thought of being jealous, as might have happened at any other time. Felicity was in her element, for she and her mother were deep in preparations for the day. Cecily and the Story Girl were excluded from these doings with indifference on Aunt Janet's part and what seemed ostentatious complacency on Felicity's. Cecily took this to heart and complained to me about it.

"I'm one of this family just as much as Felicity is," she said, with as much indignation as Cecily could feel, "and I don't think she need shut me out of everything. When I wanted to stone the raisins for the mince-meat she said, no, she would do it herself, because Christmas mince-meat was *very* particular—as if I couldn't stone raisins right! The airs Felicity puts on about her cooking just make me sick," concluded Cecily wrathfully.

"It's a pity she doesn't make a mistake in cooking once in a while herself," I said. "Then maybe she wouldn't think she knew so much more than other people."

All parcels that came in the mail from distant friends were taken charge of by Aunts Janet and Olivia, not to be opened until the great day of the feast itself. How slowly the last week passed! But even watched pots will boil in the fulness of time, and finally Christmas day came, gray and dour and frost-bitten without, but full of revelry and rose-red mirth within. Uncle Roger and Aunt Olivia and the Story Girl came over early for the day; and Peter came too, with his shining, morning face, to be hailed with joy, for we had been afraid that Peter would not be able to spend Christmas with us. His mother had wanted him home with her.

"Of course I ought to go," Peter had told me mournfully, "but we won't have turkey for dinner, because ma can't afford it. And ma always cries on holidays because she says they make her think of father. Of course she can't help it, but it ain't cheerful. Aunt Jane wouldn't have cried. Aunt Jane used to say she never saw the man who was worth spoiling her eyes for. But I guess I'll have to spend Christmas at home."

At the last moment, however, a cousin of Mrs. Craig's in Charlottetown invited her for Christmas, and Peter, being given his choice of going or staying, joyfully elected to stay. So we were all together, except Sara Ray, who had been invited but whose mother wouldn't let her come.

"Sara Ray's mother is a nuisance," snapped the Story Girl. "She just lives to make that poor child miserable, and she won't let her go to the party tonight, either."

"It is just breaking Sara's heart that she can't," said Cecily compassionately. "I'm almost afraid I won't enjoy myself for thinking of her, home there alone, most likely reading the Bible, while we're at the party."

"She might be worse occupied than reading the Bible," said Felicity rebukingly.

"But Mrs. Ray makes her read it as a punishment," protested Cecily. "Whenever Sara cries to go anywhere—and of course she'll cry tonight—Mrs. Ray makes her read seven chapters in the Bible. I wouldn't think that would make her very fond of it. And I'll not be able to talk the party over with Sara afterwards—and that's half the fun gone."

"You can tell her all about it," comforted Felix.

"Telling isn't a bit like talking it over," retorted Cecily. "It's too one-sided."

We had an exciting time opening our presents. Some of us had more than others, but we all received enough to make us feel comfortably that we were not unduly neglected in the matter. The contents of the box which the Story Girl's father had sent her from Paris made our eyes stick out. It was full of beautiful things, among them another red silk dress—not the bright, flame-hued tint of her old one, but a rich, dark crimson, with the most distracting flounces and bows and ruffles; and with it were little red satin slippers with gold buckles, and heels that made Aunt Janet hold up her hands in horror. Felicity remarked scornfully that she would have thought the Story Girl would get tired wearing red so much, and even Cecily commented apart to me that she thought when you got so many things all at once you didn't appreciate them as much as when you only got a few.

"I'd never get tired of red," said the Story Girl. "I just love it—it's so rich and glowing. When I'm dressed in red I always feel ever so much cleverer than in any other colour. Thoughts just crowd into my brain one after the other. Oh, you darling dress—you dear, sheeny, red-rosy, glistening, silky thing!"

She flung it over her shoulder and danced around the kitchen.

"Don't be silly, Sara," said Aunt Janet, a little stiffly. She was a good soul, that Aunt Janet, and had a kind, loving heart in her ample bosom. But I fancy there were times when she thought it rather hard that the daughter of a roving adventurer— as she considered him—like Blair Stanley should disport herself in silk dresses, while her own daughters must go clad in gingham and muslin—for those were the days when a feminine creature got one silk dress in her lifetime, and seldom more than one.

The Story Girl also got a present from the Awkward Man— a little, shabby, worn volume with a great many marks on the leaves.

"Why, it isn't new—it's an old book!" exclaimed Felicity. "I didn't think the Awkward Man was mean, whatever else he was."

"Oh, you don't understand, Felicity," said the Story Girl patiently. "And I don't suppose I can make you understand. But I'll try. I'd ten times rather have this than a new book. It's one of his own, don't you see—one that he has read a hundred times and loved and made a friend of. A new book, just out of a shop, wouldn't be the same thing at all. It wouldn't *mean* anything. I consider it a great compliment that he has given me this book. I'm prouder of it than of anything else I've got."

"Well, you're welcome to it," said Felicity. "I don't understand and I don't want to. *I* wouldn't give anybody a Christmas present that wasn't new, and I wouldn't thank anybody who gave me one."

Peter was in the seventh heaven because Felicity had given him a present—and, moreover, one that she had made herself. It was a bookmark of perforated cardboard, with a gorgeous red and yellow worsted goblet worked on it, and below, in green letters, the solemn warning, "Touch Not The Cup." As Peter was not addicted to habits of intemperance, not even to looking on dandelion wine when it was pale yellow, we did not exactly see why Felicity should have selected such a device. But Peter was perfectly satisfied, so nobody cast any blight on his happiness by carping criticism. Later on Felicity told me she had worked the bookmark for him because his father used to drink before he ran away.

"I thought Peter ought to be warned in time," she said.

Even Pat had a ribbon of blue, which he clawed off and lost half an hour after it was tied on him. Pat did not care for vain adornments of the body.

We had a glorious Christmas dinner, fit for the halls of Lucullus, and ate far more than was good for us, none daring to make us afraid on that one day of the year. And in the evening—oh, rapture and delight!—we went to Kitty Marr's party.

It was a fine December evening; the sharp air of morning had mellowed until it was as mild as autumn. There had been no snow, and the long fields, sloping down from the homestead, were brown and mellow. A weird, dreamy stillness had fallen on the purple earth, the dark fir woods, the valley rims, the sere meadows. Nature seemed to have folded satisfied hands to rest, knowing that her long wintry slumber was coming upon her.

At first, when the invitations to the party had come, Aunt Janet had said we could not go; but Uncle Alec interceded in our favour, perhaps influenced thereto by Cecily's wistful eyes. If Uncle Alec had a favourite among his children it was Cecily, and he had grown even more indulgent towards her of late. Now and then I saw him looking at her intently, and, following his eyes and thought, I had, somehow, seen that Cecily was paler and thinner than she had been in the summer, and that her soft eyes seemed larger, and that over her little face in moments of repose there was a certain languor and weariness that made it very sweet and pathetic. And I heard him tell Aunt Janet that he did not like to see the child getting so much the look of her Aunt Felicity.

"Cecily is perfectly well," said Aunt Janet sharply. "She's only growing very fast. Don't be foolish, Alec."

But after that Cecily had cups of cream where the rest of us got only milk; and Aunt Janet was very particular to see that she had her rubbers on whenever she went out.

On this merry Christmas evening, however, no fears or dim foreshadowings of any coming event clouded our hearts or faces. Cecily looked brighter and prettier than I had ever seen her, with her softly shining eyes and the nut brown gloss of her hair. Felicity was too beautiful for words; and even the Story Girl, between excitement and the crimson silk array, blossomed out with a charm and allurement more potent than any regular loveliness—and this in spite of the fact that Aunt Olivia had tabooed the red satin slippers and mercilessly decreed that stout shoes should be worn.

"I know just how you feel about it, you daughter of Eve," she said, with gay sympathy, "but December roads are damp, and if you are going to walk to Marrs' you are not going to do it in those frivolous Parisian concoctions, even with over-boots on; so be brave, dear heart, and show that you have a soul above little red satin shoes."

"Anyhow," said Uncle Roger, "that red silk dress will break the hearts of all the feminine small fry at the party. You'd break their spirits, too, if you wore the slippers. Don't do it, Sara. Leave them one wee loophole of enjoyment."

"What does Uncle Roger mean?" whispered Felicity.

"He means you girls are all dying of jealousy because of the Story Girl's dress," said Dan.

"I am not of a jealous disposition," said Felicity loftily, "and she's entirely welcome to the dress—with a complexion like that."

But we enjoyed that party hugely, every one of us. And we enjoyed the walk home afterwards, through dim, enshadowed fields where silvery star-beams lay, while Orion trod his stately march above us, and a red moon climbed up the black horizon's rim. A brook went with us part of the way, singing to us through the dark—a gay, irresponsible vagabond of valley and wilderness.

Felicity and Peter walked not with us. Peter's cup must surely have brimmed over that Christmas night. When we left the Marr house, he had boldly said to Felicity, "May I see you home?" And Felicity, much to our amazement, had taken his arm and marched off with him. The primness of her was indescribable, and was not at all ruffled by Dan's hoot of derision. As for me, I was consumed by a secret and burning desire to ask the Story Girl if I might see *her* home; but I could not screw my courage to the sticking point. How I envied Peter his easy, insouciant manner! I could not emulate him, so Dan and Felix and Cecily and the Story Girl and I all walked hand in hand, huddling a little closer together as we went through James Frewen's woods—for there are strange harps in a fir grove, and who shall say what fingers sweep them? Mighty and sonorous was the music above our heads as the winds of the night stirred the great boughs tossing athwart the starlit sky. Perhaps it was that æolian harmony which recalled to the Story Girl a legend of elder days.

"I read such a pretty story in one of Aunt Olivia's books last night," she said. "It was called 'The Christmas Harp.' Would you like to hear it? It seems to me it would just suit this part of the road."

"There isn't anything about—about ghosts in it, is there?" said Cecily timidly.

"Oh, no, I wouldn't tell a ghost story here for anything. I'd frighten myself too much. This story is about one of the shepherds who saw the angels on the first Christmas night. He was just a youth, and he loved music with all his heart, and he longed to be able to express the melody that was in his soul. But he could not; he had a harp and he often tried to play on it; but his clumsy fingers only made such discord that his companions laughed at him and mocked him, and called him a madman because he would not give it up, but would rather sit apart by himself, with his arms about his harp, looking up into the sky, while they gathered around their fire and told tales to wile away their long night vigils as they watched their sheep on the hills. But to him the thoughts that came out of the great silence were far sweeter than their mirth; and he never gave up the hope, which sometimes left his lips as a prayer, that some day he might be able to express those thoughts in music to the tired, weary, forgetful world. On the first Christmas night he was out with his fellow shepherds on the hills. It was chill and dark, and all, except him, were glad to gather around the fire. He sat, as usual, by himself, with his harp on his knee and a great longing in his heart. And there came a marvellous light in the sky and over the hills, as if the darkness of the night had suddenly blossomed into a wonderful meadow of flowery flame; and all the shepherds saw the angels and heard them sing. And as they sang, the harp that the young shepherd held began to play softly by itself, and as he listened to it he realized that it was playing the same music that the angels sang and that all his secret longings and aspirations and strivings were expressed in it. From that night, whenever he took the harp in his hands, it played the same music; and he wandered all over the world carrying it; wherever the sound of its music was heard hate and discord fled away and peace and good-will reigned. No one who heard it could think an evil thought; no one could feel hopeless or despairing or bitter or angry. When a man had once heard that music it entered into his soul and heart and life and became a part of him for ever. Years went by; the shepherd grew old and bent and feeble; but still he roamed over land and sea, that his harp might carry the message of the Christmas night and the angel song to all mankind. At last his strength failed him and he fell by the wayside in the darkness; but his harp played as his spirit passed; and it seemed to him that a Shining One stood by him, with wonderful starry eyes, and said to him, 'Lo, the music thy harp has played for so many years has been but the echo of the love and sympathy and purity and beauty in thine own soul; and if at any time in the wanderings thou hadst opened the door of that soul to evil or envy or selfishness thy harp would have ceased to play. Now thy life is ended; but what thou hast given to mankind has no end; and as long as the world lasts, so long will the heavenly music of the Christmas harp ring in the ears of men.' When the sun rose the old shepherd lay dead by the roadside, with a smile on his face; and in his hands was a harp with all its strings broken."

We left the fir woods as the tale was ended, and on the opposite hill was home. A dim light in the kitchen window betokened that Aunt Janet had no idea of going to bed until all her young fry were safely housed for the night.

"Ma's waiting up for us," said Dan. "I'd laugh if she happened to go to the door just as Felicity and Peter were strutting up. I guess she'll be cross. It's nearly twelve."

"Christmas will soon be over," said Cecily, with a sigh. "Hasn't it been a nice one? It's the first we've all spent together. Do you suppose we'll ever spend another together?"

"Lots of 'em," said Dan cheerily. "Why not?"

"Oh, I don't know," answered Cecily, her footsteps lagging somewhat. "Only things seem just a little too pleasant to last."

"If Willy Fraser had had as much spunk as Peter, Miss Cecily King mightn't be so low spirited," quoth Dan, significantly.

Cecily tossed her head and disdained reply. There are really some remarks a self-respecting young lady must ignore.

CHAPTER 4

NEW YEAR RESOLUTIONS

IF WE did not have a white Christmas we had a white New Year. Midway between the two came a heavy snowfall. It was winter in our orchard of old delights then,—so truly winter that it was hard to believe summer had ever dwelt in it, or that spring would ever return to it. There were no birds to sing the music of the moon; and the path where the apple blossoms had fallen were heaped with less fragrant drifts. But it was a place of wonder on a moonlight night, when the snowy arcades shone like avenues of ivory and crystal, and the bare trees cast fairy-like traceries upon them. Over Uncle Stephen's Walk, where the snow had fallen smoothly, a spell of white magic had been woven. Taintless and wonderful it seemed, like a street of pearl in the new Jerusalem.

On New Year's Eve we were all together in Uncle Alec's kitchen, which was tacitly given over to our revels during the winter evenings. The Story Girl and Peter were there, of course, and Sara Ray's mother had allowed her to come up on condition that she should be home by eight sharp. Cecily was glad to see her, but the boys never hailed her arrival with over-much delight, because, since the dark began to come down early, Aunt Janet always made one of us walk down home with her. We hated this, because Sara Ray was always so maddeningly self-conscious of having an escort. We knew perfectly well that next day in school she would tell her chums as a "dead" secret that "So-and-So King saw her home" from the hill farm the night before. Now, seeing a young lady home from choice, and being sent home with her by your aunt or mother are two entirely different things, and we thought Sara Ray ought to have sense enough to know it.

Outside there was a vivid rose of sunset behind the cold hills of fir, and the long reaches of snowy fields glowed fairily pink in the western light. The drifts along the edges of the meadows and down the lane looked as if a series of breaking waves had, by the lifting of a magician's wand, been suddenly transformed into marble, even to their toppling curls of foam.

Slowly the splendour died, giving place to the mystic beauty of a winter twilight when the moon is rising. The hollow sky was a cup of blue. The stars came out over the white glens and the earth was covered with a kingly carpet for the feet of the young year to press.

"I'm so glad the snow came," said the Story Girl. "If it hadn't the New Year would have seemed just as dingy and worn out as the old. There's something very solemn about the idea of a New Year, isn't there? Just think of three hundred and sixty-five whole days, with not a thing happened in them yet."

"I don't suppose anything very wonderful will happen in them," said Felix pessimistically. To Felix, just then, life was flat, stale and unprofitable because it was his turn to go home with Sara Ray.

"It makes me a little frightened to think of all that may happen in them," said Cecily. "Miss Marwood says it is what we put into a year, not what we get out of it, that counts at last."

"I'm always glad to see a New Year," said the Story Girl. "I wish we could do as they do in Norway. The whole family sits up until midnight, and then, just as the clock is striking twelve, the father opens the door and welcomes the New Year in. Isn't it a pretty custom?"

"If ma would let us stay up till twelve we might do that too," said Dan, "but she never will. I call it mean."

"If I ever have children I'll let them stay up to watch the New Year in," said the Story Girl decidedly.

"So will I," said Peter, "but other nights they'll have to go to bed at seven."

"You ought to be ashamed, speaking of such things," said Felicity, with a scandalized face.

Peter shrank into the background abashed, no doubt believing that he had broken some *Family Guide* precept all to pieces.

"I didn't know it wasn't proper to mention children," he muttered apologetically.

"We ought to make some New Year resolutions," suggested the Story Girl. "New Year's Eve is the time to make them."

"I can't think of any resolutions I want to make," said Felicity, who was perfectly satisfied with herself.

"I could suggest a few to you," said Dan sarcastically.

"There are so many I would like to make," said Cecily, "that I'm afraid it wouldn't be any use trying to keep them all."

"Well, let's all make a few, just for the fun of it, and see if we can keep them," I said. "And let's get paper and ink and write them out. That will make them seem more solemn and binding."

"And then pin them up on our bedroom walls, where we'll see them every day," suggested the Story Girl, "and every time we break a resolution we must put a cross opposite it. That will show us what progress we are making, as well as make us ashamed if we have too many crosses."

"And let's have a Roll of Honour in *Our Magazine,*" suggested Felix, "and every month we'll publish the names of those who keep their resolutions perfect."

"I think it's all nonsense," said Felicity. But she joined our circle around the table, though she sat for a long time with a blank sheet before her.

"Let's each make a resolution in turn," I said. "I'll lead off."

And, recalling with shame certain unpleasant differences of opinion I had lately had with Felicity, I wrote down in my best hand,

"I shall try to keep my temper always."

"You'd better," said Felicity tactfully.

It was Dan's turn next.

"I can't think of anything to start with," he said, gnawing his penholder fiercely.

"You might make a resolution not to eat poison berries," suggested Felicity.

"You'd better make one not to nag people everlastingly," retorted Dan.

"Oh, don't quarrel the last night of the old year," implored Cecily.

"You might resolve not to quarrel any time," suggested Sara Ray.

"No, sir," said Dan emphatically. "There's no use making a resolution you *can't* keep. There are people in this family you've just *got* to quarrel with if you want to live. But I've thought of one—I won't do things to spite people."

Felicity—who really was in an unbearable mood that night—laughed disagreeably; but Cecily gave her a fierce nudge, which probably restrained her from speaking.

"I will not eat any apples," wrote Felix.

"What on earth do you want to give up eating apples for?" asked Peter in astonishment.

"Never mind," returned Felix.

"Apples make people fat, you know," said Felicity sweetly.

"It seems a funny kind of resolution," I said doubtfully. "I think our resolutions ought to be giving up wrong things or doing right ones."

"You make your resolutions to suit yourself and I'll make mine to suit myself," said Felix defiantly.

"I shall never get drunk," wrote Peter painstakingly.

"But you never do," said the Story Girl in astonishment.

"Well, it will be all the easier to keep the resolution," argued Peter.

"That isn't fair," complained Dan. "If we all resolved not to do the things we never do we'd all be on the Roll of Honour."

"You let Peter alone," said Felicity severely. "It's a very good resolution and one everybody ought to make."

"I shall not be jealous," wrote the Story Girl.

"But are you?" I asked, surprised.

The Story Girl coloured and nodded. "Of one thing," she confessed, "but I'm not going to tell what it is."

"I'm jealous sometimes, too," confessed Sara Ray, "and so my first resolution will be 'I shall try not to feel jealous when I hear the other girls in school describing all the sick spells they've had.' "

"Goodness, do you want to be sick?" demanded Felix in astonishment.

"It makes a person important," explained Sara Ray.

"I am going to try to improve my mind by reading good books and listening to older people," wrote Cecily.

"You got that out of the Sunday School paper," cried Felicity.
"It doesn't matter where I got it," said Cecily with dignity.
"The main thing is to keep it."

"It's your turn, Felicity," I said.

Felicity tossed her beautiful golden head.

"I told you I wasn't going to make any resolutions. Go on yourself."

"I shall always study my grammar lesson," I wrote—I, who loathed grammar with a deadly loathing.

"I hate grammar too," signed Sara Ray. "It seems so unimportant."

Sara was rather fond of a big word, but did not always get hold of the right one. I rather suspected that in the above instance she really meant uninteresting.

"I won't get mad at Felicity, if I can help it," wrote Dan.

"I'm sure I never do anything to make you mad," exclaimed Felicity.

"I don't think it's polite to make resolutions about your sisters," said Peter.

"He can't keep it anyway," scoffed Felicity. "He's got such an awful temper."

"It's a family failing," flashed Dan, breaking his resolution ere the ink on it was dry.

"There you go," taunted Felicity.

"I'll work all my arithmetic problems without any help," scribbled Felix.

"I wish I could resolve that, too," sighed Sara Ray, "but it wouldn't be any use. I'd never be able to do those compound multiplication sums the teacher gives us to do at home every night if I didn't get Judy Pineau to help me. Judy isn't a good reader and she can't spell *at all*, but you can't stick her in arithmetic as far as she went herself. I feel sure," concluded poor Sara, in a hopeless tone, "that I'll *never* be able to understand compound multiplication."

> " 'Multiplication is vexation,
>   Division is as bad,
> The rule of three perplexes me,
>   And fractions drive me mad,' "

quoted Dan.

"I haven't got as far as fractions yet," sighed Sara, "and I hope I'll be too big to go to school before I do. I hate arithmetic, but I am *passionately* fond of geography."

"I will not play tit-tat-x on the fly leaves of my hymn book in church," wrote Peter.

"Mercy, did you ever do such a thing?" exclaimed Felicity in horror.

Peter nodded shamefacedly.

"Yes—that Sunday Mr. Bailey preached. He was so long-winded, I got awful tired, and, anyway, he was talking about things I couldn't understand, so I played tit-tat-x with one of the Markdale boys. It was the day I was sitting up in the gallery."

"Well, I hope if you ever do the like again you won't do it in *our* pew," said Felicity severely.

"I ain't going to do it at all," said Peter. "I felt sort of mean all the rest of the day."

"I shall try not to be vexed when people interrupt me when I'm telling stories," wrote the Story Girl. "but it will be hard," she added with a sigh.

"*I* never mind being interrupted," said Felicity.

"I shall try to be cheerful and smiling all the time," wrote Cecily.

"You are, anyway," said Sara Ray loyally.

"I don't believe we ought to be cheerful *all* the time," said the Story Girl. "The Bible says we ought to weep with those who weep."

"But maybe it means that we're to weep cheerfully," suggested Cecily.

"Sorter as if you were thinking, 'I'm very sorry for you but I'm mighty glad I'm not in the scrape too,' " said Dan.

"Dan, don't be irreverent," rebuked Felicity.

"I know a story about old Mr. and Mrs. Davidson of Markdale," said the Story Girl. "She was always smiling and it used to aggravate her husband, so one day he said very crossly, 'Old lady, what *are* you grinning at?' 'Oh, well, Abiram, everything's so bright and pleasant, I've just got to smile.'

"Not long after there came a time when everything went wrong—the crop failed and their best cow died, and Mrs. Davidson had rheumatism; and finally Mr. Davidson fell and broke his leg. But still Mrs. Davidson smiled. 'What in the dickens are you grinning about now, old lady?' he demanded. 'Oh, well, Abiram,' she said, 'everything is so dark and unpleasant I've just got to smile.' 'Well,' said the old man crossly, 'I think you might give your face a rest sometimes.' "

"I shall not talk gossip," wrote Sara Ray with a satisfied air.

"Oh, don't you think that's a little *too* strict?" asked Cecily anxiously. "Of course, it's not right to talk *mean* gossip, but the harmless kind doesn't hurt. If I say to you that Emmy MacPhail is going to get a new fur collar this winter, *that* is harmless gossip, but if I say I don't see how Emmy MacPhail can afford a new fur collar when her father can't pay my father for the oats he got from him, that would be *mean* gossip. If I were you, Sara, I'd put *mean* gossip."

Sara consented to this amendment.

"I will be polite to everybody," was my third resolution, which passed without comment.

"I'll try not to use slang since Cecily doesn't like it," wrote Dan.

"*I* think some slang is real cute," said Felicity.

"The *Family Guide* says it's very vulgar," grinned Dan. "Doesn't it, Sara Stanley?"

"Don't disturb me," said the Story Girl dreamily. "I'm just thinking a beautiful thought."

"I've thought of a resolution to make," cried Felicity. "Mr. Marwood said last Sunday we should always try to think beautiful thoughts and then our lives would be very beautiful. So I shall resolve to think a beautiful thought every morning before breakfast."

"Can you only manage one a day?" queried Dan.

"And why before breakfast?" I asked.

"Because it's easier to think on an empty stomach," said Peter, in all good faith. But Felicity shot a furious glance at him.

"I selected that time," she explained with dignity, "because when I'm brushing my hair before my glass in the morning I'll see my resolution and remember it."

"Mr. Marwood meant that *all* our thoughts ought to be beautiful," said the Story Girl. "If they were, people wouldn't be afraid to say what they think."

"They oughtn't to be afraid to, anyhow," said Felix stoutly. "I'm going to make a resolution to say just what I think always."

"And do you expect to get through the year alive if you do?" asked Dan.

"It might be easy enough to say what you think if you could always be sure just what you *do* think," said the Story Girl. "So often I can't be sure."

"How would you like it if people always said just what they think to you?" asked Felicity.

"I'm not very particular what *some* people think of me," rejoined Felix.

"I notice you don't like to be told by anybody that you're fat," retorted Felicity.

"Oh, dear me, I do wish you wouldn't all say such sarcastic things to each other," said poor Cecily plaintively. "It sounds so horrid the last night of the old year. Dear knows where we'll all be this night next year. Peter, it's your turn."

"I will try," wrote Peter, "to say my prayers every night regular, and not twice one night because I don't expect to have time the next,—like I did the night before the party," he added.

"I s'pose you never said your prayers until we got you to go to church," said Felicity—who had had no hand in inducing Peter to go to church, but had stoutly opposed it, as recorded in the first volume of our family history.

"I did, too," said Peter. "Aunt Jane taught me to say my prayers. Ma hadn't time, being as father had run away; ma had to wash at night same as in daytime."

"I shall learn to cook," wrote the Story Girl, frowning.

"You'd better resolve not to make puddings of—" began Felicity, then stopped as suddenly as if she had bitten off the rest of her sentence and swallowed it. Cecily had nudged her, so she had probably remembered the Story Girl's threat that she would never tell another story if she was ever twitted with the pudding she had made from sawdust. But we all knew what Felicity had started to say and the Story Girl dealt her a most uncousinly glance.

"I will not cry because mother won't starch my aprons," wrote Sara Ray.

"Better resolve not to cry about anything," said Dan kindly.

Sara Ray shook her head forlornly.

"That would be too hard to keep. There are times when I *have* to cry. It's a relief."

"Not to the folks who have to hear you," muttered Dan aside to Cecily.

"Oh, hush," whispered Cecily back. "Don't go and hurt her feelings the last night of the old year. Is it my turn again? Well, I'll resolve not to worry because my hair is not curly. But, oh, I'll never be able to help wishing it was."

"Why don't you curl it as you used to do, then?" asked Dan.

"You know very well that I've never put my hair up in curl papers since the time Peter was dying of the measles," said Cecily reproachfully. "I resolved then I wouldn't because I wasn't sure it was quite right."

"I will keep my finger-nails neat and clean," I wrote. "There, that's four resolutions. I'm not going to make any more. Four's enough."

"I shall always think twice before I speak," wrote Felix.

"That's an awful waste of time," commented Dan, "but I guess you'll need to if you're always going to say what you think."

"I'm going to stop with three," said Peter.

"I will have all the good times I can," wrote the Story Girl.

"*That's* what *I* call sensible," said Dan.

"It's a very easy resolution to keep, anyhow," commented Felix.

"I shall try to like reading the Bible," wrote Sara Ray.

"You ought to like reading the Bible without trying to," exclaimed Felicity.

"If you had to read seven chapters of it every time you were naughty I don't believe you would like it either," retorted Sara Ray with a flash of spirit.

"I shall try to believe only half of what I hear," was Cecily's concluding resolution.

"But which half?" scoffed Dan.

"The best half," said sweet Cecily simply.

"I'll try to obey mother *always,*" wrote Sara Ray, with a tremendous sigh, as if she fully realized the difficulty of keeping such a resolution. "And that's all I'm going to make."

"Felicity has only made one," said the Story Girl.

"I think it better to make just one and keep it than make a lot and break them," said Felicity loftily.

She had the last word on the subject, for it was time for Sara Ray to go, and our circle broke up. Sara and Felix departed and we watched them down the lane in the moonlight—Sara walking demurely in one runner track, and Felix stalking grimly along in the other. I fear the romantic beauty of that silver shining night was entirely thrown away on my misanthropic brother.

And it was, as I remember it, a most exquisite night—a white poem, a frosty, starry lyric of light. It was one of those nights on which one might fall asleep and dream happy dreams of gardens of mirth and song, feeling all the while through one's sleep the soft splendour and radiance of the white moon-world outside, as one hears soft, far-away music sounding through the thoughts and words that are born of it.

As a matter of fact, however, Cecily dreamed that night that she saw three full moons in the sky, and wakened up crying with the horror of it.

CHAPTER 5

THE FIRST NUMBER OF OUR MAGAZINE

THE FIRST number of Our Magazine was ready on New Year's Day, and we read it that evening in the kitchen. All our staff had worked nobly and we were enormously proud of the result, although Dan still continued to scoff at a paper that wasn't printed. The Story Girl and I read it turnabout while the others, except Felix, ate apples. It opened with a short

EDITORIAL

With this number Our Magazine makes its first bow to the public. All the editors have done their best and the various departments are full of valuable information and amusement. The tastefully designed cover is by a famous artist, Mr. Blair Stanley, who sent it to us all the way from Europe at the request of his daughter. Mr. Peter Craig, our enterprising literary editor, contributes a touching love story. (*Peter, aside, in a gratified pig's whisper:* "I never was called 'Mr.' before.") Miss Felicity King's essays on Shakespeare is none the worse for being an old school composition, as it is new to most of our readers. Miss Cecily King contributes a thrilling article of adventure. The various departments are ably edited, and we feel that we have reason to be proud of *Our Magazine.* But we shall not rest on our oars. "Excelsior" shall ever be our motto. We trust that each succeeding issue will be better than the one that went before. We are well aware of many defects, but it is easier to see them than to remedy them. Any suggestion that would tend to the improvement of *Our Magazine* will be thankfully received, but we trust that no criticism will be made that will hurt anyone's feelings. Let us all work together in harmony, and strive to make *Our Magazine* an influence for good and a source of innocent pleasure, and let us always remember the words of the poet.

"The heights by great men reached and kept
Were not attained by sudden flight,
But they, while their companions slept,
Were toiling upwards in the night."

(*Peter, impressively:*—"I've read many a worse editorial in the *Enterprise.*")

ESSAY ON SHAKESPEARE

Shakespeare's full name was William Shakespeare. He did not always spell it the same way. He lived in the reign of Queen Elizabeth and wrote a great many plays. His plays are written in dialogue form. Some people think they were not written by Shakespeare but by another man of the same name. I have read some of them because our school teacher says everybody ought to read them, but I did not care much for them. There are some things in them I cannot understand. I like the stories of Valeria H. Montague in the *Family Guide* ever so much better. They are more exciting and truer to life. *Romeo and Juliet* was one of the plays I read. It was very sad. Juliet dies and I don't like stories where people die. I like it better when they all get married especially to dukes and earls. Shakespeare himself was married to Anne Hathaway. They are both dead now. They have been dead a good while. He was a very famous man.

FELICITY KING.

(*Peter, modestly:* "I don't know much about Shakespeare myself but I've got a book of his plays that belonged to my Aunt Jane, and I guess I'll have to tackle him as soon as I finish with the Bible.")

THE STORY OF AN ELOPEMENT FROM CHURCH

This is a true story. It happened in Markdale to an uncle of my mothers. He wanted to marry Miss Jemima Parr. Felicity says Jemima is not a romantic name for a heroin of a story but I cant help it in this case because it is a true story and her name realy was Jemima. My mothers uncle was named Thomas Taylor. He was poor at that time and so the father of Miss Jemima Parr did not want him for a soninlaw and told him he was not to come near the house or he would set the dog on him. Miss Jemima Parr was very pretty and my mothers uncle Thomas was just crazy about her and she wanted him too. She cried almost every night after her father forbid him to come to the house except the nights she had to sleep or she would have died. And she was so frightened he might try to come for all and get tore up by the dog and it was a bull-dog too that would never let go. But mothers uncle Thomas was too cute for that. He waited till one day there was preaching in the Markdale church in the middle of the week because it was sacrament time and Miss Jemima Parr and her family all went because her father was an elder. My mothers uncle Thomas went too and set in the pew just behind Miss Jemima Parrs family. When they all bowed their heads at prayer time Miss Jemima Parr didnt but set bolt uprite and my mothers uncle Thomas bent over and wispered in her ear. I dont know what he said so I cant right it but Miss Jemima Parr blushed that is turned red and nodded her head. Perhaps some people may think that my mothers uncle Thomas shouldent of wispered at prayer time in church but you must remember that Miss Jemima Parrs father had thretened to set the dog on him and that was hard lines when he was a respektable young man though not rich. Well when they were singing the last sam my mothers uncle Thomas got up and went out very quietly and as soon as church was out Miss Jemima Parr walked out too real quick. Her family never suspekted anything and they hung round talking to folks and shaking hands while Miss Jemima Parr and my mothers uncle Thomas were eloping outside. And what do you suppose they eloped in. Why in Miss Jemima Parrs fathers slay. And when he went out they were gone and his slay was gone also his horse. Of course my mothers uncle Thomas didnt steal the horse. He just borrowed it and sent it home the next day. But before Miss Jemima Parrs father could get another rig to follow them they were so far away he couldent catch them before they got married. And they lived happy together forever afterwards. Mothers uncle Thomas lived to be a very old man. He died very suddent. He felt quite well when he went to sleep and when he woke up he was dead.

PETER CRAIG.

MY MOST EXCITING ADVENTURE

The editor says we must all write up our most exciting adventure for *Our Magazine.* My most exciting adventure happened a year ago last November. I was nearly frightened to death. Dan says he wouldn't of been scared and Felicity says she would of known what it was but it's easy to talk.

It happened the night I went down to see Kitty Marr. I thought when I went that Aunt Olivia was visiting there and I could come home with her. But she wasn't there and I had to come home alone. Kitty came a piece of the way but she wouldn't come any further than Uncle James Frewen's gate. She said it was because it was so windy she was afraid she would get the tooth-ache and not because she was frightened of the ghost of the dog that haunted the bridge in Uncle James' hollow. I did wish she hadn't said anything about the dog because I mightn't of thought about it if she hadn't. I had to go on alone thinking of it. I'd heard the story often but I'd never believed in it. They said the dog used to appear at one end of the bridge and walk across it with people and vanish when he got to the other end. He never tried to bite anyone but one wouldn't want to meet the ghost of a dog even if one didn't believe in him. I knew there was no such thing as ghosts and I kept saying a paraphrase over to myself and the Golden

Text of the next Sunday School lesson but oh, how my heart beat when I got near the hollow! It was so dark. You could just see things dim-like but you couldn't see what they were. When I got to the bridge I walked along sideways with my back to the railing so I couldn't think the dog was behind me. And then just in the middle of the bridge I met something. It was right before me and it was big and black, just about the size of a Newfoundland dog, and I thought I could see a white nose. And it kept jumping about from one side of the bridge to the other. Oh, I hope none of my readers will ever be so frightened as I was then. I was too frightened to run back because I was afraid it would chase me and I couldn't get past it, it moved so quick, and then it just made one spring right on me and I felt its claws and I screamed and fell down. It rolled off to one side and laid there quite quiet but I didn't dare move and I don't know what would have become of me if Amos Cowan hadn't come along that very minute with a lantern. And there was me sitting in the middle of the bridge and that awful thing beside me. And what do you think it was but a big umbrella with a white handle? Amos said it was his umbrella and it had blown away from him and he had to go back and get the lantern to look for it. I felt like asking him what on earth he was going about with an umbrella open when it wasent raining. But the Cowans do such queer things. You remember the time Jerry Cowan sold us God's picture. Amos took me right home and I was thankful for I don't know what would have become of me if he hadn't come along. I couldn't sleep all night and I never want to have any more adventures like that one.

CECILY KING.

PERSONALS

Mr. Dan King felt somewhat indisposed the day after Christmas—probably as the result of too much mince pie. (*Dan, indignantly:*—"I wasn't. I only et one piece!")

Mr. Peter Craig thinks he saw the Family Ghost on Christmas Eve. But the rest of us think all he saw was the white calf with the red tail. (*Peter, muttering sulkily:*—"It's a queer calf that would walk up on end and wring its hands.")

Miss Cecily King spent the night of Dec. 20th with Miss

Kitty Marr. They talked most of the night about new knitted lace patterns and their beaus and were very sleepy in school next day. (*Cecily, sharply:*—"We never mentioned such things!")

Patrick Grayfur, Esq., was indisposed yesterday, but seems to be enjoying his usual health today.

The King family expect their Aunt Eliza to visit them in January. She is really our great-aunt. We have never seen her but we are told she is very deaf and does not like children. So Aunt Janet says we must make ourselves scarece when she comes.

Miss Cecily King has undertaken to fill with names a square of the missionary quilt which the Mission Band is making. You pay five cents to have your name embroidered in a corner, ten cents to have it in the centre, and a quarter if you want it left off altogether. (*Cecily, indignantly:*—"That isn't the way at all.")

HOUSEHOLD DEPARTMENT

Mrs. Alexander King killed all her geese the twentieth of December. We all helped pick them. We had one Christmas Day and will have one every fortnight the rest of the winter.

The bread was sour last week because mother wouldn't take my advice. I told her it was too warm for it in the corner behind the stove.

Miss Felicity King invented a new recete for date cookies recently, which everybody said were excelent. I am not going to publish it though, because I don't want other people to find it out.

ANXIOUS INQUIRER:—If you want to remove inkstains place the stain over steam and apply salt and lemon juice. If it was Dan who sent this question in I'd advise him to stop wiping his pen on his shirt sleeves and then he wouldn't have so many stains.

FELICITY KING.

ETIQUETTE DEPARTMENT

F-l-x:—Yes, you should offer your arm to a lady when seeing her home. but don't keep her standing too long at the gate while you say good night.

(*Felix, enraged:*—"I never asked such a question.")

C-c-l-y:—No, it is not polite to use "Holy Moses" or "dodgasted" in ordinary conversation.

(Cecily had gone down cellar to replenish the apple plate, so this passed without protest.)

S-r-a:—No, it isn't polite to cry all the time. As to whether you should ask a young man in, it all depends on whether he went home with you of his own accord or was sent by some elderly relative.

F-l-t-y:—It does not break any rule of etiquette if you keep a button off your best young man's coat for a keepsake. But don't take more than one or his mother might miss them.

, DAN KING.

FASHION NOTES

Knitted mufflers are much more stylish than crocheted ones this winter. It is nice to have one the same colour as your cap.

Red mittens with a black diamond pattern on the back are much run after. Em Frewen's grandma knits hers for her. She can knit the double diamond pattern and Em puts on such airs about it, but I think the single diamond is in better taste.

The new winter hats at Markdale are very pretty. It is so exciting to pick a hat. Boys can't have that fun. Their hats are so much alike.

CECILY KING.

FUNNY PARAGRAPHS

This is a true joke and really happened.

There was an old local preacher in New Brunswick one time whose name was Samuel Clask. He used to preach and pray and visit the sick just like a regular minister. One day he was visiting a neighbour who was dying and he prayed the Lord to have mercy on him because he was very poor and had worked so hard all his life that he hadn't much time to attend to religion.

"And if you don't believe me, O Lord," Mr. Clask finished up with, "just take a look at his hands."

FELIX KING.

GENERAL INFORMATION BUREAU

DAN:—Do porpoises grow on trees or vines?
Ans. Neither. They inhabit the deep sea.

FELIX KING.

(*Dan, aggrieved:*—"Well, I'd never heard of porpoises and it sounded like something that grew. But you needn't have gone and put it in the paper."

Felix:—"It isn't any worse than the things you put in about me that I never asked at all."

Cecily, soothingly:—"Oh, well, boys, it's all in fun, and I think *Our Magazine* is perfectly elegant."

Felicity, failing to see the Story Girl and Beverley exchanging winks behind her back:—"It certainly is, though *some people* were so opposed to starting it.")

What harmless, happy fooling it all was! How we laughed as we read and listened and devoured apples! Blow high, blow low, no wind can ever quench the ruddy glow of that faraway winter night in our memories. And though *Our Magazine* never made much of a stir in the world, or was the means of hatching any genius, it continued to be capital fun for us throughout the year.

CHAPTER 6

GREAT-AUNT ELIZA'S VISIT

IT WAS a diamond winter day in February—clear, cold, hard, brilliant. The sharp blue sky shone, the white fields and hills glittered, the fringe of icicles around the eaves of Uncle Alec's house sparkled. Keen was the frost and crisp the snow over our world; and we young fry of the King households were all agog to enjoy life—for was it not Saturday, and were we not left all alone to keep house?

Aunt Janet and Aunt Olivia had had their last big "kill" of market poultry the day before; and early in the morning all our grown-ups set forth to Charlottetown, to be gone the whole day. They left us many charges as usual, some of which we remembered and some of which we forgot; but with Felicity in command none of us dared stray far out of line. The Story Girl and Peter came over, of course, and we all agreed that we would haste and get the work done in the forenoon, that we might have an afternoon of uninterrupted enjoyment. A taffy-pull after dinner and then a jolly hour of coasting on the hill field before supper were on our programme. But disappointment was our portion. We did manage to get the taffy made but before we could sample the result satisfactorily, and just as the girls were finishing with the washing of the dishes, Felicity glanced out of the window and exclaimed in tones of dismay,

"Oh, dear me, here's Great-aunt Eliza coming up the lane! Now, isn't that too mean?"

We all looked out to see a tall, gray-haired lady approaching the house, looking about her with the slightly puzzled air of a stranger. We had been expecting Great-aunt Eliza's advent for some weeks, for she was visiting relatives in Markdale. We knew she was liable to pounce down on us any time, being one of those delightful folk who like to "surprise" people, but we had never thought of her coming that particular day. It must be confessed that we did not look forward to her visit with any pleasure. None of us had ever seen her, but we knew she was very deaf, and had very decided opinions as to the way in which children should behave.

273

"Whew!" whistled Dan. "We're in for a jolly afternoon. She's deaf as a post and we'll have to split our throats to make her hear at all. I've a notion to skin out."

"Oh, don't talk like that, Dan," said Cecily reproachfully. "She's old and lonely and has had a great deal of trouble. She has buried three husbands. We must be kind to her and do the best we can to make her visit pleasant."

"She's coming to the back door," said Felicity, with an agitated glance around the kitchen. "I told you, Dan, that you should have shovelled the snow away from the front door this morning. Cecily, set those pots in the pantry quick—hide those boots, Felix—shut the cupboard door, Peter—Sara, straighten up the lounge. She's awfully particular and ma says her house is always as neat as wax."

To do Felicity justice, while she issued orders to the rest of us, she was flying busily about herself, and it was amazing how much was accomplished in the way of putting the kitchen in perfect order during the two minutes in which Great-aunt Eliza was crossing the yard.

"Fortunately the sitting-room is tidy and there's plenty in the pantry," said Felicity, who could face anything undauntedly with a well-stocked larder behind her.

Further conversation was cut short by a decided rap at the door. Felicity opened it.

"Why, how do you do, Aunt Eliza?" she said loudly.

A slightly bewildered look appeared on Aunt Eliza's face. Felicity perceived she had not spoken loudly enough.

"How do you do, Aunt Eliza," she repeated at the top of her voice. "Come in—we are glad to see you. We've been looking for you for ever so long."

"Are your father and mother at home?" asked Aunt Eliza, slowly.

"No, they went to town today. But they'll be home this evening."

"I'm sorry they're away," said Aunt Eliza, coming in, "because I can stay only a few hours."

"Oh, that's too bad," shouted poor Felicity, darting an angry glance at the rest of us, as if to demand why we didn't help her out. "Why, we've been thinking you'd stay a week with us anyway. You *must* stay over Sunday."

"I really can't. I have to go to Charlottetown tonight," returned Aunt Eliza.

"Well, you'll take off your things and stay to tea, at least," urged Felicity, as hospitably as her strained vocal chords would admit.

"Yes, I think I'll do that. I want to get acquainted with my— my nephews and nieces," said Aunt Eliza, with a rather pleasant glance around our group. If I could have associated the thought of such a thing with my preconception of Great-aunt Eliza I could have sworn there was a twinkle in her eye. But of course it was impossible. "Won't you introduce yourselves, please?"

Felicity shouted our names and Great-aunt Eliza shook hands all round. She performed the duty grimly and I concluded I must have been mistaken about the twinkle. She was certainly very tall and dignified and imposing—altogether a great-aunt to be respected.

Felicity and Cecily took her to the spare room and then left her in the sitting-room while they returned to the kitchen, to discuss the matter in family conclave.

"Well, and what do you think of dear Aunt Eliza?" asked Dan.

"S-s-s-sh," warned Cecily, with a glance at the half-open hall door.

"Pshaw," scoffed Dan, "she can't hear us. There ought to be a law against anyone being as deaf as that."

"She's not so old-looking as I expected," said Felix. "If her hair wasn't so white she wouldn't look much older than your mother."

"You don't have to be very old to be a great-aunt," said Cecily. "Kitty Marr has a great-aunt who is just the same age as her mother. I expect it was burying so many husbands turned her hair white. But Aunt Eliza doesn't look just as I expected she would either."

"She's dressed more stylishly than I expected," said Felicity. "I thought she'd be real old-fashioned, but her clothes aren't too bad at all."

"She wouldn't be bad-looking if 'tweren't for her nose," said Peter. "It's too long, and crooked besides."

"You needn't criticize our relations like that," said Felicity tartly.

"Well, aren't you doing it yourselves?" expostulated Peter.

"That's different," retorted Felicity. "Never you mind Great-aunt Eliza's nose."

"Well, don't expect me to talk to her," said Dan, "'cause I won't."

"I'm going to be very polite to her," said Felicity. "She's rich. But how are we to entertain her, that's the question."

"What does the *Family Guide* say about entertaining your rich, deaf old aunt?" queried Dan ironically.

"The *Family Guide* says we should be polite to *everybody,*" said Cecily, with a reproachful look at Dan.

"The worst of it is," said Felicity, looking worried, "that there isn't a bit of old bread in the house and she can't eat new, I've heard father say. It gives her indigestion. What will we do?"

"Make a pan of rusks and apologize for having no old bread," suggested the Story Girl, probably by way of teasing Felicity. The latter, however, took it in all good faith.

"The *Family Guide* says we should never apologize for things we can't help. It says it's adding insult to injury to do it. But you run over home for a loaf of stale bread, Sara, and it's a good idea about the rusks. I'll make a panful."

"Let me make them," said the Story Girl, eagerly. "I can make real good rusks now."

"No, it wouldn't do to trust you," said Felicity mercilessly. "You might make some queer mistake and Aunt Eliza would tell it all over the country. She's a fearful old gossip. I'll make the rusks myself. She hates cats, so we mustn't let Paddy be seen. And she's a Methodist, so mind nobody says anything against Methodists to her."

"Who's going to say anything, anyhow?" asked Peter belligerently.

"I wonder if I might ask her for her name for my quilt square?" speculated Cecily. "I believe I will. She looks so much friendlier than I expected. Of course she'll choose the five-cent section. She's an estimable old lady, but very economical."

"Why don't you say she's so mean she'd skin a flea for its hide and tallow?" said Dan. "That's the plain truth."

"Well, I'm going to see about getting tea," said Felicity, "so the rest of you will have to entertain her. You better go in and show her the photographs in the album. Dan, you do it."

"Thank you, that's a girl's job," said Dan. "I'd look nice sitting up to Aunt Eliza and yelling out that this was Uncle Jim and 'tother Cousin Sarah's twins, wouldn't I? Cecily or the Story Girl can do it."

"I don't know all the pictures in your album," said the Story Girl hastily.

"I s'pose I'll have to do it, though I don't like to," sighed Cecily. "But we ought to go in. We've left her alone too long now. She'll think we have no manners."

Accordingly we all filed in rather reluctantly. Great-aunt Eliza was toasting her toes—clad, as we noted, in very smart and shapely shoes—at the stove and looking quite at her ease. Cecily, determined to do her duty even in the face of such fearful odds as Great-aunt Eliza's deafness, dragged a ponderous, plush-covered album from its corner and proceeded to display and explain the family photographs. She did her brave best but she could not shout like Felicity, and half the time, as she confided to me later on, she felt that Great-aunt Eliza did not hear one word she said, because she didn't seem to take in who the people were, though, just like all deaf folks, she wouldn't let on. Great-aunt Eliza certainly didn't talk much; she looked at the photographs in silence, but she smiled now and then. That smile bothered me. It was so twinkly and so very un-great-aunt-Elizaish. But I felt indignant with her. I thought she might have shown a little more appreciation of Cecily's gallant efforts to entertain.

It was very dull for the rest of us. The Story Girl sat rather sulkily in her corner; she was angry because Felicity would not let her make the rusks, and also, perhaps, a little vexed because she could not charm Great-aunt Eliza with her golden voice and story-telling gift. Felix and I looked at each other and wished ourselves out in the hill field, careering gloriously adown its gleaming crust.

But presently a little amusement came our way. Dan, who was sitting behind Great-aunt Eliza, and consequently out of her view, began making comments on Cecily's explanation of this one and that one among the photographs. In vain Cecily implored him to stop. It was too good fun to give up. For the next half-hour the dialogue ran after this fashion, while Peter and Felix and I, and even the Story Girl, suffered agonies trying to smother our bursts of laughter—for Great-aunt Eliza could see if she couldn't hear:

Cecily, shouting:—"That is Mr. Joseph Elliott of Markdale, a second cousin of mother's."

Dan:—"Don't brag of it, Sis. He's the man who was asked if somebody else said something in sincerity and old Joe said 'No, he said it in my cellar.'"

Cecily:—"This isn't anybody in *our* family. It's little Xavy Gautier who used to be hired with Uncle Roger."

Dan:—"Uncle Roger sent him to fix a gate one day and scolded him because he didn't do it right, and Xavy was mad as hops and said 'How you 'spect me to fix dat gate? I never learned jogerfy.'"

Cecily, with an anguished glance at Dan:—"This is Great-uncle Robert King."

Dan:—"He's been married four times. Don't you think that's often enough, dear great-aunty?"

Cecily:—"(Dan! !) This is a nephew of Mr. Ambrose Marr's. He lives out west and teaches school."

Dan:—"Yes, and Uncle Roger says he doesn't know enough not to sleep in a field with the gate open."

Cecily:—"This is Miss Julia Stanley, who used to teach in Carlisle a few years ago."

Dan:—"When she resigned the trustees had a meeting to see if they'd ask her to stay and raise her supplement. Old Highland Sandy was alive then and he got up and said, 'If she for go let her for went. Perhaps she for marry.'"

Cecily, with the air of a martyr:—"This is Mr. Layton, who used to travel around selling Bibles and hymn books and Talmage's sermons."

Dan:—"He was so thin Uncle Roger used to say he always mistook him for a crack in the atmosphere. One time he stayed here all night and went to prayer meeting and Mr. Marwood asked him to lead in prayer. It had been raining 'most every day for three weeks, and it was just in haymaking time, and everybody thought the hay was going to be ruined, and old Layton got up and prayed that God would send gentle showers on the growing crops, and I heard Uncle Roger whisper to a fellow behind me, 'If somebody don't choke him off we won't get the hay made this summer.'"

Cecily, in exasperation:—"(Dan, shame on you for telling such irreverent stories.) This is Mrs. Alexander Scott of Markdale. She has been very sick for a long time."

Dan:—"Uncle Roger says all that keeps her alive is that she's scared her husband will marry again."

Cecily:—"This is old Mr. James MacPherson who used to live behind the graveyard."

Dan:—"He's the man who told mother once that he always made his own iodine out of strong tea and baking soda."

Cecily:—"This is Cousin Ebenezer MacPherson on the Markdale road."

Dan:—"Great temperance man! He never tasted rum in his life. He took the measles when he was forty-five and was crazy as a loon with them, and the doctor ordered them to give him a dose of brandy. When he swallowed it he looked up and says, solemn as an owl, 'Give it to me oftener and more at a time.' "

Cecily, imploringly:—"(Dan, do stop. You make me so nervous I don't know what I'm doing.) This is Mr. Lemuel Goodridge. He is a minister."

Dan:—"You ought to see his mouth. Uncle Roger says the drawing string has fell out of it. It just hangs loose—so fashion."

Dan, whose own mouth was far from being beautiful, here gave an imitation of the Rev. Lemuel's, to the utter undoing of Peter, Felix, and myself. Our wild guffaws of laughter penetrated even Great-aunt Eliza's deafness, and she glanced up with a startled face. What we would have done I do not know had not Felicity at that moment appeared in the doorway with panic-stricken eyes and exclaimed,

"Cecily, come here for a moment."

Cecily, glad of even a temporary respite, fled to the kitchen and we heard her demanding what was the matter.

"Matter!" exclaimed Felicity, tragically. "Matter enough! Some of you left a soup plate with molasses in it on the pantry table and Pat got into it and what do you think? He went into the spare room and walked all over Aunt Eliza's things on the bed. You can see his tracks plain as plain. What in the world can we do? She'll be simply furious."

I looked apprehensively at Great-aunt Eliza; but she was gazing intently at a picture of Aunt Janet's sister's twins, a most stolid, uninteresting pair; but evidently Great-aunt Eliza found them amusing for she was smiling widely over them.

"Let us take a little clean water and a soft bit of cotton," came Cecily's clear voice from the kitchen, "and see if we can't clean the molasses off. The coat and hat are both cloth, and molasses isn't like grease."

"Well, we can try, but I wish the Story Girl would keep her cat home," grumbled Felicity.

The Story Girl here flew out to defend her pet, and we four boys sat on, miserably conscious of Great-aunt Eliza, who never said a word to us, despite her previously expressed desire to become acquainted with us. She kept on looking at the photographs and seemed quite oblivious of our presence.

Presently the girls returned, having, as transpired later, been so successful in removing the traces of Paddy's mischief that it was not deemed necessary to worry Great-aunt Eliza with any account of it. Felicity announced tea and, while Cecily conveyed Great-aunt Eliza out to the dining-room, lingered behind to consult with us for a moment.

"Ought we to ask her to say grace?" she wanted to know.

"I know a story," said the Story Girl, "about Uncle Roger when he was just a young man. He went to the house of a very deaf old lady and when they sat down to the table she asked him to say grace. Uncle Roger had never done such a thing in his life and he turned as red as a beet and looked down and muttered, 'E-r-r, please excuse me—I—I'm not accustomed to doing that.' Then he looked up and the old lady said 'Amen,' loudly and cheerfully. She thought Uncle Roger was saying grace all the time."

"I don't think it's right to tell funny stories about such things," said Felicity coldly. "And I asked for your opinion, not for a story."

"If we don't ask her, Felix must say it, for he's the only one who can, and we must have it, or she'd be shocked."

"Oh, ask her—ask her," advised Felix hastily.

She was asked accordingly and said grace without any hesitation, after which she proceeded to eat heartily of the excellent supper Felicity had provided. The rusks were especially good and Great-aunt Eliza ate three of them and praised them. Apart from that she said little and during the first part of the meal we sat in embarrassed silence. Towards the last, however, our tongues were loosened, and the Story Girl told us a tragic tale of old Charlottetown and a governor's wife who had died of a broken heart in the early days of the colony.

"They say that story isn't true," said Felicity. "They say what she really died of was indigestion. The Governor's wife who lives there now is a relation of our own. She is a second cousin of father's but we've never seen her. Her name was Agnes Clark. And mind you, when father was a young man he was dead in love with her and so was she with him."

"Who ever told you that?" exclaimed Dan.

"Aunt Olivia. And I've heard ma teasing father about it, too. Of course, it was before father got acquainted with mother."

"Why didn't your father marry her?" I asked.

"Well, she just simply wouldn't marry him in the end. She got over being in love with him. I guess she was pretty fickle. Aunt Olivia said father felt awful about it for awhile, but he got over it when he met ma. Ma was twice as goodlooking as Agnes Clark. Agnes was a sight for freckles, so Aunt Olivia says. But she and father remained real good friends. Just think, if she had married him we would have been the children of the Governor's wife."

"But she wouldn't have been the Governor's wife then," said Dan.

"I guess it's just as good being father's wife," declared Cecily loyally.

"You might think so if you saw the Governor," chuckled Dan. "Uncle Roger says it would be no harm to worship him because he doesn't look like anything in the heavens above or on the earth beneath or the waters under the earth."

"Oh, Uncle Roger just says that because he's on the opposite side of politics," said Cecily. "The Governor isn't really so very ugly. I saw him at the Markdale picnic two years ago. He's very fat and bald and red-faced, but I've seen far worse looking men."

"I'm afraid your seat is too near the stove, Aunt Eliza," shouted Felicity.

Our guest, whose face was certainly very much flushed, shook her head.

"Oh, no, I'm very comfortable," she said. But her voice had the effect of making us uncomfortable. There was a queer, uncertain little sound in it. Was Great-aunt Eliza laughing at us? We looked at her sharply but her face was very solemn.

Only her eyes had a suspicious appearance. Somehow, we did not talk much more the rest of the meal.

When it was over Great-aunt Eliza said she was very sorry but she must really go. Felicity politely urged her to stay, but was much relieved when Great-aunt Eliza adhered to her intention of going. When Felicity took her to the spare room Cecily slipped upstairs and presently came back with a little parcel in her hand.

"What have you got there?" demanded Felicity suspiciously.

"A—a little bag of rose-leaves," faltered Cecily. "I thought I'd give them to Aunt Eliza."

"The idea! Don't you do such a thing," said Felicity contemptuously. "She'd think you were crazy."

"She was awfully nice when I asked her for her name for the quilt," protested Cecily, "and she took a ten-cent section after all. So I'd like to give her the rose-leaves—and I'm going to, too, Miss Felicity."

Great-aunt Eliza accepted the little gift quite graciously, bade us all good-bye, said she had enjoyed herself very much, left messages for father and mother, and finally betook herself away. We watched her cross the yard, tall, stately, erect, and disappear down the lane. Then, as often aforetime, we gathered together in the cheer of the red hearth-flame, while outside the wind of a winter twilight sang through fair white valleys brimmed with a reddening sunset, and a faint, serene, silver-cold star glimmered over the willow at the gate.

"Well," said Felicity, drawing a relieved breath, "I'm glad she's gone. She certainly is queer, just as mother said."

"It's a different kind of queerness from what I expected, though," said the Story Girl meditatively. "There's something I can't quite make out about Aunt Eliza. I don't think I altogether like her."

"I'm precious sure I don't," said Dan.

"Oh, well, never mind. She's gone now and that's the last of it," said Cecily comfortingly.

But it wasn't the last of it—not by any manner of means was it! When our grown-ups returned almost the first words Aunt Janet said were,

"And so you had the Governor's wife to tea?"

We all stared at her.

"I don't know what you mean," said Felicity. "We had

nobody to tea except Great-aunt Eliza. She came this afternoon and—"

"Great-aunt Eliza? Nonsense," said Aunt Janet. "Aunt Eliza was in town today. She had tea with us at Aunt Louisa's. But wasn't Mrs. Governor Lesley here? We met her on her way back to Charlottetown and she told us she was. She said she was visiting a friend in Carlisle and thought she'd call to see father for old acquaintance sake. What in the world are all you children staring like that for? Your eyes are like saucers."

"There was a lady here to tea," said Felicity miserably, "but we thought it was Great-aunt Eliza—she never *said* she wasn't— I thought she acted queer—and we all yelled at her as if she was deaf—and said things to each other about her nose—and Pat running over her clothes—"

"She must have heard all you said while I was showing her the photographs, Dan," cried Cecily.

"And about the Governor at tea time," chuckled unrepentant Dan.

"I want to know what all this means," said Aunt Janet sternly.

She knew in due time, after she had pieced the story together from our disjointed accounts. She was horrified, and Uncle Alec was mildly disturbed, but Uncle Roger roared with laughter and Aunt Olivia echoed it.

"To think you should have so little sense!" said Aunt Janet in a disgusted tone.

"I think it was real mean of her to pretend she was deaf," said Felicity, almost on the verge of tears.

"That was Agnes Clark all over," chuckled Uncle Roger. "How she must have enjoyed this afternoon!"

She had enjoyed it, as we learned the next day, when a letter came from her.

"Dear Cecily and all the rest of you," wrote the Governor's wife, "I want to ask you to forgive me for pretending to be Aunt Eliza. I suspect it was a little horrid of me, but really I couldn't resist the temptation, and if you will forgive me for it I will forgive you for the things you said about the Governor, and we will all be good friends. You know the Governor is a very nice man, though he has the misfortune not to be handsome.

"I had just a splendid time at your place, and I envy your

Aunt Eliza her nephews and nieces. You were all so nice to me, and I didn't dare to be a bit nice to you lest I should give myself away. But I'll make up for that when you come to see me at Government House, as you all must the very next time you come to town. I'm so sorry I didn't see Paddy, for I love pussy cats, even if they do track molasses over my clothes. And, Cecily, thank you ever so much for that little bag of pot-pourri. It smells like a hundred rose gardens, and I have put it between the sheets for my very sparest room bed, where you shall sleep when you come to see me, you dear thing. And the Governor wants you to put his name on the quilt square, too, in the ten-cent section.

"Tell Dan I enjoyed his comments on the photographs very much. They were quite a refreshing contrast to the usual ex-planations of 'who's who.' And Felicity, your rusks were per-fection. Do send me your recipe for them, there's a darling.
    "Yours most cordially,
                    "AGNES CLARK LESLEY."

"Well, it was decent of her to apologize, anyhow," commented Dan.

"If we only hadn't said that about the Governor," moaned Felicity.

"How did you make your rusks?" asked Aunt Janet. "There was no baking-powder in the house, and I never could get them right with soda and cream of tartar."

"There was plenty of baking-powder in the pantry," said Felicity.

"No, there wasn't a particle. I used the last making those cookies Thursday morning."

"But I found another can nearly full, away back on the top shelf, ma,—the one with the yellow label. I guess you forgot it was there."

Aunt Janet stared at her pretty daughter blankly. Then amaze-ment gave place to horror.

"Felicity King!" she exclaimed. "You don't mean to tell me that you raised those rusks with the stuff that was in that old yellow can?"

"Yes, I did," faltered Felicity, beginning to look scared. "Why, ma, what was the matter with it?"

"Matter! That stuff was *tooth-powder*, that's what it was.

Your Cousin Myra broke the bottle her tooth-powder was in when she was here last winter and I gave her that old can to keep it in. She forgot to take it when she went away and I put it on that top shelf. I declare you must all have been bewitched yesterday."

Poor, poor Felicity! If she had not always been so horribly vain over her cooking and so scornfully contemptuous of other people's aspirations and mistakes along that line, I could have found it in my heart to pity her.

The Story Girl would have been more than human if she had not betrayed a little triumphant amusement, but Peter stood up for his lady manfully.

"The rusks were splendid, anyhow, so what difference does it make what they were raised with?"

Dan, however, began to taunt Felicity with her tooth-powder rusks, and kept it up for the rest of his natural life.

"Don't forget to send the Governor's wife the recipe for them," he said.

Felicity, with eyes tearful and cheeks crimson from mortification, rushed from the room, but never, never did the Governor's wife get the recipe for those rusks.

CHAPTER 7

WE VISIT COUSIN MATTIE'S

ONE SATURDAY in March we walked over to Baywater, for a long-talked-of visit to Cousin Mattie Dilke. By the road, Baywater was six miles away, but there was a short cut across hills and fields and woods which was scantly three. We did not look forward to our visit with any particular delight, for there was nobody at Cousin Mattie's except grown-ups who had been grown up so long that it was rather hard for them to remember they had ever been children. But, as Felicity told us, it was necessary to visit Cousin Mattie at least once a year, or else she would be "huffed," so we concluded we might as well go and have it over.

"Anyhow, we'll get a splendiferous dinner," said Dan. "Cousin Mattie's a great cook and there's nothing stingy about her."

"You are always thinking of your stomach," said Felicity pleasantly.

"Well, you know I couldn't get along very well without it, darling," responded Dan who, since New Year's, had adopted a new method of dealing with Felicity—whether by way of keeping his resolution or because he had discovered that it annoyed Felicity far more than angry retorts, deponent sayeth not. He invariably met her criticisms with a good-natured grin and a flippant remark with some tender epithet tagged on to it. Poor Felicity used to get hopelessly furious over it.

Uncle Alec was dubious about our going that day. He looked abroad on the general dourness of gray earth and gray air and gray sky, and said a storm was brewing. But Cousin Mattie had been sent word that we were coming, and she did not like to be disappointed, so he let us go, warning us to stay with Cousin Mattie all night if the storm came on while we were there.

We enjoyed our walk—even Felix enjoyed it, although he had been appointed to write up the visit for *Our Magazine* and was rather weighed down by the responsibility of it. What mattered it though the world were gray and wintry? We walked the golden road and carried spring time in our hearts, and we beguiled our way with laughter and jest, and the tales the Story Girl told us—myths and legends of elder time.

The walking was good, for there had lately been a thaw and everything was frozen. We went over fields, crossed by spidery trails of gray fences, where the withered grasses stuck forlornly up through the snow; we lingered for a time in a group of hill pines, great, majestic tree-creatures, friends of evening stars; and finally struck into the belt of fir and maple which intervened between Carlisle and Baywater. It was in this locality that Peg Bowen lived, and our way lay near her house though not directly in sight of it. We hoped we would not meet her, for since the affair of the bewitchment of Paddy we did not know quite what to think of Peg; the boldest of us held his breath as we passed her haunts, and drew it again with a sigh of relief when they were safely left behind.

The woods were full of the brooding stillness that often precedes a storm, and the wind crept along their white, cone-sprinkled floors with a low, wailing cry. Around us were solitudes of snow, arcades picked out in pearl and silver, long avenues of untrodden marble whence sprang the cathedral columns of the firs. We were all sorry when we were through the woods and found ourselves looking down into the snug, commonplace, farmstead-dotted settlement of Baywater.

"There's Cousin Mattie's house—that big white one at the turn of the road," said the Story Girl. "I hope she has that dinner ready, Dan. I'm hungry as a wolf after our walk."

"I wish Cousin Mattie's husband was still alive," said Dan. "He was an awful nice old man. He always had his pockets full of nuts and apples. I used to like going there better when he was alive. Too many old women don't suit me."

"Oh, Dan, Cousin Mattie and her sisters-in-law are just as nice and kind as they can be," reproached Cecily.

"Oh, they're kind enough, but they never seem to see that a fellow gets over being five years old if he only lives long enough," retorted Dan.

"I know a story about Cousin Mattie's husband," said the Story Girl. "His name was Ebenezer, you know—"

"Is it any wonder he was thin and stunted looking?" said Dan.

"Ebenezer is just as nice a name as Daniel," said Felicity.

"Do you *really* think so, my angel?" inquired Dan, in honey-sweet tones.

"Go on. Remember your second resolution," I whispered to the Story Girl, who was stalking along with an outraged expression.

The Story Girl swallowed something and went on.

"Cousin Ebenezer had a horror of borrowing. He thought it was simply a dreadful disgrace to borrow *anything*. Well, you know he and Cousin Mattie used to live in Carlisle, where the Rays now live. This was when Grandfather King was alive. One day Cousin Ebenezer came up the hill and into the kitchen where all the family were. Uncle Roger said he looked as if he had been stealing sheep. He sat for a whole hour in the kitchen and hardly spoke a word, but just looked miserable. At last he got up and said in a desperate sort of way, 'Uncle Abraham, can I speak with you in private for a minute?' 'Oh, certainly,' said grandfather, and took him into the parlour. Cousin Ebenezer shut the door, looked all around him and then said imploringly, *'More private still.'* So grandfather took him into the spare room and shut that door. He was getting frightened. He thought something terrible must have happened Cousin Ebenezer. Cousin Ebenezer came right up to grandfather, took hold of the lapel of his coat, and said in a whisper, 'Uncle Abraham, *can—you—lend—me—an—axe?'* "

"He needn't have made such a mystery about it," said Cecily, who had missed the point entirely, and couldn't see why the rest of us were laughing. But Cecily was such a darling that we did not mind her lack of a sense of humour.

"It's kind of mean to tell stories like that about people who are dead," said Felicity.

"Sometimes it's safer than when they're alive though, sweetheart," commented Dan.

We had our expected good dinner at Cousin Mattie's—may it be counted unto her for righteousness. She and her sisters-in-law, Miss Louisa Jane and Miss Caroline, were very kind to us. We had quite a nice time, although I understood why Dan objected to them when they patted us all on the head and told us whom we resembled and gave us peppermint lozenges.

--------- CHAPTER 8 ---------

WE VISIT PEG BOWEN

WE LEFT Cousin Mattie's early, for it still looked like a storm, though no more so than it had in the morning. We intended to go home by a different path—one leading through cleared land overgrown with scrub maple, which had the advantage of being farther away from Peg Bowen's house. We hoped to be home before it began to storm, but we had hardly reached the hill above the village when a fine, driving snow began to fall. It would have been wiser to have turned back even then; but we had already come a mile and we thought we would have ample time to reach home before it became really bad. We were sadly mistaken; by the time we had gone another half-mile we were in the thick of a bewildering, blinding snowstorm. But it was by now just as far back to Cousin Mattie's as it was to Uncle Alec's, so we struggled on, growing more frightened at every step. We could hardly face the stinging snow, and we could not see ten feet ahead of us. It had turned bitterly cold and the tempest howled all around us in white desolation under the fast-darkening night. The narrow path we were trying to follow soon became entirely obliterated and we stumbled blindly on, holding to each other, and trying to peer through the furious whirl that filled the air. Our plight had come upon us so suddenly that we could not realize it. Presently Peter, who was leading the van because he was supposed to know the path best, stopped.

"I can't see the road any longer," he shouted. "I don't know where we are."

We all stopped and huddled together in a miserable group. Fear filled our hearts. It seemed ages ago that we had been snug and safe and warm at Cousin Mattie's. Cecily began to cry with cold. Dan, in spite of her protests, dragged off his overcoat and made her put it on.

"We can't stay here," he said. "We'll all freeze to death if we do. Come on—we've got to keep moving. The snow ain't so deep yet. Take hold of my hand, Cecily. We must all hold together. Come, now."

"It won't be nice to be frozen to death, but if we get through alive think what a story we'll have to tell," said the Story Girl between her chattering teeth.

In my heart I did not believe we would ever get through alive. It was almost pitch dark now, and the snow grew deeper every moment. We were chilled to the heart. I thought how nice it would be to lie down and rest; but I remembered hearing that that was fatal, and I endeavoured to stumble on with the others. It was wonderful how the girls kept up, even Cecily. It occurred to me to be thankful that Sara Ray was not with us.

But we were wholly lost now. All around us was a horror of great darkness. Suddenly Felicity fell. We dragged her up, but she declared she could not go on—she was done out.

"Have you any idea where we are?" shouted Dan to Peter.
"No," Peter shouted back, "the wind is blowing every which
way. I haven't any idea where home is."

Home! Would we ever see it again? We tried to urge Felicity
on, but she only repeated drowsily that she must lie down and
rest. Cecily, too, was reeling against me. The Story Girl still
stood up staunchly and counselled struggling on, but she was
numb with cold and her words were hardly distinguishable.
Some wild idea was in my mind that we must dig a hole in
the snow and all creep into it. I had read somewhere that
people had thus saved their lives in snowstorms. Suddenly Felix
gave a shout.

"I see a light," he cried.

"Where? Where?" We all looked but could see nothing.

"I don't see it now but I saw it a moment ago," shouted
Felix. "I'm sure I did. Come on—over in this direction."

Inspired with fresh hope we hurried after him. Soon we all
saw the light—and never shone a fairer beacon. A few more
steps and, coming into the shelter of the woodland on the
further side, we realized where we were.

"That's Peg Bowen's house," exclaimed Peter, stopping short
in dismay.

"I don't care whose house it is," declared Dan. "We've got
to go to it."

"I s'pose so," acquiesced Peter ruefully. "We can't freeze to
death even if she is a witch."

"For goodness' sake don't say anything about witches so close
to her house," gasped Felicity. "I'll be thankful to get in
anywhere."

We reached the house, climbed the flight of steps that led
to that mysterious second story door, and Dan rapped. The
door opened promptly and Peg Bowen stood before us, in what
seemed exactly the same costume she had worn on the mem-
orable day when we had come, bearing gifts, to propitiate her
in the matter of Paddy.

Behind her was a dim room scantly illumined by the one
small candle that had guided us through the storm; but the old
Waterloo stove was colouring the gloom with tremulous, rose-
red whorls of light, and warm and cosy indeed seemed Peg's
retreat to us snow-covered, frost-chilled, benighted wanderers.

"Gracious goodness, where did yez all come from?" exclaimed Peg. "Did they turn yez out?"

"We've been over to Baywater, and we got lost in the storm coming back," explained Dan. "We didn't know where we were till we saw your light. I guess we'll have to stay here till the storm is over—if you don't mind."

"And if it won't inconvenience you," said Cecily timidly.

"Oh, it's no inconvenience to speak of. Come in. Well, yez *have* got some snow on yez. Let me get a broom. You boys stomp your feet well and shake your coats. You girls give me your things and I'll hang them up. Guess yez are most froze. Well, sit up to the stove and git het up."

Peg bustled away to gather up a dubious assortment of chairs, with backs and rungs missing, and in a few minutes we were in a circle around her roaring stove, getting dried and thawed out. In our wildest flights of fancy we had never pictured ourselves as guests at the witch's hearthstone. Yet here we were; and the witch herself was actually brewing a jorum of ginger tea for Cecily, who continued to shiver long after the rest of us were roasted to the marrow. Poor Sis drank that scalding draught, being in too great awe of Peg to do aught else.

"That'll soon fix your shivers," said our hostess kindly. "And now I'll get yez all some tea."

"Oh, please don't trouble," said the Story Girl hastily.

"'Tain't any trouble," said Peg briskly; then, with one of the sudden changes to fierceness which made her such a terrifying personage, "Do yez think my vittels ain't clean?"

"Oh, no, no," cried Felicity quickly, before the Story Girl could speak, "none of us would ever think *that*. Sara only meant she didn't want you to go to any bother on our account."

"It ain't any bother," said Peg, mollified. "I'm spry as a cricket this winter, though I have the realagy sometimes. Many a good bite I've had in your ma's kitchen. I owe yez a meal."

No more protests were made. We sat in awed silence, gazing with timid curiosity about the room, the stained, plastered walls of which were well-nigh covered with a motley assortment of pictures, chromos, and advertisements, pasted on without much regard for order or character. We had heard much of Peg's pets and now we saw them. Six cats occupied various cosy corners; one of them, the black goblin which had so terrified us in the summer, blinked satirically at us from the centre of Peg's bed. Another, a dilapidated, striped beastie, with both ears and one eye gone, glared at us from the sofa in the corner. A dog, with only three legs, lay behind the stove; a crow sat on a roost above our heads, in company with a matronly old hen; and on the clock shelf were a stuffed monkey and a grinning skull. We had heard that a sailor had given Peg the monkey. But where had she got the skull? And whose was it? I could not help puzzling over these gruesome questions.

Presently tea was ready and we gathered around the festal board—a board literally as well as figuratively, for Peg's table was the work of her own unskilled hands. The less said about the viands of that meal, and the dishes they were served in, the better. But we ate them—bless you, yes!—as we would have eaten any witch's banquet set before us. Peg might or might not be a witch—common sense said not; but we knew she was quite capable of turning every one of us out of doors in one of her sudden fierce fits if we offended her; and we had no mind to trust ourselves again to that wild forest where we had fought a losing fight with the demon forces of night and storm.

But it was not an agreeable meal in more ways than one. Peg was not at all careful of anybody's feelings. She hurt Felix's cruelly as she passed him his cup of tea.

"You've gone too much to flesh, boy. So the magic seed didn't work, hey?"

How in the world had Peg found out about that magic seed? Felix looked uncommonly foolish.

"If you'd come to me in the first place I'd soon have told you how to get thin," said Peg, nodding wisely.

"Won't you tell me now?" asked Felix eagerly, his desire to melt his too solid flesh overcoming his dread and shame.

"No, I don't like being second fiddle," answered Peg with a crafty smile. "Sara, you're too scrawny and pale—not much like your ma. I knew her well. She was counted a beauty, but she made no great things of a match. Your father had some money but he was a tramp like meself. Where is he now?"

"In Rome," said the Story Girl rather shortly.

"People thought your ma was crazy when she took him. But she'd a right to please herself. Folks is too ready to call other folks crazy. There's people who say *I'm* not in my right mind.

Did yez ever"—Peg fixed Felicity with a piercing glance—"hear anything so ridiculous?"

"Never," said Felicity, white to the lips.

"I wish everybody was as sane as I am," said Peg scornfully. Then she looked poor Felicity over critically. "You're good-looking but proud. And your complexion won't wear. It'll be like your ma's yet—too much red in it."

"Well, that's better than being the colour of mud," muttered Peter, who wasn't going to hear his lady traduced, even by a witch. All the thanks he got was a furious look from Felicity, but Peg had not heard him and now she turned her attention to Cecily.

"You look delicate. I daresay you'll never live to grow up."

Cecily's lip trembled and Dan's face turned crimson.

"Shut up," he said to Peg. "You've no business to say such things to people."

I think my jaw dropped. I know Peter's and Felix's did. Felicity broke in wildly.

"Oh, don't mind him, Miss Bowen. He's got *such* a temper— that's just the way he talks to us all at home. *Please* excuse him."

"Bless you, I don't mind him," said Peg, from whom the unexpected seemed to be the thing to expect. "I like a lad of spurrit. And so your father run away, did he, Peter? He used to be a beau of mine—he seen me home three times from singing school when we was young. Some folks said he did it for a dare. There's such a lot of jealousy in the world, ain't there? Do you know where he is now?"

"No," said Peter.

"Well, he's coming home before long," said Peg mysteriously.

"Who told you that?" cried Peter in amazement.

"Better not ask," responded Peg, looking up at the skull.

If she meant to make the flesh creep on our bones she succeeded. But now, much to our relief, the meal was over and Peg invited us to draw our chairs up to the stove again.

"Make yourselves at home," she said, producing her pipe from her pocket. "I ain't one of the kind who thinks their houses too good to live in. Guess I won't bother washing the dishes. They'll do yez for breakfast if yez don't forget your places. I s'pose none of yez smokes."

"No," said Felicity, rather primly.

"Then yez don't know what's good for yez," retorted Peg, rather grumpily. But a few whiffs of her pipe placated her and, observing Cecily sigh, she asked her kindly what was the matter.

"I'm thinking how worried they'll be at home about us," explained Cecily.

"Bless you, dearie, don't be worrying over that. I'll send them word that yez are all snug and safe here."

"But how can you?" cried amazed Cecily.

"Better not ask," said Peg again, with another glance at the skull.

An uncomfortable silence followed, finally broken by Peg, who introduced her pets to us and told how she had come by them. The black cat was her favourite.

"That cat knows more than I do, if yez'll believe it," she said proudly. "I've got a rat too, but he's a bit shy when strangers is round. Your cat got all right again that time, didn't he?"

"Yes," said the Story Girl.

"Thought he would," said Peg, nodding sagely. "I seen to that. Now, don't yez all be staring at the hole in my dress."

"We weren't," was our chorus of protest.

"Looked as if yez were. I tore that yesterday but I didn't mend it. I was brought up to believe that a hole was an accident but a patch was a disgrace. And so your Aunt Olivia is going to be married after all?"

This was news to us. We felt and looked dazed.

"I never heard anything of it," said the Story Girl.

"Oh, it's true enough. She's a great fool. I've no faith in husbands. But one good thing is she ain't going to marry that Henry Jacobs of Markdale. He wants her bad enough. Just like his presumption,—thinking himself good enough for a King. His father is the worst man alive. He chased me off his place with his dog once. But I'll get even with him yet."

Peg looked very savage, and visions of burned barns floated through our minds.

"He'll be punished in hell, you know," said Peter timidly.

"But I won't be there to see that," rejoined Peg. "Some folks say I'll go there because I don't go to church oftener. But *I* don't believe it."

"Why don't you go?" asked Peter, with a temerity that bordered on rashness.

"Well, I've got so sunburned I'm afraid folks might take me for an Injun," explained Peg, quite seriously. "Besides, your minister makes such awful long prayers. Why does he do it?"

"I suppose he finds it easier to talk to God than to people," suggested Peter reflectively.

"Well, anyway, I belong to the round church," said Peg comfortably, "and so the devil can't catch *me* at the corners. I haven't been to Carlisle church for over three years. I thought I'd a-died laughing the last time I was there. Old Elder Marr took up the collection that day. He'd on a pair of new boots and they squeaked all the way up and down the aisles. And every time the boots squeaked the elder made a face, like he had toothache. It was awful funny. How's your missionary quilt coming on, Cecily?"

Was there anything Peg didn't know?

"Very well," said Cecily.

"You can put my name on it, if you want to."

"Oh, thank you. Which section—the five-cent one or the ten-cent one?" asked Cecily timidly.

"The ten-cent one, of course. The best is none too good for me. I'll give you the ten cents another time. I'm short of change just now—not being as rich as Queen Victory. There's her picture up there—the one with the blue sash and diamint crown and the lace curting on her head. Can any of yez tell me this— is Queen Victory a married woman?"

"Oh, yes, but her husband is dead," answered the Story Girl.

"Well, I s'pose they couldn't have called her an old maid, seeing she was a queen, even if she'd never got married. Sometimes I sez to myself, 'Peg, would you like to be Queen Victory?' But I never know what to answer. In summer, when I can roam anywhere in the woods and the sunshine—I wouldn't be Queen Victory for anything. But when it's winter and cold and I can't git nowheres—I feel as if I wouldn't mind changing places with her."

Peg put her pipe back in her mouth and began to smoke fiercely. The candle wick burned long, and was topped by a little cap of fiery red that seemed to wink at us like an impish gnome. The most grotesque shadow of Peg flickered over the wall behind her. The one-eyed cat remitted his grim watch and went to sleep. Outside the wind screamed like a ravening beast at the window. Suddenly Peg removed her pipe from her mouth, bent forward, gripped my wrist with her sinewy fingers until I almost cried out with pain, and gazed straight into my face. I felt horribly frightened of her. She seemed an entirely different creature. A wild light was in her eyes, a furtive, animal-like expression was on her face. When she spoke it was in a different voice and in different language.

"Do you hear the wind?" she asked in a thrilling whisper. "What *is* the wind? What *is* the wind?"

"I—I—don't know," I stammered.

"No more do I," said Peg, "and nobody knows. Nobody knows what the wind is. I wish I could find out. I mightn't be so afraid of the wind if I knew what it was. I *am* afraid of it. When the blasts come like that I want to crouch down and hide me. But I can tell you one thing about the wind—it's the only free thing in the world—*the—only—free—thing.* Everything else is subject to some law, but the wind is *free.* It bloweth where it listeth and no man can tame it. It's free—that's why I love it, though I'm afraid of it. It's a grand thing to be free—free—free!"

Peg's voice rose almost to a shriek. We were dreadfully frightened, for we knew there were times when she was quite crazy and we feared one of her "spells" was coming on her. But with a swift movement she turned the man's coat she wore up over her shoulders and head like a hood, completely hiding her face. Then she crouched forward, elbows on knees, and relapsed into silence. None of us dared speak or move. We sat thus for half an hour. Then Peg jumped up and said briskly in her usual tone,

"Well, I guess yez are all sleepy and ready for bed. You girls can sleep in my bed over there, and I'll take the sofy. Yez can put the cat off if yez like, though he won't hurt yez. You boys can go downstairs. There's a big pile of straw there that'll do yez for a bed, if yez put your coats on. I'll light yez down, but I ain't going to leave yez a light for fear yez'd set fire to the place."

Saying good-night to the girls, who looked as if they thought their last hour was come, we went to the lower room. It was quite empty, save for a pile of fire wood and another of clean straw. Casting a stealthy glance around, ere Peg withdrew the light, I was relieved to see that there were no skulls in sight. We four boys snuggled down in the straw. We did not expect to sleep, but we were very tired and before we knew it our eyes were shut, to open no more till morning. The poor girls were not so fortunate. They always averred they never closed an eye. Four things prevented them from sleeping. In the first place Peg snored loudly; in the second place the fitful gleams of firelight kept flickering over the skull for half the night and making gruesome effects on it; in the third place Peg's pillows and bedclothes smelled rankly of tobacco smoke; and in the fourth place they were afraid the rat Peg had spoken of might come out to make their acquaintance. Indeed, they were sure they heard him skirmishing about several times.

When we wakened in the morning the storm was over and a young morning was looking through rosy eyelids across a white world. The little clearing around Peg's cabin was heaped with dazzling drifts, and we boys fell to and shovelled out a road to her well. She gave us breakfast—stiff oatmeal porridge without milk, and a boiled egg apiece. Cecily could *not* eat her porridge; she declared she had such a bad cold that she had no appetite; a cold she certainly had; the rest of us choked our messes down and after we had done so Peg asked us if we had noticed a soapy taste.

"The soap fell into the porridge while I was making it," she said. "But,"—smacking her lips,—"I'm going to make yez an Irish stew for dinner. It'll be fine."

An Irish stew concocted by Peg! No wonder Dan said hastily, "You are very kind but we'll have to go right home."

"Yez can't walk," said Peg.

"Oh, yes, we can. The drifts are so hard they'll carry, and the snow will be pretty well blown off the middle of the fields. It's only three-quarters of a mile. We boys will go home and get a pung and come back for you girls."

But the girls wouldn't listen to this. They must go with us, even Cecily.

"Seems to me yez weren't in such a hurry to leave last night," observed Peg sarcastically.

"Oh, it's only because they'll be so anxious about us at home, and it's Sunday and we don't want to miss Sunday School," explained Felicity.

"Well, I hope your Sunday School will do yez good," said Peg, rather grumpily. But she relented again at the last and gave Cecily a wishbone.

"Whatever you wish on that will come true," she said. "But you only have the one wish, so don't waste it."

"We're so much obliged to you for all your trouble," said the Story Girl politely.

"Never mind the trouble. The expense is the thing," retorted Peg grimly.

"Oh!" Felicity hesitated. "If you would let us pay you—give you something—"

"No, thank yez," responded Peg loftily. "There is people who take money for their hospitality, I've heerd, but I'm thankful to say I don't associate with that class. Yez are welcome to all yez have had here, if yez *are* in a big hurry to get away."

She shut the door behind us with something of a slam, and her black cat followed us so far, with stealthy, furtive footsteps, that we were frightened of it. Eventually it turned back; then, and not till then, did we feel free to discuss our adventure.

"Well, I'm thankful we're out of *that,*" said Felicity, drawing a long breath. "Hasn't it just been an awful experience?"

"We might all have been found frozen stark and stiff this morning," remarked the Story Girl with apparent relish.

"I tell you, it was a lucky thing we got to Peg Bowen's," said Dan.

"Miss Marwood says there is no such thing as luck," protested Cecily. "We ought to say it was Providence instead."

"Well, Peg and Providence don't seem to go together very well, somehow," retorted Dan. "If Peg is a witch it must be the Other One she's in co. with."

"Dan, it's getting to be simply scandalous the way you talk," said Felicity. "I just wish ma could hear you."

"Is soap in porridge any worse than tooth-powder in rusks, lovely creature?" asked Dan.

"Dan, Dan," admonished Cecily, between her coughs, "remember it's Sunday."

"It seems hard to remember that," said Peter. "It doesn't seem a mite like Sunday and it seems awful long since yesterday."

"Cecily, you've got a dreadful cold," said the Story Girl anxiously.

"In spite of Peg's ginger tea," added Felix.

"Oh, that ginger tea was *awful,*" exclaimed poor Cecily. "I thought I'd never get it down—it was so hot with ginger—and there was so much of it! But I was so frightened of offending Peg I'd have tried to drink it all if there had been a bucketful. Oh, yes, it's very easy for you all to laugh! *You* didn't have to drink it."

"We had to eat two meals, though," said Felicity with a shiver. "And I don't know when those dishes of hers were washed. I just shut my eyes and took gulps."

"Did you notice the soapy taste in the porridge?" asked the Story Girl.

"Oh, there were so many queer tastes about it I didn't notice one more than another," answered Felicity wearily.

"What bothers me," remarked Peter absently, "is that skull. Do you suppose Peg really finds things out by it?"

"Nonsense! How could she?" scoffed Felix, bold as a lion in daylight.

"She didn't *say* she did, you know," I said cautiously.

"Well, we'll know in time if the things she said were going to happen do," mused Peter.

"Do you suppose your father is really coming home?" queried Felicity.

"I hope not," answered Peter decidedly.

"You ought to be ashamed of yourself," said Felicity severely.

"No, I oughtn't. Father got drunk all the time he was home, and wouldn't work and was bad to mother," said Peter defiantly. "She had to support him as well as herself and me. I don't want to see any father coming home, and you'd better believe it. Of course, if he was the right sort of a father it'd be different."

"What *I* would like to know is if Aunt Olivia is going to be married," said the Story Girl absently. "I can hardly believe it. But now that I think of it—Uncle Roger has been teasing her ever since she was in Halifax last summer."

"If she does get married you'll have to come and live with us," said Cecily delightedly.

Felicity did not betray so much delight and the Story Girl remarked with a weary little sigh that she hoped Aunt Olivia wouldn't. We all felt rather weary, somehow. Peg's predictions had been unsettling, and our nerves had all been more or less strained during our sojourn under her roof. We were glad when we found ourselves at home.

The folks had not been at all troubled about us, but it was because they were sure the storm had come up before we would think of leaving Cousin Mattie's and not because they had received any mysterious message from Peg's skull. We were relieved at this, but on the whole, our adventure had not done much towards clearing up the vexed question of Peg's witchcraft.

CHAPTER 9

EXTRACTS FROM THE FEBRUARY AND MARCH NUMBERS OF *OUR MAGAZINE*

RESOLUTION HONOUR ROLL

Miss Felicity King.

HONOURABLE MENTION

Mr. Felix King.
Mr. Peter Craig.
Miss Sara Ray.

EDITORIAL

The editor wishes to make a few remarks about the Resolution Honour Roll. As will be seen, only one name figures on it. Felicity says she has thought a beautiful thought every morning before breakfast without missing one morning, not even the one we were at Peg Bowen's. Some of our number think it not fair that Felicity should be on the honour roll (*Felicity, aside:* "That's Dan, of course.") when she only made one resolution and won't tell us what any of the thoughts were. So we have decided to give honourable mention to everybody who has kept one resolution perfect. Felix has worked all his arithmetic problems by himself. He complains that he never got more than a third of them right and the teacher has marked him away down; but one cannot keep resolutions without some inconvenience. Peter has never played tit-tat-x in church or got drunk and says it wasn't as bad as he expected. (*Peter, indignantly:* "I never said it." *Cecily, soothingly:* "Now, Peter, Bev only meant that as a joke.") Sara Ray has never talked any mean gossip, but does not find conversation as interesting as it used to be. (*Sara Ray, wonderingly:* "I don't remember of saying that.")

Felix did not eat any apples until March, but forgot and ate seven the day we were at Cousin Mattie's. (*Felix:* "I only ate five!") He soon gave up trying to say what he thought always. He got into too much trouble. We think Felix ought to change to old Grandfather King's rule. It was, "Hold your tongue when you can, and when you can't tell the truth." Cecily feels she has not read all the good books she might, because some she tried to read were very dull and the *Pansy* books were so much more interesting. And it is no use trying not to feel bad because her hair isn't curly and she has marked that resolution out. The Story Girl came very near to keeping her resolution to have all the good times possible, but she says she missed two, if not three, she might have had. Dan refuses to say anything about his resolutions and so does the editor.

PERSONALS

We regret that Miss Cecily King is suffering from a severe cold.

Mr. Alexander Marr of Markdale died very suddenly last week. We never heard of his death till he was dead.

Miss Cecily King wishes to state that she did not ask the question about "Holy Moses" and the other word in the January number. Dan put it in for a mean joke.

The weather has been cold and fine. We have only had one bad storm. The coasting on Uncle Roger's hill continues good.

Aunt Eliza did not favour us with a visit after all. She took cold and had to go home. We were sorry that she had a cold but glad that she had to go home. Cecily said she thought it wicked of us to be glad. But when we asked her "cross her heart" if she wasn't glad herself she had to say she was.

Miss Cecily King has got three very distinguished names on

her quilt square. They are the Governor and his wife and a witch's.

The King family had the honour of entertaining the Governor's wife to tea on February the seventeenth. We are all invited to visit Government House but some of us think we won't go.

A tragic event occurred last Tuesday. Mrs. James Frewen came to tea and there was no pie in the house. Felicity has not yet fully recovered.

A new boy is coming to school. His name is Cyrus Brisk and his folks moved up from Markdale. He says he is going to punch Willy Fraser's head if Willy keeps on thinking he is Miss Cecily King's beau.

(*Cecily:* "I haven't *any* beau! I don't mean to think of such a thing for at least eight years yet!")

Miss Alice Reade of Charlottetown Royalty has come to Carlisle to teach music. She boards at Mr. Peter Armstrong's. The girls are all going to take music lessons from her. Two descriptions of her will be found in another column. Felix wrote one, but the girls thought he did not do her justice, so Cecily wrote another one. She admits she copied most of the description out of Valeria H. Montague's story *Lord Marmaduke's First, Last, and Only Love; or the Bride of the Castle by the Sea,* but says they fit Miss Reade better than anything she could make up.

HOUSEHOLD DEPARTMENT

Always keep the kitchen tidy and then you needn't mind if company comes unexpectedly.

ANXIOUS INQUIRER: We don't know anything that will take the stain out of a silk dress when a soft-boiled egg is dropped on it. Better not wear your silk dress so often, especially when boiling eggs.

Ginger tea is good for colds.

OLD HOUSEKEEPER: Yes, when the baking-powder gives out you can use tooth-powder instead.

(*Felicity:* "I never wrote that! I don't care, I don't think it's fair for other people to be putting things in my department!")

Our apples are not keeping well this year. They are rotting; and besides father says we eat an awful lot of them.

PERSEVERANCE: I will give you the recipe for dumplings you ask for. But remember it is not everyone who can make dumplings, even from the recipe. There's a knack in it.

If the soap falls into the porridge do not tell your guests about it until they have finished eating it because it might take away their appetite.

FELICITY KING.

ETIQUETTE DEPARTMENT

P-r C-g:—Do not criticize people's noses unless you are sure they can't hear you, and don't criticize your best girl's great-aunt's nose in any case.

(*Felicity, tossing her head:* "Oh, my! I s'pose Dan thought that was extra smart.")

C-y K-g:—When my most intimate friend walks with another girl and exchanges lace patterns with her, what ought I to do? Ans. Adopt a dignified attitude.

F-y K-g:—It is better not to wear your second best hat to church, but if your mother says you must it is not for me to question her decision.

(*Felicity:* "Dan just copied that word for word out of the *Family Guide,* except about the hat part.")

P-r C-g:—Yes, it would be quite proper to say good evening to the family ghost if you met it.

F-x K-g:—No, it is not polite to sleep with your mouth open. What's more, it isn't safe. Something might fall into it.

DAN KING.

FASHION NOTES

Crocheted watch pockets are all the rage now. If you haven't a watch they do to carry your pencil in or a piece of gum.

It is stylish to have hair ribbons to match your dress. But it is hard to match gray drugget. I like scarlet for that.

It is stylish to pin a piece of ribbon on your coat the same colour as your chum wears in her hair. Mary Martha Cowan saw them doing it in town and started us doing it here. I always wear Kitty's ribbon and Kitty wears mine, but the Story Girl thinks it is silly.

CECILY KING.

AN ACCOUNT OF OUR VISIT TO COUSIN MATTIE'S

We all walked over to Cousin Mattie's last week. They were all well there and we had a fine dinner. On our way back a snow-storm came up and we got lost in the woods. We didn't know where we were or nothing. If we hadn't seen a light I guess we'd all have been frozen and snowed over, and they would never have found us till spring and that would be very sad. But we saw a light and made for it and it was Peg Bowen's. Some people think she is a witch and it's hard to tell, but she was real hospitable and took us all in. Her house was very untidy but it was warm. She has a skull. I mean a loose skull, not her own. She lets on it tells her things, but Uncle Alec says it couldn't because it was only an Indian skull that old Dr. Beecham had and Peg stole it when he died, but Uncle Roger says he wouldn't trust himself with Peg's skull for anything. She gave us supper. It was a horrid meal. The Story Girl says I must not tell what I found in the bread and butter because it would be too disgusting to read in *Our Magazine* but it don't matter because we were all there, except Sara Ray, and know what it was. We stayed all night and us boys slept in straw. None of us had ever slept on straw before. We got home in the morning. That is all I can write about our visit to Cousin Mattie's.

FELIX KING.

MY WORST ADVENTURE

It's my turn to write it so I suppose I must. I guess my worst adventure was two years ago when a whole lot of us were coasting on Uncle Rogers hill. Charlie Cowan and Fred Marr had started, but half-way down their sled got stuck and I run down to shove them off again. Then I stood there just a moment to watch them with my back to the top of the hill. While I was standing there Rob Marr started Kitty and Em Frewen off on his sled. His sled had a wooden tongue in it and it slanted back over the girls' heads. I was right in the way and they yelled to me to get out, but just as I heard them it struck me. The sled took me between the legs and I was histed back over the tongue and dropped in a heap behind before I knew what had happened to me. I thought a tornado had struck me. The girls couldn't stop though they thought I was killed, but Rob came tearing down and helped me up. He was awful scared but I wasn't killed nor my back wasn't broken but my nose bled something awful and kept on bleeding for three days. Not all the time but by spells.

DAN KING.

THE STORY OF HOW CARLISLE GOT ITS NAME

This is a true story to. Long ago there was a girl lived in charlotte town. I dont know her name so I cant right it and maybe it is just as well for Felicity might think it wasnt romantik like Miss Jemima Parrs. She was awful pretty and a young englishman who had come out to make his fortune fell in love with her and they were engaged to be married the next spring. His name was Mr. Carlisle. In the winter he started off to hunt cariboo for a spell. Cariboos lived on the island then. There aint any here now. He got to where it is Carlisle now. It wasn't anything then only woods and a few indians. He got awful sick and was sick for ever so long in a indian camp and only an old micmac squaw to wait on him. Back in town they all thought he was dead and his girl felt bad for a little while and then got over it and took up with another beau. The girls say that wasnt romantik but I think it was sensible but if it had been me that died I'd have felt bad if she forgot me so soon. But he hadnt died and when he got back to town he went right to her house and walked in and there she was standing up to be married to the other fellow. Poor Mr. Carlisle felt awful. He was sick and week and it went to his head. He just turned and run and run till he got back to the old micmac's camp and fell in front of it. But the indians had gone because it was spring and it didnt matter because he really was dead this time and people come looking for him from town and found him and buryed him there and called the place after him. They say the girl was never happy again and that was hard lines on her but maybe she deserved it.

PETER CRAIG.

MISS ALICE READE

Miss Alice Reade is a very pretty girl. She has kind of curly blackish hair and big gray eyes and a pale face. She is tall and thin but her figure is pretty fair and she has a nice mouth and a sweet way of speaking. The girls are crazy about her and talk about her all the time.

FELIX KING.

BEAUTIFUL ALICE

That is what we girls call Miss Reade among ourselves. She is divinely beautiful. Her magnificent wealth of raven hair flows back in glistening waves from her sun-kissed brow. (*Dan:* "If Felix had said she was sunburned you'd have all jumped on him." (*Cecily, coldly:* "Sun-kissed doesn't mean sunburned." *Dan:* "What does it mean then?" *Cecily, embarrassed:* "I—I don't know. But Miss Montague says the Lady Geraldine's brow was sun-kissed and of course an earl's daughter wouldn't be sunburned." *The Story Girl:* "Oh, don't interrupt the reading like this. It spoils it.") Her eyes are gloriously dark and deep, like midnight lakes mirroring the stars of heaven. Her features are like sculptured marble and her mouth is a trembling, curving Cupid's bow. (*Peter, aside:* "What kind of a thing is that?") Her creamy skin is as fair and flawless as the petals of a white lily. Her voice is like the ripple of a woodland brook and her slender form is matchless in its symmetry. (*Dan:* "That's Valeria's way of putting it, but Uncle Roger says she don't show her feed much." *Felicity:* "Dan! if Uncle Roger is vulgar you needn't be!") Her hands are like a poet's dreams. She dresses so nicely and looks so stylish in her clothes. Her favourite colour is blue. Some people think she is stiff and some say she is stuck-up, but she isn't a bit. It's just that she is different from them and they don't like it. She is just lovely and we adore her.

CECILY KING.

——————— C H A P T E R 10 ———————

DISAPPEARANCE OF PADDY

As I remember, the spring came late that year in Carlisle. It was May before the weather began to satisfy the grown-ups. But we children were more easily pleased, and we thought April a splendid month because the snow all went early and left gray, firm, frozen ground for our rambles and games. As the days slipped by they grew more gracious; the hillsides began to look as if they were thinking of mayflowers; the old orchard was washed in a bath of tingling sunshine and the sap stirred in the big trees; by day the sky was veiled with delicate cloud drift, fine and filmy as woven mist; in the evenings a full, low moon looked over the valleys, as pallid and holy as some aureoled saint; a sound of laughter and dream was on the wind and the world grew young with the mirth of April breezes.

"It's so nice to be alive in the spring," said the Story Girl one twilight as we swung on the boughs of Uncle Stephen's walk.

"It's nice to be alive any time," said Felicity, complacently.

"But it's nicer in the spring," insisted the Story Girl. "When I'm dead I think I'll *feel* dead all the rest of the year, but when spring comes I'm sure I'll feel like getting up and being alive again."

"You do say such queer things," complained Felicity. "You won't be really dead any time. You'll be in the next world. And I think it's horrid to talk about people being dead anyhow."

"We've all got to die," said Sara Ray solemnly, but with a certain relish. It was as if she enjoyed looking forward to something in which nothing, neither an unsympathetic mother, nor the cruel fate which had made her a colourless little nonentity, could prevent her from being the chief performer.

"I sometimes think," said Cecily, rather wearily, "that it isn't so dreadful to die young as I used to suppose."

She prefaced her remark with a slight cough, as she had been all too apt to do of late, for the remnants of the cold she had caught the night we were lost in the storm still clung to her.

"Don't talk such nonsense, Cecily," cried the Story Girl with unwonted sharpness, a sharpness we all understood. All of us, in our hearts, though we never spoke of it to each other, thought Cecily was not as well as she ought to be that spring, and we hated to hear anything said which seemed in any way to touch or acknowledge the tiny, faint shadow which now and again showed itself dimly athwart our sunshine.

"Well, it was you began talking of being dead," said Felicity angrily. "*I* don't think it's right to talk of such things. Cecily,

are you sure your feet ain't damp? We ought to go in anyhow—
it's too chilly out here for you."

"You girls had better go," said Dan, "but I ain't going in
till old Isaac Frewen goes. I've no use for him."

"I hate him, too," said Felicity, agreeing with Dan for once
in her life. "He chews tobacco all the time and spits on the
floor—the horrid pig!"

"And yet his brother is an elder in the church," said Sara
Ray wonderingly.

"I know a story about Isaac Frewen," said the Story Girl.
"When he was young he went by the name of Oatmeal Frewen
and he got it this way. He was noted for doing outlandish
things. He lived at Markdale then and he was a great, overgrown,
awkward fellow, six feet tall. He drove over to Baywater one
Saturday to visit his uncle there and came home the next
afternoon, and although it was Sunday he brought a big bag
of oatmeal in the wagon with him. When he came to Carlisle
church he saw that service was going on there, and he concluded
to stop and go in. But he didn't like to leave his oatmeal
outside for fear something would happen to it, because there
were always mischievous boys around, so he hoisted the bag
on his back and walked into church with it and right to the
top of the aisle to Grandfather King's pew. Grandfather King
used to say he would never forget it to his dying day. The
minister was preaching and everything was quiet and solemn
when he heard a snicker behind him. Grandfather King turned
around with a terrible frown—for you know in those days it
was thought a dreadful thing to laugh in church—to rebuke
the offender; and what did he see but that great, hulking young
Isaac stalking up the aisle, bending a little forward under the
weight of a big bag of oatmeal? Grandfather King was so amazed
he couldn't laugh, but almost everyone else in the church was
laughing, and grandfather said he never blamed them, for no
funnier sight was ever seen. Young Isaac turned into grandfather's pew and thumped the bag of oatmeal down on the
seat with a thud that cracked it. Then he plumped down beside
it, took off his hat, wiped his face, and settled back to listen
to the sermon, just as if it was all a matter of course. When
the service was over he hoisted his bag up again, marched out
of church, and drove home. He could never understand why

it made so much talk; but he was known by the name of Oatmeal Frewen for years."

Our laughter, as we separated, rang sweetly through the old orchard and across the far, dim meadows. Felicity and Cecily went into the house and Sara Ray and the Story Girl went home, but Peter decoyed me into the granary to ask advice.

"You know Felicity has a birthday next week," he said, "and I want to write her an ode."

"A—a what?" I gasped.

"An ode," repeated Peter, gravely. "It's poetry, you know. I'll put it in *Our Magazine.*"

"But you can't write poetry, Peter," I protested.

"I'm going to try," said Peter stoutly. "That is, if you think she won't be offended at me."

"She ought to feel flattered," I replied.

"You never can tell how she'll take things," said Peter gloomily. "Of course I ain't going to sign my name, and if she ain't pleased I won't tell her I wrote it. Don't you let on."

I promised I wouldn't and Peter went off with a light heart. He said he meant to write two lines every day till he got it done.

Cupid was playing his world-old tricks with others than poor Peter that spring. Allusion has been made in these chronicles to one, Cyrus Brisk, and to the fact that our brown-haired, soft-voiced Cecily had found favour in the eyes of the said Cyrus. Cecily did not regard her conquest with any pride. On the contrary, it annoyed her terribly to be teased about Cyrus. She declared she hated both him and his name. She was as uncivil to him as sweet Cecily could be to anyone, but the gallant Cyrus was nothing daunted. He laid determined siege to Cecily's young heart by all the methods known to love-lorn swains. He placed delicate tributes of spruce gum, molasses taffy, "conversation" candies and decorated slate pencils on her desk; he persistently "chose" her in all school games calling for a partner; he entreated to be allowed to carry her basket from school; he offered to work her sums for her; and rumour had it that he had made a wild statement to the effect that he meant to ask if he might see her home some night from prayer meeting. Cecily was quite frightened that he would; she confided to me that she would rather die than walk home with him, but that if he asked her she would be too bashful to say no. So far, however, Cyrus had not molested her out of school, nor had he as yet thumped Willy Fraser—who was reported to be very low in his spirits over the whole affair.

And now Cyrus had written Cecily a letter—a love letter, mark you. Moreover, he had sent it through the post-office, with a real stamp on it. Its arrival made a sensation among us. Dan brought it from the office and, recognizing the handwriting of Cyrus, gave Cecily no peace until she showed us the letter. It was a very sentimental and rather ill-spelled epistle in which the inflammable Cyrus reproached her in heart-rending words for her coldness, and begged her to answer his letter, saying that if she did he would keep the secret "in violets." Cyrus probably meant "inviolate" but Cecily thought it was intended for a poetical touch. He signed himself "your troo lover, Cyrus Brisk" and added in a postscript that he couldn't eat or sleep for thinking of her.

"Are you going to answer it?" asked Dan.

"Certainly not," said Cecily with dignity.

"Cyrus Brisk wants to be kicked," growled Felix, who never seemed to be any particular friend of Willy Fraser's either. "He'd better learn how to spell before he takes to writing love letters."

"Maybe Cyrus will starve to death if you don't," suggested Sara Ray.

"I hope he will," said Cecily cruelly. She was truly vexed over the letter; and yet, so contradictory a thing is the feminine heart, even at twelve years old, I think she was a little flattered by it also. It was her first love letter and she confided to me that it gives you a very queer feeling to get it. At all events— the letter, though unanswered, was not torn up. I feel sure Cecily preserved it. But she walked past Cyrus next morning at school with a frozen countenance, evincing not the slightest pity for his pangs of unrequited affection. Cecily winced when Pat caught a mouse, visited a school chum the day the pigs were killed that she might not hear their squealing, and would not have stepped on a caterpillar for anything; yet she did not care at all how much she made the brisk Cyrus suffer.

Then, suddenly, all our spring gladness and Maytime hopes were blighted as by a killing frost. Sorrow and anxiety pervaded our days and embittered our dreams by night. Grim tragedy held sway in our lives for the next fortnight.

Paddy disappeared. One night he lapped his new milk as usual at Uncle Roger's dairy door and then sat blandly on the flat stone before it, giving the world assurance of a cat, sleek sides glistening, plumy tail gracefully folded around his paws, brilliant eyes watching the stir and flicker of bare willow boughs in the twilight air above him. That was the last seen of him. In the morning he was not.

At first we were not seriously alarmed. Paddy was no roving Thomas, but occasionally he vanished for a day or so. But when two days passed without his return we became anxious, the third day worried us greatly, and the fourth found us distracted.

"Something has happened to Pat," the Story Girl declared miserably. "He never stayed away from home more than two days in his life."

"What could have happened to him?" asked Felix.

"He's been poisoned—or a dog has killed him," answered the Story Girl in tragic tones.

Cecily began to cry at this; but tears were of no avail. Neither was anything else, apparently. We searched every nook and cranny of barns and out-buildings and woods on both the King farms; we inquired far and wide; we roved over Carlisle meadows calling Paddy's name, until Aunt Janet grew exasperated and declared we must stop making such exhibitions of ourselves. But we found and heard no trace of our lost pet. The Story Girl moped and refused to be comforted; Cecily declared she could not sleep at night for thinking of poor Paddy dying miserably in some corner to which he had dragged his failing body, or lying somewhere mangled and torn by a dog. We hated every dog we saw on the ground that he might be the guilty one.

"It's the suspense that's so hard," sobbed the Story Girl. "If I just knew what had happened to him it wouldn't be *quite* so hard. But I don't know whether he's dead or alive. He may be living and suffering, and every night I dream that he has come home and when I wake up and find it's only a dream it just breaks my heart."

"It's ever so much worse than when he was so sick last fall," said Cecily drearily. "Then we knew that everything was done for him that could be done."

We could not appeal to Peg Bowen this time. In our desperation we would have done it, but Peg was far away. With the first breath of spring she was up and off, answering to the lure of the long road. She had not been seen in her accustomed haunts for many a day. Her pets were gaining their own living in the woods and her house was locked up.

CHAPTER 11

THE WITCH'S WISHBONE

WHEN A fortnight had elapsed we gave up all hope.

"Pat is dead," said the Story Girl hopelessly, as we returned one evening from a bootless quest to Andrew Cowan's where a strange gray cat had been reported—a cat which turned out to be a yellowish brown nondescript, with no tail to speak of.

"I'm afraid so," I acknowledged at last.

"If only Peg Bowen had been at home she could have found him for us," asserted Peter. "Her skull would have told her where he was."

"I wonder if the wishbone she gave me would have done any good," cried Cecily suddenly. "I'd forgotten all about it. Oh, do you suppose it's too late yet?"

"There's nothing in a wishbone," said Dan impatiently.

"You can't be sure. She told me I'd get the wish I made on it. I'm going to try whenever I get home."

"It can't do any harm, anyhow," said Peter, "but I'm afraid you've left it too late. If Pat is dead even a witch's wishbone can't bring him back to life."

"I'll never forgive myself for not thinking about it before," mourned Cecily.

As soon as we got home she flew to the little box upstairs where she kept her treasures, and brought therefrom the dry and brittle wishbone.

"Peg told me how it must be done. I'm to hold the wishbone with both hands, like this, and walk backward, repeating the wish nine times. And when I've finished the ninth time I'm to turn around nine times, from right to left, and then the wish will come true right away."

"Do you expect to see Pat when you finish turning?" said Dan skeptically.

None of us had any faith in the incantation except Peter, and, by infection, Cecily. You never could tell what might happen. Cecily took the wishbone in her trembling little hands and began her backward pacing, repeating solemnly, "I wish that we may find Paddy alive, or else his body, so that we can bury him decently." By the time Cecily had repeated this nine times we were all slightly infected with the desperate hope that something might come of it; and when she had made her nine gyrations we looked eagerly down the sunset lane, half expecting to see our lost pet. But we saw only the Awkward Man turning in at the gate. This was almost as surprising as the sight of Pat himself would have been; but there was no sign of Pat and hope flickered out in every breast but Peter's.

"You've got to give the spell time to work," he expostulated. "If Pat was miles away when it was wished it wouldn't be reasonable to expect to see him right off."

But we of little faith had already lost that little, and it was a very disconsolate group which the Awkward Man presently joined.

He was smiling—his rare, beautiful smile which only children ever saw—and he lifted his hat to the girls with no trace of the shyness and awkwardness for which he was notorious.

"Good evening," he said. "Have you little people lost a cat lately?"

We stared. Peter said "I knew it!" in a triumphant pig's whisper. The Story Girl started eagerly forward.

"Oh, Mr. Dale, can you tell us anything of Paddy?" she cried.

"A silver gray cat with black points and very fine marking?"

"Yes, yes!"

"Well, he is over at Golden Milestone."

"Alive?"

"Yes."

"Well, doesn't that beat the Dutch!" muttered Dan.

But we were all crowding about the Awkward Man, demanding where and when he had found Paddy.

"You'd better come over to my place and make sure that it really is your cat," suggested the Awkward Man, "and I'll tell you all about finding him on the way. I must warn you that he is pretty thin—but I think he'll pull through."

We obtained permission to go without much difficulty, although the spring evening was wearing late, for Aunt Janet said she supposed none of us would sleep a wink that night if we didn't. A joyful procession followed the Awkward Man and the Story Girl across the gray, star-litten meadows to his home and through his pine-guarded gate.

"You know that old barn of mine back in the woods?" said the Awkward Man. "I go to it only about once in a blue moon. There was an old barrel there, upside down, one side resting on a block of wood. This morning I went to the barn to see about having some hay hauled home, and I had occasion to move the barrel. I noticed that it seemed to have been moved slightly since my last visit, and it was now resting wholly on the floor. I lifted it up—and there was a cat lying on the floor under it. I had heard you had lost yours and I took it this was your pet. I was afraid he was dead at first. He was lying there with his eyes closed; but when I bent over him he opened them and gave a pitiful little mew; or rather his mouth made the motion of a mew, for he was too weak to utter a sound."

"Oh, poor, poor Paddy," said tender-hearted Cecily tearfully.

"He couldn't stand, so I carried him home and gave him just a little milk. Fortunately he was able to lap it. I gave him a little more at intervals all day, and when I left he was able to crawl around. I think he'll be all right, but you'll have to be careful how you feed him for a few days. Don't let your hearts run away with your judgment and kill him with kindness."

"Do you suppose any one put him under that barrel?" asked the Story Girl.

"No. The barn was locked. Nothing but a cat could get in. I suppose he went under the barrel, perhaps in pursuit of a mouse, and somehow knocked it off the block and so imprisoned himself."

Paddy was sitting before the fire in the Awkward Man's clean, bare kitchen. Thin! Why, he was literally skin and bone, and his fur was dull and lustreless. It almost broke our hearts to see our beautiful Paddy brought so low.

"Oh, how he must have suffered!" moaned Cecily.

"He'll be as prosperous as ever in a week or two," said the Awkward Man kindly.

The Story Girl gathered Paddy up in her arms. Most mellifluously did he purr as we crowded around to stroke him; with friendly joy he licked our hands with his little red tongue; poor Paddy was a thankful cat; he was no longer lost, starving, imprisoned, helpless; he was with his comrades once more and he was going home—home to his old familiar haunts of orchard and dairy and granary, to his daily rations of new milk and cream, to the cosy corner of his own fireside. We trooped home joyfully, the Story Girl in our midst carrying Paddy hugged against her shoulder. Never did April stars look down on a happier band of travellers on the golden road. There was a little gray wind out in the meadows that night, and it danced along beside us on viewless, fairy feet, and sang a delicate song of the lovely, waiting years, while the night laid her beautiful hands of blessing over the world.

"You see what Peg's wishbone did," said Peter triumphantly.

"Now, look here, Peter, don't talk nonsense," expostulated Dan. "The Awkward Man found Paddy this morning and had started to bring us word before Cecily ever thought of the wishbone. Do you mean to say you believe he wouldn't have come walking up our lane just when he did if she had never thought of it?"

"I mean to say that I wouldn't mind if I had several wishbones of the same kind," retorted Peter stubbornly.

"Of course I don't think the wishbone had really anything to do with our getting Paddy back, but I'm glad I tried it, for all that," remarked Cecily in a tone of satisfaction.

"Well, anyhow, we've got Pat and that's the main thing," said Felix.

"And I hope it will be a lesson to him to stay home after this," commented Felicity.

"They say the barrens are full of mayflowers," said the Story Girl. "Let us have a mayflower picnic tomorrow to celebrate Paddy's safe return."

CHAPTER 12

FLOWERS O' MAY

ACCORDINGLY WE went a-maying, following the lure of dancing winds to a certain westward sloping hill lying under the spirit-like blue of spring skies, feathered over with lisping young pines and firs, which cupped little hollows and corners where the sunshine got in and never got out again, but stayed there and grew mellow, coaxing dear things to bloom long before they would dream of waking up elsewhere.

'Twas there we found our mayflowers, after faithful seeking. Mayflowers, you must know, never flaunt themselves; they must be sought as becomes them, and then they will yield up their treasures to the seeker—clusters of star-white and dawn-pink that have in them the very soul of all the springs that ever were, re-incarnated in something it seems gross to call perfume, so exquisite and spiritual is it.

We wandered gaily over the hill, calling to each other with laughter and jest, getting parted and delightfully lost in that little pathless wilderness, and finding each other unexpectedly in nooks and dips and sunny silences, where the wind purred and gentled and went softly. When the sun began to hang low, sending great fan-like streamers of radiance up to the zenith, we foregathered in a tiny, sequestered valley, full of young green fern, lying in the shadow of a wooded hill. In it was a shallow pool—a glimmering green sheet of water on whose banks nymphs might dance as blithely as ever they did on Argive hill or in Cretan dale. There we sat and stripped the faded leaves and stems from our spoil, making up the blossoms into bouquets to fill our baskets with sweetness. The Story Girl twisted a spray of divinest pink in her brown curls, and told us an old legend of a beautiful Indian maiden who died of a broken heart when the first snows of winter were falling, because she believed her long-absent lover was false. But he came back in the spring time from his long captivity; and when he heard that she was dead he sought her grave to mourn her, and lo, under the dead leaves of the old year he found sweet sprays of a blossom never seen before, and knew that it was a message of love and remembrance from his dark-eyed sweetheart.

"Except in stories Indian girls are called squaws," remarked practical Dan, tying his mayflowers together in one huge, solid, cabbage-like bunch. Not for Dan the bother of filling his basket with the loose sprays, mingled with feathery elephant's-ears and trails of creeping spruce, as the rest of us, following the Story Girl's example, did. Nor would he admit that ours looked any better than his.

"I like things of one kind together. I don't like them mixed," he said.

"You have no taste," said Felicity.

"Except in my mouth, best beloved," responded Dan.

"You do think you are so smart," retorted Felicity, flushing with anger.

"Don't quarrel this lovely day," implored Cecily.

"Nobody's quarrelling, Sis. I ain't a bit mad. It's Felicity. What on earth is that at the bottom of your basket, Cecily?"

"It's a History of the Reformation in France," confessed poor Cecily, "by a man named D-a-u-b-i-g-n-y. I can't pronounce it. I heard Mr. Marwood saying it was a book everyone ought to read, so I began it last Sunday. I brought it along today to read when I got tired picking flowers. I'd ever so much rather have brought *Ester Reid*. There's so much in the history I can't understand, and it is so dreadful to read of people being burned to death. But I felt I *ought* to read it."

"Do you really think your mind has improved any?" asked Sara Ray seriously, wreathing the handle of her basket with creeping spruce.

"No, I'm afraid it hasn't one bit," answered Cecily sadly. "I feel that I haven't succeeded very well in keeping my resolutions."

"I've kept mine," said Felicity complacently.

"It's easy to keep just one," retorted Cecily, rather resentfully.

"It's not so easy to think beautiful thoughts," answered Felicity.

"It's the easiest thing in the world," said the Story Girl, tiptoeing to the edge of the pool to peep at her own arch reflection, as some nymph left over from the golden age might do. "Beautiful thoughts just crowd into your mind at times."

"Oh, yes, *at times*. But that's different from thinking one *regularly* at a given hour. And mother is always calling up the stairs for me to hurry up and get dressed, and it's *very* hard sometimes."

"That's so," conceded the Story Girl. "There *are* times when I can't think anything but gray thoughts. Then, other days, I think pink and blue and gold and purple and rainbow thoughts all the time."

"The idea! As if thoughts were coloured," giggled Felicity.

"Oh, they are!" cried the Story Girl. "Why, I can always *see* the colour of any thought I think. Can't you?"

"I never heard of such a thing," declared Felicity, "and I don't believe it. I believe you are just making that up."

"Indeed I'm not. Why, I always supposed everyone thought in colours. It must be very tiresome if you don't."

"When you think of me what colour is it?" asked Peter curiously.

"Yellow," answered the Story Girl promptly. "And Cecily is a sweet pink, like those mayflowers, and Sara Ray is very pale blue, and Dan is red and Felix is yellow, like Peter, and Bev is striped."

"What colour am I?" asked Felicity, amid the laughter at my expense.

"You're—you're like a rainbow," answered the Story Girl rather reluctantly. She had to be honest, but she would rather not have complimented Felicity. "And you needn't laugh at Bev. His stripes are beautiful. It isn't *he* that is striped. It's just the *thought* of him. Peg Bowen is a queer sort of yellowish green and the Awkward Man is lilac. Aunt Olivia is pansy-purple mixed with gold, and Uncle Roger is navy blue."

"I never heard such nonsense," declared Felicity. The rest of us were rather inclined to agree with her for once. We thought the Story Girl was making fun of us. But I believe she really had a strange gift of thinking in colours. In later years, when we were grown up, she told me of it again. She said that everything had colour in her thought; the months of the year ran through all the tints of the spectrum, the days of the week were arrayed as Solomon in his glory, morning was golden, noon orange, evening crystal blue, and night violet. Every idea came to her mind robed in its own especial hue. Perhaps that was why her voice and words had such a charm, conveying to the listeners' perception such fine shadings of meaning and tint and music.

"Well, let's go and have something to eat," suggested Dan. "What colour is eating, Sara?"

"Golden brown, just the colour of a molasses cooky," laughed the Story Girl.

We sat on the ferny bank of the pool and ate of the generous basket Aunt Janet had provided, with appetites sharpened by the keen spring air and our wilderness rovings. Felicity had made some very nice sandwiches of ham which we all appreciated except Dan, who declared he didn't like things minced up and dug out of the basket a chunk of boiled pork which he proceeded to saw up with a jack-knife and devour with gusto.

"I told ma to put this in for me. There's some *chew* to it," he said.

"You are not a bit *refined*," commented Felicity.

"Not a morsel, my love," grinned Dan.

"You make me think of a story I heard Uncle Roger telling about Cousin Annetta King," said the Story Girl. "Great-uncle Jeremiah King used to live where Uncle Roger lives now, when Grandfather King was alive and Uncle Roger was a boy. In those days it was thought rather coarse for a young lady to have too hearty an appetite, and she was more admired if she was delicate about what she ate. Cousin Annetta set out to be very refined indeed. She pretended to have no appetite at all. One afternoon she was invited to tea at Grandfather King's when they had some special company—people from Charlottetown. Cousin Annetta said she could hardly eat anything. 'You know, Uncle Abraham,' she said, in a very affected, fine-young-lady voice, 'I really hardly eat enough to keep a bird alive. Mother says she wonders how I continue to exist.' And she picked and pecked until Grandfather King declared he would like to throw something at her. After tea Cousin Annetta went home, and just about dark Grandfather King went over to Uncle Jeremiah's on an errand. As he passed the open, lighted pantry window he happened to glance in, and what do you think he saw? Delicate Cousin Annetta standing at the dresser, with a big loaf of bread beside her and a big platterful of cold, boiled pork in front of her; and Annetta was hacking off great chunks, like Dan there, and gobbling them down as if she was starving. Grandfather King couldn't resist the temptation. He stepped up to the window and said, 'I'm glad your appetite has come back to you, Annetta. Your mother needn't worry about your continuing to exist as long as you can tuck away fat, salt pork in that fashion.'

"Cousin Annetta never forgave him, but she never pretended to be delicate again."

"The Jews don't believe in eating pork," said Peter.

"I'm glad I'm not a Jew and I guess Cousin Annetta was too," said Dan.

"I like bacon, but I can never look at a pig without wondering if they were ever intended to be eaten," remarked Cecily naively.

When we finished our lunch the barrens were already wrapping themselves in a dim, blue dusk and falling upon rest in dell and dingle. But out in the open there was still much light of a fine emerald-golden sort and the robins whistled us home in it. "Horns of Elfland" never sounded more sweetly around hoary castle and ruined fane than those vesper calls of the robins from the twilight spruce woods and across green pastures lying under the pale radiance of a young moon.

When we reached home we found that Miss Reade had been up to the hill farm on an errand and was just leaving. The Story Girl went for a walk with her and came back with an important expression on her face.

"You look as if you had a story to tell," said Felix.

"One is growing. It isn't a whole story yet," answered the Story Girl mysteriously.

"What is it?" asked Cecily.

"I can't tell you till it's fully grown," said the Story Girl. "But I'll tell you a pretty little story the Awkward Man told us—told me—tonight. He was walking in his garden as we went by, looking at his tulip beds. His tulips are up ever so much higher than ours, and I asked him how he managed to coax them along so early. And he said he didn't do it—it was all the work of the pixies who lived in the woods across the brook. There were more pixy babies than usual this spring, and the mothers were in a hurry for the cradles. The tulips are the pixy babies' cradles, it seems. The mother pixies come out of the woods at twilight and rock their tiny little brown babies to sleep in the tulip cups. That is the reason why tulip blooms last so much longer than other blossoms. The pixy babies must have a cradle until they are grown up. They grow very fast, you see, and the Awkward Man says on a spring evening, when the tulips are out, you can hear the sweetest, softest, clearest, fairy music in his garden, and it is the pixy folk singing as they rock the pixy babies to sleep."

"Then the Awkward Man says what isn't true," said Felicity severely.

<hr />

CHAPTER 13

A SURPRISING ANNOUNCEMENT

"NOTHING EXCITING has happened for ever so long," said the Story Girl discontentedly, one late May evening, as we lingered under the wonderful white bloom of the cherry trees. There was a long row of them in the orchard, with a Lombardy poplar at either end, and a hedge of lilacs behind. When the wind blew over them all the spicy breezes of Ceylon's isle were never sweeter.

It was a time of wonder and marvel, of the soft touch of silver rain on greening fields, of the incredible delicacy of young leaves, of blossom in field and garden and wood. The whole world bloomed in a flush and tremor of maiden loveliness, instinct with all the evasive, fleeting charm of spring and girlhood and young morning. We felt and enjoyed it all without understanding or analyzing it. It was enough to be glad and young with spring on the golden road.

"I don't like excitement very much," said Cecily. "It makes one so tired. I'm sure it was exciting enough when Paddy was missing, but we didn't find that very pleasant."

"No, but it was interesting," returned the Story Girl thoughtfully. "After all, I believe I'd rather be miserable than dull."

"I wouldn't then," said Felicity decidedly. "And you need never be dull when you have work to do. 'Satan finds some mischief still for idle hands to do!' "

"Well, mischief is interesting," laughed the Story Girl. "And I thought you didn't think it lady-like to speak of that person, Felicity?"

"It's all right if you call him by his polite name," said Felicity stiffly.

"Why does the Lombardy poplar hold its branches straight up in the air like that, when all the other poplars hold theirs out or hang them down?" interjected Peter, who had been gazing intently at the slender spire showing darkly against the fine blue eastern sky.

"Because it grows that way," said Felicity.

"Oh I know a story about that," cried the Story Girl. "Once upon a time an old man found the pot of gold at the rainbow's end. There *is* a pot there, it is said, but it is very hard to find because you can never get to the rainbow's end before it vanishes from your sight. But this old man found it, just at sunset, when Iris, the guardian of the rainbow gold, happened to be absent. As he was a long way from home, and the pot was very big and heavy, he decided to hide it until morning and then get one of his sons to go with him and help him carry it. So he hid it under the boughs of the sleeping poplar tree.

"When Iris came back she missed the pot of gold and of course she was in a sad way about it. She sent Mercury, the messenger of the gods, to look for it, for she didn't dare leave the rainbow again, lest somebody should run off with that too. Mercury asked all the trees if they had seen the pot of gold, and the elm, oak and pine pointed to the poplar and said,

" 'The poplar can tell you where it is.'

" 'How can I tell you where it is?' cried the poplar, and she held up all her branches in surprise, just as we hold up our hands—and down tumbled the pot of gold. The poplar was amazed and indignant, for she was a very honest tree. She stretched her boughs high above her head and declared that she would always hold them like that, so that nobody could hide stolen gold under them again. And she taught all the little poplars she knew to stand the same way, and that is why Lombardy poplars always do. But the aspen poplar leaves are always shaking, even on the very calmest day. And do you know why?"

And then she told us the old legend that the cross on which the Saviour of the world suffered was made of aspen poplar wood and so never again could its poor, shaken, shivering leaves know rest or peace. There was an aspen in the orchard, the very embodiment of youth and spring in its litheness and symmetry. Its little leaves were hanging tremulously, not yet so fully blown as to hide its development of bough and twig, making poetry against the spiritual tints of a spring sunset.

"It does look sad," said Peter, "but it is a pretty tree, and it wasn't its fault."

"There's a heavy dew and it's time we stopped talking non-sense and went in," decreed Felicity. "If we don't we'll all have a cold, and then we'll be miserable enough, but it won't be very exciting."

"All the same, I wish something exciting would happen," finished the Story Girl, as we walked up through the orchard, peopled with its nun-like shadows.

"There's a new moon tonight, so may be you'll get your wish," said Peter. "My Aunt Jane didn't believe there was anything in the moon business, but you never can tell."

The Story Girl did get her wish. Something happened the very next day. She joined us in the afternoon with a quite indescribable expression on her face, compounded of triumph, anticipation, and regret. Her eyes betrayed that she had been crying, but in them shone a chastened exultation. Whatever the Story Girl mourned over it was evident she was not without hope.

"I have some news to tell you," she said importantly. "Can you guess what it is?"

We couldn't and wouldn't try.

"Tell us right off," implored Felix. "You look as if it was something tremendous."

"So it is. Listen—Aunt Olivia is going to be married."

We stared in blank amazement. Peg Bowen's hint had faded from our minds and we had never put much faith in it.

"Aunt Olivia! I don't believe it," cried Felicity flatly. "Who told you?"

"Aunt Olivia herself. So it is perfectly true. I'm awfully sorry in one way—but oh, won't it be splendid to have a real wedding in the family? She's going to have a big wedding—and I am to be bridesmaid."

"I shouldn't think you were old enough to be a bridesmaid," said Felicity sharply.

"I'm nearly fifteen. Anyway, Aunt Olivia says I have to be."

"Who's she going to marry?" asked Cecily, gathering herself together after the shock, and finding that the world was going on just the same.

"His name is Dr. Seton and he is a Halifax man. She met him when she was at Uncle Edward's last summer. They've been engaged ever since. The wedding is to be the third week in June."

"And our school concert comes off the next week," complained Felicity. "Why do things always come together like that? And what are you going to do if Aunt Olivia is going away?"

"I'm coming to live at your house," answered the Story Girl rather timidly. She did not know how Felicity might like that. But Felicity took it rather well.

"You've been here most of the time anyhow, so it'll just be that you'll sleep and eat here, too. But what's to become of Uncle Roger?"

"Aunt Olivia says he'll have to get married, too. But Uncle Roger says he'd rather hire a housekeeper than marry one, because in the first case he could turn her off if he didn't like her, but in the second case he couldn't."

"There'll be a lot of cooking to do for the wedding," reflected Felicity in a tone of satisfaction.

"I s'pose Aunt Olivia will want some rusks made. I hope she has plenty of tooth-powder laid in," said Dan.

"It's a pity you don't use some of that tooth-powder you're so fond of talking about yourself," retorted Felicity. "When anyone has a mouth the size of yours the teeth show so plain."

"I brush my teeth every Sunday," asseverated Dan.

"Every Sunday! You ought to brush them every *day*."

"Did anyone ever hear such nonsense?" demanded Dan sincerely.

"Well, you know, it really does say so in the *Family Guide*," said Cecily quietly.

"Then the *Family Guide* people must have lots more spare time than I have," retorted Dan contemptuously.

"Just think, the Story Girl will have her name in the papers if she's bridesmaid," marvelled Sara Ray.

"In the Halifax papers, too," added Felix, "since Dr. Seton is a Halifax man. What is his first name?"

"Robert."

"And will we have to call him Uncle Robert?"

"Not until he's married to her. Then we will, of course."

"I hope your Aunt Olivia won't disappear before the ceremony," remarked Sara Ray, who was surreptitiously reading *"The Vanished Bride,"* by Valeria H. Montague in the *Family Guide.*

"I hope Dr. Seton won't fail to show up, like your cousin Rachel Ward's beau," said Peter.

"That makes me think of another story I read the other day about Great-uncle Andrew King and Aunt Georgina," laughed the Story Girl. "It happened eighty years ago. It was a very stormy winter and the roads were bad. Uncle Andrew lived in Carlisle, and Aunt Georgina—she was Miss Georgina Matheson then—lived away up west, so he couldn't get to see her very often. They agreed to be married that winter, but Georgina couldn't set the day exactly because her brother, who lived in Ontario, was coming home for a visit, and she wanted to be married while he was home. So it was arranged that she was to write Uncle Andrew and tell him what day to come. She did, and she told him to come on a Tuesday. But her writing wasn't very good and poor Uncle Andrew thought she wrote Thursday. So on Thursday he drove all the way to Georgina's home to be married. It was forty miles and a bitter cold day. But it wasn't any colder than the reception he got from Georgina. She was out in the porch, with her head tied up in a towel, picking geese. She had been all ready Tuesday, and her friends and the minister were there, and the wedding supper prepared. But there was no bridegroom and Georgina was furious. Nothing Uncle Andrew could say would appease her. She wouldn't listen to a word of explanation, but told him to go, and never show his nose there again. So poor Uncle Andrew had to go ruefully home, hoping that she would relent later on, because he was really very much in love with her."

"And did she?" queried Felicity.

"She did. Thirteen years exactly from that day they were married. It took her just that long to forgive him."

"It took her just that long to find out she couldn't get anybody else," said Dan, cynically.

CHAPTER 14

A PRODIGAL RETURNS

AUNT OLIVIA and the Story Girl lived in a whirlwind of dressmaking after that, and enjoyed it hugely. Cecily and Felicity also had to have new dresses for the great event, and they talked of little else for a fortnight. Cecily declared that she hated to go to sleep because she was sure to dream that she was at Aunt Olivia's wedding in her old faded gingham dress and a ragged apron.

"And no shoes or stockings," she added, "and I can't move, and everyone walks past and looks at my feet."

"That's only in a dream," mourned Sara Ray, "but I may have to wear my last summer's white dress to the wedding. It's too short, but ma says it's plenty good for this summer. I'll be so mortified if I have to wear it."

"I'd rather not go at all than wear a dress that wasn't nice," said Felicity pleasantly.

"I'd go to the wedding if I had to go in my school dress," cried Sara Ray. "I've never been to anything. I wouldn't miss it for the world."

"My Aunt Jane always said that if you were neat and tidy it didn't matter whether you were dressed fine or not," said Peter.

"I'm sick and tired of hearing about your Aunt Jane," said Felicity crossly.

Peter looked grieved but held his peace. Felicity was very hard on him that spring, but his loyalty never wavered. Everything she said or did was right in Peter's eyes.

"It's all very well to be neat and tidy," said Sara Ray, "but *I* like a little style too."

"I think you'll find your mother will get you a new dress after all," comforted Cecily. "Anyway, nobody will notice you because everyone will be looking at the bride. Aunt Olivia will make a lovely bride. Just think how sweet she'll look in a white silk dress and a floating veil."

"She says she is going to have the ceremony performed out here in the orchard under her own tree," said the Story Girl.

"Won't that be romantic? It almost makes me feel like getting married myself."

"What a way to talk," rebuked Felicity, "and you only fifteen."

"Lots of people have been married at fifteen," laughed the Story Girl. "Lady Jane Gray was."

"But you are always saying that Valeria H. Montague's stories are silly and not true to life, so that is no argument," retorted Felicity, who knew more about cooking than about history, and evidently imagined that the Lady Jane Gray was one of Valeria's titled heroines.

The wedding was a perennial source of conversation among us in those days; but presently its interest palled for a time in the light of another quite tremendous happening. One Saturday night Peter's mother called to take him home with her for Sunday. She had been working at Mr. James Frewen's, and Mr. Frewen was driving her home. We had never seen Peter's mother before, and we looked at her with discreet curiosity. She was a plump, black-eyed little woman, neat as a pin, but with a rather tired and care-worn face that looked as if it should have been rosy and jolly. Life had been a hard battle for her, and I rather think that her curly-headed little lad was all that had kept heart and spirit in her. Peter went home with her and returned Sunday evening. We were in the orchard sitting around the Pulpit Stone, where we had, according to the custom of the households of King, been learning our golden texts and memory verses for the next Sunday School lesson. Paddy, grown sleek and handsome again, was sitting on the stone itself, washing his jowls.

Peter joined us with a very queer expression on his face. He seemed bursting with some news which he wanted to tell and yet hardly liked to.

"Why are you looking so mysterious, Peter?" demanded the Story Girl.

"What do you think has happened?" asked Peter solemnly.

"What has?"

"My father has come home," answered Peter.

The announcement produced all the sensation he could have wished. We crowded around him in excitement.

"Peter! When did he come back?"

"Saturday night. He was there when ma and I got home. It give her an awful turn. I didn't know him at first, of course."

"Peter Craig, I believe you are glad your father has come back," cried the Story Girl.

"'Course I'm glad," retorted Peter.

"And after you saying you didn't want ever to see him again," said Felicity.

"You just wait. You haven't heard my story yet. I wouldn't have been glad to see father if he'd come back the same as he went away. But he is a changed man. He happened to go into a revival meeting one night this spring and he got converted. And he's come home to stay, and he says he's never going to drink another drop, but he's going to look after his family. Ma isn't to do any more washing for nobody but him and me, and I'm not to be a hired boy any longer. He says I can stay with your Uncle Roger till the fall 'cause I promised I would, but after that I'm to stay home and go to school right along and learn to be whatever I'd like to be. I tell you it made me feel queer. Everything seemed to be upset. But he gave ma forty dollars—every cent he had—so I guess he really is converted."

"I hope it will last, I'm sure," said Felicity. She did not say it nastily, however. We were all glad for Peter's sake, though a little dizzy over the unexpectedness of it all.

"This is what I'd like to know," said Peter. "How did Peg Bowen know my father was coming home? Don't you tell me she isn't a witch after that."

"And she knew about your Aunt Olivia's wedding, too," added Sara Ray.

"Oh, well, she likely heard that from some one. Grown up folks talk things over long before they tell them to children," said Cecily.

"Well, she couldn't have heard father was coming home from any one," answered Peter. "He was converted up in Maine, where nobody knew him, and he never told a soul he was coming till he got here. No, you can believe what you like, but I'm satisfied at last that Peg is a witch and that skull of hers does tell her things. She told me father was coming home and he come!"

"How happy you must be," sighed Sara Ray romantically. "It's just like that story in the *Family Guide,* where the missing earl comes home to his family just as the Countess and Lady Violetta are going to be turned out by the cruel heir."

Felicity sniffed.

"There's some difference, I guess. The earl had been imprisoned for years in a loathsome dungeon."

Perhaps Peter's father had too, if we but realized it—imprisoned in the dungeon of his own evil appetites and habits, than which none could be more loathsome. But a Power, mightier than the forces of evil, had struck off his fetters and led him back to his long-forfeited liberty and light. And no countess or lady of high degree could have welcomed a long-lost earl home more joyfully than the tired little washerwoman had welcomed the erring husband of her youth.

But in Peter's ointment of joy there was a fly or two. So very, very few things are flawless in this world, even on the golden road.

"Of course I'm awful glad that father has come back and that ma won't have to wash any more," he said with a sigh, "but there are two things that kind of worry me. My Aunt Jane always said that it didn't do any good to worry, and I s'pose it don't, but it's kind of a relief."

"What's worrying you?" asked Felix.

"Well, for one thing I'll feel awful bad to go away from you all. I'll miss you just dreadful, and I won't even be able to go to the same school. I'll have to go to Markdale school."

"But you must come and see us often," said Felicity graciously. "Markdale isn't so far away, and you could spend every other Saturday afternoon with us anyway."

Peter's black eyes filled with adoring gratitude.

"That's so kind of you, Felicity. I'll come as often as I can, of course; but it won't be the same as being around with you all the time. The other thing is even worse. You see, it was a Methodist revival father got converted in, and so of course he joined the Methodist church. He wasn't anything before. He used to say he was a Nothingarian and lived up to it—kind of bragging like. But he's a strong Methodist now, and is going to go to Markdale Methodist church and pay to the salary. Now what'll he say when I tell him I'm a Presbyterian?"

"You haven't told him, yet?" asked the Story Girl.

"No, I didn't dare. I was scared he'd say I'd have to be a Methodist."

"Well, Methodists are pretty near as good as Presbyterians," said Felicity, with the air of one making a great concession.

"I guess they're every bit as good," retorted Peter. "But that ain't the point. I've got to be a Presbyterian, 'cause I stick to a thing when I once decide it. But I expect father will be mad when he finds out."

"If he's converted he oughtn't to get mad," said Dan.

"Well, lots o' people do. But if he isn't mad he'll be sorry, and that'll be even worse, for a Presbyterian I'm bound to be. But I expect it will make things unpleasant."

"You needn't tell him anything about it," advised Felicity. "Just keep quiet and go to the Methodist church until you get big, and then you can go where you please."

"No, that wouldn't be honest," said Peter sturdily. "My Aunt Jane always said it was best to be open and above board in everything, and especially in religion. So I'll tell father right out, but I'll wait a few weeks so as not to spoil things for ma too soon if he acts up."

Peter was not the only one who had secret cares. Sara Ray was beginning to feel worried over her looks. I heard her and Cecily talking over their troubles one evening while I was weeding the onion bed and they were behind the hedge knitting lace. I did not mean to eavesdrop. I supposed they knew I was there until Cecily overwhelmed me with indignation later on.

"I'm so afraid, Cecily, that I'm going to be homely all my life," said poor Sara with a tremble in her voice. "You can stand being ugly when you are young if you have any hope of being better looking when you grow up. But I'm getting worse. Aunt Mary says I'm going to be the very image of Aunt Matilda. And Aunt Matilda is as homely as she can be. It isn't"—and poor Sara sighed—"a very cheerful prospect. If I am ugly nobody will ever want to marry me, and," concluded Sara candidly, "I don't want to be an old maid."

"But plenty of girls get married who aren't a bit pretty," comforted Cecily. "Besides, you are real nice looking at times, Sara. I think you are going to have a nice figure."

"But just look at my hands," moaned Sara. "They're simply covered with warts."

"Oh, the warts will all disappear before you grow up," said Cecily.

"But they won't disappear before the school concert. How

am I to get up there and recite? You know there is one line in my recitation, 'She waved her lily-white hand,' and I have to wave mine when I say it. Fancy waving a lily-white hand all covered with warts. I've tried every remedy I ever heard of, but nothing does any good. Judy Pineau said if I rubbed them with toad-spit it would take them away for sure. But how am I to get any toad-spit?"

"It doesn't sound like a very nice remedy, anyhow," shuddered Cecily. "I'd rather have the warts. But do you know, I believe if you didn't cry so much over every little thing, you'd be ever so much better looking. Crying spoils your eyes and makes the end of your nose red."

"I can't help crying," protested Sara. "My feelings are so very sensitive. I've given up trying to keep *that* resolution."

"Well, men don't like cry-babies," said Cecily sagely. Cecily had a good deal of Mother Eve's wisdom tucked away in that smooth, brown head of hers.

"Cecily, do you ever intend to be married?" asked Sara in a confidential tone.

"Goodness!" cried Cecily, quite shocked. "It will be time enough when I grow up to think of that, Sara."

"I should think you'd have to think of it now, with Cyrus Brisk as crazy after you as he is."

"I wish Cyrus Brisk was at the bottom of the Red Sea," exclaimed Cecily, goaded into a spurt of temper by mention of the detested name.

"What has Cyrus been doing now?" asked Felicity, coming around the corner of the hedge.

"Doing *now!* It's *all* the time. He just worries me to death," returned Cecily angrily. "He keeps writing me letters and putting them in my desk or in my reader. I never answer one of them, but he keeps on. And in the last one, mind you, he said he'd do something desperate right off if I wouldn't promise to marry him when we grew up."

"Just think, Cecily, you've had a proposal already," said Sara Ray in an awe-struck tone.

"But he hasn't done anything desperate yet, and that was last week," commented Felicity, with a toss of her head.

"He sent me a lock of his hair and wanted one of mine in exchange," continued Cecily indignantly. "I tell you I sent his back to him pretty quick."

"Did you never answer any of his letters?" asked Sara Ray.
"No, indeed! I guess not!"

"Do you know," said Felicity, "I believe if you wrote him just once and told him your exact opinion of him in good plain English it would cure him of his nonsense."

"I couldn't do that. I haven't enough spunk," confessed Cecily with a blush. "But I'll tell you what I did do once. He wrote me a long letter last week. It was just awfully *soft,* and every other word was spelled wrong. He even spelled baking soda, 'bacon soda!' "

"What on earth had he to say about baking soda in a love-letter?" asked Felicity.

"Oh, he said his mother sent him to the store for some and he forgot it because he was thinking about me. Well, I just took his letter and wrote in all the words, spelled right, above the wrong ones, in red ink, just as Mr. Perkins makes us do with our dictation exercises, and sent it back to him. I thought maybe he'd feel insulted and stop writing to me."

"And did he?"

"No, he didn't. It is *my* opinion you can't insult Cyrus Brisk. He is too thick-skinned. He wrote another letter, and thanked me for correcting his mistakes, and said it made him feel glad because it showed I was beginning to take an interest in him when I wanted him to spell better. Did you ever? Miss Marwood says it is wrong to hate anyone, but I don't care, I hate Cyrus Brisk."

"Mrs. Cyrus Brisk *would* be an awful name," giggled Felicity.

"Flossie Brisk says Cyrus is ruining all the trees on his father's place cutting your name on them," said Sara Ray. "His father told him he would whip him if he didn't stop, but Cyrus keeps right on. He told Flossie it relieved his feelings. Flossie says he cut yours and his together on the birch tree in front of the parlour window, and a row of hearts around them."

"Just where every visitor can see them, I suppose," lamented Cecily. "He just worries my life out. And what I mind most of all is, he sits and looks at me in school with such melancholy, reproachful eyes when he ought to be working sums. I won't look at him, but I *feel* him staring at me, and it makes me so nervous."

"They say his mother was out of her mind at one time," said Felicity.

I do not think Felicity was quite well pleased that Cyrus should have passed over her rose-red prettiness to set his affections on that demure elf of a Cecily. She did not want the allegiance of Cyrus in the least, but it was something of a slight that he had not wanted her to want it.

"And he sends me pieces of poetry he cuts out of the papers," Cecily went on, "with lots of the lines marked with a lead pencil. Yesterday he put one in his letter, and this is what he marked:

> " 'If you will not relent to me
> Then must I learn to know
> Darkness alone till life be flown.

Here—I have the piece in my sewing-bag—I'll read it all to you."

Those three graceless girls read the sentimental rhyme and giggled over it. Poor Cyrus! His young affections were sadly misplaced. But after all, though Cecily never relented towards him, he did not condemn himself to darkness alone till life was flown. Quite early in life he wedded a stout, rosy, buxom lass, the very antithesis of his first love; he prospered in his undertakings, raised a large and respectable family, and was eventually appointed a Justice of the Peace. Which was all very sensible of Cyrus.

CHAPTER 15

THE RAPE OF THE LOCK

JUNE WAS crowded full of interest that year. We gathered in with its sheaf of fragrant days the choicest harvest of childhood. Things happened right along. Cecily declared she hated to go to sleep for fear she might miss something. There were so many dear delights along the golden road to give us pleasure—the earth dappled with new blossom, the dance of shadows in the fields, the rustling, rain-wet ways of the woods, the faint fragrance in meadow lanes, liltings of birds and croon of bees in the old orchard, windy pipings on the hills, sunset behind the pines, limpid dews filling primrose cups, crescent moons through darkling boughs, soft nights alight with blinking stars. We enjoyed all these boons, unthinkingly and light-heartedly, as children do. And besides these, there was the absorbing little drama of human life which was being enacted all around us, and in which each of us played a satisfying part—the gay preparations for Aunt Olivia's mid-June wedding, the excitement of practising for the concert with which our school-teacher, Mr. Perkins, had elected to close the school year, and Cecily's troubles with Cyrus Brisk, which furnished unholy mirth for the rest of us, though Cecily could not see the funny side of it at all.

Matters went from bad to worse in the case of the irrepressible Cyrus. He continued to shower Cecily with notes, the spelling of which showed no improvement; he worried the life out of her by constantly threatening to fight Willy Fraser—although, as Felicity sarcastically pointed out, he never did it.

"But I'm always afraid he will," said Cecily, "and it would be such a *disgrace* to have two boys fighting over me in school."

"You *must* have encouraged Cyrus a little in the beginning or he'd never have been so persevering," said Felicity unjustly.

"I never did!" cried outraged Cecily. "You know very well, Felicity King, that I hated Cyrus Brisk ever since the very first time I saw his big, fat, red face. So there!"

"Felicity is just jealous because Cyrus didn't take a notion to her instead of you, Sis," said Dan.

"Talk sense!" snapped Felicity.

"If I did you wouldn't understand me, sweet little sister," rejoined aggravating Dan.

Finally Cyrus crowned his iniquities by stealing the denied lock of Cecily's hair. One sunny afternoon in school, Cecily and Kitty Marr asked and received permission to sit out on the side bench before the open window, where the cool breeze swept in from the green fields beyond. To sit on this bench was always considered a treat, and was only allowed as a reward of merit; but Cecily and Kitty had another reason for wishing to sit there. Kitty had read in a magazine that sunbaths were good for the hair; so both she and Cecily tossed their long braids over the window-sill and let them hang there in the broiling sunshine. And while Cecily sat thus, diligently working a fraction sum on her slate, that base Cyrus asked permission to go out, having previously borrowed a pair of scissors from one of the big girls who did fancy work at the noon recess. Outside, Cyrus sneaked up close to the window and cut off a piece of Cecily's hair.

This rape of the lock did not produce quite such terrible consequences as the more famous one in Pope's poem, but Cecily's soul was no less agitated than Belinda's. She cried all the way home from school about it, and only checked her tears when Dan declared he'd fight Cyrus and make him give it up.

"Oh, no, you mustn't," said Cecily, struggling with her sobs. "I won't have you fighting on my account for anything. And besides, he'd likely lick you—he's so big and rough. And the folks at home might find out all about it, and Uncle Roger would never give me any peace, and mother would be cross, for she'd never believe it wasn't my fault. It wouldn't be so bad if he'd only taken a little, but he cut a great big chunk right off the end of one of the braids. Just look at it. I'll have to cut the other to make them fair—and they'll look so awful stubby."

But Cyrus' acquirement of the chunk of hair was his last triumph. His downfall was near; and, although it involved Cecily in most humiliating experience, over which she cried half the following night, in the end she confessed it was worth undergoing just to get rid of Cyrus.

Mr. Perkins was an exceedingly strict disciplinarian. No communication of any sort was permitted between his pupils during school hours. Anyone caught violating this rule was promptly punished by the infliction of one of the weird penances for which Mr. Perkins was famous, and which were generally far worse than ordinary whipping.

One day in school Cyrus sent a letter across to Cecily. Usually he left his effusions in her desk, or between the leaves of her books; but this time it was passed over to her under cover of the desk through the hands of two or three scholars. Just as Em Frewen held it over the aisle Mr. Perkins wheeled around from his station before the blackboard and caught her in the act.

"Bring that here, Emmeline," he commanded.

Cyrus turned quite pale. Em carried the note to Mr. Perkins. He took it, held it up, and scrutinized the address.

"Did you write this to Cecily, Emmeline?" he asked.

"No, sir."

"Who wrote it then?"

Em said quite shamelessly that she didn't know—it had just been passed over from the next row.

"And I suppose you have no idea where it came from?" said Mr. Perkins, with his frightful, sardonic grin. "Well, perhaps Cecily can tell us. You may take your seat, Emmeline, and you will remain at the foot of your spelling class for a week as punishment for passing the note. Cecily, come here."

Indignant Em sat down and poor, innocent Cecily was haled forth to public ignominy. She went with a crimson face.

"Cecily," said her tormentor, "do you know who wrote this letter to you?"

Cecily, like a certain renowned personage, could not tell a lie.

"I—I think so, sir," she murmured faintly.

"Who was it?"

"I can't tell you that," stammered Cecily, on the verge of tears.

"Ah!" said Mr. Perkins politely. "Well, I suppose I could easily find out by opening it. But it is very impolite to open other people's letters. I think I have a better plan. Since you refuse to tell me who wrote it, open it yourself, take this chalk, and copy the contents on the blackboard that we may all enjoy them. And sign the writer's name at the bottom."

"Oh," gasped Cecily, choosing the lesser of two evils, "I'll tell you who wrote it—it was—"

"Hush!" Mr. Perkins checked her with a gentle motion of his hand. He was always most gentle when most inexorable. "You did not obey me when I first ordered you to tell me the writer. You cannot have the privilege of doing so now. Open the note, take the chalk, and do as I command you."

Worms will turn, and even meek, mild, obedient little souls like Cecily may be goaded to the point of wild, sheer rebellion.

"I—I won't!" she cried passionately.

Mr. Perkins, martinet though he was, would hardly, I think, have inflicted such a punishment on Cecily, who was a favourite of his, had he known the real nature of that luckless missive.

But, as he afterwards admitted, he thought it was merely a note from some other girl, of such trifling sort as school-girls are wont to write; and moreover, he had already committed himself to the decree, which, like those of Mede and Persian, must not alter. To let Cecily off, after her mad defiance, would be to establish a revolutionary precedent.

"So you really think you won't?" he queried smilingly. "Well, on second thoughts, you may take your choice. Either you will do as I have bidden you, or you will sit for three days with"— Mr. Perkins' eye skimmed over the school-room to find a boy who was sitting alone—"with Cyrus Brisk."

This choice of Mr. Perkins, who knew nothing of the little drama of emotions that went on under the routine of lessons and exercises in his domain, was purely accidental, but we took it at the time as a stroke of diabolical genius. It left Cecily no choice. She would have done almost anything before she would have sat with Cyrus Brisk. With flashing eyes she tore open the letter, snatched up the chalk, and dashed at the blackboard.

In a few minutes the contents of that letter graced the expanse usually sacred to more prosaic compositions. I cannot reproduce it verbatim, for I had no after opportunity of refreshing my memory. But I remember that it was exceedingly sentimental and exceedingly ill-spelled—for Cecily mercilessly copied down poor Cyrus' mistakes. He wrote her that he wore her hare over his hart—"and he stole it," Cecily threw passionately over her shoulder at Mr. Perkins—that her eyes were so sweet and lovely that he couldn't find words nice enuf to describ them, that he could never forget how butiful she had looked in prar meeting the evening before, and that some meels he couldn't eat for thinking of her, with more to the same effect and he signed it "yours till deth us do part, Cyrus Brisk."

As the writing proceeded we scholars exploded into smothered laughter, despite our awe of Mr. Perkins. Mr. Perkins himself could not keep a straight face. He turned abruptly away and looked out of the window, but we could see his shoulders shaking. When Cecily had finished and had thrown down the chalk with bitter vehemence, he turned around with a very red face.

"That will do. You may sit down. Cyrus, since it seems you are the guilty person, take the eraser and wipe that off the board. Then go stand in the corner, facing the room, and hold your arms straight above your head until I tell you to take them down."

Cyrus obeyed and Cecily fled to her seat and wept, nor did Mr. Perkins meddle with her more that day. She bore her burden of humiliation bitterly for several days, until she was suddenly comforted by a realization that Cyrus had ceased to persecute her. He wrote no more letters, he gazed no longer in rapt adoration, he brought no more votive offerings of gum and pencils to her shrine. At first we thought he had been cured by the unmerciful chaffing he had to undergo from his mates, but eventually his sister told Cecily the true reason. Cyrus had at last been driven to believe that Cecily's aversion to him was real, and not merely the defence of maiden coyness. If she hated him so intensely that she would rather write that note on the blackboard than sit with him, what use was it to sigh like a furnace longer for her? Mr. Perkins had blighted love's young dream for Cyrus with a killing frost. Thenceforth sweet Cecily kept the noiseless tenor of her way unvexed by the attentions of enamoured swains.

CHAPTER 16

AUNT UNA'S STORY

FELICITY, AND Cecily, Dan, Felix, Sara Ray and I were sitting one evening on the mossy stones in Uncle Roger's hill pasture, where we had sat the morning the Story Girl told us the tale of the Wedding Veil of the Proud Princess. But it was evening now and the valley beneath us was brimmed up with the glow of the afterlight. Behind us, two tall, shapely spruce trees rose up against the sunset, and through the dark oriel of their sundered branches an evening star looked down. We sat on a little strip of emerald grassland and before us was a sloping meadow all white with daisies.

We were waiting for Peter and the Story Girl. Peter had gone to Markdale after dinner to spend the afternoon with his reunited parents because it was his birthday. He had left us grimly determined to confess to his father the dark secret of his Presbyterianism, and we were anxious to know what the result had been. The Story Girl had gone that morning with Miss Reade to visit the latter's home near Charlottetown, and we expected soon to see her coming gaily along over the fields from the Armstrong place.

Presently Peter came jauntily stepping along the field path up the hill.

"Hasn't Peter got tall?" said Cecily.

"Peter is growing to be a very fine looking boy," decreed Felicity.

"I notice he's got ever so much handsomer since his father came home," said Dan, with a killing sarcasm that was wholly lost on Felicity, who gravely responded that she supposed it was because Peter felt so much freer from care and responsibility.

"What luck, Peter?" yelled Dan, as soon as Peter was within earshot.

"Everything's all right," he shouted jubilantly. "I told father right off, licketty-split, as soon as I got home," he added when he reached us. "I was anxious to have it over with. I says, solemn-like, 'Dad, there's something I've got to tell you, and I don't know how you'll take it, but it can't be helped,' I says. Dad looked pretty sober, and he says, says he, 'What have you been up to, Peter? Don't be afraid to tell me. I've been forgiven to seventy times seven, so surely I can forgive a little, too?' 'Well,' I says, desperate-like, 'the truth is, father, I'm a Presbyterian. I made up my mind last summer, the time of the Judgment Day, that I'd be a Presbyterian, and I've got to stick to it. I'm sorry I can't be a Methodist, like you and mother and Aunt Jane, but I can't and that's all there is to it,' I says. Then I waited, scared-like. But father, he just looked relieved and he says, says he, 'Goodness, boy, you can be a Presbyterian or anything else you like, so long as it's Protestant. I'm not caring,' he says. 'The main thing is that you must be good and do what's right.' I tell you," concluded Peter emphatically, "father is a Christian all right."

"Well, I suppose your mind will be at rest now," said Felicity. "What's that you have in your buttonhole?"

"That's a four-leaved clover," answered Peter exultantly. "That means good luck for the summer. I found it in Markdale. There ain't much clover in Carlisle this year of any kind of leaf. The crop is going to be a failure. Your Uncle Roger says it's because there ain't enough old maids in Carlisle. There's lots of them in Markdale, and that's the reason, he says, why they always have such good clover crops there."

"What on earth have old maids to do with it?" cried Cecily.

"I don't believe they've a single thing to do with it, but Mr. Roger says they have, and he says a man called Darwin proved it. This is the rigmarole he got off to me the other day. The clover crop depends on there being plenty of bumble-bees, because they are the only insects with tongues long enough to—to—fer—fertilize—I think he called it—the blossoms. But mice eat bumble-bees and cats eat mice and old maids keep cats. So your Uncle Roger says the more old maids the more cats, and the more cats the fewer field-mice, and the fewer field-mice the more bumble-bees, and the more bumble-bees the better clover crops."

"So don't worry if you do get to be old maids, girls," said Dan. "Remember, you'll be helping the clover crops."

"I never heard such stuff as you boys talk," said Felicity, "and Uncle Roger is no better."

"There comes the Story Girl," cried Cecily eagerly. "Now we'll hear all about Beautiful Alice's home."

The Story Girl was bombarded with eager questions as soon as she arrived. Miss Reade's home was a dream of a place, it appeared. The house was just covered with ivy and there was a most delightful old garden—"and," added the Story Girl, with the joy of a connoisseur who has found a rare gem, "the sweetest little story connected with it. And I saw the hero of the story too."

"Where was the heroine?" queried Cecily.

"She is dead."

"Oh, of course she'd have to die," exclaimed Dan in disgust. "I'd like a story where somebody lived once in awhile."

"I've told you heaps of stories where people lived," retorted the Story Girl. "If this heroine hadn't died there wouldn't have been any story. She was Miss Reade's aunt and her name was Una, and I believe she must have been just like Miss Reade herself. Miss Reade told me all about her. When we went into the garden I saw in one corner of it an old stone bench arched over by a couple of pear trees and all grown about with grass and violets. And an old man was sitting on it—a bent old man with long, snow-white hair and beautiful sad blue eyes. He seemed very lonely and sorrowful and I wondered that Miss Reade didn't speak to him. But she never let on she saw him and took me away to another part of the garden. After awhile he got up and went away and then Miss Reade said, 'Come over to Aunt Una's seat and I will tell you about her and her lover—that man who has just gone out.'

" 'Oh, isn't he too old for a lover?' I said.

"Beautiful Alice laughed and said it was forty years since he had been her Aunt Una's lover. He had been a tall, handsome young man then, and her Aunt Una was a beautiful girl of nineteen.

"We went over and sat down and Miss Reade told me all about her. She said that when she was a child she had heard much of her Aunt Una—that she seemed to have been one of those people who are not soon forgotten, whose personality seems to linger about the scenes of their lives long after they have passed away."

"What is a personality? Is it another word for ghost?" asked Peter.

"No," said the Story Girl shortly. "I can't stop in a story to explain words."

"I don't believe you know what it is yourself," said Felicity.

The Story Girl picked up her hat, which she had thrown down on the grass, and placed it defiantly on her brown curls.

"I'm going in," she announced. "I have to help Aunt Olivia ice a cake tonight, and you all seem more interested in dictionaries than stories."

"That's not fair," I exclaimed. "Dan and Felix and Sara Ray and Cecily and I have never said a word. It's mean to punish us for what Peter and Felicity did. We want to hear the rest of the story. Never mind what a personality is but go on—and, Peter, you young ass, keep still."

"I only wanted to know," muttered Peter sulkily.

"I *do* know what personality is, but it's hard to explain," said the Story Girl, relenting. "It's what makes you different from Dan, Peter, and me different from Felicity or Cecily. Miss Reade's Aunt Una had a personality that was very uncommon. And she was beautiful, too, with white skin and night-black eyes and hair—a 'moonlight beauty,' Miss Reade called it. She used to keep a kind of a diary, and Miss Reade's mother used to read parts of it to her. She wrote verses in it and they were lovely; and she wrote descriptions of the old garden which she loved very much. Miss Reade said that everything in the garden, plot or shrub or tree, recalled to her mind some phrase or verse of her Aunt Una's, so that the whole place seemed full of her, and her memory haunted the walks like a faint, sweet perfume.

"Una had, as I've told you, a lover; and they were to have been married on her twentieth birthday. Her wedding dress was to have been a gown of white brocade with purple violets in it. But a little while before it she took ill with fever and died; and she was buried on her birthday instead of being married. It was just in the time of opening roses. Her lover has been faithful to her ever since; he has never married, and every June, on her birthday, he makes a pilgrimage to the old garden and sits for a long time in silence on the bench where he used to woo her on crimson eves and moonlight nights of long ago. Miss Reade says she always loves to see him sitting there because it gives her such a deep and lasting sense of the beauty and strength of love which can thus outlive time and death. And sometimes, she says, it gives her a little eerie feeling, too, as if her Aunt Una were really sitting there beside him, keeping tryst, although she has been in her grave for forty years."

"It would be real romantic to die young and have your lover make a pilgrimage to your garden every year," reflected Sara Ray.

"It would be more comfortable to go on living and get married to him," said Felicity. "Mother says all those sentimental ideas are bosh and I expect they are. It's a wonder Beautiful Alice hasn't a beau herself. She is so pretty and ladylike."

"The Carlisle fellows all say she is too stuck up," said Dan.

"There's nobody in Carlisle half good enough for her," cried the Story Girl, "except—except—"

"Except who?" asked Felix.

"Never mind," said the Story Girl mysteriously.

CHAPTER 17

AUNT OLIVIA'S WEDDING

WHAT A delightful, old-fashioned, wholesome excitement there was about Aunt Olivia's wedding! The Monday and Tuesday preceding it we did not go to school at all, but were all kept home to do chores and run errands. The cooking and decorating and arranging that went on those two days was amazing, and Felicity was so happy over it all that she did not even quarrel with Dan—though she narrowly escaped it when he told her that the Governor's wife was coming to the wedding.

"Mind you have some of her favourite rusks for her," he said.

"I guess," said Felicity with dignity, "that Aunt Olivia's wedding supper will be good enough for even a Governor's wife."

"I s'pose none of us except the Story Girl will get to the first table," said Felix, rather gloomily.

"Never mind," comforted Felicity. "There's a whole turkey to be kept for us, and a freezerful of ice cream. Cecily and I are going to wait on the tables, and we'll put away a little of everything that's extra nice for our suppers."

"I do so want to have my supper with you," sighed Sara Ray, "but I s'pose ma will drag me with her wherever she goes. She won't trust me out of her sight a minute the whole evening—I know she won't."

"I'll get Aunt Olivia to ask her to let you have your supper with us," said Cecily. "She can't refuse the bride's request."

"You don't know all ma can do," returned Sara darkly. "No, I feel that I'll have to eat my supper with her. But I suppose I ought to be very thankful I'm to get to the wedding at all, and that ma did get me a new white dress for it. Even yet I'm so scared something will happen to prevent me from getting to it."

Monday evening shrouded itself in clouds, and all night long the voice of the wind answered to the voice of the rain. Tuesday the downpour continued. We were quite frantic about it. Suppose it kept on raining over Wednesday! Aunt Olivia couldn't be married in the orchard then. That would be too bad, especially when the late apple tree had most obligingly kept its store of blossom until after all the other trees had faded and then burst lavishly into bloom for Aunt Olivia's wedding. That apple tree was always very late in blooming, and this year it was a week later than usual. It was a sight to see—a great tree-pyramid with high, far-spreading boughs, over which a wealth of rosy snow seemed to have been flung. Never had bride a more magnificent canopy.

To our rapture, however, it cleared up beautifully Tuesday evening, and the sun, before setting in purple pomp, poured a flood of wonderful radiance over the whole great, green, diamond-dripping world, promising a fair morrow. Uncle Alec drove off to the station through it to bring home the bridegroom and his best man. Dan was full of a wild idea that we should all meet them at the gate, armed with cowbells and tin-pans, and "charivari" them up the lane. Peter sided with him, but the rest of us voted down the suggestion.

"Do you want Dr. Seton to think we are a pack of wild Indians?" asked Felicity severely. "A nice opinion he'd have of our manners!"

"Well, it's the only chance we'll have to chivaree them," grumbled Dan. "Aunt Olivia wouldn't mind. *She* can take a joke."

"Ma would kill you if you did such a thing," warned Felicity. "Dr. Seton lives in Halifax and they *never* chivaree people there. He would think it very vulgar."

"Then he should have stayed in Halifax and got married there," retorted Dan, sulkily.

We were very curious to see our uncle-elect. When he came and Uncle Alec took him into the parlour, we were all crowded into the dark corner behind the stairs to peep at him. Then we fled to the moonlight world outside and discussed him at the dairy.

"He's bald," said Cecily disappointedly.

"And *rather* short and stout," said Felicity.

"He's forty, if he's a day," said Dan.

"Never you mind," cried the Story Girl loyally, "Aunt Olivia loves him with all her heart."

"And more than that, he's got lots of money," added Felicity.

"Well, he may be all right," said Peter, "but it's my opinion that your Aunt Olivia could have done just as well on the Island."

"*Your* opinion doesn't matter very much to *our* family," said Felicity crushingly.

But when we made the acquaintance of Dr. Seton next morning we liked him enormously, and voted him a jolly good fellow. Even Peter remarked aside to me that he guessed Miss Olivia hadn't made much of a mistake after all, though it was plain he thought she was running a risk in not sticking to the Island. The girls had not much time to discuss him with us. They were all exceedingly busy and whisked about at such a rate that they seemed to possess the power of being in half a dozen places at once. The importance of Felicity was quite terrible. But after dinner came a lull.

"Thank goodness, everything is ready at last," breathed Felicity devoutly, as we foregathered for a brief space in the fir wood. "We've nothing more to do now but get dressed. It's really a serious thing to have a wedding in the family."

"I have a note from Sara Ray," said Cecily. "Judy Pineau brought it up when she brought Mrs. Ray's spoons. Just let me read it to you:—

" 'DEAREST CECILY:—A *dreadful misfortune* has happened to me. Last night I went with Judy to water the cows and in the spruce bush we found a *wasps' nest* and Judy thought it was *an old one* and she *poked it with a stick.* And it was a *new one,* full of wasps, and they all flew out and *stung us terribly,* on the face and hands. My face is all swelled up and I can *hardly see* out of one eye. The *suffering* was awful but I didn't mind that as much as being scared ma wouldn't take me to the wedding. But she says I can go and I'm going. I know that I am a *hard-looking sight,* but it isn't anything catching. I am writing this so that you won't get a shock when you see me. Isn't it *so strange* to think your dear Aunt Olivia is going away? How you will miss her! But your loss will be her gain.

" '*Au revoir,*

" 'Your loving chum,

" 'SARA RAY.' "

"That poor child," said the Story Girl.

"Well, all I hope is that strangers won't take her for one of the family," remarked Felicity in a disgusted tone.

Aunt Olivia was married at five o'clock in the orchard under the late apple tree. It was a pretty scene. The air was full of the perfume of apple bloom, and the bees blundered foolishly and delightfully from one blossom to another, half drunken with perfume. The old orchard was full of smiling guests in wedding garments. Aunt Olivia was most beautiful amid the frost of her bridal veil, and the Story Girl, in an unusually long white dress, with her brown curls clubbed up behind, looked so tall and grown-up that we hardly recognized her. After the ceremony—during which Sara Ray cried all the time— there was a royal wedding supper, and Sara Ray was permitted to eat her share of the feast with us.

"I'm glad I was stung by the wasps after all," she said delightedly. "If I hadn't been ma would never have let me eat with you. She just got tired explaining to people what was the matter with my face, and so she was glad to get rid of me. I know I look awful, but, oh, wasn't the bride a dream?"

We missed the Story Girl, who, of course, had to have her supper at the bridal table; but we were a hilarious little crew and the girls had nobly kept their promise to save tid-bits for us. By the time the last table was cleared away Aunt Olivia and our new uncle were ready to go. There was an orgy of tears and leavetakings, and then they drove away into the odorous moonlight night. Dan and Peter pursued them down the lane with a fiendish din of bells and pans, much to Felicity's wrath. But Aunt Olivia and Uncle Robert took it in good part and waved their hands back to us with peals of laughter.

"They're just that pleased with themselves that they wouldn't mind if there was an earthquake," said Felix, grinning.

"It's been splendid and exciting, and everything went off well," sighed Cecily, "but, oh dear, it's going to be so queer and lonesome without Aunt Olivia. I just believe I'll cry all night."

"You're tired to death, that's what's the matter with you," said Dan, returning. "You girls have worked like slaves today."

"Tomorrow will be even harder," said Felicity comfortingly. "Everything will have to be cleaned up and put away."

Peg Bowen paid us a call the next day and was regaled with a feast of fat things left over from the supper.

"Well, I've had all I can eat," she said, when she had finished and brought out her pipe. "And that doesn't happen to me every day. There ain't been as much marrying as there used to be, and half the time they just sneak off to the minister, as if they were ashamed of it, and get married without any wedding or supper. That ain't the King way, though. And so Olivia's gone off at last. She weren't in any hurry but they tell me she's done well. Time'll show."

"Why don't you get married yourself, Peg?" queried Uncle Roger teasingly. We held our breath over his temerity.

"Because I'm not so easy to please as your wife will be," retorted Peg.

She departed in high good humour over her repartee. Meeting Sara Ray on the doorstep she stopped and asked her what was the matter with her face.

"Wasps," stammered Sara Ray, laconic from terror.

"Humph! And your hands?"

"Warts."

"I'll tell you what'll take *them* away. You get a pertater and go out under the full moon, cut the pertater in two, rub your warts with one half and say, 'One, two, three, warts, go away from me.' Then rub them with the other half and say, 'One, two, three, four, warts, never trouble me more.' Then bury the pertater and never tell a living soul where you buried it. You won't have no more warts. Mind you bury the pertater, though. If you don't, and anyone picks it up, she'll get your warts."

CHAPTER 18

SARA RAY HELPS OUT

WE ALL missed Aunt Olivia greatly; she had been so merry and companionable, and had possessed such a knack of understanding small fry. But youth quickly adapts itself to changed conditions; in a few weeks it seemed as if the Story Girl had always been living at Uncle Alec's, and as if Uncle Roger had always had a fat, jolly housekeeper with a double chin and little, twinkling blue eyes. I don't think Aunt Janet ever quite got over missing Aunt Olivia, or looked upon Mrs. Hawkins as anything but a necessary evil; but life resumed its even tenor on the King farm, broken only by the ripples of excitement over the school concert and letters from Aunt Olivia describing her trip through the land of Evangeline. We incorporated the letters in *Our Magazine* under the heading "From Our Special Correspondent" and were very proud of them.

At the end of June our school concert came off and was a great event in our young lives. It was the first appearance of most of us on any platform, and some of us were very nervous. We all had recitations, except Dan, who had refused flatly to take any part and was consequently care-free.

"I'm sure I shall die when I find myself up on that platform, facing people," sighed Sara Ray, as we talked the affair over in Uncle Stephen's Walk the night before the concert.

"I'm afraid I'll faint," was Cecily's more moderate foreboding.

"I'm not one single bit nervous," said Felicity complacently.

"I'm not nervous this time," said the Story Girl, "but the first time I recited I was."

"My Aunt Jane," remarked Peter, "used to say that an old teacher of hers told her that when she was going to recite or speak in public she must just get it firmly into her mind that it was only a lot of cabbage heads she had before her, and she wouldn't be nervous."

"One mightn't be nervous, but I don't think there would be much inspiration in reciting to cabbage heads," said the Story Girl decidedly. "I want to recite to *people,* and see them looking interested and thrilled."

"If I can only get through my piece without breaking down I don't care whether I thrill people or not," said Sara Ray.

"I'm afraid I'll forget mine and get stuck," foreboded Felix. "Some of you fellows be sure and prompt me if I do—and do it quick, so's I won't get worse rattled."

"I know one thing," said Cecily resolutely, "and that is, I'm going to curl my hair for tomorrow night. I've never curled it since Peter almost died, but I simply must tomorrow night, for all the other girls are going to have theirs in curls."

"The dew and heat will take all the curl out of yours and then you'll look like a scarecrow," warned Felicity.

"No, I won't. I'm going to put my hair up in paper tonight and wet it with a curling-fluid that Judy Pineau uses. Sara brought me up a bottle of it. Judy says it is great stuff—your hair will keep in curl for days, no matter how damp the weather is. I'll leave my hair in the papers till tomorrow evening, and then I'll have beautiful curls."

"You'd better leave your hair alone," said Dan gruffly. "Smooth hair is better than a lot of fly-away curls."

But Cecily was not to be persuaded. Curls she craved and curls she meant to have.

"I'm thankful my warts have all gone, anyway," said Sara Ray.

"So they have," exclaimed Felicity. "Did you try Peg's recipe?"

"Yes. I didn't believe in it but I tried it. For the first few days afterwards I kept watching my warts, but they didn't go away, and then I gave up and forgot them. But one day last week I just happened to look at my hands and there wasn't a wart to be seen. It was the most amazing thing."

"And yet you'll say Peg Bowen isn't a witch," said Peter.

"Pshaw, it was just the potato juice," scoffed Dan.

"It was a dry old potato I had, and there wasn't much juice in it," said Sara Ray. "One hardly knows what to believe. But one thing is certain—my warts are gone."

Cecily put her hair up in curl-papers that night, thoroughly soaked in Judy Pineau's curling-fluid. It was a nasty job, for the fluid was very sticky, but Cecily persevered and got it done. Then she went to bed with a towel tied over her head to protect the pillow. She did not sleep well and had uncanny dreams, but she came down to breakfast with an expression of triumph. The Story Girl examined her head critically and said,

"Cecily, if I were you I'd take those papers out this morning."

"Oh, no; if I do my hair will be straight again by night. I mean to leave them in till the last minute."

"I wouldn't do that—I really wouldn't," persisted the Story Girl. "If you do your hair will be too curly and all bushy and fuzzy."

Cecily finally yielded and went upstairs with the Story Girl. Presently we heard a little shriek—then two little shrieks—then three. Then Felicity came flying down and called her mother. Aunt Janet went up and presently came down again with a grim mouth. She filled a large pan with warm water and carried it upstairs. We dared ask her no questions, but when Felicity came down to wash the dishes we bombarded her.

"What on earth is the matter with Cecily?" demanded Dan. "Is she sick?"

"No, she isn't. I warned her not to put her hair in curls but she wouldn't listen to me. I guess she wishes she had now. When people haven't natural curly hair they shouldn't try to make it curly. They get punished if they do."

"Look here, Felicity, never mind all that. Just tell us what has happened Sis."

"Well, this is what has happened her. That ninny of a Sara Ray brought up a bottle of mucilage instead of Judy's curling-fluid, and Cecily put her hair up with *that*. It's in an awful state."

"Good gracious!" exclaimed Dan. "Look here, will she ever get it out?"

"Goodness knows. She's got her head in soak now. Her hair is just matted together hard as a board. That's what comes of vanity," said Felicity, than whom no vainer girl existed.

Poor Cecily paid dearly enough for *her* vanity. She spent a bad forenoon, made no easier by her mother's severe rebukes. For an hour she "soaked" her head; that is, she stood over a panful of warm water and kept dipping her head in with tightly shut eyes. Finally her hair softened sufficiently to be disentangled from the curl papers; and then Aunt Janet subjected it to a merciless shampoo. Eventually they got all the mucilage washed out of it and Cecily spent the remainder of the forenoon sitting before the open oven door in the hot kitchen drying her ill-used tresses. She felt very down-hearted; her hair was of that order which, glossy and smooth normally, is dry and harsh and lustreless for several days after being shampooed.

"I'll look like a fright tonight," said the poor child to me with trembling voice. "The ends will be sticking out all over my head."

"Sara Ray is a perfect idiot," I said wrathfully.

"Oh, don't be hard on poor Sara. She didn't mean to bring me mucilage. It's really all my own fault, I know. I made a solemn vow when Peter was dying that I would never curl my hair again, and I should have kept it. It isn't right to break solemn vows. But my hair will look like dried hay tonight."

Poor Sara Ray was quite overwhelmed when she came up

and found what she had done. Felicity was very hard on her, and Aunt Janet was coldly disapproving, but sweet Cecily forgave her unreservedly, and they walked to the school that night with their arms about each other's waists as usual.

The school-room was crowded with friends and neighbours. Mr. Perkins was flying about, getting things into readiness, and Miss Reade, who was the organist of the evening, was sitting on the platform, looking her sweetest and prettiest. She wore a delightful white lace hat with a fetching little wreath of tiny forget-me-nots around the brim, a white muslin dress with sprays of blue violets scattered over it, and a black lace scarf.

"Doesn't she look angelic?" said Cecily rapturously.

"Mind you," said Sara Ray, "the Awkward Man is here— in the corner behind the door. I never remember seeing him at a concert before."

"I suppose he came to hear the Story Girl recite," said Felicity. "He is such a friend of hers."

The concert went off very well. Dialogues, choruses and recitations followed each other in rapid succession. Felix got through his without "getting stuck," and Peter did excellently, though he stuffed his hands in his trousers pockets—a habit of which Mr. Perkins had vainly tried to break him. Peter's recitation was one greatly in vogue at that time, beginning,

> "My name is Norval; on the Grampian hills
> My father feeds his flocks."

At our first practice Peter had started gaily in, rushing through the first line with no thought whatever of punctuation—"My name is Norval on the Grampian Hills."

"Stop, stop, Peter," quoth Mr. Perkins, sarcastically, "your name might be Norval if you were never on the Grampian Hills. There's a semi-colon in that line, I wish you to remember."

Peter did remember it. Cecily neither fainted nor failed when it came her turn. She recited her little piece very well, though somewhat mechanically. I think she really did much better than if she had had her desired curls. The miserable conviction that her hair, alone among that glossy-tressed bevy, was looking badly, quite blotted out all nervousness and self-consciousness from her mind. Her hair apart, she looked very pretty. The prevailing excitement had made bright her eye and flushed her cheeks rosily—too rosily, perhaps. I heard a Carlisle woman behind me whisper that Cecily King looked consumptive, just like her Aunt Felicity; and I hated her fiercely for it.

Sara Ray also managed to get through respectably, although she was pitiably nervous. Her bow was naught but a short nod—"as if her head worked on wires," whispered Felicity uncharitably—and the wave of her lily-white hand more nearly resembled an agonized jerk than a wave. We all felt relieved when she finished. She was, in a sense, one of "our crowd," and we had been afraid she would disgrace us by breaking down.

Felicity followed her and recited her selection without haste, without rest, and absolutely without any expression whatever. But what mattered it how she recited? To look at her was sufficient. What with her splendid fleece of golden curls, her great, brilliant blue eyes, her exquisitely tinted face, her dimpled hands and arms, every member of the audience must have felt it was worth the ten cents he had paid merely to see her.

The Story Girl followed. An expectant silence fell over the room, and Mr. Perkins' face lost the look of tense anxiety it had worn all the evening. Here was a performer who could be depended on. No need to fear stage fright or forgetfulness on her part. The Story Girl was not looking her best that night. White never became her, and her face was pale, though her eyes were splendid. But nobody thought about her appearance when the power and magic of her voice caught and held her listeners spellbound.

Her recitation was an old one, figuring in one of the School Readers, and we scholars all knew it off by heart. Sara Ray alone had not heard the Story Girl recite it. The latter had not been drilled at practices as had the other pupils, Mr. Perkins choosing not to waste time teaching her what she already knew far better than he did. The only time she had recited it had been at the "dress rehearsal" two nights before, at which Sara Ray had not been present.

In the poem a Florentine lady of old time, wedded to a cold and cruel husband, had died, or was supposed to have died, and had been carried to "the rich, the beautiful, the dreadful tomb" of her proud family. In the night she wakened from her trance and made her escape. Chilled and terrified, she had made her way to her husband's door, only to be driven away brutally as a restless ghost by the horror-stricken inmates. A similar reception awaited her at her father's. Then she had wandered blindly through the streets of Florence until she had fallen exhausted at the door of the lover of her girlhood. He, unafraid, had taken her in and cared for her. On the morrow, the husband and father, having discovered the empty tomb, came to claim her. She refused to return to them and the case was carried to the court of law. The verdict given was that a woman who had been "to burial borne" and left for dead, who had been driven from her husband's door and from her childhood home, "must be adjudged as dead in law and fact," was no more daughter or wife, but was set free to form what new ties she would. The climax of the whole selection came in the line,

"The court pronounces the defendant—*Dead!*" and the Story Girl was wont to render it with such dramatic intensity and power that the veriest dullard among her listeners could not have missed its force and significance.

She swept along through the poem royally, playing on the emotions of her audience as she had so often played on ours in the old orchard. Pity, terror, indignation, suspense, possessed her hearers in turn. In the court scene she surpassed herself. She was, in very truth, the Florentine judge, stern, stately, impassive. Her voice dropped into the solemnity of the all-important line,

" 'The court pronounces the defendant—' "

She paused for a breathless moment, the better to bring out the tragic import of the last word.

"Dead," piped up Sara Ray in her shrill, plaintive little voice.

The effect, to use a hackneyed but convenient phrase, can better be imagined than described. Instead of the sigh of relieved tension that should have swept over the audience at the con-clusion of the line, a burst of laughter greeted it. The Story Girl's performance was completely spoiled. She dealt the luckless Sara a glance that would have slain her on the spot could glances kill, stumbled lamely and impotently through the few remaining lines of her recitation, and fled with crimson cheeks to hide her mortification in the little corner that had been curtained off for a dressing-room. Mr. Perkins looked things not lawful to be uttered, and the audience tittered at intervals for the rest of the performance.

Sara Ray alone remained serenely satisfied until the close of the concert, when we surrounded her with a whirlwind of reproaches.

"Why," she stammered aghast, "what did I do? I—I thought she was stuck and that I ought to prompt her quick."

"You little fool, she just paused for effect," cried Felicity angrily. Felicity might be rather jealous of the Story Girl's gift, but she was furious at beholding "one of our family" made ridiculous in such a fashion. "You have less sense than anyone I ever heard of, Sara Ray."

Poor Sara dissolved in tears.

"I didn't know. I thought she was stuck," she wailed again.

She cried all the way home, but we did not try to comfort her. We felt quite out of patience with her. Even Cecily was seriously annoyed. This second blunder of Sara's was too much even for her loyalty. We saw her turn in at her own gate and go sobbing up her lane with no relenting.

The Story Girl was home before us, having fled from the schoolhouse as soon as the programme was over. We tried to sympathize with her but she would not be sympathized with.

"Please don't ever mention it to me again," she said, with compressed lips. "I never want to be reminded of it. Oh, that little *idiot!*"

"She spoiled Peter's sermon last summer and now she's spoiled your recitation," said Felicity. "*I* think it's time we gave up associating with Sara Ray."

"Oh, don't be quite so hard on her," pleaded Cecily. "Think of the life the poor child has to live at home. I know she'll cry all night."

"Oh, let's go to bed," growled Dan. "I'm good and ready for it. I've had enough of school concerts."

CHAPTER 19

BY WAY OF THE STARS

But for two of us the adventures of the night were not yet over. Silence settled down over the old house—the eerie, whisperful, creeping silence of night. Felix and Dan were already sound asleep; I was drifting near the coast o' dreams when I was aroused by a light tap on the door.

"Bev, are you asleep?" came in the Story Girl's whisper.

"No, what is it?"

"S-s-h. Get up and dress and come out. I want you."

With a good deal of curiosity and some misgiving I obeyed. What was in the wind now? Outside in the hall I found the Story Girl, with a candle in her hand, and her hat and jacket.

"Where are you going?" I whispered in amazement.

"Hush. I've got to go to the school and you must come with me. I left my coral necklace there. The clasp came loose and I was so afraid I'd lose it that I took it off and put it in the bookcase. I was feeling so upset when the concert was over that I forgot all about it."

The coral necklace was a very handsome one which had belonged to the Story Girl's mother. She had never been permitted to wear it before, and it had only been by dint of much coaxing that she had induced Aunt Janet to let her wear it to the concert.

"But there's no sense in going for it in the dead of night," I objected. "It will be quite safe. You can go for it in the morning."

"Lizzie Paxton and her daughter are going to clean the school tomorrow, and I heard Lizzie say tonight she meant to be at it by five o'clock to get through before the heat of the day. *You* know perfectly well what Liz Paxton's reputation is. If she finds that necklace I'll never see it again. Besides, if I wait till the morning, Aunt Janet may find out that I left it there and she'd never let me wear it again. No, I'm going for it now. If you're afraid," added the Story Girl with delicate scorn, "of course you needn't come."

Afraid! I'd show her!

"Come on," I said.

We slipped out of the house noiselessly and found ourselves in the unutterable solemnity and strangeness of a dark night. It was a new experience, and our hearts thrilled and our nerves tingled to the charm of it. Never had we been abroad before at such an hour. The world around us was not the world of daylight. 'Twas an alien place, full of weird, evasive enchantment and magicry.

Only in the country can one become truly acquainted with the night. There it has the solemn calm of the infinite. The dim wide fields lie in silence, wrapped in the holy mystery of darkness. A wind, loosened from wild places far away, steals out to blow over dewy, star-lit, immemorial hills. The air in the pastures is sweet with the hush of dreams, and one may rest here like a child on its mother's breast.

"Isn't it wonderful?" breathed the Story Girl as we went down the long hill. "Do you know, I can forgive Sara Ray now. I thought tonight I never could—but now it doesn't matter any more. I can even see how funny it was. Oh, wasn't it funny? *'Dead'* in that squeaky little voice of Sara's! I'll just behave to her tomorrow as if nothing had happened. It seems so long ago now, here in the night."

Neither of us ever forgot the subtle delight of that stolen walk. A spell of glamour was over us. The breezes whispered strange secrets of elf-haunted glens, and the hollows where the ferns grew were brimmed with mystery and romance. Ghostlike scents crept out of the meadows to meet us, and the fir wood before we came to the church was a living sweetness of Junebells growing in abundance.

Junebells have another and more scientific name, of course. But who could desire a better name than Junebells? They are so perfect in their way that they seem to epitomize the very scent and charm of the forest, as if the old wood's daintiest thoughts had materialized in blossom; and not all the roses by Bendameer's stream are as fragrant as a shallow sheet of Junebells under the boughs of fir.

There were fireflies abroad that night, too, increasing the gramarye of it. There is certainly something a little supernatural about fireflies. Nobody pretends to understand them. They are akin to the tribes of fairy, survivals of the elder time when the woods and hills swarmed with the little green folk. It is still very easy to believe in fairies when you see those goblin lanterns glimmering among the fir tassels.

"Isn't it beautiful?" said the Story Girl in rapture. "I wouldn't have missed it for anything. I'm glad I left my necklace. And I am glad you are with me, Bev. The others wouldn't understand so well. I like you because I don't have to talk to you all the time. It's so nice to walk with someone you don't have to talk to. Here is the graveyard. Are you frightened to pass it, Bev?"

"No, I don't think I'm frightened," I answered slowly, "but I have a queer feeling."

"So have I. But it isn't fear. I don't know what it is. I feel as if something was reaching out of the graveyard to hold me— something that wanted life—I don't like it—let's hurry. But isn't it strange to think of all the dead people in there who were once alive like you and me. I don't feel as if I could *ever* die. Do you?"

"No, but everybody must. Of course we go on living afterwards, just the same. Don't let's talk of such things here," I said hurriedly.

When we reached the school I contrived to open a window. We scrambled in, lighted a lamp and found the missing necklace. The Story Girl stood on the platform and gave an imitation of the catastrophe of the evening that made me shout with laughter. We prowled around for sheer delight over being there at an unearthly hour when everybody supposed we were sound asleep in our beds. It was with regret that we left, and we walked home as slowly as we could to prolong the adventure.

"Let's never tell anyone," said the Story Girl, as we reached home. "Let's just have it as a secret between us for ever and ever—something that nobody else knows a thing about but you and me."

"We'd better keep it a secret from Aunt Janet anyhow," I whispered, laughing. "She'd think we were both crazy."

"It's real jolly to be crazy once in a while," said the Story Girl.

CHAPTER 20

EXTRACTS FROM *OUR MAGAZINE*

EDITORIAL

As WILL be seen there is no Honour Roll in this number. Even Felicity has thought all the beautiful thoughts that can be thought and cannot think any more. Peter has never got drunk but, under existing circumstances, that is not greatly to his credit. As for our written resolutions they have silently disappeared from our chamber walls and the place that once knew them knows them no more for ever. (*Peter, perplexedly:* "Seems to me I've heard something like that before.") It is very sad but we will all make some new resolutions next year and maybe it will be easier to keep those.

THE STORY OF THE LOCKET THAT WAS BAKED

This was a story my Aunt Jane told me about her granma when she was a little girl. Its funny to think of baking a locket, but it wasn't to eat. She was my great granma but Ill call her granma for short. It happened when she was ten years old. Of course she wasent anybodys granma then. Her father and mother and her were living in a new settlement called Brinsley. Their nearest naybor was a mile away. One day her Aunt Hannah from Charlottetown came and wanted her ma to go visiting with her. At first granma's ma thought she couldent go because it was baking day and granma's pa was away. But granma wasent afraid to stay alone and she knew how to bake the bread so she made her ma go and her Aunt Hannah took off the handsome gold locket and chain she was waring round her neck and hung it on granmas and told her she could ware it all day. Granma was awful pleased for she had never had any jewelry. She did all the chores and then was needing the loaves when she looked up and saw a tramp coming in and he was an awful villenus looking tramp. He dident even pass the time of day but just set down on a chair. Poor granma was awful fritened and she turned her back on him and went on needing the loaf cold and trembling—that is, granma was trembling not the loaf. She was worried about the locket. She didn't know how she could hide it for to get anywhere she would have to turn round and pass him.

All of a suddent she thought she would hide it in the bread. She put her hand up and pulled it hard and quick and broke the fastening and needed it right into the loaf. Then she put the loaf in the pan and set it in the oven.

The tramp hadent seen her do it and then he asked for something to eat. Granma got him up a meal and when hed et it he began prowling about the kitchen looking into everything and opening the cubbord doors. Then he went into granma's mas room and turned the buro drawers and trunk inside out and threw the things in them all about. All he found was a purse with a dollar in it and he swore about it and took it and went away. When granma was sure he was really gone she broke down and cried. She forgot all about the bread and it burned as black as coal. When she smelled it burning granma run and pulled it out. She was awful scared the locket was spoiled but she sawed open the loaf and it was there safe and sound. When her Aunt Hannah came back she said granma deserved the locket because she had saved it so clever and she gave it to her and grandma always wore it and was very proud of it. And granma used to say that was the only loaf of bread she ever spoiled in her life.

PETER CRAIG.

(*Felicity:* "Those stories are all very well but they are only true stories. It's easy enough to write true stories. *I* thought Peter was appointed fiction editor, but he has never written any fiction since the paper started. That's not *my* idea of a fiction editor. He ought to make up stories out of his own head." *Peter, spunkily:* "I can do it, too, and I will next time. And it ain't easier to write true stories. It's harder, 'cause you have to stick to facts." *Felicity:* "I don't believe you could make up a story." *Peter:* "I'll show you!")

MY MOST EXCITING ADVENTURE

It's my turn to write it but I'm *so nervous.* My worst adventure happened *two years ago.* It was an awful one. I had a striped ribbon, striped brown and yellow and *I lost it.* I was very sorry for it was a handsome ribbon and all the girls in school were

jealous of it. (*Felicity: "I* wasn't. I didn't think it one bit pretty."
Cecily: "Hush!") I hunted everywhere but I couldn't find it.
Next day was Sunday and I was running into the house by
the front door and I saw *something lying on the step* and I
thought it was my ribbon and I made a grab at it as I passed.
But, oh, it was *a snake!* Oh, I can never describe how I felt
when I felt that awful thing *wriggling in my hand.* I let it go
and *screamed and screamed,* and ma was cross at me for yelling
on Sunday and made me read seven chapters in the Bible but
I didn't mind that much after what I had come through. I
would rather *die* than have *such an experience* again.

SARA RAY.

TO FELICITY ON HER BERTHDAY

Oh maiden fair with golden hair
And brow of purest white,
Id fight for you I'd die for you
Let me be your faithful knite.

This is your berthday blessed day
You are thirteen years old today
May you be happy and fair as you are now
Until your hair is gray.

I gaze into your shining eyes,
They are so blue and bright.
Id fight for you Id die for you
Let me be your faithful knite.

A FRIEND.

(*Dan:* "Great snakes, who got that up? I'll bet it was Peter."
Felicity, with dignity: "Well, it's more than *you* could do. *You*
couldn't write poetry to save your life." *Peter, aside to Beverley:*
"She seems quite pleased. I'm glad I wrote it, but it was awful
hard work.")

PERSONALS

Patrick Grayfur, Esq., caused his friends great anxiety recently
by a prolonged absence from home. When found he was very
thin but is now as fat and conceited as ever.

On Wednesday, June 20th, Miss Olivia King was united in the bonds of holy matrimony to Dr. Robert Seton of Halifax. Miss Sara Stanley was bridesmaid, and Mr. Andrew Seton attended the groom. The young couple received many handsome presents. Rev. Mr. Marwood tied the nuptial knot. After the ceremony a substantial repast was served in Mrs. Alex King's well-known style and the happy couple left for their new home in Nova Scotia. Their many friends join in wishing them a very happy and prosperous journey through life.

A precious one from us is gone,
A voice we loved is stilled.
A place is vacant in our home
That never can be filled.

(The Story Girl: "Goodness, that sounds as if somebody had died. I've seen that verse on a tombstone. *Who* wrote that notice?" *Felicity, who wrote it:* "I think it is just as appropriate to a wedding as to a funeral!")

Our school concert came off on the evening of June 29th and was a great success. We made ten dollars for the library.

We regret to chronicle that Miss Sara Ray met with a misfortune while taking some violent exercise with a wasps' nest recently. The moral is that it is better not to monkey with a wasps' nest, new or old.

Mrs. C. B. Hawkins of Baywater is keeping house for Uncle Roger. She is a very large woman. Uncle Roger says he has to spend too much time walking round her, but otherwise she is an excellent housekeeper.

It is reported that the school is haunted. A mysterious light was seen there at two o'clock one night recently.

(The Story Girl and I exchange knowing smiles behind the others' backs.)

Dan and Felicity had a fight last Tuesday—not with fists but with tongues. Dan came off best—as usual. *(Felicity laughs sarcastically.)*

Mr. Newton Craig of Markdale returned home recently after a somewhat prolonged visit in foreign parts. We are glad to welcome Mr. Craig back to our midst.

Billy Robinson was hurt last week. A cow kicked him. I suppose it is wicked of us to feel glad but we all do feel glad because of the way he cheated us with the magic seed last summer.

On April 1st Uncle Roger sent Mr. Peter Craig to the manse to borrow the biography of Adam's grandfather. Mr. Marwood told Peter he didn't think Adam had any grandfather and advised him to go home and look at the almanac. (*Peter, sourly:* "Your Uncle Roger thought he was pretty smart." *Felicity, severely:* "Uncle Roger *is* smart. It was so easy to fool you.")

A pair of blue birds have built a nest in a hole in the sides of the well, just under the ferns. We can see the eggs when we look down. They are so cunning.

Felix sat down on a tack one day in May. Felix thinks housecleaning is great foolishness.

ADS

LOST—STOLEN—OR STRAYED—A HEART. Finder will be rewarded by returning same to Cyrus E. Brisk, Desk 7, Carlisle School.

LOST OR STOLEN. A piece of brown hair about three inches long and one inch thick. Finder will kindly return to Miss Cecily King, Desk 15, Carlisle School.

(*Cecily:* "Cyrus keeps my hair in his Bible for a bookmark, so Flossie tells me. He says he means to keep it always for a remembrance though he has given up hope." *Dan:* "I'll steal it out of his Bible in Sunday School." *Cecily, blushing:* "Oh, let him keep it if it is any comfort to him. Besides, it isn't right to steal." *Dan:* "He stole it." *Cecily:* "But Mr. Marwood says two wrongs never make a right.")

HOUSEHOLD DEPARTMENT

Aunt Olivia's wedding cake was said to be the best one of its kind ever tasted in Carlisle. Me and mother made it.

ANXIOUS INQUIRER:—It is not advisable to curl your hair with mucilage if you can get anything else. Quince juice is better. (*Cecily, bitterly:* "I suppose I'll never hear the last of that mucilage." *Dan:* "Ask her who used tooth-powder to raise biscuits?")

We had rhubarb pies for the first time this spring last week. They were fine but hard on the cream.

FELICITY KING.

ETIQUETTE DEPARTMENT

PATIENT SUFFERER:—What will I do when a young man steals a lock of my hair? Ans.:—Grow some more.

No, F-l-x, a little caterpillar is not called a kittenpillar. (*Felix, enraged:* "I never asked that! Dan just makes that etiquette column up from beginning to end!" *Felicity:* "I don't see what that kind of a question has to do with etiquette anyhow.")

Yes, P-t-r, it is quite proper to treat a lady friend to ice cream twice if you can afford it.

No, F-l-c-t-y, it is not ladylike to chew tobacco. Better stick to spruce gum.

DAN KING.

FASHION NOTES

Frilled muslin aprons will be much worn this summer. It is no longer fashionable to trim them with knitted lace. One pocket is considered smart.

Clam-shells are fashionable keepsakes. You write your name and the date inside one and your friend writes hers in the other and you exchange.

CECILY KING.

FUNNY PARAGRAPHS

Mr. Perkins:—"Peter, name the large islands of the world."

Peter:—"The Island, the British Isles and Australia." (*Peter, defiantly:* "Well, Mr. Perkins said he guessed I was right, so you needn't laugh.")

This is a true joke and really happened. It's about Mr. Samuel Clask again. He was once leading a prayer meeting and he looked through the window and saw the constable driving up and guessed he was after him because he was always in debt. So in a great hurry he called on Brother Casey to lead in prayer and while Brother Casey was praying with his eyes shut and everybody else had their heads bowed Mr. Clask got out of the window and got away before the constable got in because he didn't like to come in till the prayer was finished.

Uncle Roger says it was a smart trick on Mr. Clask's part, but I don't think there was much religion about it.

FELIX KING.

CHAPTER 21

PEG BOWEN COMES TO CHURCH

WHEN THOSE of us who are still left of that band of children who played long years ago in the old orchard and walked the golden road together in joyous companionship, foregather now and again in our busy lives and talk over the events of those many merry moons—there are some of our adventures that gleam out more vividly in memory than the others, and are oftener discussed. The time we bought God's picture from Jerry Cowan—the time Dan ate the poison berries—the time we heard the ghostly bell ring—the bewitchment of Paddy—the visit of the Governor's wife—and the night we were lost in the storm—all awaken reminiscent jest and laughter; but none more than the recollection of the Sunday Peg Bowen came to church and sat in our pew. Though goodness knows, as Felicity would say, we did not think it any matter for laughter at the time— far from it.

It was one Sunday evening in July. Uncle Alec and Aunt Janet, having been out to the morning service, did not attend in the evening, and we small fry walked together down the long hill road, wearing Sunday attire and trying, more or less successfully, to wear Sunday faces also. Those walks to church, through the golden completeness of the summer evenings, were always very pleasant to us, and we never hurried, though, on the other hand, we were very careful not to be late.

This particular evening was particularly beautiful. It was cool after a hot day, and wheat fields all about us were ripening to their harvestry. The wind gossiped with the grasses along our way, and over them the buttercups danced, goldenly-glad. Waves of sinuous shadow went over the ripe hayfields, and plundering bees sang a freebooting lilt in wayside gardens.

"The world is so lovely tonight," said the Story Girl. "I just hate the thought of going into the church and shutting all the sunlight and music outside. I wish we could have the service outside in summer."

"I don't think that would be very religious," said Felicity.

"I'd feel ever so much more religious outside than in," retorted the Story Girl.

"If the service was outside we'd have to sit in the graveyard and that wouldn't be very cheerful," said Felix.

"Besides, the music isn't shut out," added Felicity. "The choir is inside."

" 'Music has charms to soothe a savage breast,' " quoted Peter, who was getting into the habit of adorning his conversation with similar gems. "That's in one of Shakespeare's plays. I'm reading them now, since I got through with the Bible. They're great."

"I don't see when you get time to read them," said Felicity.

"Oh, I read them Sunday afternoons when I'm home."

"I don't believe they're fit to read on Sundays," exclaimed Felicity. "Mother says Valeria Montague's stories ain't."

"But Shakespeare's different from Valeria," protested Peter.

"I don't see in what way. He wrote a lot of things that weren't true, just like Valeria, and he wrote swear words too. Valeria never does that. Her characters all talk in a very refined fashion."

"Well, I always skip the swear words," said Peter. "And Mr. Marwood said once that the Bible and Shakespeare would furnish any library well. So you see he put them together, but I'm sure that he would never say that the Bible and Valeria would make a library."

"Well, all I know is, I shall never read Shakespeare on Sunday," said Felicity loftily.

"I wonder what kind of a preacher young Mr. Davidson is," speculated Cecily.

"Well, we'll know when we hear him tonight," said the Story Girl. "He ought to be good, for his uncle before him was a fine preacher, though a very absent-minded man. But Uncle Roger says the supply in Mr. Marwood's vacation never amounts to much. I know an awfully funny story about old Mr. Davidson. He used to be the minister in Baywater, you know, and he had a large family and his children were very mischievous. One day his wife was ironing and she ironed a great big nightcap with a frill round it. One of the children took it when she wasn't looking and hid it in his father's best beaver hat—the one he wore on Sundays. When Mr. Davidson went to church next Sunday he put the hat on without ever looking into the crown. He walked to church in a brown study and at the door he took off his hat. The nightcap just slipped down on his head, as if it had been put on, and the frill stood out around his face and the string hung down his back. But he never noticed it, because his thoughts were far away, and he walked up the church aisle and into the pulpit, like that. One of his elders had to tiptoe up and tell him what he had on his head. He plucked it off in a dazed fashion, held it up, and looked at it. 'Bless me, it is Sally's nightcap!' he exclaimed mildly. 'I do not know how I could have got it on.' Then he just stuffed it into his pocket calmly and went on with the service, and the long strings of the nightcap hung down out of his pocket all the time."

"It seems to me," said Peter, amid the laughter with which we greeted the tale, "that a funny story is funnier when it is about a minister than it is about any other man. I wonder why."

"Sometimes I don't think it is right to tell funny stories about ministers," said Felicity. "It certainly isn't respectful."

"A good story is a good story—no matter who it's about," said the Story Girl with ungrammatical relish.

There was as yet no one in the church when we reached it, so we took our accustomed ramble through the graveyard surrounding it. The Story Girl had brought flowers for her mother's grave as usual, and while she arranged them on it the rest of us read for the hundredth time the epitaph on Great-Grandfather King's tombstone, which had been composed by Great-Grandmother King. That epitaph was quite famous among the little family traditions that entwine every household with mingled mirth and sorrow, smiles and tears. It had a perennial fascination for us and we read it over every Sunday. Cut deeply in the upright slab of red Island sandstone, the epitaph ran as follows:—

SWEET DEPARTED SPIRIT

Do receive the vows a grateful widow pays,
Each future day and night shall hear her speak her
   Isaac's praise.
Though thy beloved form must in the grave decay
Yet from her heart thy memory no time, no change
   shall steal away.
Do thou from mansions of eternal bliss
Remember thy distressed relict.
Look on her with an angel's love—
Soothe her sad life and cheer her end
Through this world's dangers and its griefs.
Then meet her with thy well-known smiles and welcome
At the last great day.

"Well, *I* can't make out what the old lady was driving at,"
said Dan.
   "That's a nice way to speak of your great-grandmother," said
Felicity severely.
   "How does *The Family Guide* say you ought to speak of
your great-grandma, sweet one?" asked Dan.
   "There is one thing about it that puzzles me," remarked
Cecily. "She calls herself a *grateful* widow. Now, what was she
grateful for?"
   "Because she was rid of him at last," said graceless Dan.
   "Oh, it couldn't have been that," protested Cecily seriously.
"I've always heard that Great-Grandfather and Great-Grand-
mother were very much attached to each other."
   "Maybe, then, it means she was grateful that she'd had him
as long as she did," suggested Peter.
   "She was grateful to him because he had been so kind to
her in life, *I* think," said Felicity.
   "What is a 'distressed relict'?" asked Felix.
   " 'Relict' is a word I hate," said the Story Girl. "It sounds
so much like relic. Relict means just the same as widow, only
a man can be a relict, too."
   "Great-Grandmother seemed to run short of rhymes at the
last of the epitaph," commented Dan.
   "Finding rhymes isn't as easy as you might think," avowed
Peter, out of his own experience.

"I think Grandmother King intended the last of the epitaph to be in blank verse," said Felicity with dignity.

There was still only a sprinkling of people in the church when we went in and took our places in the old-fashioned, square King pew. We had just got comfortably settled when Felicity said in an agitated whisper, "Here is Peg Bowen!"

We all stared at Peg, who was pacing composedly up the aisle. We might be excused for so doing, for seldom were the decorous aisles of Carlisle church invaded by such a figure. Peg was dressed in her usual short drugget skirt, rather worn and frayed around the bottom, and a waist of brilliant turkey red calico. She wore no hat, and her grizzled black hair streamed in elf locks over her shoulders. Face, arms and feet were bare— and face, arms and feet were liberally powdered with *flour*. Certainly no one who saw Peg that night could ever forget the apparition.

Peg's black eyes, in which shone a more than usually wild and fitful light, roved scrutinizingly over the church, then settled on our pew.

"She's coming here," whispered Felicity in horror. "Can't we spread out and make her think the pew is full?"

But the manœuvre was too late. The only result was that Felicity and the Story Girl in moving over left a vacant space between them and Peg promptly plumped down in it.

"Well, I'm here," she remarked aloud. "I did say once I'd never darken the door of Carlisle church again, but what that boy there"—nodding at Peter—"said last winter set me thinking, and I concluded maybe I'd better come once in a while, to be on the safe side."

Those poor girls were in an agony. Everybody in the church was looking at our pew and smiling. We all felt that we were terribly disgraced; but we could do nothing. Peg was enjoying herself hugely, beyond all doubt. From where she sat she could see the whole church, including pulpit and gallery, and her black eyes darted over it with restless glances.

"Bless me, there's Sam Kinnaird," she exclaimed, still aloud. "He's the man that dunned Jacob Marr for four cents on the church steps one Sunday. I heard him. 'I think, Jacob, you owe me four cents on that cow you bought last fall. Rec'llect you couldn't make the change?' Well, you know, 'twould a-made a cat laugh. The Kinnairds were all mighty close, I can tell you. That's how they got rich."

What Sam Kinnaird felt or thought during this speech, which everyone in the church must have heard, I know not. Gossip had it that he changed colour. We wretched occupants of the King pew were concerned only with our own outraged feelings.

"And there's Melita Ross," went on Peg. "She's got the same bonnet on she had last time I was in Carlisle church six years ago. Some folks has the knack of making things last. But look at the style Mrs. Elmer Brewer wears, will yez? Yez wouldn't think her mother died in the poorhouse, would yez, now?"

Poor Mrs. Brewer! From the tip of her smart kid shoes to the dainty cluster of ostrich tips in her bonnet—she was most immaculately and handsomely arrayed; but I venture to think she could have taken small pleasure in her fashionable attire that evening. Some of the unregenerate, including Dan, were shaking with suppressed laughter, but most of the people looked as if they were afraid to smile, lest their turn should come next.

"There's old Stephen Grant coming in," exclaimed Peg viciously, shaking her floury fist at him, "and looking as if butter wouldn't melt in his mouth. He may be an elder, but he's a scoundrel just the same. He set fire to his house to get the insurance and then blamed *me* for doing it. But I got even with him for it. Oh, yes! He knows that, and so do I! He, he!"

Peg chuckled quite fiendishly and Stephen Grant tried to look as if nothing had been said.

"Oh, will the minister never come?" moaned Felicity in my ear. "Surely she'll have to stop then."

But the minister did not come and Peg had no intention of stopping.

"There's Maria Dean," she resumed. "I haven't seen Maria for years. I never call there for she never seems to have anything to eat in the house. She was a Clayton and the Claytons never could cook. Maria sorter looks as if she'd shrunk in the wash, now, don't she? And there's Douglas Nicholson. His brother put rat poison in the family pancakes. Nice little trick that, wasn't it? They say it was by mistake. I hope it *was* a mistake. His wife is all rigged out in silk. Yez wouldn't think to look at her she was married in cotton—and mighty thankful to get married in anything, it's my opinion. There's Timothy Patterson. He's the meanest man alive—meaner'n Sam Kinnaird even. Timothy pays his children five cents apiece to go without their suppers, and then steals the cents out of their pockets after they've gone to bed. It's a fact. And when his old father died he wouldn't let his wife put his best shirt on him. He said his second best was plenty good to be buried in. That's another fact."

"I can't stand much more of this," wailed Felicity.

"See here, Miss Bowen, you really oughtn't to talk like that about people," expostulated Peter in a low tone, goaded thereto, despite his awe of Peg, by Felicity's anguish.

"Bless you, boy," said Peg good-humouredly, "the only difference between me and other folks is that I say these things out loud and they just think them. If I told yez all the things I know about the people in this congregation you'd be amazed. Have a peppermint?"

To our horror Peg produced a handful of peppermint lozenges from the pocket of her skirt and offered us one each. We did not dare refuse but we each held our lozenge very gingerly in our hands.

"Eat them," commanded Peg rather fiercely.

"Mother doesn't allow us to eat candy in church," faltered Felicity.

"Well, I've seen just as fine ladies as your ma give their children lozenges in church," said Peg loftily. She put a peppermint in her own mouth and sucked it with gusto. We were relieved, for she did not talk during the process; but our relief was of short duration. A bevy of three very smartly dressed young ladies, sweeping past our pew, started Peg off again.

"Yez needn't be so stuck up," she said, loudly and derisively. "Yez was all of yez rocked in a flour barrel. And there's old Henry Frewen, still above ground. I called my parrot after him because their noses were exactly alike. Look at Caroline Marr, will yez? That's a woman who'd like pretty well to get married. And there's Alexander Marr. He's a real Christian, anyhow, and so's his dog. I can always size up what a man's religion amounts to by the kind of dog he keeps. Alexander Marr is a good man."

It was a relief to hear Peg speak well of somebody; but that was the only exception she made.

"Look at Dave Fraser strutting in," she went on. "That man

has thanked God so often that he isn't like other people that it's come to be true. He isn't! And there's Susan Frewen. She's jealous of everybody. She's even jealous of Old Man Rogers because he's buried in the best spot in the graveyard. Seth Erskine has the same look he was born with. They say the Lord made everybody but *I* believe the devil made all the Erskines."

"She's getting worse all the time. What *will* she say next?" whispered poor Felicity.

But her martyrdom was over at last. The minister appeared in the pulpit and Peg subsided into silence. She folded her bare, floury arms over her breast and fastened her black eyes on the young preacher. Her behaviour for the next half-hour was decorum itself, save that when the minister prayed that we might all be charitable in judgment Peg ejaculated "Amen" several times, loudly and forcibly, somewhat to the discomfiture of the young man, to whom Peg was a stranger. He opened his eyes, glanced at our pew in a startled way, then collected himself and went on.

Peg listened to the sermon, silently and motionlessly, until Mr. Davidson was half through. Then she suddenly got on her feet.

"This is too dull for me," she exclaimed. "I want something more exciting."

Mr. Davidson stopped short and Peg marched down the aisle in the midst of complete silence. Half way down the aisle she turned around and faced the minister.

"There are so many hypocrites in this church that it isn't fit for decent people to come to," she said. "Rather than be such hypocrites as most of you are it would be better for you to go miles into the woods and commit suicide."

Wheeling about, she strode to the door. Then she turned for a Parthian shot.

"I've felt kind of worried for God sometimes, seeing He has so much to attend to," she said, "but I see I needn't be, so long's there's plenty of ministers to tell Him what to do."

With that Peg shook the dust of Carlisle church from her feet. Poor Mr. Davidson resumed his discourse. Old Elder Bayley, whose attention an earthquake could not have distracted from the sermon, afterwards declared that it was an excellent and edifying exhortation, but I doubt if anyone else in Carlisle church tasted it much or gained much good therefrom. Certainly we of the King household did not. We could not even remember the text when we reached home. Felicity was comfortless.

"Mr. Davidson would be sure to think she belonged to our family when she was in our pew," she said bitterly. "Oh, I feel as if I could never get over such a mortification! Peter, I do wish you wouldn't go telling people they ought to go to church. It's all your fault that this happened."

"Never mind, it will be a good story to tell sometime," remarked the Story Girl with relish.

———————— CHAPTER 22 ————————

THE YANKEE STORM

IN AN August orchard six children and a grown-up were sitting around the pulpit stone. The grown-up was Miss Reade, who had been up to give the girls their music lesson and had consented to stay to tea, much to the rapture of the said girls, who continued to worship her with unabated and romantic ardour. To us, over the golden grasses, came the Story Girl, carrying in her hand a single large poppy, like a blood-red chalice filled with the wine of August wizardry. She proffered it to Miss Reade and, as the latter took it into her singularly slender, beautiful hand, I saw a ring on her third finger. I noticed it, because I had heard the girls say that Miss Reade never wore rings, not liking them. It was not a new ring; it was handsome, but of an old-fashioned design and setting, with a glint of diamonds about a central sapphire. Later on, when Miss Reade had gone, I asked the Story Girl if she had noticed the ring. She nodded, but seemed disinclined to say more about it.

"Look here, Sara," I said, "there's something about that ring—something you know."

"I told you once there was a story growing but you would have to wait until it was fully grown," she answered.

"Is Miss Reade going to marry anybody—anybody we know?" I persisted.

"Curiosity killed a cat," observed the Story Girl coolly. "Miss Reade hasn't told me that she was going to marry anybody. You will find out all that is good for you to know in due time."

When the Story Girl put on grown-up airs I did not like her so well, and I dropped the subject with a dignity that seemed to amuse her mightily.

She had been away for a week, visiting cousins in Markdale, and she had come home with a new treasure-trove of stories, most of which she had heard from the old sailors of Markdale Harbour. She had promised that morning to tell us of "the most tragic event that had ever been known on the north shore," and we now reminded her of her promise.

"Some call it the 'Yankee Storm,' and others the 'American Gale,'" she began, sitting down by Miss Reade and beaming, because the latter put her arm around her waist. "It happened nearly forty years ago, in October of 1851. Old Mr. Coles at the Harbour told me all about it. He was a young man then and he says he can never forget that dreadful time. You know in those days hundreds of American fishing schooners used to come down to the Gulf every summer to fish mackerel. On one beautiful Saturday night in this October of 1851, more than one hundred of these vessels could be counted from Markdale Capes. By Monday night more than seventy of them had been destroyed. Those which had escaped were mostly those which went into harbour Saturday night, to keep Sunday. Mr. Coles says the rest stayed outside and fished all day Sunday, same as through the week, and *he* says the storm was a judgment on them for doing it. But he admits that even some of them got into harbour later on and escaped, so it's hard to know what to think. But it is certain that on Sunday night there came up a sudden and terrible storm—the worst, Mr. Coles says, that has ever been known on the north shore. It lasted for two days and scores of vessels were driven ashore and completely wrecked. The crews of most of the vessels that went ashore on the sand beaches were saved, but those that struck on the rocks went to pieces and all hands were lost. For weeks after the storm the north shore was strewn with the bodies of drowned men. Think of it! Many of them were unknown and unrecognizable, and they were buried in Markdale graveyard. Mr. Coles says the schoolmaster who was in Markdale then wrote a poem on the storm and Mr. Coles recited the first two verses to me.

" 'Here are the fishers' hillside graves,
The church beside, the woods around,
Below, the hollow moaning waves
Where the poor fishermen were drowned.

" 'A sudden tempest the blue welkin tore,
The seamen tossed and torn apart
Rolled with the seaweed to the shore
While landsmen gazed with aching heart.'

"Mr. Coles couldn't remember any more of it. But the saddest of all the stories of the Yankee Storm was the one about the *Franklin Dexter*. The *Franklin Dexter* went ashore on the Markdale Capes and all on board perished, the Captain and three of his brothers among them. These four young men were the sons of an old man who lived in Portland, Maine, and when he heard what had happened he came right down to the Island to see if he could find their bodies. They had all come ashore and had been buried in Markdale graveyard; but he was determined to take them up and carry them home for burial. He said he had promised their mother to take her boys home to her and he must do it. So they were taken up and put on board a sailing vessel at Markdale Harbour to be taken back to Maine, while the father himself went home on a passenger steamer. The name of the sailing vessel was the *Seth Hall,* and the captain's name was Seth Hall, too. Captain Hall was a dreadfully profane man and used to swear blood-curdling oaths. On the night he sailed out of Markdale Harbour the old sailors warned him that a storm was brewing and that it would catch him if he did not wait until it was over. The captain had become very impatient because of several delays he had already met with, and he was in a furious temper. He swore a wicked oath that he would sail out of Markdale Harbour that night and 'God Almighty Himself shouldn't catch him.' He did sail out of the harbour; and the storm did catch him, and the *Seth Hall* went down with all hands, the dead and the living finding a watery grave together. So the poor old mother up in Maine never had her boys brought back to her after all. Mr. Coles says it seems as if it were foreordained that they should not rest in a grave, but should lie beneath the waves until the day when the sea gives up its dead."

      " 'They sleep as well beneath that purple tide
        As others under turf,' "

quoted Miss Reade softly. "I am very thankful," she added, "that I am not one of those whose dear ones 'go down to the sea in ships.' It seems to me that they have treble their share of this world's heartache."

"Uncle Stephen was a sailor and he was drowned," said Felicity, "and they say it broke Grandmother King's heart. I don't see why people can't be contented on dry land."

Cecily's tears had been dropping on the autograph quilt square she was faithfully embroidering. She had been diligently collecting names for it ever since the preceding autumn and had a goodly number; but Kitty Marr had one more and this was certainly a fly in Cecily's ointment.

"Besides, one I've got isn't paid for—Peg Bowen's," she lamented, "and I don't suppose it ever will be, for I'll never dare to ask her for it."

"I wouldn't put it on at all," said Felicity.

"Oh, I don't dare not to. She'd be sure to find out I didn't and then she'd be very angry. I wish I could get just one more name and then I'd be contented. But I don't know of a single person who hasn't been asked already."

"Except Mr. Campbell," said Dan.

"Oh, of course nobody would ask Mr. Campbell. We all know it would be of no use. He doesn't believe in missions at all—in fact, he says he detests the very mention of missions—and he never gives one cent to them."

"All the same, I think he ought to be asked, so that he wouldn't have the excuse that nobody *did* ask him," declared Dan.

"Do you really think so, Dan?" asked Cecily earnestly.

"Sure," said Dan, solemnly. Dan liked to tease even Cecily a wee bit now and then.

Cecily relapsed into anxious thought, and care sat visibly on her brow for the rest of the day. Next morning she came to me and said:

"Bev, would you like to go for a walk with me this afternoon?"

"Of course," I replied. "Any particular where?"

"I'm going to see Mr. Campbell and ask him for his name for my square," said Cecily resolutely. "I don't suppose it will do any good. He wouldn't give anything to the library last summer, you remember, till the Story Girl told him that story about his grandmother. She won't go with me this time—I don't know why. I can't tell a story and I'm frightened to death just to think of going to him. But I believe it is my duty; and besides I would love to get as many names on my square as Kitty Marr has. So if you'll go with me we'll go this afternoon. I simply *couldn't* go alone."

CHAPTER 23

A MISSIONARY HEROINE

ACCORDINGLY, THAT afternoon we bearded the lion in his den. The road we took was a beautiful one, for we went "cross lots," and we enjoyed it, in spite of the fact that we did not expect the interview with Mr. Campbell to be a very pleasant one. To be sure, he had been quite civil on the occasion of our last call upon him, but the Story Girl had been with us then and had beguiled him into good-humour and generosity by the magic of her voice and personality. We had no such ally now, and Mr. Campbell was known to be virulently opposed to missions in any shape or form.

"I don't know whether it would have been any better if I could have put on my good clothes," said Cecily, with a rueful glance at her print dress, which, though neat and clean, was undeniably faded and *rather* short and tight. "The Story Girl said it would, and I wanted to, but mother wouldn't let me. She said it was all nonsense, and Mr. Campbell would never notice what I had on."

"It's my opinion that Mr. Campbell notices a good deal more than you'd think for," I said sagely.

"Well, I wish our call was over," sighed Cecily. "I can't tell you how I dread it."

"Now, see here, Sis," I said cheerfully, "let's not think about it till we get there. It'll only spoil our walk and do no good. Let's just forget it and enjoy ourselves."

"I'll try," agreed Cecily, "but it's ever so much easier to preach than to practise."

Our way lay first over a hill top, gallantly plumed with golden rod, where cloud shadows drifted over us like a gypsying crew. Carlisle, in all its ripely tinted length and breadth, lay below us, basking in the August sunshine, that spilled over the brim of the valley to the far-off Markdale Harbour, cupped in its harvest-golden hills.

Then came a little valley overgrown with the pale purple bloom of thistles and elusively haunted with their perfume. You say that thistles have no perfume? Go you to a brook hollow where they grow some late summer twilight at dewfall; and on the still air that rises suddenly to meet you will come a waft of faint, aromatic fragrance, wondrously sweet and evasive, the distillation of that despised thistle bloom.

Beyond this the path wound through a forest of fir, where a wood wind wove its murmurous spell and a wood brook dimpled pellucidly among the shadows—the dear, companionable, elfin shadows—that lurked under the low growing boughs. Along the edges of that winding path grew banks of velvet green moss, starred with clusters of pigeon berries. Pigeon berries are not to be eaten. They are woolly, tasteless things. But they are to be looked at in their glowing scarlet. They are the jewels with which the forest of cone-bearers loves to deck its brown breast. Cecily gathered some and pinned them on hers, but they did not become her. I thought how witching the Story Girl's brown curls would have looked twined with those brilliant clusters. Perhaps Cecily was thinking of it, too, for she presently said,

"Bev, don't you think the Story Girl is changing somehow?"

"There are times—just times—when she seems to belong more among the grown-ups than among us," I said, reluctantly, "especially when she puts on her bridesmaid dress."

"Well, she's the oldest of us, and when you come to think

of it, she's fifteen,—that's almost grown-up," sighed Cecily. Then she added, with sudden vehemence, "I hate the thought of any of us growing up. Felicity says she just longs to be grown-up, but I don't, not a bit. I wish I could just stay a little girl for ever—and have you and Felix and all the others for playmates right along. I don't know how it is—but whenever I think of being grown-up I seem to feel tired."

Something about Cecily's speech—or the wistful look that had crept into her sweet brown eyes—made me feel vaguely uncomfortable; I was glad that we were at the end of our journey, with Mr. Campbell's big house before us, and his dog sitting gravely at the veranda steps.

"Oh, dear," said Cecily, with a shiver, "I'd been hoping that dog wouldn't be around."

"He never bites," I assured her.

"Perhaps he doesn't, but he always looks as if he was going to," rejoined Cecily.

The dog continued to look, and, as we edged gingerly past him and up the veranda steps, he turned his head and kept on looking. What with Mr. Campbell before us and the dog behind, Cecily was trembling with nervousness; but perhaps it was as well that the dour brute was there, else I verily believe she would have turned and fled shamelessly when we heard steps in the hall.

It was Mr. Campbell's housekeeper who came to the door, however; she ushered us pleasantly into the sitting-room where Mr. Campbell was reading. He laid down his book with a slight frown and said nothing at all in response to our timid "good afternoon." But after we had sat for a few minutes in wretched silence, wishing ourselves a thousand miles away, he said, with a chuckle,

"Well, is it the school library again?"

Cecily had remarked as we were coming that what she dreaded most of all was introducing the subject; but Mr. Campbell had given her a splendid opening, and she plunged wildly in at once, rattling her explanation off nervously with trembling voice and flushed cheeks.

"No, it's our Mission Band autograph quilt, Mr. Campbell. There are to be as many squares in it as there are members in the Band. Each one has a square and is collecting names for it. If you want to have your name on the quilt you pay five cents, and if you want to have it right in the round spot in the middle of the square you must pay ten cents. Then when we have got all the names we can we will embroider them on the squares. The money is to go to the little girl our Band is supporting in Korea. I heard that nobody had asked you, so I thought perhaps you would give me your name for my square."

Mr. Campbell drew his black brows together in a scowl.

"Stuff and nonsense!" he exclaimed angrily. "I don't believe in Foreign Missions—don't believe in them at all. I never give a cent to them."

"Five cents isn't a very large sum," said Cecily earnestly.

Mr. Campbell's scowl disappeared and he laughed.

"It wouldn't break me," he admitted, "but it's the principle of the thing. And as for that Mission Band of yours, if it wasn't for the fun you get out of it, catch one of you belonging. You don't really care a rap more for the heathen than I do."

"Oh, we do," protested Cecily. "We do think of all the poor little children in Korea, and we like to think we are helping them, if it's ever so little. We *are* in earnest, Mr. Campbell— indeed we are."

"Don't believe it—don't believe a word of it," said Mr. Campbell impolitely. "You'll do things that are nice and interesting. You'll get up concerts, and chase people about for autographs and give money your parents give you and that doesn't cost you either time or labour. But you wouldn't do anything you disliked for the heathen children—you wouldn't make any real sacrifice for them—catch you!"

"Indeed we would," cried Cecily, forgetting her timidity in her zeal. "I just wish I had a chance to prove it to you."

"You do, eh? Come, now, I'll take you at your word. I'll test you. Tomorrow is Communion Sunday and the church will be full of folks and they'll all have their best clothes on. If you go to church tomorrow in the very costume you have on at present, without telling anyone why you do so, until it is all over, I'll give you—why, I vow I'll give you five dollars for that quilt of yours."

Poor Cecily! To go to church in a faded print dress, with a shabby little old sun-hat and worn shoes! It was very cruel of Mr. Campbell.

"I—I don't think mother would let me," she faltered.

Her tormentor smiled grimly.

"It's not hard to find some excuse," he said sarcastically.

Cecily crimsoned and sat up facing Mr. Campbell spunkily. "It's *not* an excuse," she said. "If mother will let me go to church like this I'll go. But I'll have to tell *her* why, Mr. Campbell, because I'm certain she'd never let me if I didn't."

"Oh, you can tell all your own family," said Mr. Campbell, "but remember, none of them must tell it outside until Sunday is over. If they do, I'll be sure to find it out and then our bargain is off. If I see you in church tomorrow, dressed as you are now, I'll give you my name and five dollars. But I won't see you. You'll shrink when you've had time to think it over."

"I sha'n't," said Cecily resolutely.

"Well, we'll see. And now come out to the barn with me. I've got the prettiest little drove of calves out there you ever saw. I want you to see them."

Mr. Campbell took us all over his barns and was very affable. He had beautiful horses, cows and sheep, and I enjoyed seeing them. I don't think Cecily did, however. She was very quiet and even Mr. Campbell's handsome new span of dappled grays failed to arouse any enthusiasm in her. She was already in bitter anticipation living over the martyrdom of the morrow. On the way home she asked me seriously if I thought Mr. Campbell would go to heaven when he died.

"Of course he will," I said. "Isn't he a member of the church?"

"Oh, yes, but I can't imagine him fitting into heaven. You know he isn't really fond of anything but live stock."

"He's fond of teasing people, I guess," I responded. "Are you really going to church tomorrow in that dress, Sis?"

"If mother'll let me I'll have to," said poor Cecily. "I won't let Mr. Campbell triumph over me. And I *do* want to have as many names as Kitty has. And I *do* want to help the poor little Korean children. But it will be simply dreadful. I don't know whether I hope mother will or not."

I did not believe she would, but Aunt Janet sometimes could be depended on for the unexpected. She laughed and told Cecily she could please herself. Felicity was in a rage over it, and declared *she* wouldn't go to church if Cecily went in such a rig. Dan sarcastically inquired if all she went to church for was to show off her fine clothes and look at other people's; then they quarrelled and didn't speak to each other for two days, much to Cecily's distress.

I suspect poor Sis wished devoutly that it might rain the next day; but it was gloriously fine. We were all waiting in the orchard for the Story Girl who had not begun to dress for church until Cecily and Felicity were ready. Felicity was her prettiest in flower-trimmed hat, crisp muslin, floating ribbons and trim black slippers. Poor Cecily stood beside her mute and pale, in her faded school garb and heavy copper-toed boots. But her face, if pale, was very determined. Cecily, having put her hand to the plough, was not of those who turn back.

"You do look just awful," said Felicity. "I don't care—I'm going to sit in Uncle James' pew. I *won't* sit with you. There will be so many strangers there, and all the Markdale people, and what will they think of you? Some of them will never know the reason, either."

"I wish the Story Girl would hurry," was all poor Cecily said. "We're going to be late. It wouldn't have been quite so hard if I could have got there before anyone and slipped quietly into our pew."

"Here she comes at last," said Dan. "Why—what's she got on?"

The Story Girl joined us with a quizzical smile on her face. Dan whistled. Cecily's pale cheeks flushed with understanding and gratitude. The Story Girl wore her school print dress and hat also, and was gloveless and heavy shod.

"You're not going to have to go through this all alone, Cecily," she said.

"Oh, it won't be half so hard now," said Cecily, with a long breath of relief.

I fancy it was hard enough even then. The Story Girl did not care a whit, but Cecily rather squirmed under the curious glances that were cast at her. She afterwards told me that she really did not think she could have endured it if she had been alone.

Mr. Campbell met us under the elms in the churchyard, with a twinkle in his eye.

"Well, you did it, Miss," he said to Cecily, "but you should have been alone. That was what I meant. I suppose you think you've cheated me nicely."

"No, she doesn't," spoke up the Story Girl undauntedly. "She was all dressed and ready to come before she knew I was going to dress the same way. So she kept her bargain faithfully, Mr. Campbell, and I think you were cruel to make her do it."

"You do, eh? Well, well, I hope you'll forgive me. I didn't think she'd do it—I was sure feminine vanity would win the day over missionary zeal. It seems it didn't—though how much was pure missionary zeal and how much just plain King spunk I'm doubtful. I'll keep my promise, Miss. You shall have your five dollars, and mind you put my name in the round space. No five-cent corners for me."

CHAPTER 24

A TANTALIZING REVELATION

"I SHALL have something to tell you in the orchard this evening," said the Story Girl at breakfast one morning. Her eyes were very bright and excited. She looked as if she had not slept a great deal. She had spent the previous evening with Miss Reade and had not returned until the rest of us were in bed. Miss Reade had finished giving music lessons and was going home in a few days. Cecily and Felicity were in despair over this and mourned as those without comfort. But the Story Girl, who had been even more devoted to Miss Reade than either of them, had not, as I noticed, expressed any regret and seemed to be very cheerful over the whole matter.

"Why can't you tell it now?" asked Felicity.

"Because the evening is the nicest time to tell things in. I only mentioned it now so that you would have something interesting to look forward to all day."

"Is it about Miss Reade?" asked Cecily.

"Never mind."

"I'll bet she's going to be married," I exclaimed, remembering the ring.

"Is she?" cried Felicity and Cecily together.

The Story Girl threw an annoyed glance at me. She did not like to have her dramatic announcements forestalled.

"I don't say that it is about Miss Reade or that it isn't. You must just wait till the evening."

"I wonder what it is," speculated Cecily, as the Story Girl left the room.

"I don't believe it's much of anything," said Felicity, beginning to clear away the breakfast dishes. "The Story Girl always likes to make so much out of so little. Anyhow, I don't believe Miss Reade is going to be married. She hasn't any beaus around here and Mrs. Armstrong says she's sure she doesn't correspond with anybody. Besides, if she was she wouldn't be likely to tell the Story Girl."

"Oh, she might. They're such friends, you know," said Cecily.

"Miss Reade is no better friends with her than she is with me and you," retorted Felicity.

"No, but sometimes it seems to me that she's a different kind of friend with the Story Girl than she is with me and you," reflected Cecily. "I can't just explain what I mean."

"No wonder. Such nonsense," sniffed Felicity.

"It's only some girl's secret, anyway," said Dan, loftily. "I don't feel much interest in it."

But he was on hand with the rest of us that evening, interest or no interest, in Uncle Stephen's Walk, where the ripening apples were beginning to glow like jewels among the boughs.

"Now, are you going to tell us your news?" asked Felicity impatiently.

"Miss Reade *is* going to be married," said the Story Girl. "She told me so last night. She is going to be married in a fortnight's time."

"Who to?" exclaimed the girls.

"To"—the Story Girl threw a defiant glance at me as if to say, "You can't spoil the surprise of *this,* anyway,"—"to—the Awkward Man."

For a few moments amazement literally held us dumb.

"You're not in earnest, Sara Stanley?" gasped Felicity at last.

"Indeed I am. I thought you'd be astonished. But I wasn't. I've suspected it all summer, from little things I've noticed. Don't you remember that evening last spring when I went a piece with Miss Reade and told you when I came back that a story was growing? I guessed it from the way the Awkward

Man looked at her when I stopped to speak to him over his garden fence."

"But—the Awkward Man!" said Felicity helplessly. "It doesn't seem possible. Did Miss Reade tell you *herself?*"

"Yes."

"I suppose it must be true then. But how did it ever come about? He's *so* shy and awkward. How did he ever manage to get up enough spunk to ask her to marry him?"

"Maybe she asked him," suggested Dan.

The Story Girl looked as if she might tell if she would.

"I believe that *was* the way of it," I said, to draw her on.

"Not exactly," she said reluctantly. "I know all about it but I can't tell you. I guessed part from things I've seen—and Miss Reade told me a good deal—and the Awkward Man himself told me his side of it as we came home last night. I met him just as I left Mr. Armstrong's and we were together as far as his house. It was dark and he just talked on as if he were talking to himself—I think he forgot I was there at all, once he got started. He has never been shy or awkward with me, but he never talked as he did last night."

"You might tell us what he said," urged Cecily. "We'd never tell."

The Story Girl shook her head.

"No, I can't. You wouldn't understand. Besides, I couldn't tell it just right. It's one of the things that are hardest to tell. I'd spoil it if I told it—now. Perhaps some day I'll be able to tell it properly. It's very beautiful—but it might sound very ridiculous if it wasn't told just exactly the right way."

"I don't know what you mean, and I don't believe you know yourself," said Felicity pettishly. "All that I can make out is that Miss Reade is going to marry Jasper Dale, and I don't like the idea one bit. She is so beautiful and sweet. I thought she'd marry some dashing young man. Jasper Dale must be nearly twenty years older than her—and he's so queer and shy—and such a hermit."

"Miss Reade is perfectly happy," said the Story Girl. "She thinks the Awkward Man is lovely—and so he is. You don't know him, but I do."

"Well, you needn't put on such airs about it," sniffed Felicity.

"I am not putting on any airs. But it's true. Miss Reade and I are the only people in Carlisle who really know the Awkward

Man. Nobody else ever got behind his shyness to find out just what sort of a man he is."

"When are they to be married?" asked Felicity.

"In a fortnight's time. And then they are coming right back to live at Golden Milestone. Won't it be lovely to have Miss Reade always so near us?"

"I wonder what she'll think about the mystery of Golden Milestone," remarked Felicity.

Golden Milestone was the beautiful name the Awkward Man had given his home; and there was a mystery about it, as readers of the first volume of these chronicles will recall.

"She knows all about the mystery and thinks it perfectly lovely—and so do I," said the Story Girl.

"Do *you* know the secret of the locked room?" cried Cecily.

"Yes, the Awkward Man told me all about it last night. I told you I'd find out the mystery some time."

"And what is it?"

"I can't tell you that either."

"I think you're hateful and mean," exclaimed Felicity. "It hasn't anything to do with Miss Reade, so I think you might tell us."

"It has something to do with Miss Reade. It's all about her."

"Well, I don't see how that can be when the Awkward Man never saw or heard of Miss Reade until she came to Carlisle in the spring," said Felicity incredulously, "and he's had that locked room for years."

"I can't explain it to you—but it's just as I've said," responded the Story Girl.

"Well, it's a very queer thing," retorted Felicity.

"The name in the books in the room was Alice—and Miss Reade's name is Alice," marvelled Cecily. "Did he know her before she came here?"

"Mrs. Griggs says that room has been locked for ten years. Ten years ago Miss Reade was just a little girl of ten. *She* couldn't be the Alice of the books," argued Felicity.

"I wonder if she'll wear the blue silk dress," said Sara Ray.

"And what will she do about the picture, if it isn't hers?" added Cecily.

"The picture couldn't be hers, or Mrs. Griggs would have known her for the same when she came to Carlisle," said Felix.

"I'm going to stop wondering about it," exclaimed Felicity

crossly, aggravated by the amused smile with which the Story Girl was listening to the various speculations. "I think Sara is just as mean as mean when she won't tell us."

"I can't," repeated the Story Girl patiently.

"You said one time you had an idea who 'Alice' was," I said. "Was your idea anything like the truth?"

"Yes, I guessed pretty nearly right."

"Do you suppose they'll keep the room locked after they are married?" asked Cecily.

"Oh, no. I can tell you that much. It is to be Miss Reade's own particular sitting room."

"Why, then, perhaps we'll see it some time ourselves, when we go to see Miss Reade," cried Cecily.

"I'd be frightened to go into it," confessed Sara Ray. "I hate things with mysteries. They always make me nervous."

"I love them. They're so exciting," said the Story Girl.

"Just think, this will be the second wedding of people we know," reflected Cecily. "Isn't that interesting?"

"I only hope the next thing won't be a funeral," remarked Sara Ray gloomily. "There were three lighted lamps on our kitchen table last night, and Judy Pineau says that's a sure sign of a funeral."

"Well, there are funerals going on all the time," said Dan.

"But it means the funeral of somebody you know. *I* don't believe in it—*much*—but Judy says she's seen it come true time and again. I hope if it does it won't be anybody we know *very* well. But I hope it'll be somebody I know a *little,* because then I might get to the funeral. I'd just love to go to a funeral."

"That's a dreadful thing to say," commented Felicity in a shocked tone.

Sara Ray looked bewildered.

"I don't see what is dreadful in it," she protested.

"People don't go to funerals for the fun of it," said Felicity severely. "And you just as good as said you hoped somebody you knew would die so you'd get to the funeral."

"No, no, I didn't. I didn't mean that *at all,* Felicity. I don't want anybody to die; but what I meant was, if anybody I knew *had* to die there might be a chance to go to the funeral. I've never been to a single funeral yet, and it must be so interesting."

"Well, don't mix up talk about funerals with talk about weddings," said Felicity. "It isn't lucky. *I* think Miss Reade is simply throwing herself away, but I hope she'll be happy. And I hope the Awkward Man will manage to get married without making some awful blunder, but it's more than I expect."

"The ceremony is to be very private," said the Story Girl.

"I'd like to see them the day they appear out in church," chuckled Dan. "How'll he ever manage to bring her in and show her into the pew? I'll bet he'll go in first—or tramp on her dress—or fall over his feet."

"Maybe he won't go to church at all the first Sunday and she'll have to go alone," said Peter. "That happened in Markdale. A man was too bashful to go to church the first time after getting married, and his wife went alone till he got used to the idea."

"They may do things like that in Markdale but that is not the way people behave in Carlisle," said Felicity loftily.

Seeing the Story Girl slipping away with a disapproving face I joined her.

"What is the matter, Sara?" I asked.

"I hate to hear them talking like that about Miss Reade and Mr. Dale," she answered vehemently. "It's really all so beautiful—but they make it seem silly and absurd, somehow."

"You might tell me all about it, Sara," I insinuated. "I wouldn't tell—and I'd understand."

"Yes, I think you would," she said thoughtfully. "But I can't tell it even to you because I can't tell it well enough yet. I've a feeling that there's only one way to tell it—and I don't know the way yet. Some day I'll know it—and then I'll tell you, Bev."

Long, long after she kept her word. Forty years later I wrote to her, across the leagues of land and sea that divided us, and told her that Jasper Dale was dead; and I reminded her of her old promise and asked its fulfilment. In reply she sent me the written love story of Jasper Dale and Alice Reade. Now, when Alice sleeps under the whispering elms of the old Carlisle churchyard, beside the husband of her youth, that story may be given, in all its old-time sweetness, to the world.

CHAPTER 25

THE LOVE STORY OF THE AWKWARD MAN

(Written by the Story Girl)

JASPER DALE lived alone in the old homestead which he had named Golden Milestone. In Carlisle this giving one's farm a name was looked upon as a piece of affectation; but if a place must be named why not give it a sensible name with some meaning to it? Why Golden Milestone, when Pinewood or Hillslope or, if you wanted to be very fanciful, Ivy Lodge, might be had for the taking?

He had lived alone at Golden Milestone since his mother's death; he had been twenty then and he was close upon forty now, though he did not look it. But neither could it be said that he looked young; he had never at any time looked young with common youth; there had always been something in his appearance that stamped him as different from the ordinary run of men, and, apart from his shyness, built up an intangible, invisible barrier between him and his kind. He had lived all his life in Carlisle; and all the Carlisle people knew of or about him—although they thought they knew everything—was that he was painfully, abnormally shy. He never went anywhere except to church; he never took part in Carlisle's simple social life; even with most men he was distant and reserved; as for women, he never spoke to or looked at them; if one spoke to him, even if she were a matronly old mother in Israel, he was at once in an agony of painful blushes. He had no friends in the sense of companions; to all outward appearance his life was solitary and devoid of any human interest.

He had no housekeeper; but his old house, furnished as it had been in his mother's lifetime, was cleanly and daintily kept. The quaint rooms were as free from dust and disorder as a woman could have had them. This was known, because Jasper Dale occasionally had his hired man's wife, Mrs. Griggs, in to scrub for him. On the morning she was expected he betook himself to woods and fields, returning only at night-fall. During his absence Mrs. Griggs was frankly wont to explore the house from cellar to attic, and her report of its condition was always the same—"neat as wax." To be sure, there was one room that was always locked against her, the west gable, looking out on the garden and the hill of pines beyond. But Mrs. Griggs knew that in the lifetime of Jasper Dale's mother it had been unfurnished. She supposed it still remained so, and felt no especial curiosity concerning it, though she always tried the door.

Jasper Dale had a good farm, well cultivated; he had a large garden where he worked most of his spare time in summer; it was supposed that he read a great deal, since the postmistress declared that he was always getting books and magazines by mail. He seemed well contented with his existence and people let him alone, since that was the greatest kindness they could do him. It was unsupposable that he would ever marry; nobody ever had supposed it.

"Jasper Dale never so much as *thought* about a woman," Carlisle oracles declared. Oracles, however, are not always to be trusted.

One day Mrs. Griggs went away from the Dale place with a very curious story, which she diligently spread far and wide. It made a good deal of talk, but people, although they listened eagerly, and wondered and questioned, were rather incredulous about it. They thought Mrs. Griggs must be drawing considerably upon her imagination; there were not lacking those who declared that she had invented the whole account, since her reputation for strict veracity was not wholly unquestioned.

Mrs. Grigg's story was as follows:—

One day she found the door of the west gable unlocked. She went in, expecting to see bare walls and a collection of odds and ends. Instead she found herself in a finely furnished room. Delicate lace curtains hung before the small, square, broadsilled windows. The walls were adorned with pictures in much finer taste than Mrs. Griggs could appreciate. There was a bookcase between the windows filled with choicely bound books. Beside it stood a little table with a very dainty work-basket on it. By the basket Mrs. Griggs saw a pair of tiny scissors and a silver thimble. A wicker rocker, comfortable with silk cushions, was near it. Above the bookcase a woman's picture hung—a watercolour, if Mrs. Griggs had but known it—representing a pale, very sweet face, with large, dark eyes and a wistful expression under loose masses of black, lustrous hair. Just beneath the picture, on the top shelf of the bookcase, was a vaseful of flowers. Another vaseful stood on the table beside the basket.

All this was astonishing enough. But what puzzled Mrs. Griggs completely was the fact that a woman's dress was hanging over a chair before the mirror—a pale blue, silken affair. And on the floor beside it were two little blue satin slippers!

Good Mrs. Griggs did not leave the room until she had thoroughly explored it, even to shaking out the blue dress and discovering it to be a tea-gown—wrapper, she called it. But she found nothing to throw any light on the mystery. The fact that the simple name "Alice" was written on the fly-leaves of all the books only deepened it, for it was a name unknown in the Dale family. In this puzzled state she was obliged to depart, nor did she ever find the door unlocked again; and, discovering that people thought she was romancing when she talked about the mysterious west gable at Golden Milestone, she indignantly held her peace concerning the whole affair.

But Mrs. Griggs had told no more than the simple truth. Jasper Dale, under all his shyness and aloofness, possessed a nature full of delicate romance and poesy, which, denied expression in the common ways of life, bloomed out in the realm of fancy and imagination. Left alone, just when the boy's nature was deepening into the man's, he turned to this ideal kingdom for all he believed the real world could never give him. Love— a strange, almost mystical love—played its part here for him. He shadowed forth to himself the vision of a woman, loving and beloved; he cherished it until it became almost as real to him as his own personality and he gave this dream woman the name he liked best—Alice. In fancy he walked and talked with her, spoke words of love to her, and heard words of love in return. When he came from work at the close of day she met him at his threshold in the twilight—a strange, fair, starry shape, as elusive and spiritual as a blossom reflected in a pool by moonlight—with welcome on her lips and in her eyes.

One day, when he was in Charlottetown on business, he had been struck by a picture in the window of a store. It was strangely like the woman of his dream love. He went in, awkward and embarrassed, and bought it. When he took it home he did not know where to put it. It was out of place among the dim old engravings of bewigged portraits and conventional landscapes on the walls of Golden Milestone. As he pondered the matter in his garden that evening he had an inspiration. The sunset, flaming on the windows of the west gable, kindled them into burning rose. Amid the splendour he fancied Alice's fair face peeping archly down at him from the room. The inspiration came then. It should be her room; he would fit it up for her; and her picture should hang there.

He was all summer carrying out his plan. Nobody must know or suspect, so he must go slowly and secretly. One by one the furnishings were purchased and brought home under cover of darkness. He arranged them with his own hands. He bought the books he thought she would like best and wrote her name in them; he got the little feminine knick-knacks of basket and thimble. Finally he saw in a store a pale blue tea-gown and the satin slippers. He had always fancied her as dressed in blue. He bought them and took them home to her room. Thereafter it was sacred to her; he always knocked on its door before he entered; he kept it sweet with fresh flowers; he sat there in the purple summer evenings and talked aloud to her or read his favourite books to her. In his fancy she sat opposite to him in her rocker, clad in the trailing blue gown, with her head leaning on one slender hand, as white as a twilight star.

But Carlisle people knew nothing of this—would have thought him tinged with mild lunacy if they had known. To them, he was just the shy, simple farmer he appeared. They never knew or guessed at the real Jasper Dale.

One spring Alice Reade came to teach music in Carlisle. Her pupils worshipped her, but the grown people thought she was rather too distant and reserved. They had been used to merry, jolly girls who joined eagerly in the social life of the place. Alice Reade held herself aloof from it—not disdainfully, but as one to whom these things were of small importance. She was very fond of books and solitary rambles; she was not at all shy but she was as sensitive as a flower; and after a time Carlisle people were content to let her live her own life and no longer resented her unlikeness to themselves.

She boarded with the Armstrongs, who lived beyond Golden Milestone around the hill of pines. Until the snow disappeared she went out to the main road by the long Armstrong lane; but when spring came she was wont to take a shorter way, down the pine hill, across the brook, past Jasper Dale's garden, and out through his lane. And one day, as she went by, Jasper Dale was working in his garden.

He was on his knees in a corner, setting out a bunch of

roots—an unsightly little tangle of rainbow possibilities. It was a still spring morning; the world was green with young leaves; a little wind blew down from the pines and lost itself willingly among the budding delights of the garden. The grass opened eyes of blue violets. The sky was high and cloudless, turquoise-blue, shading off into milkiness on the far horizons. Birds were singing along the brook valley. Rollicking robins were whistling joyously in the pines. Jasper Dale's heart was filled to over-flowing with a realization of all the virgin loveliness around him; the feeling in his soul had the sacredness of a prayer. At this moment he looked up and saw Alice Reade.

She was standing outside the garden fence, in the shadow of a great pine tree, looking not at him, for she was unaware of his presence, but at the virginal bloom of the plum trees in a far corner, with all her delight in it outblossoming freely in her face. For a moment Jasper Dale believed that his dream love had taken visible form before him. She was like—so like; not in feature, perhaps, but in grace and colouring—the grace of a slender, lissome form and the colouring of cloudy hair and wistful, dark gray eyes, and curving red mouth; and more than all, she was like her in expression—in the subtle revelation of personality exhaling from her like perfume from a flower. It was as if his own had come to him at last and his whole soul suddenly leaped out to meet and welcome her.

Then her eyes fell upon him and the spell was broken. Jasper remained kneeling mutely there, shy man once more, crimson with blushes, a strange, almost pitiful creature in his abject confusion. A little smile flickered about the delicate corners of her mouth, but she turned and walked swiftly away down the lane.

Jasper looked after her with a new, painful sense of loss and loveliness. It had been agony to feel her conscious eyes upon him, but he realized now that there had been a strange sweetness in it, too. It was still greater pain to watch her going from him.

He thought she must be the new music teacher but he did not even know her name. She had been dressed in blue, too— a pale, dainty blue; but that was of course; he had known she must wear it; and he was sure her name must be Alice. When, later on, he discovered that it was, he felt no surprise.

He carried some mayflowers up to the west gable and put

them under the picture. But the charm had gone out of the tribute; and looking at the picture, he thought how scant was the justice it did her. Her face was so much sweeter, her eyes so much softer, her hair so much more lustrous. The soul of his love had gone from the room and from the picture and from his dreams. When he tried to think of the Alice he loved he saw, not the shadowy spirit occupant of the west gable, but the young girl who had stood under the pine, beautiful with the beauty of moonlight, of starshine on still water, of white, wind-swayed flowers growing in silent, shadowy places. He did not then realize what this meant; had he realized it he would have suffered bitterly; as it was he felt only a vague discomfort—a curious sense of loss and gain commingled.

He saw her again that afternoon on her way home. She did not pause by the garden but walked swiftly past. Thereafter, every day for a week he watched unseen to see her pass his home. Once a little child was with her, clinging to her hand. No child had ever before had any part in the shy man's dream life. But that night in the twilight the vision of the rocking-chair was a girl in a blue print dress, with a little, golden-haired shape at her knee—a shape that lisped and prattled and called her "mother;" and both of them were his.

It was the next day that he failed for the first time to put flowers in the west gable. Instead, he cut a loose handful of daffodils and, looking furtively about him as if committing a crime, he laid them across the footpath under the pine. She must pass that way; her feet would crush them if she failed to see them. Then he slipped back into his garden, half exultant, half repentant. From a safe retreat he saw her pass by and stoop to lift his flowers. Thereafter he put some in the same place every day.

When Alice Reade saw the flowers she knew at once who had put them there, and divined that they were for her. She lifted them tenderly in much surprise and pleasure. She had heard all about Jasper Dale and his shyness; but before she had heard about him she had seen him in church and liked him. She thought his face and his dark blue eyes beautiful; she even liked the long brown hair that Carlisle people laughed at. That he was quite different from other people she had under-stood at once, but she thought the difference in his favour.

Perhaps her sensitive nature divined and responded to the beauty in his. At least, in her eyes Jasper Dale was never a ridiculous figure.

When she heard the story of the west gable, which most people disbelieved, she believed it, although she did not understand it. It invested the shy man with interest and romance. She felt that she would have liked, out of no impertinent curiosity, to solve the mystery; she believed that it contained the key to his character.

Thereafter, every day she found flowers under the pine tree; she wished to see Jasper to thank him, unaware that he watched her daily from the screen of shrubbery in his garden; but it was some time before she found the opportunity. One evening she passed when he, not expecting her, was leaning against his garden fence with a book in his hand. She stopped under the pine.

"Mr. Dale," she said softly, "I want to thank you for your flowers."

Jasper, startled, wished that he might sink into the ground. His anguish of embarrassment made her smile a little. He could not speak, so she went on gently.

"It has been so good of you. They have given me so much pleasure—I wish you could know how much."

"It was nothing—nothing," stammered Jasper. His book had fallen on the ground at her feet, and she picked it up and held it out to him.

"So you like Ruskin," she said. "I do, too. But I haven't read this."

"If you—would care—to read it—you may have it," Jasper contrived to say.

She carried the book away with her. He did not again hide when she passed, and when she brought the book back they talked a little about it over the fence. He lent her others, and got some from her in return; they fell into the habit of discussing them. Jasper did not find it hard to talk to her now; it seemed as if he were talking to his dream Alice, and it came strangely natural to him. He did not talk volubly, but Alice thought what he did say was worth while. His words lingered in her memory and made music. She always found his flowers under the pine, and she always wore some of them, but she did not know if he noticed this or not.

One evening Jasper walked shyly with her from his gate up the pine hill. After that he always walked that far with her. She would have missed him much if he had failed to do so; yet it did not occur to her that she was learning to love him. She would have laughed with girlish scorn at the idea. She liked him very much; she thought his nature beautiful in its simplicity and purity; in spite of his shyness she felt more delightfully at home in his society than in that of any other person she had ever met. He was one of those rare souls whose friendship is at once a pleasure and a benediction, showering light from their own crystal clearness into all the dark corners in the souls of others, until, for the time being at least, they reflected his own nobility. But she never thought of love. Like other girls she had her dreams of a possible Prince Charming, young and handsome and debonair. It never occurred to her that he might be found in the shy, dreamy recluse of Golden Milestone.

In August came a day of gold and blue. Alice Reade, coming through the trees, with the wind blowing her little dark love-locks tricksily about under her wide blue hat, found a fragrant heap of mignonette under the pine. She lifted it and buried her face in it, drinking in the wholesome, modest perfume.

She had hoped Jasper would be in his garden, since she wished to ask him for a book she greatly desired to read. But she saw him sitting on the rustic seat at the further side. His back was towards her, and he was partially screened by a copse of lilacs.

Alice, blushing slightly, unlatched the garden gate, and went down the path. She had never been in the garden before, and she found her heart beating in a strange fashion.

He did not hear her footsteps, and she was close behind him when she heard his voice, and realized that he was talking to himself, in a low, dreamy tone. As the meaning of his words dawned on her consciousness she started and grew crimson. She could not move or speak; as one in a dream she stood and listened to the shy man's reverie, guiltless of any thought of eavesdropping.

"How much I love you, Alice," Jasper Dale was saying, unafraid, with no shyness in voice or manner. "I wonder what you would say if you knew. You would laugh at me—sweet as you are, you would laugh in mockery. I can never tell you.

I can only dream of telling you. In my dream you are standing here by me, dear. I can see you very plainly, my sweet lady, so tall and gracious, with your dark hair and your maiden eyes. I can dream that I tell you my love; that—maddest, sweetest dream of all—that you love me in return. Everything is possible in dreams, you know, dear. My dreams are all I have, so I go far in them, even to dreaming that you are my wife. I dream how I shall fix up my dull old house for you. One room will need nothing more—it is your room, dear, and has been ready for you a long time—long before that day I saw you under the pine. Your books and your chair and your picture are there, dear—only the picture is not half lovely enough. But the other rooms of the house must be made to bloom out freshly for you. What a delight it is thus to dream of what I would do for you! Then I would bring you home, dear, and lead you through my garden and into my house as its mistress. I would see you standing beside me in the old mirror at the end of the hall—a bride, in your pale blue dress, with a blush on your face. I would lead you through all the rooms made ready for your coming, and then to your own. I would see you sitting in your own chair and all my dreams would find rich fulfilment in that royal moment. Oh, Alice, we would have a beautiful life together! It's sweet to make believe about it. You will sing to me in the twilight, and we will gather early flowers together in the spring days. When I come home from work, tired, you will put your arms about me and lay your head on my shoulder. I will stroke it—so—that bonny, glossy head of yours. Alice, my Alice—all mine in my dream—never to be mine in real life—how I love you!"

The Alice behind him could bear no more. She gave a little choking cry that betrayed her presence. Jasper Dale sprang up and gazed upon her. He saw her standing there, amid the languorous shadows of August, pale with feeling, wide-eyed, trembling.

For a moment shyness wrung him. Then every trace of it was banished by a sudden, strange, fierce anger that swept over him. He felt outraged and hurt to the death; he felt as if he had been cheated out of something incalculably precious—as if sacrilege had been done to his most holy sanctuary of emotion. White, tense with his anger, he looked at her and spoke, his lips as pale as if his fiery words scathed them.

"How dare you? You have spied on me—you have crept in and listened! How dare you? Do you know what you have done, girl? You have destroyed all that made life worth while to me. My dream is dead. It could not live when it was betrayed. And it was all I had. Oh, laugh at me—mock me! I know that I am ridiculous! What of it? It never could have hurt you! Why must you creep in like this to hear me and put me to shame? Oh, I love you—I will say it, laugh as you will. Is it such a strange thing that I should have a heart like other men? This will make sport for you! I, who love you better than my life, better than any other man in the world can love you, will be a jest to you all your life. I love you—and yet I think I could hate you—you have destroyed my dream—you have done me deadly wrong."

"Jasper! Jasper!" cried Alice, finding her voice. His anger hurt her with a pain she could not endure. It was unbearable that Jasper should be angry with her. In that moment she realized that she loved him—that the words he had spoken when unconscious of her presence were the sweetest she had ever heard, or ever could hear. Nothing mattered at all, save that he loved her and was angry with her.

"Don't say such dreadful things to me," she stammered, "I did not mean to listen. I could not help it. I shall never laugh at you. Oh, Jasper"—she looked bravely at him and the fine soul of her shone through the flesh like an illuminating lamp— "I am *glad* that you love me! and I am glad I chanced to overhear you, since you would never have had the courage to tell me otherwise. Glad—glad! Do you understand, Jasper?"

Jasper looked at her with the eyes of one who, looking through pain, sees rapture beyond.

"Is it possible?" he said, wonderingly. "Alice—I am so much older than you—and they call me the Awkward Man—they say I am unlike other people"—

"You *are* unlike other people," she said softly, "and that is why I love you. I know now that I must have loved you ever since I saw you."

"I loved you long before I saw you," said Jasper.

He came close to her and drew her into his arms, tenderly and reverently, all his shyness and awkwardness swallowed up in the grace of his great happiness. In the old garden he kissed her lips and Alice entered into her own.

CHAPTER 26

UNCLE BLAIR COMES HOME

IT HAPPENED that the Story Girl and I both got up very early on the morning of the Awkward Man's wedding day. Uncle Alec was going to Charlottetown that day, and I, awakened at daybreak by the sounds in the kitchen beneath us, remembered that I had forgotten to ask him to bring me a certain schoolbook I wanted. So I hurriedly dressed and hastened down to tell him before he went. I was joined on the stairs by the Story Girl, who said she had wakened and, not feeling like going to sleep again, thought she might as well get up.

"I had such a funny dream last night," she said. "I dreamed that I heard a voice calling me from away down in Uncle Stephen's Walk—'Sara, Sara, Sara,' it kept calling. I didn't know whose it was, and yet it seemed like a voice I knew. I wakened up while it was calling, and it seemed so real I could hardly believe it was a dream. It was bright moonlight, and I felt just like getting up and going out to the orchard. But I knew that would be silly and of course I didn't go. But I kept on wanting to and I couldn't sleep any more. Wasn't it queer?"

When Uncle Alec had gone I proposed a saunter to the farther end of the orchard, where I had left a book the preceding evening. A young morn was walking rosily on the hills as we passed down Uncle Stephen's Walk, with Paddy trotting before us. High overhead was the spirit-like blue of paling skies; the east was a great arc of crystal, smitten through with auroral crimsonings; just above it was one milk-white star of morning, like a pearl on a silver sea. A light wind of dawn was weaving an orient spell.

"It's lovely to be up as early as this, isn't it?" said the Story Girl. "The world seems so different just at sunrise, doesn't it? It makes me feel just like getting up to see the sun rise every morning of my life after this. But I know I won't. I'll likely sleep later than ever tomorrow morning. But I wish I could."

"The Awkward Man and Miss Reade are going to have a lovely day for their wedding," I said.

"Yes, and I'm so glad. Beautiful Alice deserves everything good. Why, Bev—why, Bev! Who is that in the hammock?"

I looked. The hammock was swung under the two end trees of the Walk. In it a man was lying, asleep, his head pillowed on his overcoat. He was sleeping easily, lightly, and wholesomely. He had a pointed brown beard and thick wavy brown hair. His cheeks were a dusky red and the lashes of his closed eyes were as long and dark and silken as a girl's. He wore a light gray suit, and on the slender white hand that hung down over the hammock's edge was a spark of diamond fire.

It seemed to me that I knew his face, although assuredly I had never seen him before. While I groped among vague speculations the Story Girl gave a queer, choked little cry. The next moment she had sprung over the intervening space, dropped on her knees by the hammock, and flung her arms about the man's neck.

"Father! Father!" she cried, while I stood, rooted to the ground in my amazement.

The sleeper stirred and opened two large, exceedingly brilliant hazel eyes. For a moment he gazed rather blankly at the brown-curled young lady who was embracing him. Then a most delightful smile broke over his face; he sprang up and caught her to his heart.

"Sara—Sara—my little Sara! To think I didn't know you at first glance! But you are almost a woman. And when I saw you last you were just a little girl of eight. My own little Sara!"

"Father—father—sometimes I've wondered if you were ever coming back to me," I heard the Story Girl say, as I turned and scuttled up the Walk, realizing that I was not wanted there just then and would be little missed. Various emotions and speculations possessed my mind in my retreat; but chiefly did I feel a sense of triumph in being the bearer of exciting news.

"Aunt Janet, Uncle Blair is here," I announced breathlessly at the kitchen door.

Aunt Janet, who was kneading her bread, turned round and lifted floury hands. Felicity and Cecily, who were just entering the kitchen, rosy from slumber, stopped still and stared at me.

"Uncle who?" exclaimed Aunt Janet.

"Uncle Blair—the Story Girl's father, you know. He's here."

"Where?"

"Down in the orchard. He was asleep in the hammock. We found him there."

"Dear me!" said Aunt Janet, sitting down helplessly. "If that isn't like Blair! Of course he couldn't come like anybody else. I wonder," she added in a tone unheard by anyone else save myself, "I wonder if he has come to take the child away."

My elation went out like a snuffed candle. I had never thought of this. If Uncle Blair took the Story Girl away would not life become rather savourless on the hill farm? I turned and followed Felicity and Cecily out in a very subdued mood.

Uncle Blair and the Story Girl were just coming out of the orchard. His arm was about her and hers was on his shoulder. Laughter and tears were contending in her eyes. Only once before—when Peter had come back from the Valley of the Shadow—had I seen the Story Girl cry. Emotion had to go very deep with her ere it touched the source of tears. I had always known that she loved her father passionately, though she rarely talked of him, understanding that her uncles and aunts were not whole-heartedly his friends.

But Aunt Janet's welcome was cordial enough, though a trifle flustered. Whatever thrifty, hardworking farmer folk might think of gay, Bohemian Blair Stanley in his absence, in his presence even they liked him, by the grace of some winsome, lovable quality in the soul of him. He had "a way with him"—revealed even in the manner with which he caught staid Aunt Janet in his arms, swung her matronly form around as though she had been a slim schoolgirl, and kissed her rosy cheek.

"Sister o' mine, are you never going to grow old?" he said. "Here you are at forty-five with the roses of sixteen—and not a gray hair, I'll wager."

"Blair, Blair, it is you who are always young," laughed Aunt Janet, not ill pleased. "Where in the world did you come from? And what is this I hear of your sleeping all night in the hammock?"

"I've been painting in the Lake District all summer, as you know," answered Uncle Blair, "and one day I just got homesick to see my little girl. So I sailed for Montreal without further delay. I got here at eleven last night—the station-master's son drove me down. Nice boy. The old house was in darkness and I thought it would be a shame to rouse you all out of bed after a hard day's work. So I decided that I would spend the night in the orchard. It was moonlight, you know, and moonlight in an old orchard is one of the few things left over from the Golden Age."

"It was very foolish of you," said practical Aunt Janet. "These September nights are real chilly. You might have caught your death of cold—or a bad dose of rheumatism."

"So I might. No doubt it was foolish of me," agreed Uncle Blair gaily. "It must have been the fault of the moonlight. Moonlight, you know, Sister Janet, has an intoxicating quality. It is a fine, airy, silver wine, such as fairies may drink at their revels, unharmed of it; but when a mere mortal sips of it, it mounts straightway to his brain, to the undoing of his daylight common sense. However, I have got neither cold nor rheumatism, as a sensible person would have done had he ever been lured into doing such a nonsensible thing; there is a special Providence for us foolish folk. I enjoyed my night in the orchard; for a time I was companioned by sweet old memories; and then I fell asleep listening to the murmurs of the wind in those old trees yonder. And I had a beautiful dream, Janet. I dreamed that the old orchard blossomed again, as it did that spring eighteen years ago. I dreamed that its sunshine was the sunshine of spring, not autumn. There was newness of life in my dream, Janet, and the sweetness of forgotten words."

"Wasn't it strange about *my* dream?" whispered the Story Girl to me.

"Well, you'd better come in and have some breakfast," said Aunt Janet. "These are my little girls—Felicity and Cecily."

"I remember them as two most adorable tots," said Uncle Blair, shaking hands. "They haven't changed quite so much as my own baby-child. Why, she's a woman, Janet—she's a woman."

"She's child enough still," said Aunt Janet hastily.

The Story Girl shook her long brown curls.

"I'm fifteen," she said. "And you ought to see me in my long dress, father."

"We must not be separated any longer, dear heart," I heard Uncle Blair say tenderly. I hoped that he meant he would stay in Canada—not that he would take the Story Girl away.

Apart from this we had a gay day with Uncle Blair. He evidently liked our society better than that of the grown-ups, for he was a child himself at heart, gay, irresponsible, always acting on the impulse of the moment. We all found him a delightful companion. There was no school that day, as Mr. Perkins was absent, attending a meeting of the Teachers' Convention, so we spent most of its golden hours in the orchard with Uncle Blair, listening to his fascinating accounts of foreign wanderings. He also drew all our pictures for us, and this was especially delightful, for the day of the camera was only just dawning and none of us had ever had even our photographs taken. Sara Ray's pleasure was, as usual, quite spoiled by wondering what her mother would say of it, for Mrs. Ray had, so it appeared, some very peculiar prejudices against the taking or making of any kind of picture whatsoever, owing to an exceedingly strict interpretation of the second commandment. Dan suggested that she need not tell her mother anything about it; but Sara shook her head.

"I'll have to tell her. I've made it a rule to tell ma everything I do ever since the Judgment Day."

"Besides," added Cecily seriously, "the *Family Guide* says one ought to tell one's mother everything."

"It's pretty hard sometimes, though," sighed Sara. "Ma scolds so much when I do tell her things, that it sort of discourages me. But when I think of how dreadful I felt the time of the Judgment Day over deceiving her in some things it nerves me up. I'd do almost anything rather than feel like that the next time the Judgment Day comes."

"Fe, fi, fo, fum, I smell a story," said Uncle Blair. "What do you mean by speaking of the Judgment Day in the past tense?"

The Story Girl told him the tale of that dreadful Sunday in the preceding summer and we all laughed with him at ourselves.

"All the same," muttered Peter, "I don't want to have another experience like that. I hope I'll be dead the next time the Judgment Day comes."

"But you'll be raised up for it," said Felix.

"Oh, that'll be all right. I won't mind that. I won't know anything about it till it really happens. It's the expecting it that's the worst."

"I don't think you ought to talk of such things," said Felicity.

When evening came we all went to Golden Milestone. We knew the Awkward Man and his bride were expected home at sunset, and we meant to scatter flowers on the path by which she must enter her new home. It was the Story Girl's idea, but I don't think Aunt Janet would have let us go if Uncle Blair had not pleaded for us. He asked to be taken along, too, and we agreed, if he would stand out of sight when the newly married pair came home.

"You see, father, the Awkward Man won't mind us, because we're only children and he knows us well," explained the Story Girl, "but if he sees you, a stranger, it might confuse him and we might spoil the home-coming, and that would be such a pity."

So we went to Golden Milestone, laden with all the flowery spoil we could plunder from both gardens. It was a clear amber-tinted September evening and far away, over Markdale Harbour, a great round red moon was rising as we waited. Uncle Blair was hidden behind the wind-blown tassels of the pines at the gate, but he and the Story Girl kept waving their hands at each other and calling out gay, mirthful jests.

"Do you really feel acquainted with your father?" whispered Sara Ray wonderingly. "It's long since you saw him."

"If I hadn't seen him for a hundred years it wouldn't make any difference that way," laughed the Story Girl.

"S-s-h-s-s-h—they're coming," whispered Felicity excitedly.

And then they came—Beautiful Alice blushing and lovely, in the prettiest of pretty blue dresses, and the Awkward Man, so fervently happy that he quite forgot to be awkward. He lifted her out of the buggy gallantly and led her forward to us, smiling. We retreated before them, scattering our flowers lavishly on the path, and Alice Dale walked to the very doorstep of her new home over a carpet of blossoms. On the step they both paused and turned towards us, and we shyly did the proper thing in the way of congratulations and good wishes.

"It was so sweet of you to do this," said the smiling bride.

"It was lovely to be able to do it for you, dearest," whispered the Story Girl, "and oh, Miss Reade—Mrs. Dale, I mean—we all hope you'll be so, so happy for ever."

"I am sure I shall," said Alice Dale, turning to her husband. He looked down into her eyes—and we were quite forgotten by both of them. We saw it, and slipped away, while Jasper Dale drew his wife into their home and shut the world out.

We scampered joyously away through the moonlit dusk. Uncle Blair joined us at the gate and the Story Girl asked him what he thought of the bride.

"When she dies white violets will grow out of her dust," he answered.

"Uncle Blair says even queerer things than the Story Girl," Felicity whispered to me.

And so that beautiful day went away from us, slipping through our fingers as we tried to hold it. It hooded itself in shadows and fared forth on the road that is lighted by the white stars of evening. It had been a gift of Paradise. Its hours had all been fair and beloved. From dawn flush to fall of night there had been naught to mar it. It took with it its smiles and laughter. But it left the boon of memory.

CHAPTER 27

THE OLD ORDER CHANGETH

"I AM going away with father when he goes. He is going to spend the winter in Paris, and I am to go to school there."

The Story Girl told us this one day in the orchard. There was a little elation in her tone, but more regret. The news was not a great surprise to us. We had felt it in the air ever since Uncle Blair's arrival. Aunt Janet had been very unwilling to let the Story Girl go. But Uncle Blair was inexorable. It was time, he said, that she should go to a better school than the little country one in Carlisle; and besides, he did not want her to grow into womanhood a stranger to him. So it was finally decided that she was to go.

"Just think, you are going to Europe," said Sara Ray in an awe-struck tone. "Won't that be splendid!"

"I suppose I'll like it after a while," said the Story Girl slowly, "but I know I'll be dreadfully homesick at first. Of course, it will be lovely to be with father, but oh, I'll miss the rest of you so much!"

"Just think how *we'll* miss *you*," sighed Cecily. "It will be so lonesome here this winter, with you and Peter both gone. Oh, dear, I do wish things didn't have to change."

Felicity said nothing. She kept looking down at the grass on which she sat, absently pulling at the slender blades. Presently

we saw two big tears roll down over her cheeks. The Story
Girl looked surprised.

"Are you crying because I'm going away, Felicity?" she asked.

"Of course I am," answered Felicity, with a big sob. "Do
you think I've no f-f-eeling?"

"I didn't think you'd care much," said the Story Girl frankly.
"You've never seemed to like me very much."

"I d-don't wear my h-heart on my sleeve," said poor Felicity,
with an attempt at dignity. "I think you m-might stay. Your
father would let you s-stay if you c-coaxed him."

"Well, you see I'd have to go some time," sighed the Story
Girl, "and the longer it was put off the harder it would be.
But I do feel dreadfully about it. I can't even take poor Paddy.
I'll have to leave him behind, and oh, I want you all to promise
to be kind to him for my sake."

We all solemnly assured her that we would.

"I'll g-give him cream every m-morning and n-night," sobbed
Felicity, "but I'll never be able to look at him without crying.
He'll make me think of you."

"Well, I'm not going right away," said the Story Girl, more
cheerfully. "Not till the last of October. So we have over a
month yet to have a good time in. Let's all just determine to
make it a splendid month for the last. We won't think about
my going at all till we have to, and we won't have any quarrels
among us, and we'll just enjoy ourselves all we possibly can.
So don't cry any more, Felicity. I'm awfully glad you do like
me and am sorry I'm going away, but let's all forget it for a
month."

Felicity sighed, and tucked away her damp handkerchief.

"It isn't so easy for me to forget things, but I'll try," she
said disconsolately, "and if you want any more cooking lessons
before you go I'll be real glad to teach you anything I know."

This was a high plane of self-sacrifice for Felicity to attain.
But the Story Girl shook her head.

"No, I'm not going to bother my head about cooking lessons
this last month. It's too vexing."

"Do you remember the time you made the pudding—" began
Peter, and suddenly stopped.

"Out of sawdust?" finished the Story Girl cheerfully. "You
needn't be afraid to mention it to me after this. I don't mind
any more. I begin to see the fun of it now. I should think I

do remember it—and the time I baked the bread before it was raised enough."

"People have made worse mistakes than that," said Felicity kindly.

"Such as using tooth-powd—" but here Dan stopped abruptly, remembering the Story Girl's plea for a beautiful month. Felicity coloured, but said nothing—did not even *look* anything.

"We *have* had lots of fun together one way or another," said Cecily, retrospectively.

"Just think how much we've laughed this last year or so," said the Story Girl. "We've had good times together; but I think we'll have lots more splendid years ahead."

"Eden is always behind us—Paradise always before," said Uncle Blair, coming up in time to hear her. He said it with a sigh that was immediately lost in one of his delightful smiles.

"I like Uncle Blair so much better than I expected to," Felicity confided to me. "Mother says he's a rolling stone, but there really is something very nice about him, although he says a great many things I don't understand. I suppose the Story Girl will have a very gay time in Paris."

"She's going to school and she'll have to study hard," I said.

"She says she's going to study for the stage," said Felicity. "Uncle Roger thinks it is all right, and says she'll be very famous some day. But mother thinks it's dreadful, and so do I."

"Aunt Julia is a concert singer," I said.

"Oh, that's very different. But I hope poor Sara will get on all right," sighed Felicity. "You never know what may happen to a person in those foreign countries. And everybody says Paris is such a wicked place. But we must hope for the best," she concluded in a resigned tone.

That evening the Story Girl and I drove the cows to pasture after milking, and when we came home we sought out Uncle Blair in the orchard. He was sauntering up and down Uncle Stephen's Walk, his hands clasped behind him and his beautiful, youthful face uplifted to the western sky where waves of night were breaking on a dim primrose shore of sunset.

"See that star over there in the south-west?" he said, as we joined him. "The one just above that pine? An evening star shining over a dark pine tree is the whitest thing in the universe—because it is *living* whiteness—whiteness possessing a soul. How full this old orchard is of twilight! Do you know, I have been trysting here with ghosts."

"The Family Ghost?" I asked, very stupidly.

"No, not the Family Ghost. I never saw beautiful, broken-hearted Emily yet. Your mother saw her once, Sara—that was a strange thing," he added absently, as if to himself.

"Did mother really see her?" whispered the Story Girl.

"Well, she always believed she did. Who knows?"

"Do you think there are such things as ghosts, Uncle Blair?" I asked curiously.

"I never saw any, Beverley."

"But you said you were trysting with ghosts here this evening," said the Story Girl.

"Oh, yes—the ghosts of the old years. I love this orchard because of its many ghosts. We are good comrades, those ghosts and I; we walk and talk—we even laugh together—sorrowful laughter that has sorrow's own sweetness. And always there comes to me one dear phantom and wanders hand in hand with me—a lost lady of the old years."

"My mother?" said the Story Girl very softly.

"Yes, your mother. Here, in her old haunts, it is impossible for me to believe that she can be dead—that her *laughter* can be dead. She was the gayest, sweetest thing—and so young— only three years older than you, Sara. Yonder old house had been glad because of her for eighteen years when I met her first."

"I wish I could remember her," said the Story Girl, with a little sigh. "I haven't even a picture of her. Why didn't you paint one, father?"

"She would never let me. She had some queer, funny, half-playful, half-earnest superstition about it. But I always meant to when she would become willing to let me. And then—she died. Her twin brother Felix died the same day. There was something strange about that, too. I was holding her in my arms and she was looking up at me; suddenly she looked past me and gave a little start. 'Felix!' she said. For a moment she trembled and then she smiled and looked up at me again a little beseechingly. 'Felix has come for me, dear,' she said. 'We were always together before you came—you must not mind— you must be glad I do not have to go alone.' Well, who knows? But she left me, Sara—she left me."

There was that in Uncle Blair's voice that kept us silent for a time. Then the Story Girl said, still very softly:

"What did mother look like, father? I don't look the least little bit like her, do I?"

"No, I wish you did, you brown thing. Your mother's face was as white as a wood-lily, with only a faint dream of rose in her cheeks. She had the eyes of one who always had a song in her heart—blue as a mist, those eyes were. She had dark lashes, and a little red mouth that quivered when she was very sad or very happy like a crimson rose too rudely shaken by the wind. She was as slim and lithe as a young, white-stemmed birch tree. How I loved her! How happy we were! But he who accepts human love must bind it to his soul with pain, and she is not lost to me. Nothing is ever really lost to us as long as we remember it."

Uncle Blair looked up at the evening star. We saw that he had forgotten us, and we slipped away, hand in hand, leaving him alone in the memory-haunted shadows of the old orchard.

CHAPTER 28

THE PATH TO ARCADY

OCTOBER THAT year gathered up all the spilled sunshine of the summer and clad herself in it as in a garment. The Story Girl had asked us to try to make the last month together beautiful, and Nature seconded our efforts, giving us that most beautiful of beautiful things—a gracious and perfect moon of falling leaves. There was not in all that vanished October one day that did not come in with auroral splendour and go out attended by a fair galaxy of evening stars—not a day when there were not golden lights in the wide pastures and purple hazes in the ripened distances. Never was anything so gorgeous as the maple trees that year. Maples are trees that have primeval fire in their souls. It glows out a little in their early youth, before the leaves open, in the redness and rosy-yellowness of their blossoms, but in summer it is carefully hidden under a demure, silver-lined greenness. Then when autumn comes, the maples give up trying to be sober and flame out in all the barbaric splendour and gorgeousness of their real nature, making of the hills things out of an Arabian Nights dream in the golden prime of good Haroun Alraschid.

You may never know what scarlet and crimson really are until you see them in their perfection on an October hillside, under the unfathomable blue of an autumn sky. All the glow and radiance and joy at earth's heart seem to have broken loose in a splendid determination to express itself for once before the frost of winter chills her beating pulses. It is the year's carnival ere the dull Lenten days of leafless valleys and penitential mists come.

The time of apple-picking had come around once more and we worked joyously. Uncle Blair picked apples with us, and between him and the Story Girl it was an October never to be forgotten.

"Will you go far afield for a walk with me today?" he said to her and me, one idle afternoon of opal skies, pied meadows and misty hills.

It was Saturday and Peter had gone home; Felix and Dan were helping Uncle Alec top turnips; Cecily and Felicity were making cookies for Sunday, so the Story Girl and I were alone in Uncle Stephen's Walk.

We liked to be alone together that last month, to think the long, long thoughts of youth and talk about our futures. There had grown up between us that summer a bond of sympathy that did not exist between us and the others. We were older than they—the Story Girl was fifteen and I was nearly that; and all at once it seemed as if we were immeasurably older than the rest, and possessed of dreams and visions and forward-reaching hopes which they could not possibly share or understand. At times we were still children, still interested in childish things. But there came hours when we seemed to our two selves very grown up and old, and in those hours we talked our dreams and visions and hopes, vague and splendid, as all such are, over together, and so began to build up, out of the rainbow fragments of our childhood's companionship, that rare and beautiful friendship which was to last all our lives, enriching and enstarring them. For there is no bond more lasting than that formed by the mutual confidences of that magic time when youth is slipping from the sheath of childhood and beginning to wonder what lies for it beyond those misty hills that bound the golden road.

"Where are you going?" asked the Story Girl.

"To 'the woods that belt the gray hillside'—ay, and overflow beyond it into many a valley purple-folded in immemorial peace," answered Uncle Blair. "I have a fancy for one more ramble in Prince Edward Island woods before I leave Canada again. But I would not go alone. So come, you two gay youthful things to whom all life is yet fair and good, and we will seek the path to Arcady. There will be many little things along our way to make us glad. Joyful sounds will 'come ringing down the wind;' a wealth of gypsy gold will be ours for the gathering; we will learn the potent, unutterable charm of a dim spruce wood and the grace of flexible mountain ashes fringing a lonely glen; we will tryst with the folk of fur and feather; we'll hearken to the music of gray old firs. Come, and you'll have a ramble and an afternoon that you will both remember all your lives."

We did have it; never has its remembrance faded; that idyllic afternoon of roving in the old Carlisle woods with the Story Girl and Uncle Blair gleams in my book of years, a page of living beauty. Yet it was but a few hours of simplest pleasure; we wandered pathlessly through the sylvan calm of those dear places which seemed that day to be full of a great friendliness; Uncle Blair sauntered along behind us, whistling softly; sometimes he talked to himself; we delighted in those brief reveries of his; Uncle Blair was the only man I have ever known who could, when he so willed, "talk like a book," and do it without seeming ridiculous; perhaps it was because he had the knack of choosing "fit audience, though few," and the proper time to appeal to that audience.

We went across the fields, intending to skirt the woods at the back of Uncle Alec's farm and find a lane that cut through Uncle Roger's woods; but before we came to it we stumbled on a sly, winding little path quite by accident—if, indeed, there can be such a thing as accident in the woods, where I am tempted to think we are led by the Good People along such of their fairy ways as they have a mind for us to walk in.

"Go to, let us explore this," said Uncle Blair. "It always drags terribly at my heart to go past a wood lane if I can make any excuse at all for traversing it: for it is the by-ways that lead to the heart of the woods and we must follow them if we would know the forest and be known of it. When we can really feel its wild heart beating against ours its subtle life will steal into our veins and make us its own for ever, so that no matter where we go or how wide we wander in the noisy ways of cities or over the lone ways of the sea, we shall yet be drawn back to the forest to find our most enduring kinship."

"I always feel so *satisfied* in the woods," said the Story Girl dreamily, as we turned in under the low-swinging fir boughs. "Trees seem such friendly things."

"They are the most friendly things in God's good creation," said Uncle Blair emphatically. "And it is so easy to live with them. To hold converse with pines, to whisper secrets with the poplars, to listen to the tales of old romance that beeches have to tell, to walk in eloquent silence with self-contained firs, is to learn what real companionship is. Besides, trees are the same all over the world. A beech tree on the slopes of the Pyrenees is just what a beech tree here in these Carlisle woods is; and there used to be an old pine hereabouts whose twin brother I was well acquainted with in a dell among the Apennines. Listen to those squirrels, will you, chattering over yonder. Did you ever hear such a fuss over nothing? Squirrels are the gossips and busybodies of the woods; they haven't learned the fine reserve of its other denizens. But after all, there is a certain shrill friendliness in their greeting."

"They seem to be scolding us," I said, laughing.

"Oh, they are not half such scolds as they sound," answered Uncle Blair gaily. "If they would but 'tak a thought and mend' their shrew-like ways they would be dear, lovable creatures enough."

"If I had to be an animal I think I'd like to be a squirrel," said the Story Girl. "It must be next best thing to flying."

"Just see what a spring that fellow gave," laughed Uncle Blair. "And now listen to his song of triumph! I suppose that chasm he cleared seemed as wide and deep to him as Niagara Gorge would to us if we leaped over it. Well, the wood people are a happy folk and very well satisfied with themselves."

Those who have followed a dim, winding, balsamic path to the unexpected hollow where a wood-spring lies have found the rarest secret the forest can reveal. Such was our good fortune that day. At the end of our path we found it, under the pines, a crystal-clear thing with lips unkissed by so much as a stray sunbeam.

"It is easy to dream that this is one of the haunted springs of old romance," said Uncle Blair. "'Tis an enchanted spot this, I am very sure, and we should go softly, speaking low, lest we disturb the rest of a white, wet naiad, or break some spell that has cost long years of mystic weaving."

"It's so easy to believe things in the woods," said the Story Girl, shaping a cup from a bit of golden-brown birch bark and filling it at the spring.

"Drink a toast in that water, Sara," said Uncle Blair. "There's not a doubt that it has some potent quality of magic in it and the wish you wish over it will come true."

The Story Girl lifted her golden-hued flagon to her red lips. Her hazel eyes laughed at us over the brim.

"Here's to our futures," she cried, "I wish that every day of our lives may be better than the one that went before."

"An extravagant wish—a very wish of youth," commented Uncle Blair, "and yet in spite of its extravagance, a wish that will come true if you are true to yourselves. In that case, every day *will* be better than all that went before—but there will be many days, dear lad and lass, when you will not believe it."

We did not understand him, but we knew Uncle Blair never explained his meaning. When asked it he was wont to answer with a smile, "Some day you'll grow to it. Wait for that." So we addressed ourselves to follow the brook that stole away from the spring in its windings and doublings and tricky surprises.

"A brook," quoth Uncle Blair, "is the most changeful, bewitching, lovable thing in the world. It is never in the same mind or mood two minutes. Here it is sighing and murmuring as if its heart were broken. But listen—yonder by the birches it is laughing as if it were enjoying some capital joke all by itself."

It was indeed a changeful brook; here it would make a pool, dark and brooding and still, where we bent to look at our mirrored faces; then it grew communicative and gossiped shallowly over a broken pebble bed where there was a diamond dance of sunbeams and no troutling or minnow could glide through without being seen. Sometimes its banks were high and steep, hung with slender ashes and birches; again they were mere, low margins, green with delicate mosses, shelving out of the wood. Once it came to a little precipice and flung itself over undauntedly in an indignation of foam, gathering itself up rather dizzily among the mossy stones below. It was some time before it got over its vexation; it went boiling and muttering along, fighting with the rotten logs that lie across it, and making far more fuss than was necessary over every root that interfered with it. We were getting tired of its ill-humour and talked of leaving it, when it suddenly grew sweet-tempered again, swooped around a curve—and presto, we were in fairyland.

It was a little dell far in the heart of the woods. A row of birches fringed the brook, and each birch seemed more exquisitely graceful and golden than her sisters. The woods receded from it on every hand, leaving it lying in a pool of amber sunshine. The yellow trees were mirrored in the placid stream, with now and then a leaf falling on the water, mayhap to drift away and be used, as Uncle Blair suggested, by some adventurous wood sprite who had it in mind to fare forth to some far-off, legendary region where all the brooks ran into the sea.

"Oh, what a lovely place!" I exclaimed, looking around me with delight.

"A spell of eternity is woven over it, surely," murmured Uncle Blair. "Winter may not touch it, or spring ever revisit it. It should be like this for ever."

"Let us never come here again," said the Story Girl softly, "never, no matter how often we may be in Carlisle. Then we will never see it changed or different. We can always remember it just as we see it now, and it will be like this for ever for us."

"I'm going to sketch it," said Uncle Blair.

While he sketched it the Story Girl and I sat on the banks of the brook and she told me the story of the Sighing Reed. It was a very simple little story, that of the slender brown reed which grew by the forest pool and always was sad and sighing because it could not utter music like the brook and the birds and the winds. All the bright, beautiful things around it mocked it and laughed at it for its folly. Who would ever look for music in it, a plain, brown, unbeautiful thing? But one day a youth came through the wood; he was as beautiful as the spring; he cut the brown reed and fashioned it according to his liking; and then he put it to his lips and breathed on it; and, oh, the music that floated through the forest! It was so entrancing that everything—brooks and birds and winds—grew silent to listen to it. Never had anything so lovely been heard; it was the music that had for so long been shut up in the soul of the sighing reed and was set free at last through its pain and suffering.

I had heard the Story Girl tell many a more dramatic tale; but that one stands out for me in memory above them all, partly, perhaps, because of the spot in which she told it, partly because it was the last one I was to hear her tell for many years—the last one she was ever to tell me on the golden road.

When Uncle Blair had finished his sketch the shafts of sunshine were turning crimson and growing more and more remote; the early autumn twilight was falling over the woods. We left our dell, saying good-bye to it for ever, as the Story Girl had suggested, and we went slowly homeward through the fir woods, where a haunting, indescribable odour stole out to meet us.

"There is magic in the scent of dying fir," Uncle Blair was saying aloud to himself, as if forgetting he was not quite alone. "It gets into our blood like some rare, subtly-compounded wine, and thrills us with unutterable sweetnesses, as of recollections from some other fairer life, lived in some happier star. Compared to it, all other scents seem heavy and earth-born, luring to the valleys instead of the heights. But the tang of the fir summons onward and upward to some 'far-off, divine event'—some spiritual peak of attainment whence we shall see with unfaltering, unclouded vision the spires of some aerial City Beautiful, or the fulfilment of some fair, fadeless land of promise."

He was silent for a moment, then added in a lower tone,

"Felicity, you loved the scent of dying fir. If you were here tonight with me—Felicity—Felicity!"

Something in his voice made me suddenly sad. I was comforted when I felt the Story Girl slip her hand into mine. So we walked out of the woods into the autumn dusk.

We were in a little valley. Half-way up the opposite slope a brush fire was burning clearly and steadily in a maple grove. There was something indescribably alluring in that fire, glowing so redly against the dark background of forest and twilit hill.

"Let us go to it," cried Uncle Blair, gaily, casting aside his sorrowful mood and catching our hands. "A wood fire at night has a fascination not to be resisted by those of mortal race. Hasten—we must not lose time."

"Oh, it will burn a long time yet," I gasped, for Uncle Blair was whisking us up the hill at a merciless rate.

"You can't be sure. It *may* have been lighted by some good, honest farmer-man, bent on tidying up his sugar orchard, but it may also, for anything we know, have been kindled by no earthly woodman as a beacon or summons to the tribes of fairyland, and may vanish away if we tarry."

It did not vanish and presently we found ourselves in the grove. It was very beautiful; the fire burned with a clear, steady glow and a soft crackle; the long arcades beneath the trees were illuminated with a rosy radiance, beyond which lurked companies of gray and purple shadows. Everything was very still and dreamy and remote.

"It is impossible that out there, just over the hill, lies a village of men, where tame household lamps are shining," said Uncle Blair.

"I feel as if we must be thousands of miles away from everything we've ever known," murmured the Story Girl.

"So you are!" said Uncle Blair emphatically. "You're back in the youth of the race—back in the beguilement of the young world. Everything is in this hour—the beauty of classic myths, the primal charm of the silent and the open, the lure of mystery. Why, it's a time and place when and where everything might come true—when the men in green might creep out to join hands and dance around the fire, or dryads steal from their trees to warm their white limbs, grown chilly in October frosts, by the blaze. I wouldn't be much surprised if we should see something of the kind. Isn't that the flash of an ivory shoulder through yonder gloom? And didn't you see a queer little elfin face peering at us around that twisted gray trunk? But one can't be sure. Mortal eyesight is too slow and clumsy a thing to match against the flicker of a pixy-litten fire."

Hand in hand we wandered through that enchanted place, seeking the folk of elf-land, "and heard their mystic voices calling, from fairy knoll and haunted hill." Not till the fire died down into ashes did we leave the grove. Then we found that the full moon was gleaming lustrously from a cloudless sky across the valley. Between us and her stretched up a tall pine, wondrously straight and slender and branchless to its very top, where it overflowed in a crest of dark boughs against the silvery splendour behind it. Beyond, the hill farms were lying in a suave, white radiance.

"Doesn't it seem a long, long time to you since we left home this afternoon?" asked the Story Girl. "And yet it is only a few hours."

Only a few hours—true; yet such hours were worth a cycle of common years untouched by the glory and the dream.

------------------ **CHAPTER 29** ------------------

WE LOSE A FRIEND

OUR BEAUTIFUL October was marred by one day of black tragedy—the day Paddy died. For Paddy, after seven years of as happy a life as ever a cat lived, died suddenly—of poison, as was supposed. Where he had wandered in the darkness to meet his doom we did not know, but in the frosty dawnlight he dragged himself home to die. We found him lying on the doorstep when we got up, and it did not need Aunt Janet's curt announcement, or Uncle Blair's reluctant shake of the head, to tell us that there was no chance of our pet recovering this time. We felt that nothing could be done. Lard and sulphur on his paws would be of no use, nor would any visit to Peg Bowen avail. We stood around in mournful silence; the Story Girl sat down on the step and took poor Paddy upon her lap.

"I s'pose there's no use even in praying now," said Cecily desperately.

"It wouldn't do any harm to try," sobbed Felicity.

"You needn't waste your prayers," said Dan mournfully, "Pat is beyond human aid. You can tell that by his eyes. Besides, I don't believe it was the praying cured him last time."

"No, it was Peg Bowen," declared Peter, "but she couldn't have bewitched him this time for she's been away for months, nobody knows where."

"If he could only *tell* us where he feels the worst!" said Cecily piteously. "It's so dreadful to see him suffering and not be able to do a single thing to help him!"

"I don't think he's suffering much now," I said comfortingly.

The Story Girl said nothing. She passed and repassed her long brown hand gently over her pet's glossy fur. Pat lifted his head and essayed to creep a little nearer to his beloved mistress. The Story Girl drew his limp body close in her arms. There was a plaintive little mew—a long quiver—and Paddy's friendly soul had fared forth to wherever it is that good cats go.

"Well, he's gone," said Dan, turning his back abruptly to us.

"It doesn't seem as if it can be true," sobbed Cecily. "This time yesterday morning he was full of life."

"He drank two full saucers of cream," moaned Felicity, "and I saw him catch a mouse in the evening. Maybe it was the last one he ever caught."

"He did for many a mouse in his day," said Peter, anxious to pay his tribute to the departed.

" 'He was a cat—take him for all in all. We shall not look upon his like again,' " quoted Uncle Blair.

Felicity and Cecily and Sara Ray cried so much that Aunt Janet lost patience completely and told them sharply that they would have something to cry for some day—which did not seem to comfort them much. The Story Girl shed no tears, though the look in her eyes hurt more than weeping.

"After all, perhaps it's for the best," she said drearily. "I've been feeling so badly over having to go away and leave Paddy. No matter how kind you'd all be to him I know he'd miss me terribly. He wasn't like most cats who don't care who comes and goes as long as they get plenty to eat. Paddy wouldn't have been contented without me."

"Oh, no-o-o, oh, no-o-o," wailed Sara Ray lugubriously.

Felix shot a disgusted glance at her.

"I don't see what *you* are making such a fuss about," he said unfeelingly. "He wasn't *your* cat."

"But I l-l-oved him," sobbed Sara, "and I always feel bad when my friends d-do."

"I wish we could believe that cats went to heaven, like people," sighed Cecily. "Do you really think it isn't possible?"

Uncle Blair shook his head.

"I'm afraid not. I'd like to think cats have a chance for

heaven, but I can't. There's nothing heavenly about cats, delightful creatures though they are."

"Blair, I'm really surprised to hear the things you say to the children," said Aunt Janet severely.

"Surely you wouldn't prefer me to tell them that cats *do* go to heaven," protested Uncle Blair.

"I think it's wicked to carry on about an animal as those children do," answered Aunt Janet decidedly, "and you shouldn't encourage them. Here now, children, stop making a fuss. Bury that cat and get off to your apple picking."

We had to go to our work, but Paddy was not to be buried in any such off-hand fashion as that. It was agreed that we should bury him in the orchard at sunset that evening, and Sara Ray, who had to go home, declared she would be back for it, and implored us to wait for her if she didn't come exactly on time.

"I mayn't be able to get away till after milking," she sniffed, "but I don't want to miss it. Even a cat's funeral is better than none at all."

"Horrid thing!" said Felicity, barely waiting until Sara was out of earshot.

We worked with heavy hearts that day; the girls cried bitterly most of the time and we boys whistled defiantly. But as evening drew on we began to feel a sneaking interest in the details of the funeral. As Dan said, the thing should be done properly, since Paddy was no common cat. The Story Girl selected the spot for the grave, in a little corner behind the cherry copse, where early violets enskied the grass in spring, and we boys dug the grave, making it "soft and narrow," as the heroine of the old ballad wanted hers made. Sara Ray, who managed to come in time after all, and Felicity stood and watched us, but Cecily and the Story Girl kept far aloof.

"This time last night you never thought you'd be digging Pat's grave tonight," sighed Felicity.

"We little k-know what a day will bring forth," sobbed Sara. "I've heard the minister say that and it is true."

"Of course it's true. It's in the Bible; but I don't think you should repeat it in connection with a cat," said Felicity dubiously.

When all was in readiness the Story Girl brought her pet

through the orchard where he had so often frisked and prowled. No useless coffin enclosed his breast but he reposed in a neat cardboard box.

"I wonder if it would be right to say 'ashes to ashes and dust to dust,' " said Peter.

"No, it wouldn't," averred Felicity. "It would be real wicked."

"I think we ought to sing a hymn, anyway," asseverated Sara Ray.

"Well, we might do that, if it isn't a very religious one," conceded Felicity.

"How would 'Pull for the shore, sailor, pull for the shore,' do?" asked Cecily. "That never seemed to me a very religious hymn."

"But it doesn't seem very appropriate to a funeral occasion either," said Felicity.

"I think 'Lead, kindly light,' would be ever so much more suitable," suggested Sara Ray, "and it is kind of soothing and melancholy too."

"We are not going to sing anything," said the Story Girl coldly. "Do you want to make the affair ridiculous? We will just fill up the grave quietly and put a flat stone over the top."

"It isn't much like my idea of a funeral," muttered Sara Ray discontentedly.

"Never mind, we're going to have a real obituary about him in *Our Magazine*," whispered Cecily consolingly.

"And Peter is going to cut his name on top of the stone," added Felicity. "Only we mustn't let on to the grown-ups until it is done, because they might say it wasn't right."

We left the orchard, a sober little band, with the wind of the gray twilight blowing round us. Uncle Roger passed us at the gate.

"So the last sad obsequies are over?" he remarked with a grin.

And we hated Uncle Roger. But we loved Uncle Blair because he said quietly,

"And so you've buried your little comrade?"

So much may depend on the way a thing is said. But not even Uncle Blair's sympathy could take the sting out of the fact that there was no Paddy to get the froth that night at milking time. Felicity cried bitterly all the time she was straining

the milk. Many human beings have gone to their graves un-
attended by as much real regret as followed that one gray pussy
cat to his.

—————————— C H A P T E R 30 ——————————

PROPHECIES

"HERE'S A letter for you from father," said Felix, tossing it to
me as he came through the orchard gate. We had been picking
apples all day, but were taking a mid-afternoon rest around
the well, with a cup of its sparkling cold water to refresh us.

I opened the letter rather indifferently, for father, with all
his excellent and lovable traits, was but a poor correspondent;
his letters were usually very brief and very unimportant.

This letter was brief enough, but it was freighted with a
message of weighty import. I sat gazing stupidly at the sheet
after I had read it until Felix exclaimed,

"Bev, what's the matter with you? What's in that letter?"

"Father is coming home," I said dazedly. "He is to leave
South America in a fortnight and will be here in November
to take us back to Toronto."

Everybody gasped. Sara Ray, of course, began to cry, which
aggravated me unreasonably.

"Well," said Felix, when he got his second wind, "I'll be
awful glad to see father again, but I tell you I don't like the
thought of leaving here."

I felt exactly the same but, in view of Sara Ray's tears, admit
it I would not; so I sat in grum silence while the other tongues
wagged.

"If I were not going away myself I'd feel just terrible," said
the Story Girl. "Even as it is I'm real sorry. I'd like to be able
to think of you as all here together when I'm gone, having
good times and writing me about them."

"It'll be awfully dull when you fellows go," muttered Dan.

"I'm sure I don't know what we're ever going to do here

this winter," said Felicity, with the calmness of despair.

"Thank goodness there are no more fathers to come back," breathed Cecily with a vicious earnestness that made us all laugh, even in the midst of our dismay.

We worked very half-heartedly the rest of the day, and it was not until we assembled in the orchard in the evening that our spirits recovered something like their wonted level. It was clear and slightly frosty; the sun had declined behind a birch on a distant hill and it seemed a tree with a blazing heart of fire. The great golden willow at the lane gate was laughter-shaken in the wind of evening. Even amid all the changes of our shifting world we could not be hopelessly low-spirited— except Sara Ray, who was often so, and Peter, who was rarely so. But Peter had been sorely vexed in spirit for several days. The time was approaching for the October issue of *Our Magazine* and he had no genuine fiction ready for it. He had taken so much to heart Felicity's taunt that his stories were all true that he had determined to have a really-truly false one in the next number. But the difficulty was to get anyone to write it. He had asked the Story Girl to do it, but she refused; then he appealed to me and I shirked. Finally Peter determined to write a story himself.

"It oughtn't to be any harder than writing a poem and I managed that," he said dolefully.

He worked at it in the evenings in the granary loft, and the rest of us forebore to question him concerning it, because he evidently disliked talking about his literary efforts. But this evening I had to ask him if he would soon have it ready, as I wanted to make up the paper.

"It's done," said Peter, with an air of gloomy triumph. "It don't amount to much, but anyhow I made it all out of my own head. Not one word of it was ever printed or told before, and nobody can say there was."

"Then I guess we have all the stuff in and I'll have *Our Magazine* ready to read by tomorrow night," I said.

"I s'pose it will be the last one we'll have," sighed Cecily. "We can't carry it on after you all go, and it has been such fun."

"Bev will be a real newspaper editor some day," declared the Story Girl, on whom the spirit of prophecy suddenly descended that night.

She was swinging on the bough of an apple tree, with a crimson shawl wrapped about her head, and her eyes were bright with roguish fire.

"How do you know he will?" asked Felicity.

"Oh, I can tell futures," answered the Story Girl mysteriously. "I know what's going to happen to all of you. Shall I tell you?"

"Do, just for the fun of it," I said. "Then some day we'll know just how near you came to guessing right. Go on. What else about me?"

"You'll write books, too, and travel all over the world," continued the Story Girl. "Felix will be fat to the end of his life, and he will be a grandfather before he is fifty, and he will wear a long black beard."

"I won't," cried Felix disgustedly. "I hate whiskers. Maybe I can't help the grandfather part, but I *can* help having a beard."

"You can't. It's written in the stars."

"'Tain't. The stars can't prevent me from shaving."

"Won't Grandpa Felix sound awful funny?" reflected Felicity.

"Peter will be a minister," went on the Story Girl.

"Well, I might be something worse," remarked Peter, in a not ungratified tone.

"Dan will be a farmer and will marry a girl whose name begins with K and he will have eleven children. And he'll vote Grit."

"I won't," cried scandalized Dan. "You don't know a thing about it. Catch *me* ever voting Grit! As for the rest of it—I don't care. Farming's well enough, though I'd rather be a sailor."

"Don't talk such nonsense," protested Felicity sharply. "What on earth do you want to be a sailor for and be drowned?"

"All sailors aren't drowned," said Dan.

"Most of them are. Look at Uncle Stephen."

"You ain't sure he was drowned."

"Well, he disappeared, and that is worse."

"How do you know? Disappearing might be real easy."

"It's not very easy for your family."

"Hush, let's hear the rest of the predictions," said Cecily.

"Felicity," resumed the Story Girl gravely, "will marry a minister."

Sara Ray giggled and Felicity blushed. Peter tried hard not to look too self-consciously delighted.

"She will be a perfect housekeeper and will teach a Sunday

School class and be very happy all her life."

"Will her husband be happy?" queried Dan solemnly.

"I guess he'll be as happy as *your* wife," retorted Felicity reddening.

"He'll be the happiest man in the world," declared Peter warmly.

"What about me?" asked Sara Ray.

The Story Girl looked rather puzzled. It was so hard to imagine Sara Ray as having any kind of future. Yet Sara was plainly anxious to have her fortune told and must be gratified.

"You'll be married," said the Story Girl recklessly, "and you'll live to be nearly a hundred years old, and go to dozens of funerals and have a great many sick spells. You will learn not to cry after you are seventy; but your husband will never go to church."

"I'm glad you warned me," said Sara Ray solemnly, "because now I know I'll make him promise before I marry him that he will go."

"He won't keep the promise," said the Story Girl, shaking her head. "But it is getting cold and Cecily is coughing. Let us go in."

"You haven't told my fortune," protested Cecily disappointedly.

The Story Girl looked very tenderly at Cecily—at the smooth little brown head, at the soft, shining eyes, at the cheeks that were often over-rosy after slight exertion, at the little sunburned hands that were always busy doing faithful work or quiet kindnesses. A very strange look came over the Story Girl's face; her eyes grew sad and far-reaching, as if of a verity they pierced beyond the mists of hidden years.

"I couldn't tell any fortune half good enough for you, dearest," she said, slipping her arm round Cecily. "You deserve everything good and lovely. But you know I've only been in fun—of course I don't know anything about what's going to happen to us."

"Perhaps you know more than you think for," said Sara Ray, who seemed much pleased with her fortune and anxious to believe it, despite the husband who wouldn't go to church.

"But I'd like to be told my fortune, even in fun," persisted Cecily.

"Everybody you meet will love you as long as you live," said the Story Girl. "There that's the very nicest fortune I can tell you, and it will come true whether the others do or not, and now we must go in."

We went, Cecily still a little disappointed. In later years I often wondered why the Story Girl refused to tell her fortune that night. Did some strange gleam of foreknowledge fall for a moment across her mirth-making? Did she realize in a flash of prescience that there was no earthly future for our sweet Cecily? Not for her were to be the lengthening shadows or the fading garland. The end was to come while the rainbow still sparkled on her wine of life, ere a single petal had fallen from her rose of joy. Long life was before all the others who trysted that night in the old homestead orchard; but Cecily's maiden feet were never to leave the golden road.

CHAPTER 31

THE LAST NUMBER OF OUR MAGAZINE

EDITORIAL

IT IS with heartfelt regret that we take up our pen to announce that this will be the last number of *Our Magazine*. We have edited ten numbers of it and it has been successful beyond our expectations. It has to be discontinued by reason of circumstances over which we have no control and not because we have lost interest in it. Everybody has done his or her best for *Our Magazine*. Prince Edward Island expected everyone to do his and her duty and everyone did it.

Mr. Dan King conducted the etiquette department in a way worthy of the *Family Guide* itself. He is especially entitled to commendation because he laboured under the disadvantage of having to furnish most of the questions as well as the answers. Miss Felicity King has edited our helpful household department very ably, and Miss Cecily King's fashion notes were always up to date. The personal column was well looked after by Miss Sara Stanley and the story page has been a marked success under the able management of Mr. Peter Craig, to whose original story in this issue, "The Battle of the Partridge Eggs," we would call especial attention. The Exciting Adventure series has also been very popular.

And now, in closing, we bid farewell to our staff and thank them one and all for their help and co-operation in the past year. We have enjoyed our work and we trust that they have too. We wish them all happiness and success in years to come, and we hope that the recollection of *Our Magazine* will not be held least dear among the memories of their childhood.

(Sobs from the girls): "Indeed it won't!"

OBITUARY

On October eighteenth, Patrick Grayfur departed for that bourne whence no traveller returns. He was only a cat, but he had been our faithful friend for a long time and we aren't ashamed to be sorry for him. There are lots of people who are not as friendly and gentlemanly as Paddy was, and he was a great mouser. We buried all that was mortal of poor Pat in the orchard and we are never going to forget him. We have resolved that whenever the date of his death comes round we'll bow our heads and pronounce his name at the hour of his funeral. If we are anywhere where we can't say the name out loud we'll whisper it.

> "Farewell, dearest Paddy, in all the years that are
>   to be
> We'll cherish your memory faithfully."[1]

MY MOST EXCITING ADVENTURE

My most exciting adventure was the day I fell off Uncle Roger's loft two years ago. I wasn't excited until it was all over because I hadn't time to be. The Story Girl and I were looking for eggs in the loft. It was filled with wheat straw nearly to the roof and it was an awful distance from us to the floor. And wheat straw is so slippery. I made a little spring and the straw slipped from under my feet and there I was going head first

---

[1] The obituary was written by Mr. Felix King, but the two lines of poetry were composed by Miss Sara Ray.

down from the loft. It seemed to me I was an awful long time falling, but the Story Girl says I couldn't have been more than three seconds. But I know that I thought five thoughts and there seemed to be quite a long time between them. The first thing I thought was, what has happened, because I really didn't know at first, it was so sudden. Then after a spell I thought the answer, I am falling off the loft. And then I thought, what will happen to me when I strike the floor, and after another little spell I thought, I'll be killed. And then I thought, well, I don't care. I really wasn't a bit frightened. I just was quite willing to be killed. If there hadn't been a big pile of chaff on the barn floor these words would never have been written. But there was and I fell on it and wasn't a bit hurt, only my hair and mouth and eyes and ears got all full of chaff. The strange part is that I wasn't a bit frightened when I thought I was going to be killed, but after all the danger was over I was awfully frightened and trembled so the Story Girl had to help me into the house.

FELICITY KING.

THE BATTLE OF THE PARTRIDGE EGGS

Once upon a time there lived about half a mile from a forrest a farmer and his wife and his sons and daughters and a granddaughter. The farmer and his wife loved this little girl very much but she caused them great trouble by running away into the woods and they often spent haf days looking for her. One day she wondered further into the forrest than usual and she begun to be hungry. Then night closed in. She asked a fox where she could get something to eat. The fox told her he knew where there was a partridges nest and a bluejays nest full of eggs. So he led her to the nests and she took five eggs out of each. When the birds came home they missed the eggs and flew into a rage. The bluejay put on his topcoat and was going to the partridge for law when he met the partridge coming to him. They lit up a fire and commenced sining their deeds when they heard a tremendous howl close behind them. They jumped up and put out the fire and were immejutly attacked by five great wolves. The next day the little girl was rambelling through the woods when they saw her and took her prisoner. After she had confessed that she had stole the eggs they told her to raise an army. They would have to fight over the nests of eggs and whoever one would have the eggs. So the partridge raised a great army of all kinds of birds except robins and the little girl got all the robins and foxes and bees and wasps. And best of all the little girl had a gun and plenty of ammunishun. The leader of her army was a wolf. The result of the battle was that all the birds were killed except the partridge and the bluejay and they were taken prisoner and starved to death.

The little girl was then taken prisoner by a witch and cast into a dunjun full of snakes where she died from their bites and people who went through the forrest after that were taken prisoner by her ghost and cast into the same dunjun where they died. About a year after the wood turned into a gold castle and one morning everything had vanished except a piece of a tree.

PETER CRAIG.

(*Dan, with a whistle:*—"Well, I guess nobody can say Peter can't write fiction after *that*."

Sara Ray, wiping away her tears:—"It's a *very* interesting story, but it ends *so* sadly."

Felix:—"What made you call it The Battle of the Partridge Eggs when the bluejay had just as much to do with it?"

Peter, shortly:—"Because it sounded better that way."

Felicity:—"Did she eat the eggs raw?"

Sara Ray:—"Poor little thing, I suppose if you're starving you can't be very particular."

Cecily, sighing:—"I wish you'd let her go home safe, Peter, and not put her to such a cruel death."

Beverley:—"I don't quite understand where the little girl got her gun and ammunition."

Peter, suspecting that he is being made fun of:—"If you could write a better story, why didn't you? I give you the chance."

The Story Girl, with a preternaturally solemn face:—"You shouldn't criticize Peter's story like that. It's a fairy tale, you know, and anything can happen in a fairy tale."

Felicity:—"There isn't a word about fairies in it!"

Cecily:—"Besides, fairy tales always end nicely and this doesn't."

Peter, sulkily:—"I wanted to punish her for running away from home."

Dan:—"Well, I guess you did it all right."

Cecily:—"Oh, well, it was very interesting, and that is all that is really necessary in a story.")

PERSONALS

Mr. Blair Stanley is visiting friends and relatives in Carlisle. He intends returning to Europe shortly. His daughter, Miss Sara, will accompany him.

Mr. Alan King is expected home from South America next month. His sons will return with him to Toronto. Beverley and Felix have made hosts of friends during their stay in Carlisle and will be much missed in social circles.

The Mission Band of Carlisle Presbyterian Church completed their missionary quilt last week. Miss Cecily King collected the largest sum on her square. Congratulations, Cecily.

Mr. Peter Craig will be residing in Markdale after October and will attend school there this winter. Peter is a good fellow and we all wish him success and prosperity.

Apple picking is almost ended. There was an unusually heavy crop this year. Potatoes, not so good.

HOUSEHOLD DEPARTMENT

Apple pies are the order of the day.

Eggs are a very good price now. Uncle Roger says it isn't fair to have to pay as much for a dozen little eggs as a dozen big ones, but they go just as far.

FELICITY KING.

ETIQUETTE DEPARTMENT

F-l-t-y. Is it considered good form to eat peppermints in church? Ans.; No, not if a witch gives them to you.

No, F-l-x, we would not call Treasure Island or the Pilgrim's Progress dime novels.

Yes, P-t-r, when you call on a young lady and her mother offers you a slice of bread and jam it is quite polite for you to accept it.

DAN KING.

FASHION NOTES

Necklaces of roseberries are very much worn now.

It is considered smart to wear your school hat tilted over your left eye.

Bangs are coming in. Em Frewen has them. She went to Summerside for a visit and came back with them. All the girls in school are going to bang their hair as soon as their mothers will let them. But I do not intend to bang mine.

CECILY KING.

(*Sara Ray, despairingly:*—"I know ma will never let *me* have bangs.")

FUNNY PARAGRAPHS

D-n. What are details? C-l-y. I am not sure, but I think they are things that are left over.

(*Cecily, wonderingly:*—"I don't see why that was put among the funny paragraphs. Shouldn't it have gone in the General Information department?")

Old Mr. McIntyre's son on the Markdale Road had been very sick for several years and somebody was sympathizing with him because his son was going to die. "Oh," Mr. McIntyre said, quite easy, "he might as weel be awa'. He's only retarding buzziness."

FELIX KING.

GENERAL INFORMATION BUREAU

P-t-r. What kind of people live in uninhabited places? Ans.: Cannibals, likely.

FELIX KING.

CHAPTER 32

OUR LAST EVENING TOGETHER

It was the evening before the day on which the Story Girl and Uncle Blair were to leave us, and we were keeping our last tryst together in the orchard where we had spent so many happy hours. We had made a pilgrimage to all the old haunts—the hill field, the spruce wood, the dairy, Grandfather King's willow, the Pulpit Stone, Pat's grave, and Uncle Stephen's Walk; and now we foregathered in the sere grasses about the old well and feasted on the little jam turnovers Felicity had made that day specially for the occasion.

"I wonder if we'll ever all be together again," sighed Cecily.

"I wonder when I'll get jam turnovers like this again," said the Story Girl, trying to be gay but not making much of a success of it.

"If Paris wasn't so far away I could send you a box of nice things now and then," said Felicity forlornly, "but I suppose there's no use thinking of that. Dear knows what they'll give you to eat over there."

"Oh, the French have the reputation of being the best cooks in the world," rejoined the Story Girl, "but I know they can't beat your jam turnovers and plum puffs, Felicity. Many a time I'll be hankering after them."

"If we ever do meet again you'll be grown up," said Felicity gloomily.

"Well, you won't have stood still yourselves, you know."

"No, but that's just the worst of it. We'll all be different and everything will be changed."

"Just think," said Cecily, "last New Year's Eve we were wondering what would happen this year; and what a lot of things have happened that we never expected. Oh, dear!"

"If things never happened life would be pretty dull," said the Story Girl briskly. "Oh, don't look so dismal, all of you."

"It's hard to be cheerful when everybody's going away," sighed Cecily.

"Well, let's pretend to be, anyway," insisted the Story Girl. "Don't let's think of parting. Let's think instead of how much we've laughed this last year or so. I'm sure I shall never forget this dear old place. We've had so many good times here."

"And some bad times, too," reminded Felix. "Remember when Dan et the bad berries last summer?"

"And the time we were so scared over that bell ringing in the house," grinned Peter.

"And the Judgment Day," added Dan.

"And the time Paddy was bewitched," suggested Sara Ray.

"And when Peter was dying of the measles," said Felicity.

"And the time Jimmy Patterson was lost," said Dan. "Gee-whiz, but that scared me out of a year's growth."

"Do you remember the time we took the magic seed," grinned Peter.

"Weren't we silly?" said Felicity. "I really can never look Billy Robinson in the face when I meet him. I'm always sure he's laughing at me in his sleeve."

"It's Billy Robinson who ought to be ashamed when he meets you or any of us," commented Cecily severely. "I'd rather be cheated than cheat other people."

"Do you mind the time we bought God's picture?" asked Peter.

"I wonder if it's where we buried it yet," speculated Felix.

"I put a stone over it, just as we did over Pat," said Cecily.

"I wish I could forget what God looks like," sighed Sara Ray. "I can't forget it—and I can't forget what the bad place is like either, ever since Peter preached that sermon on it."

"When you get to be a real minister you'll have to preach that sermon over again, Peter," grinned Dan.

"My Aunt Jane used to say that people needed a sermon on that place once in a while," retorted Peter seriously.

"Do you mind the night I et the cucumbers and milk to make me dream?" said Cecily.

And therewith we hunted out our old dream books to read them again, and, forgetful of coming partings, laughed over them till the old orchard echoed to our mirth. When we had finished we stood in a circle around the well and pledged "eternal friendship" in a cup of its unrivalled water.

Then we joined hands and sang "Auld Lang Syne." Sara Ray cried bitterly in lieu of singing.

"Look here," said the Story Girl, as we turned to leave the old orchard, "I want to ask a favour of you all. Don't say good-bye to me tomorrow morning."

"Why not?" demanded Felicity in astonishment.

"Because it's such a hopeless sort of word. Don't let's *say* it at all. Just see me off with a wave of your hands. It won't seem half so bad then. And don't any of you cry if you can help it. I want to remember you all smiling."

We went out of the old orchard where the autumn night wind was beginning to make its weird music in the russet boughs, and shut the little gate behind us. Our revels there were ended.

-------------------- CHAPTER 33 --------------------

THE STORY GIRL GOES

THE MORNING dawned, rosy and clear and frosty. Everybody was up early, for the travellers must leave in time to catch the nine o'clock train. The horse was harnessed and Uncle Alec was waiting by the door. Aunt Janet was crying, but everybody else was making a valiant effort not to. The Awkward Man and Mrs. Dale came to see the last of their favourite. Mrs. Dale had brought her a glorious sheaf of chrysanthemums, and the Awkward Man gave her, quite gracefully, another little, old, limp book from his library.

"Read it when you are sad or happy or lonely or discouraged or hopeful," he said gravely.

"He has really improved very much since he got married," whispered Felicity to me.

Sara Stanley wore a smart new travelling suit and a blue felt hat with a white feather. She looked so horribly grown up in it that we felt as if she were lost to us already.

Sara Ray had vowed tearfully the night before that she would be up in the morning to say farewell. But at this juncture Judy Pineau appeared to say that Sara, with her usual luck, had a sore throat, and that her mother consequently would not permit her to come. So Sara had written her parting words in a three-cornered pink note.

"My *own darling friend:—Words cannot express* my feelings over not being able to go up this morning to say good-bye to one I so *fondly adore.* When I think that I cannot *see you again* my heart is almost *too full for utterance.* But mother says I cannot and I *must obey.* But I will be present *in spirit.* It just *breaks my heart* that you are going *so far away.* You have always been *so kind* to me and never hurt my feelings *as some do* and I shall miss you *so much.* But I earnestly *hope and pray* that you will be *happy and prosperous* wherever *your lot is cast* and not be seasick on *the great ocean.* I hope you will find time *among your many duties* to write me a letter *once in a while.* I shall *always remember you* and please remember me. I hope we *will meet again* sometime, but if not may we meet in *a far better world* where there are *no sad partings.*

"Your true and loving friend,

"SARA RAY."

"Poor little Sara," said the Story Girl, with a queer catch in her voice, as she slipped the tear-blotted note into her pocket. "She isn't a bad little soul, and I'm sorry I couldn't see her once more, though maybe it's just as well for she'd have to cry and set us all off. I *won't* cry. Felicity, don't you dare. Oh, you dear, darling people, I love you all so much and I'll go on loving you always."

"Mind you write us every week at the very least," said Felicity, winking furiously.

"Blair, Blair, watch over the child well," said Aunt Janet. "Remember, she has no mother."

The Story Girl ran over to the buggy and climbed in. Uncle Blair followed her. Her arms were full of Mrs. Dale's chrysanthemums, held close up to her face, and her beautiful eyes shone softly at us over them. No good-byes were said, as she wished. We all smiled bravely and waved our hands as they drove out of the lane and down the moist red road into the shadows of the fir wood in the valley. But we still stood there, for we knew we should see the Story Girl once more. Beyond the fir wood was an open curve in the road and she had promised to wave a last farewell as they passed around it.

We watched the curve in silence, standing in a sorrowful little group in the sunshine of the autumn morning. The delight of the world had been ours on the golden road. It had enticed us with daisies and rewarded us with roses. Blossom and lyric had waited on our wishes. Thoughts, careless and sweet, had visited us. Laughter had been our comrade and fearless Hope our guide. But now the shadow of change was over it.

"There she is," cried Felicity.

The Story Girl stood up and waved her chrysanthemums at us. We waved wildly back until the buggy had driven around the curve. Then we went slowly and silently back to the house. The Story Girl was gone.

Kilmeny of the Orchard

TO MY COUSIN
BEATRICE A. McINTYRE
THIS BOOK
IS AFFECTIONATELY DEDICATED

OVERLEAF: KILMENY LOOKED STRAIGHT INTO THE MIRROR
WHERE, LIKE A LOVELY PICTURE IN A GOLDEN FRAME,
SHE SAW HERSELF REFLECTED.

KILMENY looked up with a lovely grace,
But no smile was seen on Kilmeny's face;
As still was her look, and as still was her ee,
As the stillness that lay on the emerant lea,
Or the mist that sleeps on a waveless sea.
. . . .
Such beauty bard may never declare,
For there was no pride nor passion there;
. . . .
Her seymar was the lily flower,
And her cheek the moss-rose in the shower;
And her voice like a distant melodye
That floats along the twilight sea."
                    —THE QUEEN'S WAKE

CHAPTER 1

THE THOUGHTS OF SOUTH

THE SUNSHINE of a day in early spring, honey pale and honey sweet, was showering over the red brick buildings of Queenslea College and the grounds about them, throwing through the bare, budding maples and elms, delicate, evasive etchings of gold and brown on the paths, and coaxing into life the daffodils that were peering greenly and perkily up under the windows of the co-eds' dressing-room.

A young April wind, as fresh and sweet as if it had been blowing over the fields of memory instead of through dingy streets, was purring in the tree-tops and whipping the loose tendrils of the ivy network which covered the front of the main building. It was a wind that sang of many things, but what it sang to each listener was only what was in that listener's heart. To the college students who had just been capped and diplomad by "Old Charlie," the grave president of Queenslea, in the presence of an admiring throng of parents and sisters, sweethearts and friends, it sang, perchance, of glad hope and shining success and high achievement. It sang of the dreams of youth that may never be quite fulfilled, but are well worth the dreaming for all that. God help the man who has never known such dreams—who, as he leaves his alma mater, is not already rich in aerial castles, the proprietor of many a spacious estate in Spain. He has missed his birthright.

The crowd streamed out of the entrance hall and scattered over the campus, fraying off into the many streets beyond. Eric Marshall and David Baker walked away together. The former had graduated in Arts that day at the head of his class; the latter had come to see the graduation, nearly bursting with pride in Eric's success.

Between these two was an old and tried and enduring friendship, although David was ten years older than Eric, as the mere tale of years go, and a hundred years older in knowledge of the struggles and difficulties of life which age a man far more quickly and effectually than the passing of time.

Physically the two men bore no resemblance to one another, although they were second cousins. Eric Marshall, tall, broadshouldered, sinewy, walking with a free, easy stride, which was somehow suggestive of reserve strength and power, was one of those men regarding whom less-favoured mortals are tempted seriously to wonder why all the gifts of fortune should be showered on one individual. He was not only clever and good to look upon, but he possessed that indefinable charm of personality which is quite independent of physical beauty or mental ability. He had steady, grayish-blue eyes, dark chestnut hair with a glint of gold in its waves when the sunlight struck it, and a chin that gave the world assurance of a chin. He was a rich man's son, with a clean young manhood behind him and splendid prospects before him. He was considered a practical sort of fellow, utterly guiltless of romantic dreams and visions of any sort.

"I am afraid Eric Marshall will never do one quixotic thing," said a Queenslea professor, who had a habit of uttering rather mysterious epigrams, "but if he ever does it will supply the one thing lacking in him."

David Baker was a short, stocky fellow with an ugly, irregular, charming face; his eyes were brown and keen and secretive; his mouth had a comical twist which became sarcastic, or teasing, or winning, as he willed. His voice was generally as soft and musical as a woman's; but some few who had seen David Baker righteously angry and heard the tones which then issued from his lips were in no hurry to have the experience repeated.

He was a doctor—a specialist in troubles of the throat and voice—and he was beginning to have a national reputation.

He was on the staff of the Queenslea Medical College and it was whispered that before long he would be called to fill an important vacancy at McGill.

He had won his way to success through difficulties and drawbacks which would have daunted most men. In the year Eric was born David Baker was an errand boy in the big department store of Marshall & Company. Thirteen years later he graduated with high honours from Queenslea Medical College. Mr. Marshall had given him all the help which David's sturdy pride could be induced to accept, and now he insisted on sending the young man abroad for a post-graduate course in London and Germany. David had eventually repaid every cent Mr. Marshall had expended on him; but he never ceased to cherish a passionate gratitude to the kind and generous man; and he loved that man's son with a love surpassing that of brothers.

He had followed Eric's college course with keen, watchful interest. It was his wish that Eric should take up the study of law or medicine now that he was through Arts; and he was greatly disappointed that Eric should have finally made up his mind to go into business with his father.

"It's a clean waste of your talents," he grumbled, as they walked home from the college. "You'd win fame and distinction in law—that glib tongue of yours was meant for a lawyer and it is sheer flying in the face of Providence to devote it to commercial uses—a flat crossing of the purposes of destiny. Where is your ambition, man?"

"In the right place," answered Eric, with his ready laugh. "It is not your kind, perhaps, but there is room and need for all kinds in this lusty young country of ours. Yes, I am going into the business. In the first place, it has been father's cherished desire ever since I was born, and it would hurt him pretty badly if I backed out now. He wished me to take an Arts course because he believed that every man should have as liberal an education as he can afford to get, but now that I have had it he wants me in the firm."

"He wouldn't oppose you if he thought you really wanted to go in for something else."

"Not he. But I don't really want to—that's the point, David, man. You hate a business life so much yourself that you can't get it into your blessed noddle that another man might like it.

There are many lawyers in the world—too many, perhaps—but there are never too many good honest men of business, ready to do clean big things for the betterment of humanity and the upbuilding of their country, to plan great enterprises and carry them through with brain and courage, to manage and control, to aim high and strike one's aim. There, I'm waxing eloquent, so I'd better stop. But ambition, man! Why, I'm full of it—it's bubbling in every pore of me. I mean to make the department store of Marshall & Company famous from ocean to ocean. Father started in life as a poor boy from a Nova Scotian farm. He has built up a business that has a provincial reputation. I mean to carry it on. In five years it shall have a maritime reputation, in ten, a Canadian. I want to make the firm of Marshall & Company stand for something big in the commercial interests of Canada. Isn't that as honourable an ambition as trying to make black seem white in a court of law, or discovering some new disease with a harrowing name to torment poor creatures who might otherwise die peacefully in blissful ignorance of what ailed them?"

"When you begin to make poor jokes it is time to stop arguing with you," said David, with a shrug of his fat shoulders. "Go your own gait and dree your own weird. I'd as soon expect success in trying to storm the citadel single-handed as in trying to turn you from any course about which you had once made up your mind. Whew, this street takes it out of a fellow! What could have possessed our ancestors to run a town up the side of a hill? I'm not so slim and active as I was on *my* graduation day ten years ago. By the way, what a lot of co-eds were in your class—twenty, if I counted right. When I graduated there were only two ladies in our class and they were the pioneers of their sex at Queenslea. They were well past their first youth, very grim and angular and serious; and they could never have been on speaking terms with a mirror in their best days. But mark you, they were excellent females—oh, very excellent. Times have changed with a vengeance, judging from the line-up of co-eds today. There was one girl there who can't be a day over eighteen—and she looked as if she were made out of gold and roseleaves and dewdrops."

"The oracle speaks in poetry," laughed Eric. "That was Florence Percival, who led the class in mathematics, as I'm a living man. By many she is considered the beauty of her class.

I can't say that such is my opinion. I don't greatly care for that blonde, babyish style of loveliness—I prefer Agnes Campion. Did you notice her—the tall, dark girl with the ropes of hair and a sort of crimson, velvety bloom on her face, who took honours in philosophy?"

"I *did* notice her," said David emphatically, darting a keen side glance at his friend. "I noticed her most particularly and critically—for someone whispered her name behind me and coupled it with the exceedingly interesting information that Miss Campion was supposed to be the future Mrs. Eric Marshall. Whereupon I stared at her with all my eyes."

"There is no truth in that report," said Eric in a tone of annoyance. "Agnes and I are the best of friends and nothing more. I like and admire her more than any woman I know; but if the future Mrs. Eric Marshall exists in the flesh I haven't met her yet. I haven't even started out to look for her—and don't intend to for some years to come. I have something else to think of," he concluded, in a tone of contempt, for which anyone might have known he would be punished sometime if Cupid were not deaf as well as blind.

"You'll meet the lady of the future some day," said David dryly. "And in spite of your scorn I venture to predict that if fate doesn't bring her before long you'll very soon start out to look for her. A word of advice, oh, son of your mother. When you go courting take your common sense with you."

"Do you think I shall be likely to leave it behind?" asked Eric amusedly.

"Well, I mistrust you," said David, sagely wagging his head. "The Lowland Scotch part of you is all right, but there's a Celtic streak in you, from that little Highland grandmother of yours, and when a man has that there's never any knowing where it will break out, or what dance it will lead him, especially when it comes to this love-making business. You are just as likely as not to lose your head over some little fool or shrew for the sake of her outward favour and make yourself miserable for life. When you pick you a wife please remember that I shall reserve the right to pass a candid opinion on her."

"Pass all the opinions you like, but it is *my* opinion, and mine only, which will matter in the long run," retorted Eric.

"Confound you, yes, you stubborn off-shoot of a stubborn breed," growled David, looking at him affectionately. "I know that, and that is why I'll never feel at ease about you until I see you married to the right sort of a girl. She's not hard to find. Nine out of ten girls in this country of ours are fit for kings' palaces. But the tenth always has to be reckoned with."

"You are as bad as *Clever Alice* in the fairy tale who worried over the future of her unborn children," protested Eric.

"*Clever Alice* has been very unjustly laughed at," said David gravely. "We doctors know that. Perhaps she overdid the worrying business a little, but she was perfectly right in principle. If people worried a little more about their unborn children—at least, to the extent of providing a proper heritage, physically, mentally, and morally, for them—and then stopped worrying about them after they *are* born, this world would be a very much pleasanter place to live in, and the human race would make more progress in a generation than it has done in recorded history."

"Oh, if you are going to mount your dearly beloved hobby of heredity I am not going to argue with you, David, man. But as for the matter of urging me to hasten and marry me a wife, why don't you"—It was on Eric's lips to say, "Why don't you get married to a girl of the right sort yourself and set me a good example?" But he checked himself. He knew that there was an old sorrow in David Baker's life which was not to be unduly jarred by the jests even of privileged friendship. He changed his question to, "Why don't you leave this on the knees of the gods where it properly belongs? I thought you were a firm believer in predestination, David."

"Well, so I am, to a certain extent," said David cautiously. "I believe, as an excellent old aunt of mine used to say, that what is to be will be and what isn't to be happens sometimes. And it is precisely such unchancy happenings that make the scheme of things go wrong. I dare say you think me an old fogy, Eric; but I know something more of the world than you do, and I believe, with Tennyson's *Arthur,* that 'there's no more subtle master under heaven than is the maiden passion for a maid.' I want to see you safely anchored to the love of some good woman as soon as may be, that's all. I'm rather sorry Miss Campion isn't your lady of the future. I liked her looks, that I did. She is good and strong and true—and has the eyes of a woman who could love in a way that would be worth while. Moreover, she's well-born, well-bred, and well-educated—

three very indispensable things when it comes to choosing a woman to fill your mother's place, friend of mine!"

"I agree with you," said Eric carelessly. "I could not marry any woman who did not fulfil those conditions. But, as I have said, I am not in love with Agnes Campion—and it wouldn't be of any use if I were. She is as good as engaged to Larry West. You remember West?"

"That thin, leggy fellow you chummed with so much your first two years in Queenslea? Yes, what has become of him?"

"He had to drop out after his second year for financial reasons. He is working his own way through college, you know. For the past two years he has been teaching school in some out-of-the-way place over in Prince Edward Island. He isn't any too well, poor fellow—never was very strong and has studied remorselessly. I haven't heard from him since February. He said then that he was afraid he wasn't going to be able to stick it out till the end of the school year. I hope Larry won't break down. He is a fine fellow and worthy even of Agnes Campion. Well, here we are. Coming in, David?"

"Not this afternoon—haven't got time. I must mosey up to the North End to see a man who has got a lovely throat. Nobody can find out what is the matter. He has puzzled all the doctors. He has puzzled me, but I'll find out what is wrong with him if he'll only live long enough."

CHAPTER 2

A LETTER OF DESTINY

ERIC, FINDING that his father had not yet returned from the college, went into the library and sat down to read a letter he had picked up from the hall table. It was from Larry West, and after the first few lines Eric's face lost the absent look it had worn and assumed an expression of interest.

"I am writing to ask a favour of you, Marshall," wrote West. "The fact is, I've fallen into the hands of the Philistines—that is to say, the doctors. I've not been feeling very fit all winter but I've held on, hoping to finish out the year.

"Last week my landlady—who is a saint in spectacles and calico—looked at me one morning at the breakfast table and said, *very* gently, 'You must go to town tomorrow, Master, and see a doctor about yourself.'

"I went and did not stand upon the order of my going. Mrs. Williamson is She-Who-Must-Be-Obeyed. She has an inconvenient habit of making you realize that she is exactly right, and that you would be all kinds of a fool if you didn't take her advice. You feel that what she thinks today you will think tomorrow.

"In Charlottetown I consulted a doctor. He punched and pounded me, and poked things at me and listened at the other end of them; and finally he said I must stop work 'immejutly and to onct' and hie me straightway to a climate not afflicted with the north-east winds of Prince Edward Island in the spring. I am not to be allowed to do any work until the fall. Such was his dictum and Mrs. Williamson enforces it.

"I shall teach this week out and then the spring vacation of three weeks begins. I want you to come over and take my place as pedagogue in the Lindsay school for the last week in May and the month of June. The school year ends then and there will be plenty of teachers looking for the place, but just now I cannot get a suitable substitute. I have a couple of pupils who are preparing to try the Queen's Academy entrance examinations, and I don't like to leave them in the lurch or hand them over to the tender mercies of some third-class teacher who knows little Latin and less Greek. Come over and take the school till the end of the term, you petted son of luxury. It will do you a world of good to learn how rich a man feels when he is earning twenty-five dollars a month by his own unaided efforts!

"Seriously, Marshall, I hope you can come, for I don't know any other fellow I can ask. The work isn't hard, though you'll likely find it monotonous. Of course, this little north-shore farming settlement isn't a very lively place. The rising and setting of the sun are the most exciting events of the average day. But the people are very kind and hospitable; and Prince Edward Island in the month of June is such a thing as you don't often see except in happy dreams. There are some trout in the pond and you'll always find an old salt at the harbour ready and willing to take you out cod-fishing or lobstering.

"I'll bequeath you my boarding house. You'll find it comfortable and not further from the school than a good constitutional. Mrs. Williamson is the dearest soul alive; and she is one of those old-fashioned cooks who feed you on feasts of fat things and whose price is above rubies.

"Her husband, Robert, or Bob, as he is commonly called despite his sixty years, is quite a character in his way. He is an amusing old gossip, with a turn for racy comment and a finger in everybody's pie. He knows everything about everybody in Lindsay for three generations back.

"They have no living children, but Old Bob has a black cat which is his especial pride and darling. The name of this animal is Timothy and as such he must always be called and referred to. Never, as you value Robert's good opinion, let him hear you speaking of his pet as 'the cat,' or even as 'Tim.' You will never be forgiven and he will not consider you a fit person to have charge of the school.

"You shall have my room, a little place over the kitchen, with a ceiling that follows the slant of the roof down one side, against which you will bump your head times innumerable until you learn to remember that it is there, and a looking glass which will make one of your eyes as small as a pea and the other as big as an orange.

"But to compensate for these disadvantages the supply of towels is generous and unexceptionable: and there is a window whence you will daily behold an occidental view over Lindsay Harbour and the gulf beyond which is an unspeakable miracle of beauty. The sun is setting over it as I write and I see such 'a sea of glass mingled with fire' as might have figured in the visions of the Patmian seer. A vessel is sailing away into the gold and crimson and pearl of the horizon; the big revolving light on the tip of the headland beyond the harbour has just been lighted and is winking and flashing like a beacon,

> " 'O'er the foam
> Of perilous seas in faerie lands forlorn.' "

"Wire me if you can come; and if you can, report for duty on the twenty-third of May."

Mr. Marshall, Senior, came in, just as Eric was thoughtfully folding up his letter. The former looked more like a benevolent old clergyman or philanthropist than the keen, shrewd, somewhat hard, although just and honest, man of business that he really was. He had a round, rosy face, fringed with white whiskers, a fine head of long white hair, and a pursed-up mouth. Only in his blue eyes was a twinkle that would have made any man who designed getting the better of him in a bargain think twice before he made the attempt.

It was easily seen that Eric must have inherited his personal beauty and distinction of form from his mother, whose picture hung on the dark wall between the windows. She had died while still young, when Eric was a boy of ten. During her lifetime she had been the object of the passionate devotion of both her husband and son; and the fine, strong, sweet face of the picture was a testimony that she had been worthy of their love and reverence. The same face, cast in a masculine mould, was repeated in Eric; the chestnut hair grew off his forehead in the same way; his eyes were like hers, and in his grave moods they held a similar expression, half brooding, half tender, in their depths.

Mr. Marshall was very proud of his son's success in college, but he had no intention of letting him see it. He loved this boy of his, with the dead mother's eyes, better than anything on earth, and all his hopes and ambitions were bound up in him.

"Well, that fuss is over, thank goodness," he said testily, as he dropped into his favourite chair.

"Didn't you find the programme interesting?" asked Eric absently.

"Most of it was tommyrot," said his father. "The only things I liked were Charlie's Latin prayer and those pretty little girls trotting up to get their diplomas. Latin *is* the language for praying in, I do believe,—at least, when a man has a voice like Old Charlie's. There was such a sonorous roll to the words that the mere sound of them made me feel like getting down on my marrow bones. And then those girls were as pretty as pinks, now weren't they? Agnes was the finest-looking of the lot in my opinion. I hope it's true that you're courting her, Eric?"

"Confound it, father," said Eric, half irritably, half laughingly, "have you and David Baker entered into a conspiracy to hound me into matrimony whether I will or no?"

"I've never said a word to David Baker on such a subject," protested Mr. Marshall.

"Well, you are just as bad as he is. He hectored me all the way home from the college on the subject. But why are you in such a hurry to have me married, dad?"

"Because I want a homemaker in this house as soon as may be. There has never been one since your mother died. I am tired of housekeepers. And I want to see your children at my knees before I die, Eric, and I'm an old man now."

"Well, your wish is natural, father," said Eric gently, with a glance at his mother's picture. "But I can't rush out and marry somebody off-hand, can I? And I fear it wouldn't exactly do to advertise for a wife, even in these days of commercial enterprise."

"Isn't there *anybody* you're fond of?" queried Mr. Marshall, with the patient air of a man who overlooks the frivolous jests of youth.

"No. I never yet saw the woman who could make my heart beat any faster."

"I don't know what you young men are made of nowadays," growled his father. "I was in love half a dozen times before I was your age."

"You might have been 'in love.' But you never *loved* any woman until you met my mother. I know that, father. And it didn't happen till you were pretty well on in life either."

"You're too hard to please. That's what's the matter, that's what's the matter!"

"Perhaps I am. When a man has had a mother like mine his standard of womanly sweetness is apt to be pitched pretty high. Let's drop the subject, father. Here, I want you to read this letter—it's from Larry."

"Humph!" grunted Mr. Marshall, when he had finished with it. "So Larry's knocked out at last—always thought he would be—always expected it. Sorry, too. He was a decent fellow. Well, are you going?"

"Yes, I think so, if you don't object."

"You'll have a pretty monotonous time of it, judging from his account of Lindsay."

"Probably. But I am not going over in search of excitement.

I'm going to oblige Larry and have a look at the Island."

"Well, it's worth looking at, some parts of the year," conceded Mr. Marshall. "When I'm on Prince Edward Island in the summer I always understand an old Scotch Islander I met once in Winnipeg. He was always talking of 'the Island.' Somebody once asked him, 'What island do you mean?' He simply *looked* at that ignorant man. Then he said, 'Why, Prince Edward Island, mon. *What other island is there?*' Go if you'd like to. You need a rest after the grind of examinations before settling down to business. And mind you don't get into any mischief, young sir."

"Not much likelihood of that in a place like Lindsay, I fancy," laughed Eric.

"Probably the devil finds as much mischief for idle hands in Lindsay as anywhere else. The worst tragedy I ever heard of happened on a backwoods farm, fifteen miles from a railroad and five from a store. However, I expect your mother's son to behave himself in the fear of God and man. In all likelihood the worst thing that will happen to you over there will be that some misguided woman will put you to sleep in a spare room bed. And if that does happen may the Lord have mercy on your soul!"

CHAPTER 3

THE MASTER OF LINDSAY SCHOOL

ONE EVENING, a month later, Eric Marshall came out of the old, white-washed schoolhouse at Lindsay, and locked the door—which was carved over with initials innumerable, and built of double plank in order that it might withstand all the assaults and batteries to which it might be subjected.

Eric's pupils had gone home an hour before, but he had stayed to solve some algebra problems, and correct some Latin exercises for his advanced students.

The sun was slanting in warm yellow lines through the thick grove of maples to the west of the building, and the dim green air beneath them burst into golden bloom. A couple of sheep were nibbling the lush grass in a far corner of the playground; a cow-bell, somewhere in the maple woods, tinkled faintly and musically, on the still crystal air, which, in spite of its blandness, still retained a touch of the wholesome austerity and poignancy of a Canadian spring. The whole world seemed to have fallen, for the time being, into a pleasant untroubled dream.

The scene was very peaceful and pastoral—almost too much so, the young man thought, with a shrug of his shoulders, as he stood on the worn steps and gazed about him. How was he going to put in a whole month here, he wondered, with a little smile at his own expense.

"Father would chuckle if he knew I was sick of it already," he thought, as he walked across the play-ground to the long red road that ran past the school. "Well, one week is ended, at any rate. I've earned my own living for five whole days, and that is something I could never say before in all my twenty-four years of existence. It is an exhilarating thought. But teaching the Lindsay district school is distinctly *not* exhilarating—at least in such a well-behaved school as this, where the pupils are so painfully good that I haven't even the traditional excitement of thrashing obstreperous bad boys. Everything seems to go by clock work in Lindsay educational institution. Larry must certainly have possessed a marked gift for organizing and drilling. I feel as if I were merely a big cog in an orderly machine that ran itself. However, I understand that there are some pupils who haven't shown up yet, and who, according to all reports, have not yet had the old Adam totally drilled out of them. They may make things more interesting. Also a few more compositions, such as John Reid's, would furnish some spice to professional life."

Eric's laughter wakened the echoes as he swung into the road down the long sloping hill. He had given his fourth grade pupils their own choice of subjects in the composition class that morning, and John Reid, a sober, matter-of-fact little urchin, with not the slightest embryonic development of a sense of humour, had, acting upon the whispered suggestion of a roguish desk-mate, elected to write upon "Courting." His opening sentence made Eric's face twitch mutinously whenever he recalled it during the day. "Courting is a very pleasant thing which a great many people go too far with."

The distant hills and wooded uplands were tremulous and aerial in delicate spring-time gauzes of pearl and purple. The young, green-leafed maples crowded thickly to the very edge of the road on either side, but beyond them were emerald fields basking in sunshine, over which cloud shadows rolled, broadened, and vanished. Far below the fields a calm ocean slept bluely, and sighed in its sleep, with the murmur that rings for ever in the ear of those whose good fortune it is to have been born within the sound of it.

Now and then Eric met some callow, check-shirted, barelegged lad on horseback, or a shrewd-faced farmer in a cart, who nodded and called out cheerily, "Howdy, Master?" A young girl, with a rosy, oval face, dimpled cheeks, and pretty dark eyes filled with shy coquetry, passed him, looking as if she would not be at all averse to a better acquaintance with the new teacher.

Half way down the hill Eric met a shambling, old gray horse drawing an express wagon which had seen better days. The driver was a woman: she appeared to be one of those drab-tinted individuals who can never have felt a rosy emotion in all their lives. She stopped her horse, and beckoned Eric over to her with the knobby handle of a faded and bony umbrella.

"Reckon you're the new Master, ain't you?" she asked.

Eric admitted that he was.

"Well, I'm glad to see you," she said, offering him a hand in a much darned cotton glove that had once been black.

"I was right sorry to see Mr. West go, for he was a right good teacher, and as harmless, inoffensive a creetur as ever lived. But I always told him every time I laid eyes on him that he was in consumption, if ever a man was. *You* look real healthy—though you can't always tell by looks, either. I had a brother complected like you, but he was killed in a railroad accident out west when he was real young.

"I've got a boy I'll be sending to school to you next week. He'd oughter gone this week, but I had to keep him home to help me put the pertaters in; for his father won't work and doesn't work and can't be made to work.

"Sandy—his full name is Edward Alexander—called after

both of his grandfathers—hates the idee of going to school worse 'n pisen–always did. But go he shall, for I'm determined he's got to have more larning hammered into his head yet. I reckon you'll have trouble with him, Master, for he's as stupid as an owl, and as stubborn as Solomon's mule. But mind this, Master, I'll back you up. You just lick Sandy good and plenty when he needs it, and send me a scrape of the pen home with him, and I'll give him another dose.

"There's people that always sides in with their young ones when there's any rumpus kicked up in the school, but I don't hold to that, and never did. You can depend on Rebecca Reid every time, Master."

"Thank you. I am sure I can," said Eric, in his most winning tones.

He kept his face straight until it was safe to relax, and Mrs. Reid drove on with a soft feeling in her leathery old heart, which had been so toughened by long endurance of poverty and toil, and a husband who wouldn't work and couldn't be made to work, that it was no longer a very susceptible organ where members of the opposite sex were concerned.

Mrs. Reid reflected that this young man had a way with him.

Eric already knew most of the Lindsay folks by sight; but at the foot of the hill he met two people, a man and a boy, whom he did not know. They were sitting in a shabby, old-fashioned wagon, and were watering their horse at the brook, which gurgled limpidly under the little plank bridge in the hollow.

Eric surveyed them with some curiosity. They did not look in the least like the ordinary run of Lindsay people. The boy, in particular, had a distinctly foreign appearance, in spite of the gingham shirt and homespun trousers, which seemed to be the regulation, work-a-day outfit for the Lindsay farmer lads. He had a lithe, supple body, with sloping shoulders, and a lean, satiny brown throat above his open shirt collar. His head was covered with thick, silky, black curls, and the hand that hung down by the side of the wagon was unusually long and slender. His face was richly, though somewhat heavily featured, olive tinted, save for the cheeks, which had a dusky crimson bloom. His mouth was as red and beguiling as a girl's, and his eyes were large, bold and black. All in all, he was a strikingly handsome fellow; but the expression of his face was sullen, and he somehow gave Eric the impression of a sinuous, feline creature basking in lazy grace, but ever ready for an unexpected spring.

The other occupant of the wagon was a man between sixty-five and seventy, with iron-gray hair, a long, full, gray beard, a harsh-featured face, and deep-set hazel eyes under bushy, bristling brows. He was evidently tall, with a spare, ungainly figure, and stooping shoulders. His mouth was close-lipped and relentless, and did not look as if it had ever smiled. Indeed, the idea of smiling could not be connected with this man—it was utterly incongruous. Yet there was nothing repellent about his face; and there was something in it that compelled Eric's attention.

He rather prided himself on being a student of physiognomy, and he felt quite sure that this man was no ordinary Lindsay farmer of the genial, garrulous type with which he was familiar.

Long after the old wagon, with its oddly assorted pair, had gone lumbering up the hill, Eric found himself thinking of the stern, heavy browed man and the black-eyed, red-lipped boy.

CHAPTER 4

A TEA TABLE CONVERSATION

The Williamson place, where Eric boarded, was on the crest of the succeeding hill. He liked it as well as Larry West had prophesied that he would. The Williamsons, as well as the rest of the Lindsay people, took it for granted that he was a poor college student working his way through as Larry West had been doing. Eric did not disturb this belief, although he said nothing to contribute to it.

The Williamsons were at tea in the kitchen when Eric went in. Mrs. Williamson was the "saint in spectacles and calico" which Larry West had termed her. Eric liked her greatly. She was a slight, gray-haired woman, with a thin, sweet, high-bred face, deeply lined with the records of outlived pain. She talked little as a rule; but, in the pungent country phrase she never spoke but she said something. The one thing that constantly puzzled Eric was how such a woman ever came to marry Robert Williamson.

She smiled in a motherly fashion at Eric, as he hung his hat on the white-washed wall and took his place at the table. Outside of the window behind him was a birch grove which, in the westering sun, was a tremulous splendour, with a sea of undergrowth wavered into golden billows by every passing wind.

Old Robert Williamson sat opposite to him, on a bench. He was a small, lean old man, half lost in loose clothes that seemed far too large for him. When he spoke his voice was as thin and squeaky as he appeared to be himself.

The other end of the bench was occupied by Timothy, sleek and complacent, with a snowy breast and white paws. After old Robert had taken a mouthful of anything he gave a piece to Timothy, who ate it daintily and purred resonant gratitude.

"You see we're busy waiting for you, Master," said old Robert. "You're late this evening. Keep any of the youngsters in? That's a foolish way of punishing them, as hard on yourself as on them. One teacher we had four years ago used to lock them in and go home. Then he'd go back in an hour and let them out—if they were there. They weren't always. Tom Ferguson kicked the panels out of the old door once and got out that way. We put a new door of double plank in that they couldn't kick out."

"I stayed in the schoolroom to do some work," said Eric briefly.

"Well, you've missed Alexander Tracy. He was here to find out if you could play checkers, and, when I told him you could, he left word for you to go up and have a game some evening soon. Don't beat him too often, even if you can. You'll need to stand in with him, I tell you, Master, for he's got a son that may brew trouble for you when he starts in to go to school. Seth Tracy's a young imp, and he'd far sooner be in mischief than eat. He tries to run on every new teacher and he's run two clean out of the school. But he met his match in Mr. West. William Tracy's boys now—you won't have a scrap of bother with *them*. They're always good because their mother tells them every Sunday that they'll go straight to hell if they don't behave in school. It's effective. Take some preserve,

Master. You know we don't help things here the way Mrs. Adam Scott does when she has boarders, 'I s'pose you don't want any of this—nor you—nor you?' Mother, Aleck says old George Wright is having the time of his life. His wife has gone to Charlottetown to visit her sister and he is his own boss for the first time since he was married forty years ago. He's on a regular orgy, Aleck says. He smokes in the parlour and sits up till eleven o'clock reading dime novels."

"Perhaps I met Mr. Tracy," said Eric. "Is he a tall man, with gray hair and a dark, stern face?"

"No, he's a round, jolly fellow, is Aleck, and he stopped growing pretty much before he'd ever begun. I reckon the man you mean is Thomas Gordon. I seen him driving down the road too. *He* won't be troubling you with invitations up, small fear of it. The Gordons ain't sociable, to say the least of it. No, sir! Mother, pass the biscuits to the Master."

"Who was the young fellow he had with him?" asked Eric curiously.

"Neil—Neil Gordon."

"That is a Scotchy name for such a face and eyes. I should rather have expected Guiseppe or Angelo. The boy looks like an Italian."

"Well, now, you know, Master, I reckon it's likely he does, seeing that that's exactly what he is. You've hit the nail square on the head. Italyun, yes, sir! Rather too much so, I'm thinking, for decent folks' taste."

"How has it happened that an Italian boy with a Scotch name is living in a place like Lindsay?"

"Well, Master, it was this way. About twenty-two years ago— *was* it twenty-two, Mother or twenty-four? Yes, it was twenty-two—'twas the same year our Jim was born and he'd have been twenty-two if he'd lived, poor little fellow. Well, Master, twenty-two years ago a couple of Italian pack peddlers came along and called at the Gordon place. The country was swarming with them then. I useter set the dog on one every day on an average.

"Well, these peddlers were man and wife, and the woman took sick up there at the Gordon place, and Janet Gordon took her in and nursed her. A baby was born the next day, and the woman died. Then the first thing anybody knew the father skipped clean out, pack and all, and was never seen or heard tell of afterwards. The Gordons were left with the fine youngster on their hands. Folks advised them to send him to the Orphan Asylum, and 'twould have been the wisest plan, but the Gordons were never fond of taking advice. Old James Gordon was living then, Thomas and Janet's father, and he said he would never turn a child out of his door. He was a masterful old man and liked to be boss. Folks used to say he had a grudge against the sun 'cause it rose and set without his say so. Anyhow, they kept the baby. They called him Neil and had him baptized same as any Christian child. He's always lived there. They did well enough by him. He was sent to school and taken to church and treated like one of themselves. Some folks think they made too much of him. It doesn't always do with that kind, for 'what's bred in bone is mighty apt to come out in flesh,' if 'taint kept down pretty well. Neil's smart and a great worker, they tell me. But folks hereabouts don't like him. They say he ain't to be trusted further'n you can see him, if as far. It's certain he's awful hot tempered, and one time when he was going to school he near about killed a boy he'd took a spite to—choked him till he was black in the face and Neil had to be dragged off."

"Well now, father, you know they teased him terrible," protested Mrs. Williamson. "The poor boy had a real hard time when he went to school, Master. The other children were always casting things up to him and calling him names."

"Oh, I daresay they tormented him a lot," admitted her husband. "He's a great hand at the fiddle and likes company. He goes to the harbour a good deal. But they say he takes sulky spells when he hasn't a word to throw to a dog. 'Twouldn't be any wonder, living with the Gordons. They're all as queer as Dick's hat-band."

"Father, you shouldn't talk so about your neighbours," said his wife rebukingly.

"Well now, Mother, you know they are, if you'd only speak up honest. But you're like old Aunt Nancy Scott, you never say anything uncharitable except in the way of business. You know the Gordons ain't like other people and never were and never will be. They're about the only queer folks we have in Lindsay, Master, except old Peter Cook, who keeps twenty-five cats. Lord, Master, think of it! What chanct would a poor mouse have? None of the rest of us are queer, leastwise, we hain't found it out if we are. But, then, we're mighty uninteresting, I'm bound to admit that."

"Where do the Gordons live?" asked Eric, who had grown used to holding fast to a given point of inquiry through all the bewildering mazes of old Robert's conversation.

"Away up yander, half a mile in from Radnor road, with a thick spruce wood atween them and all the rest of the world. They never go away anywheres, except to church—they never miss that—and nobody goes there. There's just old Thomas, and his sister Janet, and a niece of theirs, and this here Neil we've been talking about. They're a queer, dour, cranky lot, and I *will* say it, Mother. There, give your old man a cup of tea and never mind the way his tongue runs on. Speaking of tea, do you know Mrs. Adam Palmer and Mrs. Jim Martin took tea together at Foster Reid's last Wednesday afternoon?"

"No, why, I thought they were on bad terms," said Mrs. Williamson, betraying a little feminine curiosity.

"So they are, so they are. But they both happened to visit Mrs. Foster the same afternoon and neither would leave because that would be knuckling down to the other. So they stuck it out, on opposite sides of the parlour. Mrs. Foster says she never spent such an uncomfortable afternoon in all her life before. She would talk a spell to one and then to t'other. And they kept talking *to* Mrs. Foster and *at* each other. Mrs. Foster says she really thought she'd have to keep them all night, for neither would start to go home afore the other. Finally Jim Martin came in to look for his wife, 'cause he thought she must have got stuck in the marsh, and that solved the problem. Master, you ain't eating anything. Don't mind my stopping; I was at it half an hour afore you come, and anyway I'm in a hurry. My hired boy went home today. He heard the rooster crow at twelve last night and he's gone home to see which of his family is dead. He knows one of 'em is. He heard a rooster crow in the middle of the night onct afore and the next day he got word that his second cousin down at Souris was dead. Mother, if the Master don't want any more tea, ain't there some cream for Timothy?"

CHAPTER 5

A PHANTOM OF DELIGHT

SHORTLY BEFORE sunset that evening Eric went for a walk. When he did not go to the shore he liked to indulge in long tramps through the Lindsay fields and woods, in the mellowness of "the sweet o' the year." Most of the Lindsay houses were built along the main road, which ran parallel to the shore, or about the stores at "The Corner." The farms ran back from them into solitudes of woods and pasture lands.

Eric struck southwest from the Williamson homestead, in a direction he had not hitherto explored, and walked briskly along, enjoying the witchery of the season all about him in earth and air and sky. He felt it and loved it and yielded to it, as anyone of clean life and sane pulses must do.

The spruce wood in which he presently found himself was smitten through with arrows of ruby light from the setting sun. He went through it, walking up a long, purple aisle where the wood-floor was brown and elastic under his feet, and came out beyond it on a scene which surprised him.

No house was in sight, but he found himself looking into an orchard; an old orchard, evidently long neglected and forsaken. But an orchard dies hard; and this one, which must have been a very delightful spot once, was delightful still, none the less so for the air of gentle melancholy which seemed to prevade it, the melancholy which invests all places that have once been the scenes of joy and pleasure and young life, and are so no longer, places where hearts have throbbed, and pulses thrilled, and eyes brightened, and merry voices echoed. The ghosts of these things seem to linger in their old haunts through many empty years.

The orchard was large and long, enclosed in a tumbledown old fence of longers bleached to a silvery gray in the suns of many lost summers. At regular intervals along the fence were tall, gnarled fir trees, and an evening wind, sweeter than that which blew over the beds of spice from Lebanon, was singing in their tops, an earth-old song with power to carry the soul back to the dawn of time.

Eastward, a thick fir wood grew, beginning with tiny treelets

459

just feathering from the grass, and grading up therefrom to the tall veterans of the mid-grove, unbrokenly and evenly, giving the effect of a solid, sloping green wall, so beautifully compact that it looked as if it had been clipped into its velvet surface by art.

Most of the orchard was grown over lushly with grass; but at the end where Eric stood there was a square, treeless place which had evidently once served as a homestead garden. Old paths were still visible, bordered by stones and large pebbles. There were two clumps of lilac trees; one blossoming in royal purple, the other in white. Between them was a bed ablow with the starry spikes of June lilies. Their penetrating, haunting fragrance distilled on the dewy air in every soft puff of wind. Along the fence rosebushes grew, but it was as yet too early in the season for roses.

Beyond was the orchard proper, three long rows of trees with green avenues between, each tree standing in a wonderful blow of pink and white.

The charm of the place took sudden possession of Eric as nothing had ever done before. He was not given to romantic fancies; but the orchard laid hold of him subtly and drew him to itself, and he was never to be quite his own man again. He went into it over one of the broken panels of fence, and so, unknowing, went forward to meet all that life held for him.

He walked the length of the orchard's middle avenue between long, sinuous boughs picked out with delicate, rose-hearted bloom. When he reached its southern boundary he flung himself down in a grassy corner of the fence where another lilac bush grew, with ferns and wild blue violets at its roots. From where he now was he got a glimpse of a house about a quarter of a mile away, its gray gable peering out from a dark spruce wood. It seemed a dull, gloomy, remote place, and he did not know who lived there.

He had a wide outlook to the west, over far hazy fields and misty blue intervales. The sun had just set, and the whole world of green meadows beyond swam in golden light. Across a long valley brimmed with shadow were uplands of sunset, and great sky lakes of saffron and rose where a soul might lose itself in colour. The air was very fragrant with the baptism of the dew, and the odours of a bed of wild mint upon which he had trampled. Robins were whistling, clear and sweet and sudden, in the woods all about him.

"This is a veritable 'haunt of ancient peace,' " quoted Eric, looking around with delighted eyes. "I could fall asleep here, dream dreams and see visions. What a sky! Could anything be diviner than that fine crystal eastern blue, and those frail white clouds that look like woven lace? What a dizzying, intoxicating fragrance lilacs have! I wonder if perfume could set a man drunk. Those apple trees now—why, what is that?"

Eric started up and listened. Across the mellow stillness, mingled with the croon of the wind in the trees and the flute-like calls of the robins, came a strain of delicious music, so beautiful and fantastic that Eric held his breath in astonishment and delight. Was he dreaming? No, it was real music, the music of a violin played by some hand inspired with the very spirit of harmony. He had never heard anything like it; and, somehow, he felt quite sure that nothing exactly like it ever had been heard before; he believed that that wonderful music was coming straight from the soul of the unseen violinist, and translating itself into those most airy and delicate and exquisite sounds for the first time; the very soul of music, with all sense and earthliness refined away.

It was an elusive, haunting melody, strangely suited to the time and place; it had in it the sigh of the wind in the woods, the eerie whispering of the grasses at dewfall, the white thoughts of the June lilies, the rejoicing of the apple blossoms; all the soul of all the old laughter and song and tears and gladness and sobs the orchard had ever known in the lost years; and besides all this, there was in it a pitiful, plaintive cry as of some imprisoned thing calling for freedom and utterance.

At first Eric listened as a man spellbound, mutely and motionlessly, lost in wonderment. Then a very natural curiosity overcame him. Who in Lindsay could play a violin like that? And who was playing so here, in this deserted old orchard, of all places in the world?

He rose and walked up the long white avenue, going as slowly and silently as possible, for he did not wish to interrupt the player. When he reached the open space of the garden he stopped short in new amazement and was again tempted into thinking he must certainly be dreaming.

Under the big branching white lilac tree was an old, sagging, wooden bench; and on this bench a girl was sitting, playing on an old brown violin. Her eyes were on the faraway horizon and she did not see Eric. For a few moments he stood there and looked at her. The picture she made photographed itself on his vision to the finest detail, never to be blotted from his book of remembrance. To his latest day Eric Marshall will be able to recall vividly that scene as he saw it then—the velvet darkness of the spruce woods, the overarching sky of soft brilliance, the swaying lilac blossoms, and amid it all the girl on the old bench with the violin under her chin.

He had, in his twenty-four years of life, met hundreds of pretty women, scores of handsome women, a scant half dozen of really beautiful women. But he knew at once, beyond all possibility of question or doubt, that he had never seen or imagined anything so exquisite as this girl of the orchard. Her loveliness was so perfect that his breath almost went from him in his first delight of it.

Her face was oval, marked in every cameo-like line and feature with that expression of absolute, flawless purity, found in the angels and Madonnas of old paintings, a purity that held in it no faintest stain of earthliness. Her head was bare, and her thick, jet-black hair was parted above her forehead and hung in two heavy lustrous braids over her shoulders. Her eyes were of such a blue as Eric had never seen in eyes before, the tint of the sea in the still, calm light that follows after a fine sunset; they were as luminous as the stars that came out over Lindsay Harbour in the afterglow, and were fringed about with very long, soot-black lashes, and arched over by most delicately pencilled dark eyebrows. Her skin was as fine and purely tinted as the heart of a white rose. The collarless dress of pale blue print she wore revealed her smooth, slender throat; her sleeves were rolled up above her elbows and the hand which guided the bow of her violin was perhaps the most beautiful thing about her, perfect in shape and texture, firm and white, with rosy-nailed taper fingers. One long, drooping plume of lilac blossom lightly touched her hair and cast a wavering shadow over the flower-like face beneath it.

There was something very child-like about her, and yet at least eighteen sweet years must have gone to the making of

FOR A FEW MOMENTS, HE STOOD THERE AND LOOKED AT HER.

her. She seemed to be playing half unconsciously, as if her thoughts were far away in some fair dreamland of the skies. But presently she looked away from "the bourne of sunset," and her lovely eyes fell on Eric, standing motionless before her in the shadow of the apple tree.

The sudden change that swept over her was startling. She sprang to her feet, the music breaking in mid-strain and the bow slipping from her hand to the grass. Every hint of colour fled from her face and she trembled like one of the wind-stirred June lilies.

"I beg your pardon," said Eric hastily. "I am sorry that I have alarmed you. But your music was so beautiful that I did not remember you were not aware of my presence here. Please forgive me."

He stopped in dismay, for he suddenly realized that the expression on the girl's face was one of terror—not merely the startled alarm of a shy, childlike creature who had thought herself alone, but absolute terror. It was betrayed in her blanched and quivering lips and in the widely distended blue eyes that stared back into his with the expression of some trapped wild thing.

It hurt him that any woman should look at him in such a fashion, at him who had always held womanhood in such reverence.

"Don't look so frightened," he said gently, thinking only of calming her fear, and speaking as he would to a child. "I will not hurt you. You are safe, quite safe."

In his eagerness to reassure her he took an unconscious step forward. Instantly she turned and, without a sound, fled across the orchard, through a gap in the northern fence and along what seemed to be a lane bordering the fir wood beyond and arched over with wild cherry trees misty white in the gathering gloom. Before Eric could recover his wits she had vanished from his sight among the firs.

He stooped and picked up the violin bow, feeling slightly foolish and very much annoyed.

"Well, this is a most mysterious thing," he said, somewhat impatiently. "Am I bewitched? Who was she? *What* was she? Can it be possible that she is a Lindsay girl? And why in the name of all that's provoking should she be so frightened at the mere sight of me? I have never thought I was a particularly hideous person, but certainly this adventure has not increased my vanity to any perceptible extent. Perhaps I have wandered into an enchanted orchard, and been outwardly transformed into an ogre. Now that I have come to think of it, there is something quite uncanny about the place. Anything might happen here. It is no common orchard for the production of marketable apples, that is plain to be seen. No, it's a most unwholesome locality; and the sooner I make my escape from it the better."

He glanced about it with a whimsical smile. The light was fading rapidly and the orchard was full of soft, creeping shadows and silences. It seemed to wink sleepy eyes of impish enjoyment at his perplexity. He laid the violin bow down on the old bench.

"Well, there is no use in my following her, and I have no right to do so even if it were of use. But I certainly wish she hadn't fled in such evident terror. Eyes like hers were never meant to express anything but tenderness and trust. Why—why—*why* was she so frightened? And who—who—*who*—can she be?"

All the way home, over fields and pastures that were beginning to be moonlight silvered, he pondered the mystery.

"Let me see," he reflected. "Mr. Williamson was describing the Lindsay girls for my benefit the other evening. If I remember rightly he said that there were four handsome ones in the district. What were their names? Florrie Woods, Melissa Foster—no, Melissa Palmer—Emma Scott, and Jennie May Ferguson. Can she be one of them? No, it is a flagrant waste of time and gray matter supposing it. That girl couldn't be a Florrie or a Melissa or an Emma, while Jennie May is completely out of the question. Well, there is some bewitchment in the affair. Of that I'm convinced. So I'd better forget all about it."

But Eric found that it was impossible to forget all about it. The more he tried to forget, the more keenly and insistently he remembered. The girl's exquisite face haunted him and the mystery of her tantalized him.

True, he knew that, in all likelihood, he might easily solve the problem by asking the Williamsons about her. But somehow, to his own surprise, he found that he shrank from doing this. He felt that it was impossible to ask Robert Williamson and probably have the girl's name overflowed in a stream of petty gossip concerning her and all her antecedents and collaterals to the third and fourth generation. If he had to ask any one it should be Mrs. Williamson; but he meant to find out the secret for himself if it were at all possible.

He had planned to go to the harbour the next evening. One of the lobstermen had promised to take him out cod-fishing. But instead he wandered southwest over the fields again.

He found the orchard easily—he had half expected *not* to find it. It was still the same fragrant, grassy, wind-haunted spot. But it had no occupant and the violin bow was gone from the old bench.

"Perhaps she tiptoed back here for it by the light o' the moon," thought Eric, pleasing his fancy by the vision of a lithe, girlish figure stealing with a beating heart through mingled shadow and moonshine. "I wonder if she will possibly come this evening, or if I have frightened her away for ever. I'll hide me behind this spruce copse and wait."

Eric waited until dark, but no music sounded through the orchard and no one came to it. The keenness of his disappointment surprised him, nay more, it vexed him. What nonsense to be so worked up because a little girl he had seen for five minutes failed to appear! Where was his common sense, his "gumption," as old Robert Williamson would have said? Naturally a man liked to look at a pretty face. But was that any reason why he should feel as if life were flat, stale, and unprofitable simply because he could not look at it? He called himself a fool and went home in a petulant mood. Arriving there, he plunged fiercely into solving algebraical equations and working out geometry exercises, determined to put out of his head forthwith all vain imaginings of an enchanted orchard, white in the moonshine, with lilts of elfin music echoing down its long arcades.

The next day was Sunday and Eric went to church twice. The Williamson pew was one of the side ones at the top of the church and its occupants practically faced the congregation. Eric looked at every girl and woman in the audience, but he saw nothing of the face which, setting will power and common sense flatly at defiance, haunted his memory like a star.

Thomas Gordon was there, sitting alone in his long, empty pew near the top of the building; and Neil Gordon sang in the choir which occupied the front pew of the gallery. He had a powerful and melodious, though untrained voice, which dominated the singing and took the colour out of the weaker, more commonplace tones of the other singers. He was well-dressed in a suit of dark blue serge, with a white collar and tie. But Eric idly thought it did not become him so well as the working clothes in which he had first seen him. He was too obviously dressed up, and he looked coarser and more out of harmony with his surroundings.

For two days Eric refused to let himself think of the orchard. Monday evening he went cod-fishing, and Tuesday evening he went up to play checkers with Alexander Tracy. Alexander won all the games so easily that he never had any respect for Eric Marshall again.

"Played like a feller whose thoughts were wool gathering," he complained to his wife. "He'll never make a checker player— never in this world."

CHAPTER 6

THE STORY OF KILMENY

WEDNESDAY EVENING Eric went to the orchard again; and again he was disappointed. He went home, determined to solve the mystery by open inquiry. Fortune favoured him, for he found Mrs. Williamson alone, sitting by the west window of her kitchen and knitting at a long gray sock. She hummed softly to herself as she knitted, and Timothy slept blackly at her feet. She looked at Eric with quiet affection in her large, candid eyes. She had liked Mr. West. But Eric had found his way into the inner chamber of her heart, by reason that his eyes were so like those of the little son she had buried in the Lindsay churchyard many years before.

"Mrs. Williamson," said Eric, with an affectation of carelessness, "I chanced on an old deserted orchard back behind the woods over there last week, a charming bit of wilderness. Do you know whose it is?"

"I suppose it must be the old Connors orchard," answered Mrs. Williamson after a moment's reflection. "I had forgotten all about it. It must be all of thirty years since Mr. and Mrs. Connors moved away. Their house and barns were burned down and they sold the land to Thomas Gordon and went to live in town. They're both dead now. Mr. Connors used to be very proud of his orchard. There weren't many orchards in Lindsay then, though almost everybody has one now."

"There was a young girl in it, playing on a violin," said Eric, annoyed to find that it cost him an effort to speak of her, and that the blood mounted to his face as he did so. "She ran away in great alarm as soon as she saw me, although I do not think I did or said anything to frighten or vex her. I have no idea who she was. Do you know?"

Mrs. Williamson did not make an immediate reply. She laid down her knitting and gazed out of the window as if pondering seriously some question in her own mind. Finally she said, with an intonation of keen interest in her voice,

"I suppose it must have been Kilmeny Gordon, Master."

"Kilmeny Gordon? Do you mean the niece of Thomas Gordon of whom your husband spoke?"

"Yes."

"I can hardly believe that the girl I saw can be a member of Thomas Gordon's family."

"Well, if it wasn't Kilmeny Gordon I don't know who it could have been. There is no other house near that orchard and I've heard she plays the violin. If it was Kilmeny you've seen what very few people in Lindsay have ever seen, Master. And those few have never seen her close by. I have never laid eyes on her myself. It's no wonder she ran away, poor girl. She isn't used to seeing strangers."

"I'm rather glad if that was the sole reason of her flight," said Eric. "I admit I didn't like to see any girl so frightened of me as she appeared to be. She was as white as paper, and so terrified that she never uttered a word, but fled like a deer to cover."

"Well, she couldn't have spoken a word in any case," said Mrs. Williamson quietly. "Kilmeny Gordon is dumb."

Eric sat in dismayed silence for a moment. That beautiful

creature afflicted in such a fashion—why, it was horrible! Mingled with his dismay was a strange pang of personal regret and disappointment.

"It couldn't have been Kilmeny Gordon, then," he protested at last, remembering. "The girl I saw played on the violin exquisitely. I never heard anything like it. It is impossible that a deaf mute could play like that."

"Oh, she isn't deaf, Master," responded Mrs. Williamson, looking at Eric keenly through her spectacles. She picked up her knitting and fell to work again. "That is the strange part of it, if anything about her can be stranger than another. She can hear as well as anybody and understands everything that is said to her. But she can't speak a word and never could, at least, so they say. The truth is, nobody knows much about her. Janet and Thomas never speak of her, and Neil won't either. He has been well questioned, too, you can depend on that; but he won't ever say a word about Kilmeny and he gets mad if folks persist."

"Why isn't she to be spoken of?" queried Eric impatiently. "What is the mystery about her?"

"It's a sad story, Master. I suppose the Gordons look on her existence as a sort of disgrace. For my own part, I think it's terrible, the way she's been brought up. But the Gordons are very strange people, Mr. Marshall. I kind of reproved father for saying so, you remember, but it is true. They have very strange ways. And you've really seen Kilmeny? What does she look like? I've heard that she was handsome. Is it true?"

"I thought her very beautiful," said Eric rather curtly. "But *how* has she been brought up, Mrs. Williamson? And why?"

"Well, I might as well tell you the whole story, Master. Kilmeny is the niece of Thomas and Janet Gordon. Her mother was Margaret Gordon, their younger sister. Old James Gordon came out from Scotland. Janet and Thomas were born in the Old Country and were small children when they came here. They were never very sociable folks, but still they used to visit out some then, and people used to go there. They were kind and honest people, even if they were a little peculiar.

"Mrs. Gordon died a few years after they came out, and four years later James Gordon went home to Scotland and brought a new wife back with him. She was a great deal younger than he was and a very pretty woman, as my mother often told me. She was friendly and gay and liked social life. The Gordon place was a very different sort of place after she came there, and even Janet and Thomas got thawed out and softened down a good bit. They were real fond of their stepmother, I've heard. Then, six years after she was married, the second Mrs. Gordon died too. She died when Margaret was born. They say James Gordon almost broke his heart over it.

"Janet brought Margaret up. She and Thomas just worshipped the child and so did their father. I knew Margaret Gordon well once. We were just the same age and we set together in school. We were always good friends until she turned against all the world.

"She was a strange girl in some ways even then, but I always liked her, though a great many people didn't. She had some bitter enemies, but she had some devoted friends too. That was her way. She made folks either hate or love her. Those who did love her would have gone through fire and water for her.

"When she grew up she was very pretty—tall and splendid, like a queen, with great thick braids of black hair and red, red cheeks and lips. Everybody who saw her looked at her a second time. She was a little vain of her beauty, I think, Master. And she was proud, oh, she was very proud. She liked to be first in everything, and she couldn't bear not to show to good advantage. She was dreadful determined, too. You couldn't budge her an inch, Master, when she once had made up her mind on any point. But she was warm-hearted and generous. She could sing like an angel and she was very clever. She could learn anything with just one look at it and she was terrible fond of reading.

"When I'm talking about her like this it all comes back to me, just what she was like and how she looked and spoke and acted, and little ways she had of moving her hands and head. I declare it almost seems as if she was right here in this room instead of being over there in the churchyard. I wish you'd light the lamp, Master. I feel kind of nervous."

Eric rose and lighted the lamp, rather wondering at Mrs. Williamson's unusual exhibition of nerves. She was generally so calm and composed.

"Thank you, Master. That's better. I won't be fancying now that Margaret Gordon's here listening to what I'm saying. I had the feeling so strong a moment ago.

"I suppose you think I'm a long while getting to Kilmeny, but I'm coming to that. I didn't mean to talk so much about Margaret, but somehow my thoughts got taken up with her.

"Well, Margaret passed the Board and went to Queen's Academy and got a teacher's license. She passed pretty well up when she came out, but Janet told me she cried all night after the pass list came out because there were some ahead of her.

"She went to teach school over at Radnor. It was there she met a man named Ronald Fraser. Margaret had never had a beau before. She could have had any young man in Lindsay if she had wanted him, but she wouldn't look at one of them. They said it was because she thought nobody was good enough for her, but that wasn't the way of it at all, Master. I knew, because Margaret and I used to talk of those matters, as girls do. She didn't believe in going with anybody unless it was somebody she thought everything of. And there was nobody in Lindsay she cared that much for.

"This Ronald Fraser was a stranger from Nova Scotia and nobody knew much about him. He was a widower, although he was only a young man. He had set up store-keeping at Radnor and was doing well. He was real handsome and had the taking ways women like. It was said that all the Radnor girls were in love with him, but I don't think his worst enemy could have said he flirted with them. He never took any notice of them; but the very first time he saw Margaret Gordon he fell in love with her and she with him.

"They came over to church in Lindsay together the next Sunday and everybody said it would be a match. Margaret looked lovely that day, so gentle and womanly. She had been used to hold her head pretty high, but that day she held it drooping a little and her black eyes cast down. Ronald Fraser was very tall and fair, with blue eyes. They made as handsome a couple as I ever saw.

"But old James Gordon and Thomas and Janet didn't much approve of him. I saw that plain enough one time I was there and he brought Margaret home from Radnor Friday night. I guess they wouldn't have liked anybody, though, who come after Margaret. They thought nobody was good enough for her.

"But Margaret coaxed them all round in time. She could do pretty near anything with them, they were so fond and proud of her. Her father held out the longest, but finally he give in and consented for her to marry Ronald Fraser.

"They had a big wedding, too—all the neighbours were asked. Margaret always liked to make a display. I was her bridesmaid, Master. I helped her dress and nothing would please her, she wanted to look that nice for Ronald's sake. She was a handsome bride; dressed in white, with red roses in her hair and at her breast. She wouldn't wear white flowers; she said they looked too much like funeral flowers. She looked like a picture. I can see her this minute, as plain as plain, just as she was that night, blushing and turning pale by turns, and looking at Ronald with her eyes of love. If ever a girl loved a man with all her heart Margaret Gordon did. It almost made me feel frightened. She gave him the worship it isn't right to give anybody but God, Master, and I think that is always punished.

"They went to live at Radnor and for a little while everything went well. Margaret had a nice house, and was gay and happy. She dressed beautiful and entertained a good deal. Then—well, Ronald Fraser's first wife turned up looking for him! She wasn't dead after all.

"Oh, there was terrible scandal, Master. The talk and gossip was something dreadful. Every one you met had a different story, and it was hard to get at the truth. Some said Ronald Fraser had known all the time that his wife wasn't dead, and had deceived Margaret. But I don't think he did. He swore he didn't. They hadn't been very happy together, it seems. Her mother made trouble between them. Then she went to visit her mother in Montreal, and died in the hospital there, so the word came to Ronald. Perhaps he believed it a little too readily, but that he *did* believe it I never had a doubt. Her story was that it was another woman of the same name. When she found out Ronald thought her dead she and her mother agreed to let him think so. But when she heard he had got married again she thought she'd better let him know the truth.

"It all sounded like a queer story and I suppose you couldn't blame people for not believing it too readily. But I've always felt it was true. Margaret didn't think so, though. She believed that Ronald Fraser had deceived her, knowing all the time that he couldn't make her his lawful wife. She turned against him and hated him just as much as she had loved him before.

"Ronald Fraser went away with his real wife, and in less

than a year word came of his death. They said he just died of a broken heart, nothing more nor less.

"Margaret came home to her father's house. From the day that she went over its threshold, she never came out until she was carried out in her coffin three years ago. Not a soul outside of her own family ever saw her again. I went to see her, but Janet told me she wouldn't see me. It was foolish of Margaret to act so. She hadn't done anything real wrong; and everybody was sorry for her and would have helped her all they could. But I reckon pity cut her as deep as blame could have done, and deeper, because you see, Master, she was so proud she couldn't bear it.

"They say her father was hard on her, too; and that was unjust if it was true. Janet and Thomas felt the disgrace, too. The people that had been in the habit of going to the Gordon place soon stopped going, for they could see they were not welcome.

"Old James Gordon died that winter. He never held his head up again after the scandal. He had been an elder in the church, but he handed in his resignation right away and nobody could persuade him to withdraw it.

"Kilmeny was born in the spring, but nobody ever saw her, except the minister who baptized her. She was never taken to church or sent to school. Of course, I suppose there wouldn't have been any use in her going to school when she couldn't speak, and it's likely Margaret taught her all she could be taught herself. But it was dreadful that she was never taken to church, or let go among the children and young folks. And it was a real shame that nothing was ever done to find out why she couldn't talk, or if she could be cured.

"Margaret Gordon died three years ago, and everybody in Lindsay went to the funeral. But they didn't see her. The coffin lid was screwed down. And they didn't see Kilmeny either. I would have loved to see *her* for Margaret's sake, but I didn't want to see poor Margaret. I had never seen her since the night she was a bride, for I had left Lindsay on a visit just after that, and when I came home the scandal had just broken out. I remembered Margaret in all her pride and beauty, and I couldn't have borne to look at her dead face and see the awful changes I knew must be there.

"It was thought perhaps Janet and Thomas would take Kilmeny out after her mother was gone, but they never did, so I suppose they must have agreed with Margaret about the way she had been brought up. I've often felt sorry for the poor girl, and I don't think her people did right by her, even if she was mysteriously afflicted. She must have had a very sad, lonely life.

"That is the story, Master, and I've been a long time telling it, as I dare say you think. But the past just seemed to be living again for me as I talked. If you don't want to be pestered with questions about Kilmeny Gordon, Master, you'd better not let on you've seen her."

Eric was not likely to. He had heard all he wanted to know and more.

"So this girl is at the core of the tragedy," he reflected, as he went to his room. "And she is dumb! The pity of it! Kilmeny! The name suits her. She is as lovely and innocent as the heroine of the old ballad. 'And oh, Kilmeny was fair to see.' But the next line is certainly not so appropriate, for her eyes were anything but 'still and steadfast'—after she had seen me, at all events."

He tried to put her out of his thoughts, but he could not. The memory of her beautiful face drew him with a power he could not resist. The next evening he went again to the orchard.

--- CHAPTER 7 ---

A ROSE OF WOMANHOOD

WHEN HE emerged from the spruce wood and entered the orchard his heart gave a sudden leap, and he felt that the blood rushed madly to his face. She was there, bending over the bed of June lilies in the centre of the garden plot. He could see only her profile, virginal and white.

He stopped, not wishing to startle her again. When she lifted her head he expected to see her shrink and flee, but she did not do so; she only grew a little paler and stood motionless, watching him intently.

Seeing this, he walked slowly towards her, and when he was so close to her that he could hear the nervous flutter of her breath over her parted, trembling lips, he said very gently,

"Do not be afraid of me. I am a friend, and I do not wish to disturb or annoy you in any way."

She seemed to hesitate a moment. Then she lifted a little slate that hung at her belt, wrote something on it rapidly, and held it out to him. He read, in a small distinctive handwriting,

"I am not afraid of you now. Mother told me that all strange men were very wicked and dangerous, but I do not think you can be. I have thought a great deal about you, and I am sorry I ran away the other night."

He realized her entire innocence and simplicity. Looking earnestly into her still troubled eyes he said,

"I would not do you any harm for the world. All men are not wicked, although it is too true that some are so. My name is Eric Marshall and I am teaching in the Lindsay school. You, I think, are Kilmeny Gordon. I thought your music so very lovely the other evening that I have been wishing ever since that I might hear it again. Won't you play for me?"

The vague fear had all gone from her eyes by this time, and suddenly she smiled—a merry, girlish, wholly irresistible smile, which broke through the calm of her face like a gleam of sunlight rippling over a placid sea. Then she wrote, "I am very sorry that I cannot play this evening. I did not bring my violin bow with me. But I will bring it tomorrow evening and play for you if you would like to hear me. I should like to please you."

Again that note of innocent frankness! What a child she was—what a beautiful, ignorant child, utterly unskilled in the art of hiding her feelings! But why should she hide them? They were as pure and beautiful as herself. Eric smiled back at her with equal frankness.

"I should like it more than I can say, and I shall be sure to come tomorrow evening if it is fine. But if it is at all damp or unpleasant you must not come. In that case another evening will do. And now won't you give me some flowers?"

She nodded, with another little smile, and began to pick some of the June lilies, carefully selecting the most perfect among them. He watched her lithe, graceful motions with delight; every movement seemed poetry itself. She looked like a very incarnation of Spring—as if all the shimmer of young leaves and glow of young mornings and evanescent sweetness of young blossoms in a thousand springs had been embodied in her.

When she came to him, radiant, her hands full of the lilies, a couplet from a favourite poem darted into his head—

> "A blossom vermeil white
> That lightly breaks a faded flower sheath,
> Here, by God's rood, is the one maid for me."

The next moment he was angry with himself for his folly. She was, after all, nothing but a child—and a child set apart from her fellow creatures by her sad defect. He must not let himself think nonsense.

"Thank you. These June lilies are the sweetest flowers the spring brings us. Do you know that their real name is the white narcissus?" She looked pleased and interested.

"No, I did not know," she wrote. "I have often read of the white narcissus and wondered what it was like. I never thought of it being the same as my dear June lilies. I am glad you told me. I love flowers very much. They are my very good friends."

"You couldn't help being friends with the lilies. Like always takes to like," said Eric. "Come and sit down on the old bench—here, where you were sitting that night I frightened you so badly. I could not imagine who or what you were. Sometimes I thought I had dreamed you—only," he added under his breath and unheard by her, "I could never have dreamed anything half so lovely."

She sat down beside him on the old bench and looked unshrinkingly in his face. There was no boldness in her glance—nothing but the most perfect, childlike trust and confidence. If there had been any evil in his heart—any skulking thought, he was afraid to acknowledge—those eyes must have searched it out and shamed it. But he could meet them unafraid. Then she wrote,

"I was very much frightened. You must have thought me very silly, but I had never seen any man except Uncle Thomas and Neil and the egg peddler. And you are different from them—oh, very, very different. I was afraid to come back here the next evening. And yet, somehow, I wanted to come. I did not want you to think I did not know how to behave. I sent Neil back for my bow in the morning. I could not do without it. I cannot speak, you know. Are you sorry?"

"I am very sorry for your sake."

"Yes, but what I mean is, would you like me better if I could speak like other people?"

"No, it does not make any difference in that way, Kilmeny. By the way, do you mind my calling you Kilmeny?"

She looked puzzled and wrote, "What else should you call me? That is my name. Everybody calls me that."

"But I am such a stranger to you that perhaps you would wish me to call you Miss Gordon."

"Oh, no, I would not like that," she wrote quickly, with a distressed look on her face. "Nobody ever calls me that. It would make me feel as if I were not myself but somebody else. And you do not seem like a stranger to me. Is there any reason why you should not call me Kilmeny?"

"No reason whatever, if you will allow me the privilege. You have a very lovely name—the very name you ought to have."

"I am glad you like it. Do you know that I was called after my grandmother and she was called after a girl in a poem? Aunt Janet has never liked my name, although she liked my grandmother. But I am glad you like both my name and me. I was afraid you would not like me because I cannot speak."

"You can speak through your music, Kilmeny."

She looked pleased. "How well you understand," she wrote. "Yes, I cannot speak or sing as other people can, but I can make my violin say things for me."

"Do you compose your own music?" he asked. But he saw she did not understand him. "I mean, did any one ever teach you the music you played here that evening?"

"Oh, no. It just came as I thought. It has always been that way. When I was very little Neil taught me to hold the violin and the bow, and the rest all came of itself. My violin once belonged to Neil, but he gave it to me. Neil is very good and kind to me, but I like you better. Tell me about yourself."

The wonder of her grew upon him with every passing moment. How lovely she was! What dear little ways and gestures she had—ways and gestures as artless and unstudied as they were effective. And how strangely little her dumbness seemed to matter after all! She wrote so quickly and easily, her eyes and smile gave such expression to her mobile face, that voice was hardly missed.

They lingered in the orchard until the long, languid shadows of the trees crept to their feet. It was just after sunset and the distant hills were purple against the melting saffron of the sky in the west and the crystalline blue of the sky in the south. Eastward, just over the fir woods, were clouds, white and high heaped like snow mountains, and the westernmost of them shone with a rosy glow as of sunset on an Alpine height.

The higher worlds of air were still full of light—perfect, stainless light, unmarred of earth shadow; but down in the orchard and under the spruces the light had almost gone, giving place to a green, dewy dusk, made passionately sweet with the breath of the apple blossoms and mint, and the balsamic odours that rained down upon them from the firs.

Eric told her of his life, and the life in the great outer world, in which she was girlishly and eagerly interested. She asked him many questions about it—direct and incisive questions which showed that she had already formed decided opinions and views about it. Yet it was plain to be seen that she did not regard it as anything she might ever share herself. Hers was the dispassionate interest with which she might have listened to a tale of the land of fairy or of some great empire long passed away from earth.

Eric discovered that she had read a great deal of poetry and history, and a few books of biography and travel. She did not know what a novel meant and had never heard of one. Curiously enough, she was well informed regarding politics and current events, from the weekly paper for which her uncle subscribed.

"I never read the newspaper while mother was alive," she wrote, "nor any poetry either. She taught me to read and write and I read the Bible all through many times and some of the histories. After mother died Aunt Janet gave me all her books. She had a great many. Most of them had been given to her as prizes when she was a girl at school, and some of them had been given to her by my father. Do you know the story of my father and mother?"

Eric nodded.

"Yes, Mrs. Williamson told me all about it. She was a friend of your mother."

"I am glad you have heard it. It is so sad that I would not like to tell it, but you will understand everything better because you know. I never heard it until just before mother died. Then she told me all. I think she had thought father was to blame for the trouble; but before she died she told me she believed that she had been unjust to him and that he had not known. She said that when people were dying they saw things more clearly and she saw she had made a mistake about father. She said she had many more things she wanted to tell me, but she did not have time to tell them because she died that night. It was a long while before I had the heart to read her books. But when I did I thought them so beautiful. They were poetry and it was like music put into words."

"I will bring you some books to read, if you would like them," said Eric.

Her great blue eyes gleamed with interest and delight.

"Oh, thank you, I would like it very much. I have read mine over so often that I know them nearly all by heart. One cannot get tired of really beautiful things, but sometimes I feel that I would like some new books."

"Are you never lonely, Kilmeny?"

"Oh no, how could I be? There is always plenty for me to do, helping Aunt Janet about the house. I can do a great many things"—she glanced up at him with a pretty pride as her flying pencil traced the words. "I can cook and sew. Aunt Janet says I am a very good housekeeper, and she does not praise people very often or very much. And then, when I am not helping her, I have my dear, dear violin. That is all the company I want. But I like to read and hear of the big world so far away and the people who live there and the things that are done. It must be a very wonderful place."

"Wouldn't you like to go out into it and see its wonders and meet those people yourself?" he asked, smiling at her.

At once he saw that, in some way he could not understand, he had hurt her. She snatched her pencil and wrote, with such swiftness of motion and energy of expression that it almost seemed as if she had passionately exclaimed the words aloud,

"No, no, no. I do not want to go anywhere away from home.

I do not want ever to see strangers or have them see me. I could not bear it."

He thought that possibly the consciousness of her defect accounted for this. Yet she did not seem sensitive about her dumbness and made frequent casual references to it in her written remarks. Or perhaps it was the shadow on her birth. Yet she was so innocent that it seemed unlikely she could realize or understand the existence of such a shadow. Eric finally decided that it was merely the rather morbid shrinking of a sensitive child who had been brought up in an unwholesome and unnatural way. At last the lengthening shadows warned him that it was time to go.

"You won't forget to come tomorrow evening and play for me," he said, rising reluctantly. She answered by a quick little shake of her sleek, dark head, and a smile that was eloquent. He watched her as she walked across the orchard,

"With the moon's beauty and the moon's soft pace,"

and along the wild cherry lane. At the corner of the firs she paused and waved her hand to him before turning it.

When Eric reached home old Robert Williamson was having a lunch of bread and milk in the kitchen. He looked up, with a friendly grin, as Eric strode in, whistling.

"Been having a walk, Master?" he queried.

"Yes," said Eric.

Unconsciously and involuntarily he infused so much triumph into the simple monosyllable that even old Robert felt it. Mrs. Williamson, who was cutting bread at the end of the table, laid down her knife and loaf, and looked at the young man with a softly troubled expression in her eyes. She wondered if he had been back to the Connors orchard—and if he could have seen Kilmeny Gordon again.

"You didn't discover a gold mine, I s'pose?" said old Robert, dryly. "You look as if you might have."

CHAPTER 8

AT THE GATE OF EDEN

WHEN ERIC went to the old Connors orchard the next evening he found Kilmeny waiting for him on the bench under the white lilac tree, with the violin in her lap. As soon as she saw him she caught it up and began to play an airy delicate little melody that sounded like the laughter of daisies.

When it was finished she dropped her bow, and looked up at him with flushed cheeks and questioning eyes.

"What did that say to you?" she wrote.

"It said something like this," answered Eric, falling into her humour smilingly. "Welcome, my friend. It is a very beautiful evening. The sky is so blue and the apple blossoms so sweet. The wind and I have been here alone together and the wind is a good companion, but still I am glad to see you. It is an evening on which it is good to be alive and to wander in an orchard that is fine and white. Welcome, my friend."

She clapped her hands, looking like a pleased child.

"You are very quick to understand," she wrote. "That was just what I meant. Of course I did not think it in just those words, but that was the *feeling* of it. I felt that I was so glad I was alive, and that the apple blossoms and the white lilacs and the trees and I were all pleased together to see you come. You are quicker than Neil. He is almost always puzzled to understand my music, and I am puzzled to understand his. Sometimes it frightens me. It seems as if there were something in it trying to take hold of me—something I do not like and want to run away from."

Somehow Eric did not like her references to Neil. The idea of that handsome, low-born boy seeing Kilmeny every day, talking to her, sitting at the same table with her, dwelling under the same roof, meeting her in the hundred intimacies of daily life, was distasteful to him. He put the thought away from him, and flung himself down on the long grass at her feet.

"Now play for me, please," he said. "I want to lie here and listen to you."

"And look at you," he might have added. He could not tell which was the greater pleasure. Her beauty, more wonderful

481

than any pictured loveliness he had ever seen, delighted him. Every tint and curve and outline of her face was flawless. Her music enthralled him. This child, he told himself as he listened, had genius. But it was being wholly wasted. He found himself thinking resentfully of the people who were her guardians, and who were responsible for her strange life. They had done her a great and irremediable wrong. How dared they doom her to such an existence? If her defect of utterance had been attended to in time, who knew but that it might have been cured? Now it was probably too late. Nature had given her a royal birthright of beauty and talent, but their selfish and unpardonable neglect had made it of no account.

What divine music she lured out of the old violin—merry and sad, gay and sorrowful by turns, music such as the stars of morning might have made singing together, music that the fairies might have danced to in their revels among the green hills or on yellow sands, music that might have mourned over the grave of a dead hope. Then she drifted into a still sweeter strain. As he listened to it he realized that the whole soul and nature of the girl were revealing themselves to him through her music—the beauty and purity of her thoughts, her childhood dreams and her maiden reveries. There was no thought of concealment about her; she could not help the revelation she was unconscious of making.

At last she laid her violin aside and wrote,

"I have done my best to give you pleasure. It is your turn now. Do you remember a promise you made me last night? Have you kept it?"

He gave her the two books he had brought for her—a modern novel and a volume of poetry unknown to her. He had hesitated a little over the former; but the book was so fine and full of beauty that he thought it could not bruise the bloom of her innocence ever so slightly. He had no doubts about the poetry. It was the utterance of one of those great inspired souls whose passing tread has made the kingdom of their birth and labour a veritable Holy Land.

He read her some of the poems. Then he talked to her of his college days and friends. The minutes passed very swiftly. There was just then no world for him outside of that old orchard with its falling blossoms and its shadows and its crooning winds.

Once, when he told her the story of some college pranks wherein the endless feuds of freshmen and sophomores figured, she clapped her hands together according to her habit, and laughed aloud—a clear, musical, silvery peal. It fell on Eric's ear with a shock of surprise. He thought it strange that she could laugh like that when she could not speak. Wherein lay the defect that closed for her the gates of speech? Was it possible that it could be removed?

"Kilmeny," he said gravely after a moment's reflection, during which he had looked up at her as she sat with the ruddy sunlight falling through the lilac branches on her bare, silky head like a shower of red jewels, "do you mind if I ask you something about your inability to speak? Will it hurt you to talk of the matter with me?"

She shook her head.

"Oh, no," she wrote, "I do not mind at all. Of course I am sorry I cannot speak, but I am quite used to the thought and it never hurts me at all."

"Then, Kilmeny, tell me this. Do you know why it is that you are unable to speak, when all your other faculties are so perfect?"

"No, I do not know at all why I cannot speak. I asked mother once and she told me it was a judgment on her for a great sin she had committed, and she looked so strangely that I was frightened, and I never spoke of it to her or any one else again."

"Were you ever taken to a doctor to have your tongue and organs of speech examined?"

"No. I remember when I was a very little girl that Uncle Thomas wanted to take me to a doctor in Charlottetown and see if anything could be done for me, but mother would not let him. She said it would be no use. And I do not think Uncle Thomas thought it would be, either."

"You can laugh very naturally. Can you make any other sound?"

"Yes, sometimes. When I am pleased or frightened I have made little cries. But it is only when I am not thinking of it at all that I can do that. If I *try* to make a sound I cannot do it at all."

This seemed to Eric more mysterious than ever.

"Do you ever try to speak—to utter words?" he persisted.

"Oh, yes, very often. All the time I am saying the words in my head, just as I hear other people saying them, but I never can make my tongue say them. Do not look so sorry, my friend. I am very happy and I do not mind so very much not being able to speak—only sometimes when I have so many thoughts and it seems so slow to write them out, some of them get away from me. I must play to you again. You look too sober."

She laughed again, picked up her violin, and played a tinkling, roguish little melody as if she were trying to tease him, looking at Eric over her violin with luminous eyes that dared him to be merry.

Eric smiled; but the puzzled look returned to his face many times that evening. He walked home in a brown study. Kilmeny's case certainly seemed a strange one, and the more he thought of it the stranger it seemed.

"It strikes me as something very peculiar that she should be able to make sounds only when she is not thinking about it," he reflected. "I wish David Baker could examine her. But I suppose that is out of the question. That grim pair who have charge of her would never consent."

CHAPTER 9

THE STRAIGHT SIMPLICITY OF EVE

FOR THE next three weeks Eric Marshall seemed to himself to be living two lives, as distinct from each other as if he possessed a double personality. In one, he taught the Lindsay district school diligently and painstakingly; solved problems; argued on theology with Robert Williamson; called at the homes of his pupils and took tea in state with their parents; went to a rustic dance or two and played havoc, all unwittingly, with the hearts of the Lindsay maidens.

But this life was as a dream of workaday. He only *lived* in the other, which was spent in an old orchard, grassy and overgrown, where the minutes seemed to lag for sheer love of the spot and the June winds made wild harping in the old spruces.

Here every evening he met Kilmeny; in that old orchard they garnered hours of quiet happiness together; together they went wandering in the fair fields of old romance; together they read many books and talked of many things; and, when they were tired of all else, Kilmeny played to him and the old orchard echoed with her lovely, fantastic melodies.

At every meeting her beauty came home afresh to him with the old thrill of glad surprise. In the intervals of absence it seemed to him that she could not possibly be as beautiful as he remembered her; and then when they met she seemed even more so. He learned to watch for the undisguised light of welcome that always leaped into her eyes at the sound of his footsteps. She was nearly always there before him and she always showed that she was glad to see him with the frank delight of a child watching for a dear comrade.

She was never in the same mood twice. Now she was grave, now gay, now stately, now pensive. But she was always charming. Thrawn and twisted the old Gordon stock might be, but it had at least this one offshoot of perfect grace and symmetry. Her mind and heart, utterly unspoiled of the world, were as beautiful as her face. All the ugliness of existence had passed her by, shrined in her double solitude of upbringing and muteness.

She was naturally quick and clever. Delightful little flashes of wit and humour sparkled out occasionally. She could be whimsical—even charmingly capricious. Sometimes innocent mischief glimmered out in the unfathomable deeps of her blue eyes. Sarcasm, even, was not unknown to her. Now and then she punctured some harmless bubble of a young man's conceit or masculine superiority with a biting little line of daintily written script.

She assimilated the ideas in the books they read, speedily, eagerly, and thoroughly, always seizing on the best and truest, and rejecting the false and spurious and weak with an unfailing intuition at which Eric marvelled. Hers was the spear of Ithuriel, trying out the dross of everything and leaving only the pure gold.

In manner and outlook she was still a child. Yet now and

again she was as old as Eve. An expression would leap into her laughing face, a subtle meaning reveal itself in her smile, that held all the lore of womanhood and all the wisdom of the ages.

Her way of smiling enchanted him. The smile always began far down in her eyes and flowed outward to her face like a sparkling brook stealing out of shadow into sunshine.

He knew everything about her life. She told him her simple history freely. She often mentioned her uncle and aunt and seemed to regard them with deep affection. She rarely spoke of her mother. Eric came somehow to understand, less from what she said than from what she did not say, that Kilmeny, though she had loved her mother, had always been rather afraid of her. There had not been between them the natural beautiful confidence of mother and child.

Of Neil, she wrote frequently at first, and seemed very fond of him. Later she ceased to mention him. Perhaps—for she was marvellously quick to catch and interpret every fleeting change of expression in his voice and face—she discerned what Eric did not know himself—that his eyes clouded and grew moody at the mention of Neil's name.

Once she asked him naïvely,

"Are there many people like you out in the world?"

"Thousands of them," said Eric, laughing.

She looked gravely at him. Then she gave her head a quick decided little shake.

"I do not think so," she wrote. "I do not know much of the world, but I do not think there are many people like you in it."

One evening, when the far-away hills and fields were scarfed in gauzy purples, and the intervales were brimming with golden mists, Eric carried to the old orchard a little limp, worn volume that held a love story. It was the first thing of the kind he had ever read to her, for in the first novel he had lent her the love interest had been very slight and subordinate. This was a beautiful, passionate idyl exquisitely told.

He read it to her, lying in the grass at her feet; she listened with her hands clasped over her knee and her eyes cast down. It was not a long story; and when he had finished it he shut the book and looked up at her questioningly.

"Do you like it, Kilmeny?" he asked.

Very slowly she took her slate and wrote,

"Yes, I like it. But it hurt me, too. I did not know that a person could like anything that hurt her. I do not know why it hurt me. I felt as if I had lost something that I never had. That was a very silly feeling, was it not? But I did not understand the book very well, you see. It is about love and I do not know anything about love. Mother told me once that love is a curse, and that I must pray that it would never enter into my life. She said it very earnestly, and so I believed her. But your book teaches that it is a blessing. It says that it is the most splendid and wonderful thing in life. Which am I to believe?"

"Love—real love—is never a curse, Kilmeny," said Eric gravely. "There is a false love which is a curse. Perhaps your mother believed it was that which had entered her life and ruined it; and so she made the mistake. There is nothing in the world—or in heaven either, as I believe—so truly beautiful and wonderful and blessed as love."

"Have you ever loved?" asked Kilmeny, with the directness of phrasing necessitated by her mode of communication which was sometimes a little terrible. She asked the question simply and without any embarrassment. She knew of no reason why love might not be discussed with Eric as other matters—music and books and travel—might be.

"No," said Eric—honestly, as he thought, "but every one has an ideal of love whom he hopes to meet some day—'the ideal woman of a young man's dream.' I suppose I have mine, in some sealed, secret chamber of my heart."

"I suppose your ideal woman would be beautiful, like the woman in your book?"

"Oh, yes, I am sure I could never care for an ugly woman," said Eric, laughing a little as he sat up. "Our ideals are always beautiful, whether they so translate themselves into realities or not. But the sun is going down. Time does certainly fly in this enchanted orchard. I believe you bewitch the moments away, Kilmeny. Your namesake of the poem was a somewhat uncanny maid, if I recollect aright, and thought as little of seven years in elfland as ordinary folk do of half an hour on upper earth. Some day I shall waken from a supposed hour's lingering here and find myself an old man with white hair and ragged coat, as in that fairy tale we read the other night. Will you let me give you this book? I should never commit the sacrilege of reading it in any other place than this. It is an old book, Kilmeny. A new book, savouring of the shop and market-place, however beautiful it might be, would not do for you. This was one of my mother's books. She read it and loved it. See—the faded rose leaves she placed in it one day are there still. I'll write your name in it—that quaint, pretty name of yours which always sounds as if it had been specially invented for you— 'Kilmeny of the Orchard'—and the date of this perfect June day on which we read it together. Then when you look at it you will always remember me, and the white buds opening on that rosebush beside you, and the rush and murmur of the wind in the tops of those old spruces."

He held out the book to her, but, to his surprise, she shook her head, with a deeper flush on her face.

"Won't you take the book, Kilmeny? Why not?"

She took her pencil and wrote slowly, unlike her usual quick movement.

"Do not be offended with me. I shall not need anything to make me remember you because I can never forget you. But I would rather not take the book. I do not want to read it again. It is about love, and there is no use in my learning about love, even if it is all you say. Nobody will ever love me. I am too ugly."

"You! Ugly!" exclaimed Eric. He was on the point of going off into a peal of laughter at the idea when a glimpse of her half averted face sobered him. On it was a hurt, bitter look, such as he remembered seeing once before, when he had asked her if she would not like to see the world for herself.

"Kilmeny," he said in astonishment, "you don't really think yourself ugly, do you?"

She nodded, without looking at him, and then wrote,

"Oh, yes, I know that I am. I have known it for a long time. Mother told me that I was very ugly and that nobody would ever like to look at me. I am sorry. It hurts me much worse to know I am ugly than it does to know I cannot speak. I suppose you will think that is very foolish of me, but it is true. That was why I did not come back to the orchard for such a long time, even after I had got over my fright. I hated to think that *you* would think me ugly. And that is why I do not want to go out into the world and meet people. They would look at me as the egg peddler did one day when I went out with

Aunt Janet to his wagon the spring after mother died. He stared at me so. I knew it was because he thought me so ugly, and I have always hidden when he came ever since."

Eric's lips twitched. In spite of his pity for the real suffering displayed in her eyes, he could not help feeling amused over the absurd idea of this beautiful girl believing herself in all seriousness to be ugly.

"But, Kilmeny, do you think yourself ugly when you look in a mirror?" he asked smiling.

"I have never looked in a mirror," she wrote. "I never knew there was such a thing until after mother died, and I read about it in a book. Then I asked Aunt Janet and she said mother had broken all the looking glasses in the house when I was a baby. But I have seen my face reflected in the spoons, and in a little silver sugar bowl Aunt Janet has. And it *is* ugly—very ugly."

Eric's face went down into the grass. For his life he could not help laughing; and for his life he would not let Kilmeny see him laughing. A certain little whimsical wish took possession of him and he did not hasten to tell her the truth, as had been his first impulse. Instead, when he dared to look up he said slowly,

"I don't think you are ugly, Kilmeny."

"Oh, but I am sure you must," she wrote protestingly. "Even Neil does. He tells me I am kind and nice, but one day I asked him if he thought me very ugly, and he looked away and would not speak, so I knew what he thought about it, too. Do not let us speak of this again. It makes me feel sorry and spoils everything. I forget it at other times. Let me play you some good-bye music, and do not feel vexed because I would not take your book. It would only make me unhappy to read it."

"I am not vexed," said Eric, "and I think you will take it some day yet—after I have shown you something I want you to see. Never mind about your looks, Kilmeny. Beauty isn't everything."

"Oh, it is a great deal," she wrote naïvely. "But you do like me, even though I am so ugly, don't you? You like me because of my beautiful music, don't you?"

"I like you very much, Kilmeny," answered Eric, laughing a little; but there was in his voice a tender note of which he was unconscious. Kilmeny was aware of it, however, and she picked up her violin with a pleased smile.

He left her playing there, and all the way through the dim resinous spruce wood her music followed him like an invisible guardian spirit.

"Kilmeny the Beautiful!" he murmured, "and yet, good heavens, the child thinks she is ugly—she with a face more lovely than ever an artist dreamed of! A girl of eighteen who has never looked in a mirror! I wonder if there is another such in any civilized country in the world. What could have possessed her mother to tell her such a falsehood? I wonder if Margaret Gordon could have been quite sane. It is strange that Neil has never told her the truth. Perhaps he doesn't want her to find out."

Eric had met Neil Gordon a few evenings before this, at a country dance where Neil had played the violin for the dancers. Influenced by curiosity he had sought the lad's acquaintance. Neil was friendly and talkative at first; but at the first hint concerning the Gordons which Eric threw out skilfully his face and manner changed. He looked secretive and suspicious, almost sinister. A sullen look crept into his big black eyes and he drew his bow across the violin strings with a discordant screech, as if to terminate the conversation. Plainly nothing was to be found out from him about Kilmeny and her grim guardians.

CHAPTER 10

A TROUBLING OF THE WATERS

ONE EVENING in late June Mrs. Williamson was sitting by her kitchen window. Her knitting lay unheeded in her lap, and Timothy, though he nestled ingratiatingly against her foot as he lay on the rug and purred his loudest, was unregarded. She rested her face on her hand and looked out of the window, across the distant harbour, with troubled eyes.

"I guess I must speak," she thought wistfully. "I hate to do it. I always did hate meddling. My mother always used to say that ninety-nine times out of a hundred the last state of a meddler and them she meddled with was worse than the first. But I guess it's my duty. I was Margaret's friend, and it is my duty to protect her child any way I can. If the Master does go back across there to meet her I must tell him what I think about it."

Overhead in his room, Eric was walking about whistling. Presently he came downstairs, thinking of the orchard, and the girl who would be waiting for him there.

As he crossed the little front entry he heard Mrs. Williamson's voice calling to him.

"Mr. Marshall, will you please come here a moment?"

He went out to the kitchen. Mrs. Williamson looked at him deprecatingly. There was a flush on her faded cheek and her voice trembled.

"Mr. Marshall, I want to ask you a question. Perhaps you will think it isn't any of my business. But it isn't because I want to meddle. No, no. It is only because I think I ought to speak. I have thought it over for a long time, and it seems to me that I ought to speak. I hope you won't be angry, but even if you are I must say what I have to say. Are you going back to the old Connors orchard to meet Kilmeny Gordon?"

For a moment an angry flush burned in Eric's face. It was more Mrs. Williamson's tone than her words which startled and annoyed him.

"Yes, I am, Mrs. Williamson," he said coldly. "What of it?"

"Then, sir," said Mrs. Williamson with more firmness, "I have got to tell you that I don't think you are doing right. I have been suspecting all along that that was where you went every evening, but I haven't said a word to any one about it. Even my husband doesn't know. But tell me this, Master. Do Kilmeny's uncle and aunt know that you are meeting her there?"

"Why," said Eric, in some confusion, "I—I do not know whether they do or not. But Mrs. Williamson, surely you do not suspect me of meaning any harm or wrong to Kilmeny Gordon?"

"No, I don't, Master. I might think it of some men, but never of you. I don't for a minute think that you would do her or any woman any wilful wrong. But you may do her great harm for all that. I want you to stop and think about it. I guess you haven't thought. Kilmeny can't know anything about the world or about men, and she may get to thinking too much of you. That might break her heart, because you couldn't ever marry a dumb girl like her. So I don't think you ought to be meeting her so often in this fashion. It isn't right, Master. Don't go to the orchard again."

Without a word Eric turned away, and went upstairs to his room. Mrs. Williamson picked up her knitting with a sigh.

"That's done, Timothy, and I'm real thankful," she said. "I guess there'll be no need of saying anything more. Mr. Marshall is a fine young man, only a little thoughtless. Now that he's got his eyes opened I'm sure he'll do what is right. I don't want Margaret's child made unhappy."

Her husband came to the kitchen door and sat down on the steps to enjoy his evening smoke, talking between whiffs to his wife of Elder Tracy's church row, and Mary Alice Martin's beau, the price Jake Crosby was giving for eggs, the quantity of hay yielded by the hill meadow, the trouble he was having with old Molly's calf, and the respective merits of Plymouth Rock and Brahma roosters. Mrs. Williamson answered at random, and heard not one word in ten.

"What's got the Master, Mother?" inquired old Robert, presently. "I hear him striding up and down in his room 'sif he was caged. Sure you didn't lock him in by mistake?"

"Maybe he's worried over the way Seth Tracy's acting in school," suggested Mrs. Williamson, who did not choose that her gossipy husband should suspect the truth about Eric and Kilmeny Gordon.

"Shucks, he needn't worry a morsel over that. Seth'll quiet down as soon as he finds he can't run the Master. He's a rare good teacher—better'n Mr. West was even, and that's saying something. The trustees are hoping he'll stay for another term. They're going to ask him at the school meeting tomorrow, and offer him a raise of supplement."

Upstairs, in his little room under the eaves, Eric Marshall was in the grip of the most intense and overwhelming emotion he had ever experienced.

Up and down, to and fro, he walked, with set lips and clenched hands. When he was wearied out he flung himself on a chair by the window and wrestled with the flood of feeling.

Mrs. Williamson's words had torn away the delusive veil with which he had bound his eyes. He was face to face with the knowledge that he loved Kilmeny Gordon with the love that comes but once, and is for all time. He wondered how he could have been so long blind to it. He knew that he must have loved her ever since their first meeting that May evening in the old orchard.

And he knew that he must choose between two alternatives— either he must never go to the orchard again, or he must go as an avowed lover to woo him a wife.

Worldly prudence, his inheritance from a long line of thrifty, cool-headed ancestors, was strong in Eric, and he did not yield easily or speedily to the dictates of his passion. All night he struggled against the new emotions that threatened to sweep away the "common sense" which David Baker had bade him take with him when he went a-wooing. Would not a marriage with Kilmeny Gordon be an unwise thing from any standpoint?

Then something stronger and greater and more vital than wisdom or unwisdom rose up in him and mastered him. Kilmeny, beautiful, dumb Kilmeny was, as he had once involuntarily thought, "the one maid" for him. Nothing should part them. The mere idea of never seeing her again was so unbearable that he laughed at himself for having counted it a possible alternative.

"If I can win Kilmeny's love I shall ask her to be my wife," he said, looking out of the window to the dark, southwestern hill beyond which lay his orchard.

The velvet sky over it was still starry; but the water of the harbour was beginning to grow silvery in the reflection of the dawn that was breaking in the east.

"Her misfortune will only make her dearer to me. I cannot realize that a month ago I did not know her. It seems to me that she has been a part of my life for ever. I wonder if she was grieved that I did not go to the orchard last night—if she waited for me. I wonder if she cares for me. If she does, she does not know it herself yet. It will be my sweet task to teach her what love means, and no man has ever had a lovelier, purer, pupil."

At the annual school meeting, the next afternoon, the trustees asked Eric to take the Lindsay school for the following year. He consented unhesitatingly.

That evening he went to Mrs. Williamson, as she washed her tea dishes in the kitchen.

"Mrs. Williamson, I am going back to the old Connors orchard to see Kilmeny again tonight."

She looked at him reproachfully.

"Well, Master, I have no more to say. I suppose it wouldn't be of any use if I had. But you know what I think of it."

"I intend to marry Kilmeny Gordon if I can win her."

An expression of amazement came into the good woman's face. She looked scrutinizingly at the firm mouth and steady gray eyes for a moment. Then she said in a troubled voice,

"Do you think that is wise, Master? I suppose Kilmeny is pretty; the egg peddler told me she was; and no doubt she is a good, nice girl. But she wouldn't be a suitable wife for you— a girl that can't speak."

"That doesn't make any difference to me."

"But what will your people say?"

"I have no 'people' except my father. When he sees Kilmeny he will understand. She is all the world to me, Mrs. Williamson."

"As long as you believe that there is nothing more to be said," was the quiet answer, "I'd be a little bit afraid if I was you, though. But young people never think of those things."

"My only fear is that she won't care for me," said Eric soberly.

Mrs. Williamson surveyed the handsome, broad-shouldered young man shrewdly.

"I don't think there are many women would say you 'no,' Master. I wish you well in your wooing, though I can't help thinking you're doing a daft-like thing. I hope you won't have any trouble with Thomas and Janet. They are so different from other folks there is no knowing. But take my advice, Master, and go and see them about it right off. Don't go on meeting Kilmeny unbeknownst to them."

"I shall certainly take your advice," said Eric, gravely. "I should have gone to them before. It was merely thoughtlessness on my part. Possibly they do know already. Kilmeny may have told them."

Mrs. Williamson shook her head decidedly.

"No, no, Master, she hasn't. They'd never have let her go on meeting you there if they had known. I know them too well to think of that for a moment. Go you straight to them and say to them just what you have said to me. That is your best plan, Master. And take care of Neil. People say he has a notion of Kilmeny himself. He'll do you a bad turn if he can, I've no doubt. Them foreigners can't be trusted—and he's just as much a foreigner as his parents before him—though he *has* been brought up on oatmeal and the shorter catechism, as the old saying has it. I feel that somehow—I always feel it when I look at him singing in the choir."

"Oh, I am not afraid of Neil," said Eric carelessly. "He couldn't help loving Kilmeny—nobody could."

"I suppose every young man thinks that about his girl—if he's the right sort of young man," said Mrs. Williamson with a little sigh.

She watched Eric out of sight anxiously.

"I hope it'll all come out right," she thought. "I hope he ain't making an awful mistake—but—I'm afraid. Kilmeny must be very pretty to have bewitched him so. Well, I suppose there is no use in my worrying over it. But I do wish he had never gone back to that old orchard and seen her."

CHAPTER 11

A LOVER AND HIS LASS

KILMENY WAS in the orchard when Eric reached it, and he lingered for a moment in the shadow of the spruce wood to gloat over her beauty.

The orchard had lately overflowed in waves of old-fashioned caraway, and she was standing in the midst of its sea of bloom, with the lace-like blossoms swaying around her in the wind. She wore the simple dress of pale blue print in which he had first seen her; silk attire could not better have become her loveliness. She had woven herself a chaplet of half open white rosebuds and placed it on her dark hair, where the delicate blossoms seemed less wonderful than her face.

When Eric stepped through the gap she ran to meet him with outstretched hands, smiling. He took her hands and looked into her eyes with an expression before which hers for the first time faltered. She looked down, and a warm blush stained the ivory curves of her cheek and throat. His heart bounded, for in that blush he recognized the banner of love's vanguard.

"Are you glad to see me, Kilmeny?" he asked, in a low significant tone.

She nodded, and wrote in a somewhat embarrassed fashion, "Yes. Why do you ask? You know I am always glad to see you. I was afraid you would not come. You did not come last night and I was so sorry. Nothing in the orchard seemed nice any longer. I couldn't even play. I tried to, and my violin only cried. I waited until it was dark and then I went home."

"I am sorry you were disappointed, Kilmeny. I couldn't come last night. Some day I shall tell you why. I stayed home to learn a new lesson. I am sorry you missed me—no, I am glad. Can you understand how a person may be glad and sorry for the same thing?"

She nodded again, with a return of her usual sweet composure.

"Yes, I could not have understood once, but I can now. Did you learn your new lesson?"

"Yes, very thoroughly. It was a delightful lesson when I once understood it. I must try to teach it to you some day. Come over to the old bench, Kilmeny. There is something I want to say to you. But first, will you give me a rose?"

She ran to the bush, and, after careful deliberation, selected a perfect half-open bud and brought it to him—a white bud with a faint, sunrise flush about its golden heart.

"Thank you. It is as beautiful as—as a woman I know," Eric said.

A wistful look came into her face at his words, and she walked with a drooping head across the orchard to the bench.

"Kilmeny," he said, seriously, "I am going to ask you to do something for me. I want you to take me home with you and introduce me to your uncle and aunt."

She lifted her head and stared at him incredulously, as if he had asked her to do something wildly impossible. Understanding from his grave face that he meant what he said, a look of dismay dawned in her eyes. She shook her head almost violently and seemed to be making a passionate, instinctive effort to speak. Then she caught up her pencil and wrote with feverish haste:

"I cannot do that. Do not ask me to. You do not understand.

They would be very angry. They do not want to see any one coming to the house. And they would never let me come here again. Oh, you do not mean it?"

He pitied her for the pain and bewilderment in her eyes; but he took her slender hands in his and said firmly,

"Yes, Kilmeny, I do mean it. It is not quite right for us to be meeting each other here as we have been doing, without the knowledge and consent of your friends. You cannot now understand this, but—believe me—it is so."

She looked questioningly, pityingly into his eyes. What she read there seemed to convince her, for she turned very pale and an expression of hopelessness came into her face. Releasing her hands, she wrote slowly,

"If you say it is wrong I must believe it. I did not know anything so pleasant could be wrong. But if it is wrong we must not meet here any more. Mother told me I must never do anything that was wrong. But I did not know this was wrong."

"It was not wrong for you, Kilmeny. But it was a little wrong for me, because I knew better—or rather, should have known better. I didn't stop to think, as the children say. Some day you will understand fully. Now, you will take me to your uncle and aunt, and after I have said to them what I want to say it will be all right for us to meet here or anywhere."

She shook her head.

"No," she wrote, "Uncle Thomas and Aunt Janet will tell you to go away and never come back. And they will never let me come here any more. Since it is not right to meet you I will not come, but it is no use to think of going to them. I did not tell them about you because I knew that they would forbid me to see you, but I am sorry, since it is so wrong."

"You must take me to them," said Eric firmly. "I am quite sure that things will not be as you fear when they hear what I have to say."

Uncomforted, she wrote forlornly,

"I must do it, since you insist, but I am sure it will be no use. I cannot take you tonight because they are away. They went to the store at Radnor. But I will take you tomorrow night; and after that I shall not see you any more."

Two great tears brimmed over in her big blue eyes and splashed down on her slate. Her lips quivered like a hurt child's.

Eric put his arm impulsively about her and drew her head down upon his shoulder. As she cried there, softly, miserably, he pressed his lips to the silky black hair with its coronal of rosebuds. He did not see two burning eyes which were looking at him over the old fence behind him with hatred and mad passion blazing in their depths. Neil Gordon was crouched there, with clenched hands and heaving breast, watching them.

"Kilmeny, dear, don't cry," said Eric tenderly. "You shall see me again. I promise you that, whatever happens. I do not think your uncle and aunt will be as unreasonable as you fear, but even if they are they shall not prevent me from meeting you somehow."

Kilmeny lifted her head, and wiped the tears from her eyes.

"You do not know what they are like," she wrote. "They will lock me into my room. That is the way they always punished me when I was a little girl. And once, not so very long ago, when I was a big girl, they did it."

"If they do I'll get you out somehow," said Eric, laughing a little.

She allowed herself to smile, but it was a rather forlorn little effort. She did not cry any more, but her spirits did not come back to her. Eric talked gaily, but she only listened in a pensive, absent way, as if she scarcely heard him. When he asked her to play she shook her head.

"I cannot think any music tonight," she wrote. "I must go home, for my head aches and I feel very stupid."

"Very well, Kilmeny. Now, don't worry, little girl. It will all come out all right."

Evidently she did not share his confidence, for her head drooped again as they walked together across the orchard. At the entrance of the wild cherry lane she paused and looked at him half reproachfully, her eyes filling again. She seemed to be bidding him a mute farewell. With an impulse of tenderness which he could not control, Eric put his arm about her and kissed her red, trembling mouth. She started back with a little cry. A burning colour swept over her face, and the next moment she fled swiftly up the darkening lane.

The sweetness of that involuntary kiss clung to Eric's lips as he went homeward, half-intoxicating him. He knew that it had opened the gates of womanhood to Kilmeny. Never again, he felt, would her eyes meet his with their old unclouded frankness.

When next he looked into them he knew that he should see there the consciousness of his kiss. Behind her in the orchard that night Kilmeny had left her childhood.

———————— CHAPTER 12 ————————

A PRISONER OF LOVE

WHEN ERIC betook himself to the orchard the next evening he had to admit that he felt rather nervous. He did not know how the Gordons would receive him and certainly the reports he had heard of them were not encouraging, to say the least of it. Even Mrs. Williamson, when he had told her where he was going, seemed to look upon him as one bent on bearding a lion in his den.

"I do hope they won't be very uncivil to you, Master," was the best she could say.

He expected Kilmeny to be in the orchard before him, for he had been delayed by a call from one of the trustees; but she was nowhere to be seen. He walked across it to the wild cherry lane; but at its entrance he stopped short in sudden dismay.

Neil Gordon had stepped from behind the trees and stood confronting him, with blazing eyes, and lips which writhed in emotion so great that at first it prevented him from speaking.

With a thrill of dismay Eric instantly understood what must have taken place. Neil had discovered that he and Kilmeny had been meeting in the orchard, and beyond doubt had carried the tale to Janet and Thomas Gordon. He realized how unfortunate it was that this should have happened before he had had time to make his own explanation. It would probably prejudice Kilmeny's guardians still further against him. At this point in his thoughts Neil's pent up passion suddenly found vent in a burst of wild words.

"So you've come to meet her again. But she isn't here— you'll never see her again! I hate you—I hate you—I hate you!"

His voice rose to a shrill scream. He took a furious step nearer Eric as if he would attack him. Eric looked steadily in his eyes with a calm defiance, before which his wild passion broke like foam on a rock.

"So you have been making trouble for Kilmeny, Neil, have you?" said Eric contemptuously. "I suppose you have been playing the spy. And I suppose that you have told her uncle and aunt that she has been meeting me here. Well, you have saved me the trouble of doing it, that is all. I was going to tell them myself, tonight. I don't know what your motive in doing this has been. Was it jealousy of me? Or have you done it out of malice to Kilmeny?"

His contempt cowed Neil more effectually than any display of anger could have done.

"Never you mind why I did it," he muttered sullenly. "What I did or why I did it is no business of yours. And you have no business to come sneaking around here either. Kilmeny won't meet you here again."

"She will meet me in her own home then," said Eric sternly. "Neil, in behaving as you have done you have shown yourself to be a very foolish, undisciplined boy. I am going straightway to Kilmeny's uncle and aunt to explain everything."

Neil sprang forward in his path.

"No—no—go away," he implored wildly. "Oh, sir—oh, Mr. Marshall, please go away. I'll do anything for you if you will. I love Kilmeny. I've loved her all my life. I'd give my life for her. I can't have you coming here to steal her from me. If you do—I'll kill you! I wanted to kill you last night when I saw you kiss her. Oh, yes, I saw you. I was watching—spying, if you like. I don't care what you call it. I had followed her—I suspected something. She was so different—so changed. She never would wear the flowers I picked for her any more. She seemed to forget I was there. I knew something had come between us. And it was you, curse you! Oh, I'll make you sorry for it."

He was working himself up into a fury again—the untamed fury of the Italian peasant thwarted in his heart's desire. It overrode all the restraint of his training and environment. Eric, amid all his anger and annoyance, felt a thrill of pity for him. Neil Gordon was only a boy still; and he was miserable and beside himself.

"Neil, listen to me," he said quietly. "You are talking very foolishly. It is not for you to say who shall or shall not be Kilmeny's friend. Now, you may just as well control yourself and go home like a decent fellow. I am not at all frightened by your threats, and I shall know how to deal with you if you persist in interfering with me or persecuting Kilmeny. I am not the sort of person to put up with that, my lad."

The restrained power in his tone and look cowed Neil. The latter turned sullenly away, with another muttered curse, and plunged into the shadow of the firs.

Eric, not a little ruffled under all his external composure by this most unexpected and unpleasant encounter, pursued his way along the lane which wound on by the belt of woodland in twist and curve to the Gordon homestead. His heart beat as he thought of Kilmeny. What might she not be suffering? Doubtless Neil had given a very exaggerated and distorted account of what he had seen, and probably her dour relations were very angry with her, poor child. Anxious to avert their wrath as soon as might be, he hurried on, almost forgetting his meeting with Neil. The threats of the latter did not trouble him at all. He thought the angry outburst of a jealous boy mattered but little. What did matter was that Kilmeny was in trouble which his heedlessness had brought upon her.

Presently he found himself before the Gordon house. It was an old building with sharp eaves and dormer windows, its shingles stained a dark gray by long exposure to wind and weather. Faded green shutters hung on the windows of the lower story. Behind it grew a thick wood of spruces. The little yard in front of it was grassy and prim and flowerless; but over the low front door a luxuriant early-flowering rose vine clambered, in a riot of blood-red blossom which contrasted strangely with the general bareness of its surroundings. It seemed to fling itself over the grim old house as if intent on bombarding it with an alien life and joyousness.

Eric knocked at the door, wondering if it might be possible that Kilmeny should come to it. But a moment later it was opened by an elderly woman—a woman of rigid lines from the hem of her lank, dark print dress to the crown of her head, covered with black hair which, despite its few gray threads, was still thick and luxuriant. She had a long, pale face somewhat worn and wrinkled, but possessing a certain harsh comeliness of feature which neither age nor wrinkles had quite destroyed; and her deep-set, light gray eyes were not devoid of suggested kindliness, although they now surveyed Eric with an unconcealed hostility. Her figure, in its merciless dress, was very angular; yet there was about her a dignity of carriage and manner which Eric liked. In any case, he preferred her unsmiling dourness to vulgar garrulity.

He lifted his hat.

"Have I the honour of speaking to Miss Gordon?" he asked.

"I am Janet Gordon," said the woman stiffly.

"Then I wish to talk with you and with your brother."

"Come in."

She stepped aside and motioned him to a low brown door opening on the right.

"Go in and sit down. I'll call Thomas," she said coldly, as she walked out through the hall.

Eric walked into the parlour and sat down as bidden. He found himself in the most old-fashioned room he had ever seen. The solidly made chairs and tables, of some wood grown dark and polished with age, made even Mrs. Williamson's "parlour set" of horsehair seem extravagantly modern by contrast. The painted floor was covered with round braided rugs. On the centre table was a lamp, a Bible and some theological volumes contemporary with the square-runged furniture. The walls, wainscoted half way up in wood and covered for the rest with a dark, diamond-patterned paper, were hung with faded engravings, mostly of clerical-looking, bewigged personages in gowns and bands.

But over the high, undecorated black mantel-piece, in a ruddy glow of sunset light striking through the window, hung one which caught and held Eric's attention to the exclusion of everything else. It was the enlarged "crayon" photograph of a young girl, and, in spite of the crudity of execution, it was easily the centre of interest in the room.

Eric at once guessed that this must be the picture of Margaret Gordon, for, although quite unlike Kilmeny's sensitive, spirited face in general, there was a subtle, unmistakable resemblance about brow and chin.

The pictured face was a very handsome one, suggestive of velvety dark eyes and vivid colouring; but it was its expression rather than its beauty which fascinated Eric. Never had he seen a countenance indicative of more intense and stubborn will power. Margaret Gordon was dead and buried; the picture was a cheap and inartistic production in an impossible frame of gilt and plush; yet the vitality in that face dominated its surroundings still. What then must have been the power of such a personality in life?

Eric realized that this woman could and would have done whatsoever she willed, unflinchingly and unrelentingly. She could stamp her desire on everything and everybody about her, moulding them to her wish and will, in their own despite and in defiance of all the resistance they might make. Many things in Kilmeny's upbringing and temperament became clear to him.

"If that woman had told me I was ugly I should have believed her," he thought. "Ay, even though I had a mirror to contradict her. I should never have dreamed of disputing or questioning anything she might have said. The strange power in her face is almost uncanny, peering out as it does from a mask of beauty and youthful curves. Pride and stubbornness are its salient characteristics. Well, Kilmeny does not at all resemble her mother in expression and only very slightly in feature."

His reflections were interrupted by the entrance of Thomas and Janet Gordon. The latter had evidently been called from his work. He nodded without speaking, and the two sat gravely down before Eric.

"I have come to see you with regard to your niece, Mr. Gordon," he said abruptly, realizing that there would be small use in beating about the bush with this grim pair. "I met your— I met Neil Gordon in the Connors orchard, and I found that he has told you that I have been meeting Kilmeny there."

He paused. Thomas Gordon nodded again; but he did not speak, and he did not remove his steady, piercing eyes from the young man's flushed countenance. Janet still sat in a sort of expectant immovability.

"I fear that you have formed an unfavourable opinion of me on this account, Mr. Gordon," Eric went on. "But I hardly think I deserve it. I can explain the matter if you will allow me. I met your niece accidentally in the orchard three weeks ago and heard her play. I thought her music very wonderful and I fell into the habit of coming to the orchard in the evenings to hear it. I had no thought of harming her in any way, Mr.

Gordon. I thought of her as a mere child, and a child who was doubly sacred because of her affliction. But recently I— I—it occurred to me that I was not behaving quite honourably in encouraging her to meet me thus. Yesterday evening I asked her to bring me here and introduce me to you and her aunt. We would have come then if you had been at home. As you were not we arranged to come tonight."

"Yes, she told us so," said Thomas Gordon slowly, speaking in a strong, vibrant voice. "We did not believe her. But your story agrees with hers, and I begin to think that we were too harsh with her. But Neil's tale had an ugly sound and made us very angry. We have no reason to be over-trustful in the case of strange men, Master. Perhaps you meant no harm. I am willing to believe that, sir. But there must be no more of it."

"I hope you will not refuse me the privilege of seeing your niece, Mr. Gordon," said Eric eagerly. "I ask you to allow me to visit her here. But I do not ask you to receive me as a friend on my own recommendations only. I will give you references—men of standing in Charlottetown and Queenslea. If you refer to them—"

"I don't need to do that," said Thomas Gordon, quietly. "I know more of you than you think, Master. I know your father well by reputation and I have seen him. I know you are a rich man's son, whatever your whim in teaching a country school may be. Since you have kept your own counsel about your affairs I supposed you didn't want your true position generally known, and so I have held my tongue about you. I know no ill of you, Master, and I think none, now that I believe you were not beguiling Kilmeny to meet you unknown to her friends of set purpose. But all this doesn't make you a suitable friend for her, sir—it makes you all the more unsuitable. The less she sees of you the better."

Eric almost started to his feet in an indignant protest; but he swiftly remembered that his only hope of winning Kilmeny lay in bringing Thomas Gordon to another way of thinking. He had got on better than he had expected so far; he must not now jeopardize what he had gained by rashness or impatience.

"Why do you think so, Mr. Gordon?" he asked, regaining his self-control with an effort.

"Well, plain speaking is best, Master. If you were to come here and see Kilmeny often she'd most likely come to think too much of you. I mistrust there's some mischief done in that direction already. Then when you went away she might break her heart—for she is one of those who feel things deeply. She has been happy enough. I know folks condemn us for the way she has been brought up, but they don't know everything. It was the best way for her, all things considered. And we don't want her made unhappy, Master."

"But I love your niece and I want to marry her if I can win her love," said Eric steadily.

He surprised them out of their self possession at last. Both started, and looked at him as if they could not believe the evidence of their ears.

"Marry her! Marry Kilmeny!" exclaimed Thomas Gordon incredulously. "You can't mean it, sir. Why, she is dumb—Kilmeny is dumb."

"That makes no difference in my love for her, although I deeply regret it for her own sake," answered Eric. "I can only repeat what I have already said, Mr. Gordon. I want Kilmeny for my wife."

The older man leaned forward and looked at the floor in a troubled fashion, drawing his bushy eyebrows down and tapping the calloused tips of his fingers together uneasily. He was evidently puzzled by this unexpected turn of the conversation, and in grave doubt what to say.

"What would your father say to all this, Master?" he queried at last.

"I have often heard my father say that a man must marry to please himself," said Eric, with a smile. "If he felt tempted to go back on that opinion I think the sight of Kilmeny would convert him. But, after all, it is what I say that matters in this case, isn't it, Mr. Gordon? I am well educated and not afraid of work. I can make a home for Kilmeny in a few years even if I have to depend entirely on my own resources. Only give me the chance to win her—that is all I ask."

"I don't think it would do, Master," said Thomas Gordon, shaking his head. "Of course, I dare say you—you"—he tried to say "love," but Scotch reserve balked stubbornly at the terrible word—"you think you like Kilmeny now, but you are only a lad—and lads' fancies change."

"Mine will not," Eric broke in vehemently. "It is not a fancy, Mr. Gordon. It is the love that comes once in a lifetime and once only. I may be but a lad, but I know that Kilmeny is the one woman in the world for me. There can never be any other. Oh, I'm not speaking rashly or inconsiderately. I have weighed the matter well and looked at it from every aspect. And it all comes to this—I love Kilmeny and I want what any decent man who loves a woman truly has the right to have— the chance to win her love in return."

"Well!" Thomas Gordon drew a long breath that was almost a sigh. "Maybe—if you feel like that, Master—I don't know— there are some things it isn't right to cross. Perhaps we oughtn't— Janet, woman, what shall we say to him?"

Janet Gordon had hitherto spoken no word. She had sat rigidly upright on one of the old chairs under Margaret Gordon's insistent picture, with her knotted, toil-worn hands grasping the carved arms tightly, and her eyes fastened on Eric's face. At first their expression had been guarded and hostile, but as the conversation proceeded they lost this gradually and became almost kindly. Now, when her brother appealed to her, she leaned forward and said eagerly,

"Do you know that there is a stain on Kilmeny's birth, Master?"

"I know that her mother was the innocent victim of a very sad mistake, Miss Gordon. I admit no real stain where there was no conscious wrong doing. Though, for that matter, even if there were, it would be no fault of Kilmeny's and would make no difference to me as far as she is concerned."

A sudden change swept over Janet Gordon's face, quite marvellous in the transformation it wrought. Her grim mouth softened and a flood of repressed tenderness glorified her cold gray eyes.

"Well, then," she said almost triumphantly, "since neither that nor her dumbness seems to be any drawback in your eyes I don't see why you should not have the chance you want. Perhaps your world will say she is not good enough for you, but she is—she is"—this half defiantly. "She is a sweet and innocent and true-hearted lassie. She is bright and clever and she is not ill looking. Thomas, I say let the young man have his will."

Thomas Gordon stood up, as if he considered the responsibility off his shoulders and the interview at an end.

"Very well, Janet, woman, since you think it is wise. And may God deal with him as he deals with her. Good evening, Master. I'll see you again, and you are free to come and go as suits you. But I must go to my work now. I left my horses standing in the field."

"I will go up and send Kilmeny down," said Janet quietly.

She lighted the lamp on the table and left the room. A few minutes later Kilmeny came down. Eric rose and went to meet her eagerly, but she only put out her right hand with a pretty dignity and, while she looked into his face, she did not look into his eyes.

"You see I was right after all, Kilmeny," he said, smiling. "Your uncle and aunt haven't driven me away. On the contrary they have been very kind to me, and they say I may see you whenever and wherever I like."

She smiled, and went over to the table to write on her slate.

"But they were very angry last night, and said dreadful things to me. I felt very frightened and unhappy. They seemed to think I had done something terribly wrong. Uncle Thomas said he would never trust me out of his sight again. I could hardly believe it when Aunt Janet came up and told me you were here and that I might come down. She looked at me very strangely as she spoke, but I could see that all the anger had gone out of her face. She seemed pleased and yet sad. But I am glad they have forgiven us."

She did not tell him how glad she was, and how unhappy she had been over the thought that she was never to see him again. Yesterday she would have told him all frankly and fully; but for her yesterday was a lifetime away—a lifetime in which she had come into her heritage of womanly dignity and reserve. The kiss which Eric had left on her lips, the words her uncle and aunt had said to her, the tears she had shed for the first time on a sleepless pillow—all had conspired to reveal her to herself. She did not yet dream that she loved Eric Marshall, or that he loved her. But she was no longer the child to be made a dear comrade of. She was, though quite unconsciously, the woman to be wooed and won, exacting, with sweet, innate pride, her dues of allegiance.

CHAPTER 13

A SWEETER WOMAN NE'ER DREW BREATH

THENCEFORWARD Eric Marshall was a constant visitor at the Gordon homestead. He soon became a favourite with Thomas and Janet, especially the latter. He liked them both, discovering under all their outward peculiarities sterling worth and fineness of character. Thomas Gordon was surprisingly well read and could floor Eric any time in argument, once he became sufficiently warmed up to attain to fluency of words. Eric hardly recognized him the first time he saw him thus animated. His bent form straightened, his sunken eyes flashed, his face flushed, his voice rang like a trumpet, and he poured out a flood of eloquence which swept Eric's smart, up-to-date arguments away like straws in the rush of a mountain torrent. Eric enjoyed his own defeat enormously, but Thomas Gordon was ashamed of being thus drawn out of himself, and for a week afterwards confined his remarks to "Yes" and "No," or, at the outside, to a brief statement that a change in the weather was brewing.

Janet never talked on matters of church and state; such she plainly considered to be far beyond a woman's province. But she listened with lurking interest in her eyes while Thomas and Eric pelted each other with facts and statistics and opinions, and on the rare occasions when Eric scored a point she permitted herself a sly little smile at her brother's expense.

Of Neil, Eric saw but little. The Italian boy avoided him, or if they chanced to meet passed him by with sullen, downcast eyes. Eric did not trouble himself greatly about Neil; but Thomas Gordon, understanding the motive which had led Neil to betray his discovery of the orchard trysts, bluntly told Kilmeny that she must not make such an equal of Neil as she had done.

"You have been too kind to the lad, lassie, and he's got presumptuous. He must be taught his place. I mistrust we have all made more of him than we should."

But most of the idyllic hours of Eric's wooing were spent in the old orchard; the garden end of it was now a wilderness of roses—roses red as the heart of a sunset, roses pink as the early flush of dawn, roses white as the snows on mountain peaks, roses full blown, and roses in buds that were sweeter than anything on earth except Kilmeny's face. Their petals fell in silken heaps along the old paths or clung to the lush grasses among which Eric lay and dreamed, while Kilmeny played to him on her violin.

Eric promised himself that when she was his wife her wonderful gift for music should be cultivated to the utmost. Her powers of expression seemed to deepen and develop every day, growing as her soul grew, taking on new colour and richness from her ripening heart.

To Eric, the days were all pages in an inspired idyl. He had never dreamed that love could be so mighty or the world so beautiful. He wondered if the universe were big enough to hold his joy or eternity long enough to live it out. His whole existence was, for the time being, bounded by that orchard where he wooed his sweetheart. All other ambitions and plans and hopes were set aside in the pursuit of this one aim, the attainment of which would enhance all others a thousand fold, the loss of which would rob all others of their reason for existence. His own world seemed very far away and the things of that world forgotten.

His father, on hearing that he had taken the Lindsay school for a year, had written him a testy, amazed letter, asking him if he were demented.

"Or is there a girl in the case?" he wrote. "There must be, to tie you down to a place like Lindsay for a year. Take care, master Eric; you've been too sensible all your life. A man is bound to make a fool of himself at least once, and when you didn't get through with that in your teens it may be attacking you now."

David also wrote, expostulating more gravely; but he did not express the suspicions Eric knew he must entertain.

"Good old David! He is quaking with fear that I am up to something he can't approve of, but he won't say a word by way of attempting to force my confidence."

It could not long remain a secret in Lindsay that "the Master" was going to the Gordon place on courting thoughts intent. Mrs. Williamson kept her own and Eric's counsel; the Gordons said nothing; but the secret leaked out and great was the surprise and gossip and wonder. One or two incautious people ventured to express their opinion of the Master's wisdom to the Master himself; but they never repeated the experiment. Curiosity was rife. A hundred stories were circulated about Kilmeny, all greatly exaggerated in the circulation. Wise heads were shaken and the majority opined that it was a great pity. The Master was a likely young fellow; he could have his pick of almost anybody, you might think; it was too bad that he should go and take up with that queer, dumb niece of the Gordons who had been brought up in such a heathenish way. But then you never could guess what way a man's fancy would jump when he set out to pick him a wife. They guessed Neil Gordon didn't like it much. He seemed to have got dreadful moody and sulky of late and wouldn't sing in the choir any more. Thus the buzz of comment and gossip ran.

To those two in the old orchard it mattered not a whit. Kilmeny knew nothing of gossip. To her, Lindsay was as much of an unknown world as the city of Eric's home. Her thoughts strayed far and wide in the realm of fancy, but they never wandered out to the little realities that hedged her strange life around. In that life she had blossomed out, a fair, unique thing. There were times when Eric almost regretted that one day he must take her out of her white solitude to a world that, in the last analysis, was only Lindsay on a larger scale, with just the same pettiness of thought and feeling and opinion at the bottom of it. He wished he might keep her to himself for ever, in that old, spruce-hidden orchard where the roses fell.

One day he indulged himself in the fulfilment of the whim he had formed when Kilmeny had told him she thought herself ugly. He went to Janet and asked her permission to bring a mirror to the house that he might have the privilege of being the first to reveal Kilmeny to herself exteriorly. Janet was somewhat dubious at first.

"There hasn't been such a thing in the house for sixteen years, Master. There never was but three—one in the spare room, and a little one in the kitchen, and Margaret's own. She broke them all the day it first struck her that Kilmeny was going to be bonny. I might have got one after she died maybe. But I didn't think of it; and there's no need of lasses to be always prinking at their looking glasses."

But Eric pleaded and argued skilfully, and finally Janet said,

"Well, well, have your own way. You'd have it anyway I think, lad. You are one of those men who always get their own way. But that is different from the men who *take* their own way—and that's a mercy," she added under her breath.

Eric went to town the next Saturday and picked out a mirror that pleased him. He had it shipped to Radnor and Thomas Gordon brought it home, not knowing what it was, for Janet had thought it just as well he should not know.

"It's a present the Master is making Kilmeny," she told him.

She sent Kilmeny off to the orchard after tea, and Eric slipped around to the house by way of the main road and lane. He and Janet together unpacked the mirror and hung it on the parlour wall.

"I never saw such a big one, Master," said Janet rather doubtfully, as if, after all, she distrusted its gleaming, pearly depth and richly ornamented frame. "I hope it won't make her vain. She is very bonny, but it may not do her any good to know it."

"It won't harm her," said Eric confidently. "When a belief in her ugliness hasn't spoiled a girl a belief in her beauty won't."

But Janet did not understand epigrams. She carefully removed a little dust from the polished surface, and frowned meditatively at the by no means beautiful reflection she saw therein.

"I cannot think what made Kilmeny suppose she was ugly, Master.

"Her mother told her she was," said Eric, rather bitterly.

"Ah!" Janet shot a quick glance at the picture of her sister. "Was that it? Margaret was a strange woman, Master. I suppose she thought her own beauty had been a snare to her. She *was* bonny. That picture doesn't do her justice. I never liked it. It was taken before she was—before she met Ronald Fraser. We none of us thought it very like her at the time. But, Master, three years later it was like her—oh, it was like her then! That very look came in her face."

"Kilmeny doesn't resemble her mother," remarked Eric, glancing at the picture with the same feeling of mingled fascination and distaste with which he always regarded it. "Does she look like her father?"

"No, not a great deal, though some of her ways are very like his. She looks like her grandmother—Margaret's mother, Master. Her name was Kilmeny too, and she was a handsome, sweet woman. I was very fond of my stepmother, Master. When she died she gave her baby to me, and asked me to be a mother to it. Ah well, I tried; but I couldn't fence the sorrow out of

Margaret's life, and it sometimes comes to my mind that maybe I'll not be able to fence it out of Kilmeny's either."

"That will be my task," said Eric.

"You'll do your best, I do not doubt. But maybe it will be through you that sorrow will come to her after all."

"Not through any fault of mine, Aunt Janet."

"No, no, I'm not saying it will be your fault. But my heart misgives me at times. Oh, I dare say I am only a foolish old woman, Master. Go your ways and bring your lass here to look at your plaything when you like. I'll not make or meddle with it."

Janet betook herself to the kitchen and Eric went to look for Kilmeny. She was not in the orchard and it was not until he had searched for some time that he found her. She was standing under a beech tree in a field beyond the orchard, leaning on the longer fence, with her hands clasped against her cheek. In them she held a white Mary-lily from the orchard. She did not run to meet him while he was crossing the pasture, as she would once have done. She waited motionless until he was close to her. Eric began, half laughingly, half tenderly, to quote some lines from her namesake ballad:

> " 'Kilmeny, Kilmeny, where have you been?
> Long hae we sought baith holt and den,—
> By linn, by ford, and greenwood tree!
> Yet you are halesome and fair to see.
> Where got you that joup o' the lily sheen?
> That bonny snood o' the birk sae green,
> And those roses, the fairest that ever was seen?
> Kilmeny, Kilmeny, where have you been?'

"Only it's a lily and not a rose you are carrying. I might go on and quote the next couplet too—

> " 'Kilmeny looked up with a lovely grace,
> But there was nae smile on Kilmeny's face.'

Why are you looking so sober?"

Kilmeny did not have her slate with her and could not answer; but Eric guessed from something in her eyes that she was bitterly contrasting the beauty of the ballad's heroine with her own supposed ugliness.

"Come down to the house, Kilmeny. I have something there to show you—something lovelier than you have ever seen before," he said, with boyish pleasure shining in his eyes. "I want you to go and put on that muslin dress you wore last Sunday evening, and pin up your hair the same way you did then. Run along—don't wait for me. But you are not to go into the parlour until I come. I want to pick some of those Mary-lilies up in the orchard."

When Eric returned to the house with an armful of the long stemmed, white Madonna lilies that bloomed in the orchard Kilmeny was just coming down the steep, narrow staircase with its striped carpeting of homespun drugget. Her marvellous loveliness was brought out into brilliant relief by the dark wood work and shadows of the dim old hall.

She wore a trailing, clinging dress of some creamy tinted fabric that had been her mother's. It had not been altered in any respect, for fashion held no sway at the Gordon homestead, and Kilmeny thought that the dress left nothing to be desired. Its quaint style suited her admirably; the neck was slightly cut away to show the round white throat, and the sleeves were long, full "bishops," out of which her beautiful, slender hands slipped like flowers from their sheaths. She had crossed her long braids at the back and pinned them about her head like a coronet; a late white rose was fastened low down on the left side.

> " 'A man had given all other bliss
> And all his worldly wealth for this—
> To waste his whole heart in one kiss
> Upon her perfect lips,' "

quoted Eric in a whisper as he watched her descend. Aloud he said,

"Take these lilies on your arm, letting their bloom fall against your shoulder—so. Now, give me your hand and shut your eyes. Don't open them until I say you may."

He led her into the parlour and up to the mirror.

"Look," he cried, gayly.

Kilmeny opened her eyes and looked straight into the mirror

where, like a lovely picture in a golden frame, she saw herself reflected. For a moment she was bewildered. Then she realized what it meant. The lilies fell from her arm to the floor and she turned pale. With a little low, involuntary cry she put her hands over her face.

Eric pulled them boyishly away.

"Kilmeny, do you think you are ugly now? This is a truer mirror than Aunt Janet's silver sugar bowl! Look—look—look! Did you ever imagine anything fairer than yourself, dainty Kilmeny?"

She was blushing now, and stealing shy radiant glances at the mirror. With a smile she took her slate and wrote naïvely,

"I think I am pleasant to look upon. I cannot tell you how glad I am. It is so dreadful to believe one is ugly. You can get used to everything else, but you never get used to that. It hurts just the same every time you remember it. But why did mother tell me I was ugly? Could she really have thought so? Perhaps I have become better looking since I grew up."

"I think perhaps your mother had found that beauty is not always a blessing, Kilmeny, and thought it wiser not to let you know you possessed it. Come, let us go back to the orchard now. We mustn't waste this rare evening in the house. There is going to be a sunset that we shall remember all our lives. The mirror will hang here. It is yours. Don't look into it too often, though, or Aunt Janet will disapprove. She is afraid it will make you vain."

Kilmeny gave one of her rare, musical laughs, which Eric never heard without a recurrence of the old wonder that she could laugh so when she could not speak. She blew an airy little kiss at her mirrored face and turned from it, smiling happily.

On their way to the orchard they met Neil. He went by them with an averted face, but Kilmeny shivered and involuntarily drew nearer to Eric.

"I don't understand Neil at all now," she wrote nervously. "He is not nice, as he used to be, and sometimes he will not answer when I speak to him. And he looks so strangely at me, too. Besides, he is surly and impertinent to Uncle and Aunt."

"Don't mind Neil," said Eric lightly. "He is probably sulky because of some things I said to him when I found he had spied on us."

LIKE A LOVELY PICTURE IN A GOLDEN FRAME,
SHE SAW HERSELF REFLECTED.

That night before she went up stairs Kilmeny stole into the parlour for another glimpse of herself in that wonderful mirror by the light of a dim little candle she carried. She was still lingering there dreamily when Aunt Janet's grim face appeared in the shadows of the doorway.

"Are you thinking about your own good looks, lassie? Ay, but remember that handsome is as handsome does," she said, with grudging admiration—for the girl with her flushed cheeks and shining eyes was something that even dour Janet Gordon could not look upon unmoved.

Kilmeny smiled softly.

"I'll try to remember," she wrote, "but oh, Aunt Janet, I am so glad I am not ugly. It is not wrong to be glad of that, is it?"

The older woman's face softened.

"No, I don't suppose it is, lassie," she conceded. "A comely face is something to be thankful for—as none know better than those who have never possessed it. I remember well when I was a girl—but that is neither here nor there. The Master thinks you are wonderful bonny, Kilmeny," she added, looking keenly at the girl.

Kilmeny started and a scarlet blush scorched her face. That, and the expression that flashed into her eyes, told Janet Gordon all she wished to know. With a stifled sigh she bade her niece good night and went away.

Kilmeny ran fleetly up the stairs to her dim little room, that looked out into the spruces, and flung herself on her bed, burying her burning face in the pillow. Her aunt's words had revealed to her the hidden secret of her heart. She knew that she loved Eric Marshall—and the knowledge brought with it a strange anguish. For was she not dumb? All night she lay staring wide-eyed through the darkness till the dawn.

CHAPTER 14

IN HER SELFLESS MOOD

ERIC NOTICED a change in Kilmeny at their next meeting—a change that troubled him. She seemed aloof, abstracted, almost ill at ease. When he proposed an excursion to the orchard he thought she was reluctant to go. The days that followed convinced him of the change. Something had come between them. Kilmeny seemed as far away from him as if she had in truth, like her namesake of the ballad, sojourned for seven years in the land "where the rain never fell and the wind never blew," and had come back washed clean from all the affections of earth.

Eric had a bad week of it; but he determined to put an end to it by plain speaking. One evening in the orchard he told her of his love.

It was an evening in August, with wheat fields ripening to their harvestry—a soft violet night made for love, with the distant murmur of an unquiet sea on a rocky shore sounding through it. Kilmeny was sitting on the old bench where he had first seen her. She had been playing for him, but her music did not please her and she laid aside the violin with a little frown.

It might be that she was afraid to play—afraid that her new emotions might escape her and reveal themselves in music. It was difficult to prevent this, so long had she been accustomed to pour out all her feelings in harmony. The necessity for restraint irked her and made of her bow a clumsy thing which no longer obeyed her wishes. More than ever at that instant did she long for speech—speech that would conceal and protect where dangerous silence might betray.

In a low voice that trembled with earnestness Eric told her that he loved her—that he had loved her from the first time he had seen her in that old orchard. He spoke humbly but not fearfully, for he believed that she loved him, and he had little expectation of any rebuff.

"Kilmeny, will you be my wife?" he asked finally, taking her hands in his.

Kilmeny had listened with averted face. At first she had

blushed painfully but now she had grown very pale. When he had finished speaking and was waiting for her answer, she suddenly pulled her hands away, and, putting them over her face, burst into tears and noiseless sobs.

"Kilmeny, dearest, have I alarmed you? Surely you knew before that I loved you. Don't you care for me?" Eric said, putting his arm about her and trying to draw her to him. But she shook her head sorrowfully, and wrote with compressed lips,

"Yes, I do love you, but I will never marry you, because I cannot speak."

"Oh, Kilmeny," said Eric smiling, for he believed his victory won, "that doesn't make any difference to me—you know it doesn't, sweetest. If you love me that is enough."

But Kilmeny only shook her head again. There was a very determined look on her pale face. She wrote,

"No, it is not enough. It would be doing you a great wrong to marry you when I cannot speak, and I will not do it because I love you too much to do anything that would harm you. Your world would think you had done a very foolish thing and it would be right. I have thought it all over many times since something Aunt Janet said made me understand, and I know I am doing right. I am sorry I did not understand sooner, before you had learned to care so much."

"Kilmeny, darling, you have taken a very absurd fancy into that dear black head of yours. Don't you know that you will make me miserably unhappy all my life if you will not be my wife?"

"No, you think so now; and I know you will feel very badly for a time. Then you will go away and after awhile you will forget me; and then you will see that I was right. I shall be very unhappy, too, but that is better than spoiling your life. Do not plead or coax because I shall not change my mind."

Eric did plead and coax, however—at first patiently and smilingly, as one might argue with a dear foolish child; then with vehement and distracted earnestness, as he began to realize that Kilmeny meant what she said. It was all in vain. Kilmeny grew paler and paler, and her eyes revealed how keenly she was suffering. She did not even try to argue with him, but only listened patiently and sadly, and shook her head. Say what he would, entreat and implore as he might, he could not move her resolution a hairs-breadth.

Yet he did not despair; he could not believe that she would adhere to such a resolution; he felt sure that her love for him would eventually conquer, and he went home not unhappily after all. He did not understand that it was the very intensity of her love which gave her the strength to resist his pleading, where a more shallow affection might have yielded. It held her back unflinchingly from doing him what she believed to be a wrong.

———————— CHAPTER 15 ————————

AN OLD, UNHAPPY, FAR-OFF THING

THE NEXT day Eric sought Kilmeny again and renewed his pleadings, but again in vain. Nothing he could say, no argument which he could advance, was of any avail against her sad determination. When he was finally compelled to realize that her resolution was not to be shaken, he went in his despair to Janet Gordon. Janet listened to his story with concern and disappointment plainly visible on her face. When he had finished she shook her head.

"I'm sorry, Master. I can't tell you how sorry I am. I had hoped for something very different. *Hoped!* I have *prayed* for it. Thomas and I are getting old and it has weighed on my mind for years—what was to become of Kilmeny when we would be gone. Since you came I had hoped she would have a protector in you. But if Kilmeny says she will not marry you I am afraid she'll stick to it."

"But she loves me," cried the young man, "and if you and her uncle speak to her—urge her—perhaps you can influence her—"

"No, Master, it wouldn't be any use. Oh, we will, of course, but it will not be any use. Kilmeny is as determined as her mother when once she makes up her mind. She has always been good and obedient for the most part, but once or twice we have found out that there is no moving her if she does resolve upon anything. When her mother died Thomas and I wanted to take her to church. We could not prevail on her to go. We did not know why then, but now I suppose it was because she believed she was so very ugly. It is because she thinks so much of you that she will not marry you. She is afraid you would come to repent having married a dumb girl. Maybe she is right—maybe she is right."

"I cannot give her up," said Eric stubbornly. "Something must be done. Perhaps her defect can be remedied even yet. Have you ever thought of that? You have never had her examined by a doctor qualified to pronounce on her case, have you?"

"No, Master, we never took her to anyone. When we first began to fear that she was never going to talk Thomas wanted to take her to Charlottetown and have her looked to. He thought so much of the child and he felt terrible about it. But her mother wouldn't hear of it being done. There was no use trying to argue with her. She said that it would be no use—that it was her sin that was visited on her child and it could never be taken away."

"And did you give in meekly to a morbid whim like that?" asked Eric impatiently.

"Master, you didn't know my sister. We *had* to give in— nobody could hold out against her. She was a strange woman— and a terrible woman in many ways—after her trouble. We were afraid to cross her for fear she would go out of her mind."

"But, could you not have taken Kilmeny to a doctor unknown to her mother?"

"No, that was not possible. Margaret never let her out of her sight, not even when she was grown up. Besides, to tell you the whole truth, Master, we didn't think ourselves that it would be much use to try to cure Kilmeny. It *was* a sin that made her as she is."

"Aunt Janet, how can you talk such nonsense? Where was there any sin? Your sister thought herself a lawful wife. If Ronald Fraser thought otherwise—and there is no proof that he did—*he* committed a sin, but you surely do not believe that it was visited in this fashion on his innocent child!"

"No, I am not meaning that, Master. That wasn't where Margaret did wrong; and though I never liked Ronald Fraser over much, I must say this in his defence—I believe he thought himself a free man when he married Margaret. No, it's something else—something far worse. It gives me a shiver whenever I think of it. Oh, Master, the Good Book is right when it says the sins of the parents are visited on the children. There isn't a truer word in it than that from cover to cover."

"What, in heaven's name, is the meaning of all this?" exclaimed Eric. "Tell me what it is. I must know the whole truth about Kilmeny. Do not torment me."

"I am going to tell you the story, Master, though it will be like opening an old wound. No living person knows it but Thomas and me. When you hear it you will understand why Kilmeny can't speak, and why it isn't likely that there can ever be anything done for her. She doesn't know the truth and you must never tell her. It isn't a fit story for her ears, especially when it is about her mother. Promise me that you will never tell her, no matter what may happen."

"I promise. Go on—go on," said the young man feverishly.

Janet Gordon locked her hands together in her lap, like a woman who nerves herself to some hateful task. She looked very old; the lines on her face seemed doubly deep and harsh.

"My sister Margaret was a very proud, high-spirited girl, Master. But I would not have you think she was unlovable. No, no, that would be doing a great injustice to her memory. She had her faults as we all have; but she was bright and merry and warm-hearted. We all loved her. She was the light and life of this house. Yes, Master, before the trouble that came on her Margaret was a winsome lass, singing like a lark from morning till night. Maybe we spoiled her a little—maybe we gave her too much of her own way.

"Well, Master, you have heard the story of her marriage to Ronald Fraser and what came after, so I need not go into that. I know, or used to know Elizabeth Williamson well, and I know that whatever she told you would be the truth and nothing more or less than the truth.

"Our father was a very proud man. Oh, Master, if Margaret was too proud she got it from no stranger. And her misfortune cut him to the heart. He never spoke a word to us here for more than three days after he heard of it. He sat in the corner there with bowed head and would not touch bite or sup. He had not been very willing for her to marry Ronald Fraser; and when she came home in disgrace she had not set foot over the threshold before he broke out railing at her. Oh, I can see her there at the door this very minute, Master, pale and trembling, clinging to Thomas' arm, her great eyes changing from sorrow and shame to wrath. It was just at sunset and a red ray came in at the window and fell right across her breast like a stain of blood.

"Father called her a hard name, Master. Oh, he was too hard—even though he was my father I must say he was too hard on her, broken-hearted as she was, and guilty of nothing more after all than a little wilfulness in the matter of her marriage.

"And father was sorry for it—Oh, Master, the word wasn't out of his mouth before he was sorry for it. But the mischief was done. Oh, I'll never forget Margaret's face, Master! It haunts me yet in the black of the night. It was full of anger and rebellion and defiance. But she never answered him back. She clenched her hands and went up to her old room without saying a word, all those mad feelings surging in her soul, and being held back from speech by her sheer, stubborn will. And, Master, never a word did Margaret say from that day until after Kilmeny was born—not one word, Master. Nothing we could do for her softened her. And we were kind to her, Master, and gentle with her, and never reproached her by so much as a look. But she would not speak to anyone. She just sat in her room most of the time and stared at the wall with such awful eyes. Father implored her to speak and forgive him, but she never gave any sign that she heard him.

"I haven't come to the worst yet, Master. Father sickened and took to his bed. Margaret would not go in to see him. Then one night Thomas and I were watching by him; it was about eleven o'clock. All at once he said,

"'Janet, go up and tell the lass'—he always called Margaret that—it was a kind of pet name he had for her—'that I'm deein' and ask her to come down and speak to me afore I'm gone.'

"Master, I went. Margaret was sitting in her room all alone in the cold and dark, staring at the wall. I told her what our father had said. She never let on she heard me. I pleaded and wept, Master. I did what I had never done to any human creature—I kneeled to her and begged her, as she hoped for mercy herself, to come down and see our dying father. Master, she wouldn't! She never moved or looked at me. I had to get up and go downstairs and tell that old man she would not come."

Janet Gordon lifted her hands and struck them together in her agony of remembrance.

"When I told father he only said, oh, so gently,

" 'Poor lass, I was too hard on her. She isna to blame. But I canna go to meet her mother till our little lass has forgie'n me for the name I called her. Thomas, help me up. Since she winna come to me I must e'en go to her.'

"There was no crossing him—we saw that. He got up from his deathbed and Thomas helped him out into the hall and up the stair. I walked behind with the candle. Oh, Master, I'll never forget it—the awful shadows and the storm wind wailing outside, and father's gasping breath. But we got him to Margaret's room and he stood before her, trembling, with his white hairs falling about his sunken face. And he prayed Margaret to forgive him—to forgive him and speak just one word to him before he went to meet her mother. Master"—Janet's voice rose almost to a shriek—"she would not—she would not! And yet she *wanted* to speak—afterwards she confessed to me that she wanted to speak. But her stubbornness wouldn't let her. It was like some evil power that had gripped hold of her and wouldn't let go. Father might as well have pleaded with a graven image. Oh, it was hard and dreadful! She saw her father die and she never spoke the word he prayed for to him. *That* was her sin, Master,—and for that sin the curse fell on her unborn child. When father understood that she would not speak he closed his eyes and was like to have fallen if Thomas had not caught him.

" 'Oh, lass, you're a hard woman,' was all he said. And they were his last words. Thomas and I carried him back to his room, but the breath was gone from him before we even got him there.

"Well, Master, Kilmeny was born a month afterwards, and when Margaret felt her baby at her breast the evil thing that had held her soul in its bondage lost its power. She spoke and wept and was herself again. Oh, how she wept! She implored us to forgive her and we did freely and fully. But the one against whom she had sinned most grievously was gone, and no word of forgiveness could come to her from the grave. My poor sister never knew peace of conscience again, Master. But she was gentle and kind and humble until—until she began to fear that Kilmeny was never going to speak. We thought then that she would go out of her mind. Indeed, Master, she never was quite right again.

"But that is the story and it's a thankful woman I am that the telling of it is done. Kilmeny can't speak because her mother wouldn't."

Eric had listened with a gray horror on his face to the gruesome tale. The black tragedy of it appalled him—the tragedy of that merciless law, the most cruel and mysterious thing in God's universe, which ordains that the sin of the guilty shall be visited on the innocent. Fight against it as he would, the miserable conviction stole into his heart that Kilmeny's case was indeed beyond the reach of any human skill.

"It is a dreadful tale," he said moodily, getting up and walking restlessly to and fro in the dim spruce-shadowed old kitchen where they were. "And if it is true that her mother's wilful silence caused Kilmeny's dumbness, I fear, as you say, that we cannot help her. But you may be mistaken. It may have been nothing more than a strange coincidence. Possibly something may be done for her. At all events, we must try. I have a friend in Queenslea who is a physician. His name is David Baker, and he is a very skilful specialist in regard to the throat and voice. I shall have him come here and see Kilmeny."

"Have your way," assented Janet in the hopeless tone which she might have used in giving him permission to attempt any impossible thing.

"It will be necessary to tell Dr. Baker why Kilmeny cannot speak—or why you think she cannot."

Janet's face twitched.

"Must that be, Master? Oh, it's a bitter tale to tell a stranger."

"Don't be afraid. I shall tell him nothing that is not strictly necessary to his proper understanding of the case. It will be quite enough to say that Kilmeny may be dumb because for several months before her birth her mother's mind was in a very morbid condition, and she preserved a stubborn and unbroken silence because of a certain bitter personal resentment."

"Well, do as you think best, Master."

Janet plainly had no faith in the possibility of anything being done for Kilmeny. But a rosy glow of hope flashed over Kilmeny's face when Eric told her what he meant to do.

"Oh, do you think he can make me speak?" she wrote eagerly.

"I don't know, Kilmeny. I hope that he can, and I know he will do all that mortal skill can do. If he can remove your defect will you promise to marry me, dearest?"

She nodded. The grave little motion had the solemnity of a sacred promise.

"Yes," she wrote, "when I can speak like other women I will marry you."

CHAPTER 16

DAVID BAKER'S OPINION

THE NEXT week David Baker came to Lindsay. He arrived in the afternoon when Eric was in school. When the latter came home he found that David had, in the space of an hour, captured Mrs. Williamson's heart, wormed himself into the good graces of Timothy, and become hail-fellow-well-met with old Robert. But he looked curiously at Eric when the two young men found themselves alone in the upstairs room.

"Now, Eric, I want to know what all this is about. What scrape have you got into? You write me a letter, entreating me in the name of friendship to come to you at once. Accordingly I come post haste. You seem to be in excellent health yourself. Explain why you have inveigled me hither."

"I want you to do me a service which only you can do, David," said Eric quietly. "I didn't care to go into the details by letter. I have met in Lindsay a young girl whom I have learned to love. I have asked her to marry me, but, although she cares for me, she refuses to do so because she is dumb. I wish you to examine her and find out the cause of her defect, and if it can be cured. She can hear perfectly and all her other faculties are entirely normal. In order that you may better understand the case I must tell you the main facts of her history."

This Eric proceeded to do. David Baker listened with grave attention, his eyes fastened on his friend's face. He did not betray the surprise and dismay he felt at learning that Eric had fallen in love with a dumb girl of doubtful antecedents; and the strange case enlisted his professional interest. When he had heard the whole story he thrust his hands into his pockets and strode up and down the room several times in silence. Finally he halted before Eric.

"So you have done what I foreboded all along you would do—left your common sense behind you when you went courting."

"If I did," said Eric quietly, "I took with me something better and nobler than common sense."

David shrugged his shoulders.

"You'll have hard work to convince me of that, Eric."

"No, it will not be difficult at all. I have one argument that will convince you speedily—and that is Kilmeny Gordon herself. But we will not discuss the matter of my wisdom or lack of it just now. What I want to know is this—what do you think of the case as I have stated it to you?"

David frowned thoughtfully.

"I hardly know what to think. It is very curious and unusual, but it is not totally unprecedented. There have been cases on record where pre-natal influences have produced a like result. I cannot just now remember whether any were ever cured. Well, I'll see if anything can be done for this girl. I cannot express any further opinion until I have examined her."

The next morning Eric took David up to the Gordon homestead. As they approached the old orchard a strain of music came floating through the resinous morning arcades of the spruce wood—a wild, sorrowful, appealing cry, full of indescribable pathos, yet marvellously sweet.

"What is that?" exclaimed David, starting.

"That is Kilmeny playing on her violin," answered Eric. "She has great talent in that respect and improvises wonderful melodies."

When they reached the orchard Kilmeny rose from the old bench to meet them, her lovely luminous eyes distended, her face flushed with the excitement of mingled hope and fear.

"Oh, ye gods!" muttered David helplessly.

He could not hide his amazement and Eric smiled to see it. The latter had not failed to perceive that his friend had until now considered him as little better than a lunatic.

"Kilmeny, this is my friend, Dr. Baker," he said.

Kilmeny held out her hand with a smile. Her beauty, as she stood there in the fresh morning sunshine beside a clump of her sister lilies, was something to take away a man's breath. David, who was by no means lacking in confidence and generally had a ready tongue where women were concerned, found himself as mute and awkward as a school boy, as he bowed over her hand.

But Kilmeny was charmingly at ease. There was not a trace of embarrassment in her manner, though there was a pretty shyness. Eric smiled as he recalled *his* first meeting with her. He suddenly realized how far Kilmeny had come since then and how much she had developed.

With a little gesture of invitation Kilmeny led the way through the orchard to the wild cherry lane, and the two men followed.

"Eric, she is simply unutterable!" said David in an undertone. "Last night, to tell you the truth, I had a rather poor opinion of your sanity. But now I am consumed with a fierce envy. She is the loveliest creature I ever saw."

Eric introduced David to the Gordons and then hurried away to his school. On his way down the Gordon lane he met Neil and was half startled by the glare of hatred in the Italian boy's eyes. Pity succeeded the momentary alarm. Neil's face had grown thin and haggard; his eyes were sunken and feverishly bright; he looked years older than on the day when Eric had first seen him in the brook hollow.

Prompted by a sudden compassionate impulse Eric stopped and held out his hand.

"Neil, can't we be friends?" he said. "I am sorry if I have been the cause of inflicting pain on you."

"Friends! Never!" said Neil passionately. "You have taken

Kilmeny from me. I shall hate you always. And I'll be even with you yet."

He strode fiercely up the lane, and Eric, with a shrug of his shoulders, went on his way, dismissing the meeting from his mind.

The day seemed interminably long to him. David had not returned when he went home to dinner; but when he went to his room in the evening he found his friend there, staring out of the window.

"Well," he said, impatiently, as David wheeled around but still kept silence, "What have you to say to me? Don't keep me in suspense any longer, David. I have endured all I can. Today has seemed like a thousand years. Have you discovered what is the matter with Kilmeny?"

"There is nothing the matter with her," answered David slowly, flinging himself into a chair by the window.

"What do you mean?"

"Just exactly what I say. Her vocal organs are all perfect. As far as they are concerned, there is absolutely no reason why she should not speak."

"Then why can't she speak? Do you think—do you think—"

"I think that I cannot express my conclusion in any better words than Janet Gordon used when she said that Kilmeny cannot speak because her mother wouldn't. That is all there is to it. The trouble is psychological, not physical. Medical skill is helpless before it. There are greater men than I in my profession; but it is my honest belief, Eric, that if you were to consult them they would tell you just what I have told you, neither more nor less."

"Then there is no hope," said Eric in a tone of despair. "You can do nothing for her?"

David took from the back of his chair a crochet antimacassar with a lion rampant in the centre and spread it over his knee.

"*I* can do nothing for her," he said, scowling at that work of art. "I do not believe any living man can do anything for her. But I do not say—exactly—that there is no hope."

"Come, David, I am in no mood for guessing riddles. Speak plainly, man, and don't torment me."

David frowned dubiously and poked his finger through the hole which represented the eye of the king of beasts.

"I don't know that I can make it plain to you. It isn't very plain to myself. And it is only a vague theory of mine, of course. I cannot substantiate it by any facts. In short, Eric, I think it is possible that Kilmeny may speak sometime—if she ever wants to badly enough."

"Wants to! why, man, she wants to as badly as it is possible for any one to want anything. She loves me with all her heart and she won't marry me because she can't speak. Don't you suppose that a girl under such circumstances would 'want' to speak as much as any one could?"

"Yes, but I do not mean that sort of wanting, no matter how strong the wish may be. What I do mean is—a sudden, vehement, passionate inrush of desire, phsyical, psychical, mental, all in one, mighty enough to rend asunder the invisible fetters that hold her speech in bondage. If any occasion should arise to evoke such a desire I believe that Kilmeny would speak—and having once spoken would thenceforth be normal in that respect—ay, if she spoke but the one word."

"All this sounds like great nonsense to me," said Eric restlessly. "I suppose you have an idea what you are talking about, but I haven't. And, in any case, it practically means that there is no hope for her—or me. Even if your theory is correct it is not likely such an occasion as you speak of will ever arise. And Kilmeny will never marry me."

"Don't give up so easily, old fellow. There *have* been cases on record where women have changed their minds."

"Not women like Kilmeny," said Eric miserably. "I tell you she has all her mother's unfaltering will and tenacity of purpose, although she is free from any taint of pride or selfishness. I thank you for your sympathy and interest, David. You have done all you could—but, heavens, what it would have meant to me if you could have helped her!"

With a groan Eric flung himself on a chair and buried his face in his hands. It was a moment which held for him all the bitterness of death. He had thought that he was prepared for disappointment; he had not known how strong his hope had really been until that hope was utterly taken from him.

David, with a sigh, returned the crochet antimacassar carefully to its place on the chair back.

"Eric, last night, to be honest, I thought that, if I found I could not help this girl, it would be the best thing that could happen, as far as you were concerned. But since I have seen her—well, I would give my right hand if I could do anything for her. She is the wife for you, if we could make her speak: yes, and by the memory of your mother"—David brought his fist down on the window sill with a force that shook the casement,—"she is the wife for you, speech or no speech, if we could only convince her of it."

"She cannot be convinced of that. No, David, I have lost her. Did you tell her what you have told me?"

"I told her I could not help her. I did not say anything to her of my theory—that would have done no good."

"How did she take it?"

"Very bravely and quietly—'like a winsome lady.' But the look in her eyes—Eric, I felt as if I had murdered something. She bade me a mute good-bye with a pitiful smile and went upstairs. I did not see her again, although I stayed to dinner at her uncle's request. Those old Gordons are a queer pair. I liked them, though. They are strong and staunch—good friends, bitter enemies. They were sorry that I could not help Kilmeny, but I saw plainly that old Thomas Gordon thought that I had been meddling with predestination in attempting it."

Eric smiled mechanically.

"I must go up and see Kilmeny. You'll excuse me, won't you, David? My books are there—help yourself."

But when Eric reached the Gordon house he saw only old Janet, who told him that Kilmeny was in her room and refused to see him.

"She thought you would come up, and she left this with me to give you, Master."

Janet handed him a little note. It was very brief and blotted with tears.

"Do not come any more, Eric," it ran. "I must not see you, because it would only make it harder for us both. You must go away and forget me. You will be thankful for this some day. I shall always love and pray for you.

                                        "KILMENY."

"I *must* see her," said Eric desperately. "Aunt Janet, be my friend. Tell her she must see me for a little while at least."

Janet shook her head but went upstairs. She soon returned.

"She says she cannot come down. You know she means it,

Master, and it is of no use to coax her. And I must say I think she is right. Since she will not marry you it is better for her not to see you."

Eric was compelled to go home with no better comfort than this. In the morning, as it was Saturday, he drove David Baker to the station. He had not slept and he looked so miserable and reckless that David felt anxious about him. David would have stayed in Lindsay for a few days, but a certain critical case in Queenslea demanded his speedy return. He shook hands with Eric on the station platform.

"Eric, give up that school and come home at once. You can do no good in Lindsay now, and you'll only eat your heart out here."

"I must see Kilmeny once more before I leave," was all Eric's answer.

That afternoon he went again to the Gordon homestead. But the result was the same; Kilmeny refused to see him, and Thomas Gordon said gravely,

"Master, you know I like you and I am sorry Kilmeny thinks as she does, though maybe she is right. I would be glad to see you often for your own sake and I'll miss you much; but as things are I tell you plainly you'd better not come here any more. It will do no good, and the sooner you and she get over thinking about each other the better for you both. Go now, lad, and God bless you."

"Do you know what it is you are asking of me?" said Eric hoarsely.

"I know I am asking a hard thing for your own good, Master. It is not as if Kilmeny would ever change her mind. We have had some experience with a woman's will ere this. Tush, Janet, woman, don't be weeping. You women are foolish creatures. Do you think tears can wash such things away? No, they cannot blot out sin, or the consequences of sin. It's awful how one sin can spread out and broaden, till it eats into innocent lives, sometimes long after the sinner has gone to his own accounting. Master, if you take my advice, you'll give up the Lindsay school and go back to your own world as soon as may be."

CHAPTER 17

A BROKEN FETTER

ERIC WENT home with a white, haggard face. He had never thought it possible for a man to suffer as he suffered then. What was he to do? It seemed impossible to go on with life— there was *no* life apart from Kilmeny. Anguish wrung his soul until his strength went from him and youth and hope turned to gall and bitterness in his heart.

He never afterwards could tell how he lived through the following Sunday or how he taught school as usual on Monday. He found out how much a man may suffer and yet go on living and working. His body seemed to him an automaton that moved and spoke mechanically, while his tortured spirit, pent-up within, endured pain that left its impress on him for ever. Out of that fiery furnace of agony Eric Marshall was to go forth a man who had put boyhood behind him for ever and looked out on life with eyes that saw into it and beyond.

On Tuesday afternoon there was a funeral in the district and, according to custom, the school was closed. Eric went again to the old orchard. He had no expectation of seeing Kilmeny there, for he thought she would avoid the spot lest she might meet him. But he could not keep away from it, although the thought of it was an added torment, and he vibrated between a wild wish that he might never see it again, and a sick wonder how he could possibly go away and leave it—that strange old orchard where he had met and wooed his sweetheart, watching her develop and blossom under his eyes, like some rare flower, until in the space of three short months she had passed from exquisite childhood into still more exquisite womanhood.

As he crossed the pasture field before the spruce wood he came upon Neil Gordon, building a longer fence. Neil did not look up as Eric passed, but sullenly went on driving poles. Before this Eric had pitied Neil; now he was conscious of feeling sympathy with him. Had Neil suffered as he was suffering? Eric had entered into a new fellowship whereof the passport was pain.

The orchard was very silent and dreamy in the thick, deep tinted sunshine of the September afternoon, a sunshine which

532

seemed to possess the power of extracting the very essence of all the odours which summer has stored up in wood and field. There were few flowers now; most of the lilies, which had queened it so bravely along the central path a few days before, were withered. The grass had become ragged and sere and unkempt. But in the corners the torches of the goldenrod were kindling and a few misty purple asters nodded here and there. The orchard kept its own strange attractiveness, as some women with youth long passed still preserve an atmosphere of remembered beauty and innate, indestructible charm.

Eric walked drearily and carelessly about it, and finally sat down on a half fallen fence panel in the shadow of the over-hanging spruce boughs. There he gave himself up to a reverie, poignant and bitter sweet, in which he lived over again everything that had passed in the orchard since his first meeting there with Kilmeny.

So deep was his abstraction, that he was conscious of nothing around him. He did not hear stealthy footsteps behind him in the dim spruce wood. He did not even see Kilmeny as she came slowly around the curve of the wild cherry lane.

Kilmeny had sought the old orchard for the healing of her heartbreak, if healing were possible for her. She had no fear of encountering Eric there at that time of the day, for she did not know that it was the district custom to close the school for a funeral. She would never have gone to it in the evening, but she longed for it continually; it, and her memories, were all that was left her now.

Years seemed to have passed over the girl in those few days. She had drunk of pain and broken bread with sorrow. Her face was pale and strained, with bluish, transparent shadows under her large wistful eyes, out of which the dream and laughter of girlhood had gone, but into which had come the potent charm of grief and patience. Thomas Gordon had shaken his head bodingly when he had looked at her that morning at the breakfast table.

"She won't stand it," he thought. "She isn't long for this world. Maybe it is all for the best, poor lass. But I wish that young Master had never set foot in the Connors orchard, or in this house. Margaret, Margaret, it's hard that your child should have to be paying the reckoning of a sin that was sinned before her birth."

Kilmeny walked through the lane slowly and absently like a woman in a dream. When she came to the gap in the fence where the lane ran into the orchard she lifted her wan, drooping face and saw Eric, sitting in the shadow of the wood at the other side of the orchard with his bowed head in his hands. She stopped quickly and the blood rushed wildly over her face.

The next moment it ebbed, leaving her white as marble. Horror filled her eyes,—blank, deadly horror, as the livid shadow of a cloud might fill two blue pools.

Behind Eric Neil Gordon was standing tense, crouched, murderous. Even at that distance Kilmeny saw the look on his face, saw what he held in his hand, and realized in one agonized flash of comprehension what it meant.

All this photographed itself in her brain in an instant. She knew that by the time she could run across the orchard to warn Eric by a touch it would be too late. Yet she must warn him—she *must*—she MUST! A mighty surge of desire seemed to rise up within her and overwhelm her like a wave of the sea,—a surge that swept everything before it in an irresistible flood. As Neil Gordon swiftly and vindictively, with the face of a demon, lifted the axe he held in his hand, Kilmeny sprang forward through the gap.

"Eric, Eric, look behind you—look behind you!"

Eric started up, confused, bewildered, as the voice came shrieking across the orchard. He did not in the least realize that it was Kilmeny who had called to him, but he instinctively obeyed the command.

He wheeled around and saw Neil Gordon, who was looking, not at him, but past him at Kilmeny. The Italian boy's face was ashen and his eyes were filled with terror and incredulity, as if he had been checked in his murderous purpose by some supernatural interposition. The axe, lying at his feet where he had dropped it in his unutterable consternation on hearing Kilmeny's cry, told the whole tale. But before Eric could utter a word Neil turned, with a cry more like that of an animal than a human being, and fled like a hunted creature into the shadow of the spruce wood.

A moment later Kilmeny, her lovely face dewed with tears and sunned over with smiles, flung herself on Eric's breast.

"Oh, Eric, I can speak,—I can speak! Oh, it is so wonderful! Eric, I love you—I love you!"

AS NEIL GORDON LIFTED THE AXE HE HELD IN HIS HAND,
KILMENY SPRANG FORWARD.

CHAPTER 18

NEIL GORDON SOLVES HIS OWN PROBLEM

"IT IS a miracle!" said Thomas Gordon in an awed tone.

It was the first time he had spoken since Eric and Kilmeny had rushed in, hand in hand, like two children intoxicated with joy and wonder, and gasped out their story together to him and Janet.

"Oh, no, it is very wonderful, but it is not a miracle," said Eric. "David told me it might happen. I had no hope that it would. He could explain it all to you if he were here."

Thomas Gordon shook his head. "I doubt if he could, Master—he, or any one else. It is near enough to a miracle for me. Let us thank God reverently and humbly that he has seen fit to remove his curse from the innocent. Your doctors may explain it as they like, lad, but I'm thinking they won't get much nearer to it than that. It is awesome, that is what it is. Janet, woman, I feel as if I were in a dream. Can Kilmeny really speak?"

"Indeed I can, Uncle," said Kilmeny, with a rapturous glance at Eric. "Oh, I don't know how it came to me—I felt that I *must* speak—and I did. And it is so easy now—it seems to me as if I could always have done it."

She spoke naturally and easily. The only difficulty which she seemed to experience was in the proper modulation of her voice. Occasionally she pitched it too high—again, too low. But it was evident that she would soon acquire perfect control of it. It was a beautiful voice—very clear and soft and musical.

"Oh, I am so glad that the first word I said was your name, dearest," she murmured to Eric.

"What about Neil?" asked Thomas Gordon gravely, rousing himself with an effort from his abstraction of wonder. "What are we to do with him when he returns? In one way this is a sad business."

Eric had almost forgotten about Neil in his overwhelming amazement and joy. The realization of his escape from sudden and violent death had not yet had any opportunity to take possession of his thoughts.

"We must forgive him, Mr. Gordon. I know how I should feel towards a man who took Kilmeny from me. It was an evil impulse to which he gave way in his suffering—and think of the good which has resulted from it."

"That is true, Master, but it does not alter the terrible fact that the boy had murder in his heart,—that he would have killed you. An over-ruling Providence has saved him from the actual commission of the crime and brought good out of evil; but he is guilty in thought and purpose. And we have cared for him and instructed him as our own—with all his faults we have loved him! It is a hard thing, and I do not see what we are to do. We cannot act as if nothing had happened. We can never trust him again."

But Neil Gordon solved the problem himself. When Eric returned that night he found old Robert Williamson in the pantry regaling himself with a lunch of bread and cheese after a trip to the station. Timothy sat on the dresser in black velvet state and gravely addressed himself to the disposal of various tid-bits that came his way.

"Good night, Master. Glad to see you're looking more like yourself. I told the wife it was only a lover's quarrel most like. She's been worrying about you; but she didn't like to ask you what was the trouble. She ain't one of them unfortunate folks who can't be happy athout they're everlasting poking their noses into other people's business. But what kind of a rumpus was kicked up at the Gordon place, tonight, Master?"

Eric looked amazed. What could Robert Williamson have heard so soon?

"What do you mean?" he asked.

"Why, us folks at the station knew there must have been a to-do of some kind when Neil Gordon went off on the harvest excursion the way he did."

"Neil gone! On the harvest excursion!" exclaimed Eric.

"Yes, sir. You know this was the night the excursion train left. They cross on the boat tonight—special trip. There was a dozen or so fellows from hereabouts went. We was all standing around chatting when Lincoln Frame drove up full speed and Neil jumped out of his rig. Just bolted into the office, got his ticket and out again, and on to the train without a word to any one, and as black looking as the Old Scratch himself. We was all too surprised to speak till he was gone. Lincoln couldn't give us much information. He said Neil had rushed up to their place about dark, looking as if the constable was after him, and offered to sell that black filly of his to Lincoln for sixty dollars if Lincoln would drive him to the station in time to catch the excursion train. The filly was Neil's own, and Lincoln had been wanting to buy her but Neil would never hear to it afore. Lincoln jumped at the chance. Neil had brought the filly with him, and Lincoln hitched right up and took him to the station. Neil hadn't no luggage of any kind and wouldn't open his mouth the whole way up, Lincoln says. We concluded him and old Thomas must have had a row. D'ye know anything about it? Or was you so wrapped up in sweethearting that you didn't hear or see nothing else?"

Eric reflected rapidly. He was greatly relieved to find that Neil had gone. He would never return and this was best for all concerned. Old Robert must be told a part of the truth at least, since it would soon become known that Kilmeny could speak.

"There was some trouble at the Gordon place tonight, Mr. Williamson," he said quietly. "Neil Gordon behaved rather badly and frightened Kilmeny terribly,—so terribly that a very surprising thing has happened. She has found herself able to speak, and can speak perfectly."

Old Robert laid down the piece of cheese he was conveying to his mouth on the point of a knife and stared at Eric in blank amazement.

"God bless my soul, Master, what an extraordinary thing!" he ejaculated. "Are you in earnest? Or are you trying to see how much of a fool you can make of the old man?"

"No, Mr. Williamson, I assure you it is no more than the simple truth. Dr. Baker told me that a shock might cure her,— and it has. As for Neil, he has gone, no doubt for good, and I think it well that he has."

Not caring to discuss the matter further, Eric left the kitchen. But as he mounted the stairs to his room he heard old Robert muttering, like a man in hopeless bewilderment,

"Well, I never heard anything like this in all my born days— never—never. Timothy, did *you* ever hear the like? Them Gordons are an unaccountable lot and no mistake. They couldn't act like other people if they tried. I must wake mother up and tell her about this, or I'll never be able to sleep."

CHAPTER 19

VICTOR FROM VANQUISHED ISSUES

Now that everything was settled Eric wished to give up teaching and go back to his own place. True, he had "signed papers" to teach the school for a year; but he knew that the trustees would let him off if he procured a suitable substitute. He resolved to teach until the fall vacation, which came in October, and then go. Kilmeny had promised that their marriage should take place in the following spring. Eric had pleaded for an earlier date, but Kilmeny was sweetly resolute, and Thomas and Janet agreed with her.

"There are so many things that I must learn yet before I shall be ready to be married," Kilmeny had said. "And I want to get accustomed to seeing people. I feel a little frightened yet whenever I see any one I don't know, although I don't think I show it. I am going to church with Uncle and Aunt after this, and to the Missionary Society meetings. And Uncle Thomas says that he will send me to a boarding school in town this winter if you think it advisable."

Eric vetoed this promptly. The idea of Kilmeny in a boarding school was something that could not be thought about without laughter.

"I can't see why she can't learn all she needs to learn after she is married to me, just as well as before," he grumbled to her uncle and aunt.

"But we want to keep her with us for another winter yet," explained Thomas Gordon patiently. "We are going to miss her terrible when she does go, Master. She has never been away from us for a day—she is all the brightness there is in our lives. It is very kind of you to say that she can come home whenever she likes, but there will be a great difference. She will belong to your world and not to ours. That is for the best—and we wouldn't have it otherwise. But let us keep her as our own for this one winter yet."

Eric yielded with the best grace he could muster. After all, he reflected, Lindsay was not so far from Queenslea, and there were such things as boats and trains.

"Have you told your father about all this yet?" asked Janet anxiously.

No, he had not. But he went home and wrote a full account of his summer to old Mr. Marshall that night.

Mr. Marshall, Senior, answered the letter in person. A few days later, Eric, coming home from school, found his father sitting in Mrs. Williamson's prim, fleckless parlour. Nothing was said about Eric's letter, however, until after tea. When they found themselves alone, Mr. Marshall said abruptly,

"Eric, what about this girl? I hope you haven't gone and made a fool of yourself. It sounds remarkably like it. A girl that has been dumb all her life—a girl with no right to her father's name—a country girl brought up in a place like Lindsay! Your wife will have to fill your mother's place,—and your mother was a pearl among women. Do you think this girl is worthy of it? It isn't possible! You've been led away by a pretty face and dairy maid freshness. I expected some trouble out of this freak of yours coming over here to teach school."

"Wait until you see Kilmeny, father," said Eric, smiling.

"Humph! That's just exactly what David Baker said. I went straight to him when I got your letter, for I knew that there was some connection between it and that mysterious visit of his over here, concerning which I never could drag a word out of him by hook or crook. And all *he* said was, 'Wait until you see Kilmeny Gordon, sir.' Well, I *will* wait till I see her, but I shall look at her with the eyes of sixty-five, mind you, not the eyes of twenty-four. And if she isn't what your wife ought to be, sir, you give her up or paddle your own canoe. I shall not aid or abet you in making a fool of yourself and spoiling your life."

Eric bit his lip, but only said quietly,

"Come with me, father. We will go to see her now."

They went around by way of the main road and the Gordon lane. Kilmeny was not in when they reached the house.

"She is up in the old orchard, Master," said Janet. "She loves that place so much she spends all her spare time there. She likes to go there to study."

They sat down and talked awhile with Thomas and Janet. When they left, Mr. Marshall said,

"I like those people. If Thomas Gordon had been a man like Robert Williamson I shouldn't have waited to see your

Kilmeny. But they are all right—rugged and grim, but of good stock and pith—native refinement and strong character. But I must say candidly that I hope your young lady hasn't got her aunt's mouth."

"Kilmeny's mouth is like a love-song made incarnate in sweet flesh," said Eric enthusiastically.

"Humph!" said Mr. Marshall. "Well," he added more tolerantly, a moment later, "I was a poet, too, for six months in my life, when I was courting your mother."

Kilmeny was reading on the bench under the lilac trees when they reached the orchard. She stood up and came shyly forward to meet them, guessing who the tall, white-haired old gentleman with Eric must be. As she approached Eric saw with a thrill of exultation that she had never looked lovelier. She wore a dress of her favourite blue, simply and quaintly made, as all her gowns were, revealing the perfect lines of her lithe, slender figure. Her glossy black hair was wound about her head in a braided coronet, against which a spray of wild asters shone like pale purple stars. Her face was flushed delicately with excitement. She looked like a young princess, crowned with a ruddy splash of sunlight that fell through the old trees.

"Father, this is Kilmeny," said Eric proudly.

Kilmeny held out her hand with a shyly murmured greeting. Mr. Marshall took it and held it in his, looking so steadily and piercingly into her face that even her frank gaze wavered before the intensity of his keen old eyes. Then he drew her to him and kissed her gravely and gently on her white forehead.

"My dear," he said, "I am glad and proud that you have consented to be my son's wife—and my very dear and honoured daughter."

Eric turned abruptly away to hide his emotion and on his face was a light as of one who sees a great glory widening and deepening down the vista of his future.